DIRTY

THE COMPLETE SERIES

ELLA MILES

Copyright © 2018 by Ella Miles

EllaMiles.com

Ella@ellamiles.com

Editor: Jovana Shirley, Unforeseen Editing, www.unforeseenediting.com

Cover Designer: © Cara Garrison

❀ Created with Vellum

DIRTY BEGINNING

1

NINA

I CAN'T GO after him.

Not because I'm in Italy for only one month, so there is no way anything but a fling could happen between us.

I can't *kiss* him.

Not because his lips aren't kissable. I writhe and ache, imagining what his lips would feel like pressed up against my lips as our tongues tangled together in a passionate kiss.

I can't *think* about him.

Not because I should be studying for my exams. I could pass those whether or not I was thinking about ripping his shirt off and running my fingers across every hard inch of him.

I sure as hell can't *sleep* with him.

Not because I don't want to.

Not because he wouldn't be the most life-altering sex I'd ever had.

Not because he's out of my league.

Not because he doesn't want me.

I can't have Arlo Carini because he's *dangerous*. And I'm *obsessed*.

I can't keep my eyes off him as Arlo gives me and thirty other grad students a tour of his historic mansion. I can't keep my heart from racing. Or my mind from thinking dirty thoughts of all the ways and places we could have sex in this mansion.

On the couch in the sitting room, on the grand staircase, against the stone wall in the foyer.

I can't stop the obsession once it starts. And, right now, I'm full-on obsessed as he guides us through more and more rooms, the whole time ignoring everyone else and staring directly at me. It's clear that he might be a little obsessed or at least curious about me, which only makes me crazier.

I can't do this. I'm not really obsessed. Just infatuated. He's just a hot guy that I want to fuck. The same thought that every other woman here is thinking.

Arlo leads us outside and I try to do my best to focus on other things. That's what my years of therapy has taught me; distraction is key. I focus on the blooming flowers that are so large that they would hold my interest if this were any other time. Just not when there is one of the hottest warm-blooded males I've ever seen standing only a few feet away from me.

I try listening to the birds. I try focusing on the beautiful statues and fountains. I try ogling the men in my class but they all look like boys compared to Arlo.

Nothing works.

I just have to get through this and then I'll find a nice Italian man to distract me tonight. I just haven't had sex in a while. That's it.

The class starts walking again. So I do too. But when I take a step I feel nothing beneath my foot.

Shit.

I don't have time to react. I feel my body falling and then I feel the water soaking me as I fall into the pool. I let my body sink to the bottom because drowning sounds better than reappearing on the surface and facing my embarrassment.

I open my eyes under the water as a body jumps into the pool. My eyes widen and my heart sinks as Arlo swims toward me. He grabs hold of my waist and pushes me toward the surface.

We both break through the surface sucking in air like we'd been underwater for minutes instead of just seconds. He jumped in to save me. He thought I was drowning, not just dying from embarrassment. And he saved me.

I begin to swim toward the stairs, but Arlo doesn't let me go. He scoops me into his arms, as he swims, and then carries me out of the pool.

The class applauds instead of laughing, like Arlo is a hero or something.

He ignores them and carries me as he walks into what looks like a pool house a few yards away from where the class is gathered.

He sits me down gently in a chair and grabs a towel, draping it over my shoulders.

"You okay?" he asks. His voice is sweet and caring, such a stark difference from the hard and cold exterior he has been all afternoon.

"You saved me."

He smiles for the first time today. "I wouldn't say that. Just saved you from embarrassment."

I shake my head. "No, you saved me. I'm forever in your debt. How can I repay you?"

With a date, please.

His hard expression returns. He removes his gray jacket, tie, vest, and shirt leaving it on the floor while I ogle every hard muscle on his body. He realizes his mistake and takes a towel from the rack. He begins drying his hair as he walks back out without a word.

I close my eyes as I sit alone in the pool house, trying to push the familiar feelings down. I was strong enough before to resist. Before he was just a hot stranger, that with enough distraction, I could have left alone. Now he's the sexy stranger that saved my life. That's too much temptation for me to resist.

I can't obsess about him though. The last time I was obsessed with a guy, I ended up with months of therapy and a restraining order. I got more therapy after I chased and almost ran a guy off the road. I self-medicated with alcohol after I flunked a semester while dating another guy. I started doing drugs after I ruined a married man's life.

I know what men do to me. They make me obsessed. They make me insane. Addicted. I don't have a life when I'm with a man.

I've been through it time and time again. More than a dozen times with a dozen different men. I know the only cure is to stay away from men. I'm like an alcoholic who can't go into a bar. I can't go anywhere near hot, attractive, powerful men.

But Arlo Carini is different. He's hot, sure. He's tall with unruly, dark hair and muscles that I can't wait to have on top of me, overpowering me and controlling me. I didn't have to wait for him to undress to see his muscles. I can see every single one. The gray three-piece suit did nothing to contain them.

He's sexy as hell. But I've gone after sexy men before.

And there is more to him than a hot body.

He's powerful. I know from the way he's demanded everyone's attention from the second we entered the mansion. But so do hundreds of other men who run companies, and I've vied for their attention, too.

He's filthy rich. I know that from the enormous mansion I'm currently standing in, which is owned by the Carini family. But I have plenty of money myself, and I've gone after men with money before.

What makes me want Arlo more than any man I've wanted in the last three months of sobriety is the intensity with which he stares at me and no one else in the room, both before and after he saved me. It's the way he never grins or lets any emotion through. It's the mystery that surrounds him and the whole Carini family. The town hasn't stopped talking about his family since I arrived.

I want to know everything about him.

What does he do?

Who has he slept with?

What would it feel like to kiss him?

How much dick is he hiding beneath those tight slacks?

Does he know how to handle a woman in bed?

Is he a playboy, or is he looking for a wife?

Does he have freckles, moles, birthmarks?

Does he prefer coffee or tea?

Night owl or early riser?

I want to know *everything.*

My mind goes crazy, already trying to fill in the answers. I'm sure I have guessed right on most. I've studied enough people in the past to know. But I don't like guessing.

I like obsessing. I like the chase. The hunt. I like knowing everything and making a man mine. I like control. I like being wrapped up in a man who I would rather die for than give up. Something I've almost done three times now while chasing a man.

I know I can't go down that road. I promised my father on his deathbed that I would give it up. Get help. And I've kept my promise for eighty-nine days now. It was getting easier to give men up. I threw myself into grad school. Got into a one-month study abroad program in Italy.

But one attempt at saving my life, and I've forgotten all about my sobriety.

Maybe my grief made it easier for me. Maybe I wasn't doing so well after all.

I'm here for only one month. Not even that. Four weeks. Twenty-eight days. Maybe it'd be okay to sleep with him. Get the thrill of fucking a guy again out of my system so that life will be easier when I go home. I can't obsess when I'm four thousand miles away, back in Vermont.

I run back outside to join the group, after doing my best at drying off.

"My cousin, Paola, will be continuing your tour of the grounds. It was a pleasure meeting you all," Arlo says, his eyes falling on me one last time before he turns and walks toward the house. Most likely, to get out of his wet clothes.

I turn my head to his beautiful cousin who has long brown curls for days as she leads the class outside. But I can't listen to her. I can't be so far away from Arlo so soon after meeting him.

"You okay? That was quite a fall," Eden asks.

I nod. "I'm going to see if they have any dry clothes for me to wear." I dart inside and turn in the direction I saw Arlo walk. I have to walk only two doors down when I find him standing inside the office he showed us earlier.

My stomach twists in knots as my anxiety builds when I enter his office, uninvited. We can fuck right here on his desk, or maybe he'll sneak me off to his bedroom upstairs. Or maybe he'll whisk me off to some special room in the mansion that he didn't show us yet.

"You can't be in here," Arlo says, staring at me with dark eyes that overwhelm me. I have no idea what he is feeling or thinking when he looks at me, but I hope it's the same need I feel when I look at him. Surely, he felt a connection to me after he saved me, even if it is just lust. But his voice is so different than it was in the pool house. Before he was sweet. Now he's angry and cold.

I grin and take a step forward, making sure to push my breasts out as I walk toward him. The V-neck shirt I'm wearing isn't that revealing, even wet, but it's enough to get him to glance down at my breasts.

"I think this is exactly where I need to be," I say as I twist a dark brown strand of hair, which fell out of my ponytail, around my finger.

His eyes dart to where my finger is twisting my hair.

I grin wider. He can tell me I shouldn't be in here all he wants, but his interest in my body says differently.

He grabs my wrist, and I stop moving. His touch sends a shock wave through my body, unnerving me. His grip is firm, giving me a hint of just how rough he could be in bed.

"You. Aren't. Allowed. In. Here," he says slowly and sternly without raising his voice.

I reach my other hand out to touch the stubble on his cheek. His hand grabs my other wrist. This time, more roughly.

I'm not worried about both my wrists being trapped in his hands. Although I should be. His eyes have darkened. He looks like he's about to kill someone. And I'm the only one in the room for him to take his anger out on.

"You don't know who I am," Arlo says, still holding on to my wrists.

"I know you're Arlo Carini, basically royalty in this town." I take a deep breath. "And I know that you want to fuck me."

He grips my wrists tighter and pulls me toward him until our bodies are pressed together. I can't breathe. All I can think about is the pain he is inflicting on my wrists. It's making my head spin. But I kind of like it.

"You have no idea who I am. You, on the other hand, I know exactly who you are."

I smirk. *I doubt it.*

"You're Nina Young. Twenty-something grad student who is majoring in art history because you love it even though it's going to lead to a dead-end job that pays you nothing. That means, you have family money to make up the difference or are planning on marrying a rich lawyer or doctor as soon as you return to the US. But none of that matters. What matters is that you are a spoiled, rich little girl who gets to come to Italy and will do anything to bang every hot Italian man she can find, so when you return home, you can relive the excitement and adventure instead of dealing with the reality of your pathetic life."

He loosens his grip just a little on my wrist, and I breathe.

"Your life is perfect. But you're living in a dream world."

I open my mouth to tell him that my life is anything but perfect, but Arlo's eyes shut me up before I even start.

"You don't know me, and you don't want to. I ruin women. I destroy them. I mean that literally. Stay away from me, Nina. No, run away. And don't ever look back." He says it like he means it. His eyes beg me to stay.

He releases my wrists, but I don't move. I can't move. I have so many questions.

Why don't I want to know him? What does he mean about destroying women? How does he know my name?

"Go," he growls at me when I don't move.

I turn, startled at his growl, and begin to leave the room. Much slower than I'm sure he wants me to. But I know that I'm not going to get anywhere with him right now.

I will. I'll get him to fuck me. I'll get him to obsess about me. Love me. Marry me if I want him to. He can be my last obsession. He's perfect. He would make the best husband.

I glance back at him when I reach the door. He's nothing but a hot stranger to me. He was just supposed to be a man giving me and my classmates a tour of his mansion, which is full of history. Nothing more. Definitely not the object of my new obsession.

9

He smiles smugly at me. He thinks he's won. That I'll leave him alone after he scared me. But he's wrong. He's just made me more obsessed than ever before.

2

NINA

"ARE YOU SICK?" my roommate, Eden, asks.

"Yes," I answer as I stare into the tiny mirror in the bathroom.

"A stomach bug? Migraine? Hangover? What?" Eden asks.

"Migraine," I answer, hoping that it will be enough to get her to stop talking.

I love Eden. She is my best friend. I've known her my whole life. We do everything together. We are in the same classes. Lived in the same towns. But I regret living with her, even for a few weeks. She is nosy and isn't afraid to tell me like it is. Even when I don't want to hear it.

"I'll get you some Advil," she says, her heels clicking on the hardwood floor as she walks away from the bathroom door.

I exhale slowly while I glance at my watch. I have to leave in two hours if I want to get to Carini's party at a decent time. I've been anxious about going ever since I overheard some townspeople talking about it last night. I haven't started getting ready at all. I didn't bring a fancy dress with me. I'll have to find something in one of the local shops since I can't ask Eden to let me borrow a dress of hers. If I do, she will grow suspicious that I'm not really sick. And it takes me hours to get my stick-straight brown hair to curl and resemble anything other than a boring mop of hair.

Eden's heels start clicking along the old, hard floor that gives and squeaks as she walks across it, making me cringe with each step. She knocks on the bathroom door, and the rattling of the rickety door is enough to drive me insane.

"I couldn't find the Advil in your purse. Is it in the medicine cabinet?" she asks.

I open the cabinet and pick up the small container of Advil. I dump the contents into the toilet and then flush.

"Yes, but it's empty." I open the door. "I'll have to go to the store to get some more."

I walk past Eden, ignoring her critical stare. I know she cares about me, and that is the reason for her studied look, but she doesn't have to make me feel so guilty all the time.

"I can get you some Advil before I go to the lecture tonight," Eden says, following me to my bedroom.

I walk over to my closet, find my black leather jacket, and put it on. "No need. I know you want to get a front row seat since Professor Patrizio is your favorite. Take good notes for me. I'll pick up some food and put it in the fridge for you. You can warm it up when you get back. I'm going to just take a bath, after I get some medicine and food, and then go to bed early."

I grab my purse and start to walk past her. Eden steps in front of me, preventing me from leaving.

I tuck a strand of hair behind my ear while I try to stay calm even though I can practically hear the second hand of my watch ticking loudly, reminding me that each second is another one I'm missing Arlo's attention at his party.

"Do you need me to pick up something for you at the store while I'm there?" I ask, attempting to act casual even though I can hear the annoyance dripping off every word I say, and I know Eden doesn't miss it either.

"I don't believe you."

I narrow my eyes. "What don't you believe? I have a migraine. I'm going to the store and then to the bakery on the corner to get something to eat, and then I'm going to bed."

Eden smirks. "You really think I'm going to fall for your act? You do realize that I know you better than that."

"I have a migraine! And every second that I have to stay here and hear your voice or your heels clicking on the floor or your music pounding through the apartment is making the migraine a million times worse. Now, get out of my way so that I can go get more Advil," I say, trying to push past Eden.

She doesn't budge though. She stands firm.

We are almost identical in height and strength. The only real visible difference between the two of us is hair color. Hers is black while mine is brown. But both of our hair is long and straight, hitting mid back. Our eyes are both dark, and our skin is olive brown. Almost everyone who meets us assumes we are sisters.

If I try again, it's going to lead to a fight, which is going to make me far too late for Arlo's party. I close my eyes and then slowly open them to try to keep from doing just that.

"Just tell me what you want to say, so we can get whatever fight is about to happen over with," I say.

"I'm not going to fight with you, Nina. I love you, and I want to make sure you are okay. You've been doing so well these last few months, and I just don't want one misstep to ruin everything."

I smile. "Don't worry. I'm fine. Promise. I have a migraine."

She shakes her head. "I took some Advil yesterday. We had almost a full bottle."

I frown.

"And I saw you yesterday..." Eden says.

I narrow my eyes, trying to understand. "What do you mean?"

"I saw you with Mr. Carini in his office. I know you, Nina. He's hot and mysterious and rich. And you want him. He turned you down, and now, you won't stop until you've fucked him every which way. You'll stop going to classes. You'll only think about him."

There is no point in lying to Eden. "So, I'm obsessed. I've been good for months now, and we are here for only four weeks. What damage could I really do?"

"A lot of damage. He's dangerous, Nina. The whole town says so."

"I can't fight it, Eden. He pulls me in just like all the rest of them. Every day that I resist, the pain gets worse. My stomach is in knots, and I really do have a migraine."

Eden stares into my eyes with a sadness that I haven't seen since my father's funeral. "I know."

"Then, you know that I have to see him again."

She sighs. "I know."

"I have to fuck him."

"I know."

"Maybe, after I do, I'll be able to leave him alone."

Eden nods even though I know she doesn't believe me. She tightly hugs me.

"I'll be careful," I promise.

She lets me go. "And I'll be here to pick up the pieces when you aren't careful enough."

I smile, and this time, when I try to walk past Eden, she lets me.

"You can borrow my dress. The black lace one that makes your boobs look amazing."

"Thank you," I say.

She knows me too well and is willing to help me even though she knows the trouble I'm about to get myself into. She's been there when I've fallen apart and almost ruined my life. I know she'll keep her promise to pick up the pieces that I leave in my wake. I just wish, for once, I could keep my promise and be careful.

3

NINA

I COULD STAND OUTSIDE the Carini mansion all night, staring at it. For an art history major like me, it doesn't get any better than the Carini mansion. It is full of architecture and structures that simply aren't built like this anymore. But, as much as I would love to study every inch of the outside, study how every brick was formed and how every vine grew up the front of the building, it's what is inside that really has me intrigued.

I got the tour of the mansion only yesterday, two days after we arrived, but there was so much more that I wanted to ingrain in my memory forever. So much more that I wanted to know about the history behind every room, every painting, every person who'd ever lived in the Carini mansion.

The mansion's history alone would be enough for me to skip out on another lecture about the Italian Renaissance and come to the party here to get a chance to soak it all in. But that isn't why I'm here.

I'm here to get Arlo to want me.

I see the security guard standing at the door, and I panic. I don't have an invite. There is no reason he should let me into the party. But then I look down at one of the sexiest dresses I have ever worn. Just act like I belong, and there is no way I won't get in. I've been let into parties and bars, wearing clothing that doesn't reveal anywhere near as much cleavage as this dress.

I walk up the long flight of stairs that lead up to the entrance. I wink at the security guard and then begin walking through the door.

I freeze. The guard's hand firmly holds on to my shoulder as I move through the door.

"Let me escort you to your seat, Ms. Young," the guard says, letting go of my shoulder and holding his arm out to me.

My eyes widen when he says my name. I try to smile and act like I belong, but I can't help myself. I have to know. "How do you know my name? How do I have a seat? I wasn't invited."

The man continues to hold his arm out to me and now smiles calmly instead of the serious look that was on his face a moment before. "It's my job to know who you are. And, as far as being invited or not goes, it's irrelevant. Mr. Carini said you would come and saved you a seat at the main table."

I stop blinking. I stop breathing. This can't be right. This has to be a mistake.

"Arlo made it perfectly clear that I was not supposed to see him again. You must be mistaken," I say.

"Are you Nina Young?"

I nod.

"Do you want to attend this party tonight or not?"

"I want to attend," I say hesitantly.

"Then, I'm not mistaken. Mr. Carini said you would come. He saved you a place at the table. Would you like me to escort you to your seat now?" he asks again, growing impatient.

I stare down at the stranger's arm and then slowly smile. I must have made an impression on Arlo if he knew I would be coming tonight and then saved me a seat.

I finally loop my arm through the guard's extended bent arm. "Take me to my seat."

He nods, and then his smile disappears as he starts guiding me through the large entryway and down a long passageway that is filled with paintings I didn't get to see on my tour of the mansion. I try to focus on keeping my poise, thinking about what I'm going to say when

I see Arlo, but the paintings draw my attention. One of the paintings is of a man dressed in clothing from decades ago who looks a lot like Arlo. The next one resembles someone who could be his grandmother. They are all family members. All share a history that is rich in culture and tradition. They all live in Italy. They all have lived inside these walls. All have kept family jobs that the rest of the town either doesn't know about or doesn't talk about. I could learn a lot from the paintings. Or at least, I could learn what the painter thought of the family.

But the guard who is walking me to my seat doesn't seem to know that he should slow down so that I can get a good look at each painting as we walk by. He is set on his mission, and his mission is to get me to my seat as fast as possible.

We get to the end of the hallway when my escort stops abruptly.

He glances at me. "The dinner has already started. Be prepared," he says as he reaches for the door.

"Be prepared for what?" I ask.

But, before he answers me, the door swings open, and I have hundreds of eyes staring at me.

I swallow, but I don't have time to panic as I'm guided into the room. It is so silent, I can hear my own heart thumping in my chest despite all the people in the large dining hall. I stare around at all the men and women who are dressed in clothing that is far fancier than what I am wearing. I thought I would be in the sexiest dress here, easily demanding Arlo's attention, but the clothes the women are wearing are far more revealing.

What I don't understand is why everyone is staring at me. I didn't realize that it was a dinner party.

But so what if it is?

What dinner party with this many people cares if one person shows up late?

I expect the escort to stop at any of the tables toward the back, which have a few empty seats, but that is not where I am led. We walk toward a table at the front of the room, which sits high up on a stage where everyone else can see the people sitting at the table.

I feel my face warm as we walk. I've embarrassed myself plenty throughout my life. But I've never felt so judged by so many people at once. It seems the entire town has turned up for this party. It's a rather small town, I've learned since coming here. One in which everyone knows everyone else's business. And I'm sure that this moment will be the talk of the town tomorrow. I'm not supposed to be here, and it appears that everyone knows it.

Finally, my escort stops at an empty seat at the far end of the head table. He pulls out my chair, sliding it across the marble floor, and it makes a high-pitched scrape against the floor. I wince. And then I quickly take my seat, hoping the moment will finally stop.

"Thank you," I say in barely a whisper, but my escort is already gone.

I feel everyone's eyes around the room slowly leave me—if for no other reason than these people are rich and used to acting polite, and staring for this long is anything but polite. The noise in the room slowly builds to where I'm sure it was before I entered. Loud. But not obnoxiously so. But, while everyone else has returned to eating, everyone seated at my table is staring at me, waiting for me to say something.

"Sorry I'm late," I say as I look around at the best-dressed people in the room, all dripping in expensive jewelry that is beyond anything I could ever imagine.

Most of the eyes quickly go back to their food, and they begin eating and chatting again. But three sets of eyes remain on me. A young girl of maybe fifteen or sixteen sitting on my left, an older gentleman in his sixties sitting toward the far end of the table, and Arlo, who is sitting three seats down from me.

His eyes are the only ones I care about. I hope to learn everything from him just by looking at him. But his gaze doesn't tell me anything. He doesn't seem surprised that I'm here, nor does he seem happy or upset. Just indifferent.

"You must be Nina," the young woman to my left says.

I nod and smile weakly.

"I'm Gia. My brother said you would be coming and that you would probably be late due to your classes."

"It's nice to meet you, Gia. I'm sorry I'm so late. I didn't realize that it would cause such a break in the meal."

Gia laughs. "Don't apologize. It's just because everyone has been waiting to see the special guest my brother has invited to sit at the family table for dinner tonight."

I open my mouth to tell her that he didn't really invite me, but then I stop as a delicious plate of pasta is placed in front of everyone. I'm sure I missed the first few courses, and for that, I will forever regret being late because just the smell of the pasta is enough for me to forget about anything other than how hungry I am.

I dig in without thinking, shoveling the glorious pasta into my mouth. I moan when the buttery, creamy sauce hits my tongue. It's the most delicious thing I have ever tasted. I shovel another bite into my mouth and then another after that, not able to get enough.

A throat clears next to me, and I stop. I feel the liquid spill down my lip, but I'm too embarrassed to wipe it away.

I look up and see more than a dozen eyeballs staring at me. I've caught the attention of the entire table. Again. I feel my cheeks burn as some of the richest and most powerful people in the city stare at me while Alfredo sauce drips down my face. I quickly grab my napkin, and I wipe my lip and chin before trying to muster a smile onto my face.

I hear Gia giggle softly to my left, and I try to let her joy fill me instead of the disgust that everyone else has on their faces. But her laughter isn't enough to overcome my own shame.

A few more seconds pass before people at the table return to eating their meals in perfect precision, almost as if they were performing a dance. I finally chance a glance up across the table to see what Arlo thinks of me, only to find him gone. I sink back in my chair even though I know that my bad posture will be enough to get a couple of disgusted looks from others at the table.

"My brother never stays long at these dinners," Gia says.

"Where did he go?" I ask.

Gia shrugs and then takes another bite of her pasta.

I glance around the room filled with beautiful people, including more than enough handsome men my age who I could spend one night with. But none of them are what I want.

"Excuse me," I say, getting up from my chair.

"Where are you going?" she asks.

I don't bother answering her. She seems like a smart girl who is fully capable of figuring out where I'm going. And, if I tell her, all she's going to do is try to stop me.

I'm sure that everyone's eyes are on me again as I storm out of the dining hall, but I don't stop to look. My entire focus is on Arlo. And how I'm going to try to find him despite the fact that I'm sure there are guards throughout the mansion to prevent unwanted guests like me from entering the private spaces. Not to mention, there are over fifty rooms in this house, and it's either going to take an extreme chance of luck for me to find Arlo or take all night for me to search through all the rooms.

But surely he would want to be found by me? He made sure I had a seat at his table. He wants me.

When we were getting the tour, we were only granted permission to about a dozen or so of the rooms. I'm going to assume he is not in any of those, so when I get back to the hallway that I know leads me toward the main areas of the house, I take a right instead of a left. Down a much darker hallway that isn't lit up, meant to be as uninviting as possible.

I walk past door after door. I don't stop to look inside any of the rooms, even the ones that have lights on and voices inside. I take a left and then a right as I feel myself getting closer to Arlo. I don't know how I know where to go. Call it a sixth sense, intuition, or chance. Maybe it is plain dumb luck. Call it whatever you want, but when my feet stop automatically in front of a set of double wooden doors, I know that Arlo is behind it. Knocking would be the proper thing to do, but I've never been about doing the proper thing. And I know my chances with Arlo are slim. This might even be my last chance with him. I need to surprise him, throw him off guard.

I hear music pumping mildly behind the closed doors. It's not the quiet, classical stuff that was playing downstairs, but it's not a song I recognize either. Something fast. Pop music with a little bit of rock. I take a deep breath, trying to slow the pounding in my heart that matches the speed of the music, but it does nothing. The music, if anything, entices me further, making me want him more. Making me want to fuck Arlo to this very song.

I grab both handles of the closed doubled doors, push down on the levers, and then swing the doors wide open.

My heart jumps in my chest when I see Arlo. My eyes glow with lust, and I feel my panties soak.

I should be shocked at what I see. I should gasp or blush or run away. But, instead, I'm just incredibly turned on.

Arlo doesn't widen his eyes or even raise an eyebrow when he sees me. He looks at me like I belong in his doorway. Maybe he put a spell on me that led me directly to his door. He's sitting in a fancy chair that looks like a throne. His shirt is unbuttoned, letting me see every ripple of muscle on his chest down to the V that hides his cock beneath his tux pants. His eyes are fixated on me. I have no idea how I can be capturing any of his attention when he has three almost naked women around him with their hands all over his body. Their lips kissing and worshipping every inch of him. Their bodies willingly providing a very seductive show, only for him.

I force my eyes to tear from his and really look at the women surrounding him. Two are blondes with fair skin. One rather curvy, the other as thin as a rail. The third woman has jet-black hair and skin darker than night, her curves sitting somewhere in the middle of the other two. It doesn't seem that he has a type.

None of the women care that I intruded on them. In fact, they act like I'm not even here. One continues kissing Arlo while another dances over his lap, and the third kisses his neck.

They don't look like strippers or hookers to me. They look happy, like their purpose is to please Arlo.

It's just a guess though. Arlo could be paying them. But by the jewels on their necks and dripping off their ears, the lace covering their bras, and the fancy dresses draped over various furniture in the room, they seem to come from their own wealth. Or Arlo pays his hookers like queens.

I take a second to decide my next move. No one has kicked me out, but no one has invited me in either. Other than Arlo's intense gaze still locked on me, I might as well not be here.

But I have to decide. *Do I want to turn away and take my chances at getting him alone by myself, or do I join them now and share him with three other women?*

Both.

I'll join in on the fun now and try to get him on my own later.

I take a step forward, and then I close the doors behind me. When I turn back, his eyes are still on me.

This is going to be too easy, I think.

I reach behind me and find the zipper on my dress, quickly pulling it down. I slip my arms out of the straps and let the dress slink down my body. I shimmy it over my hips before it falls to pile on the floor. I step out of the dress and start walking toward Arlo.

I've never had a threesome before, let alone a fivesome or whatever this is. But I don't lack confidence when it comes to my body or sex. And, from the hint of surprise in Arlo's eyes when I stepped out of the dress, I know that he appreciates my body, too.

I walk forward until I reach the blond, who is still dancing in Arlo's lap. I grab her hand, and I move my body close to hers until I'm rubbing up against her, dancing with her in front of Arlo. His eyes intensify even more, but he still doesn't say anything. I turn to the blond and put a finger under her chin. I pull her toward me, off Arlo's lap so that I can trade places with her. And then I firmly kiss her on the lips, letting our tongues tangle together and then slowly part. I keep my eyes on Arlo, showing him what I plan on doing to him when I get my turn with him.

When I stop the kiss, I see that Arlo is deeply frowning at me. I smile. Maybe he does really want me all to himself. I move from the blond and toward Arlo, facing him as I climb up onto his lap. I hover my lips over his, prepared to tease him first until he's begging me to kiss him.

A second later though, I feel my body being slammed against the wall across the room with Arlo firmly holding on to my arm with one hand. He holds on to my chin with his other hand as he stares at me, breathing hard.

I bite my lip to keep from smiling.

He wants me all to himself, I think.

"Excuse me, ladies. I have to deal with some business," Arlo says.

Not bothering to look at them as he drags me through another door and into a dark room.

"I knew you wanted me," I say.

Arlo throws me into the room, releasing my arm as he does. I fall to the cold tiled floor, off-balance from my heels and the force he used to push me inside.

He leaves the lights off, but I can still make him out as he walks back to the door.

"You have no idea what I want," he says matter-of-factly before shutting the door.

Then, I hear the door lock.

I slowly get off the floor, feeling my hands around until I find cabinets. I pull myself up and find a sink, mirror, shower, and toilet. I move in the dark until I find the door, but the knob doesn't budge.

That motherfucker locked me in the bathroom with no clothes.

I can already hear him grunting and moaning with the women outside while I'm trapped, listening to him fuck other women. I'm no longer sure that he's going to come back and fuck me after.

That bastard.

4

NINA

I'M GOING MAD. The sound of Arlo fucking those whores is making me crazy. I've tried to distract myself by going through the drawers and cabinets in his bathroom. But I'm pretty sure that this isn't the main bathroom he uses. All I've found are a few towels, a full bottle of soap, and a box of condoms. Nothing really to go through to learn about Arlo. Nothing to reorganize and distract myself with.

Now, every moan, every groan, every grunt is going to forever be burned into my memory. I'm never going to forget the sound that Arlo makes when he's had his turn with each of the women. The sound of their bodies banging together, completed with vivid images from my own imagination. My jealousy at not getting to be one of his girls consumes me.

I don't understand why Arlo won't let me fuck him like all the rest of the women. *How am I any different?* But, on the other hand, I also don't understand why he let me go as far as I did before he stopped me. *Why did he let me strip for him? Why did he let me dance on his lap? Why did he stop me only when I went in for a kiss?*

I don't have the answers, only questions. Questions that are driving me mad. I have no idea how long they fuck, but it seems like hours pass until they stop. They don't talk when they're done. Not a,

Was that good for you?, *Did you come?*, or, *I'll walk you out*. They just stop.

And then there's nothing for me to hear but silence. And, somehow, this feels worse than listening to them fuck. I feel empty and abandoned.

I wait a few seconds for the door to open, but it doesn't open.

I walk over to it and try the doorknob again, hoping that, this time, it will somehow be unlocked. But the doorknob doesn't budge. Pushing on the door doesn't help either. Despite the house being hundreds of years old, the door is solid. There is no way I'm breaking the door or the lock.

I walk back to the rug in front of the bathtub, and I sit down. I shiver immediately from the cold. I remove my heels, setting them on the floor next to me, so that I can be as comfortable as I can while I wait. And then I hug my legs against my chest to try to stay warm.

Waiting for Arlo to unlock the door.

Waiting for Arlo to give me answers.

Waiting to plan my revenge.

I consider yelling for help, but I don't think it would do me any good. Arlo seems like a stubborn man who takes complete control. Screaming would just leave me exhausted and worn out.

So, instead of screaming, I try to come up with a plan to make him as jealous and angry as he's made me. I rest my head against the wall and close my eyes, letting my mind drift off as I imagine ways that I can make him jealous.

I quickly sit up, startled by the sound of footsteps.

I smile slowly. *Finally*.

But the footsteps don't come toward my door. Instead, more footsteps join them. Followed by sounds of kissing, of spit being swapped, of tongues tangling, and of bodies joining together with sweat and lust.

Bastard is fucking them. Again.

I'm not going to let him get to me.

So, I close my eyes and drop my hand down my body to where my panties are soaking wet. Despite how angry and jealous I am, I've never been more turned on by a man in my life. I won't let him break me. I don't know why, but I know that's what he's doing. I won't let him win. My fingers slip inside my panties and I pleasure myself to the sound of his groans, pretending he's fucking me instead of them.

———

The door opens, and I jump awake. I must have drifted off to sleep in the cold bathroom after making myself come on the floor—twice.

"Why does it smell like sex in here?" Arlo asks as he steps into the dark bathroom.

With lust-filled eyes, I look up at him from my spot on the floor. "I was turned on and had no one to help me, so I took care of myself."

He smirks. "Feel better now?"

I want to lie to him. I want to tell him, *Yes, I feel perfectly satisfied now,* but the way he looks at me makes it impossible for me to lie to him.

"No."

"Get up," he says.

I do.

"Get dressed." He tosses my dress at me, and then he turns and walks out of the bathroom.

I put the dress on, but I don't zip it up. For one, it's almost impossible to zip up by myself, and two, I want him to have to touch my body. I don't bother with my shoes either. I just pick them up and then carry them out of the bathroom. It feels like defiance while still following his command. I love it.

He disapprovingly looks at me but doesn't say anything about the fact that my dress is still unzipped.

"How did you know that I would come tonight?" I ask.

He walks over to a small bar I didn't see before in the corner of the bedroom and pours himself what looks like scotch from the decanter on the table. He doesn't offer me any as he walks back to me. He's fully dressed again in his tuxedo, as if the last few hours didn't even happen. The girls are gone. The only remaining clue that they were ever here is the lingering smell of sex still clinging to the room. The smell alone makes me infuriated, but I will not let him know that. He doesn't get to know how jealous or angry he made me. Not until he pays for what he did to me.

"Because it's my business to know everything about everyone in this town, including spoiled, rich girls who are only here for four weeks."

I take a deep breath, but I can't help but glare at him. Everything about him drives insane. I have so many questions left to ask, but I know his patience won't last long. And my patience has completely run dry.

"Why didn't you let me fuck you like the others?"

He looks at me straight on without blinking. "Because you're not in my debt."

"What...what does that mean?"

He sips his scotch, completely unfazed by my questions. "I run a business that loans out money and services along with many other things. I accept many forms of payment for the debt. Those women were just paying me back."

I blink rapidly as my brain tries to understand what he just said.

"I'm in your debt. You saved me, now I owe you."

"No. I didn't save you. I just wanted an excuse to stop having to give the tour. Pretending to save you was that excuse. You owe me nothing."

"But—"

"No. You are not in my debt. I'll admit that, that day you infatuated me. I had to touch you. But then I came to my senses after I jumped in that pool after you."

I hesitate. "And what if I want to be in your debt?"

He frowns. "You can't. You will never be in my debt."

I grimace, completely confused. "But, if that's your business, then why don't you want me in your debt?"

His lip twitches. "You don't get to know that. You need to forget about me. Forget about this place. Find yourself another Italian boy to satisfy you for the next couple of weeks. That man won't be me."

I don't understand, but it's clear that I'm not going to get any more answers out of him tonight. But I've got enough for now. Enough to form a plan because I'd do anything to be in his debt. Even after he tortured me by locking me in the bathroom. I still want a chance to fuck the man that saved me one second and then has done everything to keep me away from him the next. A man that could have just told his guards not to let me in, but instead put me on the guest list and then locked me away when I came for him. I want to know what kind of man does something so contradictory.

"Zip me up," I say instead of asking more questions.

I turn around and wait. To my surprise, his hands firmly grip the zipper, and he slowly zips up my dress. I can feel his hot breath on my neck, and his grip on my hip makes me think that he wants to be unzipping my dress instead of zipping it up.

When he's done, he turns me around and grabs me by the neck, tightening his grip so that I truly can't breathe.

"Stop, Nina. You don't know what you're getting yourself into. Stop flirting. Stop coming after me. Or I'll make you stop."

He releases my throat, and I cough.

"Gregorio Manuel," Arlo says.

A man enters the room, who I recognize as the security guard from before. He's been waiting outside the door for who knows how long.

Did he follow me the whole way to Arlo's room?

"Escort Miss Young away, please, and make sure she doesn't return for the night," Arlo says before walking out of the room.

The security guard looks at me and then grabs me by the arm. He escorts me out into the empty hallway. Arlo has already disappeared. My mind races with everything he said as the guard leads me down hallways. I assume he is taking me out of the mansion. But that's not what happens. Instead of leading me back out, he takes me down a staircase and into a dark room.

"What are you doing?" I ask.

"As Mr. Carini instructed, making sure you don't return tonight or ever again."

He pushes me into the dark room, which looks like a dungeon, and closes the door. He locks it, trapping me for the second time tonight.

5

NINA

THE LIGHT BEAMS in as the door to the room is flung open. I sharply
turn my head away, trying to avoid the pain in my eyes from the
sudden brightness. I don't know why I bother though when a slight
pain from the light is nothing compared to the pain I feel in my body.

"Let me help you up," Gregorio, the guard, says.

I don't respond. I don't look at him. I don't move. I just sit like I
have been sitting all night. I clutch my legs tight against my chest with
my arms wrapped around them for warmth while I sit on the dirt-
covered floor, freezing. It turns out, a dark dungeon without air-condi-
tioning, even with my clothes on, is much colder than a heated bathroom without my clothes.

"Get up, Nina," he says as he reaches toward my hand.

When his rough fingers brush the skin on my arm, I jump.

"Don't touch me," I say as I push his arm away and stand up on
my own.

I stare at the man who has held me captive all night.

I spent the first hour shouting at him through the bars in the door
to let me out, that he couldn't do this to me, that it wasn't legal. But
the man never broke. He just stood there, silently guarding me, not
getting any sleep either. He should be just as sleep-deprived and

agitated as I am, but he doesn't seem to be that way. He seems so calm, cool, and collected.

But the guard isn't really the man I should be angry with because he isn't my captor. Arlo is. And, unlike this man in front of me, I feel completely broken. All it took to break me was one night alone in the cold dungeon, but I'm a fast healer. And it has just made me even more determined to get what I want.

"There is a car waiting to take you home."

I start walking toward the door. "Tell Arlo—"

"I will tell Mr. Carini nothing but the answer to the one question he wanted me to ask. Will you leave Mr. Carini and his whole family alone now?"

I pause for a second, staring into his eyes that although dark also seem kind. He's just a man doing his job. He is just the messenger. There is not the same touch of evil in his eyes like there is in Arlo's. I should say yes and not let him know my plans. But I tried surprise before, and he was already one step ahead of me.

"No," I say.

He sighs. "Mr. Carini said that you would say that."

"Then, why did you even bother asking?"

"Because I hoped you were smarter than the rest of them." He releases his grip on my arm. "Your ride is waiting out front. I'll escort you."

He leads me out front, and the warm sun beats down on us. I don't know what time it is, but I guess it's eight, maybe nine o'clock, in the morning. The bastard left me in there for close to ten hours.

He opens the door to the black town car, and I climb in without a word. He slowly closes the door after climbing in next to me, and continues to stare at me as the driver begins to drive off without me saying a word of where I live, but of course, he already knows.

I'm angry, and my whole body aches with pain from the cold and lack of sleep. I want nothing but revenge. And that revenge is going to be sleeping with Arlo.

For a split second, the guard's expression holds my attention. He looks like he just witnessed a death.

I smirk. Maybe he did because I sure as hell don't feel like the same person.

I don't want Arlo anymore because he's the hot, mysterious man who has threesomes in his fancy mansion. I'm obsessed with Arlo because he tried to get rid of me by leaving me broken and helpless. I will never be that girl again. I plan on destroying him. The first step is getting him to fuck me because, for some reason, I think it would hurt him a lot more than it would hurt me. Make him fall for me. Then I'll rip out his heart.

———

"What the hell happened to you?" Eden asks when I walk into our apartment.

"You don't want to know," I say, walking past her.

"Please tell me that it was some filthy sex thing that you and Arlo did in the woods, and now, he's out of your system."

I laugh. "Something like that."

"Well, whatever it is, we'll have to talk about it later. We needed to leave for class, like, five minutes ago, so get changed, and let's go."

I'm exhausted. I look down at my filthy dress. I touch my hair and feel the grease and oil from not having washed my hair, and I'm sure my mascara and eyeshadow are now smudged all over my face.

"I—"

"You are not skipping class. You are going to go wash your face and put your hair up in a ponytail while I go pick out some clothes for you. Got it?"

I nod and walk to the bathroom. I start trying to wash off the makeup that is now caked onto my face. Before I even finish half of my face, Eden is back with jeans, a T-shirt, and new underwear. She stands in the bathroom doorway, waiting for me to finish washing my face before thrusting the clothes into my hands.

"Put them on now."

I get dressed, and then Eden basically drags me to class about five blocks away. We step into the lecture room that's already filled with the thirty other study abroad students, and we end up taking the only two seats left in the back.

"Thank God Italians run on a much more relaxed schedule than we do in America," Eden says. "It would've been so embarrassing to walk into a class that had already started."

I give her a fake smile. She has no idea what being embarrassed really means.

An older gentleman with frazzled hair and tiny, rimmed glasses walks toward the front of the room. "Welcome, everyone. I hope you've been enjoying your time in Italy so far. I'm Professor Gianpaolo Tullio, and I'll be teaching you everything I can while you're here."

The professor rambles for a little bit about the importance of art and history and what his areas of expertise are before he says, "But the best way I find to learn about art is to create it yourself."

Several small moans can be heard throughout the room. There is a reason most of us are art history majors instead of artists.

He motions for us to stand up, so we do. Then, we follow him to another room where easels are set up throughout the room.

"Take a seat. We are going to work on two paintings. The first will be of an object, and the second will be of a person."

I sigh. I'm a horrible painter. I've tried countless times, but it's just not a skill I've ever learned to harness. I love art, and I love history. I would love to be able to contribute something meaningful to this world, but I realized that I would never be the kind of person who could paint, draw, or do anything artistic. I'm the kind of person who will study it and teach others how to use their gifts and learn from the past.

"Start by painting this beautiful bouquet of flowers."

That's all the direction he gives us after showing us the vase of flowers, and then he sits in the front of the room. I don't understand what we are supposed to learn from this class if he's not going to give us any amount of instruction. I could attempt a crappy painting of some flowers at home anytime. But I should be happy because it gives me time to mindlessly think about Arlo.

"So, are you going to tell me what happened last night?" Eden asks five minutes after we've started painting.

"Not today."

I get lost in painting until I have a picture that resembles a vase of flowers that a five-year-old could have painted.

"You're a good painter," a man sitting to my right says.

I raise an eyebrow. He's got to be kidding. Most people looking at my painting wouldn't even be able to make out that I painted a vase of flowers. I turn my attention back to the boy on my right. He is very good-looking with light, sandy blond hair and a bright smile. I'm sure most girls immediately fall for his charm.

Why can't I go after someone like him?

Because he's a boy, not a man. Because he's easy, not hard. Because I can already guess every boring thing about him. He's not the excitement that I crave.

I open my mouth to say, *Thank you for being so nice, but I know you're just trying to sleep with me*, when I hear a deep voice say, "It looks like shit. You should tell her that if you want to get into her pants. I'm sure she'd spread her legs for a good-looking boy like you."

My mouth drops as I look up and see Arlo standing over us with a wicked grin on his face.

"He's right; it does look like shit. While I appreciate you trying to give me a compliment, my painting skills are not what you should be complimenting me on. And, as far as sleeping with me goes, he's right."

I watch both men's eyes grow wide.

"The only men I don't sleep with are those who lock me in a dungeon and think they can control me," I say, glaring up at Arlo.

"Oh, Mr. Carini, you made it," our professor—I already forgot his name—says as he runs over to Arlo and kisses him on each cheek.

Arlo walks to the front of the room as the professor says, "Everybody, this is Mr. Carini. He will be helping us with our paintings this afternoon."

I watch as Arlo removes his black leather jacket and hangs it over the back of a chair. My mouth waters, and my cheeks flush when he begins unbuttoning the dark blue shirt that he is wearing underneath his jacket.

I turn my attention back to the professor, who's still rambling, but I do manage to catch his last word.

Nude.

We will be painting Arlo in the nude.

Arlo smirks as I realize that I'm going to see him naked and be forced to attempt to paint him naked while keeping my composure. I'm sure I won't be the only one who struggles with painting a naked man. I glance around the room, but no one else seems to be blushing or fidgeting in their seat like I am.

Arlo continues to undress with his eyes locked on me. Today, he seems to be in a better mood, probably because he got a good night's sleep while I attempted to sleep on a dungeon floor. I've seen him almost naked before, but somehow, him undressing in front of us makes it all the more intimate, especially when his eyes stay on me the entire time he's doing it.

My cheeks flush a bright shade of pink when he pulls down his pants and briefs all in one motion, and his cock springs free. I try not to stare even though I know every other warm-blooded female in the room is doing the same.

God, his body still draws me to him just as much today as it did before he locked me up.

"Paint. Free your mind, and just paint," the professor says, breaking the spell that I've been under since Arlo came into the classroom.

I stare down at the canvas in front of me, and I start painting, knowing full well that there is no way my painting is going to look anything like Arlo. I paint, hardly ever looking up at Arlo. Every time I do, his eyes are always watching me, making me nervous or so filled with lust that I can't think straight. So, I just paint, mostly from memory, not that it matters anyway.

I look over to see how Eden is doing. Her painting looks exactly like Arlo. I'm going to have to steal hers later when I'm thinking dirty thoughts about him.

"It doesn't look that bad," Eden says, lying to me.

"Really?" I ask.

"Okay, it looks horrible. How did you manage to make him look like a mix between a rhinoceros and a gorilla?"

I laugh and shrug as I look at the painting. "It's a talent, I guess."

"Let's all thank Mr. Carini for being the inspiration for all your paintings today. We'll be going through everyone's paintings over the next few weeks, and at the end of your time here, we will paint again and see how things have changed in your appreciation of what's important to capture in your painting."

I frown. "This guy does realize this is art history, not a class about how to paint, right?" I ask Eden.

She shrugs. "Well, at least I'll get an A."

"I might as well drop out now because I'm going to fail this class."

I begin to gather my things as Arlo walks out of the room. It's the wrong decision. I know it the second my feet leave the ground to start running after him. But I've never been good at doing what is good for me.

"You really think I look like a hippo, Miss Young?" Arlo asks as he continues to walk forward without looking behind himself to know who is following. He just knows, or at least presumes, it is me.

"No, I think you look more like an ass. Too bad I'm not a skilled enough artist to convey it."

He chuckles and stops, waiting for me to catch up to him.

I'm shocked that he's talking to me, but maybe he feels that he's warned me enough, and any decision I make from this moment on is mine to make.

"Why did you let art history students paint you? Surely, they could have paid some college student who needed a buck or two instead of having you get naked in front of a room full of strangers."

"I did that because it was fun—the same reason I do everything in my life." He turns and starts walking.

"Arlo!" I shout.

He stops and turns, studying me.

"Why would you do that after everything you did last night? You made it your mission to keep me as far away from you as possible. Yet here you are, showing up in my classroom the next day."

He grins. And then he leans down and firmly kisses me on the lips. It's a sweet, chaste kiss with only a bit of his tongue and a tease of what more he could give me. But it's enough to make my craving for him uncontrollable.

He pulls away. "Maybe it's because I want you."

I blush. "I want you too. I want to come to one of your parties and actually be invited this time."

"No, you don't. The only way you become one of the women is if you become indebted to me."

The wheels start turning in my head again. I still don't know what he means by being in his debt.

"Stop thinking about it. You'll never be indebted to me."

"Fuck me, and I'll stop thinking about it."

"Why? So that you could become even more obsessed? Clingy? No, thanks. I have more than enough women who fawn over me."

And then Arlo leaves me alone. Confused and frustrated.

I want him more than I've ever wanted a man before.

But, right now, I'll have to relive the kiss over and over again while I make sense of his bizarre behavior. *What kind of man kisses me, but won't fuck me unless I'm in his debt?* Some sort of twisted, messed up man that's who. A man that makes me want to know everything about him.

6

NINA

"What is up with you? You've either been a bitch to anyone who talks to you or you have been completely silent all week," Eden says when she walks into the living room where I'm curled up on the couch.

"From that description, seems like I'm my usual self."

Eden grabs the quilt off my body.

I growl, "Give it back! It's freezing, and I'm taking a nap."

"You are not napping on our first of only three free weekends that we have here."

I close my eyes. "I'm taking a nap."

I don't want to walk around the town. Everything will just remind me of Arlo again. All I can think about is his damn kiss anyway. He's the most confusing, infuriating man I've ever met. I'm frustrated that I have already let a week pass without trying to come up with a plan for revenge. I'm way out of my league. So, my new plan is to sulk and stay away from him until I leave. It's a good plan that will get me into less trouble anyway.

Eden storms off.

I smile slightly. I've won. She'll leave me alone and let me nap while she goes and makes the best of this trip by exploring all that Italy has to offer.

"Here," Eden says, throwing a lump of something soft on me.

I glance down and find a small pile of clothes. I look back up at Eden, baffled as to why she threw me one of her shirts and pants.

"This shirt makes your boobs look great, and those pants make your ass look even better. Put them on, and let's go."

"I already told you, I'm not going."

Eden grins with her hands on her hips. "You are going. We can do this the easy way or the hard way."

I slowly sit up to see what she thinks I should wear. "Oh my God! This is your Versace shirt. This thing is over a thousand dollars. You never let me wear it."

She smirks. "Easy way, it is. It's yours if you leave with me now."

Damn it! This woman knows the way to my heart. Expensive designer clothes and shoes.

I pick up the clothes. "What about shoes?"

"You can have my Gucci black heels."

I grin and run to my bedroom to get changed. I poke my head back out. "What was the hard way going to be?" I ask.

Eden walks to her bedroom and then reappears in the hallway with her black heels. She holds them out to me, and I take them.

"I'm not telling. I might need to use the hard way later."

I quickly get ready and then reappear.

"You look smoking hot. Damn it, you should be happy that I like you; otherwise, I would never let you leave, looking better than me."

I roll my eyes as I look at Eden's dark jeans and low V-neck top. "You look amazing. I don't know what you are talking about."

Eden throws me a leather jacket. "Put this on. Your current look is a little too revealing for daylight hours."

I put the jacket on. She's probably right even though I have no idea what we are doing. But I hate to cover up the gorgeous gray lace shirt I'm wearing.

I loop my arm through Eden's arm. "Let's go, friend, to wherever you are taking me."

Eden's grin brightens. "We are going to a lecture."

My excitement drains. Leave it to my studious friend who has a body of a model and the brains of a rocket scientist to get us all dressed up and then take us to a lecture.

————

We walk into the large auditorium already filled with fifty or so people. The one nice thing about auditoriums here versus the US is that, here, they have beautiful balconies, chandeliers, sculptures, and paintings around the room. It's full of history even if the lecture that she brought me to is going to be boring as hell.

I look at the words on the screen as we take a seat in the front row.

"Why are we at a lecture for entrepreneurs of the future? We don't want to start a business. We want to teach or work in a library or museum or gallery. Our future is the exact opposite of starting a business or something new. Our jobs are very old."

Eden rolls her eyes. "There is nothing wrong with keeping our options open. What if we want to start our own business someday?"

"We won't."

"Well, that's not keeping an open mind."

"I don't care about the future. I care about the past. About the beauty in the world. About how to keep it alive. Not how to start some tech company that just cares about making money. Neither of us needs money. How long is this thing anyway?"

"Three hours."

"Three hours!"

A group of college students sitting next to us stares at us.

I glare at them, and they turn away. If only it were that easy to make everyone stop looking at me.

"Three hours? Are you serious?" I ask a little quieter.

"Yes."

"And what are you going to do for me after we get out of this three-hour torture?"

She turns her attention to the front as someone with a mic starts talking.

"You are going to find a way to thank me for bringing you."

"Why in the world would I thank you?" I hiss.

Eden nods her head toward the stage.

I face forward. She's right; I'm going to have to find a way to thank her after this.

"I would like to introduce you to our speaker for today. He's an Oxford grad, he runs a multibillion-dollar company, and the ladies tell me he's one good-looking man."

Women start screaming like they are at a rock concert.

"Let me introduce you to Mr. Carini."

Everyone applauds as Arlo walks onto the stage. He's dressed in a three-piece gray suit, his hair is tousled artfully on his head, and he has a nice five o'clock shadow going.

"Thank you. I know you are all here to listen to me talk about what it takes to be a young entrepreneur. You want to know the secret to making billions of dollars. Or as my friend Vito Abele said, you are here to swoon over my body. But I'm not going to talk to you about any of those things today."

Arlo's eyes dart to mine.

I hold my breath. I don't know how he found me so quickly in a room full of people. The last time I saw him, he kissed me. I look for something to show me that he wants me as badly as I want him. That he has been a complete mess of need and lust since our kiss, just like I have. That he is desperate for me, just like I am to have his lips on me again.

I see no sign of any sort of desperation. He does what he always does. Pretends I don't exist while making me his entire focus.

"I'm here to talk to you about why you should never be in anyone's debt."

I swallow. I glance down at the program that Eden is holding. It says he's here to talk about how to start a company. The keys to success. Not about not being in debt. This lecture is entirely for me.

"Asking someone for help shows them your weaknesses. It shows them how reckless you are. Be very careful who you show your weaknesses to. If you pick the wrong person or company, it could lead to your death," he says.

The only problem is, I can't pay attention to any of his words when he is staring at me so intently. He has to know that, if he is trying to get me to listen and leave him alone, this is the absolute worst way to do it. Because all I can see are his eyes. Occasionally, my eyes are able to break from his spell long enough to drift down to his lips. I imagine his lips on me. Kissing me again, but harder, more passionately. The kind of kiss that makes me forget about everything but him.

"Owing anyone anything will take away what little freedom you have. You should never be willing to give up your freedom in exchange for some help. Be stronger than that. Figure things out yourself. Giving up your freedom is never worth it," he continues.

Focus. Just listen to his words. They are important.

"Never be in debt to anyone who already has more power than you do. It will be the end of you," he says.

But his lips are so good-looking when he talks, it's distracting.

"You won't just owe the person who helped you. You'll owe everyone who had anything to do with the debt you incurred. And paying them back will never end. You will be trapped forever."

Trapped forever—got it.

But then he looks at me with his beautiful, dark eyes, and I forget.

"And, most importantly, if you do become indebted, run and hide. It's the only thing you can do. Fighting won't ever work. You will lose. So, run and hope that what you owe isn't worth going after. And maybe it will keep you safe."

After an hour and a half, he gives us a break and disappears from the stage. I exhale probably for the first time since he started talking.

"He couldn't stop staring at you. What did you do to him? That must have been some freaking amazing sex."

"We haven't had sex."

Eden scrunches her nose. "What? I thought you said..."

"You assumed."

"Well, I don't think it would be hard for you to convince him to sleep with you. And, if you aren't interested, I am. Maybe he has a brother or something for me?"

"He has an annoying, sweet younger sister."

She sighs. "Too bad. So, what's your plan?"

"I don't have a plan."

Eden laughs. "You always have a plan. That's part of your obsessive tendencies. You plan because you enjoy the planning almost as much as you enjoy the chase."

I shrug. "All my plans so far have failed miserably. I'm going to try going with the flow this time."

7

NINA

I WILL NOT MAKE A PLAN. I will not make a plan...

I keep repeating those words over and over again as Arlo finishes the second half of his presentation.

I don't hear a single word that he's said because of the constant replaying of those words in my head.

Occasionally, I switch to, *I will not let his smirk or the look in his eyes control me.* All while I try to seem confident and poised and not the least bit concerned with whatever Arlo is trying to convince me of.

"Excuse me."

I look up to see three men standing in front of Eden and me.

"A bunch of us are going out for drinks and dancing. Would you two like to join us?" one of the men asks with the greenest eyes I've ever seen. He knows how to work his eyes, too. They would make me say yes to anything.

"Yes!" Eden says almost automatically.

The man looks to me, reaching down to my soul with his eyes.

"And what about you?" he asks.

I should say no. These men are complete strangers who haven't even introduced themselves to us. If we go with them, it's going to be a night of drinking and bad decisions that will inevitably end up with us

43

doing a walk of shame in the morning. But I'm wearing one of the most expensive shirts I have ever worn. I look hot, and I need a fun night.

I feel more eyes on me. I glance up and see Arlo staring at me. He shakes his head ever so slightly at me. He doesn't want me to go.

I smirk. He doesn't control me. He doesn't get to tell me to stay away from him one second and then kiss me the next. And he definitely doesn't get to tell me not to go to a party with some hot men either.

"Yes," I answer defiantly.

"Great! It's just two blocks away. If you are ready, we can walk you over. I'm Clive by the way," he says.

"I'm Nina."

"And I'm Eden," Eden says, pushing herself between me and Clive. "Nina is currently in a complicated relationship. I, on the other hand, am completely free."

I shoot a look to Eden.

Eden grabs on to Clive's arm. "What? You are."

I frown. "These guys don't need to know that. And I'm not in a relationship anyway," I hiss into Eden's ear.

Eden rolls her eyes and then turns to the other two men who are equally as hot as Clive. "You," she says, pointing to the next hottest man, "escort my friend, and buy her a drink."

The man she pointed to smiles and holds out his arm. He's almost as good-looking as Clive but not even in the same ballpark as Arlo.

"I'm Erick."

I smile as I take the man's arm, and I am escorted out of the auditorium as Erick tells me all about himself. He's a college student. Business major. He grew up in England and moved to Italy for school.

I turn back to give Arlo one last smirk, but he's no longer on the stage. I glance around at the crowd on the floor of the auditorium, but he's not there either. He's just gone. And I'm left alone, realizing that Erick is my best chance at getting laid tonight. And, after being sexually frustrated from watching Arlo lecture me onstage while the entire time still feeling his kiss on my lips, I can't take it any longer. If Arlo won't have sex with me, then I'll take the next best thing.

———

"Can I get you another drink?" Erick shouts into my ear over the loud music, which has overtaken everything else in the bar.

I nod.

He smiles and then slowly moves through the crowd, toward the bar in the center of the room. It will be at least twenty minutes before he returns. This bar is completely insane. I've never been to a bar this crowded before.

Eden holds up her empty drink and points to her date, Clive. He nods and follows Erick over to the bar.

Eden and I start dancing together, which basically just consists of us moving our hips a little from side to side while keeping our feet planted in place. There isn't enough room to do much more.

Eden shouts something at me, but I have no idea what she said.

She tries again.

I shrug and shake my head.

She frowns.

I smile as I take her hand and dance some more. I feel much better after having a couple of drinks. The only thing bringing me down is the fact that I keep thinking that I see Arlo. Everywhere.

I see him in the face of every man dancing around me. Every time they turn and look at me, I see him.

I see him in the face of every bartender.

I see him lurking on the side of the dance floor, holding a scotch.

He haunts me.

Eden grabs my arm and pulls me close to her so that my ear is just below her mouth. "Arlo is here!"

I pull back and rub my ear from the pain of her screaming into it. I'm going to be deaf by the end of the night if we keep this up.

I laugh as I shake my head and go back to dancing. Now, I've convinced Eden that Arlo is everywhere too.

Eden grabs my cheeks and turns my attention toward the far wall.

"What?"

"Arlo!"

I catch my breath when the crowd parts just enough for me to see a tall, dark man leaning against the wall with an amber-colored liquid in a glass. His eyes are fixated on me with a deep grimace on his face.

"He's here," I say slowly, looking at Eden.

She nods.

"Why is he here?" I ask.

She laughs. "Because he likes you."

I bite my lip and then grab Eden's arm. I head straight toward the restroom, weaving and pushing people aside. I have to talk to her. Now.

When I see the line outside the woman's restroom, my heart sinks. *Of course there is a line.*

Instead, I pull her into the men's room.

"Hey, ladies," one of the men at the urinal says as we enter.

"Get out!" I say. I walk over to the stalls. "Everyone, out. Now!"

The men start exiting the stalls, some still zipping up their pants. Some look at me amused, but I just glare at them, and they realize just how serious I am. They all leave.

When I've ensured that we are alone, I lock the door to the entrance of the restroom.

Eden raises an eyebrow. "Why have you brought me to the men's restroom? Do you really need to pee that bad?"

I shake my head and take a deep breath. "I need to talk to you."

Eden blinks a couple of times as I try to figure out where to start, but I have no idea.

"Well...spill," Eden says.

"I've been obsessed with Arlo since the first time I saw him when we were touring his mansion for art class when he saved me. He told me to leave him alone, but of course, I couldn't do that. I snuck into his party, but he was expecting me to. After dinner, I followed him to his room where he was making out with three other women. I tried to join in. He locked me in his bathroom. He told me to leave him alone. I told him I couldn't and that I wanted to be in his debt like the other women. He locked me in a dungeon for the night and told me to forget about him. Then, he got naked in front of the whole class. I went after him. And he kissed me. Then, he gave a lecture that was directed at me to never be in his debt. And, now, he's here." I take a deep breath after not breathing through telling her everything.

Eden just stands there, staring at me.

"Well?" I ask.

"And the problem is?" she asks with a smile.

I narrow my eyes. "What do you mean, and the problem is? This guy is a bigger mess than I am. One second, he is pushing me away, and the next, he is going after me. You are supposed to give me advice. What should I do?"

Eden smiles. "I don't know. But it sounds to me like it's the beginning of some epic love affair."

"I'm only here for three more weeks. It can't be that epic."

"Sure it can."

"You still haven't told me what I'm supposed to do. I've been obsessing about him like I haven't any other man before. He's making me lose my mind."

"Maybe that's a good thing. All the other men you have obsessed about before weren't playing games with you. They were ordinary men. Arlo, on the other hand, has his own issues. I don't know what they are yet, but it's clear that he is just as messed up as you."

I frown.

"Stop frowning. He will never want you like that."

"So, what do I do?"

Eden laughs. "You already know the answer to that. You flirt with Erick. You make Arlo jealous. You play your game and let him come to you."

Someone pounds on the door.

"I gotta piss! Let me in, you assholes!" a man shouts.

Eden and I walk to the mirror where we fluff our hair and reapply lipstick. I take the jacket off that I've been wearing because there was no place to put it. But, now, I'm ready to turn the heat on.

The man knocks louder on the door.

Eden rolls her eyes at me. "Men and their small bladders."

We both walk over to the door, and Eden opens it. There are men standing outside, and their jaws drop when they see us.

"Restroom's yours, gentlemen," I say as we both strut out of the restroom.

I spot Arlo as we walk back to the center of the dance floor. His scowl deepens at the sight of me in a shirt that barely covers my breasts and is see-through enough that you can see the points of my nipples. I flip my hair from side to side and then blow Arlo a kiss, letting him know that I see him and I don't care what he thinks. He can either come and get me or I'm going to start flirting with every guy here.

Erick and Clive have returned with our drinks, and I take the margarita out of Erick's hand and down it.

I'm rewarded with shouts of excitement from both of the men.

"Dance with me!"

Erick starts dancing with me as Clive dances with Eden. I let Erick go further this time than I did the last time he was dancing with me. I let his hands touch all over the curves of my body as I move. Feeling every inch of me. His hands venture up higher to where my shirt is barely covering my chest.

He hesitates, and I grab his hands and push them onto the curves of my breasts.

Erick grins. "You're the hottest woman I've ever danced with!"

I give him a wicked grin and then shout into his ear as I look at Arlo still watching us, "I'm about to be the hottest woman you've slept with, too."

I pull away, and Erick's face lights up. But I don't care about him.

Arlo looks even angrier than before. I'm sure he has no idea what I just whispered into Erick's ear, but just the thought of me saying anything clearly pisses him off. It makes me want to take things even further.

I'm drunk and sexually frustrated and obsessed. It doesn't make for a very good combination.

I see a table toward the front of the dance floor, and I pull Erick toward it. He follows like a puppy trailing after his owner.

"Help me up!"

His eyes light up as he grabs my hips and boosts me up onto the table.

I start swaying my hips, and I dance wildly on top of the table. Everyone's eyes fall on me. I don't think about how this is breaking all the rules and that, at any second, an employee is going to come and ruin my fun. Instead, I just dance.

I'm handed a shot by one of the guys next to me, and I drink it without thinking, letting the tequila quickly slip down my throat, not even feeling the burn.

I wiggle my finger at Eden when she walks over, telling her to join me on the table.

She smiles and then is helped up by two men. We seductively dance together, turning on every man in the room. If Arlo can still resist me after this, then he has more discipline than I've given him credit for.

I don't see Arlo anymore, but Erick is definitely more than into me. His hands are all over me as I move.

I look down again, and I see Arlo standing in front of me. He doesn't look angry, just unpleased. I don't see any lust in his eyes, just a man on a mission. A man who is in complete control. I just wish I knew how to get him to give up that control.

He holds out his hand to me. "Get down," he says firmly without shouting.

I don't know how I hear him over the noise of the crowd and the music, but I do. I'm so connected to him that I just know what he is saying.

"Why should I?" I ask as I up my dancing, grinding all over Eden.

"Get down, Nina."

I grin with my eyes. "Only if you dance with me."

Arlo continues to hold his hand out to me.

I take it, and he leads me away from the table and over to the dance floor.

He starts dancing with me. His hands go to my hips, firmly holding me as we move together. He leads, and I have no choice but to follow. He's a good dancer without even trying. His moves are smooth and seductive without coming across as desperate, like when I was dancing with Erick.

We don't speak. We just dance. It's all I want to do all night. I just want to feel his strong hands on me, guiding me and promising that there is more to come.

I feel safe. I feel special. I feel cared for.

And, damn it, do I want Arlo to care for me all night long like he cared for me when he rescued me from the pool.

"Hey, man, she's my date," Erick says drunkenly to Arlo.

Arlo's frown returns, his shoulders stiffen, and his eyes look dangerous as he slows our dancing and gives Erick his attention. "Well, she's not yours anymore. She's mine. Go find another woman to try your slick come-on lines with," Arlo says.

My heart races in my chest. Arlo called me his. And, although I don't like the macho male need to claim me like a possession, I do like that he feels any claim over me. If I admit it to myself, I want to be Arlo's. I want to be his to fuck. His to tease. His to even love. I want it all.

But I can't let Arlo win that easily. Not after everything he put me through this last week.

"Excuse me," I say, pushing back out of Arlo's arms. "I am not yours any more than I am Erick's. I'll be deciding who I will dance with and who I will go home with tonight. You don't get to decide that."

Both men turn their attention to me. I can feel the anger pulsating off Arlo at the same time I can feel the testosterone and lust exuding off Erick. If I'm not careful, this night is going to end in a fight.

"You're not going home with Erick," Arlo says calmly.

"Oh, yeah? You don't get to control me. I'll go home with Erick if I want to," I say sassily.

Eden and her date walk over. "Wow, there is a lot of testosterone floating around right now."

I give her a look, and she shuts up, but it doesn't stop her from undressing Arlo with her eyes. I hate that she and half of the class got to see him naked earlier.

I dart my eyes back and forth between the two men. "I haven't decided who I want tonight. Maybe I want you both. But, for now, Erick, get me a drink while I finish dancing with Arlo. Then, it will be your turn."

Erick studies us both for a second but then slowly walks off to the bar to go get me a drink.

"Dance with me," I say to Arlo.

He doesn't.

"Dance with me," I say again.

"What are you doing, Nina?"

"I'm trying to dance with you."

He shakes his head and still stands firmly, refusing to dance with me. I watch as Eden dances with Clive next to us.

Why can't this be easy, like with Eden? Why can't I just dance with a guy and then go home and fuck him? Why does everything have to be so damn complicated?

"What are you doing with Erick? You aren't really going to go home with him. You aren't going to let him fuck you. So, what are you doing with him?" He cocks his head to one side. "Are you trying to make me jealous?"

I flip my hair over my shoulder and watch Arlo's eyes follow my every movement. He might have a lot more experience than me at playing calm, cool, and collected, but he's still a man. He still wants a hot woman like me when I'm dressed like this. He can't completely hide his urges.

"I'm either sleeping with you or Erick. I haven't decided yet."

His lip twitches just a little. "I'm not sleeping with you."

I grin and shrug. "Well, that makes my decision easy. Erick, it is."

I turn to go find Erick at the bar, but Arlo pulls me back to him.

"You aren't sleeping with Erick either. You're drunk. You and Eden just need to go home."

I laugh. "You don't think I've fucked men while drunk before? You told me to go find a nice Italian man to fuck while I'm here. Sure, Erick isn't Italian—he's English, I think—but he's hot, and he'll do for tonight."

"You aren't fucking him, Nina," Arlo says firmly.

I roll my eyes. "You aren't the boss of me. I can fuck whoever I want, whenever I want."

"No, you can't."

"Why not?"

He shakes his head.

"The better question is, what are you doing here? You like me, and you want me, don't you? That's why you are here. You can't stay away."

He pulls me closer to him. "No. I'm here because you need me. You'd get hurt if it wasn't for me."

I laugh. "The only danger I'm in is getting my brains fucked out by Erick."

"I'm here to protect you; that's it."

"I don't believe you. You kissed me. You want me."

His eyes widen for just a second, and then he says, "That was a mistake."

"I don't care what you say it was; it was the truth. You want me." I glance over to where Erick has my drink sitting on the bar. I turn back to Arlo. "But, if you aren't ready to admit that yet, then Erick, it is."

I walk over to Eden. "I'm going home with Erick. Stay safe," I say to her.

"I always do. You, too."

I nod and then start walking toward Erick, leaving Arlo alone on the dance floor. And then I see it. Erick slips something into my drink. I don't think he did it with any of my previous drinks. If he did, I don't feel anything, and it must not be very strong, but he definitely did it now.

I suck in a breath. Arlo was right. Erick is dangerous.

Still, I keep walking toward Erick as I try to decide what my next move will be.

"Why are you hanging out with a Carini?" Erick asks.

"I'm not. He approached me. I only know him from when he gave us a tour of his place and from the lecture tonight."

"You need to stay away from him, Nina. His whole family is considered royalty in this town but not for good reasons. They live above the law and do things that destroy anyone who owes them anything. Most are never seen again, and those that are go mad."

I frown as I take in the new information. "Don't worry; I won't ever owe Arlo anything."

Erick studies me, not sure if he believes me. But it doesn't matter if I'm telling the truth or not. Arlo has made it perfectly clear that I will never be in his debt. That he won't ever let me even when I should be.

"Does that mean you are choosing me over that asshole?"

I shrug. "Maybe."

Erick smiles and then picks up the two shot glasses of tequila. He hands me the glass that he slipped something into.

I take the glass out of his hand.

He raises his glass. "To choosing the right guy who is going to rock your world tonight."

I raise my glass to his, planning on just dumping the contents over my shoulder when he downs his drink.

"Nina!" Arlo shouts at me over the crowd.

I turn and look at him trying to work his way through the crowd that is thick, making it impossible for him to quickly get to me.

"Don't!" he half-commands and half-begs.

I look back to Erick whose smile is faltering and then back to Arlo. Arlo knows. He saw Erick slip something into my drink. He knows that, if I drink this shot, I'm going to be drugged with God-knows-what substance that I'm sure will give Erick complete control over me.

I absolutely should not drink this shot. I'm not going to drink this shot.

But I like seeing the worry in Arlo's eyes. He cares about me. I don't know exactly what other feelings he has for me, but I know one thing. Arlo doesn't want me to get hurt. He won't let me get hurt. He proved that the first time he saved me.

If I take this shot, he'll protect me. He'll save me.

My heart beats wildly in my chest as the plan forms in my head. If I drink it, Erick will try to drag me away before Arlo can get to me. But Arlo is only twenty feet away. He can get to us before anything bad happens to me.

And, if Arlo saves me, then I will owe him. I'll be in his debt, and I'll finally get to repay him with sex and find out the truth behind all the mysterious whispers about his family that the townspeople talk about.

I'll get exactly what I want.

Only one question remains. If I drink this, will Arlo actually save me?

I study everything about him. The way he is pushing people out of the way in an uncontrollable and savage way to get to me faster. The tightness of his jaw as he focuses on stopping me. The desperation in his eyes as he inches closer to me. But the one thing that convinces me above everything is the emotion and pain dripping off his voice when he yelled for me.

I could be wrong. I could drink this, and Arlo might not give a shit about me. He could let Erick do whatever he wanted to me. If I drink this, Erick could rape me. He could kill me.

"Don't, Nina!" Arlo shouts again, begging me with everything that he has for me not to do this. *Please*, he mouths.

I suck in a breath. Arlo will save me.

This is the most reckless thing I've ever done. I've been obsessed with countless men, but I've never risked my life for a man on quite this level before.

But I do it anyway.

I throw the shot back in my throat while I look Arlo dead in the eyes and plead for him to save me.

8

NINA

I OPEN MY EYES, but it still feels like I'm asleep. It's dark. The pitch black kind. In-the-middle-of-the-night, in-the-middle-of-nowhere dark.

I try to sit up, but I immediately fall back down onto the dirt floor. The pain in my head is dizzying. I've never felt anything like it before. I grab my head with both hands, trying to remember what happened that made me feel this bad.

It's all a haze. I remember Eden. I remember strange boys. I remember dancing. And Arlo. There was something important that happened with Arlo.

Pain. It's all I feel right now, making it impossible to sort out everything floating around in my head.

My head is pounding. My whole body aches. My stomach is queasy.

I'm naked. I don't have any clothing. Not my bra, not my panties, not an oversize shirt to cover me. There is just nothing.

I was raped.

It all comes flooding back to me. I took the shot. I passed out. Erick raped me. Arlo didn't save me. I made a gigantic mistake. And, now, I just have to hope that I can escape before he kills me.

I push through the pounding in my head and the ache all over my body and manage to sit up. It's incredibly dark, and I have no idea where the door is to make my escape. It doesn't help that my head is spinning the longer I sit up.

"Drink." A cup is thrust in front of me, seemingly out of nowhere.

I'm not going to be drugged again. I'm not going to let him rape me again. Not so easily. Not without a fight.

I push the cup away and force myself up. I start running in the opposite direction of the cup. There has to be an exit somewhere.

"Nina, stop," I hear Arlo's voice command.

I stop.

My heart stops beating. I stop breathing.

I wasn't raped. At least, not by Erick.

I turn slowly and can faintly make out Arlo walking toward me with a cup in his hand.

"It's just water. Drink. It will make your head stop aching."

I take the cup out of his hand and drink until every last drop of water is gone.

"Sit down."

I slowly sit back down on the dirt ground. I lean against the cold stone wall for support. Arlo does the same, sitting down next to me.

"Where's Eden?"

"She's safe. My driver took her home."

I take a deep breath and let my shoulders relax. I believe him when he says that she is safe. She's the only person in my world that matters. I can't lose her.

"Why am I naked?" I ask.

"You don't get to ask any stupid questions. Not after what you did last night."

Instant anger overtakes any rational thoughts. "I sure as hell get to ask any damn question that I want! You got me into this fucking mess! If it wasn't for you, I would never have taken any drugs."

"I got you into this mess? You have got to be fucking kidding me! I told you not to drink it. You didn't listen to me. You disobeyed me."

"I'm not an idiot! I knew that he'd spiked the drink with something."

"Then, why did you drink it? That sounds pretty idiotic to me!"

"I wasn't going to drink it. I was just going to make him think I did. But then you had to get all bossy and demanding, showing that you cared about me."

"You think I care about you?" He laughs. "Oh, man, Nina. Your worldview is definitely wrong. I don't care about you. But acting like royalty in this town has its disadvantages. I couldn't have a club full of people see you get drugged and disappear with a man without me interfering and saving you. One of the main reasons my family maintains so much power in this town is because we protect the town. Sorry that I was desperate not to have to spend my whole night fighting to keep you safe from some loser."

"Erick didn't rape me?"

"Of course he didn't rape you."

I clear my throat and then whisper, "Did you rape me?"

He laughs.

"It's not funny. Did you rape me?"

He continues laughing, like it's the funniest thing he's ever heard. "No, Nina, I didn't rape you. I don't have to. You were willing to risk your life to try to get me to notice you. You've practically thrown yourself at me every chance you've gotten. I don't need to rape you in order to have my way with you."

"Then, why am I naked?"

Arlo sighs. "Because you threw up on yourself countless times as the drugs took effect and were leaving your system. I thought it would be easier to hose you down if you were naked."

I frown. "You could have left my underwear on."

He rolls his eyes. "I could have. But then what enjoyment would that have brought me? I thought it was my reward—to finally see you naked after saving your life and taking care of you all night."

"I'm in your debt now," I say with a small smile on my face.

"I want to wipe that damn smile off your face. You could have died last night, Nina. You did die last night. I had to perform CPR at one point because you weren't breathing on your own. Whatever that asshole Erick gave you was strong shit. You would have died if it wasn't for me."

"But you did save me."

He runs his hand through his hair. "I've never met a woman so frustrating as you, Nina. I want to punish you so that you will never do something so stupid again in your life, but I'm not convinced you will learn your lesson."

The pain in my head is gone. My body is flush and warm with thoughts of Arlo. I have to have him. And I don't care what words he says. He cares about me. He can lie to himself all he wants.

"Punish me."

"Be careful what you ask for, Nina."

"Fuck me. Punish me. Then, fuck me again. You know you want to."

He growls, "You don't get to make decisions anymore, Nina. You make shitty decisions."

"Then, you decide. Am I in your debt or not?"

His eyes glow bright with anger.

A second later, I feel the full force of his anger as he pushes me onto the dirty ground, face-first, his body crushing me.

"You fucked up, Nina. Today is the last time you will ever fuck up like this. Do you understand?"

I can't answer him. He's squishing my lungs too much for me to be able to breathe, let alone answer him.

"Answer me!"

"Yes," I croak out as I struggle to breathe.

"You will do exactly what I say, Nina. You will not hesitate. I'm going to punish you. I'm going to fuck you. I'm going to control you like I couldn't last night. And, if you don't obey me, you will only be punished harder. Understand?"

"Yes," I breathe out, exhaling what feels like the last amount of breath in my body.

Scathing pain. That's all I can think about. He slapped me hard on the ass as I answered, and I feel the tears already stinging my eyes.

I've been fucked by dozens of men. Most were boring men who wanted meaningful, monotonous sex. Some would occasionally slap me on the ass. But none have ever brought anything close to the pain that Arlo just gave me.

He slaps my ass again, and I try to cry but can't from his crushing weight.

He strikes me again, and the tears that were simply falling before are rolling down my cheeks in waves.

"You will never disobey me again, Nina. You will never forget tonight."

He hits me one more time before rolling me over. The sting of the dirt hitting my raw ass makes me cry again.

Arlo's hand sinks between my legs, furiously rubbing me. "You're so wet. You liked that, didn't you? You can't even get punished properly. You like it too much."

I moan as he moves my wetness over my folds.

He's right. The pain was intense, but it turned me on. I like being punished. I like being controlled. *What's wrong with me?*

His hand moves from my folds and to his button and zipper on his slacks.

I watch with wide eyes as he slowly undoes the button and zipper until his cock springs free from his slacks and briefs.

It's just as long and thick as I remember it being when I attempted to paint it and failed miserably.

My hands reach out to touch it, to feel how hard and big it really is, but he grabs my hands and forces them above my head.

"You don't get to do anything without my permission. You don't get to touch. You don't get to speak. You don't get to move."

My eyes grow so wide that I'm afraid they are going to pop out of my head. *How am I supposed to ask permission if I can't even speak?*

I nod though. It feels safer than speaking.

He continues to hold my hands high above my head while he moves his cock until it is resting on my lips. I don't move. I try not to even breathe on him even though I'm desperate to take his dick in my mouth. I must taste it.

I don't. I just look up at him with big eyes.

"Suck me."

Finally.

I open my mouth, and his cock instantly fills me. He tastes as good as he looks. And, when his eyes roll back in his head as I run my tongue over the tip, I can't help but feel good. He might think he has all the control, but the second he surrendered his cock to me was the second that I gained a little of that control back.

"Suck all of me."

I lift my head up off the ground, trying to get all of him into my mouth. I've never tried fitting a man fully into my mouth before, but then again, I've never wanted to or been asked to.

I move his cock deeper into my mouth until I start gagging.

He shakes his head and grabs the back of my head. "Take all of me."

He pushes my head up onto his cock until I'm gagging again, and tears are streaming down my face.

"Relax."

I do, and he slides in a little bit further. And the look on his face is like nothing I've ever seen before. He's lost all control to me now that I have all of him in my throat. I get braver and start pumping faster with my mouth. I move until he is almost fully out of my mouth and then take him all the way in again, holding his cock there until I can't take it any longer.

"Fuck, Nina!" Arlo growls.

I take him all the way in again, and I feel the warm, salty liquid pouring down my throat. I stay relaxed so that I don't choke as Arlo keeps his cock deep in my throat until he has finished spilling inside of me.

"Good girl," he says as he removes his cock.

I cough a little, but I'm desperate to do it again. I've never been so turned on. I've never felt so in control or dirty.

I stare down at the clothes that Arlo is still wearing. I want him naked.

One of my hands slips out of his grasp and grabs at his shirt.

He seizes it almost instantly and thrusts it back over my head. "You don't learn, do you, Nina?"

I grin. "Maybe you need to teach me another lesson."

"No. I already taught you one lesson for today. It's not my fault you don't listen."

He keeps my hands high over my head as he tightens his grip on my wrists, not letting me disobey him again.

"Spread your legs."

I do.

I feel his cock move to my entrance that is soaking and begging for him to fuck me.

"I shouldn't fuck you, Nina. It's what you want."

I pout and moan a little as I ache, waiting to see if he is actually going to fuck me or not.

His thumb glides over my clit, making me purr, as he teases me while he decides what he's going to do.

"You haven't learned your lesson, have you? You would still risk your life in order to get me to fuck you?"

I nod. "Please," I whisper.

He shakes his head, and then he plunges inside me.

I exhale a groan I was holding in as he pushes me open wide.

He doesn't take his time. He moves fast, expertly filling every inch of me while also making me feel incredibly good. I can't take it. It's too much and not enough at the same time.

The sex is amazing. My hands are held high above my head as he fucks me on the dirty floor, like the slut that I am.

But I want more.

His head bends down, and he roughly takes my nipple into his mouth, giving me the *more* that I crave as he fucks me.

I don't know if it is the fact that I risked my life to have sex with him, the drug, or the anticipation of finally fucking him, but everything that I have becomes lost in him as he fucks me. I've never been so into a man before. I've never been so fully lost. Never this obsessed.

But, now that I've had him, I'm not sure how I can ever not have him again.

"Kiss me," I whisper.

He releases my nipple and moves his lips over mine as he slows his thrusts inside me. All I have to do to feel his lips on mine again is move up an inch. But I want him to kiss me. Claim me fully.

"No," he says.

Then, his lips are gone, and he's thrusting so hard that I can't think about the fact that he's not kissing me. All I can do is try to hang on while he takes me to a place that I didn't know was possible to reach.

He spills inside me, not waiting for me to come, but his cum filling me combined with the deep growls leaving his throat are enough to make me come. When I do come, I lose it. I lose everything I was holding on to, and I just feel.

I feel the pain and the intense pleasure. Sex with Arlo is everything I ever imagined and more. It's a ride I never want to get off of.

But, before I even have a chance to come down off my high, he slips out of me and is gone, leaving me alone on the floor of the same dungeon he left me alone in before. Dirty and spent and naked.

I take a deep breath as I lay motionless on the floor, and a slow smile creeps over my face. It was worth it. It was all worth it.

Shit. We didn't use a condom. I'm on birth control, but still, that was risky. And exciting. And I want more.

A second later, his hands grab at my wrists again, and I'm being pulled along the dirt floor, hitting every rock, stinging my ass.

I don't know if I have the energy to go again, but I want to. More than anything, I want him to fuck me again.

He stops and releases me. "Stand up."

It takes everything that I have, but I stand up and stare into his dark eyes.

He grabs one of my wrists again and places a cold metal shackle on it. Then, he does the same to the other. I bite my lip as I try to anticipate what he's going to do next. I try not to show how giddy I am, but I'm also exhausted.

I test the shackles once he has them on, and once he attaches them, I know I won't be able to get free. He will have full control over me. And it excites me and terrifies me at the same time.

He begins to attach a chain to both of the shackles without saying a word to me or looking me in the eye. And then, without warning, he pulls hard on the chain.

I begin falling as my arms are pulled forward and downward in front of me.

I can't catch my fall with my arms, but instead of landing on the dirt below me, my face and chest land on something hard a few feet off the ground.

My arms are tied to a pole at one end of an apparatus while my face and breasts are smashed against a wooden apparatus below me.

Arlo moves to my back. "Spread your legs."

I do, barely able to touch the ground. I feel another cold shackle go around each ankle, and then Arlo spreads my legs to my limit.

"Arch your back."

I do the best I can, and my ass is thrust into the air.

He slaps it again. I was expecting it, but the sting still hurts after all the hits before.

"I love you like this. So helpless and spread wide, just for me."

He's right. I'm completely helpless, and I'm afraid I love it just as much as he does.

I take a deep breath as I wait for what he is going to do next.

"I have to taste you first."

I feel his tongue on my folds as he buries his face in my ass. His tongue darts in and out of my pussy, alternating with licking my clit. As I'm stretched wide for him, I'm so close to coming, it's ridiculous.

"You don't get to come without my permission."

I clench my teeth, trying my best to keep from coming, while his tongue continually dances over my clit. I squeeze my hands into fists and curl my toes, but it can't stop the inevitable.

I come.

Hard.

And uncontrollably.

I scream, "Arlo!"

He smacks my ass harder than he ever has, and tears immediately sting my eyes again.

"I told you not to come. You have a lot to learn, Nina."

And then, before I can breathe, his cock slides into my ass without warning. He fucks me hard and fast in the ass—a place I've never been fucked before. He's ruthless in his thrusts, not caring how hard it is for me to keep up with him.

I try to hold on as best as I can as he thrusts inside me, but I can't.

The intensity is too much. I'm tied too tightly. I'm just here for the ride.

So, I let go, and when I do, I feel myself inching closer to that blissful feeling he gave me earlier. The feeling that I will never get enough of.

"Come, Nina."

I come.

He comes.

And I will never be the same.

He pulls out and then slowly unlocks the shackles on my ankles before moving and undoing the shackles on my wrists.

I can't move even though I'm free.

I have no energy, no ability to move.

I feel Arlo's arms go around me, and he scoops me up into his arms. He carefully places me down on the floor, leaning against the cold wall. He leans down and firmly kisses me on the lips, claiming me with his mouth.

And then he returns to the darkness while I sit, confused at what just happened.

He returns a few minutes later and throws my clothes to me. "You can get dressed now."

I'm surprised that he didn't command me like he had for the last hour that we'd been having sex.

I slowly begin putting my clothes on, starting with my panties and jeans. I have to stand to put them on, and when I do, I come face-to-face with Arlo again. It's an intimate moment, coming face-to-face with a man who has just changed everything I knew about having sex with men.

"Did I just repay my debt, or do we get to do that again?" I ask as my cheeks flush. *Please tell me we get to do that again and again and again.*

He frowns. "You don't get it, do you? You aren't even close to repaying your debt. I saved your life. Now, you have to pay the ultimate price for me giving the ultimate sacrifice. You have to pay me back with your life."

I narrow my eyes, not understanding. "Didn't you just punch Erick or something and then scoop me up and bring me here?"

He laughs. "You have no idea what I had to do to get you here."

"So, I have to pay you back with my life? What does that mean?"

"You are mine to do what I want with."

"Until?"

He shrugs. "Your death."

I shake my head. "So, what? You are going to hold me captive here and force me to do all sorts of things against my will? That's illegal."

He laughs. "It doesn't matter what is legal or not. I own this town and most of the country. No one cares what my family or I do as long as we keep pumping money into the towns and protect them. Then, they look the other way to what we do in our spare time or how we make our money."

"I'm not scared of you."

"You should be."

"I'm not," I say, but my voice falters.

"I'm not the only one you should be afraid of. When you are in my debt, you are in my entire family's debt. My sister is not as sweet as she looks. My father is more controlling than you could ever imagine. And my brother doesn't have the same charm that I do."

"You have a brother?"

"Yes."

I don't know why I didn't know that before, but it doesn't matter now. He'll rape me or make me do unthinkable things, the same as Arlo. The difference is, I want Arlo to do those things to me. His brother, not so much.

"So, what? They will all rape me? Make me have sex with them?"

"My father and brother probably will. My sister will find other ways to torture you and make you pay us back for going through the trouble of saving you. Trust me, it was a family effort to save you. I couldn't have done it on my own. As much as you think I'm some type of superman who can save you from anything, I'm not, and I can't. I'm human. The same as you."

I wrap my arms across my bare chest. I still haven't bothered to put my shirt back on.

"I warned you to stay away. Several times. But you couldn't resist. And, now, you will pay the price. You have just entered a world that you couldn't even imagine. A world where the men in my family will fight over you. The women will punish you. We will all make you love us and hate us at the same time until it drives you mad. We will play games with your mind, heart, and soul. We are twisted, dirty people who have learned to control people in the only way we know how. By putting you in our debt. Then, we can do whatever we want."

"I don't believe you. I've met your sister. She's nice. You aren't even as evil as you seem."

He shakes his head. "Then, you're naive. You thought Erick was bad. We are worse. We'll rape you and threaten to kill you; one of us might even follow through on that threat. We control you. You are our plaything, Nina. A game to entertain us when we are bored. A game that you won't even understand the rules of until you have already lost. You've just entered a dirty, dark world without any escape."

His words are twisted and wrong. Nothing makes sense. I don't know how a family could get away with raping and murdering for years without getting prosecuted. I don't even know if what he is saying is true or if he is just messing with me.

I'm scared.

Just enough to not want to be here anymore. He's scared me enough to believe that at least part of it is true.

If his brother or father is anything like him, then they will try to control me. Rape me if they want. And I won't let them.

I run.

Through the darkness, not even fully dressed, I run. I get to the door and throw it open shocked that is isn't locked and run out into the sunlight. To freedom. But I still hear his threat ringing in my ear behind me.

"Run, Nina! Don't ever stop running! We love the chase. Don't ever stop running. Because, when you do, we will own you. Forever."

9

ARLO

"WE'VE FOUND HER. Our number seven," my brother says, stepping out of the shadows.

I nod, staring at the empty black hole stretched in front of me, while Nina runs away from me. I did everything I could to keep her safe. Everything I could to scare her into running and hiding, but it won't be enough. I have to find another way to save her. She may be in debt to my family, but I'm in her debt too. She's already saved my life, even though she doesn't realize it yet. I will spend my own life paying her back. Protecting her. Caring for her. And doing everything I can to not fall in love with her. She deserves better than the love of a monster.

"She will make the perfect end to our twisted game," he says.

"I doubt we will make it that far, Matteo. I might win the first four rounds, and then the game will stop," I say.

Matteo walks over and turns the lights on while he laughs. "You know that will never happen. The family is split on who they want to win. It will come down to Nina."

I frown as I stare at my twin brother, who is a spitting image of me. Even our own family has a hard time telling us apart. I've played games against him my entire life, but the stakes have never been this high.

I have to win before it gets to Nina. It's the only way to keep her from the truth. It's the only way to protect her.

She's mine. Not his. I will do whatever it takes to make that true.

DIRTY OBSESSION

1

NINA

SEVEN YEARS IS a long time to live in fear. It's an even longer time to exist without really being alive.

But it's what I've been doing for most of the seven years since I fled Italy and the Carini family. I've been running, afraid. Never staying in one place too long.

Today is the day I stop running.

Today, I start living for the first time in seven years.

Knock, knock, knock.

I grin as I get up from the balcony chair of my hotel room that overlooks the ocean and walk toward the door. I've been waiting to hear that knock for the last half hour. When I get to the door, I don't unlock it right away. Instead, I look through the peephole to verify that my best friend, Eden, is on the other side and hasn't been followed by anyone.

She's alone.

I take a deep breath and slide the chain over on the top of the door. Then, I slowly undo the deadbolt. It's a habit I've developed these last few years. My door is always locked, and I always check who is behind the door before I unlock it.

I open the door, and my face lights up as Eden steps into my hotel room. We automatically hug each other.

She raises an eyebrow when she pulls away. "What is going on? I get a cryptic text message after over a year of not hearing from you, and a plane ticket suddenly appears at my office."

I cringe. "Do you want a drink first?"

"Do you even have to ask?" she says as she rolls her suitcase into the hotel suite.

"Margarita okay? Or do you want something else?"

"If it has alcohol in it, then it's a yes," she says, still eyeing me as I walk to the kitchenette to get the premade margarita mix out of the mini fridge.

Eden's dressed in a suit. Dark navy pants paired with a light-blue jacket. Her hair is up in a perfect bun. She looks like a lawyer. Not at all like the Eden I used to know.

She must think I'm a slob who doesn't even have a job from the way I'm dressed. I glance down at my gray sweatpants that have a hole in the right knee. I'm wearing a black tank top, and my hair is up in a messy bun.

She must think I'm in danger. That I'm desperate, and she's going to have to give me money to bail me out of my troubles.

I wish my life were that simple. I wish that money were all it would take to fix all my problems.

I pour each of us a margarita into the two glasses.

Eden watches every movement I make. Judging me, trying to figure out what is going on. I hand her one of the glasses.

"Want to sit out on the balcony with me?"

She chuckles. "No, I want to know what the hell I'm doing here, Nina. But, if you want to sit out on the balcony, then I will go out there with you."

"I'm getting married. Today."

As the last word leaves my mouth, Eden's eyes widen, and she drops her glass.

My eyes fall with the glass as it hits the floor and breaks into pieces, spilling sticky lime margarita mix all over the hard carpet.

I find the small trash can in the corner of the room and pick it up. Then, I carry it over to where the broken glass is on the floor. I bend down and begin putting the pieces into the trash can, just needing something to do while Eden deals with the shock of what I just told her.

She slowly bends down and grabs my hand before I can pick up another piece.

"What do you mean, you are getting married? You didn't even have a boyfriend the last time I talked to you a year ago. How could you be getting married? I haven't even met the man! I mean...this is just crazy. Who summons their best friend to a hotel room and then tells them they are getting married?" Eden stands and starts pacing as she continues to ramble nonsense, trying to make sense of me.

I pick up the last piece of broken glass, leaving behind the margarita goop on the floor as I stand up.

"Sit outside with me. The ocean air will calm you down. I'll answer all of your questions then," I say, walking outside, hoping that Eden is going to follow me.

I take a deep breath when the air hits my face. I should move to the beach. I'd have a lot less anxiety if I lived here.

Eden takes her time in coming outside. We both stand, leaning against the railing, as we look out at the view of the ocean.

"This is better, isn't it?"

Eden looks at me seriously. "No, it isn't. Now, spill, Young."

I sigh. "I'm eloping. I'm tired of running, Eden. I need a fresh start. I need to fight. I need to live again."

"You should stop running. I told you, you were crazy for running in the first place. Arlo wasn't going to fly thousands of miles to come after a woman he slept with one time. I don't care that he saved your life. Anyone who does anything like that is just crazy."

"Arlo's crazy."

Eden shakes her head. "No, he isn't. He scared you. He messed with your head because he knew that you were easy to mess with. He knew that you had obsessive tendencies and that you would fall for it. That's it. Arlo Carini is not coming after you. He isn't going to *kidnap* you. He isn't going to hold you *captive*. And he definitely isn't going to *kill* you."

I nod. I don't believe her, but there is no reason to worry her.

"I know. That's why I'm going to start living now instead of running."

"Good. But why are you getting married? Do you even know the guy you are marrying, or is this just another one of your obsessions?"

"Of course I know the guy! Geesh, Eden, who do you think I am?"

Eden takes my hands and turns me to look at her. "You are my best friend. I love you, and I would do anything for you. But you're also a little messed up. You're obsessive. You grew up without a mother. You watched your father die a slow, torturous death. You're fucked up, Nina, and I just want to protect you as much as I can."

I laugh to keep from crying. "You know me so well."

"I want to know what the hell you are doing, getting married, Nina."

"I love him. Isn't that a good enough reason?"

"For normal people, yes. For you, no."

I sigh and then slump into one of the two plastic chairs outside.

Eden takes a seat in the other. "Who is this guy, Nina?"

"His name is Heath. He's an artist. He's tall, blond, and handsome. He understands me. He knows that I have obsessive tendencies, and he loves me anyway. The sex is amazing. And he wants to spend the rest of his life with me. He wants to marry me. We are going to travel the world together."

"Why haven't I met this wonderful Heath before?"

"Because I was scared. I was running. I didn't want Arlo to find out."

"I don't believe you. When did you and Heath meet?"

"We met at an art gallery. We both loved the same painting. It was the first time I'd been to an art gallery in years. It was like a sign from the universe that we were meant to be together."

"Stop stalling, Nina. I don't care where you met. I want to know *when*. How long have you and Heath been together?"

I should lie. But Eden always knows when I'm lying.

"We met six days ago."

Eden doesn't even react. She knew. Somehow, she knew that Heath and I hadn't been together for very long.

"You aren't getting married today, Nina."

"You're not my mother, Eden. You don't get to tell me what to do."

"Yes, I do. I get to tell you what to do when you are being crazy!"

"I'm not acting crazy. People elope all the time. What's the worst that could happen anyway? A couple of years down the road, we will get divorced. At least we can be happy and do something spontaneous now."

Eden shakes her head. "Divorce isn't as easy as you think it is. It's messy. You have to divide everything. Fight over everything. Money, possessions, pets. Not to mention, if you decide to have a baby together because you are married. Marriage is meant for people who love each other and know each other well enough to at least know things like how he takes his coffee, where he grew up, and who his family is."

I frown. "Those things don't matter. I love him."

"No. You are obsessed with him. There's a difference."

"I just met him. Give him a chance. I'm getting married no matter what, and I'd love it if my best friend in the whole world was there."

Eden rolls her eyes. "Fine. But you can't use the best-friend thing as a reason ever again."

I smile. "Deal."

———

I take Eden to meet Heath by the pool at the hotel. When I point him out to her, her mouth drops.

"If you aren't going to marry him, I am," Eden says.

I smile. "Nope. He's taken," I say as we both ogle Heath as he swims toward us.

He flips his shoulder-length blonde hair back as he climbs out of the pool and starts walking toward us, revealing every ripple of his abs and hard muscles of his biceps.

"How old is he?" Eden asks.

"Twenty-five."

Eden raises an eyebrow as she looks at me.

"Okay, fine. He's twenty-one," I say, throwing my hands up like I give up. "But look at him! He's gorgeous. He doesn't act twenty-one. He's a man through and through. Trust me."

Eden laughs. "You don't know him well enough outside of the bedroom to know."

I grin. "Well, he's definitely a man in the bedroom, so that's all that matters."

Eden's face scrunches up as she judges me for marrying a man eight years younger than me.

"Just talk to him. He's perfect for me."

"I'm here. I'll talk to him. But I'm never going to think that marrying him is a good idea. It can't lead to anything but heartache."

Heath stops in front of us, dripping wet. He sweeps me into his arms and kisses me, getting me soaked in all the right places.

When he's done kissing me, he turns his attention to Eden. "You must be Nina's best friend, Eden. I've heard a lot about you. I know you think this is crazy, and it is. But just know, I will never do anything to hurt Nina. I love her too much to ever hurt her. I promise that, no matter what happens, I will always protect her, just as you would."

He pulls Eden into a wet hug even though she is still wearing her expensive suit, which I'm going to have to ask about later.

Eden looks to me as Heath hugs her. "Okay, I approve."

My face lights up, and I wrap my arms around both of them.

"I still think you are both crazy, but if I've learned anything from my years with Nina, it's not to fight when she gets a harebrained idea. She's going to do it anyway, so I might as well go along for the crazy ride."

Eden pulls away from our group hug, so it's just Heath wrapping his arms around my shoulders.

"But, if you hurt her or don't do everything possible to protect her, I will come after you, Heath. You will be a dead man. You understand?"

Heath smiles and looks down at me. "I'll protect her, no matter who or what comes after her."

I can breathe a little easier for the first time in seven years. Because I'm no longer running alone. Now, I have a partner I love, who will fight with me, no matter what happens. I have someone on my side, and I plan on fighting anyone who stands in our way.

2

ARLO

I'VE WAITED seven long years for this. At the same time, I've fought for seven years to keep this from happening. I wasn't strong enough. I lost the first round. But I won't lose again. I can't.

"Can I trust you to bring her back here safely?" Matteo asks.

I feel my anger boiling already, and I haven't even left yet. I just have to focus on what the end of this year is going to bring. I'm going to finally have what is mine. What I was destined to have. I won't have to fight anymore.

"Yes," I snap, not able to keep the anger out of my voice.

Matteo laughs. "This is going to be fun, isn't it?"

I glare at him.

"Do you think this is a joke, Matteo?" our father, Enrico Carini, says.

"No, I think it's funny though. I want this just as badly as Arlo does. Just because I don't mope with the same intensity that he does, it doesn't mean that I'm not taking this seriously."

Our father nods. "Good."

Miami.

I was on a plane for ten hours to get to her. And, of all the wonderful places in the US where she could be—New York, LA, Seattle, Rockport—she had to choose the hottest damn place in the country in the summertime.

I started sweating profusely the second I got off the plane in my dark suit. And I haven't stopped since.

If she wanted to get married on a beach, she should have gone to Italy or Greece; both are beautiful this time of year. Not Miami.

I should have gone and gotten her when she was hiding in Boston. It's not my favorite US city, but at least it isn't as hot as Miami.

I walk over to the front desk in the hotel where Nina is staying. It's adequate but not nice enough for a wedding.

"Excuse me, where is the Young and West wedding taking place today?" I ask the young woman standing behind the desk.

She stares at me for far longer than she should. I'm used to women devouring me with their eyes. I'm used to the awkwardness that follows. But I don't have time to deal with this woman today.

"The wedding?" I ask again, demanding her to answer me.

She swallows hard, trying to push down her embarrassment. "Um... let me see here. Um...are you one of the guests?"

My patience immediately vanishes. "Yes," I hiss.

The woman tries to force a smile on her face. "It's out on the terrace at one thirty P.M."

I frown. "Not on the beach?"

She looks at her computer screen again. "Uh...nope, it says the terrace."

I turn and walk away from the woman without a thank-you. I hate people who are incompetent at their jobs. No, I hate all people. I hate being in crowds. I hate dealing with people's stupid problems. I just want to be left alone.

I glance at my watch. It's one twenty. I head in the direction of the terrace, planning on just slipping into the crowd of wedding well-wishers and guests. But, as I approach the terrace, there is no one on site.

I get to the door that leads outside where a hotel worker is standing.

"This is reserved for a private wedding. The terrace will be available again in about thirty minutes," the friendly woman says.

I glance around her and see no guests or seats set up for guests. Just a simple arch with flowers on the green grass and the ocean far in the distance.

I nod and keep walking past. Nina isn't getting married; she's eloping. Like getting married at all is going to protect her.

I turn right and then start walking up the stairs to one of the guest rooms that seems to overlook the terrace. I knock on the first door, and a man comes out.

"Yes?" he asks.

"Sorry, wrong room," I say, walking past him and to the next door.

I knock again.

No answer.

I try one more time, and then I pop the door open. These old hotel rooms are far too easy to break into. It's one of the reasons I never stay at places like this.

I walk into the hotel room; it has suitcases and clothes thrown all over the floor.

I sigh. I picked the messiest room in the hotel, I'm sure. But I don't care. I walk to the balcony, open the sliding door, and step outside.

When I glance down, I see two men standing under the arch. One is the officiant, and the other looks to be about eighteen, maybe twenty.

I try to think back to everything I know about Nina. She doesn't have a brother or a cousin as far as I know. She has no family left.

I have no idea who this douchebag is.

I glance at the door leading out to the terrace, waiting for the groom to finally make his appearance so that I can see just what type of man Nina has picked to marry—not that she's allowed to make such decisions for her life anymore.

Instead of the groom though, Eden walks out. She looks nice, as she always does, in a simple black dress. Not really appropriate clothing for a wedding. It looks like she is going to a funeral or business meeting instead of a wedding.

I turn my gaze back to the door just in time to see Nina walking through.

My heart stops. My chest aches. My whole body hardens at the sight of her.

She's beautiful. I forgot how beautiful she truly is. Her hair is a little longer than it was seven years ago. Her skin is a little tanner, like she has recently been spending plenty of time on the beach. She has a bit of a glow around her body as she walks.

She looks better than I remember. And the lace dress she is wearing makes it even harder for me to stay up here instead of jumping off the balcony to claim her now.

I grab on to the railing of the balcony, forcing myself to stay here. To watch her marry another man. It will make it so much better to take her from him. She will fight harder to get back to him.

Nina stops when she reaches the arch. Eden softly kisses her on the cheek before she takes the flowers out of Nina's hands.

Nina turns and holds on to the boy's hands as she looks him in the eyes.

I laugh. A full-on belly laugh that is completely uncontrollable. She can't be serious. She's marrying a boy that looks like a teenager. I thought she was smarter than this.

She's desperate. She must be if she is willing to elope with a man that has to be almost ten years younger than her.

The boy starts talking, and I assume they are saying their vows to each other. I can't hear a damn thing from up here though.

The boy stops talking, and it seems it's Nina's turn. She opens her mouth and then stops. She glances up, and I know she sees me. Her entire gaze focuses on me. Her eyes turn to fire as she looks at me, and then she smiles. She knew I would be here. She was expecting me to be here. This is her trying to take control back.

She grins with her perfect red lips and then turns back to the boy. She says, "I do," slowly and deliberately, making sure that I can read her lips and know exactly what she said. That, even though she knows

I'm here, she is still willing to marry a boy she barely knows rather than be taken by me.

She's going to fight. I know that. She's not like the others who were much more willing to go along with our games as long as it meant getting to fuck some of the hottest and wealthiest men in the world. Nina is going to fight for her life.

My cock is rock hard as I think about her fighting me while I fuck her. Last time we were together was fantastic, but she didn't fight. She enjoyed how dirty I fucked her. This time though, she is going to fight back, and I can't fucking wait.

Nina glances back up at me again with a sly smile on her face before she lets the boy kiss her. She thinks it is going to make me mad to see her kissing someone else. Maybe it would piss me off a bit if she were kissing someone I actually saw as a threat. But I doubt it.

I wanted her to get married. I wanted her to move on with her life before I came for her. It'll make it all the more enjoyable for me when I rip her from him.

Eden whoops and hollers when the officiant pronounces them husband and wife, and then her groom sweeps her off her feet and leads her down to the beach and into the ocean.

I shake my head, watching him. He's such a kid. No woman wants to be dunked in the ocean after getting married. I'm sure plenty of *girls* might enjoy that. Nina might have even enjoyed that seven years ago. But she is all woman now, and I can see behind her eyes and fake smile that she doesn't want a boy to play with. She wants a man to protect her.

Too bad she couldn't find one in time.

I hear the door to the hotel room open as I walk back inside.

"Who are you?" a man asks as he stands next to who I assume is his girlfriend. He doesn't bother to protect her at all from me. He just stands there, confused as to why I'm in his room.

I walk past them. "You should have your door lock looked at. Otherwise, anyone could get in here."

———

I wait until dark to find her again.

I give her a few hours with her new husband to realize what a mistake she just made. And to think about me.

I wanted to give her time to obsess. To try to formulate a plan and realize that there is nothing she can do to prevent me from getting to her. That, by the end of the night, she is going to be *mine*, not *his*. And that she is going to be the one who chooses me over him. She will have no one to blame but herself.

I walk down to the main dance club near the hotel. I know that is where Nina and her boy toy went. I know they want to celebrate their newfound love. And that is the only place nearby where they could go.

It's not a smart move. It makes it far too easy for me to find her, but she's tired of running. I know that because it was easy to find her before, but now, even an idiot would be able to find her. She used to only pay with cash, she never used her real name, and she did nothing that tied her to her old life. This time, she used a credit card and her real name.

I walk into the dance club that is far too loud for my taste and filled with far too many people. I will never understand why people enjoy going to places like this. Is it the attention they get? The desperate need to forget about their pathetic lives? I don't get it. I would rather stay at home and drink alone than be here.

I smirk. But then again, I don't drink alone very often. There is always a woman in my bed to drink off of.

I immediately spot Nina and her boy in the middle of the dance floor. She is dancing wildly, like the night I saved her. She is acting just as foolish as she was that night.

I shake my head. She might be all grown up, but she still has a lot to learn.

I get a glass of scotch while I wait to make my move. They dance for a long time, clueless that I'm here. Finally, the boy leaves Nina alone to go get them more drinks. I down the rest of mine and then walk over to her.

I grab her waist and pull her to me.

"I wasn't sure if you were ever going to come. But then again, it's you, and you always did just have one move," she hisses angrily into my ear before I spin her around and take her in my arms to dance with.

"And it seems you only have one move yourself, my beautiful Nina. Why dance if you knew this was where I would come for you?"

"It's my wedding night. Why shouldn't I dance?"

I move her in my arms to the beat of the music. Her body fitting perfectly.

"Because it's stupid. Just like getting married was stupid. Just like running or standing your ground and fighting. You are not going to win, no matter what you do."

She frowns. "I might not win, but I'm not going to make it easy for you to take me."

I grin. "Good. I'm counting on it."

"You should go. Heath is going to be back with my drink soon."

I laugh. "His name is Heath, huh? I had him pegged for a Bobby or something. What are you doing with him, Nina?"

I hold her close to me, so I can get a clear answer out of her.

"I love him—"

"Bullshit."

She doesn't react. It isn't the first time someone has told her their true thoughts about him. *Where is her friend Eden?* I glance around the club, but I don't see her. She always seemed like the honest type.

I pull Nina closer to me so that her eyes are just inches away from me.

She doesn't pull away like I expected. In fact, she hasn't fought me the entire time I have been holding her in my arms. She said she would fight, but I'm not convinced yet. I need her to fight. *Hard.* Like her life depends on it.

"What are you doing with the boy?" I ask again.

Her eyes smile just a little, like she is hiding a secret I will never understand.

"I. Love. Him."

"Bullshit."

She cocks her head to the side. "You can believe what you want, but it's the truth."

"Your friend Eden doesn't believe you either, does she?"

She frowns and pulls away a little. I've hit a nerve.

"It doesn't matter what Eden thinks."

"Where is Eden? She must be around here somewhere. She wouldn't have left you alone, not tonight. Not after you saw me at your wedding."

Her eyes widen, and I can feel the fear pulsating off her body.

"I didn't see you at my wedding."

"Stop lying, Nina. You looked me in the eye—twice. You were putting on a show for me at your wedding."

"I...didn't..." She looks down and then defiantly back up at me. "I didn't know it was you at the time. I thought it was my imagination. But, of course, you were there on the balcony. Stalking me. Obsessing about me."

I grin. "I'm not the only one obsessing, Nina. You've been obsessing about me from the second you saw me."

She tries to rip her arms out of mine, but I hold her tightly, loving the feeling of her body pressed up against mine. Loving the feeling of her struggling in my arms.

"And it's clear you've been obsessing about me for the last seven years."

She struggles harder in my arms. "Let me go, you jerk. I have not been obsessing."

I laugh. "Stop lying, Nina. I know you too well for you to lie to me."

"You don't know me at all. We fucked one time. You barely talked to me before that. And, even if you had, don't you think I've changed in the seven years since?"

She hasn't changed in seven years, but I have. I've turned into more of a monster than I ever thought possible. She is no longer safe, not even with me.

I let her go for just a second, playing with her, letting her think she has a chance against me. And then I grab her back, firmly pulling her into my arms.

"I know everything about you, Nina. I know you never finished your grad classes. I know you haven't taken a job even remotely related to art history. I know you never stay in any one place for longer than six months. You've been to Texas, Maine, Vermont, Montana, Oregon, Nebraska, South Carolina, Mexico, Canada, Massachusetts, and now Florida. You had a cat for about a year before he died of cancer; that was bad luck since you got the cat to keep you company. And I know you have known Heath for only six days and that he's at least ten years younger than you."

"Eight years. He's only eight years younger than me."

I raise an eyebrow.

"But you've made your point. You have been following me for seven years."

"I know more about you than you do. I've studied you, prepared for seven years for the moment when I could finally claim you as mine."

"I will never be yours or any other man's. I am not property. I'm a woman who is fully capable of taking care of herself."

I cock my head to the side. "That might have been the truth. You were a very capable woman who had a whole future ahead of her at one point. But not anymore. You used to belong to yourself. Now, you belong to me and my family."

"You're an evil monster, you know that?"

My lips twitch a little and then curl up into a dark smile. "I'm much worse than you could ever imagine. But you have no one to blame but yourself."

"No. I never asked for this. All I wanted was a good fuck. Not to be kidnapped forever and used as your plaything against my will."

She tries to pull away, but she still doesn't understand that she will never have that option again.

"You don't get to pretend that I'm the bad guy and that you have no blame in any of this. I warned you multiple times to stay away. You started all of this, not me."

Nina just stares at me. She knows I'm telling her the truth, and that's why it's so hard for her. Her obsession got her into trouble.

She glances over my shoulder. "Heath is coming back soon."

"He can't protect you."

"What?"

"The boy can't protect you. That's why you married him, isn't it?

86

You were tired of running, tired of being alone. You thought, if you were married, then I would leave you alone. Or at least, if I came, you would have someone to protect you. Someone who would call the police when I kidnapped you. Someone who would never stop searching for you."

She doesn't say anything.

I grin. "You don't fight me when I'm right. It's how I know that I've figured out the truth."

"The truth is that I love Heath, and he loves me. That's it. We eloped because we love each other, and there was no reason not to get married."

"He can't save you. No one can."

"You're wrong."

I raise an eyebrow. "Yeah? How am I wrong, Nina?"

"Because one person can save me."

"And who is that?"

"Me."

3

NINA

HOW CAN Arlo know me even better than I know myself? I hate that he knows me so well.

I hate that he already thinks he has my whole plan figured out.

I hate that he thinks I don't love Heath.

I hate how he is holding me so close, like I'm his to do what he pleases with.

I hate how he looks at me like he can control me with just his eyes.

I hate the smell of his aftershave, how it is the only smell I will remember from tonight.

But, most of all, I hate how my body still reacts to his. Every nerve inside me is on fire, begging for him to touch me, hold me closer. My heart is fluttering far too fast in my chest for what is healthy for me. My breathing is uneven, making it hard for me to think. My body loves him even though I hate him. And I don't know how to get my body in line with my heart.

"Leave me alone, Arlo. I'm not afraid of you anymore. I might have been, but it was because I was a scared little girl who still believed in horror stories. I don't anymore."

Arlo pulls me closer every time I say something he disagrees with. I should stop provoking him; it just makes him hold on to me tighter.

But I can't stop myself because I hate him and also because I love it when he holds me closer. I can feel more of his hard body, and it gives me a better angle to rip his throat out if I so choose.

"Oh, my Nina, you have no idea what horrors truly exist in the world. But you are going to find out."

He's going to make his move soon. I know it.

I beg Heath to get back to me soon. To stay with me. To protect me. But I know he can't really protect me. I know the only person who truly can is me. I just have no idea if I'm strong enough.

"Bullshit," I say, repeating his word from earlier.

His eyes search mine, looking for something but I don't know what. Is he looking for fear? The fear is oozing out of every single one of my pores, so it shouldn't be hard for him to find.

"Kidnap me, Arlo, and show me how horrible you are. Show me exactly what kind of evil monster you are."

I need to keep my mouth shut. Nothing I say is going to improve my situation. But it makes me feel better. It makes me feel like I have some amount of control even though I have none.

Arlo shakes his head. "No, Nina, I'm not going to kidnap you. You are going to come with me willingly."

And then he lets me go and disappears into the night, leaving me alone on the dance floor.

What the hell was that?

I wait for Heath to return with our drinks while I search to find where Arlo went, but I can't find him. Anywhere.

I head over to the bar to look for Heath, but he isn't where I last saw him. I fibbed when I told Arlo that Heath was coming back. He was still waiting at the bar for our drinks.

I walk all the way around the circular bar. He's gone. I know it. I feel it, but I can't let him go.

"Excuse me," I say to the bartender.

He ignores me and continues to serve the dozens of people who were here before me. I glance down at my wedding dress that is covered in sand and seawater after being dunked in the ocean. I look like a mess, but I'm still a bride, damn it. It's still my wedding day, and I think I deserve something for that.

"Excuse me! Today's my wedding day, and I could really use your help," I say, fed up and frustrated.

The bartender finally turns his attention to me, and when he sees that I am in fact wearing a wedding dress, he rushes over.

"How may I help you?"

"My husband came over to get our drinks about ten minutes ago. He was standing right here at the bar, and then he just disappeared. He's dressed in a dirty tux. He's the hottest man in the bar—tall, fit, and blond. Have you seen him?"

He nods. "He just left with one of the other hottest men in the bar tonight."

My heart stops. Arlo. He has him. I don't know how, in the split second that he disappeared into the crowd, he managed to get Heath. But he did.

He's testing my love.

I could just leave. I could run again and let Arlo have Heath. That's what Arlo wants to see. If I love Heath.

Damn it!

There is no way he is getting away with this. He will not take Heath from me. He's mine.

I run out of the bar even though I have no idea where to run. I have no idea where Arlo took Heath.

I pull out my phone and call Heath's phone.

It rings once.

Twice.

Three times.

"What can I do for you, Nina?" Arlo's voice answers.

"Where is Heath?"

"You lost your husband already and on the first day? That's not a good sign, Nina."

"I know you have him, Arlo. I know you kidnapped him. Now, where is he, and what do you want? I'm not in the mood to play games, Arlo."

"Oh, but I am, Nina. All I do is play games. So, you'd better get used to it."

"Where is he?"

"Relax. He's right here, Nina."

"Run, Nina! Go to the police. Run away. I'll be fine. Just run while you still can!" Heath shouts into the phone.

"See? He's completely fine, Nina," Arlo says.

"Let him go."

"Now, what fun would that be?"

"Let him go. I'll do whatever you want. Just don't hurt him."

I can practically hear Arlo smirk on the other end of the phone.

"I don't think you should do that, Nina."

"What do you mean? I'm giving up. You win. Don't hurt him."

"I think you should listen to your husband and run."

"No."

"Are you sure, Nina? Are you sure that Heath is worth saving when you could still save yourself? Isn't that what you said you were going to do anyway? Save yourself? So, do it."

"No."

Arlo sighs. "So, you really do love Heath then? Is that it?"

"Yes."

"Well then, meet me at the SPB private airfield in ten minutes, but just know you can save only one person. You can either save Heath or you can save yourself."

The phone call ends, and I shiver despite it not being the least bit cold outside. It's not even a question of whom I'm going to save. I already know, and so does Arlo. I'm going to save Heath.

4

ARLO

I ALREADY KNOW whom she's going to save. I hope like hell that I'm wrong because the boy isn't worth saving. I know that. He knows that. Even Nina knows that.

But I know her too well.

I know she is going to get in the first cab she can find and race over to the airfield to save the day.

I glance over at the boy who is riding in the backseat of the blacked out Mercedes with me. He doesn't deserve her love or her saving.

But, somehow, I think she does love the boy. I just don't understand how.

Stay away, Nina.

Save yourself.

It's your last chance.

If you get on the flight, you have no chance left.

Save yourself. Because, once you are back in Italy, I can't protect you anymore.

5

NINA

THE CAB PULLS UP in the airfield parking lot.

He tells me what the fee is, but I don't hear him. I just pull out all the cash I have, well over a hundred dollars, and hand it to him, knowing that it is more than enough to cover the fare.

I climb out of the car and expect my heart to be racing. I expect my legs to be so weak and shaky that I'll struggle walking out to the plane. None of that happens though.

Instead, I feel calm. I feel like I was meant to do this. I feel ready.

I walk into the small building that sits outside the airfield.

"I'm here to meet Arlo Carini," I tell the receptionist behind the desk when she sees me.

She smiles at me. "Going on your honeymoon?" she asks, looking at me in my dress.

"Something like that," I say without smiling.

She nods. "He's already on the plane. It's the first one on the right. I can walk you out."

"That won't be necessary. Thank you," I say and walk away. I go through the double glass doors and then out to the first plane on the right.

I don't know if it is a large plane or a small one. If it's painted white or red or green. I couldn't tell you one detail about it. My sole focus is getting on the plane and saving Heath because I fell in love with him the moment I saw him.

———

"Can I get a whiskey gorgeous?" a man asks from behind me.

I sigh. Being a bartender sucks. I have to talk to people all day and get hit on constantly, which wouldn't be a problem if I actually could focus on any man. I can't. All I can think about is running from Arlo. Doesn't matter how good looking the man hitting on me is, I don't want anything to do with them. I need to find a job that doesn't involve having to deal with annoying men all day.

I grab the whiskey and pour it into a glass and then turn around to disappoint my latest charmer.

My jaw drops when I see him.

He's tall, muscular, has long blond hair, but so have plenty of the other men that have gone after me. What's different is his eyes. They are large and bright and caring. I wasn't expecting kindness when I turned around. I was expecting another drunk man that I would have to fend off.

"Here's your whiskey," I say setting the glass down on the counter.

He grins handing me some cash. "Keep the change."

I smile and nod and try to look away from him. It should be easy since there is a whole bar full of people waiting for me to get them drinks, but I can't. I'm drawn to this man in a way that I haven't felt in seven years. I feel a hint of my old self back. The tingling in my hands when I look at him, my cheeks flush, and my heart races. I forget about everything but this man for just a second. My obsession with a complete stranger takes over giving my body a break from constantly obsessing about when Arlo is going to come for me.

I thought my obsessive tendencies were a curse. When I want something, I will do anything to make it happen. It just so happens that most of my life, my obsessive tendencies have focused on men. I obsessed briefly over saving my father when he got sick, but when he died, my feelings locked on to the man in my life. Any man that I found attractive and wanted.

When Arlo threatened my life, my obsession changed to surviving. Living a life in fear. But looking at this man, for the first time, I feel something other than fear. Something other than the need to survive. I want to live again. I want to love. Feel loved. I want him.

I close my eyes. I can't have him. I can't drag anyone else into my nightmare of a life. But it feels good to know that the old me is still in there somewhere. That I can do something other than be on high alert that Arlo and his family are going to come bursting through the door and kidnap me.

When I open my eyes, the man is staring at me.

"Here," *he says holding the drink out to me.*

"Is something wrong with it?"

"No, but I think you need this more than me."

I take the whiskey from him and drink it. I should have learned my lesson to not drink drinks from a stranger. He could have put anything into the drink when I had my eyes closed. But I'm tired of always being on edge. Always fearing that the world is out to get me.

"Feel better?" *he asks.*

I nod. "Thank you."

He grins. "I'm Heath."

"Nina."

"Nina," *he says, grinning even brighter.* "Do you trust me, Nina?"

My heart stops. Did Arlo send some stranger here to kidnap me? I look into Heath's eyes though and I know he isn't dangerous. He's the opposite of Arlo. He's light where Arlo is dark.

"Yes," *I say.*

"Good. Let's get the hell out of here and do something fun," *he says holding his hand out to me.*

I frown. "I can't. I have to work. I need the money."

His face brightens and I know he is hiding something.

"What?" *I ask.*

"My uncle actually owns this bar."

I smile. "So you just come in here and hit on the bartenders and tell them that you'll make sure they don't get in trouble when they play hooky?"

"No."

"No?"

"Fine, my uncle doesn't own this bar. Everything I just said was a lie, but I really think you should come with me. You look very sad, and you are far too beautiful and smart of a woman to spend her days sad."

He holds out his hand again.

I stare at it. This is trouble. I shouldn't do this. I need the money. I shouldn't take a risk like this.

But I take his hand anyway.

The electricity that pours into me when I do is beyond anything I've ever felt before.

He grins. I grin.

"See, you're happier already," he says.

"So where are you taking me?" I ask.

He pulls me to him into his arms. I love being in his arms.

"Does it matter?"

"No."

My heart speeds up again as he holds me in his arms. I haven't felt this alive in years. It's like he flipped a switch inside me.

"What are you doing to me?"

He tucks a strand of my hair behind my ear. "I'm falling in love with you and giving you the happily ever after you deserve."

I raise an eyebrow. "You can't fall in love with me. You don't even know me."

"I don't. But I have good instincts and I know that you are beautiful, smart, and fierce. I know that you are running from something and I want to be the man that saves you from that if you'll let me."

I bite my lip. Heath can't be real. A man like this doesn't exist. I shouldn't let someone else into my fucked up life, but I can't resist his grin.

"I'll let you fall in love with me," I say because I'm pretty sure I'm already falling for him.

———

He fell in love with me just like he promised. And I fell in love with him. Call it lust. Call it insta-love. Call it my obsession. A distraction. Whatever others might see when they look at us doesn't matter. Because right now, it's real. Real love. We may not have been together long. But it doesn't change how I feel about him.

I'll give my life to save Heath because he helped me escape a lifetime of running scared. He let me find happiness again if only for a few days. He showed me I could love again. I'll do anything to save him.

The door is open, and the stairs leading up to the plane are down. I quickly climb up, not thinking about anything but making sure that Heath is okay.

And then I see Heath. He's sitting calmly in the second seat on the plane. I run over to him and throw my arms around his neck. He embraces me just as passionately, like we haven't seen each other in years instead of only minutes.

I pull away enough to check him over. He doesn't look hurt, not a visible scratch on him, and he isn't tied up.

"Get out of here, Heath," I say, trying to get him to get up.

"No."

"Please, this isn't your battle to fight." I grab on to his neck, needing him to go. Needing him to be safe.

"I'm not leaving without you."

"Well, isn't this sweet?" Arlo says from behind me.

I turn and see him standing in the doorway of the plane.

"Neither of you will leave without the other. And I thought you got married because of the free gifts."

I frown. "Let him go, Arlo."

Arlo grins and steps aside from the doorway, holding his arm out. "He's free to go. A deal's a deal."

I grab Heath's hand and pull him up. "Go."

"Not. Without. You."

Arlo's eyes narrow, and I know he is growing impatient. If we aren't careful, he won't let either of us go. One of us needs to survive this.

I turn to look at Heath and kiss him like I've never kissed him before. A kiss to last us both a lifetime. A kiss to top all other kisses. I don't do it to put on a show for Arlo. I don't even do it for Heath. I do it for myself. I need to have something to hold on to, to get me through whatever is ahead.

When I stop, I look deep into Heath's eyes, and then I pull him in for one last embrace. I say, "Go. If you don't, he will take us both, and one of us will be dead by the end of the night. I need you to go. It's the only way you have a chance at saving me later. If you come with us now, you'll be dead before the night is over."

I pull away and firmly look him in the eyes again. The words I said aren't for me. I know he can't come rescue me. He won't even know where to start looking. The words I spoke are for him. To get him to leave. It's the only way I can protect him.

Heath thinks about going, but it's still not enough. He still can't leave me.

"I love you," I say as tears flow down my cheeks. "I won't lose you. I wouldn't survive it. I need you to go. It's the only way I have a chance at getting through this."

Heath kisses each of my cheeks, taking my tears in his mouth. "I love you, Nina. You're strong. The strongest woman I know. Just stay alive. I'll come after you. I promise."

And then I let go of his hand. I take a step back, and I watch him walk down the aisle of the plane. Heath hesitates at the door.

Because I have no voice left to speak, I mouth, *I love you. Go.*

"I'm going to find you. I'm going to save you. I promise."

Heath walks off the plane, and I'm alone.

I don't move as Arlo closes the door on the plane after the pilots step on and into the cockpit. I don't move as Arlo enters the cockpit to talk to them, leaving me by myself in the back of the plane.

I should move. I should make a run for it. There is no one stopping me. But I'm tired of running. I will not run anymore.

The only things that move are the tears dripping down my face.

Arlo reappears. "Take a seat, Nina. We will be taking off soon."

I sit. I want to fight, but I'll have plenty of time to do that soon enough. For now, I need to mourn. I need to feel the pain of losing someone I wanted to spend my whole life with, but instead, I didn't even get one night as husband and wife. I just lost the only man I've ever loved, and I need to deal with that first before I can handle anything else.

Arlo takes a seat next to me. "Buckle your seatbelt," he says.

I don't. I can't move anymore. I can't function. I just need to deal with everything.

Arlo stands up and reaches across my body. He buckles me in before taking his own seat next to me again.

I feel the engines purr to life. The plane starts moving forward, and it won't be long before we are up in the air.

I lean my head against the window, looking out into the dark sky that is getting darker with every second that passes, just like the pain in my heart. I let the pain and darkness wash over me. I let it harden my heart, and then I push it out, so I don't have to feel it.

And then I close my eyes as the tears continue down my cheeks. The plane takes off, and it all becomes real. Heath is my husband. I love him, yet I will never see him again.

But he's safe. I saved him. And, if it was the last thing I got to decide in my life, it was the best choice I'd ever made. Because Heath deserves to live. He deserves to be saved. He deserves to be loved. And there is no greater way to show my love than by saving him.

I wake up with a startle.

It takes me a second to realize where I am. Kidnapped and on a plane with Arlo, headed back to Italy. Except, unlike my last trip to Italy, I don't think this one is going to be as nice.

I look around the plane and find Arlo sitting next to me, looking at me with careful eyes.

"How long was I asleep?" I ask, hoping we only have minutes left on the flight. Because, if we still have hours left, then it gives me too much time to deal with the anxiety and fear as I think about what is going to happen next. I want to be there now. I just want to figure out what my new life is and start fighting.

"A couple of hours," he says.

I exhale deeply. We have several hours left.

"Do you want anything to eat or drink?" Arlo asks.

My eyes shoot daggers over at him. "I thought that kidnappers were supposed to be cruel to those they kidnapped."

Arlo stands up and goes over to the small bar area at the front of the plane. I watch as he pours a glass of wine and picks up a meat and cheese tray. He walks back and places both in front of me on the table that he pulled out from the wall.

He then takes a seat across from me.

"I didn't kidnap you. I kidnapped Heath. You chose to take his place."

I don't want to eat or drink anything that Arlo has given me, but I'm hungry, and the alcohol will help with the pain. I pop a piece of cheese into my mouth and then start on the wine. I frown the whole time, showing him how displeased I am with this situation, but the second the wine touches my tongue, I melt just a little. The wine is the most extravagant thing I have ever tasted. It's delicious, and I know I'm going to drink the entire bottle before we get to Italy.

Arlo smiles, satisfied, as I drink the wine.

I hate him.

But it doesn't stop me from drinking.

"Feel better?" he asks.

"No, I don't feel better. You just ruined my life. You took me away from the only person I've ever loved. I hate you. I will never feel better until you are dead and I'm free again. When will that be?"

He continues to study me with his frigid eyes. "Sooner than you think."

I narrow my eyes, not understanding anything.

Arlo takes a drink from his scotch. "You really loved him, didn't you?"

I don't want to tell him anything. He doesn't deserve to know anything personal about me.

But I can't help but answer his question, "Yes, I really loved him. I'll always love him."

Arlo rubs his neck. "Why? You barely knew each other."

I look out the window and into the dark night. I know we are somewhere over the ocean, but I can't make out the water from so high up. It all looks the same. One dark void that I will never escape from.

I shake my head. No. I will escape. I will find a way through what seems like the impossible. I will not let him win.

I hear Arlo stand up and walk the two feet toward me.

"Why, Nina? Why him? Did your obsessive tendencies get you into trouble again? Is that what this is? You're just obsessed, not really in love?"

His hand touches my cheek, and I flinch. It was the lightest touch, and I already can't stand it.

Arlo pulls back a second, and then he pushes harder. "Do you even know what love is, Nina?"

He strokes my neck, and I can't help the shivers going up and down my spine.

He grins. "I don't think you do. Whatever you and Heath had, it wasn't love. It's not going to save you."

He lowers his lips, and I know he is going to kiss me. I can't take it. I can't just let him kiss me. Not tonight.

I know it's stupid, but I do it anyway.

I pull the gun out of my purse, and I aim it at Arlo.

The fucker grins as he slowly puts his hands up, but he doesn't move more than a few inches away from my face.

"I wouldn't grin if I were you. I could blow your brains out in a split second. I might still have to face the wrath of your family when I get to Italy, but I can kill you now."

He nods slowly. "I don't doubt that you could, Nina. In fact, maybe you should. It would make my life a whole lot easier. But I promise you, your life would become much worse if you killed me. You would no longer just be in my family's debt; you would owe my family *every-thing*. You would never stop paying with your life."

I feel my arms shaking ever so slightly as I aim the gun at Arlo's heart. *Shoot him*, I keep telling myself in my head. I squeeze my finger tighter over the trigger, but I still can't make myself actually pull it.

"Shoot me."

Damn it. I shouldn't have done this. I shouldn't have revealed my cards so soon. He didn't know I had a gun. I could have killed his entire family in their sleep instead of just taking out Arlo.

Heath's face flashes before my eyes. *Kill him*, he says to me.

I do. I squeeze the trigger and hear the pop of the gun as a bullet explodes out. I've spent the last seven years learning how to shoot a gun properly, but I've never actually shot at anyone before.

I feel the gun being ripped out of my hands before I even have time to react. And then I feel Arlo's body on top of me, holding me down so that I can't move.

We both breathe heavily as he pushes me down in my seat. I expect I'm about to be punished for what I just did. I'm going to be hit and beaten until I'm barely standing when we make it to Italy. But I welcome the pain. It will distract me from the pain I feel in my heart.

"Where did you learn to shoot?"

I frown. "Why does it matter?"

"You don't get to avoid my questions anymore. Answer me. Where did you learn to shoot?"

"I hired several different men at various shooting ranges to teach me."

He sighs. "Well, you wasted your money. That was horrible. I'll have to teach you how to shoot properly."

My eyes widen. *Why would he teach me how to shoot? Why would he do anything for me?*

He laughs at my expression. "Your new life isn't going to be as bad as you think it will be, Nina, no matter how short of time you have left. You will still be able to do some enjoyable things."

"I'm not going to survive my time with your family, am I? Even if you teach me how to shoot? Even if I do everything right, I'm still going to die, aren't I?"

Arlo lets go of my body, releasing me. "That depends on you."

He stands up and starts undoing his buttoned-down shirt. He's going to shoot me and kill me right here. He's just acting calm to keep me calm.

I watch as he removes his shirt, and I think his abs might be even more magnificent than they were seven years ago. He looks even stronger, more powerful. And I thought he was strong before. Now, he looks invincible.

I suck in a breath. He's going to rape me. I know it.

And then I see the blood as he removes his shirt. It spills out of his left shoulder. He doesn't flinch or even seemed fazed by the blood pouring out of his shoulder.

He doesn't seem angry or afraid that he's about to die from blood loss. He doesn't go to the front of the plane to signal an emergency landing when we get back over land. Instead, he walks to the back of the plane as he throws his bloodied shirt on the floor. He opens the door at the back and disappears inside, leaving me alone.

I take a deep breath as I realize that I might have missed his heart, but I hit him. I shot someone. And it could still result in his death.

I spot my gun lying carelessly on the floor. I pop out of my seat and run over to pick it up. It's still loaded. I still have a chance to take Arlo out.

I hold the gun in my hand and start walking toward the back of the plane until I get to the door. I hesitate, but I don't understand why. He's already wounded. I don't have to shoot him clearly in the heart. I just need to wound him again. The blood loss over the next few hours would do the rest. And then I could be free of at least one Carini. The worst of them anyway. The one who got me into this whole mess.

I throw the door open, shocked that he didn't lock it, and see Arlo lounging on the bed. I glance at his shoulder and see the staples that he somehow placed there, already closing the wound I'd created. It's no longer bleeding. The only risk of death now is an infection. And that could take weeks to kill him.

I aim the gun at him as he smirks.

"Come to kill me again?"

"Yes."

"You're never going to kill me, holding the gun like that. You can't even tell what you are aiming at."

"I shot you once. I can do it again. And again and again. For as many times as it takes to kill you."

Arlo sits up just a little. "What's this fascination with killing me? I know you don't like me. I know I took you away from your true love or whatever. But, really, have I done anything that horrible to you other than give you the best sex of your life? Because I know Heath never fucked you like I did. I know that, even at his best, you still thought of me when you fucked him."

I'm angry. My blood is boiling. My heart is racing as I point the gun at Arlo.

"You're evil. You think I spent the last seven years just running and living in fear? No. I studied everything I could about your family. I read everything. I know exactly who you are, and I know exactly how to take you down. I'm not a naïve, obsessed girl anymore. I'm a woman scorned who will not be defeated."

Arlo cocks his head to one side as he lies back. "And what are we? What makes us so bad that we deserve to be killed before we even lay a hand on you?"

"You are traffickers. You kidnap women and sell them as slaves. You are the worst kind of people."

Arlo purses his lips as he nods. "You're right. We are the worst kind of people. But we aren't traffickers. We would never sell a person to another. What enjoyment would we get out of that?"

"You would get money."

Arlo laughs. "And what would we do with the money? We already have more money than we know what to do with. We don't need more money."

I feel my hands drop a little, lowering the gun the tiniest bit, and then I quickly force my arms to rise again.

He raises an eyebrow. "You maybe should have worked on your arm strength a little more along with your shooting skills if your plan was to smuggle in a gun and shoot us all to death."

I ignore his remark. I'm stronger than he thinks. That's all that matters. Not his goading.

"You're evil people who traffic women. You all deserve to die."

"No, we are a powerful, ruthless family who has fought long and hard to earn the money and power that we control in Italy. We don't always play by the rules. We don't always fight fair. But, when it comes to taking someone's life, we only take what is owed to us. We only take when a debt is owed."

"And you saving my life means I have to give it up to you?"

"Yes. When we had to do what we did to save you, then yes. You have no idea how much you owe us."

"Then, tell me."

He laughs. "You'll know plenty soon enough."

My hands start shaking from holding the weight of the gun.

"Now, are you going to shoot me or not? Because I'd like to try to get some sleep before we land."

I continue to hold the gun out, aiming it at his heart.

He sighs. "Well, at least step closer. If you are going to shoot me again, I'd rather you get a clean shot to the heart that instantly kills me instead of having to deal with the pain of getting shot over and over again in the arm or leg or wherever else your horrible aims lends itself."

I step closer.

"Closer, Nina," he commands.

I do. I climb onto the edge of the bed, and I aim at his heart. My hands tremble though, and I know I won't get a clean shot off.

"Closer, Nina."

I move closer to him. This is foolish. Stupid. But I keep moving closer until he grabs on to the barrel of the gun and places it against his chest, right over his heart.

I fall forward as he jerks the gun to him. My legs are straddling his hips, and my face hovers over his face as my hands clutch the gun to his heart.

"Shoot me. Kill me, Nina. End this before it even starts."

When he speaks, he seems so sincere. He seems so hurt. Like he's in so much unbearable pain that he can't stand to live another second. Yet he patched up the wound on his arm. He won't kill himself, but he won't stop me from killing him. I wouldn't be killing him for me. I would be killing him to end his pain.

"No," I say, dropping the gun on the floor.

"That is the most foolish thing you have done yet, Nina."

"You're probably right. But then again, I've done a lot of foolish things in my life."

I feel his cock harden beneath me. I'm turning him on. I should move off of him. Retreat to my seat on the plane. But I need to understand more about Arlo. I need to understand what makes him tick, and then maybe it will be enough to save myself.

But, before I can say anything, he rolls me over and pins me to the bed beneath him.

"I'm not going to fuck you, if that's what you think is happening."

"That is not what I think is happening. You're not going to fuck me because I won't let you."

He laughs. "You can keep telling yourself that if you want to, but we both know it isn't true. You want me to fuck you."

"No, I don't."

I take a deep breath in and out, trying to slow my racing heart. I'm just anxious, worked up because I shot him. Because he's on top of me, holding me down. Because I'm in a dangerous situation, and he could kill me at any second. That's all I'm feeling.

He lowers his mouth, and I think he's going to kiss me. I don't know whether to spit in his face or beg for his lips to caress mine. His lips move at the last second though, and he nips forcefully at my ear, tugging and pulling until I think he is going to rip my ear off.

It should make me more afraid. But it doesn't. I feel my nipples perk to attention, and there's a stirring deep in my belly as I wish that he would never stop.

"You want me, Nina. You want me desperately."

He moves to my other ear, giving it the same treatment.

"No," I say in barely a whisper.

He grins. "Are you sure, Nina? Are you sure you don't want me to fuck you? I'm sure that Heath tried his best these past few days, but did he satisfy you like I did?"

"Stop," I say.

He cocks his head to the side as he stares down at me. "Fine. If that's what you really want, I'll stop. I'm not evil, Nina. And, unlike you, I've had plenty of sex these last seven years. Plenty of dirty, filthy sex that would put what we did last time to shame. I don't need you."

Arlo gets off of me and takes a step back.

He starts removing his pants.

"I said no."

He laughs. "Then, get out. No one is stopping you. I'm going to drink a couple of glasses of scotch to deal with the pain-in-the-ass wound you created in my shoulder, and then I'm going to sleep until we get to Italy. And I happen to sleep in the nude. So, either join me or get the fuck out."

I jump off the bed, intending to get out of there as quickly as possible, but I stop at the door. I don't know why. He's letting me go. I can spend the rest of the flight planning what I'm going to do once we get to Italy. How I'm going to escape. But, instead of leaving, I want to stay.

He's right in thinking that I want him to fuck me. I shouldn't. It's the absolutely wrong thing. I just married another man. But I can't get the last time we were together out of my head. I can't forget about the rope tied around my wrists. I can't stop thinking about how he controlled me. How having no control made me want him more. I can't stop thinking about that damn night.

It's just because that was the night my life changed. That was the night I had to start running instead of living.

"Go, Nina," Arlo says, standing in nothing but his underwear. "You don't want this. Save yourself, like you promised."

I open the door and disappear back into the main part of the plane. But I can't get the sadness and pain that I felt from Arlo out of my head. He cares about me. I know that. It's why he saved me. But everything else, I don't understand.

Save myself.

That's what Arlo wants me to do. He's given me chance after chance tonight to save myself. I could have let Heath go in my place. I could have shot and killed Arlo twice. And I got to leave his bedroom instead of letting him fuck me. I'm still alive and unhurt. Other than ripping Heath out of my life, Arlo really hasn't done anything that bad to me.

Save myself.

That's what he wants. But what if, by leaving his bedroom, I just lost an opportunity to save myself? Because I think the best way to save myself is through Arlo. He's the key to my freedom. I need to make him fall in love with me, and then he'll save me.

6

ARLO

NINA IS TOO easy to seduce. She's still too obsessed after all these years. She loves Heath. That's clear, but it would have been all too easy for me to get into her pants if I had truly wanted to last night.

She is going to fuck up all my plans before we even get home at this rate. I can't let that happen.

I haven't seen her in hours though. For all I know, she's found a way to put us both out of our misery.

We are landing soon, so it's time for me to get off my ass and go figure out what to do with her. I roll off the bed to start to get dressed. I should shower, as it would make me feel better, but I don't. I don't want to feel better. Maybe, if I let the pain consume me, I can do what I need to do.

I put my pants back on and then grab a clean shirt from the closet. I begin to put it on and feel the stabbing pain in my shoulder as I slip my arm in the sleeve. She got me good in the shoulder. It will take me several weeks to fully heal.

Good. I need to remember that she's no angel. That she's a fighter even if she is a terrible shot. I'll have to remedy that situation soon.

I finish getting dressed, and then I step back into the main part of the airplane to face her.

I expect her to be asleep or planning her revenge on me and my family, but I find her doing neither.

She smiles at me brightly.

"Don't do that."

"Don't do what?" she asks with a smile still plastered on her sweet face.

"Don't pretend that everything is okay when it isn't. Stop smiling. You shouldn't be smiling."

"So, now, you get to tell me that I can't even smile? I don't think that's fair."

"Life isn't fair. Get used to it."

I walk toward the front of the plane to check in with the pilots to figure out when we are landing. When I return, Nina still has a bright smile on her face.

"Buckle your seatbelt. We will be landing soon."

She smiles as she buckles her seatbelt. "When we get back to your home, will I be able to shower and change? This dress is uncomfortable and dirty."

I stare at her with wide eyes. I don't know what she is doing, but she needs to stop. Pretending like she isn't being kidnapped against her will and about to step into a completely different world where she will be tested in ways she could never imagine is useless. It won't help anything.

I ignore her and look out the window as we land. She doesn't understand it, but it's the last time I will have any freedom either. At least, until this is all over.

In the backseat of the car, I watch Nina's eyes as we pull up in front of my house. Her eyes grow just as big and wide with wonderment as they did the first time she entered my house when her class was getting a tour for her art history lesson for the day. I don't see any fear.

"What is your fascination with my house?"

She blinks rapidly, like I just turned into a monkey or something. "It's not just a fascination; it's an obsession. Your house is beautiful.

It's the most beautiful home I've ever had the pleasure of stepping foot inside of. It has architecture and history unlike so many homes in America that are just built for convenience. This home was built to be beautiful, just for beauty's sake. It was spared no expense and has lasted hundreds of years. Through all the changes in the world. What isn't there to love about it? Don't tell me you don't think your home is magical."

I shake my head and then rub my neck. Nina looks very much like a woman, and for the most part, she acts like it, but she has a long way to go in understanding how things really work.

"I don't think my home is magical or beautiful. And it's definitely not something you should obsess over. It was built on the backs of slaves, like most of the world's greatest buildings were. It served as a dungeon for many. A place of oppression for others. That history you speak so fondly of is nothing more than pain and suffering of other people. It's nothing to be obsessed over."

She frowns as she narrows her eyes at me. "It's also your home, and it carries your family's history and that of generations of people before you. It also represented hope and love for a lot of people. It represented freedom and a chance at a better life. It gave employment to some. Shelter to others. It was a place of fancy parties and people falling in love. Every place has a negative history. But you can't focus on the dark without also seeing the light. Everything has two sides."

When she speaks, I know she isn't talking about the house anymore. She is talking about me. She thinks I have a light side along with the dark. She's wrong. I haven't had a drop of goodness in me in years. It died the day Nina's life effectively ended. I've had a very different mission ever since.

The driver parks the car outside the mansion that holds more secrets than I will ever know. I can see how she finds it beautiful, but she's just letting her naïveté through.

I step out of the car, and Nina follows. She looks like a mess in her wedding dress that is covered in dirt and filth. Her makeup is smeared all over her face. She looks broken already. Maybe that's a good thing. Maybe it will make my family think she is weaker than she actually is, and they'll underestimate her.

I step back into my home that might as well be my own prison cell. That's what it feels like every time I walk inside, but in a few months, that will all change. I will own everything. I will become the ruler instead of the captive.

I keep walking through hallways and past large rooms that hold beautiful paintings and history that Nina used to stare at like it was perfection when, in fact, they are nothing more than paint and canvas.

"Where are we going?" Nina asks as we wind down hallways and up staircases that she wasn't privy to on her tour.

"To prove to my father that you are here and to learn the terms of your debt."

I hear her gasp, but I don't turn to look at her. I need to turn off my humanity now. If I have a chance at winning this fight, I need to not feel anything. Not her pain, fear, or excitement. Not my own heart racing or even the ache in my shoulder. I need to feel nothing.

I keep walking until I get to the family room in the back of the house. When I gave the tour seven years ago, I only showed the students rooms that were practically never used. I never showed the rooms that actually mattered. The rooms that we actually live in.

I open the double doors and enter the family room where my father is sitting in a large chair by the fireplace, waiting for me.

He cocks his head to one side to look past me to where Nina is standing in the doorway.

He nods his approval at me, and then he stands up and walks toward Nina.

"My beautiful Nina. It is so good of you to finally join us. Let me introduce myself. I'm Enrico Carini. You sat at the dinner table with me once before, but you weren't really concerned with meeting me at the time. Now, I think you should be very concerned with learning who I am."

Nina narrows her eyes at my father as she walks proudly into the family room. "No, I'm not particularly concerned with who you are other than learning enough to point you out to the police when I escape. Or, at least, remember your face when I put a bullet between your eyes."

My father chuckles as he turns to me. "You weren't lying about this one."

I nod but don't react otherwise. Just keep my composure. Get through tonight, and then I will have some freedom.

My father forcefully grabs Nina's hand. I can see the pain and disgust in her eyes as my father holds on to her arm and guides her over to the table.

She looks to me like I'm going to save her, but I don't do anything. The sooner she learns that I will do nothing to save her, the better.

"Take a seat, Nina," Enrico says, pushing her down into a chair at the table.

"This is illegal, you know. You can't just kidnap me. You will pay for this. My husband won't stop until he gets me back."

Enrico laughs. "I don't doubt that he will. But he will fail, as have hundreds of husbands before him."

Nina's eyes widen. "You've done this hundreds of times before? You're sicker than I thought."

Enrico nods. "It's a tradition that has gone back hundreds of years. You just happened to get caught up in it. But you have one thing very wrong if you think this is illegal. What we are doing is very legal."

He glances to the piece of paper in front of Nina. She jumps up in her seat when she sees her signature at the bottom of the paper.

"You forged my signature on some document. So what? It doesn't mean anything."

"We didn't forge anything, Nina."

"I would have never agreed to anything as twisted as whatever this is," Nina says.

"Fear will make a person do things they never dreamed of," I say, stepping forward.

She won't believe it if it comes from my father. I know that much. But, for some stupid reason, she trusts me.

Nina shakes her head, but I already see the hint of realization at what the truth is hidden beneath her long, dark lashes.

My eyes guide hers back to the document she signed seven years ago. The document that saved her yet sentenced her to death at the same time. All it did was prolong her life.

She starts reading and realizes all the things that I already know the document contains.

That she offered up her freedom for seven years in exchange for my family saving her from Clive and Erick's family the night that they put something in her drink and tried to kidnap her themselves. That she had two choices. Pay seven million dollars or pay with seven years of her life. She doesn't have seven million dollars. She doesn't even have one million dollars.

Nina skips most of the fine print of the document, her fingers tracing her signature that rests on the bottom of the page along with my signature and the rest of my family's signatures.

I know the moment it finally sinks in that she can't escape this. That this is completely legal even if the law wouldn't really support it. We have enough power in this country to get away with anything. Including owning her for seven years.

She takes a deep breath as she realizes that she is the one who got herself into this twisted mess. I tried to warn her. I tried to keep her out of this, but she didn't listen. Now, she has to pay the consequences.

She looks back at the document.

"It even says the date you would come for me. It has yesterday's date on it." She rubs her head, trying to remember. "That night is fuzzy." She stands up from the chair and starts walking around the room, trying to remember that night.

"I remember drinking the shot that had the drugs in it. I remember your face of terror as I drank it," Nina says, looking at me.

But all I see is my father's disappointment on his face.

She rubs her head some more. "I remember you all being there. And I remember yesterday's date. It's why..." She hesitates.

I smirk. "It's why you picked yesterday as your wedding day."

She nods and wraps her arms around herself, trying to comfort herself. Like that is going to help. She doesn't understand that she is surrounded by monsters.

And that she can't save herself anymore. She had her chance seven years ago. But she let her obsession with me get the best of her.

"So, the document is real. Now what? You're going to rape me and make me your slave for seven years?" Nina looks directly at me.

My father laughs. "Basically. But you aren't just Arlo's slave. You belong to all of us."

Nina's eyes don't hide the fear well. If she is going to survive here, she needs to hide her fears better than that. My family lives for fear. They love twisting and playing with others' minds. They love the control they wield over people. And they won't stop until they destroy her. That's the game.

"Matteo, why don't you introduce yourself to Nina? I don't think she remembers you," Enrico says.

I watch as Nina looks at my brother. She doesn't recognize him even though she has met him before. I can tell from the shock in her face of seeing another man who is almost identical to me. Matteo has longer hair now, and he took a knife to the face that left him with a bad scar under his eye, making it easy for people to tell us apart now, unlike when we were younger. It makes him look menacing. Terrifying. And he is. But that's not his game. He won't seem terrifying to Nina. He'll convince her that he's sweet and loving, unlike me.

I look deep into Nina's eyes as she stares at my brother. I see the instant lust and obsession starting in her eyes—the same way it did with me the first time she saw me. She wants him just as badly as she wants me even if she will never admit it. And I can't stay here and watch her obsession begin. I love my brother. I would do anything for him. But the pain of watching her fall for my brother is too much for me to bear.

I feel my blood rushing fast through my body as my anger and jealousy creep to the surface. I glance down at my shoulder and see that my wound is opening again. I should have it properly looked at and closed. But I won't. I relish this kind of pain. It will keep me from doing something incredibly stupid.

Nina doesn't look at me when the blood spills out onto my shirt. She's too infatuated with my brother and the thought of having sex with him to care about anything else.

I sigh and leave before I have to witness anymore. She's strong. I know that. But I'm still afraid that her obsession is going to be the end of her.

7

MATTEO

I FORGOT how beautiful Nina really is.

I don't know how that is possible when she's the sexiest woman I've ever seen. I don't know what it is about her that makes her seem so beautiful. Is it her piercing brown eyes, luscious red lips, her unbelievable curves, or her legs that go on for days?

Maybe it's the fierceness in her eyes. The obsessiveness that, when she sets her heart on something, she does everything to make it happen. Even at the expense of herself.

Whatever it is, I can't believe I forgot. And, now, I'm just as obsessed with her as my brother. He can pretend she's not all he wants. That he's just playing along with the game, just like he has with all the ones before. But he's lying. I know him better than that. I practically am him. So, I definitely know what he's thinking.

And he already knows what I'm thinking. That's the problem after doing this six other times. He already knows all my tricks. I'll have to play this game differently if I want to win.

"I'm Matteo Carini, Arlo's twin brother," I say, walking over to Nina and softly kissing her on each cheek. I get hard from just kissing her on the damn cheek. Man, I'm in trouble if this woman can control my dick that easily.

Nina just keeps staring at me, wide-eyed. "Have we met before?" she asks.

I nod. "I was there the night we saved you."

She frowns but still says, "Thank you."

I laugh. "I wouldn't be thanking me yet. If you think my brother is bad, I'm worse."

She studies me out of the corner of her eye, and I'm not sure she believes me. I thought my scar would make me look like more of a badass than Arlo could ever dream of being. But, apparently, it still isn't enough. His broodiness makes it impossible for me to compete with him.

I hold out my arm to her, and she apprehensively looks at it.

"Let me give you a tour of our house and where you will be staying."

She doesn't put her hand on my arm like I want her to.

"I figured I would be staying in the dungeon again."

I laugh. "And why would we do that?"

"Because I'm your prisoner, and that's where you keep prisoners."

I shrug. "We could, but then we'd have to go down to the dungeons ourselves every time we needed something from you, and that would get tiring. It's much better if you just stay up here. Don't you agree?" I say with a sexy grin.

I watch as her cheeks blush just the tiniest bit at the attention I'm giving her.

"You're right. What was I thinking? I wouldn't want to inconvenience you when you want to rape me," she says, every word dripping with sarcasm.

I grin. "Exactly," I say, liking her spunk. "Now, take my arm so that I can show you around."

"No, thanks. Arlo already gave me a tour the last time I was here."

I roll my eyes. "He didn't show you the good parts. Hold onto my arm or stay here and take your chances with what my father will need from you."

Disgust and fear cover her gorgeous eyes. And rightly so. If she is smart, she will do everything in her power to stay away from my father. She might hate Arlo and me now, but she'll learn soon enough that we are the lesser of the evils in this family.

She puts her hand in the crook of my arm. "I hate you. You can't force me to do anything. I'm not your slave."

I shake my head, laughing a little to myself. She's something else. If putting her hand on my arm pisses her off, she isn't going to like what the future holds for her.

"I'm not forcing you to do anything. I'm giving you a choice. Me or my father."

"That's not a choice."

"It is a choice. I think you will find that my family is more than fair when it comes to giving you free will while you stay with us even though you owe us a huge debt," I say, leading her out of the family room.

"A debt that your family manipulated me into having."

I stop. "You can hate my family, but you don't get to blame us for the predicament you are in. If I remember correctly, my brother even tried to warn you. This is on you. You had a choice to drink or not even though you knew it was spiked. You had the choice to be saved or to stay with them. You chose us. Now, deal with it."

She pouts but doesn't argue about it any longer, so I keep walking. I show her the kitchen, our family's private dining room, our offices, the library, and then the art gallery.

It's clear when we enter the library that also holds walls of art that this room is her favorite. She runs her hands over the spines of the books and studies each and every painting we pass.

I should have done more research before she came. I know Arlo knows everything about her. I should have been better prepared.

"Do you like art? Books?" I ask before realizing how stupid I sound.

She nods. "I like history. I like learning about the past. Art captures the imperfections of people's pasts, and books tell their stories. What isn't there to love?"

"Are you an artist?"

She laughs. It's a beautiful sound that I want to hear over and over again.

"No. I've tried, but that isn't where my talent lies."

I step closer to her, closing the space between us, testing to see how uncomfortable I make her. She doesn't step back.

"Why would I tell you what my talents are? Why would I tell you anything about myself? You are just going to use it against me."

I smile, liking how fierce she is when she speaks. It's adorable that she thinks she has any control in this situation.

"Because it might make your stay easier if you were my friend and not just the woman I fuck when I'm bored."

She narrows her eyes but doesn't say anything. She isn't going to tell me anything about herself. I'll just have to find the file that I know my obsessive, organized brother has on her. I'll find out everything I need to know from that.

But, from the look in her eyes, I know where to find her if I ever need her. She'll be here, enveloped in a story about medieval times or some shit like that. I'm sure books are interesting, but I prefer to make history rather than read about it in some book.

"Come on. Let me show you to your room," I say, again holding out my arm to her.

She doesn't want to take it. She doesn't want to do anything that she is told. I'll have to remember that tidbit. She needs to feel in control.

"You hold on to my arm, or I'll hold on to your ass. Your choice."

She frowns but takes my arm. I can practically feel the blood pulsing through her body just from the touch of her hand. She's excited or nervous or turned on. I can't tell which. Arlo is better at reading people than I am.

"You should really cheer up, sweetheart. Things could be a lot worse than they are."

"How could they be any worse? I've been kidnapped. I'm a slave. I just got married, and I don't even get to have a life with my new husband. I think this is about as bad as it gets."

I shake my head. "No. You made the right decision when you chose us over Erick seven years ago."

"And why would you say that? From what I've seen, you are both scum."

"For one, we are much fairer than Erick's family. We keep to our word and will give you back your freedom after you've paid your fair debt off. But he wouldn't ever give you your life back even though you didn't owe them anything."

I walk her up the stairs to the highest room in the mansion. I open the door and lead her inside.

"And, two, we have a lot more money than them, which means you have much better accommodations while you stay here."

I watch as her mouth drops at the gorgeous room I just brought her into. The room is circular with a large window circling the whole room, providing plenty of light. An oversize bed sits in the center of the room along with a curved couch on another wall, looking out over the gardens. A single other door leads from the room to her bathroom that is almost as large as this room, complete with a chandelier over the bathtub. I'm sure it is the best room she has ever stayed in.

"This room is mine?"

"Yes, it's yours while you stay here. No one will touch you while you're in this room. No one will come in here without your permission. It's the only safe place you have. Remember that."

She turns to me after studying the room. "Why would you give me a safe place to go? I could just stay in this room, and no one would ever touch me."

"For one, you would starve if you stayed in here the whole time. No one will bring you food as long as you stay in here. And, two, even if you were to get someone to bring you food, you would go crazy, staying in here. Seven years is a long time not to speak to anyone. People go crazy in solitary confinement. Even confinement that is as beautiful as this."

She frowns. "If this is my safe place, then why are you in here?"

"Because I was invited."

"I didn't invite you."

I sigh. "Fine, I'll leave. But, first, you need to know the rules since I'm sure you didn't read the whole document you signed very carefully."

She rolls her eyes. "No, I was more concerned with the fact that I'd willingly signed my life away."

"Not your life. Only seven years."

"Seven years is a long time."

I nod. "But it's not forever."

Her eyes bore into mine, like she is trying to figure out if I'm telling the truth or not. "Why should I believe you? Why should I believe that I'm ever going to be free again?"

"Because this is how my family keeps our power. We are honest. We do what we say. Our word means everything. When I tell you something, believe me. When Arlo tells you something, believe him. My family tells the truth above all else."

"Are you going to rape me?" she asks.

I can't tell if she wants me to or not from the way she says it. She's not afraid; I know that much.

I grin. "Not today." I pull a bracelet out of my pocket. "Now, for the rules. Hold out your arm."

She folds her arms across her chest.

I laugh, loving her fire. "Nina, will you please hold out your arm so that I can place this bracelet on your wrist, or would you rather I take you to the dungeons instead?"

She frowns but holds out her left wrist to me. I place this bracelet on her wrist.

"What is it?"

"It has a tracking device in it. That way, we can figure out where you are and allow you the freedom to move around in our home. Or you can stay in the dungeon. I heard you and Arlo fucked there, so maybe that's really what you prefer."

"The bracelet is fine," she says, shooting fire with her eyes.

She studies the bracelet, already trying to figure out a way to take it off. She's going to struggle to get it off herself. Once closed, it doesn't open, except with wire cutters.

"Don't even think about taking it off."

She rubs her wrist. "Why?"

"Just don't. You don't want to know what will happen to you if you take it off."

She studies the bracelet. "Is there poison or explosives or something in it?"

I shrug. "Just don't."

"I thought you didn't lie."

"I don't. But that doesn't mean I have to answer all of your questions either."

I don't have to tell her that the bracelet won't hurt her in any way if she removes it. It will fuck with her brain though to think that there is a possibility that it might. The punishment would come after we hunted her down and found her.

She sighs. "So, what are the rules? I'm tired, and I just want to sleep."

"Simple. Stay in the mansion or on the main grounds. Don't take the bracelet off. Stay in your room if you don't want to be ordered around. Come out, and you're free game to any of my family members to do what they feel is fair for you to pay back the debt you owe us. Stay away from Enrico if you don't want to experience any pain." I pause. "Well, the kind of pain that comes with no enjoyment for you anyway. Rinse and repeat until your time is up. If you follow the rules, then you'll survive long enough to go back to that husband of yours. Any questions?"

She folds her arms across her chest. "No."

"Don't follow the rules, and there will be consequences that you can't imagine. Including your death. Do you understand?" I say as nicely and calmly as I can.

I don't want to scare her, but she needs to know that I'm serious when I say she can't run.

She nods.

"I need to hear you say that you understand."

"I understand," she says, willing to give in without a fight because it's clear she just wants me gone.

I turn to walk toward the door. "Oh, one more thing."

She exhales deeply, like she can't take any more.

"If you want hot, can't-walk-for-a-week, life-shattering sex, then come to me, not my brother, okay? I know you think sex with him was amazing, but trust me, he has no imagination, and all he does is brood. You don't want that. You want me. I'm much more fun."

She smiles the tiniest bit, but her smile vanishes so quickly that I'm not sure if I dreamed it or if it was really there.

"I won't be going to either of you for sex. You kidnapped me, remember? You will have to rape me if you want sex. And don't forget; I put up a good fight. Just ask your brother about his shoulder."

I smile, thrilled that she caused my brother pain. I'm sure the asshole deserved it.

"Have a good night, beautiful. My room is three doors down if you need me," I say with a wink.

I watch her roll her eyes at me.

This is going to be too much fun. She's the perfect number seven.

8

NINA

I'VE SPENT the last three days in my room. And, just as Matteo said, I've been left completely alone. No one has come to check on me. No one has barged in and demanded sex. No one has hurt me.

I'm completely forgotten about as long as I stay in this room.

It's the most beautiful room I have ever stayed in. And, if I wasn't in my current predicament, then I would actually appreciate sleeping in a room like this. I would breathe in every smell, study every stone, and enjoy the gorgeous sunlight pouring in through all the large windows in the room. I would pretend I was a princess in the highest room of the castle and enjoy the warmth of the fireplace while snuggled in Arlo's arms.

But, instead, I've spent the last three days afraid of every sound in the mansion. My body shakes when I hear footsteps outside, seemingly growing closer to me. I tremble and search for anything I can use to defend myself against an intruder, but I don't have many options. The room has been stripped of anything that might be used as a weapon.

Every time the footsteps stop, I am safe again. It's taken me three days to realize that Matteo was telling the truth. That, as long as my foot doesn't cross the threshold of the door, then I am safe.

But I am also *trapped*.

Trapped in a charming prison cell with no one and nothing to keep me company. Matteo was right that, if the lack of food didn't kill me, the boredom would. There isn't a TV in the room. Not a single book. Not even a piece of art to savor. The only entertainment I've had these past three days are the birds in the garden below and the sound of footsteps.

I've tried coming up with a plan to escape, but the bracelet wrapped around my wrist concerns me. Matteo didn't tell me exactly what would happen if I ran. But I believed him when he said it wouldn't be good. I'd rather die than be someone's slave even if there is the possibility of freedom again one day. I can't handle being controlled.

I've spent seven years training for today. I'm in the best shape of my life. All I would have to do is slip out in the middle of the night and run into town. The town isn't more than ten miles away from here. I could easily run that before anyone noticed I was gone.

But then what? Would the bracelet explode and kill me?

Even if it didn't, I have no doubt that they would hunt me down and kill me. I'm sure I read something in that document about reasons that they can kill me. And running away from them is one of them.

Death. It would be a sweet release compared to whatever they have in store for me. But I can't do that to Eden. I can't do that to Heath. I have people who love me. People who are looking for me. I have to find a way to escape that doesn't end in my death. At least, at first; maybe, later, I will feel differently. But I owe it to them to fight.

I walk to the window as the sun rises. I haven't slept in three days. The fear of the unknown has overcome any need for sleep. Making me unsure if the memories that keep coming back from that night when Arlo saved me are real or imagined. They are most likely just hallucinations, but still, I can't get them out of my head.

I see Arlo everywhere.

I see his face from when I took the drink.

I see the worried expression as he lifted my broken body in his arms.

I remember the smell of his cologne as he stayed with me all night long until I came to.

But I remember others, too. The entire family there. I remember signing something. And I remember a date. I think I've always known the date. It's why I was so desperate to get married on that day. I needed to feel in control. That it was my date to claim instead of waiting for them to come for me.

My stomach growls again, and the pains of not eating are real and constant. I know that I can't survive alone in here much longer.

I just can't bring myself to venture out of this room. I thought that maybe—

I shake my head. I can't think like that. Arlo is not my friend. He's not my lover. He's nothing. He doesn't care about me, and he won't save me. He made that perfectly clear on the plane and then again when he left me alone with his father and brother.

His father scares me to death. I have no doubt that I should stay clear of him. But Matteo intrigues me. Maybe it's just because he looks so much like Arlo. It's just the attraction that I feel to them that makes my heart soften just a little toward both of them. But Matteo does seem to have a soft spot. He's not like Arlo. He might actually have a heart.

He might be the one I should aim my plan at. If I can get him to fall in love with me, then maybe he'll save me from this mess. Maybe the rest of the family will leave me alone then. I just have to get over my disgust at any man, even a man as good-looking as Matteo, touching me.

My stomach growls again, and I can't stand it any longer. The sun has just risen, so hopefully, the rest of the family isn't awake yet. I can sneak down to the kitchen, swing by the library to grab a couple of books, and then be back up in my room before anyone else is even awake. It will give me more time to figure out an escape plan that doesn't involve selling my body to save my soul.

I creep to the door and listen for footsteps, but I hear none. I grab the handle of the doorknob and slowly turn it, afraid that it might be locked and that I will be trapped in here forever, dying a slow death or at least locked away to weaken me until I'm broken.

But it's not locked.

I slowly open the door and look down the long, dark hallway. I don't see or hear anyone.

I start walking quickly down the hallway, my heart beating wildly in my chest and my breathing quick, terrified that I'm going to be caught at any second.

I round a corner and about run into a maid. I freeze, afraid that she is going to hurt me. But she doesn't. She just ignores me, walking past me down the hallway like I'm invisible.

Maybe I am.

I keep walking down the hallway and then down the stairs toward the kitchen that Matteo showed me yesterday. I gather my nerve, and I walk into the dining room that leads to the kitchen. I'm just going to grab anything that I can and then run back upstairs.

I walk inside, planning on doing just that, when I freeze. Eight pairs of eyes look up at me all at once from the table.

Shit.

The entire Carini family is sitting at the dining table along with a couple of other men I don't recognize. It can't be much past six in the morning, yet there they all sit. Like they knew today was the day that I would finally make my appearance. None of them seem surprised to see me.

But my plan to grab food and run no longer seems possible. I don't really know what to do. I try to ignore them and walk to the kitchen. No one has given me a command. No one has ordered that I strip in front of them. They haven't done anything that deserves any fear. It was probably just all talk anyway to mess with my head. I'll just spend my time cleaning or working for them. They won't actually rape me. The plan is still the same. I will just grab some food and head back to my room to eat it.

When I enter the kitchen, I find a buffet table of food. The servants all seem to ignore me as I walk over and grab a plate of food. That's when I realize they might be slaves, too. People who owe a debt to the Carini family.

I walk over to a young woman who can't be more than twenty. "Are you a slave, too?" I ask.

She smiles sweetly as she continues to chop vegetables. "No, ma'am. I'm a servant. The Carini family is a good employer that pays well. I gladly work for them."

I sigh. "I'm a slave. Help me escape."

She smiles. "You owe them a debt. You can leave when it's been paid back."

I frown. This woman won't help me.

"Are there more like me?"

"Of course there are more people who owe the Carini family a debt. But you are the only one who owes such a steep price."

I don't know what the hell she means, but I'm not going to stay here and figure it out. I start walking back out of the kitchen, hating that it is connected to the dining room and that I'm going to have to walk back through it to get to my room.

I step out and feel everyone's eyes on me again, but I don't make eye contact back. I keep my head held high as I walk through the dining room.

"Sit down, slave," Enrico says.

I freeze and turn to him, hating the command even though it is a simple one to follow. I won't do it because he commanded me to.

"I'm eating in my room."

He laughs. "No, you aren't. You are eating with us."

I shake my head and then keep walking when I hear a snap of fingers, and two men I don't know rush over. One grabs my plate of food out of my hands while the other grabs hold of me and drags me to the table, forcing me into a seat.

"Thank you for joining us for breakfast, *slave*," Enrico says, laughing.

I try to get up again, but the man forces me back into my seat.

"You eat with us, or you don't eat at all."

I want to be defiant. I want to say that I won't eat, but I can't. I need the food. If I'm going to fight any bigger battles, I need my strength. And I have nothing left after not eating or sleeping for the last few days.

So, I stay in my seat, and I start eating quickly, hoping that the faster I eat, the less time I have to spend with these disgusting people.

I see Arlo sitting at the far end of the table. He looks at me in disgust and then gets up from the table. He doesn't save me. He doesn't care.

I keep eating, and I'm again mostly ignored. I don't know why I was forced to eat at the table when none of them seem to care that I'm even here.

Enrico finally gets up from the table, as do a couple of the men. He walks over to me, and my heart stops.

"Enjoy the rest of your breakfast, *slave.*"

He grabs my chin and licks the side of my face while I freeze, not expecting him to touch me. My heart races, and my face turns red, but my body doesn't react.

"I can't wait to have you for breakfast. We have some work to do, but I will see you again soon, *slave.*"

He lets go of my chin and walks out of the room while I'm left to deal with his saliva on my face along with the threat of what tomorrow could bring. My anger grows as I wipe my face with a napkin. He knows I hate being controlled, and he is using it against me. Pushing my buttons so that he can do whatever he wants to me.

I try to remain calm. I don't have the strength now to fight him. It's not worth it. Let him do what he wants, call me what he wants. I'm not a slave, and no matter what I signed, I don't owe him or his family anything. It was their choice to save me. They should have let me die.

When the men are gone, I finish shoveling in my breakfast. There are a few other women still sitting at the table. None of them seem to give a shit about what just happened. They just continue eating. It takes me a second to notice the one person left at the table who might care—Gia. She stares at me the whole time I eat. She's not a little girl anymore like she was the last time I saw her. She's a woman. A beautiful woman who might be on my side.

Does she think what is happening to me is wrong? Will she help me escape?

If I were alone with her, I would ask. She seemed to have a heart the last time we were together. But I don't dare ask her now with others in the room who could report back to Enrico.

I finish eating every last drop of food on my plate, and then I get up. Knowing that, even if Gia commands me to do something, she has no way of enforcing me to do it. Not with the men gone. She would be foolish to command anything of me and show what little control she actually had over me. So, when I get up from the table, she says nothing.

My plan was to grab some books from the library and then run back to my room. But, after breakfast, I can't handle the thought of spending another second trapped in this house, replaying that moment with the disgusting slobber on my face over and over again.

So, instead of going back to my room, I do something impulsive. Something stupid. But it's the only thing I know how to do after years of doing just that. I run.

———

I know the fastest way out of the house. I memorized the path when Matteo gave me the tour of the house. I never thought I would run.

I was done running.

But, right now, I'm running for my life.

It doesn't take me long to run out of the house. Just three rooms and two doors were all it took for me to be outside. I'm sure I ran by staff, other members of the family, someone. But, if I did, I didn't see them.

All I could focus on was getting outside as fast as my legs would take me.

When the warm air hits my face, my mind starts swirling, thinking about what I just did. The bracelet is warm on my wrist, reminding me of Matteo's threat. My heels catch on the stone floor, and I trip, falling to the ground, rubbing even more dirt into my wedding dress.

There were plenty of clothes that I could have changed into in the closet. I had access to a full bathroom to shower in. But I did neither. That would have meant that I was giving in. That would have meant that they won. And I can't have that.

If I'm still wearing the clothes from the night Arlo captured me, then it means I still believe that I'm going to escape.

But, as I lie on the stone floor, already feeling a bit broken and trapped, I realize I should have changed. I should have eaten sooner. Maybe then I wouldn't feel so weak.

"You shouldn't run."

I turn and look at the woman standing over me—Gia. I was hoping to get a second alone with her. She will free me. She isn't heartless like everyone else.

"I wasn't running," I say, starting to slowly stand up. My body is too weak and sore to move very quickly.

Gia extends her hand to me, and I take it. She tightens her grip.

"You won't escape. Not on your own."

I smile. "But you'll help me. You know what your family is doing is wrong."

I see the change in her eyes, and it scares me.

"No. I won't help you. My brother won't help you. My father sure as hell won't help you. So, stop thinking that you are going to survive this. You aren't. The sooner your life ends, the sooner I get my family back. You put my family through hell, so you deserve what is coming to you, bitch."

She lets go of my hand, and I fall back to the ground. Gia walks away, leaving me on the ground. I felt every ounce of emotion dripping off of every word that Gia said. She's hurt. She's in pain. A pain that I don't have to imagine because I live with the same pain every day. And, for some reason, she thinks that I hurt her.

I thought Gia would be my savior. I thought she had a heart, but her heart is too broken to help me.

She's grown up a lot in the past seven years. She's no longer a sweet teenager. She's a woman scorned, and I'd do my best to steer clear of her, just like her father. It hurts that not even Gia cares about me. The maids don't care about me. It's clear that Arlo doesn't care about me. And, whatever Matteo feels about me, he's just going to try to butter me up, so he can get in my pants. I'm all alone in saving myself from this madness.

I look up at the sun beating down on me. I'll just spend my day here, soaking up the sun. It's not really freedom, but it will give me the illusion of freedom, unlike the tower that I've spent the last few days trapped in.

I close my eyes, trying to think of someplace nice to take me away from here. I dream of Heath and me on a far-off beach somewhere on our honeymoon. I pretend that, instead of here, I'm lying in his arms.

———

"I love you, Nina. I'll love you forever," Heath whispers into my hair.

I laugh. "You don't have to spend our entire honeymoon telling me that. I know you love me. That's what the wedding was about."

"But I want to. I need to tell you every single day for forever so that you don't forget it."

"I'll never forget it," I say, kissing his soft lips. "Now, go get me a drink. I'm thirsty."

He smiles and rolls off the lounger we have been lying on together while I spread out.

"What do you want, gorgeous?"

I scrunch my nose like I'm thinking real hard. "Anything that comes with one of those umbrella things."

He chuckles. "Everything comes with those here."

I smile. "Exactly. As long as it's fruity and it has alcohol in it, then I'm happy."

Heath nods and leaves to get me a drink while I nap in the warm sun.

"What are you dreaming about?" he asks when he returns.

"You." I grin. "Your muscles wrapped around me, your cock pushing against my belly, my hands tangled in your dark hair—"

———

"Dark hair, huh? I thought your husband was a blond."

My eyes shoot open, and I see Matteo standing over me with a sexy grin on his face. It's the same one I've seen from Arlo—except, unlike Arlo, Matteo smiles much more freely. Arlo spends most of his day with an intense brooding and a serious expression on his face. Matteo, on the other hand, lives life more freely. Like, if today were his last day, he would live it being happy.

I quickly sit up. "My husband is a blond."

Matteo raises an eyebrow. "Then, whom were you dreaming about if it wasn't your dear husband? It couldn't have been a sexy Italian, could it?"

I frown. Matteo's right. I was dreaming about a sexy Italian at the end. I was dreaming of Arlo.

Even though he was the one to bring me into this nightmare, my subconscious is still obsessed with him. I might be able to control my thoughts during the day. I might be able to stop thinking about him. But the sex I had with Arlo is too much for my body to stop obsessing about. It is still the best sex I've ever had. And I don't know how to stop it from happening again. Whatever happens here, I won't hurt Heath. I won't willingly fuck any of these men. I will fight until I kill them rather than let them fuck me.

"What do you want, Matteo?" I ask instead of answering his question.

He chuckles as he runs his hand through his long Italian hair. "If you don't answer me, I'm just going to assume you were having a dirty dream about me."

"Assume all you want; it doesn't make it true."

"It doesn't make it not true either."

I frown, not giving in. It won't help to tell Matteo the truth or to lie to him. He won't be happy that I was dreaming about his brother and not him. And I'm not a good enough liar to convince him that I was dreaming about him.

Matteo seems to let it go though. "I came for you."

I take a deep breath, trying not to add fear to his words. It was an innocent statement. He didn't say he was going to rape me or beat me. Just that he came for me.

"I'm a little busy at the moment," I say, closing my eyes again.

Matteo's heart might not be completely pure, but so far, he's always given me a choice. He hasn't forced me to do anything. He's the only hope I have left that he might eventually help me.

"Well, you are going to have to change *your* plans. Because I need you. Now."

The way he says *I need you* makes me ache deep in my belly. It's only been a couple of days since I've had sex, but being surrounded by sexy

Italians is going to turn me into a sex-craving lunatic even if they are keeping me here against my will. It still doesn't change the fact that, when they speak, I lose my mind.

"No, you need to change your plans."

"You don't get a say in this, beautiful. Your choices are, you come with me freely, or I'll carry you. Now, which will it be? Because I really would like to get my hands on you again."

My eyes shoot open. I don't like Matteo's choices game that he plays with me. It's never really a choice. Just like choosing to become this family's slave or dying wasn't really a choice either.

"I'll walk," I say as I slowly get up.

Matteo respects my wishes and keeps his hands off me.

As soon as I'm standing, I run.

This time, instead of running away from the house, I run toward it. Matteo said that, as long as I was in my bedroom, I wouldn't be touched. If Matteo is going to give me some choice between him forcefully fucking me in the ass or me willingly sucking his dick, he's got another thing coming. I will do no such thing. I just have to make it up to the bedroom. And then I'll spend the rest of my time hiding out there and sneaking out in the middle of the night for food.

Unless Matteo was lying.

But it's the best shot I have.

So, I run full force into the mansion and down hallways until I get to the staircase that leads up to my room. I don't hear Matteo running after me anymore. He should have been able to catch me in my heels. But he either has given up or he knows that he is going to come into my room even if it breaks the "rules."

But I keep running up the stairs. I keep running down the long, dark hallway until I'm feet from the door.

When I see Enrico, I try to stop. But I'm not prepared to stop. I run straight into him.

I try to turn and run the other way, but his hands grab my shoulders.

"Let me go!" I scream, trying to get out of his arms.

He's old and out of shape, and I know I can overtake him.

He shakes his head. "You should be black and blue by now. You should be broken and curled up into a ball in your room. But you're not."

I grin. "Because I'm stronger than you think. And I'm not some plaything that you can beat when you want."

Enrico smiles. "No. You're not strong. You're weak. Just like my sons. They think that playing some game with your head first is how they are going to win this fight. But you aren't like the rest. You're a fighter; I'll give you that. Feisty. You won't give up anything easily. That is why you need to be broken."

I stop fighting for just a second as I try to understand his words. "What do you mean?"

"It means that I'm going to be the one who breaks you. My sons need to learn a lesson. I'm going to beat you until you can't move, slave. I'm going to fuck you until all you can think about is my cock. I'm going to break you. And, when I'm done, my sons will have their turns."

The panic quickly turns into survival.

I knee him hard in the crotch, and he immediately releases me, not able to deal with the pain.

"You won't fucking touch me. I'm not your slave!" I scream at him as I run back down the stairs.

I had it right the first time. I need to get the fuck away from these deranged people.

I make it three steps down when I see two men walking up the stairs with the intent to grab me. I know from how they are dressed in dark clothes that they are Enrico's men.

The adrenaline takes over, and I run full force at them. I punch the first man as hard as I can in the nose, getting just a glimpse of the blood that pours out of him, before I get to the second man. I kick him as hard as I can in the crotch, but he grabs my leg before I make contact.

I fall onto the stairs, hitting my head against the wrought iron railing before I land on the ground. I don't have to see the blood to know that my head is fucked up. I want to keep fighting. I don't want them to take me so easily, but the world starts spinning. My head feels like it's about to explode from the pressure and pain.

I spent seven years preparing. Trying my best to take every self-defense class I could. I learned how to use a gun. I learned how to control my obsessions.

But nothing was ever going to be enough. I'm still going to get raped. Beaten. I'm still going to be a slave. Because I'm not strong enough to save myself from any of it.

9

ARLO

It's been one week since I last saw Nina.

And, every day that goes by, my heart hurts a little more. I thought that keeping my distance would make it easier for me to do what would have to be done, but it didn't. I know I don't have real feelings for her. That's not what this is. I just want to fuck her again. She was the best fuck of my life. Her pussy was tight and inviting. Her body had curves in all the right places. But what I loved the most was how she craved my control. She wanted it. She's fucked up, like me. She got off on acting like my slave.

And I'm desperate to feel that again. Even though I've had real slaves, none of them have done anything for me like what Nina did for me that one night. I've often pictured her face on the other whores while fucking them. But that doesn't do anything for me either.

I want to fuck Nina again. Now. I want to rape her for real. I want to hear her cry when I stretch her open while she secretly wants more of my cock. I want it so bad that I can't even focus on work, the only thing I give a shit about in this world.

The last time I saw Nina was in the dining room when my father slobbered all over her gorgeous face. She looked at me like she needed me to save her. I can't fuck her until she realizes that I won't save her.

When she finally stops looking at me like a sad puppy dog that needs rescuing, then I'll fuck her.

But I need to see her. I need to give a fresh face to my dirty dreams. I need to see her so that, when I jack off, I have a new image of her to get off to.

She's probably still hiding in her bedroom. Matteo fed her some stupid lie about how she was safe in her bedroom. Maybe from him, but the rest of us won't give her much space.

I should be heading off to work. I have a new deal that I'm working on closing that could bring us billions in weapons to sell, but I can't. Not until I see her face.

I run up the stairs to her bedroom and then hesitate. Should I knock first or just barrel inside like I own the place? I choose the latter.

I push the door open, surprised that she doesn't have it locked.

I don't see her when I go inside. She's not in the bed. Not on the bench overlooking the gardens below. She's not in the bathroom. She's not here.

I sigh. Matteo might have finally decided it was time to break her. Good. Let him. He can do the dirty work, and then I'll be able to do what I need to.

But I guess I'll have to wait until later to see her.

I run back down the stairs, knowing that I only have twenty minutes before I'm supposed to be at my meeting.

"Checking in on our guest? Isn't it a bit early for you to make your move? You usually let me do all the dirty work first," Matteo says, sipping his coffee in the dining room.

I frown. She's not with him.

"Where's Gia?" I ask.

He shrugs. "I think she went shopping."

Matteo turns his attention back to the newspaper he's reading.

I shake my head. *Who reads newspapers anymore?*

But he's old school. He'll never stop trying to impress our father.

Father.

He's the only one unaccounted for. And he's been dying to get his hands on a slave for months. He usually has his own playthings to keep him occupied. But he broke his last one too quickly. She didn't survive long. Only a month. She found his gun and killed herself before he could touch her again.

Nina is stronger than her, but I have no idea how long he's had her as his slave. A few hours? A day? Or the whole week?

If it's been a week, Nina will be close to the point where she'd rather die than deal with another second of my father. And I let it happen.

I run through the mansion, leaving my idiot brother sitting, clueless, in the dining room. My father's quarters are on the complete opposite side from Nina's. Matteo and I made sure of that. We tried to protect her from him, but we've failed in the first week. We never thought he would go for her so quickly. But he must have lost his patience with us after the last one.

I expect to see the usual guards at the door, but there are none. That means he doesn't think she has enough strength to escape anymore. He thinks he has her under his complete control. If there is one thing I know about Nina, it is, no matter what he does to her, she will never be controlled.

I burst into his room, and my stomach curls when I see her. She's tied to the bed, face up. Blood covers every inch of her face. Bruises and more blood stain her body. Her arms and legs are spread wide as ropes tie her to each bedpost, but I'm not sure the restraints are necessary. Her body is so broken that she couldn't possibly have the strength to fight him off her or even stand on her own.

My father walks into the room, his dick in his hand, sticking out of his slacks. "Come to watch the show?" he asks.

"No, I've come to have my turn."

He grins. "You don't like them bloody though. You like them fighting."

He's right. I don't like fucking helpless women like he does. I'm not a coward. I fuck them against their will, sure, but only when that's what they want. I'm not my father.

I look at Nina. Her eyes finally find me in the room. I expect the same help-me look in her eyes that she gives me every time I am in the same room with her. But her eyes don't ask for help. They expect nothing from me.

"Get out of here. You can have her when I'm finished with her," my father says, turning his attention to her.

My stomach churns at the thought of my father fucking her like this. I can taste the bile in my mouth. It's gone on for far too long.

I should have known.

I should have tried to stop it.

But I never have before. What makes me want to save Nina when I haven't saved so many before?

I look at her long brown hair and her beat-up body. She's beautiful, even in her current state. But it's more than just her beauty that attracts me to her. It's her obsession with me. I've never been the center of someone's world. No one has ever cared about only me ever. Not even my own mother. That must be all it is. The fascination with a woman who is obsessed with me.

She's not obsessed anymore.

She hates my guts.

I watch as my father walks toward her, and I can't take it. I don't know how to stop it, but I can't let it happen. I can't let him hurt her.

I grab my father's shoulder, and I push him against the wall.

"What the fuck are you doing? You'll have your turn with our slave. Wait, or I'll make you wait your turn, you asshole," he says.

I don't even flinch when he calls me an asshole. He's called me everything in the book. I'm not a son to him, and I never will be.

He looks at me in disgust. "Get out of here. You don't have the balls to be half the man that I am."

He throws me off of him even though I have three times the strength that he does. He's in control here, not me. He has the power over the men who stand guard and are ready at his beck and call. Not me. I don't have any power yet. But I will soon enough.

I grab his arm again, stopping him from touching Nina.

"Let go of me now. Or I'll make you. I'll whip your ass like when you were a kid, and maybe then, you'll finally learn some manners."

I tighten my grip on his arm, still not sure of what my next move will be. All I know is, I won't let him touch her. He moves to punch me, but I block him, which only makes him angrier.

"Whipping your ass won't be enough. I'll lock you in the dungeon, and you'll never see the light of day again if you keep defying me, boy."

"I want her. Now. I can't wait. I want to know what it's like to fuck a woman who's broken and beaten. I want the taste of blood in my mouth."

He stops a second and looks at me, trying to tell if I'm lying or not. "I don't believe you. You never want their blood unless they willingly give it to you. You're weak—"

"I want her blood. I want to make this slave pay for what she did."

He smiles when I use the word *slave*. "Be my guest then."

I watch him slowly walk out of the room, leaving her to me. He might not be in the room any longer, but I know he is still watching. The sick fucker has video cameras everywhere so that he can relive his disgusting fantasies, even after the women are long gone.

And watching his son finally become a man in his eyes is going to make my twisted father jack off more times than I want to imagine.

I turn to Nina as she moans quietly to herself on the bed. It's all she can do. And even her soft moans leave her exhausted.

I walk toward her and pull my knife from my back pocket. I begin slicing the ropes holding her in place. They're all completely useless anyway. She can't run; she's only hours away from dying from her wounds or loss of blood. I've never seen my father brutalize a woman like he has Nina. I don't know what she did to piss him off, but what-ever it was, it was personal.

I finish cutting the last rope and watch as her arm falls free to the bed. I want her fingers digging into my back with her sharp nails drawing blood. I want her to use that arm to push and shove and fight with everything that she has to get away from me. I don't want this emptiness.

She looks up at me like I'm a monster, and I am. Just a different kind than my father.

I take her and flip her over so that she doesn't have to look me in the eye. And then I climb on top of her.

She moans as I let my weight settle onto her body. But she doesn't fight. She can't fight. She has nothing left.

I pull my shirt off my body, and then I undo my pants, letting my hard cock spring free. I really am a monster. I shouldn't be hard at the sight of a woman in this much pain.

But, instead, I've never been harder. I push my cock against her ass. She flinches at just the touch of my cock against her ass.

I want her to feel good, but I also can't control myself once I start. I don't know if it's possible to make her feel good when she's in this state. I should just focus on being fast, and then I'll get her out of here.

I need to taste her. My lips kiss her neck. I love her sweet smell that still lingers mixed with her blood, sweat, and tears. She doesn't move when I kiss her. No reaction at all. But it doesn't stop me. I move down her body, kissing every inch of her back, trying to make the pain go away from each scar my father caused. Even once they heal, they will always be present on her body. She will never escape this. She will take this week with her forever.

If only she had a forever.

Kissing her neck and back isn't enough to satisfy me. I want to taste every inch of her body. I need it more than I need air.

I know I need to be rough with her, and I will be. But, first, I need to be sweet. As much for her as for me.

I grab her hips and pull her up onto all fours. She moves, but she doesn't have the strength to hold herself up. I have to hold her up.

I spread her legs and move underneath her. I suck each of her nipples first. Loving how they harden under my tongue. It's the first reaction I've gotten from her. I watch her chest rise and fall a little as I suck on one, her breathing slowly picking up.

She's excited.

I kiss down her smooth stomach as I hold her up with my arms, as her arms are doing nothing to keep her up. My tongue slips down to her pussy. I forgot how good she tastes. I feel the slickness that has already formed there. I expertly move my tongue around her folds and over her clit, and I feel more liquid pool. And I lap every drop that I can, loving that, even though she is in this much pain, I can still turn her body on.

Her body wants me even if she doesn't.

I continue licking a few seconds more until I finally get the one word I was hoping to get from her.

"Yes," she moans ever so quietly. So quietly that I'm not even sure I heard it or if I just wanted to hear it.

But I take that as my cue that she wants this. Maybe not exactly like this, but she still wants me. And this is much better than the alternative.

"I'm going to fuck you so hard, Nina, that you are going to forget about everything other than me," I say as I move from underneath her to behind her again.

I let her hips rest back down as I push my cock against her ass. This time, when I do, she doesn't moan; she whimpers in an I-need-you kind of way.

I spread her legs further, and then I push my cock into her pussy, just letting the head rest inside her.

Her slickness welcomes me, pushing me deeper inside. I don't want gentle though, and I don't think Nina does either.

I slap her ass hard as I drive my cock inside her.

She screams, and my cock hardens more.

I slap her again as I thrust inside.

She screams, but it's not a terrifying or painful scream. It's a God-please-don't-stop scream.

It drives me mad, and I forget about everything else other than fucking her. My beautiful, imperfect, obsessive Nina.

I move faster, pushing her so hard into the bed that I'm sure it's impossible for her to breathe. I grab her hair, pulling it roughly, lifting her head up so that I can see her face.

I slap her ass again, but this time, I get no response.

I slip my hand around to find her clit and rub furiously, bringing her back to life.

"Stay with me, Nina," I whisper into her ear.

She comes to life.

I feel her hips move against mine just ever so slightly. I feel her whimpers pick up as I fuck her harder. Her whole body comes alive, like I was the shock her body needed to remember to keep fighting. To keep living.

I push harder until I'm about to come, finally letting her have some relief. I hit her ass hard. Her pussy clinches my cock as she comes, barely whispering my name.

Her coming takes me to a whole different level. When I come, it's an explosion that I was never expecting. But then nothing with Nina has been expected. Nothing.

I roll off of her and tuck my cock back into my pants. Then, I lift her from the bed before my father has a chance to say anything different.

She's limp in my arms. I'm not even sure how she managed to stay awake the whole time I was fucking her. In a way, I wish she had passed out so that she wouldn't remember me raping her. Because, as much as I want to tell myself that she wanted that, it isn't true. No woman wants what I just did. No woman wants to be fucked while completely broken.

My father doesn't stop me when I leave his quarters. I see a couple of his men as I pass, but they don't say anything either, and if they did, I would fight them to the death. No one is touching her. No one.

I feel my phone buzz in my pants pocket, but it can wait. I don't give a shit who is calling me right now. I just want to get Nina somewhere safe. And she's no longer safe with me.

I keep walking until I get to the one door I never thought I would knock on for help. I knock loudly, making it clear that he'd better get his ass to the door as quickly as possible.

Matteo does. He opens the door seconds later and looks just as confused to see me standing at his door as I am to be standing here. We might all live under the same roof, but the mansion is so big that we basically have our own homes within its walls. We each have half a dozen or more rooms that are our own and are blocked off from everything else, giving us a feeling of having our own house.

I push past him without saying a word and carry Nina to his bed. I lay her down on the bed as gingerly as I can.

"What the hell happened? I've never seen you beat a woman like this before," Matteo says.

"It wasn't me."

Matteo's eyes widen, but he doesn't ask any more questions. He knows who caused the scars all over her body.

"How did you get her out?" he asks.

"I became a monster, just like him." I don't look at him when I say it. I don't want his judgmental stare.

I know what I did was wrong. I swore I would never become him, but maybe this is how it starts. It starts by pretending like you are saving someone, and then it's a slippery slope from there. I liked hurting her when she couldn't fight back.

"She needs medical help," I say.

"I can handle it."

I nod. I know Matteo will heal her wounds. That's why I brought her here. He's the best with medical care.

He goes over to a dresser where he pulls out a syringe and medicine, and then he injects it into her arm. "That should take away most of her pain. At least temporarily," Matteo says.

I nod.

"You're bleeding. Do you want me to stitch you up? You always suck at it, which is why you keep bleeding."

"No. Just take care of her," I say, not bothering to look down at the scar that has opened up again and is bleeding profusely. It's nothing compared to what she has gone through.

My phone buzzes again, and I know it's the arms dealer I'm supposed to be meeting with. I press Decline, but I can't actually ignore it.

"I need to go," I say for more than one reason.

"You shouldn't go. She might not make it through the night. She's lost a lot of blood."

Fuck, and I've made it that much worse.

"I have to go."

Matteo frowns. "No, you fucking don't, man. The deal can wait a couple of days."

I stare into Matteo's eyes, and he knows it isn't about the deal. I can't face myself around Nina. Not when I've caused her as much pain as my father. Not when I couldn't save her from my father before he ever laid a hand on her.

"She's strong. The strongest. She will survive this and more if she has to."

Matteo glares at me. "She shouldn't fucking have to. That wasn't the plan."

Matteo and I haven't always gotten along, but I don't want to fight now.

"I trust that you will keep her safe."

"Of course," Matteo says.

Nina stirs, looking at Matteo. He takes her hand in his, comforting her.

"You saved me," she croaks out.

Matteo grins. "Of course I saved you. I shouldn't have ever let you get hurt in the first place. I'm sorry, beautiful."

Nina gives him a faint smile, and then she begins to fade again. She doesn't look at me. She doesn't even know that I'm in the same room as her.

She's going to hate me.

Forever.

I've done something unforgivable.

She's going to love Matteo.

She thinks he saved her.

I made the right choice in bringing her to Matteo. He might actually be strong enough to save her. He can put an end to this madness. He can put an end to it all.

10

MATTEO

SHE THINKS I SAVED HER.

Usually, I would welcome her thinking that. I want her to think of me as her protector. I want her to think I care. I want her to let her guard down.

That's when I'll really be able to control her. When she thinks she can trust me.

But I don't like benefiting from my brother's mistake.

I look down at the woman in my bed. She's been sleeping for three days straight.

I wasn't sure she would even survive the first night. And, as much as my dumb-ass brother thinks he doesn't care, he does. I don't know what he was thinking, leaving her alone with me.

If she hadn't survived the night, he never would have forgiven himself.

Now that she has, I'll have to beat his ass later.

I walk over to her and sit on the edge of the bed next to her. I take the bandage in my hand and change the one on her forehead, checking the wound that is the worst.

The stitches are healing nicely. I check the others on her stomach and arm, along with all the bruises covering her body. Everything is slowly healing, but there is no way to know how bad the damage is inside her body.

I tuck her hair behind her ear and stroke her cheek. I can't stand not to touch her. Even in her bruised and beaten state, she's still as gorgeous as she was the first time I saw her.

She opens her eyes and smiles up at me like I'm her favorite person in the whole world.

"How are you feeling?" I ask.

"You saved me."

"That doesn't matter right now. How do you feel? Do you need more pain medicine? You must be starving. Can I get you something to eat or drink?"

"You saved me. Why?" she asks, trying to sit up in bed before she realizes how much of a mistake that is. Her arms aren't strong enough to push herself up, and just the movement of her head makes her sick and dizzy.

"Whoa. Just lie down, beautiful. You've been through a heck of a lot these past few days. You need to relax."

She doesn't argue with me, so I take that as a sign that she agrees with me. When she lies back down, I stroke her cheek again.

"Now, answer my questions first, and then I'll answer whatever questions you want me to. How do you feel?"

"Like I've just been hit by a train," she says, closing her eyes, hating to show any weakness.

I feel the anger rising in my chest at the thought of her feeling weak after surviving this. She is anything but weak.

I get up and walk over to the medicine cabinet and pull out a bottle of pills. I walk back and take her hand where I pour four pills.

"Take these, it will help with the pain."

She looks at the pills and then at me before she pops them all into her mouth at once. I hand her a glass of water from my nightstand, and she washes the pills down, not at all hesitating to take them. She didn't question the amount or if I was drugging her. She just took the pills.

"Good girl. Now, are you hungry, or do you need anything else right now?"

She slowly shakes her head.

I nod. "Now, I need you to tell me what happened."

I don't really. I already know what happened, but I need to know what she remembers. The pain might have completely wiped away her memory.

She looks away for a second, and when she turns her gaze back, I know that she remembers everything. Every. Fucking. Thing.

The horror.

The pain.

The fight for her life.

All of it.

"Your father raped me. He beat me. He had his men tie me up because he was too chickenshit to do it himself. And then he raped me over and over. Trying to break me." She looks down at her beaten body. "Seems like he won."

I place a finger under her chin so that I can see her endearing dark eyes that are full of fight despite everything she has already been through. "He didn't win. You have plenty of fight left in you. You aren't broken yet."

I cock my head to the side and grin because I know she will smile, too. She does. She can't help herself; my grin is infectious even in her broken state.

"He might have broken your body but not your spirit. I have no doubt that, if you had a gun or a knife tucked in your pajamas, you would still try to kill me right now to get your freedom. Even in your weakened state."

She smiles. "Others, yes. But I wouldn't try to kill *you*."

I smirk even though I know she doesn't know what she's talking about. I'm not her friend. I'm just as dangerous as the rest of my family. Just because I kept her alive for a few days doesn't make me a saint. I'm a monster, like everyone else. I might even be worse because I'm the devil who hides behind his charms.

"Anything else happen?" I probe.

I feel the anger rising to the surface. Her eyes look like she is about to rip someone's head off, and her body is flush with rage.

"It wasn't just your father. It was your brother, too. He raped me. I thought he was like you. I thought, deep down, he cared and would never do anything to really hurt me." I see the tears welling up in her eyes. "But I was wrong. He's just as vile as your father; he just didn't have the balls to try to break me himself. He let his father do all the dirty work."

I take her hand and interlock my fingers with hers, letting her think that I would never be as awful as either my father or brother.

She exhales deeply when I hold her hand. "I hate him. He's a monster," she says, thinking back to what Arlo did to her.

But there is something other than hate in her eyes. *Lust.* As much as she hates Arlo, she still enjoyed herself. She still wants him to fuck her again.

I smile. "And what do you think of me?"

Nina looks at me with the same glimmer of lust still in her eyes. "I have some hope that you are a better man than your father or brother."

I laugh. "Well, that's not hard to do. My brother is an idiot, and my father is the devil."

"Why did you save me?"

I sigh and then move closer to her. Our eyes are locked, and our lips are millimeters from touching. "What kind of monster wouldn't save a gorgeous girl like you?"

She closes the gap whether intentionally or unintentionally. Her lips press against mine. Her breathing is still heavy and labored, so I know I can't let the kiss last long. But her lips are so soft and plump that I don't want the kiss to ever end. The second our lips touch, a spell comes over me, and I become just as obsessed with her as my brother is.

I stop the kiss when I hear the tiniest wheeze in her throat. I sit back up and let her breathe as I cherish the kiss.

"What was that for?" I ask.

She sinks back into the bed, her eyes closing from the exhaustion again. It's amazing that she was even able to stay awake this long. It's going to take weeks for her to heal enough to leave this room. I'll have her in my bed for weeks. I'll become her friend, her confidant, and maybe even her lover. She'll be mine if I want before Arlo even has a chance to change his mind.

"Because you saved me and I wanted to," she says, opening her eyes for one more second. And then her heavy eyelids quickly fall, and she drifts back off to sleep.

I lean forward and kiss her forehead, needing more of her scent. *Nina Young, what are you doing to me?*

I watch her sleep. I won't leave her alone for a second. Not now. Not ever.

I won't let anyone else hurt her. I'm the only one who will get her pain.

11

NINA

I want to kill Enrico.

That's the main focus of all my dreams. Finding a way to kill Enrico before he touches me again. I've never felt such pain before. And I made a promise to myself with every lash of the whip, every bruise and broken rib that formed from his beatings, and every rip from his cock tearing me wide open that I would do everything I could before letting that happen again.

Even kill myself.

I can't go through that again.

Not even for Heath and Eden.

I have a new obsession, and right now, it's finding the most painful way to end their father's life.

"How are you feeling?" Matteo asks for the millionth time this week, like he always does when he enters the room.

I smile. "Better."

I am better. I can actually stay awake for hours at a time. I can sit up in bed. My appetite has returned, and the pain is slowly subsiding. I just don't have much strength left. I can barely walk. I can barely lift a fork to my mouth.

Matteo sits on the edge of the bed as he tucks a strand of my hair behind my ear. I love the feel of his hand against my cheek. Just like I love when Matteo asks me how I'm feeling. I love how he makes me laugh. I love how he holds me while I sleep to keep my nightmares away. I feel safe with him.

"Good. I brought you more books to read," Matteo says, setting a large stack of books on the nightstand next to me.

"Thank you," I say as Matteo stands up from my bed. "Where are you going?"

"I need to shower, and then I'm going to crash. It's been a long night."

I study Matteo further and realize that he is a dirty mess. I know, before I spent all my nights in his bed, he spent his nights away doing God knows what for the family business. But last night was the first night he spent away since I joined him in bed. I hated it.

"Crash here," I say, needing him near me to push away the demons.

His eyes search mine a second—for what, I don't know. But I let him in and show him how much I need him. I need him to lie next to me, so I can get some sleep. I need to feel his steady heartbeat and the calm inside him that washes over me whenever he's close.

But I've become obsessed with the feel of him against my skin. I can't sleep without him. If I'm not thinking of revenge against his father, I'm thinking about him. It's probably stupid. I shouldn't trust Matteo so easily, not when he is related to such monsters, but I do. He's the only one I can trust. I need to trust someone if I'm going to survive here.

Matteo stands and kicks off his shoes. Then, he lifts his shirt over his head. I soak in his hard abs and chest, which are almost identical to Arlo's. His long hair and scar on his face are the main differences between the two. That's not true. Matteo is caring while Arlo is just as bad as his father.

He slides his pants down until he is standing in just his briefs. I try not to stare. I try not to think about what lies beneath the briefs. But my eyes automatically go there.

His smirk tells me he knows exactly what I'm thinking.

Damn it!

I shouldn't feel this way, even about Matteo. I'm married.

But I need to make Matteo care enough about me to help me escape. And the only way to do that is to pretend like I care about him, too. Heath will forgive me for whatever happens while I'm here. He already knew my whole story when he married me. He knew this was a possibility. And, while he swore to do everything to protect me, he made me promise to do whatever it took to save myself. He didn't specify what he meant. Now, I know.

I swallow down the lump in my throat. *He'll forgive me, but will I ever forgive myself?*

Matteo walks over to the other side of the bed and pulls the sheets back before climbing into the bed next to me. "What are you thinking about, beautiful?"

I smile weakly as I fidget with the covers. "You."

Again, Matteo searches my eyes for the truth, and when he finds what he thinks is the truth, he moves closer to me. His hand goes to the base of my neck, and his lips press against mine. He tenderly kisses me, carefully touching me only on the places that aren't bruised. He draws me into his kiss and makes me forget about everything. I feel the familiar ache deep in my belly, and I pull away for a second, stopping the kiss.

I thought I was in control, but my body continues to disobey me. I'm not supposed to actually feel anything for these men. I'm not supposed to be turned on by Matteo's kiss. I wasn't supposed to come when Arlo fucked me.

Matteo kisses me on the forehead, and I melt a little. He's so sweet and caring to me.

How could I not fall a little for him?

"It's okay to want me. There is nothing wrong with wanting more than one man," Matteo says, reading my mind.

"I only want Heath."

"I know." But his smirk says otherwise.

I frown. He thinks I want Arlo, too. He couldn't be further from the truth. I don't want a man who raped me. Ever. No matter how obsessed and attracted to him I was before, there is no way I will ever want him again now.

Matteo pulls me close to him while he softly kisses me everywhere that I'm not bruised. My mind twists with thoughts of Arlo, Matteo, and Heath. I want the nightmares back. It would be better than what my twisted mind is thinking. Instead, I drift off to sleep in Matteo's arms while I think of two other men.

———

My eyes fly open, and I see Arlo standing over my bed. Matteo's arms wrap around me tighter as he lazily opens his eyes.

"Well, don't you two look cozy? I didn't mean to intrude," Arlo says.

"I bet you didn't," I snarl at him.

Arlo raises an eyebrow at me, not expecting my snarkiness. But he hasn't seen anything yet.

Matteo doesn't seem the least bit concerned to have his brother standing in his bedroom while he was sleeping with me.

"Relax, brother. I've just been taking care of Nina here since you couldn't deal with the sight of her so broken. Don't worry; she still cares about you," Matteo says, casually leaning back on the bed with his arms behind his head.

I give Matteo a dirty look that shows him just how insane I think what he just said is.

"I don't care about Arlo." I turn my attention back to Arlo. "I don't care about you. The tiniest feelings that I had for you before vanished when you raped me."

Arlo closes his eyes when I say *raped me*. If I didn't know him so well, I would just say that he was blinking. It happened so fast. But me saying that he raped me stung him. I don't understand why, but it did.

I want to talk to him about what happened. Because, clearly, I'm missing something, just like I'm missing everything else.

"You don't care about Arlo?" Matteo says with a raised eyebrow.

"No."

Matteo nods. "You're feeling better, aren't you, beautiful? Much stronger?"

I nod, not sure where he is going with this.

"Good. Then, I think it's time you show Arlo here that your feelings have shifted."

I cock my head to the side as I look at Matteo.

"I'll give you a choice. Suck me, or suck Arlo."

I freeze. I knew that, eventually, Matteo would want something sexual from me. He is a man after all and a man who supposedly owns me for the next seven years. But I didn't think he would be so crass about it. I thought that, someday, we would have sex, but it would be on *my* terms. Not *his*.

"No."

Matteo smiles. "It wasn't a yes or no question. It was a choice. Just like every other time. Suck me, or suck Arlo."

"No," I say again. I will not suck either of these men. Not until I'm ready.

"Choose, beautiful. Arlo needs to see that you don't care about him anymore. He needs to see that I'm the one you think about when you sleep. He needs to see that you've only been here a few weeks, and he's already lost."

I turn from Matteo to Arlo and then back. "No. You won't force me. You won't hurt me. I won't do it."

Matteo nods. "I would never hurt you, beautiful." He strokes my cheek. "You know that. But Arlo won't show you the same courtesy. You need to choose. Suck me or him."

I look back to Arlo, and I see the hardness that was there when he raped me creeping back into his eyes. I don't have any doubt that he will do it all over again in a second if I don't obey his brother's command.

I grab Matteo's hair and forcefully kiss him, passionately putting everything I can into the kiss. I suck on his tongue. His lips. Everything, letting him know exactly how I want him to think I feel about him.

And then I break away from him. I see his cocky smirk slowly vanish as I get out of the bed. My legs are a little shaky since I've barely used them this week. But I stand and walk over to where Arlo is standing at the foot of the bed.

It takes all of my strength to take each step, both physically and mentally, because I want to walk almost anywhere but toward Arlo. But I won't let him or anyone else break me again.

I stumble on the last step, and Arlo grabs me, keeping me from falling face-first into the ground. I don't know why he does it. He likes seeing me in pain while on the ground, whimpering in front of him. Maybe it's the small piece of him that still cares. The small piece that is like his brother.

"Let me go." I don't want his help. I'd rather hit the floor.

"You don't have to do this."

I nod my head. "Yes, I do."

I won't let him punish me for not listening to him.

Arlo carefully lets me go as he tests to make sure that I can stand on my own.

I take my time, and as I slowly kneel in front of Arlo. It might look like a weakness, but it feels more like my strongest moment. Matteo wanted me to suck him. He thought I'd choose him, but I will never choose someone who forces me to do anything. I feel defiant and strong.

Sucking Arlo will do nothing to me. It means nothing to me. I've already fucked him. And, if I'm completely honest with myself, he has a good cock that I would love to taste and feel again, if it were my decision. On my terms. And if I didn't have a husband waiting for me.

This is on my terms, I think.

Arlo didn't ask for this. I can take something from him, just like he took something from me.

I undo the button on his gray slacks and then push them down over his hips. I grab his briefs and pull them down, too, trying to keep my balance as his cock springs free.

I smirk. It's already hard.

He wants me.

I turn him on.

That's power.

I just need to figure out the best way to use my power over the Carini men, and then maybe I'll find my freedom.

I sway just a little, getting dizzy from being out of bed. I grab his hips for support to keep myself upright. I'm not strong enough to even kneel without having to hold myself up. But I'm not going to let the pain, bruises, or weakness stop me.

I take his cock into my mouth, and I'm rewarded with his groan.

I have the power.

I take him further in as I taste his pre-cum already dripping down my throat. I love the taste. I love the feel of his cock in my throat even though I hate him.

So wrong.

I suck him all the way in until his cock is deep in my throat, and I almost gag from the fullness in my mouth.

Arlo's hand tangles in my hair, and his eyes roll back in his head.

I run my lips all the way back to his tip and then back to his base. I get into a rhythm, using only my lips and my tongue to suck his hard cock. I feel powerful with each grunt and groan. That I can make him feel this way with just my mouth.

Arlo is not a man who loses control easily, but with my mouth around his dick, he does.

He's not thinking about what he's doing. He's not thinking about how his brother is watching him. Or that I'm nothing more than his slave who is getting him off. I'm not his lover or his friend. I'm a slave who will do anything to get free.

Even play with his mind. I'll slash his throat in his sleep or shoot him straight in the heart in the daylight. I don't care, but he'll be dead along with most of his family by the time I leave here.

I move my lips faster, not letting his pleasure last longer than I want it to. I milk him until his warm cum pours deep into my throat.

When I finally release him, he looks shocked. I took something from him without asking, and it felt good. Even if the thing I took brought him immense pleasure, it was a start.

He lets go of my hair and quickly tucks himself back into his pants. I have to grab on to the floor to keep my balance.

Arlo angrily looks at me. "I just came to tell you that you're safe.

Enrico is out of town for the next month. You can leave Matteo's room whenever you want. You'll be safe."

Arlo turns and leaves without another word.

He doesn't get to have the last word. Not like that. He doesn't get to tell me that I'm safe when he's still lurking in the next room. I won't be safe until I'm back in Heath's arms.

He doesn't get to leave.

I run after him. Not allowing him to just leave.

12

ARLO

I HEAR her running after me. She's not quiet on a normal day, and her injuries have made her that much louder, making it impossible for her to sneak up on me.

I could easily outrun her. Especially when she's so weak. But I don't. For no other reason than I want to be close to her.

I stop abruptly and turn just in time to catch her from falling again.

"You have to stop doing that," she says as she pushes herself off my chest but not before I get a whiff of her shampoo and the feel of her body against mine again.

"Stop doing what? Stop saving you?"

She frowns, and her cheeks flush bright red with anger. "You have never saved me. Stop pretending that you actually care. You don't give a shit about me!"

I wait for a second for her to get her anger out. She takes several deep breaths, and when I think she has calmed down, I say, "Are you finished lecturing me? I have some places I need to be."

"No, I'm not finished. Not even close. You don't get to tell me I'm safe. I'm not safe! I won't ever be safe again, not until I'm home in my own bed. Stop trying to save me one second and then fuck me the

159

next. You don't get to pretend you care. The only person who cares about me is Matteo."

I laugh. "You think Matteo cares about you more than I do? He's just as fucked up as I am. He's messing with your head. Can't you see that? He wants to fuck you and control you, just like every other man in this house. He's just like me. He just plays the game differently."

"What fucking game? You think getting your jollies by messing with me like a play toy is a game? I'm not a game. This is my life you are messing with!"

"And it was our lives you messed with when you took that drink, knowing full well that I would save you. I warned you. I told you not to. You did it anyway. And, now, you have to pay the consequences."

I start walking away, but she half-runs and half-stumbles after me.

"Stop!"

I run my hand through my hair, hating obeying anyone's commands, even hers.

"What do you want from me? You think I have the power to rescue you. You think I have a heart that will make me let you go. That's what you want, right? For me to save you?"

She freezes with her eyes wide.

"You're fucking wrong if you think I have that kind of power. Or that, even if I did, I would want to save you. You're nothing to me. Just another slave I have to deal with until you finally leave. You're just another distraction from getting my work done."

"You're a monster. I already knew that."

I nod. "My father's a monster. Same with my sister. Even my brother won't save you."

"He's not a monster," she whispers, but I can hear it in her voice that she doesn't even believe herself. She just wishes it were true.

I smirk. "Matteo didn't save you from my father. I did."

Her eyes widen again. "You didn't save me. You raped me! Matteo was the one who took care of me. He healed me. He dressed my wounds. He gave me pain medicine. He fed me. He stayed with me through sleepless nights and took away my nightmares. He saved me."

I laugh. "Matteo took advantage of the situation. He took care of you because that is what he does. He plays games with your head. He makes women let their guards down, and then he pounces when they least suspect. He's playing you."

She shakes her head like it can't be true, but I see the realization buried in her eyes. She knows what I'm saying is true.

"He's still a better man than you will ever be!" she yells at me like it's an insult.

I smile. "You're probably right. He is a better man than I will ever be. It doesn't change the fact that I saved you, not him."

She folds her arms across her chest, and I see the shaking in her legs. She's trying to act strong, but she's fading fast. Matteo did a good job of taking care of her. Almost too good of a job. He let her get weak instead of building her stronger.

"You didn't save me."

"Why do you think I fucked you?"

"You didn't fuck me. You raped me!"

"I raped you to save you from my father. He wouldn't have stopped until you were dead. He hates you more than he hates most of the slaves."

"Why does he hate me so much?"

"It doesn't matter. What matters is that I did the only thing that would get you out of there. I pretended to be just like him."

"You *are* just like him."

I sigh. "You're right; I am. But you're alive because of me, not Matteo."

"I still hate you," she whispers.

"I know. You should hate me. But you should also hate Matteo."

She narrows her eyes, not following my logic.

"I didn't force you to suck my dick. Matteo did. He's not your friend any more than I am. If you hate me, you should hate him, too."

She smirks. "What makes you think I've ever felt anything more than hate toward him?"

I step closer to her until I'm towering over her, letting her know that, as much as she was in control when she was sucking my dick, I'm in control now.

"Because you kissed him and sucked me. You think of him as a possible lover and me as your owner. Don't let anyone play with your mind, Nina. Not him. Not my family. Not even me."

I want to kiss her. I want to fuck her. I want to protect her. But I can't.

If she wants out of the contract she signed, then she has to do it herself. I have to stick to my plan. I have to save myself.

13

NINA

I MADE A MISTAKE.

I thought Arlo or Matteo cared about me.

I thought I was the one in control and playing games. But Arlo's words have made me realize what a mistake that was. I have no control. And, as far as games go, they are the ones who are playing games.

I just don't understand why. Or even what game they are playing.

Why aren't they all treating me like a slave? Why aren't they fucking me whenever they want? Beating me like their father did?

I don't understand any of it.

Arlo might be done talking, but Matteo isn't.

I walk back to Matteo's room. Every step draining more and more energy out of my body until I have hardly anything left when I make it back to his bedroom.

I'm panting and sweaty, and I can't focus on anything because of the pain. That's all I feel—the pain. In my legs, my arms, my head. Everything hurts.

I bend over and put my hands on my knees, like I just ran a marathon. I hate what that bastard did to me. I've never felt so weak in my entire life.

I feel Matteo's hand on my shoulder before I see him.

"You should get back into bed. You pushed yourself to your limit, and now, you just need to rest and gather your strength for tomorrow," he says gently to me.

I take a couple of more breaths, and then I stand up and see that Matteo is fully dressed in a suit. He's barely worn any clothes this last week since I've been here. So, it's weird, seeing him clothed, much less so sharply dressed.

Matteo nods toward his bed, and I don't argue. I let him lead me toward his bed. He helps me in, and the pain slowly starts to subside. The weakness stays with me though.

"Better?"

I nod. "Why are you wearing a suit?"

He smiles, although I can see a hint of sadness in his eyes that I haven't seen before.

"Because, believe it or not, I have a job that doesn't involve lying in bed all day and night with you."

"When do you have to leave?"

"Five minutes," he says without looking at his watch.

I frown. Even though I'm pissed at him, I still don't want to be alone.

He laughs at my pout. "Don't pretend that you care if I'm here or not. You clearly prefer my brother to me. I'm just your protector. I get it. As soon as all your wounds have healed, I'll send you to his bed."

I carefully consider my next words. I don't want him to know that I know they are both just playing games with me. But I need to have my questions answered. Until I have more information, I need to stick to my original plan. To get them all to care about me. Maybe even fall in love with me. So that they will let me go. I know love is stronger than anything. Make them fall in love with me, and then I'll be free.

"I care about Arlo," I say.

Matteo cocks his head to one side. "You're obsessed with him, is what I heard."

I nod. "I'm obsessed. Even though he's done horrible things to me. Stolen me from my husband. Raped me. And didn't even bother to take care of me afterward. I still care about him. I'm obsessed. It's my personality. I can't control it. Just like I can't control my feelings toward you either. Even though you made me suck your brother's dick."

He raises an eyebrow. "And what are your feelings toward me?"

"I'm becoming obsessed with you, too."

He laughs. "I don't believe you, beautiful. You gave me a chaste kiss and sucked him."

"With Arlo, it's just about sex. That's all the obsession has ever been. Wanting to get into his pants. But, with you, we started differently. You became my friend, my caretaker, my protector. I didn't want to suck you off just because you commanded me to. With you, I want our first time to be special," I say, pushing all thoughts of Heath out of my mind. I can't think about how much I might be hurting him. All I can think about is getting free at any cost.

Matteo studies me with his arms folded across his chest. "I don't believe you, beautiful. I think you want Arlo and no one else."

"I kissed you. I didn't kiss him. We have something different. Something that I will never have with Arlo."

"Prove it," he says with a dare in his eyes.

I crook my finger at him. "Come here."

Matteo takes a seat on the edge of the bed, like he always does when he is about to take care of me.

I hesitate as the smell of his cologne washes over me. It's sexy and manly, and it immediately makes me want him. But I feel so weak that I'm not sure I can even lift my head off the bed again, much less hit on Matteo or have sex with him.

And do I want to have sex with him?

So far, I've done nothing on my own. I've always been ordered or raped. I've never had the choice. The decision being mine should make it easier for me, but it doesn't. It makes me feel *dirty*.

It's wrong.

I shouldn't fuck any of these men. I'm married. But it might be my only chance. Make them fall for me, and then I can return to my husband.

I grab Matteo's neck, and I pull him down so that I can kiss him. The kiss is rough, not like our previous kisses. It's full of moans and growls, tugging of lips and sucking of tongues. It feels desperate. It's my attempt at taking back control. But Matteo feels just as desperate for the kiss as I am.

When I kiss Matteo, I try to pretend like I'm kissing Heath, but I quickly realize how much of a mistake that is. Heath's kisses were perfect. But Matteo's kisses take everything to another level. His kisses rock my whole body, making me feel the kiss deep in my belly.

My body knows that it isn't Heath kissing me. So, why pretend?

"What do you want?" Matteo asks between kisses, his breathing heavy and his eyes full of lust.

"Hmm," I say as I'm still feeling every tingling sensation from the kiss.

Matteo grins as he kisses my lips again before biting my bottom lip hard enough to draw just enough blood to bring me back to reality.

I shake my head. "What did you say?"

"What do you want, beautiful? You said you wanted our first time to be special, so what do you want? I know you're too weak to do much, but what do you want? Do you want me to fuck you hard and fast now? Do you want me to wait until you're stronger? Do you want me to take you out onto the balcony and make love slow and sweet in the sunlight? Or hard and fast in the dark? Tell me what you want."

My heartbeat picks up. He's giving me the illusion of control while really taking it all away. But, still, I get to decide this one thing—how and when I want to have sex with Matteo for the first time.

I grab the nape of his neck and force him to kiss me again. Right now, I want more kisses. So many more kisses. Arlo hasn't kissed me since I came here. And it's always my favorite part about being intimate with another person.

I get lost in his kisses again. When Matteo kisses me, he really kisses me. Like it might be the last time he ever gets to kiss me, so he gives me everything he has. It makes it easy to think that he cares about me even though I know he doesn't. I'm going to have to do a lot more to get him to actually care about me. And a heck of a lot to get him to fall in love with me.

He stops kissing me, and I know what he is asking. I don't get any more kisses until I decide.

I can't stop kissing him. I can't stop wanting him. He's turned me on, and I don't have an off button.

I don't care about how weak I am. I don't care about how I just sucked his brother's dick. I don't care that I came back to him, so he could answer my questions, not to fuck him. I need him to fuck me. I need the obsession to go away.

"Fuck me. Make me forget everything but you."

I see the switch turn on in Matteo's eyes when I give him permission to fuck me. Although he and Arlo look so similar, they are very different. Arlo saved me in his own way. He did what had to be done even though he knew I would hate him afterward. Arlo wants the control. He enjoyed me being weak. Matteo wants me to choose him. I know he's just messing with my head. Both are going to cause me years of therapy if I survive this.

Matteo stands up and undoes the button on his jacket. Removing it, he neatly places it on the chair in the corner. He kicks off his shoes while he slowly undoes the buttons on his shirt and then lays the shirt on top of his jacket. He slacks are next, and he takes just as much time with them as he did the rest of his clothes, making me crazy while I lie in the bed, unable to get up and hurry him up. He folds his pants and then puts them on the chair where the rest of his clothes lie.

When he turns to me, the smirk on his face tells me he knows exactly what he is doing to me. He's driving me wild with need and want for him. I can't remember the last time I wanted a man's cock like I do right now.

"I told you to fuck me. Not take your sweet-ass time in undressing."

He rips the covers off the bed and then climbs up on top of me, careful not to touch any part of my body as he does. His eyes travel over every inch of my body that he has already seen countless times. I'm just wearing underwear and a bra. We've slept like this all week long. But it feels different when his eyes devour me like they are now.

"Oh, beautiful, I'm going to take my sweet time with you. I don't trust that you will ever give yourself to me again. So, I'm going to make this last for as long as I can."

I suck in a breath to try to keep from panting and showing him exactly how much I want this. It's embarrassing—how much I want him to fuck me. I want him to show me just how in control he is. Just how sweet he can make me feel. He makes me feel cared for when he heals me. I can only imagine how he will care for me when he fucks me.

"I'm going to make you forget about every drop of pain," Matteo says, taking my hand and kissing over the bruises and cuts from my fingertips to my shoulder. He takes my other arm and repeats the motion. Not letting one cut, scrape, or bruise be left untouched by his lips.

He's intoxicatingly slow and careful as he kisses me. Ensuring he doesn't miss one place that could be causing me pain while, at the same time, hitting every spot that brings me pleasure.

"Tell me what hurts, beautiful," he says.

I point to the deep bruises on my stomach.

His lips move to my stomach, kissing and licking over every spot. My fingers and toes curl as I try not to fully let go and give in to him. But it's an impossible task. Everything that he does is turning me on. Even if I want to be in control, I'm not. He can do anything he wants to my body. He can turn me on, and I can't stop him. He can make me come, and I'm powerless.

When I started this, I thought I could gain some power back by pretending like I care. But I'm not sure there is a difference between me pretending and actually enjoying myself.

I feel my panties getting wetter with each kiss and lap of his tongue. I squirm as he continues to kiss my stomach, and then he moves to my legs, kissing every place there, except where I really want him to. I want him to rip my underwear and bra off. I want him to be rough. Tie me up. Slap my ass. Something. I can't wait to see what he will do.

He smirks and grabs my thighs, holding them down so that I stop squirming beneath him. "Impatient, are we?"

"Yes," I breathe. "Very impatient."

He shakes his head and starts kissing my thigh again, but I've had enough of his teasing. I push his head down between my legs and on top of my panties, hoping he will take the hint.

He grins against my panties. He's not going to move any faster than he wants to. I'm going to die a slow, torturous death from being turned on but never getting any release.

I feel his teeth scrape against my stomach, and then he pulls my panties down with his teeth. My mouth drops open just a little at the sight of him actually doing what I want him to do.

"Lick me," I command.

He does. He licks my pussy like it's the best goddamn thing he's ever tasted.

My toes curl again, and my hands grab on to his long mane of hair as he licks me like he kisses me, giving me everything he has. Making me feel everything that I want to feel.

He doesn't slow when he hears me moaning and growing close to coming. He makes me come with just his tongue, and I scream from the release.

But he doesn't stop when I come. He keeps licking and kissing me, building me again. I come. And then he does it again. And again. As I come over and over. I don't think I've ever come so quickly so many times in a row. And I don't think I can take anymore.

I grab his hair, pulling him off of my pussy. "I can't take anymore," I pant.

He grins. "You never said to stop."

"Stop," I say with a grin, happy that I never told him to stop.

He makes it clear that, right now, he will do anything that I ask of him. I just have to figure out what I want.

And, despite coming half a dozen times, my body still craves his. I still want to feel his cock throbbing and stretching me as he fucks me. I want him to make me feel dirty. I want him to mark me as his, just like his brother did.

"You're not very good with directions then. Because I already told you to fuck me. I want it hard and fast, making me feel like the dirty whore that I am. Got it?"

He smiles. "Don't worry, sweetheart. I'll fuck you until you forget about any other man other than me."

I run my tongue across my bottom lip. "Good luck. You might have pulled the most orgasms out of me. But, when your brother fucked me, he fucked me so hard that I will never forget how his cock felt in my pussy. So far, I think he's winning."

I don't add that the reason he did that was to make me forget about what his father had done. As much as I hate Arlo for taking my choices away, I'm thankful for what he did. He got me out of there and replaced the terrible memories with him.

Matteo growls. "Take it back."

I grin. "Not until you prove you can fuck me better than he did," I say, taunting him. Hoping I'm hitting a nerve.

Before I know what's happening, he has my hands tied high above my head. His hips have my legs pinned to the bed. And my bra is off, lying on the floor. I'm completely naked and completely at his will. It's what I've been craving all along even though I don't understand why. I usually love the control but not when it comes to the Carini men.

He firmly kisses me on the lips, taking my breath away, before I feel my panties being shoved in my mouth, followed by what I think is his tie going around my mouth and then being tied behind my head to keep me from pushing the panties out.

"That's better. Now, I don't have to listen to any more talk about how my brother fucks you better than I do." Matteo smirks as he looks down at me all tied up. "I don't think you are ready for me. I think you need some time to think about my cock instead of my brother's," he says, stroking his own thick cock.

My eyes grow wide, looking at him as he climbs off me.

I moan, pleading with him to fuck me. I don't want to wait. I want to feel his cock deep inside me.

He just smirks. "Sorry, sweetheart. If you play games with me, you'd better be prepared for the consequences. You won't win. I'll be back in an hour, maybe two." He touches my pussy that is dripping with my own cum and that needs to be fucked, and then he licks his finger clean.

He walks over and grabs his clothes. Then, he walks out of the room, leaving me tied to the bed and full of need.

That asshole. If he thinks it's just going to make me want him more, then he's right. *Fuck him!*

If only I could.

14

ARLO

IT'S BEEN a long twenty-four hours. I should learn to always be prepared for the unexpected, but it's not something you ever get used to. I'll never get used to taking someone else's life. Even someone who deserves to die. It's still hard. It's something that stays with me forever, and it makes me that much more of a monster than I already am.

Matteo walks over to me and puts his hand on my shoulder. "Thanks, man, I owe you. I didn't see him."

I just nod. He owes me dozens of times now for saving his life. If he was anyone else other than my brother, I would have made him sign a contract showing exactly how much he owed me and how he would be paying me back. But he's my brother. He'd do the same for me.

Matteo starts to remove the bullets from his gun.

I grab his hand, annoyed that I have to explain things to him for the millionth time. "You are never safe. You are always a target. The second you let your guard down is the second that you die. As much as you annoy the fuck out of me, I'd prefer it if you wouldn't die."

Matteo smiles like he always does. Like this is all just one big game to him.

I sigh and shake my head. That's why I need to be in control of the family. I have to protect him and everyone else. Enrico used to care enough to do it, but he doesn't anymore. He turned cynical after my mother died. And Matteo doesn't take anything seriously.

He glances down at my shirt where the blood is pouring out. "Come on, let me stitch you up anyway."

"I can do it myself," I say, frustrated. All I really want to do is go find Nina and fuck her senseless. I desperately need a distraction.

Matteo laughs. "No, you can't. This is the one thing I'm better than you at. Let me stitch you up. I need you to stay alive and not die from an infection or some shit so that you can protect me in the future."

I roll my eyes. I don't need anyone to take care of me. Least of all my brother. But I don't really have a choice. The bullet went through my stomach and out my back. I can deal with the stomach wound, but I can't really do much about the wound on my back.

"Fine," I say and follow Matteo to his section of the house.

The second I step into the hallway, I can smell Nina. The light perfume smell that still lingers from the day she applied it on her wedding day and the tiniest hint of fear but mostly sex. She smells like sex.

"What did you do?" I glare at my brother as I run into his bedroom. The whole time, I think that Enrico broke in because Matteo forgot to lock the damn door or tell security to alert us the second that Enrico returned. All I can think about is her body and soul being broken again. And I can't handle it. Not so soon after the last time it happened.

I burst through the door to the bedroom and see Nina tied to the bed. Naked.

My cock hardens automatically at the sight of her naked body. It doesn't do that for just any woman. I've walked in on countless naked women before. But there is something about Nina that my cock just can't resist.

I quickly look around the room for my father or one of his minions, but I find no one in the room.

Nina's eyes travel from mine to the man behind me. I glance back and see Matteo standing in the doorway with a smirk on his face.

"It looks like I forgot about someone. Oops," Matteo says, although he doesn't sound the least bit apologetic.

She's been tied to the bed for at least twenty-four hours. She's not going to be happy.

I walk over to the bed, pull out my knife, and cut the ropes that Matteo used to tie her to the bedposts.

Her hands immediately go to the tie around her mouth, undoing it, and then she spits out the panties in her mouth. "You asshole!"

It's not entirely clear which one of us she is calling an asshole.

"Sorry, sweetheart. Why don't you suck me off while I clean up Arlo's wounds? And then I'll fuck you. Was it hard and fast that you wanted or slow and sweet? I can't really remember," Matteo says, laughing.

I take a step back after already getting a piece of Nina's rage and knowing better than to be near her when she's this pissed.

She smiles sweetly as she walks toward Matteo, but I know that her feelings beneath the surface are anything but sweet. She acts like she is about to kneel in front of Matteo to suck his dick, but instead, she knees him as hard as she can in the goods.

I smile. *Good girl*, I think, but I don't dare say it because I don't want to be the next target of her wrath.

Matteo doubles over in pain.

"Let's get one thing clear," she says as she stands, completely naked and unashamed in front of us. "I'm done playing both of your stupid games. I understand that, for whatever stupid reason, I am in your debt for the next seven years. Something that I plan on getting changed ASAP. But, in the meantime, I will do normal things that people do to pay back a debt. I will clean for you. Do your laundry. Cook for you. Work for you. But there will be no more sex unless I say so. Got it?" Her voice is raspy after not having anything to drink for twenty-four hours, and her eyes are dark.

Her body shakes a little as she stands, and I know, despite how tough she is acting, she doesn't even have the strength to stand much longer.

"No," I say.

Nina turns her glare toward me. "No?"

"No," I say again. "You are ours. We can fuck you whenever we want."

She smirks. "You can, but you won't. I don't know why you two don't rape me like your father did, but I know that you won't."

I take a step toward her. "Are you sure about that? I've fucked you before against your will."

She pushes back. "That was because you were protecting me."

"Was I? Or did I just tell you that to get you to trust me?"

"Enough with the games. I know that you both have some sort of truce. I've figured that much out. I don't understand what it is or why, but I do know that neither of you will fuck me again without my expressed permission to do so. You can't hurt me."

Matteo finally pulls himself off the ground where he was writhing in pain. "You sure? Or do you just wish that it were true? Because the thought of either of us fucking you against your will like our father did is too much for you to bear?"

Her eyes dart back and forth between us. She crosses her arms over her chest. "You won't hurt me. I'm going to go get a drink, food, and clothes, and then you two are going to start explaining. Everything."

Nina storms past both of us and into the kitchen inside Matteo's rooms.

We both let her go. Both amused and turned on by the fact that she thinks she has any control over us. She thinks she has everything figured out, but she doesn't. She's not even close to the truth. Still, she has figured out a lot of things much sooner than most women who have been enslaved to us.

Matteo and I follow her into the kitchen where she has already pulled out a bottle of water and is quickly downing it. When she finishes the bottle of water, she starts pulling everything she can find out of the small fridge. Pizza, chicken, and pasta. She opens the box with the pizza and starts eating it cold.

She looks at Matteo. "Clothes. Now," she demands.

He smiles as he pulls his own filthy button-down shirt off his body and tosses it to her. She catches it.

"You think you're funny, don't you? But I haven't showered in weeks, so I really don't care. I'm just tired of you two staring at my boobs and ass."

She puts the shirt on, making sure to button it all the way up so that we can no longer see any skin before she continues eating her pizza while sitting on the counter.

She opens her mouth as she looks to me, about to say something but then stops when she sees the blood. She hops down from the counter she was sitting on and hobbles over to me. Her muscles must be sore from being tied up and still weak from my father's beatings.

Nina grabs the hem of my shirt and lifts it up, and her eyes go wide from what she sees. "You were shot," she says calmly, still staring at my wound.

I nod. "I don't expect much sympathy from you since you already shot me."

She looks up at my eyes with a narrowed stare that might almost mirror concern if I didn't know her better. She looks back at my wound. "What happened?"

I push my shirt down. "Just a normal day at work. It's nothing."

"It's not nothing. It looks worse than when I shot you."

"I'm fine."

Nina looks over at Matteo. "Can you help him?"

He nods.

"Then, what are you waiting for? Stitch him up before he bleeds to death. I want you both alive because I still plan on killing you both myself before I finally get out of here."

I smile a little at her sass. She doesn't understand what power she holds. If she commanded me to do anything but rescue her, I probably would just because I couldn't help but give in to her smart mouth.

Matteo smiles, too, as he walks to his dresser to get the supplies he needs to stitch me up. She has both of us under her spell. She could get either of us to do practically anything she wanted. If only she understood what was really at stake. That this is much bigger than her.

I take off my bloodied shirt, tossing it to the floor of the kitchen, as I take a seat on one of the backless barstools at the counter. Nina stares at me the whole time with wide eyes that I'm even still standing and not about to pass out on the floor from blood loss. The wound isn't good, and it hurts every time I breathe, but it is far from lethal. It's worse than the graze that Nina caused in my shoulder, but it's nothing compared to what Nina went through with my father. She could have died. I'm merely in a lot of pain.

Matteo returns with a box of supplies and sets them on the counter next to me. I can tell he's still concerned about my wound from the grimace he has on his face every time he looks at me, but he's trying to act like it's no big deal. Matteo starts pulling out the different equipment.

"Are you sure he doesn't need to see a doctor?" Nina asks Matteo as she stares at my deep wound.

Matteo opens his mouth to answer, but I don't want them to join sides and gang up on me. I'm not going to a doctor. I never have and never will.

"I don't need to see a doctor. Matteo is the best. He did a good job of taking care of you, didn't he?"

Nina nods.

"He has always been the best when it comes to medical care. He would have been a doctor if it wasn't for being born into this messed up family."

"You weren't allowed to become a doctor? Why?"

Matteo brushes off her question. "I can teach you how to stitch him up. It is a good skill to learn. We could use more than one person in this family who knows the basics about medical care for as often as someone gets shot around here."

Nina's eyes narrow as she looks back and forth between us, obviously wanting more answers but too concerned with my wound to distract either of us by asking them. "What if I mess up?"

Matteo laughs. "Then, you get to cause my brother here a little more pain. But, since you hate him as much as you hate me, that shouldn't be a problem."

Nina smiles a little at that while I give my brother an I'll-kill-you look because my jealousy is going crazy right now. It makes no sense. I have no claim to Nina any more than he does. He helped me save her. She's never been mine. But, still, my jealousy rages inside like a fire I will never be free of.

Matteo starts cleaning my wound while I memorize every freckle, every look, and every scar on Nina's face.

"First, you want to make sure the wound is clean of debris before you stitch it up."

Matteo pours cold, sterile liquid onto the wound, making me wince at the sudden sting.

"Shouldn't you give him pain medicine first?" Nina asks.

Matteo chuckles. "Do you want me to give you pain medicine?"

He cocks his head to the side with a sly grin because he already knows my answer. I've said it countless times before.

"No."

"My dear brother is a bit of a martyr. He thinks he deserves every bullet he takes and deserves to feel the pain. That it is the only way he will care enough to stop the bullets in the future. I vehemently disagree with him. Not even you, dickhead, deserve to feel this kind of pain," Matteo jokes as he starts pulling debris out of the wound.

I growl when he does. This is the worst fucking part, and he's intentionally making it worse to prove a point. He thinks he's stronger because he knows his limits when it comes to pain. I think I'm stronger because I can take any amount of pain.

He hands the tweezers to Nina. "Your turn. Dig around and see if you can get anything else out."

Nina takes the tweezers from him but hesitates.

"Go on. I know you want to hurt me for stealing you and fucking you. Now is your chance for a little payback."

She places her left hand on my stomach, holding the wound open, as her big brown eyes stare into mine. I don't know what she is feeling. She's closed off whatever it is to me. But, when she digs the tweezers into my wound, I know.

I growl loudly at the sharp pain that feels like being shot over and over again in the stomach.

"Does that hurt?" she asks sassily even though she already knows the answer from the growls leaving my body and the stinging tears in my eyes. "Good. Now, you know how I felt when you fucked me even though it was for my own good. It still hurt like hell." She pulls the tweezers out along with a small piece of the bullet. "I think I got everything," she says.

Matteo studies my wound with a smirk on his face, happy that Nina is just as pissed off at me as she is with him. He takes the supplies he needs out of the box and moves to my back where he begins stitching.

He's done this countless times, and he knows just how to move the needle so that I can barely feel the sting as he pushes it through my body. The sting of a Novocain shot would be worse than his stitches.

Nina closely studies him as he shows her how to stitch up a wound. I can't see either of them, and Nina doesn't say anything as she watches Matteo. It leaves me alone with no distraction.

I try to distract myself by counting the wine glasses hanging beneath the cabinet, but it's not enough to keep me here.

I feel the adrenaline rush through my body as I'm brought back to earlier tonight. To the bullets whizzing by. Our men dropping as they were hit by bullets. Loyal men who would do anything for us. Men with wives and children dying, all to keep me and Matteo safe. I see the five men I killed. I see every single one of their faces. The terror right before they died. I feel their anger and their fear. Even the last guy who was about to put a bullet in Matteo's heart. I shot him without a second thought at the time. I would do anything for my brother. But, every time I kill, it makes me want it more. It turns me into more of a monster. Even though I feel their pain, I want more of it. I like the control, the power.

"Arlo?" Nina says, standing in front of me.

I open my eyes that I didn't even realize I had closed and look at the most beautiful woman I have ever seen. A woman who is strong and defiant. The only woman I've ever met who has a chance at actually surviving. Maybe she can put an end to this. Finally.

"I need you to sit up straight so that I can stitch up your wound on your stomach."

I sit up so that Nina has better access to my wound. She pierces my skin with the needle, and I feel it. I don't groan or growl or even grimace. I welcome the pain because it keeps me here instead of with the pain of earlier tonight.

She moves slowly with unpracticed fingers, allowing me to feel every pierce and pull of the skin as she closes my wound. After every stitch, she pauses and looks at me.

"Maybe you should finish, Matteo. I think he's suffered enough."

She begins to hand the needle to Matteo, but I grab her wrist.

"No. I need you to finish."

She blinks a couple of times as she considers my command and then does as I wish. Every time her hand brushes against my skin, I grow hard, thinking about her naked body. About how strong she feels beneath me. How much she enjoys me in control, even when she says she doesn't. She loves being tied up and fucked hard.

When she finally finishes, she takes a step back to look at her work. "How is that?"

I don't look down to see how good of a job she did. I can't think of anything other than her. And, if I do try to think about something other than her, it's going to lead to a dark path that I can't go down.

"I want to fuck you," I say.

Nina chuckles a little as she puts the needle and thread back into the box. "You're funny."

"I'm not joking. I've never wanted anything more than to fuck you right now."

Nina looks at Matteo. "As I said before, I'm not fucking either of you."

My heart pounds in my chest, and my cock hardens at just the thought of taking her right now. Tying her up and fucking her even though she said no. I would win. I could have her and everything I'd ever wanted.

I stand up like I'm about to do just that.

"No," Nina says without a drop of fear.

I stop. I can't help but do what she says, and she knows it.

She doesn't smile snarkily, like she should now that she controls me. Her face is sad. She wants to be controlled. It's the only way to keep her obsessions at bay.

"I want to know what the fuck is going on. What games are you playing? What really happened that night that made me sign my life away to your family? What do you really do for a living? I need answers to everything. Now."

"You won't get answers from me. You don't need answers. All you need to focus on is surviving so that you don't get hurt again," I say, staring at the scars and bruises still visible all over her body. A few I'm sure I caused myself when I raped her.

Nina crosses her arms as she glares at Matteo, like one look is going to be enough to get him to talk. But, when I look at Matteo and the softness in his eyes when he stares at Nina, I'm afraid that's all it will take. Even though it would ruin everything and put Nina at risk even more than she already is. Something that I know Matteo doesn't want. I'm not sure he can resist her charms anymore. Not after taking care of her this last week.

"I'll answer your questions. My brother will, too."

I glare at him. I'm going to kill him if he tells her anything that ends up hurting her.

"We will answer one question for every time you have sex with one of us."

I grin. Most of the time, I hate my brother. But I'll owe him the rest of my life for coming up with this idea.

15

MATTEO

I DON'T KNOW NEARLY ENOUGH about Nina, but I do know one thing for sure. She likes sex just as much as I do. But the only way she will give it to me or my brother is on her own terms.

"No," she says, but it's a weak no. It's the kind of no you say so that people know you aren't so easily swayed.

I grin. "Fine. I won't try to change your mind. I have plenty of other women who will gladly fuck me." I circle her, enjoying how crazy I'm making her. "You might want to sleep in your own room tonight though. The women can get pretty loud when I fuck them, and I wouldn't want you to have to deal with that."

She rolls her eyes at me. "If that were true, you would have had women over every night this last week, but you didn't. You didn't because you want me, not some other woman. Admit it."

I shrug. "I wanted you, but you're not really worth all of this. I'll just wait until my father breaks you, and then you'll be begging me to fuck you instead of him."

She slaps me hard on the cheek. "Stop acting like you don't give a shit when I know you do. Both of you."

Arlo just looks at her like she is a queen. She might be a queen that my brother will do anything for, but she doesn't have quite the same power over me. She doesn't have me under her spell as much as she thinks she does.

"You're wrong, sweetheart. I couldn't care less about you."

"Fine, you don't care about me. Arlo does."

She walks over toward him, swaying her hips as she does. Her ass peeks out just beneath the hem of my shirt that she is wearing. She's testing me. And I'm about to fail.

When she gets to Arlo, she softly, tenderly kisses him on the cheek. And then his neck. His chest. Down his stomach, carefully kissing his wound as she kneels.

I see it in his eyes. He's about to give in and give her anything she wants. He's usually one of the strongest men I know. But not when it comes to Nina.

I understand. I've quickly come to care about her much more than I would ever like to admit to her. But he can't break.

"Fine, you win. I don't want to fuck anyone else but you tonight," I say. It's not a lie. It's the fucking truth. The whole time I was supposed to be focused on not getting shot and killed, all I could think about was Nina tied up in my bed and how much I wished I had fucked her before I left.

She keeps kissing him. She didn't even hear me; she's so lost in him as he tangles his hand in her hair, the other pulling at my shirt that she's wearing.

I grab her arm, trying to pull her away from him, but Arlo firmly holds her in place. We are fighting over her like we used to fight over our Hot Wheels cars when we were kids.

Nina smirks and stands up, pulling her arms away from both of us. "That's what I thought. You both want me." She crosses her arm. "So, who will give me the better deal? I'll fuck one of you if you answer all of my questions tonight."

Arlo looks at me, and I can already read his thoughts. He thinks I'm going to be the one who gives in to her. But I'm not the one to be worried about. It's clear she has him wrapped around her finger, willing to do anything for her.

"No. The deal is one question for one fuck. I can't give you more than that. And don't act like you won't enjoy getting every answer out of me."

She sighs but doesn't argue with him. She knows that anything she says isn't going to be true. Her cheeks are already flushed from her just thinking about fucking him. She wants him just as much as he wants her.

"What about you Matteo? I won't fuck Arlo ever again. Just you. We can fuck all night long and the rest of the time I'm here if you answer all of my questions. Tonight."

I look over at my saint of a brother. To most people, he is anything but a saint. But that's exactly what he is. He's the responsible one in the family. He's literally taken a bullet for me on more than one occasion. Here's my chance to fuck him over. I could steal the girl he cares about. Make him suffer. Take everything he's spent his whole life fighting for.

"One fuck a day for one question a day. That's my final offer."

Nina pouts, but she knows it will do her no good.

"What do you say?"

Nina looks back and forth between us. "So, the most I can get is one question a day answered?"

I nod.

She looks at me, and then she looks at Arlo. "What if I fuck you both? At the same time? Do I get two questions then?"

I was expecting her to give in to my demands. I was expecting her to fuck whoever she thought she could get more answers out of that day. Or whoever pissed her off less. I wasn't expecting her to say she wanted us both.

16

NINA

I DON'T KNOW why I said that.

I've never been with two men before in the same night.

And definitely not at the same time.

But I'm desperate.

For answers. And, as much as I don't want to admit it, for mind-blowing sex.

Sex with Arlo has been the best of my life. Even when he fucked me against my will.

Sex with Matteo would be just as amazing.

Sex with both of them? I can't even imagine how I would ever recover from that.

Arlo answers first, "No, I won't share you. You fuck me or him tonight. Tomorrow, you can change your mind and fuck the other. But not tonight. Tonight, you are either mine or his." When he says *mine*, I know that's what he wants. He wants me to be his tonight.

I want to be his. But I also want Matteo.

How the hell did I go from hating them both to wanting them both? I think my hormones have just gone crazy after I was turned on and then tied to a bed all night long.

Matteo laughs as he always does. Never taking anything too seriously. "No. We have never been very good at the whole sharing thing. You have to choose."

I look back and forth at each man who both look like they are ready to devour me and kill each other. It suddenly hits me as I'm standing here, being forced to choose between two men, that I both hate and want them at the same time. I don't know why I never realized that before.

"You're both lying. You've shared a woman before."

Matteo laughs.

"You're right. We've shared women who don't matter to us. We've never shared a woman we both actually want," Arlo says. He always tells me the truth.

So, I look Arlo dead in the eye when I say, "You've shared *me* before."

Arlo looks at me and then at Matteo. "You fucked her the night I brought her to you? The night she almost died!" His rage is more than I've ever seen before. His body instantly turns red, every vein pops out on his body, and his nostrils flare.

I know he was just shot, but right now, if they decide to fight, I'd put my money on Arlo.

Arlo does get a punch in before Matteo can tell him the truth. Right to the eyeball. I watch as blood pours from Matteo's eye and Arlo's wound. Maybe, if they kill each other, I will be free of my debt.

"I didn't fuck her, man. Other than a few kisses and tasting her pussy, I haven't touched her," Matteo says, clearly not willing to fight his brother right now.

Arlo stops his fist midair, his breathing fast and heavy, not willing to fully back down.

Matteo turns to me. "Have I fucked you?"

"Yes, you both fucked me. After you saved me. You both fucked me the night in the dungeon. You were each there, and you each had your turn. You look so alike. But, after knowing each of you, I know you each had your turn with me that night," I say testing them to see if my hunch is correct. I don't have any evidence or reason why to guess that they both fucked me that night. Just a gut instinct.

They look at each other and then at me.

"I didn't fuck you that night. I wish I had, but Arlo wouldn't let me anywhere near you," Matteo says.

I narrow my eyes. "I don't believe you."

Matteo turns to Arlo.

"I don't think he fucked you that night. He didn't when I was there at least. So, unless he went after you and fucked you after you ran..." Arlo looks to Matteo to answer him.

Matteo puts his hand up. "I didn't fuck her. You're the only one who fucked her against her will. All I ever did was kiss her when she thought I was you after art class."

I wince because I know what is about to happen. Arlo punches Matteo again.

"What did I do? It was funny, man. Nina thinks so, don't you?"

I exhale. "I'm not getting in the middle of whatever this is." I point back and forth between them.

"Then, what are you doing?" Matteo asks.

"Waiting to see who is going to fuck me." I cross my arms.

They are already pissed at each other. Now, let them fight it out for me.

Arlo walks over to the first aid kit and pulls out some gauze and a bandage. He tosses them to Matteo. Matteo begins dressing his wound on his head while Arlo wipes off the blood on his stomach and hand.

Neither of them speaks, and I don't know if I'm going to get my way or not. If I have to choose, I have no idea who to pick. Even if I feel my heart going one way, my pussy will go another. And, as far as which one is smartest to pick to help me get out of here, there isn't a clear answer. If I choose one, the other is going to be hurt. He's going to distance himself from me. I can't take the chance of choosing the wrong brother. I need them both to care for me. Both to fall in love with me. It would double my chances at getting my freedom back.

So, I do the only thing I can. I start unbuttoning the shirt I'm wearing without looking at either one of them. When I get to the last button, I push the shirt off my shoulders and let it fall to the floor. They have seen me naked before, but I've never felt so exposed as I do right now.

I'm asking for them both to fuck me.

This is wrong. So, so wrong. They think of me as their property even if they are too chicken to do anything about it.

But here is their chance. To fuck me with my permission.

Both men come to me in a second.

I grin. I have power. My body is powerful. And my mind is stronger. I'm going to be free again because I know how to use both.

"What do you want, Nina?" Arlo asks.

He's never asked me what I wanted before. He's always commanded me to do everything. It's strange—hearing him ask me what I want. Even Matteo hasn't ever asked me what I wanted. He gives me a choice, sure, but he doesn't let me decide anything. This is my chance to get exactly what I want. The problem is, I don't know what I want.

"Beautiful?" Matteo asks.

I turn back and forth between the two men. Both the same yet so different. One calls me Nina. The other beautiful or sweetheart but never Nina. I don't know which I prefer.

But I do know what I want right now.

"Control me. Make me yours," I command, my voice strong.

I like being in control ninety percent of the time. But not when it comes to sex. They are two powerful, strong men, who know my body better than I do. I want them to take control.

Both men smirk, their features almost identical to each other. Matteo grabs my hips and turns me toward him. His mouth devours mine as his hand tangles in my hair. My legs grow shaky as he kisses me. I've gained a lot of my strength back, but being kissed by Matteo makes me weak. He demands every part of me when he kisses me. So much of me that I can barely stand.

Arlo sweeps me off my feet just before I feel myself crashing to the floor, lacking strength to stand another second. He looks down at me like I'm his. His expression with his dark eyes and deep grimace shows me how much he hated watching his brother kiss me.

I reach up to his neck to pull his face toward mine so that I can kiss him. He lowers his lips but kisses my neck instead of my lips. I close my eyes as his lips and tongue kiss me slowly and deliberately, turning me on more and more with each perfectly crafted kiss. To the point that, by the time he drops me on the bed, I'm already ready for his cock.

He just smirks as he looks at me lying naked on the bed. He knows exactly how much he's turned me on.

Matteo walks in and stares at me with almost the same intensity that his brother does. He doesn't wait to see what his brother does. He pushes me up the bed and starts kissing every inch of me. My toes, my ankle, my thigh. He worships my body with his kisses, just like he did before, because he knows how much it turns me on.

Matteo keeps my eyes focused on his as he kisses me, again demanding all of my attention so that I don't give his brother any.

Arlo doesn't let Matteo get all of my attention so easily. He takes my hand, drawing small circles in my palm that I can feel all the way to deep in my stomach. I glance over at Arlo, who is looking at me like he would do anything for me. He glances up at the ropes still tied to the bed, and I know, as much as he wants to tie me to the bed, he thinks better of it. He doesn't want to tie me up again, not so soon after I spent the night that way.

It disappoints me a little. I like being tied up. I like the roughness. But the way both men are kissing me show me that neither of them is going to be rough with me. Not tonight. We are all injured. All recovering from injuries, both physically and emotionally. Tonight is about healing. Together.

Arlo glances at Matteo for just a moment, but it's enough to change the tension that was there just a second ago. Instead of fighting for me, they change to giving me everything.

Arlo kisses my neck and my ear, and then he slowly moves down to my breasts. Matteo kisses my ankle and my thigh, inching closer to my pussy. I'm in heaven as both men kiss every sensitive part of my body. Healing me, caring for me in a way I didn't think was possible.

The more they kiss me, the more I stop feeling like a slave and more like their queen. I close my eyes rather than choose between whom to look at. My skin warms with each kiss, my toes curl, and my heart beats uncontrollably for both men.

My eyes dart open when they both ignite my pussy and nipples at the same time. Both men have their tongues dancing over my most sensitive of areas, and it's too much for me to handle. I grab on to Arlo's hair to keep from losing myself completely while I stare into Matteo's eyes. His eyes are deep with a need to make me come, to make me feel good, and a hint of need to make himself feel good as well while maybe stealing a little bit of me from Arlo.

Arlo bites my nipple harder than I was expecting, and my eyes go back to his. His are much the same, but there is something more broken in his eyes than what I saw in Matteo's. Something that I haven't figured out about him yet.

They intensify their movements, kissing me harder, flicking their tongues faster, building me closer.

"God, that feels so good," I moan, careful not to say either of their names. Not that I can choose who is bringing me more pleasure. It's impossible for me to decide. To choose.

Arlo stops sucking on my nipple and moves behind my shoulder, sitting me up as his hands massage my breasts and his lips turn me on with every nibble and flick on my neck. I was expecting a dick in my mouth and the other in my pussy. But, instead, I have two men taking care of my needs before their own. I never thought either would be capable of being so selfless.

Matteo licks my clit until I'm dripping wet, my pussy begging for his cock to enter me. Only then does he move his cock to my entrance. He's never fucked me before, and he takes his time in sliding his cock over my folds, gathering my liquid on his thick cock before he pushes gently inside me at the same time that Arlo nibbles on my ear while flicking my nipple between his thumb and finger.

Matteo's thumb moves over my clit while he thrusts inside me, hitting me in all the right places.

"Yes," I moan, unable to get more than the single word out.

Matteo moves slowly, taking his time as he fucks me. He watches every expression, every sound, everything I do as he fucks me. Watching for cues of what I need more or less of before he gives it to me.

"Are you close, beautiful?" Matteo asks.

"Yes," I breathe.

My panting grows louder, my body on fire, as they both do everything they can to bring me pleasure.

Matteo moves a little faster. Arlo kisses me harder.

"Fuck, Matteo!" I scream, coming around his cock.

He slows his movements almost immediately even though he hasn't come. While Arlo's kisses on my neck soften as my body tries to recover from the intense sensation.

"What do you want?" Arlo asks, already able to tell that I need more.

I'm not sure if the deal we made is fair. Not if they are going to fuck me like this, giving in to my needs and ignoring their own. That's the problem with how they fuck me. They need to get something out of this so that I can get my questions answered faster. The sooner I get my questions answered, the sooner I can get out of here.

"I want both of you," I say, staring into Arlo's eyes.

Matteo can make me laugh. He's taken care of my wounds and emotional needs better than anyone. But he hasn't had the same experience with my body that Arlo has. Arlo knows exactly what I crave.

I want more. Faster, harder. I want more intensity pushing me to an edge that I don't know I can go over. Even if we all need a certain amount of gentle, healing, I still need even more than what they have given me so far.

Arlo looks at Matteo, and a silent exchange happens that I don't understand. A connection between them that I'm not privy to.

Arlo grabs my hips and spins me toward him. "You get whatever you ask for, Nina."

He lifts me onto his already hard cock.

I moan and grab on to hair and shoulders as he fills me completely.

He growls as he enters me. Needing to be inside me as much as I need him to be. He needs to be in control. That's where he feels most himself. He gave up that control to me and even a little bit to Matteo, but it's clear he's done giving me any more control. I asked for more, and that's what I'm getting.

Arlo slaps my ass in the way only he ever has. With a bite and a sting, but it leaves me soaked and so turned on that I can come again just from that if I don't try to regain some amount of control over my body.

Arlo kisses down my neck, and he thrusts inside me. But his kisses are more like harsh nibbles, much harder than how he was kissing me before.

I feel new hands on my ass, and then Matteo's cock is teasing the entrance to my ass. Arlo made me forget that Matteo was still here. But I'm quickly brought back to the real world as Matteo pushes harder at my entrance until he slips inside.

I bite Arlo's shoulder to keep from screaming or crying as I'm completely filled with both men. I've never been stretched so fully. I feel the sting as my ass is slapped again as both men start moving inside me again.

Both kiss my neck. Both growl. Both fuck me like it's the last time, and they don't hold anything back.

"Your ass is so tight," Matteo says.

I moan as he fucks me harder.

"I want to make you scream until you can't remember either of our names," Arlo growls.

"Impossible," I say through clenched teeth.

Arlo's eyes light up at the challenge, and I'm sure Matteo's doing the same behind me.

Because everything changes.

They fuck me harder. Faster. At the same time, they slow their kisses to tenderness all over my body just to cause a sting of their hand, their bite on my nipple, or their sucking on my neck all the more intense.

I don't have control over my body anymore. Arlo takes control of my front. Matteo, my back. And both men have my heart and soul in their grasp.

Thoughts of their father disappear into the night.

Memories of my freedom vanish.

Any thoughts of anything but these two men are ripped from me and replaced with two men I need desperately.

I can't imagine not feeling this good ever again. I need them both.

I need the laughter and the seriousness. The pleasure and the pain. The control and giving myself up.

I need everything they both give me. I want it all. I don't want to give it up. Not even for my freedom.

"Come, beautiful," Matteo commands.

I feel him come in my ass. I come right along with him.

"Fuck, Matteo," I cry as we come together.

I grab on to Arlo's shoulders as I come, barely able to keep myself upright even though both men are holding me up. Arlo's cock is still in my pussy as I come, but his mouth devours every inch it can reach. My neck, my ear, my nipple.

Matteo pulls out when he's finished filling me, and I slowly come down off my high. The second that I do, Arlo starts thrusting again into my pussy.

"I can't," I cry, not sure I can come again.

"You can, Nina," Arlo growls.

The deep growl combined with his thumb on my clit is all I need to start again. I feel myself growing wetter again and climbing with him. Matteo gathers my hair in a ponytail behind my head. Tugging gently as he kisses my neck.

But Arlo is in control now. He fucks me harder than he ever has before. Quickly moving us with a need in his eyes to make me come one last time.

I move to kiss him, but Arlo kisses my neck instead. Matteo grabs my neck and turns me toward him before he kisses my lips.

"Come, Nina," Arlo commands.

I let go of Matteo's lips and look deep into Arlo's eyes.

"Arlo," I cry out as I come around his dick as his warm cum fills my pussy.

My body is exhausted after I come for the third time tonight. Arlo slowly lifts me off his cock and then lays me down on the bed. Matteo already has a warm washcloth that he uses to wash between my legs before Arlo covers me with warm blankets.

My eyes quickly close from exhaustion as so many things swirl around in my head. *Who are these men really? Monsters or lovers? Do they really care about me? Even love me?*

Why wouldn't Arlo kiss me? But Matteo would?

I think back to the first time that Arlo fucked me. *Did he kiss me then? Or was it Matteo?* I shake my head. Arlo wouldn't lie. But Matteo might. *Or is nothing as it seems?*

And why the hell did I think this was better than my freedom?

Because it is, that sneaky voice in my head says.

Maybe it is if I can make them love me. Whether I want to stay or leave, I need them to love me. Or at least one of them.

I have so many questions but no strength left to ask them. I frown slightly as I drift off to sleep. That was their plan all along—to fuck me until I couldn't do anything but sleep, and then they wouldn't have to answer any questions.

17

ARLO

I'VE SHARED women with my brother before but never one I cared if they lived or died. Never one who had captured my soul like Nina has.

I knew that I would have to eventually share her with him. It was one of the reasons that I couldn't bear for her to be involved in our twisted games. But I at least thought I wouldn't have to see him fuck her. I never thought I would have to hear her call out his name instead of mine.

The pain was worse than the bullet in my stomach. It was the worst pain I've ever felt.

Matteo begins to climb into bed next to her. We are so exhausted that all we need to do is sleep. We could sleep for twenty-four hours straight, and I'm not sure if it would be enough.

"What are you doing?" Matteo asks, eyeing me.

"I have a couple of things to check up on, and then I'll go get some sleep."

He rolls his eyes. "We both just fucked her at the same time. My dick was inches from yours. I think we can share a bed with her in the middle."

I sigh as I look down at Matteo's oversized king bed. I want nothing more than to curl up next to Nina and pass out for hours even if I do have to share her with my idiotic brother. I don't give a fuck about having to sleep near my brother. I just can't. I wish I were like Matteo. I wish I could develop feelings for Nina. Care for her, even love her.

I can't though.

And, the more time I spend with her, the more I leave my heart open to feeling something that I can't feel.

I put my underwear and slacks back on.

"I have to go check on the men," I say as I lean down and kiss Nina on the forehead.

Matteo rolls his eyes. "No, you don't. You're just chickenshit."

He's right. He knows that. I don't argue with him. I always tell the truth. I hate lies almost as much as I hate killing. Well, used to hate killing.

"Keep her warm. And don't leave her tied up again. It brings back too many painful memories for her."

Matteo glances from me to her and then curls his body around her. As much as I want to stay, I know that Matteo will take good care of her. Better than I can.

I should let him have her. Let him win. It would be better for her. He's a better man than I am. He isn't quite as corrupted.

I feel the familiar pain in my chest as I turn and walk out of Matteo's rooms and back into the hallway of the mansion. I close the door as the pain in my chest almost consumes me.

I feel the buzzing in the back pocket of my pants, bringing me back to the present. I pull the phone out of my pocket and answer, already knowing what it is. Another painful reminder of who I am.

———

It's been two days since I saw Nina. I haven't been avoiding her exactly. My work has taken me away for most of the time, and the rest of the time, I've spent recovering in my room, trying to sleep through the nightmares.

I sense her as I lie in my bed. I know she's close. I pull out my phone and turn to the security cameras outside my quarters.

She's found me.

She's showered and changed into a white sundress. Her hair is clean again, long and straight. She looks like an angel. An angel who should not be knocking at my door right now.

I should just stay in bed. My body is broken. I'm exhausted. I won't be able to think straight right now. I know why she's here. To get her question, which is owed to her. But I don't want her here.

I roll out of bed, my body creaking in pain while, at the same time, my cock is growing hard, just thinking about her.

I walk slowly out of my bedroom, down the long hallway, and to the front door of my quarters. I throw the door open as she knocks again.

Her jaw drops, making me smirk, as she looks over my body. I didn't bother putting a shirt on. My gray sweatpants hang low on my hips. My cock strains against them the second I see her.

"Can I help you?" I raise an eyebrow as she continues to stand with her jaw open.

She quickly closes it.

"You're hurt again. Why are you always hurt?" she asks as she reaches out to my chest, feeling the new wound, gingerly touching it.

"Is that your one question?" I ask.

She sighs and pulls her hand away. But she doesn't stop looking at the wound or the dozens of others that have healed but cover my chest and arms. Her eyes grow heavy as she sees just how many there are. Until I see a tear roll down her cheek.

I narrow my eyes as I wipe away the tear. "Why are you crying?"

I don't understand what I did to hurt her.

She grabs my wrist as I wipe the tear. She closes her eyes for a second as she holds my hand against her face.

"Because I can feel your pain, and I don't like seeing it."

I frown and pull my hand away. "You shouldn't feel my pain. It's nothing compared to what you have been through."

She bites her lip to keep her from saying whatever is on her mind.

"Can I come in?" she finally asks.

"No," is my automatic response.

I don't let anyone in my personal quarters. Not my brother or sister. Not any of the women I've fucked. No one but me and occasionally the maids are ever allowed in. It's my personal retreat, something that is mine and mine alone. I need the space. I need a place where I can pretend the outside world doesn't matter. If I let her in, then the place will no longer be mine. It will be the place where Nina asked me her question. Where Nina sat, stood, breathed. It will become all about Nina, and I'm not sure I can handle that.

"You're here to ask me the question that I owe you, right?"

She nods slowly, not sure if that is why she is here or not.

"How about I show you how to shoot properly, and you can ask the question?"

I thought she might enjoy doing something that could lead her closer to being free, but if she's excited by the idea, she doesn't show it.

"Give me one second, and I'll meet you out back in the gardens."

Her eyes narrow, but she nods as she walks away.

I hurry back inside and change into jeans, a gray shirt, and dark jacket. Then, I run outside to find her sitting on the edge of one of the retaining walls that contains bright red roses.

"You look beautiful," I say without meaning to when I see her.

Her cheeks blush a little.

I chuckle. "So, me calling you beautiful embarrasses you, but my brother and I fucking you at the same time doesn't?"

That earns me a grin. "Sex is meaningless; it just feels good. But calling me beautiful means something."

"What do you think it means?"

She shrugs. "That you think I look beautiful right now. It's not surprising since I showered for the first time since I came here and am wearing something other than a dirty wedding dress."

I shake my head. "No, it's not that. You've always been gorgeous, but today, you seem different. You carry yourself with your head held higher. You have an aura around you."

She blushes again, and I find myself wanting to make her blush again and again.

"Come on, let me show you how to shoot a gun properly, so if you are ever given the chance to shoot me again, you won't miss."

She jumps off the ledge. "Hey! That's not fair. I didn't miss."

I smirk. "So, you were aiming to just graze my shoulder? Because it looked like you wanted to kill me."

"It was just a threat. I wanted to know where we stood. That's all."

"Uh-huh," I say as I lead her to the outdoor shooting range down the hill.

She follows, happily skipping along. I don't know why she is so happy. Maybe she thinks, if she gets her hand on a gun, she can kill me and finally make her escape. But, whatever it is, it's contagious. I can't help but smile at her and how happy she seems today.

"Why are you in such a good mood?"

"It's a nice day outside, and I get two questions answered by my two new favorite guys."

"Anyone, I know?"

She cocks her head to the side. "Why are you in such a good mood?"

"Because I get to spend part of it fucking you."

She laughs. "What makes you think I'm going to let you or Matteo fuck me again? I'm going to ask such good questions that I will be out of here in no time."

"Because you want to be fucked."

She frowns at that and turns her attention to the gun range spread in front of us.

I walk into a small building, which is a locker for some of our guns, leaving Nina behind in the sunshine. I almost always have a gun on me, but I need one for Nina, and she doesn't get to see how to access the guns. Not yet anyway.

I pull out a handgun for Nina along with plenty of ammo and then walk back out to where Nina is waiting for me.

I place her gun and ammo on the table and take out my gun as well.

I nod to her. "Show me what you've got."

She seems a little nervous as she reaches for the gun.

"You're just going to let me hold a gun? Easy as that?"

I laugh. "I know how well you shoot, remember? I'm not in any fear for my life."

I grab my own gun and load it. Then, I shoot off a few rounds, hitting the bull's-eye with ease. Out of the corner of my eye, I watch Nina grab the gun and begin loading it.

She aims it at the bull's-eye and starts shooting. She hits the target more times than not but never the center of the bull's-eye and never the same place more than once.

"Who taught you how to shoot?" I ask.

She shrugs. "I went to the local shooting range wherever I lived. They usually had people around who could give me a few pointers."

I shake my head. "Well, they taught you all wrong."

"Then, show me how to shoot right."

I smile, loving her sass today. I put my gun down on the table and walk over so that I can stand behind her. I position her hips square and change her grip on the gun so that it fits her hand more comfortably.

"What do you look at when you aim?" I ask.

"My target," she says confidently.

I laugh. "Yes, but what part specifically?"

"The heart."

"You should aim just below the heart. You almost always miss high."

She nods, adjusting her aim to the stomach of the fake target.

"Now, try."

She does. Shooting a couple of shots that are more centered on the target.

She smiles at her improvement.

"That's better." I walk back over and put my hands on her shoulders, which are still much too tense to get a good shot off. I feel her shoulders relax automatically in my grasp. "You have to stay relaxed when you shoot. If you tense up, you will miss every time. Staying relaxed ensures your aim is on target."

She takes a deep breath, trying to stay as relaxed as she can.

"Lastly, you need to want to hit your target."

She turns and looks at me. "What do you mean?"

"When you tried to shoot me on the plane, you weren't committed. You didn't really want to shoot me. The only way you actually shoot someone is with intention. You have to want to shoot them."

She frowns. "But I did want to shoot you on the plane."

I sigh. "Maybe a small part of you didn't. Is that possible?"

"Maybe."

"Then, that's your biggest problem. You will never shoot someone you don't want to shoot. It's harder than you think."

"How do I want to shoot someone?"

"Hopefully, you won't have to. But you have to find the one thing that drives you to pull the trigger. The one thing that is worth you saving. That is worth more than that person's life."

She nods.

"Try again."

She turns back to the cutout of a man across from her. I keep my hands on her shoulders until she relaxes again. And then I take a step back. She takes a few seconds to gather whatever she thinks is enough to get her to actually hit her target.

And then she fires. Over and over and over until she has used all of the bullets in the gun.

She tosses her gun down on the table and turns to me with the largest grin I've seen on her face. She throws her arms around my neck as she tries to kiss me. I evade her kiss and just tightly hold her in my arms, taking in the smell of her hair as I do. A smell I will never forget. I love having her in my arms, and it's a feeling I'm not used to. I'm not used to having a woman or anyone hugging me for any reason.

She slowly pulls away with the same smile on her face. "Thank you. I think I can finally shoot someone now if I want it badly enough."

I nod as I look at where she perfectly hit the cutout in the chest every single time she shot. "I think you could. Even me, if you wanted it badly enough."

She shrugs. "Don't be snarky. I just might do that."

I smile. "If I hurt you again, you'd better shoot me."

Her frown slowly dissolves off her face.

I lift her chin for her to look at me. "What's wrong?"

"Why won't you kiss me?"

I smile at how adorable she looks. "Is that your one question?"

She scrunches her face. "No...yes. I don't know."

I laugh. "Well, you have to decide first before I answer you."

She sighs. "It's really not fair, you know. I answer all of your questions."

"Sorry, I never said that this would be fair."

"I need a few minutes to decide what I want to ask."

"I'll answer whatever question you want. And then I'll fuck you, and you can ask me another question."

She laughs. "We will see about that."

"No, I know that is exactly what is going to happen."

She frowns. "No, you wish."

"Fine, I wish. I wish every single day that you would let me fuck you."

Nina walks over to the edge of the hill that looks down on the vast empty space sitting behind our mansion.

I try to give her space to decide what question she wants to ask, it's not in my nature to not try to control her. She needs to ask me why I don't kiss her. It would be a waste of a question, but then I can fuck her again. And hopefully again and again until she figures out the truth.

I put my hands in the pockets of my jeans to keep from obsessively wrapping my arms around her. But I don't keep my distance. I stand practically on top of her as she looks out at the beautiful world below her that she is no longer a part of. I intently stare at her as she closes her eyes, just feeling the sun beaming down on her. I don't know how she can find any pleasure in the world anymore. She has to hate it after what it's done to her.

The wind starts blowing, and her hair gets caught in it, blowing wildly in front of her face. When it slows, I can't help but tuck her hair behind her ear again.

She opens her eyes. Her eyes that were full of brightness a second ago have turned to a darkness of concern.

"Why haven't you kissed me?" she says without hesitation.

I pause, waiting to make sure that is really the one question she wants to ask me. "Because kissing does nothing for me and means everything to you."

She scrunches her nose as she stares at me.

"I don't want you so that I can kiss you. I want you, so I can fuck you. That might seem harsh, but I don't want you for the fairy tale. I'm not your savior. I'm not even a good guy. Good guys kiss the girls they are with. They bring them flowers, take them on dates, care for them. I do none of those things, so why would I do the first?"

She sighs. "What about the kiss means everything to me? Why wouldn't you want to take my kisses from me if they mean so much to me and you want to own me?"

"I think you having one piece of yourself that I don't steal means that you still have hope. And, when you have hope that you will escape, it makes the sex that much better."

She frowns. "I think you are lying."

"I don't lie."

She nods. "You don't lie to me, only to yourself."

"What?"

She shakes her head. "Why do you only call me Nina?"

"Because that's your name. Why bother spending time coming up with something else?"

"Because you care about me. Your brother calls me beautiful, sweetheart, pretty. It's not that hard to just say how you feel."

"I do say how I feel. I just don't feel much. And Matteo is a better man than me."

"So, you don't care about me?"

"Nope. Other than I want you alive to fuck, I don't care."

Nina faces forward again so that I can't see her face. She's mad; I'm sure of it.

"I told you that you would end up fucking me today. You wasted your question. You learned nothing new, even after I answered your follow up questions, they were all a waste."

She crosses her arms as she looks at me with a grin that I wasn't expecting. "What makes you think I learned nothing useful? I don't think I wasted my question at all."

I laugh. "You're delusional if you think knowing why I won't kiss you is helpful at all."

She shrugs. "Maybe the game I'm playing is different than the game you are playing."

I sigh and watch her as she starts walking back toward the house. "Where are you going?"

"To get my question answered by Matteo."

I frown. She hasn't asked Matteo her question yet even though it's been two days since we fucked.

What has she been doing? Or has she fucked Matteo again since she fucked us both?

I stand frozen as I watch her skip happily back into the mansion like she doesn't have a care in the world. I know what game she is playing. I know why she is so happy.

She has feelings for both of us. Her obsessive tendencies haven't left even though she's been trying to harness them for years. They are still there, bubbling under the surface.

She cares about us. Maybe even loves us. At the very least, she's beginning to obsess about us. That much is clear. And that can't happen. She can't have both of us. Eventually, she will have to choose. Not just between us but a chance at life again beyond her obsession with us.

18

MATTEO

ME AND MY stupid games within the game. I don't like sharing Nina—not with my brother, not anyone. So, why the hell did I bring up the idea of her fucking us for questions?

Because I was thinking with my cock instead of my head—as usual.

The only pleasure the new rule brings me is that it must be making Arlo fucking mad to have to share her with me. He's never admitted that he has any feelings toward her, but I know that he does. How could he not?

I have fucking feelings toward her. I want her all to myself. I want to care for her. I want to own her. I want to love her even. But I have no idea how to get out of this ridiculous mess that we are in to make any of my feelings come true. I'm afraid that, no matter how this works out, I'm going to lose her.

I'm not okay with that. I won't let her lose her life because I care about her. I don't have any idea how to save her, but I want to save her. Almost as much as I want to win the game that my brother and I play.

I already know that Nina left my bed hours ago, but still, I glance over to her spot in my bed, hoping that she is there.

She isn't.

I groan. What's the point of getting out of bed then if she isn't going to be here?

She's probably chasing my fucking brother. I hear a knock on the main door to my quarters. I groan again. Guess she's not off, fucking my brother. Because I'm sure it's my damn brother at the door, coming to complain that I didn't do something right or that I should be practicing shooting or working out or training or preparing the team for our next meeting in case it involves the use of firearms, as they all inevitably end up.

I don't want to deal with him today. I'm already as prepared as I'm going to be for our next fight. If we are smart, we will lay low for a while before we try to push any further. They are our biggest enemies for a reason. We need time to recover, and as much as Arlo thinks he is invincible, he's not. He needs to heal before we try to negotiate with them again.

When the knocking gets louder, I finally roll out of bed. The man never sleeps. If I'd gotten shot in the stomach, I would be out cold, recovering, for at least a week. Not my fucking brother though. He doesn't believe in rest.

I continue to grumble to myself until I get to the door and throw it open.

My annoyance changes to joy when I see Nina standing in the doorway instead of Arlo.

"You know you don't need to knock before entering, right? You have practically made my quarters yours. Just come in. I was in bed. You can join me if you want?"

She smiles, and her whole body lights up. I haven't seen her this happy or healthy in a long time. A good fuck and couple of days of rest have done wonders for her.

"If I were here to fuck you, I would have just let myself in."

I frown, not liking this at all. "Why are you here?"

"You owe me an answer to a question, if I recall."

I sigh and nod, letting her in.

"Do you want to put some clothes on?" she asks, staring down at my naked body.

"No."

She laughs. "Put some clothes on."

"You're not the boss of me."

"You sure about that?"

"Yes."

"Put some clothes on, or I'm leaving."

I groan. "Fine. But I'm still going to fuck you after I answer your question."

She shakes her head and walks over to the living room couch where she takes a seat. "That's what your brother said."

I narrow my eyes, not liking this conversation at all. "And?"

"And what?" she says casually even though she knows damn well what I'm talking about.

"And...did he fuck you?"

She grins and twists a strand of her hair around her finger. "That sounds like you have a question of your own. I'm tired of answering questions when I have to work so hard to get my own questions answered."

I growl. "I'll put clothes on if you answer my question. Did you fuck him?"

"No," she says, grinning like she just won.

She did.

My nostrils stop flaring, my heart stops pounding, and my body stops shaking the second the word leaves her mouth. She has a lot more power over me than I like. It's not going to end well if she has all the power and none of the information. She can't be in control.

I walk to my bedroom and throw on sweatpants and a T-shirt before returning to find Nina stretched out on the couch. I lift her legs up and take a seat before placing her legs on my lap. It feels so natural to have her legs on mine like this. This is how normal couples behave.

But we aren't a couple. Or normal.

She's my family's slave. I can't have feelings for her. It would only lead to heartbreak.

"So, what's your question?"

She opens her mouth and then closes it.

I huff. "You know I don't have all day to sit here while you think of what question to ask."

She raises an eyebrow as she folds her arms across her chest, becoming more closed off. "Oh, really? You could have fooled me. It seems like you sleep all day while your brother does the real work."

I shrug as I put my arm around the back of the couch. "My brother works too hard for his own good. I work when I need to. But I make sure I get good rest in between the hard work I do."

"So, what work..." She trails off, stopping herself. She takes a deep breath. "Why do you never call me by my name? Why do you always call me sweetheart or beautiful? Why do you kiss me?"

"That's your question?"

"Yes."

"You know, technically, that's three questions."

She glares at me, making me laugh.

"But, fine, I'll answer all three."

She couldn't have given me more of a softball question if she tried. But it doesn't take a genius to realize why she is asking the question. My brother. She wants to know why we are different. If either of us has real feelings for her. But that's impossible. Arlo is far too ambitious to care for a woman who would affect his career, and I don't take life seriously enough to let a woman into it.

"I never call you by your name because that makes you a real person whom I have to show respect. I prefer beautiful or sweetheart because it groups all of you together. I don't have to remember your name or think of you as anything but property."

Her face doesn't change as I speak. I thought she would slap me for talking about her like property, but she doesn't. And, if she's angry with me, she is holding it inside well.

"And why do I kiss you? Because I can, and I want to. Same reason I do anything else in my life."

She again doesn't say anything or move.

"Why haven't you slapped me or yelled at me, saying you aren't my property or slave?"

She sighs. "Because I'm too busy beating myself up for asking you a question I already knew the answer to."

"You thought I would say it was because I owned you?"

"You and your brother are pretty predictable."

"Oh, yeah?"

She nods.

I don't like being predictable. And I know Arlo doesn't like it either. If she thinks we are predictable, then she doesn't know us very well.

"Do you want more questions answered since you asked such awful ones?"

"Do I get to ask questions for free?"

"No."

She looks away from me while she decides. She doesn't want me to know how she really feels, but it's clear to me, no matter how hard she tries to hide her feelings. Turning her head away won't make me not notice how her breathing has grown heavy, her cheeks have flushed pink, and her eyes have darkened at the thought of me and Arlo fucking her again. She can pretend it's payment all she wants, but she enjoys it as much as we do.

Last time, she couldn't hide her cries of joy. She didn't try to hide her moans. Her wetness. Her cum. Everything we did to her, she enjoyed. She begged for more.

And just the thought of us doing it again is getting her excited.

"I think I need more time to figure out what questions to ask before I earn them."

She licks her bottom lip as she looks at me. I don't think she realizes she did it, but I do. I notice everything.

"You can earn another question whenever you want."

"Two questions," she clarifies.

I nod. "Yes, two questions. From me and Arlo."

Her eyes darken, and her lips part. She thinks she has control and power but not when it comes to sex. She loses a little of her power every time she willingly gives herself to us. She knows it. It's why she tries to resist. But her body betrays her. She doesn't have the strength to resist. Especially both of us.

"Arlo!" I shout behind me down the hallway to where I'm sure my brother is lurking, trying to decide what his next move is.

He walks down the hallway that leads to my guest rooms. I raise an eyebrow when he enters my living room. I didn't see him enter my quarters, but I knew he was here even though he shouldn't be. But then again, he thinks he owns everything in this house. Including me. So, I'm not that surprised he entered without an invitation. I am surprised that he snuck in, unnoticed.

I don't bother to show my disgust. I have other more important things on my mind. And, from the look in Arlo's eyes, he has the same thing on his mind.

We both look at Nina; she has the same look.

"We are going to fuck you," I say even though it's really a question. If she says no or stops us, we will stop.

"Yes," she breathes.

19

NINA

I SAW Arlo enter before Matteo even realized he was there. I shouldn't have. He was silent as he opened the door, and if he wanted to, he could have easily disappeared down the hallway before I ever saw him. But I felt him near before he opened the door. And he couldn't help but stare at me before he snuck down the hallway.

I thought I would have more time to make a plan before we had sex again. Not just to prepare more questions. Honestly, it doesn't matter what I ask for at least the next week or two. I just want them to let their guards down and start answering me honestly. Then, I can hit them with the questions that I really want.

I thought I would have more time to recover from the last time. I thought I would have more time to prepare my mind. And, more importantly, my heart. I thought I would have time to figure out how not to let me fall any more than I already have for either of these men. But it seems my time is up because I can't say no.

I don't have the strength.

I didn't have time to think before Matteo asked me.

And the word just fell from my lips.

I open my mouth to lay down the law. Have some sort of rules for what I want. But both men move far too quickly for me to come up with any.

Arlo grabs my mouth, covering it so that I can't speak, until I can barely breathe. He scoops me up under my arms, and Matteo grabs my legs, lifting me up.

They quickly and efficiently move me without speaking a word to me or each other about what they are doing. It's how they work together, I realize. They each know exactly what the other is thinking. Whatever they do when they aren't trying to fuck me must make them an inseparable team.

I don't squirm as they carry me. They hold me so firmly that I'm not sure it would do much good even if I did actually want to escape from them. My eyes widen a little when they don't lead me to Matteo's bed. Instead, they carry me out of his quarters and into the hallway where anyone could see us.

Not that it matters. I've already discovered that the staff doesn't care about what the family does to me. So, wherever they are taking me, even in the precarious position I'm in, they won't even bat an eye.

What if they want to fuck me in a public place?

My heart speeds up at the thought of any of the staff walking in on us. I'm not sure that I'd care if anyone walked in on us. Both men would keep too much of my attention for me to notice anyway.

But the Carini brothers don't stop at any of the places I expect. Not the living room or study. They don't turn down toward Arlo's quarters. Or up toward my room. Instead, they carry me all the way across the house...

My heart stops when I finally realize where they are taking me. And I won't have it. I don't know what kind of game they are trying to pull or if I trusted them when I absolutely shouldn't have, but there is no way they are getting me to go into Enrico's quarters.

I start fighting.

I try to kick Matteo with my legs, and I dig my nails into Arlo's arms, doing everything I can to get him to let me go. Arlo's hand is still covering my mouth, but I try my best to scream for help anyway even though I know screaming won't help me at all.

Matteo tightens his grip on my thighs, and Arlo's hand squeezes my nose shut as well as my mouth, silencing my moaned attempt at screaming.

I can't breathe while Arlo's hand is covering both my nose and mouth. I fight harder, digging my nails until I draw blood, ripping at his skin. I fight until I feel myself about to pass out from lack of oxygen. That's when Arlo finally lets me breathe again.

I only get two breaths in before he covers my mouth again, but this time, he leaves my nose uncovered. I try to focus on my breathing as they carry me through hallways and down to Enrico's bedroom.

My eyes search the room for Enrico. He must be here somewhere. That's why they are bringing me back. I haven't asked the question yet because I already know the answer. That Enrico is definitely the head of the household. That Matteo and Arlo will do anything that he tells them to. It doesn't matter if they care about me. It doesn't matter if they don't want to. If Enrico tells them to, it will be done.

He controls everything.

And I'm done with being controlled.

My eyes keep darting around the room, looking for him to be lurking in the shadows somewhere, but I don't see him or any of his guards that he used to control me.

"He's not here. He's gone," Arlo says, answering the question in my eyes.

I close my eyes, trying to get the nightmares that are over-whelming me to disappear. But, every time I open my eyes and see something else that Enrico used on me, I panic, and they come back. I don't know what they are thinking, bringing me here. But I won't let them fuck me here.

"You said yes. You can do this. Let us do this. Let us help you," Arlo says.

Arlo's words are calm and strong. He's not asking me; he's commanding me, as he always does. It's what I need. For him to reas-sure me. I'm not sure why, but I trust him. I've always trusted him. That's why I ran for seven years. I knew he was telling me the truth. That I needed to hide for as long as I could.

His eyes are the last things I see before a blindfold goes over my eyes, blocking everything from me.

Why he couldn't do that before he brought me into the torture chamber, I don't know. But I take Arlo's eyes with me into the darkness.

His hand is gone from my mouth, and then my body is placed on the bed. My first reaction is to run, to fight. Because, even though I do trust Arlo and even Matteo to keep me safe, I don't want to be fucked again in this room. Even if I agreed to be fucked, I don't want to be fucked here.

The second their hands leave my body, I make a run for it. I jump off the bed and reach for the blindfold. I feel their hands back on me in an instant. I can't help from fighting. Hard. I elbow one of them hard in the nose, making him let me go. But the other one grabs me and drags me back to the bed. I feel the cuffs going on my wrists and ankles, just like before.

I scream because I don't know what else to do. I can't handle this. I can't be raped on this bed again.

I feel his lips on mine, and I stop screaming. His tongue presses into my mouth, leaving me no room to scream.

"I want you, Nina. I want to fuck you everywhere. I want to control you. Fuck you until all the memories you have are of me and my brother. Until you have nothing left," Arlo says while Matteo kisses me.

Both men are trying to control me. One with a kiss and another with a command.

It works.

I feel my breathing change to one of excitement instead of fear. Arlo's sexy, growly voice combined with Matteo's deep kisses make me forget that I'm tied to Enrico's bed.

"Such a pretty dress," Matteo says before he rips the dress off my body.

I gasp as the cool air hits my almost naked body.

I feel leather against my skin, and I tense. It travels from my toes to up my leg, over my panties, then stomach, and bra. I suck in a breath, waiting for the painful sting that I know will come from the whip-like tool in one of their hands. But it doesn't come. At least, not as quickly as I expect.

"No," I whisper, "I'm not ready. I can't do this."

I feel a light whip against my stomach. Not enough to cause any real pain, just enough to grab all my attention.

"You crave this, Nina. You can lie to me and yourself all you want, but your body wants this. You want to feel the sting of the flogger as it hits all the right places on your body. You want us to control you. It turns you on to be controlled and owned."

"No," I whisper again as the flogger harshly hits my inner thigh. I feel the sting radiate through my body. My body curls as my arms and legs pull against their restraints.

He strikes me again on my inner thigh, and my panties are soaked.

He strikes me over my stomach, and my toes curl, as I need more.

He strikes me over my pussy, and I come undone.

I bite my lip to keep from coming right then. I don't understand why my body betrays me. Why it responds to the pain. It never responded to the pain like this when Enrico hurt me, only when Arlo does. I crave it. I seek it. I never want him to stop.

Suddenly, he stops, and I hear nothing but silence. I don't know what Matteo and Arlo are doing. I don't know if they are preparing to hurt me more. Or fuck me. Or leave me stranded again, like Matteo did.

"Please," I cry when I can't take the waiting any longer. I pray to God they haven't tricked me into getting fucked by their father or some other perverted member of their family.

"What do you want, beautiful?" Matteo asks. "I thought you didn't like it when we hurt you."

"No...I mean...I need..."

"What do you need?" Matteo asks. His breath hot and heavy on my ear.

"I need you to hurt me, control me, fuck me."

I can feel his mouth turn into a grin, but I don't feel anything. No pain. No pleasure. Nothing.

I try to focus on calming my breathing. I try to relax while I wait helplessly for them to fuck me.

I can't calm my breathing though.

"Please," I cry again, this time more persistent than the last.

Still, nothing.

"Matteo, please," I cry loudly.

Nothing.

"Arlo, I need you to fuck me. Please."

Only then do I finally get a response. No words. Just the crack of some sort of whip as he strikes my thigh again.

My bra is ripped off, and something warm begins to drip onto my breasts. Every drip brings a pleasant bite of pain I wasn't expecting. My nipples harden, and my back arches, begging for more of the warm wax to cover my body.

"Yes," I moan as I get what I want.

I feel the whip again, this time against my panties. Again and again and again. Making me more sensitive with each crack of the whip. They have barely even touched me, and already, I'm about to come.

They keep going. The whip getting harder, the wax becoming more intense. My panties are ripped from me, and I'm completely naked, lying on the bed.

The leather hits my bare pussy again.

"Yes," I cry.

They stop. Again. Leaving me panting and full of need, aching for more.

I feel Arlo's hands on my thighs as he spreads me apart. I suck in a breath, expecting another strike of the whip. Instead, his tongue gently moves over my folds.

"Come, beautiful," Matteo says.

I come. Hard and long. I scream. I writhe. I forget where I am. My arms pull hard against my restraints.

One soft touch was all it took after they tormented me.

I try to slow my breathing, I try to control the sensations still pulsating throughout my body, but I can't. I have no control, and I can't stop my body from coming again when Matteo sucks on my nipple.

I feel his grin against my nipple when I come and don't care about how cocky he feels at making me come so easily.

"I think we need to give her more time before we fuck her. I don't want her to come on my dick before I've even had my fill of her," Matteo says.

"No," I whisper as I come down off my high.

"No, she will listen to us if we command her to."

I feel Arlo walk closer to me and climb onto the bed. His cock pushes at my entrance. I don't know how I know when it's Arlo or Matteo. They don't always make it clear or tell me with their voices. But I know them well enough to just know. Or my brain guesses, and I never know if I'm right or wrong.

He pushes the tip of his cock in just a little, and I feel my body come alive again from the sensation.

"Don't come, Nina. Not until I tell you to," Arlo commands.

I suck in a breath as he pushes inside me, and I try to will my body not to come. I'm not sure I can do it. I feel the familiar feelings, and I can't hold them back. My body is so sensitive that I can come again and again. I want to come again. It feels too good not to.

"Don't come. If you come, I will punish you," Arlo says.

Something about his voice makes me believe that the punishment won't be something I like. But then again, I like everything the Carini brothers have given me.

"Nina," Arlo warns as he slips his cock fully inside me, stretching me wide.

I squeeze my hands into fists to keep the sensations locked inside instead of coming out like I want.

"Good girl," Arlo says as he fucks me, making my eyes tear up as I feel everything rolling through my body.

It hurts to keep everything inside yet makes everything so intense that I never want to release the feeling.

I feel clamps latch on to my nipples.

"Careful, beautiful," Matteo says as I arch my back.

I purse my lips, trying to get out just a tiny bit of what is pulsing through my veins. It doesn't help.

I bite my lip to keep from screaming because, if I scream, I know it will be calling out one of the Carinis' names as I come.

"Let me help you with that," Matteo says.

I feel his large, thick cock pushing against my lips. My lips part, welcoming his cock into my mouth. I hope that pleasuring him will be a pleasant distraction from what Arlo is doing to my pussy.

For just a second, I get lost, licking his cock and feeling his pre-cum drip onto my tongue. But that's all the distraction I get as Arlo thrusts deep into my pussy, his grip on my thighs tightening to an almost unbearable grip.

I move my lips, sucking more of Matteo's cock as he thrusts in and out of my mouth.

I can't hold on much longer.

I try to distract myself.

I try to focus on counting their thrusts in and out of my mouth and pussy.

I try to count my breathing.

I try squeezing my hands into fists and curling my toes.

But I feel myself losing the fight. They are both turning me on more and more with every thrust. I feel every thrust hit me everywhere in my body. I can't focus. I can't think. I can't hold back any longer.

I come.

My pussy clenches around Arlo's cock, and my mouth cries around Matteo's dick.

They both stop as I come.

There was no way for me to hide it.

No way for them not to notice I didn't follow their command.

Neither of them has come. Neither of them has gotten what they want.

Both of them rip their cocks from my body.

"I'm sorry."

I can feel Arlo's deep stare. I can see Matteo's sexy grin.

Even with the blindfold on, I know that is what both of them are doing.

"You're going to be sorry," Arlo says.

"I already am."

"No, you aren't. But you will be."

Arlo and Matteo grab on to my arms and legs, ripping me from the bed. They don't carry me far, only a few feet away. My feet are placed on the ground, my legs spread apart, as the restraints are tied to something. My arms are pulled high over my head.

If it wasn't for the restraints holding me up, I'm not sure I could stand. I'm so exhausted from coming and being in fear.

I hear the vibrator before I feel it, but it doesn't take me long before I feel it throughout my whole body as it is pressed against my pussy.

I cry out in pleasure as I come quickly.

And then again.

I bite my bottom lip to keep it from pulling another orgasm out of me so easily.

"Now, for your punishment since you can't control your own body. You are going to come. Over and over. All night long. Until you can't stand the thought of coming again," Arlo says.

That sounds like the best punishment ever.

"I would wipe that smile off your lips, beautiful. You will quickly learn how this is the worst kind of punishment," Matteo says.

I let go and come as the vibrator continues its punishing pace against my clit.

As soon as I do, Matteo replaces the vibrator with his cock. He thrusts inside me while he kisses me, punishing me with his teeth on my lip. His pace is fast as he thrusts, his mouth equally as brutal on my lips. My hands grab on to the ropes as I feel the familiar feeling growing closer.

"Come, sweetheart," Matteo says.

I do as his cum fills my pussy.

He slips out of me while I try to recover from the pounding my body just took, but I don't get a break. Arlo's cock replaces Matteo's in seconds.

His cock hits deep inside me, hitting a spot that makes me crazy. I feel his lips on my ear, and I prepare for him to torture me in the same way that Matteo just did. But he doesn't.

Instead, he whispers into my ear, "You may control me usually. But you don't have any control when my cock is buried in your pussy. Now, I'm in control. You do whatever I say."

I breathe in.

"Now, come," Arlo says.

I come.

My body hangs down, my arms stretching long as my body pulls on the restraints, unable to hold myself up. But Matteo quickly replaces Arlo, holding me up as he fucks me in the ass this time.

I can't handle this. Not if they keep this pace up. I'll die by being over fucked.

But, at least, if I do, I'll die a sweet death.

20

ARLO

WE FUCKED her all night long, just like I'd promised we would.

She almost broke several times, but she never did. It only showed me and her how strong she truly was.

I thought the endless sex would finally be what broke down her walls. But it didn't.

She thought we were fucking her all night to destroy any memory of Enrico in her head. And that was definitely part of it.

Nina is invincible. She knows exactly how strong she is now.

If she survived a night of fucking in every position possible, she could survive anything. We beat her, scarred her body, and fucked her pussy so hard that she slept for an entire week after without moving.

Matteo and I took turns in watching over her. We brought her back to Matteo's room because, despite having her own beautiful room, his room was where she felt safe. She did nothing but sleep.

We slept, too, but not like her.

Every day, we both ached for her to wake up to have a chance to fuck her again because, after having her so many times in a row, it felt impossible to go a second without having her. But it was dangerous for us to feel that way about her. Far too dangerous because it became far too close to us developing feelings for her.

When she did finally wake up, we both thought she wouldn't want to have sex again for a long time. But I'd learned to be surprised when it came to Nina.

She asked her stupid questions.

Something about if Matteo and I were close, growing up. What kind of stupid question was that? Of course we were close, growing up. If she couldn't tell that by just being with us, then she wasn't as smart as she looked.

But then it became clear. I discovered her plan after the third softball question about where my favorite place to visit was. She was softening me up, hoping that I would fall in love with her, and when she asked the really hard questions, I'd save her.

She doesn't understand that I can't. That her plan will never work. I tried her plan before, and it backfired in my face. I won't do that again. I won't risk her life like that.

So, every day that she asks, I fuck her with Matteo and pray that it isn't the day she stops asking the easy questions and starts asking the hard questions. Because I can't lie to her. And I'm afraid the only thing left that can break her is the truth.

21

MATTEO

ARLO TEXTS me that he needs me to go with him to deliver our latest weapon tonight.

It's not a question. It's a command. I'm supposed to go with him. That's what we do. He tells me what to do, and I follow.

But not this time.

I'm tired of doing everything that Arlo tells me to do.

These last few months have been amazing, but I can feel the pressure in our bubble building. And I know that it's going to pop soon. I can feel it.

I don't bother to text him back.

He's going to be pissed, but I don't care. I climb off the couch and go find Nina reading a book in my bed.

She smiles up at me when she sees me standing in the doorway.

I grin back as I fold my arms across my chest and lean in the doorway. Nina has quickly become my everything. All I can do is think about her. What she's doing. What she needs. I think about her body. Her smart mouth. I think about fucking her. Talking to her. Holding her.

I can't stop.

She used to be the one who was obsessed. But not anymore. Now, I'm just as obsessed with her as she is with me.

I can't stop. And I don't want to. I want her every second of every day. And, if Arlo thinks I'm going to be willing to leave her alone for one second in this house, even to go do work, he's crazy. He knows how I feel about her. He sees it in my eyes every night when we fuck her together. Always fucking together.

We have each tried to get her on her own, but the other is always there. Nina always pulls us both in. But it can't last forever. Eventually, whatever is going on is going to stop. Someone is bound to develop feelings. And, even if I know that Arlo has developed feelings for Nina, I know him well enough to know that he will never act on those feelings.

"What?" Nina asks, looking at me with her big brown eyes.

I step into the room and walk over to her, taking the book out of her hands and laying it on the nightstand next to the bed.

"I want you," I say.

Her eyes grow heavy. "Okay, where's Arlo?"

I shake my head. "No, not with him."

She raises an eyebrow at me as I climb on top of her in bed, pinning her down. She doesn't fight me; she just seems amused. We've fucked too many times for her to fear me.

"Where is Arlo?" she asks.

"He's working. He never has to know. Just fuck me alone, just this once."

I lean down and kiss her, tasting the sweet wine on her lips that I didn't notice she was drinking. I kiss her hard, slipping my tongue into her mouth, making it impossible for her to say no to me.

"Don't you have to work, too, then?" she asks.

"No, I don't. Not tonight. Tonight, the only thing I want is to fuck you."

She bites her lip as she looks in my eye. She hasn't fucked either of us in two days. That's the longest we have gone without sex. We were both gone working yesterday, and when we got back, she was already asleep. We all slept in, doing various things today, and then Arlo wanted me to work again tonight instead of having her. I can't go that long without having her. Not now. Not ever again.

"Come on, beautiful. Let me fuck you. You know you want it as badly as I do," I purr into her neck. I begin kissing her neck, surprised that she hasn't stopped me already.

"Yes."

"Yes?" I say, immediately stopping my kisses to look her in the eyes to make sure she is serious.

"Yes, but I have one condition."

"Anything!" I say, already thinking about where I want to have sex with her.

"Afterward, I get to ask you any questions I want, and you have to answer honestly."

I search her eyes, trying to figure out what her plan is, but it isn't hard to figure out. She's been asking easy questions for weeks, just waiting for the right time to get her real questions answered. Apparently, today is that day.

I'm ready though. I know how to answer any question to keep her safe and mine. This is the day I've been waiting for, too.

"I'll tell you anything you want."

Her face lights up at that. "I'm yours then."

I hang on to her words. They were exactly what I wanted to hear. What I needed to hear.

I grab her hand and pull her out of bed, needing to come up with the perfect place to fuck her. Now.

She laughs as I pull her out of my bed with urgency. "Where are we going? I thought you would want to fuck me in your bed."

I shake my head. That is absolutely the last place I want to fuck her. Too many memories of Arlo and me fucking her there. I want her someplace I can claim her as mine. A place where Arlo will know that I won. That she chose me over him.

She doesn't move fast enough for me, so I scoop her up in my arms as I run out of my quarters.

She giggles again as she kisses my neck. "Someone's in a rush."

I growl when she kisses my neck. "Stop distracting me, woman."

She bites her lip as I carry her through the mansion to Arlo's rooms. I get to the door to his quarters and test it just in case he left it unlocked. But, of course, he didn't.

I can't pick the lock; I've tried countless times. The door is basically bulletproof, but Arlo does claim one other room that he doesn't keep behind lock and key. The room he takes women to when he wants to fuck them.

I walk to the double doors at the end of the hallway and push them open as I carry Nina in. I don't bother shutting the doors behind me. The maids know well enough to stay far away, and if Arlo comes home, I want him to see me with her.

But where to fuck her first? I've had her every way possible, and I can't possibly choose a favorite. Every position. Every way.

I look at Nina, and I see her eyes light up when we enter the room. I don't know what history she has in this room, and I'm not sure I want to know, but I don't have a choice. I have to know.

"Did Arlo fuck you in this room?"

She motions for me to put her down. I reluctantly do, and I watch her sway her hips as she walks over to a large chair that looks more like a throne sitting in the corner of the room.

"No, I tried to get Arlo to fuck me. But he fucked three other whores instead."

I smirk. I definitely chose the right room to claim her as mine.

She runs her hand over the velvet chair, most likely remembering that night.

"I want to ride you while you sit in this chair," she says, standing behind it and pointing to it.

I suck in a breath, trying to control myself or this moment is going to end far too soon. She looks gorgeous, standing behind the chair like that. She's completely irresistible. She doesn't even have to try to be sexy; she just is. She's wearing jeans and a dark gray shirt. Her hair is pulled back in a ponytail, but her confidence is what makes all the difference. It's something she has always had, but as the weeks have gone by, especially since that night in Enrico's room, she has changed into the strongest woman I've ever seen.

"Gladly," I say with a smirk as I walk over and take a seat in the chair.

Her hands rub my shoulders, and I groan, loving her working for me for once. She slowly makes her way in front of me and begins to put on a show for me as she undresses, starting with her shirt.

"I wish I had some music to dance for you," she says.

I smile. "That, I can give you." I turn toward Arlo's sound system. "Play us a song to fuck to."

A sexy pop song comes on, and Nina starts moving her body to the music. She strips her shirt, shoes, and pants. I grip the chair, forcing myself to stay in it and wait for her to come to me, but waiting has never been my strong suit. As soon as she gets closes enough for me to touch, I grab her hips and pull her into my lap.

"I'm not a patient man."

She kisses me, pulling my bottom lip into her mouth. "I know."

"Then, what are you doing?"

"Making you crazy," she says with a wink and then starts grinding her hips against my cock that is still trapped in my pants.

I growl and pull my shirt off, needing to feel her skin against mine. She gives in immediately, running her hands over my chest. I'm not used to her touching me. Most of the times I've fucked her, she's been tied up or had to split her attention between me and Arlo. But, tonight, I get all of her attention. Her hands travel over my body, feeling every inch of me as my cock grows larger for her.

"Take off my pants," I command.

She grins as she kneels in front of me. "Someone's still bossy."

"Always."

She grabs my waistband, unbuttons my pants, undoes the zipper, and pulls my pants down along with my underwear until my cock is free.

Her large eyes get bigger, telling me exactly how much she really does want my cock. She runs her tongue across her bottom lip before devouring my cock with her mouth.

I close my eyes and let my head roll back as she wraps her lips around my cock. The way she moves her mouth over me makes it clear how much she wants this and that she is enjoying herself as much as I am.

I open my eyes, needing to see hers. She grins around my cock when I do, knowing exactly what she is doing to me.

I grab her chin, stopping her from fucking me with her mouth. As much as I want to shoot my cum down her throat, I want to feel her pussy pulsating around me more.

I pull her back up onto my lap, and her legs automatically go around me, startling me, as her lips lower to my mouth, kissing me hard and fast. One hand grabs her long mane of hair, and the other grabs her breast as her nipple hardens beneath my hand.

She moans, and the sound hardens my cock even more, pushing against her entrance. I want to fuck her now. But I need to hear her say my name first. I need her to want me as badly as I want her.

I bite her lip, bringing it into my mouth, as she purrs deep in her throat.

I grab her hips and grind them against me as she bites her lip to keep from screaming.

I lower my mouth to her nipple and suck at the same time I push my cock inside her.

"Fuck, Matteo," she moans.

Finally.

She pushes my head back the second I enter her and takes the control back. She grinds up and down on my cock, riding me like it is her favorite thing to do.

I want the control back but not nearly as much as I want her to keep doing what she is doing.

"You like my cock, beautiful?" I ask.

She nods and licks her lips as she keeps fucking me, unable to say anything.

I thrust hard against her, meeting her thrust for thrust, as her grip on my shoulders tightens. Her nails dig into my shoulders as she holds on, trying to keep from coming.

"Come, beautiful."

She keeps riding me harder, increasing her pace, as I barely contain my own orgasm.

"No."

I growl, "Come. Now."

"No."

She rides me harder, and I can't hold back another second.

"Nina," I growl.

She milks an orgasm out of me.

Only then does Nina finally come.

She collapses onto my body, and I wrap my arms around her, loving having her body pressed up so closely against mine.

We stay that way for a long time, both passed out and just holding each other.

Then, Nina slowly lifts her head with a grin on her face. "Now, I have some questions for you."

I firmly kiss her on the lips, slipping my tongue into her mouth, begging her to have sex with me again.

"But, first, you want me to fuck you again?"

She takes a deep breath and bites her lip, still grinning. "Yes."

———

"As much as I want to do that again, my body can't take much more," Nina says, lying on Arlo's bed in his playroom while I lie next to her, completely spent.

I nod. "I guess that means it's time for me to stop stalling and answer your questions."

She nods.

But neither of us says anything else as we just lie in bed, staring at each other. The sex was great. Nina and I share a connection like no one else. But it still doesn't mean we have any sort of future together once we leave this room. I don't know what feelings she has for Arlo. I'm sure she still hopes that she can find a way out of this mess and end up back with her husband. And, even if she does choose me out of all the men in her life, I'm not sure that we could have a future together. So, this might be it. The last moment I can claim her as mine and mine alone.

She knows it, too.

I can see it in the way she tries to slow her breathing down to really cherish me. I can feel it in the stillness. She doesn't move or speak right away; she just is. Her eyes don't look anywhere but mine. She's just present with me, taking everything in.

"What questions do you want to ask me?" I finally ask, breaking our perfect moment that could have lasted forever.

She takes another deep breath, staring at me while I tuck a strand of her hair behind her ear.

"What do you and your family do for a living? How do you make money? Why does Arlo come home, covered in blood almost every night? Where is Enrico? How did your family gain so much power?"

I nod. I knew my family would be at the center of her questions even though she has probably guessed enough to know most of the truth. She needs to know about my family.

So, I tell her, "My family has lived in Italy for hundreds of years. We never had any power, no noble blood, nothing to tie us to royalty.

"But the story goes, one of the first members of my family had a son who was strong and good. He lived his life as a soldier, fighting for good. One day, he and his brother were traveling back to town when they came across a horse without a rider. The brothers searched and searched until they finally found the rider. A woman had fallen off in a nearby creek. They rescued the woman and brought her to the nearest town. That woman was the princess.

"The king knew he owed a great debt that could never be repaid to the brothers, but he vowed to give the brothers whatever they wanted. Jewels, money, power. But the brothers were more interested in his daughter than the money."

"Naturally," Nina says as she rolls over onto her stomach, resting her head on her hands as she listens to my story.

"The brothers fought over the beautiful princess. But, ultimately, she chose neither of them. She chose an actual prince to marry. The brothers were heartbroken and grew to resent each other until, one day, the king sent them money as payment.

"That money turned into more money. More jewels were sent. And those jewels turned into power. People would turn up at their doorstep, asking for their help. Giving them money. Giving them women. Giving them everything they could ever want.

"They soon learned the power they wielded if they had the richest people in the country in their debt. So, that is exactly what they did. Soon, they became as powerful as the king himself.

"My family continued the tradition for years, becoming more corrupt and evil as each descendant took power until here we sit."

Nina bites her lip to keep from laughing.

"What's so funny?"

"Oh, come on! You don't really expect me to believe that crazy story you so clearly just made up, do you? You just made up that story as an attempt to get me to choose one of you."

I grin. "You can think I'm a liar all you want. I'm not. Now, do you want me to finish answering your questions or not?"

She sighs. "Continue with your lies."

"My family still carries on with the old tradition of getting powerful men—"

"And powerful women," Nina interjects.

I smile and nod. "And powerful women to owe us a debt, therefore giving us power over them. Our regular business and sources of income are building and selling powerful weapons. But we never give our enemies any weapons more powerful than what we already have. We build the weapons mainly for ourselves as a way to gain more power. We use it to protect our homeland here, which the Italian government allows us to do pretty much whatever we want with."

"So, basically, you became the unofficial kings of Italy," Nina says.

I smile, liking the thought of us as kings.

"Our work requires us to do a lot of different things. We have meetings during the daylight, negotiating terms of the debt our clients owe us or discussing weapons that we will sell or gain. At night is when we make the trades or deal with clients who think they don't owe us a debt. We make it clear that no one gets away without paying back their debt."

I watch her eat up every word I say even if she thinks part of it is a lie. Or all of it. But she still hangs on to every word.

"Sometimes, those meetings don't go so well, and we have to use force to ensure the meetings go our way."

She frowns. "But why does Arlo always end up hurt, and you never end up with much more than a scratch on you?"

"Because I'm that much better at avoiding getting shot than he is."

She raises an eyebrow. "Really?"

"Fine. You already know the answer anyway. Arlo is a martyr who will take a bullet for someone he cares about. He won't let me get shot even if it would do me some good to realize that I'm not invincible."

Nina laughs. When her laughter settles down, she asks, "And Enrico?"

"He went to America to negotiate a trade we have been working on for some time. It's tricky negotiations. He won't be back for several months yet."

She sucks in a breath and nods. I watch her as she opens her mouth to ask another question and then stops as she looks past me. I don't have to turn around to know who she is looking at.

Arlo.

22

ARLO

I STAND in the doorway of the room where I first saw Nina naked, and now, I find her naked in the bed that I desperately wanted to fuck her on the first time I saw her. I should be thrilled. I should be thanking God that my dreams have finally been answered, but instead, I feel like a dagger has been shoved into my heart and then twisted over and over again.

I shouldn't care that she is naked in my bed with my brother. But I am.

If he thinks I will protect his sorry ass again after what he just did to me, he'd better think again.

"How did the meeting go?" Matteo asks with a smirk on his face.

"It clearly doesn't matter to you. I do all the work in this family anyway."

"It definitely matters to me since I most likely won."

I laugh. "The game isn't over yet."

Matteo turns his attention back to Nina. "Do you want to go back to my room now? You can finish asking all the questions you still have for me."

Nina doesn't look at him. She looks at me. "No."

Matteo frowns. "I thought you had more questions for me?"

"No, I don't have any more questions for you. But I do have more questions for Arlo."

Nina's eyes sear into my soul when she says she wants to ask me questions, probably because she didn't get the honest answers she was hoping for out of my brother. But she doesn't get to play games with us both. I'm done playing games after she's made it perfectly clear what games she is playing. And whom she really wants.

Nina stands up and begins walking toward me. I can't get the image out of my head of the last time we were in this room, and she walked toward me like that. My cock hardens as my body remembers how badly I wanted her then and how much more I want her now. Last time, I fucked three other women while trying to imagine they were her. It didn't work. She didn't get out of my head. And, even now, after fucking her countless times, she's still not out of my head. And I'm afraid she's buried herself deeper into heart than I ever thought possible.

She reaches her hand out to touch my face, and I grab her wrist, stopping her.

"I'm not answering your questions. You made your choice; now, live with it."

She laughs and jerks her hand away. "I never said I made a choice. I made a deal with Matteo. I fucked him by himself, and in return, he offered to answer any question I had. I'm offering you the same deal. I'll fuck you. If you promise to answer my questions."

I shake my head. "I'm done answering your questions."

She bites her lip that I'm desperate to taste, bite, lick, suck. But I won't.

Nina reaches out and grabs my hand, pulling it to her mouth and slowly sucking on my index finger. "Are you sure you can't be persuaded?"

I close my eyes because I can't look her in the eyes and say what I need to say. "I'm not answering your questions."

She sighs. "Fine. Matteo—"

Damn it.

I grab her naked body and throw her over my shoulder. I carry her out of the room before she has a chance to offer to fuck Matteo. I can't answer more of her questions, but I can't be the reason she fucks Matteo again.

I don't know what I'm doing, but I carry her toward my section of the house. When I get to the door, I pause, not sure if I really want to let her into my personal space. I've never let anyone in, but I'm desperate, and for the first time ever, I want someone to share my space with, if only for a few hours.

I open the door and carry her inside. I throw her naked ass down onto the circular couch in the center of the main room while I stand, not believing what I just did.

Nina looks around with her mouth wide open. I don't know what she is thinking, and I'm too fucking nervous to ask. *Why do I care about what she thinks of my personal space?*

"Wow," she says.

I look around the room, trying to see it like she does, but I'm not sure I can. I have no idea if she loves it or hates it. Is disgusted by it or engrossed by it. And I don't have the balls to ask.

She looks back at me. "Did you paint all of these?"

I look around the circular room that is covered with paintings.

I nod.

She looks up at them. "Wow, they are incredible."

She stands up and walks over to the closest one. She hovers her fingers over the portrait of a man, getting as close as she can without actually touching the painting. "I can feel everything that you felt when you painted this man. Hatred. Fear. Heartache. Pain."

I walk over and stand behind her as I look at the painting she's looking at.

"Who is it a picture of?"

"A memory that I will never forget."

She narrows her eyes a little when she looks at me and then walks to the next picture. "And this one?" she asks, looking at a painting of a woman and her child.

"Same."

She nods, looking at them and then at me. "They are paintings of people you've hurt."

I nod.

She sucks in a breath. "They're beautiful."

"They aren't beautiful. They are paintings of pain and torture. Paintings that show me at my absolute worst."

They're my nightmares that haunt me every night when I sleep. I thought painting them would allow me some peace, but it didn't. Nothing helps.

She turns back to me, and I see the tears in her eyes. She hates me for killing them. There are dozens of paintings in the room, and they aren't even all the ones I've done, just the ones that haunt me the most. I'm the devil. She's finally realizing that one of the men she has been fucking for weeks is the monster she was trying to avoid.

She can't forgive me for what I've done.

I turn away because I can't see her cry from the pain I've caused these people. I can't deal with her hurting, too.

I feel her hand on my face, and I immediately push it away, not willing to face her right now.

She grabs my face and turns me toward her. "They're beautiful."

She leans her head against my forehead, and I feel her tears roll from her eyes to down my cheeks.

I suck in a breath, not liking being so close to someone. Not liking sharing someone's pain like this. I hate it, but I also never want it to end.

Nina pulls away and looks up at me with tears still in her eyes.

"Kiss me."

I narrow my eyes, not understanding why in the hell she would want to kiss me.

"No."

"Kiss me."

"No."

Her eyes search mine, but she'll find nothing but emptiness there.

"Kiss me."

"No."

"Please."

"Why? You don't want me. You're playing games. And, after seeing the pain I've caused, you can't possibly want anything to do with me."

She shakes her head. "It doesn't matter that I'm playing games. You're playing games with me just as much as I am with you."

"Exactly. You don't want me! You just want me to fall for you so that I will save you."

"And what's so wrong with that? Maybe I don't want to die or be held captive for seven years. Seven years is a long fucking time!"

"What's wrong with that? What's wrong is that I can't fucking save you! Even if you succeed in making me fall in love with you, I can't do a damn thing about it!"

She grabs my face and kisses me.

And, in that moment, my world stops. I've never wanted anything more. I also hate myself for wanting this and letting it happen. But, now that it is, I'll never stop kissing her.

My hands wrap around her body while my tongue tangles with hers. She tastes just as sweet as I've always imagined. Her lips are just as luscious. And the moment is even better than I could have ever imagined.

I grab her legs as she wraps them around me, and I push her against a wall as I continue to kiss her. Her hands wrap tightly around my neck, not letting me stop the kiss even if I wanted to. I don't. I don't ever want this kiss to end.

I kiss her deeper and listen to the beautiful purr in her throat as I do. Her kisses are everything.

And, as much as I try to stop my mind from going there, I think they are everything to her, too. She might still love her husband. She might even have feelings for Matteo. But there is no denying that she doesn't have feelings for me as well. No one kisses like this and doesn't love the other person.

I don't want to hear the words fall from her mouth, and I'll kiss her all night long to keep her from saying something so stupid as that she's fallen in love with a man like me. But there is no denying that is how she feels.

"I need you to fuck me," Nina says with her lips still pressed against mine, not allowing me to stop the kiss even though she is speaking.

I've never agreed more with her. I can't stop kissing her, and it's clear she won't stop kissing me either.

She's already naked, and my cock is already hard against my jeans.

Nina grabs the button and swiftly undoes it with one hand without breaking our kiss. She pushes my pants down along with my underwear until my cock is free. I push inside her, knowing how wet she is.

"Arlo," she growls against my lips as I enter her.

I'll never get tired of hearing my name fall from her lips. I'll never get tired of anything Nina does. I need to fuck her against every surface in my room. That way, when she's gone, I'll never be able to forget her.

She bites my lip hard as I thrust inside her, holding on to her ass with my hands. I love how she bites my lip before lapping up the blood. I love how she craves my body just as much as I want hers.

"Don't stop," she whimpers as I fuck her harder against the wall.

"Never," I growl back.

I can't stop. Even though I usually crave sex where I have all the power, I like tying women up. Making them suffer, causing them pain. Even though this is the complete opposite of that—it's vanilla sex—it's the best sex I've ever had.

"I...uh..." Nina says.

I won't let her get words out. She can talk to me afterward. Right now, I want her body that is saying plenty to me.

I kiss her hard. I fuck her with everything I have, and I know it still won't be enough. I'll still crave her forever after tonight is over. I will never get enough.

What started out as her obsession with me has turned into my own ridiculous obsession with her. I don't understand it or even how to make it stop, but I'm overcome by it.

Nina tugs at my lip again, and I get lost again as I fuck her. I watch her face change, and I know she will come soon and that I will come shortly afterward. I know we will both pass out and then do this again and again. But I know, soon, this will be over. This will end. And she'll be gone. And what will be left of me?

———

"Do you paint anything other than your nightmares?" Nina asks, carefully choosing her words as she lies against my bare chest.

"Not usually, no." I tense, not liking wherever this conversation is going. I don't want her to cry again.

"Don't get me wrong. I love them. I think they are very therapeutic for you, and it's good to remember your darkest side, but you would be more balanced and maybe have a more positive outlook on the world if you also painted your dreams, too."

I suck in a breath, trying to decide if I should show her or not. My heart races, and my body tenses.

"What's wrong?" she asks, able to pick up on the changes in my body as easily as I'm able to pick up on how she is feeling.

"I want to show you something."

She smiles and stands. I get up and take her hand, leading her toward my bedroom.

"You shouldn't be nervous. I doubt there is anything you can show me that is worse than what I already know about you," she teases.

I continue walking, ignoring her, which only makes her more nervous. I open the door, flip the switch, and lead her to the single painting in my bedroom.

She gasps when she sees it, immediately dropping my hand as she slowly walks over to the large mural.

I stand back, watching her, letting her take it in before I probe her to see what she thinks.

But she takes her damn time before saying anything, and I'm not a patient man.

"What do you think?"

"I think you should have been a painter instead of a debt collector, weapons dealer, and killer."

I chuckle. "I know art, and it isn't that good. It's only good because of who I painted."

She raises an eyebrow. "Are you serious? It's amazing. I would do anything to be able to paint as well as you do."

I shake my head. "What do you think about what I painted though?"

She bites her lip as she looks at me. "I think you are as obsessed about me as I am about you."

My eyes deepen when she says that about the naked painting that I painted of Nina.

"So, am I your nightmare or dream?" she asks.

"A little of both."

She grins. "Good."

She turns back to the painting as I walk behind her and wrap my arms around her body. I can feel it the second that everything changes. And I prepare for her to finally ask what she's been wanting to ask since she first came here.

"How does the game end?"

I suck in a breath because I still don't know what to tell her.

She turns her head to look up at me. "I've figured out what the game is—or at least, I think I know."

I nod, encouraging her to continue to tell me what she knows while I figure out how to save her from it.

"There have been women before me. Women who have been tricked into owing a debt to your family. And, once she is here, you and your brother play a game with her life. A game where she has to choose a winner between the two of you."

I shake my head, realizing how close she is but also how far. I don't know when I decide to tell her the truth or if I even really decide, but it all starts spilling out, and I can't stop.

"We don't trick the women. They owe us a real debt. That's how we chose the seven women."

"Seven? Why seven?"

"We needed an odd number. So, it would guarantee a winner."

"Between you and Matteo?"

I nod.

"What are you playing for?"

"The winner will take our father's place. He gets to become head of the family and will decide to continue the traditions started years before him—"

"Or not," Nina finishes for me.

I nod.

239

"How do you win?"

"Enrico chooses the winner each round. The rules aren't entirely clear, which makes it more difficult to win each round. You're number seven, but up until this point, Enrico has basically given equal rounds to Matteo and me to ensure that we go the full seven rounds."

"He wants you to be more like him."

I nod.

"And have you?"

I take a deep breath. "With some of the women, yes."

She frowns. "But not me?"

I shrug. "I've tried to make it look like I have with you."

She looks away and walks out of my arms. "Enrico has been watching us with cameras, hasn't he?"

I nod. "He has cameras in certain areas of the house that he watches."

"Not here?"

"No."

"Matteo's rooms?"

"No."

She takes a deep breath. "I remember."

"What?"

"I remember that night you saved me. It's taken me seven years of pushing the memories away, trying to pretend like they weren't real, but I remember."

My eyes widen. I wish she didn't remember that night.

"I remember not being able to control my body. My muscles going weak. I remember not staying conscious for it all though. I was awake as Erick and Clive took me from the bar when you weren't able to get to me. I remember the fear on your face as they dragged me out of the bar. You were devastated."

I take a deep breath, trying to keep the feelings I felt that night at bay.

"I thought you were devastated because you knew what they were capable of. But you were equally devastated because you knew that my life would be no better off if you saved me."

I feel the rage returning, billowing up inside me, the same feeling that I felt that night.

"I remember them trying to rape me. I remember you and your family barging in, guns drawn. I remember Clive saying that I was theirs, not yours. That you couldn't do anything to save me. It would ruin the deal you had with them."

My nostrils flare, and my whole body is on fire, thinking about it.

"You started firing. All of you, even Enrico, came to save me. I remember Enrico getting shot. Matteo was stabbed. You were the only one who wasn't hurt. You got me out of there but not before they made threats against your family, against Gia."

I can't relive any more of the night. "Stop."

Her eyes widen.

We both just stand for a while, looking at each other, both breathing heavily, both reliving that night.

"I remember signing the contract. It was just you and me. I was terrified. Traumatized. I thought I had just seen your brother and father die. Your sister's life threatened. I was almost raped. You gave me the choice to sign, and I signed without a second thought. That was the last thing I remember. Signing."

"You passed out from exhaustion after that."

She nods.

We stare at each other a moment longer.

"What I don't understand is, why would you do that? Risk your whole family's life for me? I know you needed a number seven, and I'm guessing you have saved other women from similar predicaments, only to be met with an equally bad situation. But why did you choose me? Why didn't you just let them have me and rape me and, most likely, kill me?"

I don't answer.

She takes a step toward me and looks me dead in the eye.

"Do you love me?"

I knew she would ask that question, too. She thinks I did it all because I love her. But she doesn't understand that I am incapable of love. And, even if I was, she is better off with someone else. Someone good.

241

I didn't do it because I loved her. I saved her because she'd saved me, and I couldn't watch her die even if I was saving her then, only to watch her die now.

"What do you think?" I say, not answering her.

She takes a deep breath but doesn't answer me.

"Why did you drink it? Why did you marry Heath? Why fuck my brother?"

She takes a step back, not answering me either.

But I answered all of her questions, except one. She needs to answer my questions now. I grab her arm and pull her back to me, firmly kissing her on the lips like it is the last time I'll ever be able to.

She pulls away. "Because I was obsessed with you. I've always been obsessed when it comes to men. I like sex. I want the attention. Blame it on my deadbeat father who died a slow, torturous death after his drinking finally caught up with him."

"Why did you marry Heath?"

"Because I loved him. I know you don't understand it, but when I fall, I fall hard. I can't always control it. Maybe part of it was the fear of being ripped away from my reality and needing something to keep me grounded. But, whatever it was, it felt a heck of a lot like love. It still does."

I see the tears when she says it.

"Why did you fuck my brother?"

"Because I hated you. Because I wanted to get back at you. Because I thought I could make him love me if you wouldn't."

"And who do you want now? Who do you dream about at night? Who makes you obsessed?"

She sucks back her tears. "What do you think?"

I hate her answer. But it's payback for my answer. And, honestly, I don't think she can answer my question yet. We've played with her mind too much these past weeks. And I think she can be obsessed with more than one man at a time. I think, if she were to answer honestly, she would have to say all three of us: Heath, Matteo, and me for different reasons. But, if she could choose whom she wanted most, it would still be Heath. He's the only one who hasn't fucked her against her will. It will always be Heath.

"How does the game end?" she finally asks.

I know what she's asking. Will she die? And it's a question I can't answer definitively. But, if I go off of what happened to the other women, then yes, she doesn't stand a chance. Two killed themselves rather than deal with being someone's slave. Three, my father killed. And one, I killed out of mercy. None of them even lasted a year even though they were all given the same length of time—seven years.

She sees the answer in my eyes, and her whole body slumps.

I walk over and wrap my arms around her, surprised that she will let me hold her when I just told her she will probably die and I won't do anything to save her.

"You're strong though. The strongest. You can survive."

And then I kiss her because I need to feel her lips on me again. I don't know how much time I have left with her. Another second. Another hour. Another day.

Or much longer. Weeks, months, years. But, now that I have one tiny bit of her heart, I will do anything to keep it for as long as I can.

23

NINA

I FINALLY HAVE THE TRUTH.

It's what I've wanted this whole time. To know everything. Then, I would be on an equal playing field. But, now that I know everything, I'm afraid it was a mistake. I'm more terrified than I ever was before.

Arlo was terrified to tell me the truth. He was afraid it would break me. It would make me stop fighting. Or that he was effectively signing my death sentence by telling me all of the family secrets.

His fear made my fear worse.

But it's easy to forget about all of that when I'm wrapped in his sexy arms, in his bed, and I haven't dealt with any real pain in weeks. Both of the Carini brothers have done everything to take care of me these last few weeks. And my life has become pleasant, if not enjoyable. I've had plenty of food, plenty of company, and plenty of sex.

Enrico hasn't returned, and I've been driven into a false sense of security. But last night changed all of that. I fucked them separately and got all of my questions answered. I can't go back to just fucking them both. They won't allow it. They will want me to choose one of them. And, if I don't, what will happen?

I don't know. But, whatever happens, going forward, a change is coming. And I'm afraid that change is never good.

I sit up in bed and feel my body ache from being fucked all night. It's a good kind of soreness but one I'd rather sleep off while curled in Arlo's arms for the foreseeable future. If I'm asleep, I don't have to make decisions. Nothing has to change.

But I can't face Arlo's questions when he wakes up. So, I force myself to leave his arms and his bed. I get up and go to his closet to find a pair of pants and a T-shirt that smells the least like him that I can. His closet is a perfectly organized array of dark shirts and pants. There isn't a single color outside of the gray or black family.

I grab a T-shirt and one of only two pairs of sweatpants and put them on before sneaking back out into his bedroom. I look back at him peacefully sleeping in the bed before turning my attention one last time to the painting of me. It's strange—seeing such a beautiful painting of myself. I look strong, powerful, albeit a little bit sad. It's how he sees me. I want to be that strong, powerful woman he painted. Maybe that woman has a chance to survive.

I walk out of his bedroom and stop one more time to look at all of his striking paintings that show so many feelings. I would have never thought of him as a painter. Just like I would have never imagined Matteo as a doctor before he stitched up Arlo and took care of me. But, now that I know this is who they are, I want to know more about them. Who are they really, and what have they been hiding about themselves from me and the rest of the world?

Instead of staying around to find answers, I leave Arlo's safe haven and go back into the real world. Or, at least, the shitty world that I currently exist in. My stomach growls immediately, and I know the answer to where my first stop will be. I don't have to worry about running into Matteo. Both brothers are night owls and rarely up before noon. The only time I've seen either of them up early is when their father is around.

I head to the kitchen where I scramble some eggs and make toast before taking my plate of food to the library. I haven't spent nearly enough time there, and I want to get a few books to take with me while I hide out in my room for a while until I figure out my next plan. I enter the room and almost drop my plate when I see Gia sitting in the corner of the room.

She glances over at me when I enter, but she doesn't really look at me. She looks through me.

I haven't seen her since the first day I came here. She's kept her distance, and I've spent most of my time in one of her brother's beds.

I don't know what to do. *Should I go talk to her? Should I ignore that she's here? Turn and walk back out?*

I choose to continue on with what I'm doing and ignore that she is here. If she wants to talk to me, she will. Otherwise, I should leave her alone. I don't want to cause her any more pain than I already have.

I walk over to the mystery section of the library and pick up the first couple of books that look interesting. I take them over to the small chair in the corner to look through while I eat my breakfast. Reading a mystery might help me get some ideas of how to get out of the current mess I'm in or at least keep my mind occupied for a little while.

"You made a mistake," Gia says.

I look up from the book I was staring at, and I wait for her to say more.

"You shouldn't have gone after both of them."

I frown. "I didn't."

She laughs. "Of course you did. Don't think I didn't watch you. I know everything that happened. I know you were fucking both of them, hoping that one of them would fall in love with you."

I sigh. I don't know whether to be nice or mean to her. "It worked. They both fell for me."

She shakes her head and goes back to staring out the window. But, now that she started, I have to know why she thinks it was a mistake.

"Why was it a mistake?" I ask.

Gia sharply turns her head back to me. "You ruined my life! You know that? I shouldn't help you. It's because of you that I'm always locked up in this house. I hardly ever get to go anywhere, and if I do, it has to be with a full security team. I'm a prisoner in my own house. All because Arlo had to save you, and now, I've had to live my life, always worrying if Erick or Clive or any of their men are out to get me. Ready to steal me at any second."

My heart breaks. She's lived my life for the last seven years almost exactly like I did. The difference is that I ran while she has been hiding. I got kidnapped while she's still safe—for now.

"I'm sorry," I say, my voice genuinely sorry for her. I would never wish my predicament on anyone, and it seems that Gia is living the same nightmare that I was. "If I could go back in time and make a different decision, I would. But I can't. At least you have men who want to protect you. They will do anything to keep you safe. At least your prison is beautiful and with family. At least you haven't been stolen."

I wish I knew how to help her, but there is really nothing I can do. And it's clear she doesn't think I'm worth saving.

I take my stack of books, and I get up, intending to leave her alone, when she says, "You made a mistake in trying to get them both to go after you. You should have chosen just one. Now, they are both in love with you. Feelings that neither of them has ever experienced before. You can't have them both. They will fight each other to make you theirs and destroy everyone in the process."

I suck in a breath, knowing that she's right—at least, in part. I'm not sure if either brother really loves me or if I've just become a new plaything that they don't want to share anymore. But, whatever their true feelings are, I know that the fight to claim me as theirs is about to get ugly. And I have no idea how to stay out of the crossfire.

"What do I do?"

Her eyes are blank stares. I see an emptiness there that I've felt many times before.

"Hide or run."

I swallow. Neither of those options has worked for me before. If I hide in my room, I'll eventually have to come out to eat, to survive, and when I do, all of my problems will still be there.

And, if I run...I glance down at the bracelet that Matteo threatened me with the first day I came here.

The story he told me about it was easy for me to believe then when the fear was fresh, but now, I'm not as afraid. I know that Matteo rarely tells me the truth—or at least, the whole truth. He likes to play games with my head. I look down at the thin bracelet that I'm sure holds a tracker, but what else is inside?

I glance up at Gia to ask, but she has turned her attention back to staring outside. I doubt she would know what my bracelet contains anyway. She doesn't seem to care about anything anymore.

It comes down to if I believe if Matteo was telling me the whole truth or not. I know he lied when he told me the story about the brothers who saved the princess. And I've caught him in several fibs. But would he fib about something like this? And is it worth the risk?

I could die if I take it off.

I could die if I stay.

Two choices, just like Matteo always gives me. Either way, it's my decision. Neither has great odds of me surviving. But one would end much faster than the other.

I drop the books and what's left of my breakfast, and I head outside into the warm sun that I haven't seen in days. The sun has just barely started coming up. The Carini brothers aren't awake. Enrico is gone. And Gia won't come after me. Now's my chance. If I can get rid of the tracker, then I can actually escape. I know the direction of town. I can run. I can be free again.

I look down at the bracelet that I forgot was even on my wrist; it's so lightweight. There is no way there is a bomb inside. Poison maybe, but I doubt poison touching my skin would actually kill me.

I find the fastener and click the latch, surprised that it opens with ease. I watch as the bracelet falls to the ground, and then I run.

24

NINA

MY LUNGS BURN from my heavy breathing as I run as fast as I can through the field and into the forest behind their house. I haven't exercised once since I arrived here—unless you count sex. And, while the sex was definitely enjoyable and kept up some of my stamina, it's not the same as running. My legs are clumsy from using muscles that I haven't used in weeks. Arlo's sweatpants slide down my body with each step I take since they are far too big for my slim body. And my feet ache with each step. I didn't even bother to put shoes on before I started running.

None of that will stop me though. Despite all of it, I run faster than I ever have in my life.

When I dart into the forest, I feel a false sense of safety wash over me. I know that no one can see me from the house now that I'm covered by the trees. But that doesn't mean I'm safe. I will probably never be safe again, but at least, I can be free.

Ten miles stand between me and a chance at freedom. Not an easy feat for an experienced runner, much less someone who hasn't run in months. But I have something that no other runner has. I have the adrenaline and anger that has built up inside me every day since I was kidnapped propelling me forward. I have more determination and need to succeed than any professional runner. I won't fail. I can't.

I glance up at the sun overhead. It's still early in the morning. I have all day to run before it gets dark. I just don't know how long it will take Arlo or Matteo to realize I'm gone. Did they realize the second I took the bracelet off? Are they already on my tail? And, even if they realized I was gone, would them come after me? Or would they let me have my only chance at freedom?

I don't know.

I don't know if they are already trailing behind me.

I don't know if they are still in bed.

I don't know if they have let me go.

But, until I know otherwise, I'm going to assume they discovered I was gone only minutes after I left. So, I keep running, knowing that I will eventually make it to town. To someone with a cell phone. To someone who cares enough to protect me from these monsters.

I will get to see Heath again. I will get to see Eden again. I might even get a life again if I can just run fast enough.

I use them as a motivation, but as much as I run for them, I run mostly for me. I run to save myself. Not for any other person, just me.

Images of Heath, Eden, Matteo, Arlo, Gia, and Enrico pop into my head from time to time. But I don't let any of them in. I just feel the power of my body, and I let that propel me forward.

I run and I run and I run.

I run until I start to see buildings in the distance and hear the faint sounds of cars. I'm close, so close. I don't let my legs slow down as I run. Even though my body aches with pain and exhaustion, I won't let myself stop now. Not until I'm on a plane back to America will I allow myself to slow down. Even when I get to town, I will have to carefully choose whom I speak to since I'm sure half of the town is indebted to the Carini family.

I make it to the edge of the woods and finally to a street that leads into town. All have to do is follow the road for a quarter mile, and I will have made it.

It feels a bit dangerous, coming out of the woods and out into the clearing, but it also feels empowering. I can make it.

I stop suddenly as I see a car drive by, heading into town. I could try to flag a car down, but who would stop for me, and what would I tell them if they did stop? I can't tell them the truth. No one would believe me, and those who did might try to take me back to get a reward or get their owns debts erased. I can't trust anyone. I just need to borrow a phone to let Heath or Eden know I'm safe, and then I need to get to an airport. That's it.

I let the car pass, and then I walk out of the woods and begin following along the side of the road toward town. I continue to jog, hoping that anyone who sees me will just assume I'm a jogger and not think anything about it even though I'm dressed poorly and covered in dirt and sweat.

Car after car passes me without a second glance back. I keep running until I finally make it to the center of town. I bend over for a second to catch my breath as I glance around, trying to figure out how I'm going to get someone to let me borrow a phone without drawing too much attention to myself.

I decide to duck into the church up the street. It will get me off the street, and they will probably just think I'm a homeless person. Surely, they will let me borrow a phone and get me a cab ride to the airport.

I start walking up the hill to the church, hating walking at a normal pace but feeling like I need to in order to not completely stick out in the crowd. My heartbeat quickens more with every step as my excitement builds because this nightmare is almost over. Just feet from now, I could be one step closer to being free. Just one last step, and I'm there.

I stop for a second, waiting for the streetlight to change. The second that it does, I begin lightly jogging across the street.

I feel the danger before I see it. I hear the tires. And then I feel the force of the car hitting me.

25

NINA

"WAKE UP, SLAVE," I hear Enrico's voice echo through my ears.

I don't want to wake up. And, even if I did, I'm not sure I can.

I feel a hand slap me hard across the cheek, and I jolt my eyes open from the stinging pain. That was a mistake. The second my eyes open, it all becomes real. The pain and terror explode all over my body.

I try to figure out where the pain is coming from. My head? My chest? My stomach? My legs? Where? It doesn't take me long to realize that I feel the pain everywhere. It's not in one place where I can focus and then forget about as I realize how strong the rest of my body is. It's everywhere. Just like it was after Enrico raped and beat me.

I take a deep breath. I've dealt with pain like this before and survived. I can deal with this, too. But just breathing is almost unbearable. My chest is on fire with every breath. Every rib in my body feels broken.

I need something to focus on that isn't my body. My eyes turn to Enrico standing over me.

"I really appreciate you running. It made it that much easier to capture you. I thought about stopping you after the first mile, but what fun would that have been?"

"How did you track me?"

He smirks. "I'm not giving up family secrets."

I frown.

"But then again, you are most likely going to be dead by the end of tonight, so what harm would it do?" His eyes glare into mine every time he speaks. Trying to push more terror into my soul. Trying to play the game and control me.

He won't ever control me again. I won't let that happen. His sons won't let that happen. I'd die first rather than let him touch me.

"We injected you with a tracker years ago. It was all in the contract. That way, we could always find you. That silly little bracelet of yours was Matteo's idea. He thought it would be a fun way to mess with your head."

I take a deep breath rather than react. I don't care about what Matteo did to hurt me when I first arrived. He's more than made up for it since. I know how he feels about me. He won't hurt me.

"Speaking of my sons..." Enrico turns, and that's when I see a dozen men standing around the room.

He motions to one of them. The man turns and walks to the door in what I finally realize is Enrico's bedroom. I should have known where I was from the disgusting stench I smelled the first time I entered.

He opens the door, and then Matteo and Arlo walk into the room, both scanning the room, trying to assess the situation as best as they can. I don't see any emotion in either of their eyes, which is probably a good thing since there is no chance I will survive.

"What are we doing here?" Arlo asks his father. "I have a meeting set up for this evening, so this had better be quick." His voice is ice-cold, like he feels nothing.

I try not to look at him as he talks so that it doesn't hurt me. I know he won't save me. He's already said as much numerous times, but I can't keep it from stinging me when he speaks and doesn't even bother looking at me.

I look down at my body instead, where blood is pouring out from who knows where, and bruises cover every inch of skin that is visible. Enrico didn't even bother tying me up as I lie in a broken pile on the floor, and even if he had, there is no way that I could fight off the dozen men in the room.

"Your meeting doesn't matter. We are here to finish the game and crown a new Carini leader."

I glare at him because I don't have many options for anything else. I knew that was why I was here. Everyone knew already, even Arlo; it just had to be said.

Arlo narrows his eyes as he looks at his father. "Why now? Our time isn't up yet. Are you really ready to give up being the head of the family?"

Enrico glares at his son. "I'm ready to finally see one of my sons step up into the role he was born to do. I'm tired of having to deal with the daily grind. I want to be around long enough to see one of you bring this family to the next level." He looks back and forth between his sons, both standing strong and silently.

Enrico smiles as he turns his attention back to me. "I'm sure, by now, my sons have told you plenty about why you're here, but I doubt they told you the whole truth. It's time you learned your place in all of this, slave."

I feel my heartbeat speed up every time he uses the word *slave*, my rage building slowly. But I don't let him know that he can affect me with just a word. I sit as silently as his sons stand.

"Many years ago, my beautiful wife told me she was pregnant with twin boys. You don't know how much that thrilled me to have two heirs to take over for me and continue the empire that I and generations of Carinis before me have worked hard to build.

"The night that my sons were born, I was away in America, signing a deal that would bring this family more money than it had ever seen. When I came back, I had two beautiful sons. Two heirs.

"I soon realized that I had a problem. Two men couldn't run this empire. It is impossible for two sons to work together. There has to be one leader.

"It was a simple problem though, solved by whichever son was born first. He would be my heir, and I would groom him to take over for me. But my wife was a smart woman. She knew that whatever son was born second wouldn't receive the same attention from me as the firstborn. She wanted to give her sons an equal chance at ruling and knew that would also be what was best for our family—if I raised both men to take over for me and then chose when they were old enough to take over for me.

"Well, that time has finally come."

When Enrico speaks, the whole room is silent. All of the attention is on him, and he relishes it. He lives for moments like this. I can't believe that he is willing to give it up to either of his sons. He looks invincible when he speaks, except for something in his eyes when he speaks of his wife. When he speaks of her, I see the tiniest hint of pain.

"What happened to your wife?" I ask because I think it might be a sore spot, a wound that I might be able to reopen. And, since I have nothing left to lose, I might as well.

He shakes his head. "You are definitely different than all the rest of the slaves. Maybe I'll keep you alive after all. At least until I've had my fill of you."

I can't hold back my disgust. "I would rather die."

He laughs. "I think you would. But, to answer your question, my wife died of cancer."

I shake my head. "I doubt that. See, after spending so much time with your family for this long, one thing I know is when you lie."

He frowns as he walks over to where I sit on the ground.

I glare at him.

And then he punches me in the face. My head whips to the side.

I turn back to look at him and spit the blood filling my mouth out at him. Whatever happened to his wife, it wasn't cancer.

"Now, where was I? Oh, yes, determining a winner of my twisted game. If I recall, the game is tied three to three. Each of you has won equally. You've both shown me just how powerful of a leader of this family you can be when it comes to taking debts from those who deserve it. But, today, I have one final test for you."

I suck in a breath, not liking where this is going.

Enrico walks back to me and kicks me hard in the stomach for no reason. I grab my stomach that feels like I've just been hit by a car. I cry out from the amount of pain that I feel radiating throughout my body. Tears fall, and I can't do a damn thing to stop them.

Enrico laughs, and his sons stand, frozen, acting like I'm not even here. Maybe I'm not. Maybe this is all my imagination. Maybe I'm already dead.

Please, let me be dead.

"For your first test, show me how much control you have over her," Enrico says to his sons.

They nod like they knew this was coming. *Is this how all the other women's lives ended? In a twisted game like this? Or did some of the women find a way to stop the game before it got to this?*

Matteo starts walking toward me, his eyes focused on me. I don't know what he's going to make me do. Or try to make me do. But, as he walks toward me, he winks.

I don't react, pretending like I didn't see it because I'm not sure I did. I try to think what it could mean. But I don't have a clue.

Matteo stops walking when he's standing, towering, in front of me. He looks down at me, and for a second, I can see a hint of the playful Matteo in his eyes.

"Suck me, slave," he says, commanding me.

He never uses the word *slave*. He never commands me. He always gives me a choice.

It doesn't take me long to realize that he is putting on a performance for his father. I don't know if this performance involves keeping me safe or not, but at least, it will buy me more time. I don't mind sucking his dick. I just don't want to do it in front of all these people. But it might be the last pleasant thing I ever experience.

I keep my eyes locked on Matteo as I raise my aching arms to his pants. I roughly undo the button and zipper until I reach inside and pull out his cock. I pretend like no one else is there as I wrap my mouth around his cock and suck. I can hardly move my head at all; my head hurts so much. But it doesn't matter. I'm doing what Matteo says, and within seconds, Matteo shoots his load down my throat.

I quickly pull away, and Matteo puts his dick back in his pants as he walks back over to where his brother stands.

Enrico smiles at his son.

Disgusting.

Arlo steps forward and starts walking toward me while I swallow down Matteo's cum, prepared to take Arlo's cum as well. But, when he approaches me, he gives me no sign that he is on my side, like Matteo did. In fact, even though he is looking at me, it's more like he is staring through me.

When he gets to me, he doesn't command me like Matteo did. Instead, he picks up my broken body and throws me over his shoulder. My whole body screams as he touches me and carries me to the bed. He tosses me down like I'm nothing. I close my eyes, wishing I could become nothing.

Arlo undoes his pants, and I watch as his cock hardens before my eyes. He sits up on the bed, leaning against the headboard.

"Strip and then fuck me, slave."

I defiantly stare into his eyes. I don't have the strength to stand, yet he wants me to fuck him. He's insane. But I see the hardening in his eyes, and I know it's what he wants. I don't know if he is on my side like Matteo is, but I can't take a chance that he's not.

He's only inches away from me, but it's going to take all the strength I have left to undress, let alone fuck him. I grab the hem of the T-shirt and gingerly pull it over my head, trying to keep it away from my skin but feel it scrape against every wound on my body. It takes all the energy I have left to push my pants down. I begin to inch toward Arlo, clawing at his chest as I try to use my arms to pull closer to him, my legs in too much pain to move.

Arlo watches me for a moment like he doesn't give a shit about me, and then he grabs my hips and pulls me on top of him, my pussy coming down on his cock. His eyes sear into me as he thrusts inside me. I don't know if the look is meant to comfort me or let me know that my life is over, but either way, it doesn't do much to comfort me.

My body, on the other hand, responds automatically to his cock. I get wetter with each thrust, just like I do every time he fucks me. I dig my nails into his shoulders, trying to keep myself upright while he fucks me. I don't look around at all the men who are ogling my body right now. I don't think about how degrading it is. All I think about is, despite all the pains in my body, it still feels good to have his cock inside me, just like it felt good to give Matteo a tiny bit of pleasure.

"Come," Arlo says.

We've barely fucked at all. Maybe it's the situation I'm in, or maybe I need to feel something good so desperately that I can force my body to do something that I'm not ready for, but I come easily, quietly screaming his name. He thrusts once more and comes as well, pouring his cum deep inside me.

When he's done, he pushes me off onto the bed, gets up, tucks his cock back into his pants, and walks back to where his brother is.

I take a deep breath as I lie on the bed, completely naked and exposed, but at least now, I'm on a comfortable bed instead of on the dirty floor. I feel a little more alive than I did before he fucked me. I don't know how that's possible, but it is.

Enrico laughs. "Very good. You have both made it clear that you have control over the slave. But who cares if she lives or dies?"

Enrico grabs my hair, pulling me toward him. But I'm tired of being hit and beaten. I let his sons touch me because I wanted them to. I won't let him touch me as easily.

I fight back with everything I have. But he's stronger than me. I try going for the sensitive areas. His eyes and balls. But he grabs both of my arms, holding me down, as he climbs up on top of me. Panic rises in my eyes as I realize that I'm about to be raped by this disgusting man again while more than a dozen men watch. Only to die minutes or seconds later. I can't handle it. I won't let him do it.

I keep fighting. But I can't. I'm not strong enough.

I glance over at the only two men who might be able to save me.

I look at Arlo, who looks just as cold as he has from the second he walked into the room. I turn to Matteo, begging him to stop this. Kill me if he has to, but don't let me get raped again. He stands cold as well, but when he sees my eyes, he closes his, trying to block out the pain I'm feeling.

Enrico laughs and looks in their direction, too. "Which of my sons will save you?" He shakes his head. "I'm not sure that either of them will save you, but one sure does care more than he is letting on."

Panic rises in my chest. I don't know what game within the game

Arlo and Matteo are playing. I don't know whom they want to win or if they are both actively trying to beat each other. I know they are competitive. But I don't know if they would turn on the other in order to win. I should know what their game plan is, but I don't. I never asked, and now, I have no idea how to help them defeat their father, if that is even the plan.

I look into Enrico's eyes, and I see the anger he has toward his sons. I'm just not sure if they see it. I'm not sure if he ever intended on choosing a successor tonight or if he's just teaching them both a lesson.

I might already be dead, but I won't let him kill either of them. I glance one last time at the two men I've grown to care about more than I would ever like to admit, and then I find the strength to kick Enrico as hard as I can in the balls. I strike just the right spot with enough force to make him loosen his grasp on my wrists.

I pull one free and reach for the back of his pants, the spot where I know all the Carini men carry their guns. I grab it, aim straight at Enrico's heart, and pull the trigger.

Enrico steps back, laughing, as no bullet exits the gun.

I try again.

Nothing.

I quickly examine the gun and realize there are no bullets in the gun.

Enrico takes a step back, still laughing. And then, a second later, he has me pinned to the bed again with more rage than I ever imagined possible.

"You bitch. You think I don't know what games you have been playing? You think I don't know that you messed with my sons' minds? That you made them weak by making them fall for a bitch like you? That's why I hate you more than all the rest of the women we played with before. I hoped your fire would make them hate you more, but instead, you made them fall for you. The other women got to end their debt early but not you. You will pay the full seven years before I release you. By the time I'm through with you, you will be begging for death."

"Her debt has already been paid," Arlo says suddenly.

Shut up, I want to scream. It doesn't matter if I've already paid my debt or not. He's not making anything better.

"What did you say?" Enrico glares at Arlo while still holding me down.

"Her debt has already been paid. She finished paying her debt two weeks ago," Matteo finishes for Arlo.

Enrico searches his son's eyes. "How?"

"The contract said the terms of seven years started the first day we forced her to do anything against her will," Arlo says.

"That was the day you kidnapped her," Enrico says.

"No, it wasn't," Arlo says.

"It was the first day I raped her against her will. The same day she signed the contract," Matteo finishes.

I knew it. I knew he had fucked me that night in the dungeon. They were trying to protect me this whole time. Not that it matters. We are all going to die anyway.

Enrico turns from them to me. His nostrils are flared, his face is raging red, and veins are about to pop out of his body. But it's his eyes that tell me this is the moment it all ends.

"She's free to go. If you have taught us anything, it's that we honor our contracts," Arlo says, staring at me with the tiniest drop of hope in his eyes.

But I don't return his hope when I look back at him. He might think his father is an honorable person who cares about things like contracts. But I've seen the real monster inside of Enrico. He doesn't give a shit about anything, except what he wants.

Enrico grabs my hair and rips me off the bed, throwing me onto the floor.

I don't even think about the pain anymore because I know this is all over.

"You're right. She's free to go as soon as she fulfills one final contractual obligation."

Arlo and Matteo each raise an eyebrow.

Enrico laughs. "Oh, you didn't read the contract very well then, boys. I thought I taught you better than that, as you say." He shakes his head. "I hoped for stronger sons than what you have turned out to be. You shouldn't give a shit about her; she's nothing to you. You might love her, but she doesn't love you in return! She has just said or done anything that she could to survive. To get you to love her. So that you would save her in the end."

He walks over to one of his guards who has remained completely silent this whole time, watching this ridiculous scene unfold, trying to figure out who their new boss will be. Enrico holds out his hand, and the man hands him a gun.

He walks back to me, and I know this is when my life ends. He's going to shoot me. He's going to kill me.

He grabs me by the hair again, and I close my eyes, waiting for death to quickly take me.

Enrico shakes me, and my eyes open automatically as I try to figure out what the hell he's doing.

"My sons are right. I have a contractual obligation to release you. Carinis keep their promises. Ask any of my men, and they will tell you as much. Ask any person in town. That is why we are given so much respect. You might have just won, Nina. You played us all well."

He looks at his sons, who are both standing there far too smugly.

"You get to choose if you walk free or if you die."

My heart beats fast in my chest, but I settle it quickly.

He's lying. These are all lies. Don't let your guard down. He's still going to try to kill you.

"You get to pick which of my sons will replace me as heir and which of my sons will die," Enrico says, pointing his gun in the general direction of his sons.

Both men freeze. Both men stare at the gun and then their father. Neither seems that shocked that their father is currently aiming a gun at them.

"No."

Enrico glares at me. "No is not an answer. You don't get to tell me no. You must choose."

"No."

"Then, you die." He aims the gun at my head, and the brothers take a step forward. "Take another step, and she dies."

They both stop.

"I'm giving you all the power, Nina. Isn't that what you wanted? That's what you've been saying you wanted this whole fucking time. Now's your chance. Save yourself by choosing which of my sons lives and which dies. Or I'll kill you."

My body trembles. One of us isn't going to survive this. One is going to die. Because of me.

I look at both of the men I love. *Love* is such a strange word and an even stranger feeling. It's not something I've admitted to either of them. Or even to myself. But, right now, when our lives are truly on the line, it makes it easier to admit it. I love them both. I don't know how it's possible to truly love more than one person at a time, but it's how I feel. I won't question it.

"Time is ticking, Nina, and I'm not a very patient man. Who is worthy of becoming my next heir?" He pauses, smiling. "Or, better yet, whom do you love? Whom can't you live without?" He laughs to himself. "Maybe you aren't about to leave so quickly after all. If you truly didn't care about my sons, you would have already chosen. You would have killed one of them without a second thought if it meant your freedom. So, which of my sons has won by stealing your heart?"

I look at both men standing in front of me. Neither of them deserves to die. I can't choose.

But I don't deserve to die either.

I feel the tears in my own eyes as I look to both of them like one of them will have the answer. Matteo smiles with his eyes. He loves me; I can see it in his eyes. He tells me with his whole body how much he loves me. But he doesn't tell me not to shoot him.

I look into Arlo's eyes. He doesn't tell me anything. In fact, he barely looks at me, seeming indifferent, even though I know, deep down, he cares about me.

The way they look at me is the same way they are toward me. Both men are so different, yet I love both of them.

They both tried to save me. They both deserve to live.

I close my eyes. I deserve to live, too. Words pop into my head. *Save yourself, like you promised.*

More tears pour down my cheeks as I know what I have to do. My eyes dart back and forth between the two men. I bite my lip, and then I let the words start pouring out of me.

"I promised I would save myself." I take a deep breath as I look at Arlo. "And I keep my promises."

Arlo takes a deep breath as I stare at him. I made a promise to him that I would save myself. And the only way I can live with myself after tonight is to honor that promise.

I swallow hard, and then I say, "I choose to save Matteo."

26

MATTEO

NINA SAYS MY NAME, and I rejoice and about die at the same time.

She is saving me.

But she's just killed my brother.

I don't know whether to love her or kill her.

But I don't have time to think about that. I look at Enrico, who has a shocked expression on his face. He was expecting her to choose death rather than choose one of us to kill. But, now that she's chosen, it's only a matter of seconds before he follows through.

He turns, aiming the gun at Arlo.

Arlo takes a deep breath.

"No!" I scream, trying to stop him, running toward Arlo.

I hear the pop of the gun and watch as Arlo moves, trying to avoid the bullet, but he doesn't move far enough. It hits him square in the chest. I continue running to him as he falls to the ground.

Nina screams, sobbing behind me, but I don't turn to look at her. I'll deal with her later. Right now, all I can think about is Arlo.

I get to him in seconds, immediately applying pressure to his wound to try to stop the bleeding.

"Just hold on, Arlo. You're going to be okay," I say, not really believing my own words. Of all the times Arlo has been shot, this is the least safe I have felt when saying those words. Not just because his wound is in one of the worst places for it to be, but also because, at any second, Enrico could shoot him again.

Arlo winces as he tries to move.

"Relax. Just stay still, and let me take care of you."

He closes his eyes and then opens them. "You..."

"Shh, just rest."

"You have power now," Arlo barely gets out.

It takes me a second to realize what Arlo is saying. But he's right. I have power now. Nina gave it to me the second she saved me.

"Move aside, Matteo. If he's not dead already, I need to finish the job," Enrico says as he walks toward me.

I stand slowly, putting my body between Enrico and Arlo. "No."

"You don't get to tell me no. Now, move," Enrico says.

"No, you don't have any power anymore. I have all the power. Nina chose me. Now, back off."

Enrico glares at me while holding the gun, aiming it at my heart.

Instantly, the men in the room all aim their guns at Enrico. They are my men now, and they will protect me without me having to say a word. Even from their old master.

Enrico lowers the gun and takes a step back. I exhale. I have power. Now, I just have to get Arlo to a hospital, and he'll survive.

But, before I can give the order for my men to transport him to a hospital as fast as they can, shots ring out.

They stop almost as fast as they started. But, when the smoke clears, it's easy to determine what happened. Enrico shot Nina, and my men shot Enrico. My heart drops when I see them both lying on the floor. Both possibly dead in a second.

I walk past Enrico. I will deal with whatever is left of him later. It hurts to walk past him. He was, after all, my father. But I have two more important people that I need to ensure stay alive.

I run to Nina. He shot her in her already damaged leg, but it was enough to knock her unconscious and make her breathing weak. She won't survive much longer without immediate help.

"Get Nina and Arlo to the hospital. Now," I give the command and watch as the men immediately break into two groups, one group going to each of them.

I walk back to Arlo, mainly because he's awake and I'm not sure how I feel about Nina at the moment. I still love her, but right now, she's pissed me off for making such a stupid decision.

"No..." Arlo croaks.

"Shh, I don't know what your deal is with going to the hospital, but you are going whether you like it or not. You need to be in surgery. I can't save you."

Arlo shakes his head. "Nina. Make sure she's safe."

I smile at my brother. *Always the martyr.* "I'll protect her to the ends of the earth. She's safe. Always," I say, keeping the same promise I made to Arlo when he came to me almost seven years ago.

———

"You are the worst patient ever, you know that?" I say to Arlo as he tries to climb out of bed for the hundredth time this week.

"I don't give a shit. I need to see her," he says as he stumbles out of bed, probably popping his stitches in the process.

I grab hold of him to keep him from falling. "Fine. I'll take you to her if you let me push you in a wheelchair."

He grumbles.

"It's not like you have a choice, not in your state, and even if you were healthy, I have the power now. I have dozens of men who will keep you in this bed forever if I told them to," I joke.

He glares at me, not appreciating my joke.

I sigh and go get the wheelchair. I help him into it before wheeling him down the hallway toward Nina's room. I'm not sure why he wants to see her so badly anyway. She's not awake yet.

That was a stupid thought. I know exactly why he wants to see her. The same reason I've spent all of my time split between both of their rooms. Because he loves her as much as I do.

I open her door and wheel him over to her bedside while I go around and sit on the other side of her bed. We each hold on to her hand, both willing her to wake up. To survive. We didn't go through all of this mess, only for her to die.

We sit like this as the minutes tick on. Neither of us speaks out loud, silently begging her to wake up.

Her eyes open. And she smiles, squeezing both of our hands.

Arlo and I exhale, relieved that she is awake.

"How do you feel?" I ask.

"Like I just got hit by a car, a train, and an airplane, all at the same time," she says.

"I will have the nurse increase your pain medications."

She nods.

But that's all any of us says as more minutes pass. None of us can find the right words for this situation. There are no right words. Only wrong ones.

"So, who do you want? Me or my brother?" I tease, although I'm not really teasing. I need her to choose one of us. I need her to choose me. Controlling the Carini empire means nothing to me without her by my side.

I expect her to smile, like she always does. She knows that I made a joke to try to lighten the mood, but she doesn't smile. Her eyes go back and forth between both of us.

"I want to go home."

My heart sinks. That was the one answer I wasn't expecting. I wanted her to choose me. But I don't understand her choice.

"I thought you saved me because you..." I can't finish.

"Because you thought I loved you more?" Nina finishes for me.

I nod.

She closes her eyes a second as a wave of pain hits her.

"I saved myself. That's all it was. I didn't want either of you to die. But it ultimately wasn't about either of you. I chose one of you to save and one to die because I had to save myself. Arlo had been shot the most, and I felt he had the best chance of surviving."

My eyes widen. My heart has just been ripped from my body. I thought she loved me. *How stupid was I?*

I look across to Arlo, who seems just as hurt. Not surprised. Just in pain.

She really did play us all.

"Of course," Arlo finally answers for us because I'm too angry to say anything. "As soon as you are well enough to fly, we will have you on the first flight home. But you do need to know that, when you leave here, you aren't safe. You need to hire the best protection you can."

"What do you mean, I'm not safe?" Nina asks.

Arlo sighs. "We think Enrico survived. We think some of the guards were still sympathetic toward their old master and saved him. It's also possible that Erick and Clive want you. Not as likely, but they aren't happy that we took you from them. If they realize that we let you go, they might come after you. Or any number of our enemies. Promise me that you will protect yourself."

"I promise," Nina says.

Arlo drops her hand and begins to wheel himself out of the room. I follow, not even able to look at Nina right now.

When I get to the hallway though, I explode. "We are not going to just fucking let her go. Not after everything we went through!"

"Yes, we are," Arlo says.

"Like hell we are! She almost killed you. And she played both of us to save herself. She..." I can't even finish.

"We are letting her go."

I glare at him. "You aren't the boss. I am. You can thank that stupid little cunt in there for that."

"She ripped out my heart, too, but keeping her would make us as bad as Enrico. We aren't the best people in the world, but we are better than him." He pauses. "But, ultimately, that decision is up to you."

I look at him with a raised eyebrow. "So, you are going to respect that I am the new head of the family?"

He nods. "Do I still have a job, working for you, or do I need to find employment elsewhere?"

I smile as Arlo and I shake on our new arrangement. I turn my attention toward my heartache in the hospital bed on the other side of the door. I don't want to keep being a monster, so I'll let her go. But I feel my heart harden as I think about Nina. My heart closes off a little more to the world.

My father used to always say that my mother betraying him was what he needed to become the leader that he was. He needed that heartbreak to become a stronger, more powerful leader. And I think, for the first time, that he might be right.

27

NINA

MY HEART RACES much too fast as the plane lands in Miami. In just a few minutes, I will get to be in my husband's arms again. This is the moment I never thought would happen. But somehow is.

It seems like forever passes, but finally, it's my turn to depart the plane. I stand up, my body still aching and painful from my injuries. I'll have scars the rest of my life. Not all of them visible, but they will always stay with me and remind me of my time in Italy.

I walk off the plane, following behind the people in front of me. I don't have a bag, nothing but the clothes on my back, and my nerves make me want to run past the slow people in front of me, but I don't. I'm patient. I've waited this long. I can wait a few more seconds.

But, when I walk off the plane, I can't hold back any longer. I quickly run through the airport, scanning the signs so that I can find the way out of the secure area and to where I know Heath and Eden are waiting for me.

The stupid signs are confusing as hell, but I finally start running in the right direction. Minutes pass as I run through the airport until I finally see them standing there.

They start running toward me at the same time that I run toward them. Alarms start going off as they run into the secured area without permission. A security guard stops Eden, but Heath gets through.

We collide together. My arms go around his neck while he lifts me up into his arms.

Tears stream down both of our faces.

And we have no words.

None are needed to express how we are feeling.

We are back together, and that's all that matters.

Eventually, Heath starts carrying me back to the unsecured area where we are met with guards giving Heath dirty looks.

"You would do the same if you'd just gotten the woman you loved back after thinking she was dead," Heath says.

The guards slowly back off. That's when I see Eden trying to hold herself back because she wants me and Heath to have a moment together. But she can't.

She throws her arms around both of us.

"I'm so glad you are safe," Eden sobs.

We all sob.

"We tried so hard to get to you. But we weren't even allowed into the country," Eden says.

I wipe her tears and Heath's and then my own. I shake my head. Of course the Carinis told the government to keep them out of the country.

"I'm glad you didn't succeed in getting into Italy. I just wanted you both to be safe. You couldn't have saved me anyway. I had to save myself."

They don't question me. They just hold me, wrapping me in their love.

"I love you so much, Nina. I'm never going to let you go again," Heath says.

"I know all you want to do is fuck her, Heath, but good luck getting me to let her go anytime soon," Eden says.

We all laugh.

"I love you both so much. Let's go home," I say.

I do love them both, but I also can't help but think of the two other men I also love. Men I love just because they saved me. That's it.

It will eventually disappear. I just need to get back to normal. Whatever that is. Then, my love for them will fade while my love for Heath and Eden takes over.

———

"You can fuck me harder than that," I say as I roll off of Heath.

He sighs. "I don't know how I can fuck you much harder than that, Nina, without hurting you."

"You won't hurt me. But I like it rough."

"I know, but all I think about when I have rough sex with you is what you must have gone through."

I frown. "Maybe I want you to erase those memories by making new, darker ones."

"What if I can't erase them?" he asks.

I exhale. It's the fifth time he's asked me that in the last six months. My wounds have mostly healed, but it's clear that Heath's have not. I know I should be just as patient with him as he is with me, but it's hard. I'm ready to live life to the fullest while he is more cautious than ever before.

I hear a knock on the door and groan. Heath gives me a look that tells me to be nice, but I still grumble as I grab a robe and walk to the door.

"Yes, Jeffrey," I say to the most cautious member of my security team.

"I heard a loud noise and wanted to check and make sure you were okay, ma'am."

I sigh. "I'm clearly fine. Heath and I were having sex. You don't have to check on me when I'm having sex. We've already had this conversation."

"I'm sorry, ma'am. It won't happen again. Have a good night."

"Good night, Jeffrey," I say, closing the door before taking off my robe and heading back to bed. "Are you sure we can't hire someone else?" I ask, climbing back into bed with Heath.

"He's the best."

"He's overly cautious, and I can't do anything. I don't feel normal."

Heath frowns. "The only thing that matters to me is that you are always safe. I can't lose you again. You're too important to me."

I nod. "Snuggle with me."

Heath obliges me, wrapping his arms around me as the conversation ends. Within minutes, Heath is asleep while I do everything to stay awake, thinking about my new life. A life where I feel almost as trapped as I did at the Carini mansion. Trapped by Heath's worries. Trapped by my own security team.

The only place I can escape is in my dreams. Dreams I shouldn't be having. But they are the only place where I feel free.

––––––––––

"You aren't happy," Eden says as she munches on her pizza.

"Of course I'm happy. I'm with a man I love. I'm safe. What more could I need?"

"Heath isn't happy either."

My heart stops when she says that. "What do you mean?"

He's never shown me any signs that he's unhappy.

"He loves you. He always will, and he will never tell you this because he loves you so much and doesn't want to lose you, but his whole life has become about you. He obsesses about you. He doesn't work anymore. He doesn't have hobbies or friends. All he does is worry if you are safe. You have to set him free."

I swallow hard just as Heath walks over. He said he would let me go to lunch with just Eden and my security team to ensure that I was safe. But he can't even do that.

Eden turns and sees him, too. "I'm going to take my pizza to go." Eden gives Heath a sweet smile and me a knowing look before she leaves.

"She didn't have to go," Heath says.

"She needed to. Can we talk?" I ask.

"Of course." He takes Eden's seat across from me.

"I don't know how to start this." I swallow and then say some of the hardest words of my life, "I love you, Heath. That will never, ever change, no matter what happens. You don't know how happy I am that

273

I found you before I was kidnapped. Knowing that I had you to return to kept me alive more than once, and for that, I'm forever grateful. And, if I hadn't had been kidnapped, I'm sure that we would have spent a lifetime being happy together. But I was kidnapped. And it's changed us both."

"What are you saying?"

"That we both feel trapped right now. And that's no way to live. I want us to be free."

Heath narrows his eyes at me as he tries to understand what I'm saying. "I love you, Nina. I'll do anything for you."

I smile. "I know you will. It's one of the reasons I love you so much. But this isn't healthy. Neither of us is really living. We are just worrying that something is going to happen to the other. We are living in fear. And I can't have that. I think we need a break. Not necessarily a breakup. But just some time to live on our own."

"No, I don't want to be without you."

I feel the knot in my stomach. I could lose him if I do this. But I need some time on my own. I need some time to figure out who I am without a man again. I need some time to figure out where my heart lies.

"I'm not saying forever. Just give me one month. One month apart, and then you tell me how you feel. Then, you tell me what you want."

He scowls.

"I'll have the security team with me the whole time. You can still get daily reports. And I'll call you often. I just need to be alone for a little while. And I think you need some time to find yourself again without me."

He narrows his eyes, but I see he understands.

"Can you agree to that?"

"One month?"

I nod.

"I'm going to miss you like hell. But, yes, I'll always give you what you need."

Thirty days go by far faster than I ever thought it could.

I've spent my time doing everything I never thought I would. I rented a tiny shack in the middle of nowhere, and I spent my time reading, going to the shooting range, and painting. Even though my paintings always turned out horrible, they were therapeutic to paint.

I talked to Heath several times over the month, and every time I did, he sounded happier. Freer. He started working again. Hanging out with friends. Living again.

I'm starting to be happy again, too. I still don't know what my future holds, but I do know that I don't need a man to take care of me to be happy. I can find happiness in myself.

Today is the last day of our month apart. We haven't talked about what we are going to do on our first day back together. We haven't talked about how we are going to be reunited, but I'm sure Heath will call later tonight to make a plan.

I hear a knock on the front door of the cabin I'm renting. I walk to the door, already knowing it's Jeffrey.

I open the door. "What's up?"

"I have a letter for you, ma'am."

"Thank you," I say, taking the letter from him and heading back to my sofa as I stare at the letter that I know is from Heath.

I slowly open the letter while trying to guess what's inside. *Tickets to Hawaii? He's always talked about wanting to go there for our honeymoon that we never had. A love letter? Something naughty, like maybe a picture of his dick?*

But what falls out of the envelope isn't any of those things. I unfold the legal document and read the attached small note.

To my beautiful Nina,

I love you more than life itself. I will always love you, and I know you will always love me. But that doesn't mean we are meant to be together forever, just to love each other forever.

You set me free when I needed it the most. I couldn't see how it was for the best at the time. Now, I do. And, now, it's my turn to return the favor.

Love forever,

Heath

I glance back to the legal document. Divorce papers. I flip to the last page where Heath signed the document.

A single tear drips down my face and onto the document. He loves me, and I love him, but sometimes, love isn't enough. Not when I spend all my nights dreaming of another.

28

ARLO

MY LIFE IS MISERABLE. I live a pathetic existence. But, at least, I have a life. I never thought I would be okay with giving up control to anyone, least of all my brother. But that is where I've found myself.

He makes most of the big decisions about the direction of our family while I run the day-to-day business. I handle the meetings and the tactical team. Basically, my life is the same as it was before, but instead of taking orders from Enrico, I take them from Matteo. My life is a little better but only slightly.

Right now, all I want to do is go back to my bedroom, sleep, and try to forget about everything. I'll have to drink a fifth of whiskey to have any shot of sleeping without dreaming about Nina. But that's what I'll have to do tonight. I need a dreamless sleep.

I unlock my door and walk inside. I still immediately. Someone is here.

Enrico?

Clive?

Erick?

Or any number of my enemies. Someone is here to hurt me. I pull my gun out, ready to take out whoever is here. I might not be happy, but I don't want to die. Not anymore.

I silently search my rooms, looking for the intruder, but I don't find anyone. My heart beats faster as I go from room to room until I only have my bedroom left. I creep to the door and throw it open with my gun aimed. Then, I see my target standing in the center of the room.

Nina.

I close my eyes and open them again because I'm sure that my mind is playing tricks on me. Someone else is standing in my bedroom. Not Nina.

"Hello," she says in her sweet voice.

Then, I know she's real.

I lower my gun. "You can't be here."

She nods. "I won't stay long."

Please stay, my heart begs.

"How did you get in here?" I ask, hoping that Matteo doesn't know she's here.

He has been dealing with her rejection worse than I have.

"I snuck in. I know I shouldn't have, but I needed to see you alone."

I exhale, trying to seem unaffected by her presence. "Matteo has been a mess without you. He says he has his shit together. But he's lying."

"I'm sorry I hurt your brother."

I stare into her eyes, searching for why she is here. *Revenge? Closure? What?*

"I was hoping you would answer a few questions that I have left."

I feel the tightness in my chest when she speaks. I would do anything for her. I'd die for her. I almost did. But the way she said that has brought up too many memories of her exchanging questions for sex. It's not fair—what her words do to me—and she knows it.

"Of course," I say instead of trying to keep my shit together.

She bites her lip. She's nervous. As nervous as I am. But I don't know why when she has all the control. She has all the power she always has.

"Why did you save me?" she asks.

"Because you saved me first."

"How did I save you?"

"I hated my life before I saw you. I was tired of my father's games. I was depressed. I wanted to kill myself. I was going to kill myself that night. I thought it was for the best. If I were gone, my father would have no choice but to let Matteo inherit everything. But then you fell into my pool. I saw how obsessed you were with me, and it intrigued me. It gave me something to live for. I was curious about you, about your obsession, and I couldn't kill myself without knowing more about you even though, for your safety, I knew I needed to stay far away. Your obsession with me kept me alive."

I closely study her, but she guards her feelings well.

"What do you dream about?" she asks.

"You."

"Who do you love?"

"You."

Seconds pass before she does anything, but slowly, a grin creeps up on her face. "Good. Because you are the only one I dream about. It doesn't make sense to me. I don't understand why my heart aches for you when I love so many others. I love Heath. I love Matteo. But I don't dream of either of them. I don't obsess about either of them. I love them, but I love you more."

I run to her. Wrap her in my arms. And kiss her with everything I have. It doesn't feel real until she kisses me back just as hard, holding nothing back. Our tongues push into each other's mouths, begging each other for more. Our hands dig into each other, promising never to let go. We are never going to be able to stop, but we can't stay here.

I force myself to stop.

"What are you doing?" she asks, panting hard.

I grin, soon planning on never stopping. I'll fuck her forever if she lets me.

"We can't stay here."

"Why not?"

"Because Matteo will kill one or both of us if he finds out that you chose me over him."

She frowns. "Are you sure?"

I nod. "He's not in a good place right now. We need to leave."

"But can you really leave your brother? Can you really leave your life and everything behind to run away with me? To live a life of always hiding, always running, never being safe?"

I pull her back to me, threatening our safety with another kiss. I'm not sure that, once I start kissing her, I'll be able to stop ever again. She draws me back in, promising that she doesn't ever want to stop either.

"I'll gladly give up everything for you. I love you, Nina. I've always loved you. Even when I wouldn't allow myself to feel it, it was there. I love you. You are my obsession. You are the reason I'm living. I'd rather run and hide with you forever than live a life alone here. The only chance of ever being happy is with you."

She grins and quickly kisses me again. "Good answer. I love you, too. I'll run with you forever. It's the only way I'll ever be free."

I kiss her one last time, and then we run. Hopefully, we won't have to run forever. Matteo is going to be pissed that Nina chose me. That I'm abandoning him now. But he'll soon forgive me. He's the least of our worries. One day, we will have to stop running. We will have to face our enemies. But that day is far into the future. Right now, I will enjoy running. I'll enjoy living for the first time in a long time. I'm free as long as I have Nina by my side. Forever.

EPILOGUE

NINA

I FEEL THE EMPTINESS. I don't have to reach over in bed to know that Arlo isn't there.

We've been running for a year, but it feels more like traveling. Like one long vacation that never ends. It's wonderful. I love every second that Arlo and I get to spend together. I'm in love. I'm happy.

But it's not enough.

Every day that passes makes me realize that more and more. That we can't continue on like this. Arlo loves me, but he isn't truly happy. He still has nightmares every night. He still thinks about his family every day. And as in love as we are, just existing together doesn't give his life enough purpose. Not when he was used to a life far more exciting than what our life has been the last year.

I just don't know how to bring purpose back into his life again.

I sit up and see Arlo sitting outside on the patio of the villa we are staying in.

I sigh. I already know what he is doing. Painting another one of his nightmares by moonlight.

I get out of bed and walk out to him.

"Can't sleep again?" I ask.

He nods as he sits in his boxers behind an easel looking out over the ocean.

I walk behind him and put my arms around his bare chest, wishing that I could take away his nightmares like he takes away mine. I look at the picture he's painting, expecting another horrible image of a person he feels guilty for killing, but it's not. Instead, he's painting a beautiful picture of us. Together. Happy.

I smile.

"You're painting us?"

"Yes, I had a good dream." He grabs my arms and brings me around until I'm sitting in his lap.

"Why don't you sleep when you have good dreams?"

He grins. "Because this dream was so good that I was afraid I would forget it."

I narrow my eyes to look at him, not sure I believe him. "Are you happy, really? I know this year has been hard for you. I know you don't like running. I know you miss your brother and sister. I know you miss having a purpose."

His smile disappears. "Is that what you think? That I'm not happy?"

I nod slowly.

He shakes his head. "Are you crazy? I've never been happier."

"But you're depressed. You still have nightmares almost every night. You are away from your family. How can you be happy?"

He tucks a strand of my hair behind my ear as his other arm wraps tighter around me. "Because I have you. I love you, Nina. Yes, running has its downsides. The life that I used to live has consequences that I live with daily. But I wouldn't give up the last year I've had with you for anything. I wouldn't give up the future we will have together either."

I hear his words, but I still worry. I want our life together to be amazing. I want him to follow his dreams. I want to not live in fear of our enemies coming after us. I don't want to worry that Enrico or his men are hiding behind every corner.

"Stop it."

"Stop what?"

"Stop worrying. We have each other. Nothing else matters."

"I just want you to have more than just me. I want you to live out your dreams."

He dips me back in his arms as his lips hover over me. "You're my dream, Nina. All I want is you and our future together."

He lowers his lips to mine and kisses me. Butterflies form in my stomach and my heart beats wildly as his tongue pushes deep into my mouth. Every kiss does this to me. A year of kisses has done nothing but make me fall more in love with him. If I was uncertain of which man I loved before, now I know. No other man makes me feel like Arlo does. My love for him is more than an obsession. This is what love feels like.

His lips leave mine and our eyes meet. Dirty thoughts read across his eyes.

I bite my lip. I never get tired of sex with Arlo. No amount of sex ever fully satisfies us. We both need more. Constantly. In some ways, it's probably a good thing that we spend our whole life together just living like we are on vacation because I don't think either of us could hold down a job.

"Care for a midnight swim?" he asks.

I don't know why he asks. He already knows my answer. Probably to make up for all of his controlling behavior before. Now the only time he gets to control me is during sex. And even then, only when I let him.

I nod.

He lifts me into his arms as he runs down the beach to the ocean. I kiss his neck as I anticipate what he's going to do. Sex with him is never the same. I'm never prepared for how far he takes me or what he's going to do. He always takes me right to my limit when it comes to what I'm comfortable with without ever going over what I can handle. He knows my body better than I know myself.

I stare into his eyes trying to guess what kind of mood he's in as he carries me into the cool water.

I squeal as the water hits my toes and Arlo laughs, splashing more water on me as he carries me deeper into the water. He's definitely in a playful, happy mood tonight.

I wrap my arms around his neck as he dunks us both into the water. I immediately try to swim toward the surface to get some of my body out of the cool water and to breathe again.

Arlo holds me under.

I try to remain calm even though I didn't take much of a breath before he pulled me under. But the seconds pass and I feel my chest aching for a breath.

I can't breathe.

I try to swim toward the surface but Arlo's arms hold me down under the water.

I panic.

I fight his arms trying to let him know that I need a breath now but he only holds onto me harder.

I open my eyes pleading with him for a breath. When I see his eyes staring at me though I immediately relax. He moves forward and places his lips over mine giving me a breath.

His eyes tell me to trust him. That he will never hurt me.

I love you, I mouth.

He grins and then his mouth moves down my body as he pulls my nightgown off over my head. His lips take my nipple into my mouth as he continues to hold me under the water.

I gasp, releasing some of the air he gave me leaving me little left.

But my body doesn't panic. I trust him completely. He knows when I need air and when I don't. And his lips on my body when he's in complete control makes everything more intense.

He pushes us up toward the surface just before I feel my air running out.

We both take a deep breath when we hit the surface before he kisses me again taking all my air.

He grabs my hips and lifts me until my legs hang over his shoulders and his lips hover over my pussy.

"I can never get enough of you," he says.

I moan as he licks my sensitive area.

"Lick me," I command, liking that now that I'm on top I have some control over him.

He grins as he does what I say.

"God, Arlo, that feels so good."

"You like that baby?" Arlo says.

I grab his hair and suck in a breath when he calls me baby. Every time he calls me by a term of endearment I get wet for him and he knows it. It's what I wanted for so long and now that I have it, I lose my mind when he does it.

"I'm still in control baby. Take a breath."

I suck in a breath and grab his hair firmly before he dunks me under the water again still licking my pussy as I go under backward. He holds me down, massaging my breasts and holding my head under water, while keeping my pussy and legs wrapped around his head above the surface.

That's what I focus on. Him. The feeling of him bringing me intense pleasure. He moves his tongue faster while I'm under water and I can't keep from coming much longer. But I also need air. It's an intense feeling that I don't know what I want more. Air or coming.

I choose coming.

I scream under the water as my pussy pulses around his tongue.

Not until I stop does he let me back up from the water.

I breathe heavily and quickly, gripping onto his head as he gently lowers my body into the water until we are at eye level with each other.

He sucks my lip into his mouth while I catch my breath.

"I meant what I said. I can never get enough of you, Nina. I want to fuck you every way I can. I want a life with you. Kids with you. I want it all with you. That's all I want."

I raise an eyebrow. "Kids? You want kids with me?"

He grins. "I want to see what your body is like pregnant. I can't imagine how big your breasts will get."

I laugh. "After the pregnancy comes a baby that you have to take care of."

"I know. I still want it."

I grin. "How about we just figure out to find our own happily ever, just the two of us, first?"

He nods and then kisses me and I know things are about to get dirty again.

"How about we get to dry land again before you have your way with me again?" We've tried having sex in the ocean, but it is never as good as dry land.

He grins and carries me out of the water and back into the villa. When we are back inside, he tosses me a towel. I catch it and begin to dry myself off while he does the same.

I walk over to my dresser to find a new nightgown to sleep in when I see my phone has a missed voicemail from Eden.

I smile and pick up the phone.

"Eden called."

Arlo growls as he grabs my waist and begins kissing me again. I get lost in the kiss for a second before he pulls away.

"Fine, call her back. But I'm only giving you ten minutes before I'm coming after you and having my way with you so make it quick," he says with a gleam in his eyes.

I laugh and take my phone back out on the patio as I listen to Eden's voicemail.

I wait for Eden's voice to speak, but she never does. Instead, I hear a much more terrifying voice.

I wrap my towel around me tighter as I listen. My eyes immediately scanning my surroundings, afraid that our lives are now in danger. My body shakes with a mix of fear and anger with every word that I listen to.

This can't be happening.

I lower the phone from my ear just as Arlo comes to get me.

"I know I said I would give you ten minutes, but I came up with an idea for how I want to fuck you and I can't wait."

Arlo wraps his arms around my waist before he realizes that something is wrong.

"What did she say?"

I can't speak. I can't say anything. I must be in shock.

"Nina, what's wrong?"

I don't hear him. I can't think about him. I'm too scared of what I just heard.

Arlo comes around to my front and forces me to look at him. "Nina! What's wrong? You're scaring me."

I blink, finally able to see him, but I can't say the words. If I tell him then it's true. Instead, a tear falls down my cheek.

He wipes it, looking as scared as I look.

I hear some rustling in a bush behind him and I jump.

"It's just a lizard Nina. Nothing is going to get you. I have you," Arlo says holding onto me.

I look over his shoulder at the beautiful painting he started of us. Except it's not just us. I didn't notice before but now I can't believe I missed it. It's a painting of me pregnant, with another child riding Arlo's back. We are a family. That was what his dream was. That is what he wants. Us to have kids. Us living our happily ever after.

Except we can't. We might not ever get our happily ever after. Because our enemies are always going to be one step ahead of us.

I can't hold back the tears any longer. I hate that I can't give him that. I can't give him his dream, not while we live our lives in danger.

Arlo squeezes me tighter. "Tell me, Nina. Let me take the pain away."

"You can't."

"Sure I can. That's what we do for each other. We save each other. We heal each other. We take the pain away."

I cry until I can't anymore. Until I'm hiccuping because I can't cry anymore.

"What did Eden say?"

"She didn't say anything. She wasn't the one that called. Matteo did."

"Matteo?"

I nod.

"He said he has Eden. He's had her this whole time. The whole time we have been having the time of our lives, she has been living a nightmare locked up as Matteo's slave."

"Matteo wouldn't do that. He's a good man."

I look at Arlo and he knows what I'm saying is true. I don't know what happened to Matteo after we left. If Enrico got to him or the pain of us leaving did. But he's a different person now.

I touch the painting of the dream that Arlo had for us. A dream that I now realize is exactly what I want but will probably never have.

"And if I ever want to see Eden alive again, we have to go back. He's going to kill her if I don't give myself back to him."

Arlo holds me tighter. He won't give me up without a fight. But this is Eden we are talking about. He knows I will do anything for her. She's my best friend. I love her. I should have been there for her this last year.

I've talked to her countless times on the phone and every time she protected me instead of asking me to save her. She kept me away. She saved me, now it's my turn to save her.

DIRTY ADDICTION

PROLOGUE

NINA

ONE YEAR.

That's how long Eden has been gone.

Taken.

Stolen.

That's how long I've been living my life, blissfully ignorant while I was enjoying my new life with my new love, she was going through hell.

One year.

That's how long Matteo has had her.

Matteo used to be caring. A man that I even loved, although never as much as Arlo.

But Arlo and I leaving changed him. Hardened him again. And now who knows what he is capable of.

One year.

That's how long Eden has been with Matteo.

Was she beaten?

Tortured?

Raped?

Or did she soften Matteo's heart, the way Arlo softened his with me?

One year is a long time. I'm a horrible friend for not realizing she was hurting. She needed me, and I wasn't there. I'll never forgive myself if Matteo hurt Eden.

Eden's strong. She'll survive another few hours until Arlo and I get to Italy to rescue her. Arlo didn't want me to go. He wanted to go alone. But there was no way I won't be there for my friend, now that I know she needs me.

Eden's strong, but I know how being stolen affects people. Makes you addicted. To getting better. To proving you haven't changed. To life.

But sometimes, you get addicted to the darkness and let it consume you. With no hope to escape.

1

EDEN

ONE YEAR Earlier

My life is perfect.

I have the perfect body, which I work hard to keep in shape every day.

I have the perfect condo with an oceanfront view in Los Angeles, California.

I date the perfect guys. They are all impeccable gentlemen, taking me on fancy dates and treating me like a queen in the bedroom.

And most importantly, I have the perfect job.

"Will the defendant rise for sentencing?" the judge asks, staring at the accused and his lawyers.

I look over at Ivan, the suspect and soon to be prisoner, with a smirk on my face. I toss my hair back and hold my head high as the monster stands before the court for judgment. He's a terrifying man. The kind of man who can just glance at you and strike fear into the deepest confines of your soul. His entire body exudes evil and dark. Even the suit his lawyers bought for him doesn't hide his cruelty.

They could have put him in a bunny costume, and it wouldn't have hidden the monster inside him. The dark suit he's wearing reflects the darkness of his soul. His hair is shaved short, revealing the tattoos inked into his scalp. The long jacket sleeves can't contain the tattoos, nor the scars, that blanket his arms and hands. But it's not only his general appearance that makes him menacing. It's the glare in his eyes, the arrogance in his strut, and the vulgar venom in his speech. Everything about him makes it clear he doesn't give a shit about anyone but himself. He'll hurt anyone who dares to cross him.

Right now, he's terrified. He no longer stands proud and strong, like no one can touch him. His body trembles a little as he stands and his bottom lip quivers. He tries to hold back the tears staining his bulging eyes. He knows he's lost. He knows he's going to prison for the rest of his life at the very least, or he's going to die on death row.

This is my favorite part. The part where the bad guys realize they're not untouchable. They are weak. And by locking them away, I'm saving countless other souls from these evil savages.

"Ivan Shaw, on the count of murder in the first degree, this court has found you guilty."

I cock my head to the side as I stare at Ivan. Gazing at him as the single tear rolls down his cheek. I watch as the handcuffs go around his wrists and he is lead out of the courtroom. Before he's pulled out of the courtroom entirely, he turns his head and gives me one last dirty, sullen stare, his face shining red and jaw clenching. But it does nothing to intimidate me. In fact, it warms my insides to see him dragged away, never to see freedom again.

"You're fucking amazing," Jules, my assistant, says next to me as she begins gathering up the files of papers we had laid out across the courtroom table.

I put a couple of the files into my briefcase and snap the leather case shut. "I'm not that incredible. My work is important, so I have to get it right. If not, a man like Ivan could go back out on the streets and kill dozens of other innocent people. I'm the last line of defense to ensure he doesn't hurt another person."

Jules smiles and shrugs. "You're still freaking awesome. Ivan left no evidence. His men were utterly loyal to him. The fact that you got one of his men to flip and give you the gun used to commit the murder, with Ivan's fingerprints all over it, is astonishing. No other lawyer would have gotten anyone loyal to him to say so much as a single syllable against him. Any other lawyer would have lost the case."

Exhaling, I turn and walk out of the courtroom with Jules on my heels. She's young and inexperienced, but she's well on her way to becoming my mini-me. I hope to train as many people as I can to do my job, so we can apprehend more evil creatures and protect this city.

"How do I look?" I ask before exiting the courtroom, preparing myself to face the reporters outside.

Jules scrutinizes me up and down, peering down my dark red skirt and jacket, up to my pin straight black hair, and across my face to examine my makeup. "You're flawless and perfect as usual. Not a lipstick smudge or glisten of sweat visible."

I nod. "Good."

Plastering a smug expression on my face, a warning to all other convicts out there that I'm coming for you and I'm going to win, I step out into the lobby of the courtroom. The flashes should blind me, but I'm used to it by now. Bristles from the microphone booms brush against my cheek. The attention should make me uneasy, but instead, I find it as easy as talking to a close friend.

"How were you able to lock away one of LA's worst criminals, abating the police and court system for decades?" one of the reporters asks.

I stare directly at the camera that is pointed at me. "I surround myself with the best team, and I have dedicated my life to making our world a little safer. I'll do whatever it takes to ensure the bad guy goes to jail every single time. Ivan Shaw was a villain. It may take some time, but in the end, good always conquers evil."

"This case seemed impossible. How were you able to convince the key witness, in this case, to cooperate with you?"

I turn my head towards the next camera. "Because impossible doesn't exist. Not really. Every one of these people are human. They all have wants and desires of their own. No one wants to go to prison for the rest of their lives. No one wants to be responsible for the criminal going free. So it's a matter of having a heart-to-heart conversation with someone, human to human. After that, the witness was more than willing to talk."

I glance around all the reporters. "I'll take one more question."

"What's next? You prosecute more cases than anyone in the state. Are you going to take a much-needed vacation?"

I laugh. "I'll take a vacation when all the bad guys are locked up, and there are none left to terrorize this city."

I start walking again, and the reporters reluctantly part for me, still firing off questions despite me saying I was only taking one more question. I walk fast in my stiletto heels, keeping ahead of the reporters and Jules who are trailing behind me.

I don't like admitting it, but I like the attention winning a case brings. I like the afterglow and the feeling that I did something helpful for the world. I feel like a rock star, and hopeful that maybe, this was the time I locked away the last criminal. Tomorrow I'll wake up and sleep in, instead of getting a call about yet another murder that happened while I slept. This will be the time I never get that call. All of the horrible people will have somehow been eradicated from the world, or at least my small part of it.

But I know it's just a dream, a fantasy. Tomorrow I'll wake up to a phone call asking if I want to take another case on. I know I will accept the new case because this is my life, and despite how hard it can be, it's also precisely what I want for my life. I have a perfect record when it comes to defeating wicked, cruel beasts, and I don't plan on giving up the reins anytime soon.

I walk out of the courtroom and over to my red Ferrari. I climb in and roll down the window to talk to Jules one last time before I head home.

"Do you want to get a drink or something tonight to celebrate?" Jules asks.

"Sorry, but I have —"

Jules rolls her eyes as she crosses her arms and leans against my car. "You have a date with one of your Mr. Perfect's, don't you?"

I grimace. "Am I that predictable?"

"Yes," she huffs. She glances over at the reporters who are now busy interviewing the families. I look away, unable to watch the families. I don't feel sorry for the criminal's family. As for the victim's family, I can never do enough to get the haunting, sickening feeling to leave my stomach.

"You should take some time off Jules."

She smirks. "I will if you will."

"It doesn't work that way. I'm telling you as your boss to take next week off."

"And what happens tomorrow if you accept a case for the second most evil person in the world, after that bastard, and I'm sitting on the beach somewhere?"

"Then I guess I'll have to do the initial groundwork without you. Now go. Have fun tonight, and go spend some time relaxing on the beach this week. Turn off your phone and the world, and enjoy life away from all this." I wave my hands out motioning to the courthouse and the chaos surrounding it.

She nods slowly, pulling out her phone. "I'll turn my phone off as soon as I hear about how your date with Mr. Incredible goes tonight. You know I love hearing all the juicy details."

I laugh. "No, you can hear about them when you come back."

She pouts.

I laugh again, and snatch her phone from her hand as she squeals. I turn it off before handing it back to her.

"I mean it. Keep this thing off so no one at work will bother you for a week."

"Fine."

She will probably turn it back on as soon as she is out of eyesight of me, but I can hope at least one person in my office is going to get a much-needed break from this life.

I can't take a break. I couldn't live with myself if I took a break and someone went free because I wasn't here leading the charge to lock the criminal up. Jules is still young and doesn't have the responsibility of the world on her shoulders. She should enjoy herself.

She walks back to her car a few aisles over as I start my own car and drive off. Blasting the radio as I drive home, I try to drown out my thoughts and forget about work so I can enjoy my hot blind date tonight.

I was set up by Jack, a guy I work with. My blind date's name is Saul. He's a businessman, doing something with real estate, hotels, and condos. From what I'm told, he's smart, a gentleman, and a hottie. Exactly what I'm looking for tonight. He's taking me to one of the newest and hottest restaurants in LA. It will be nice to sit back with a cocktail, delicious food, and hopefully interesting conversation with a sexy man to ogle.

My mind wanders to my usual thoughts whenever I'm not focusing on work: *Nina*.

I haven't heard from her in weeks. She usually checks in at least once a month and lets me know that she's safe and Arlo is still treating her well. Because if he's not, he knows I'll come for him and lock him up like I do all the other criminals.

But every time Nina calls, she seems happy, no, better than happy. She acts like herself, like this is where her life was leading her all this time. So as much as I want to go to Arlo and knock his balls clean off his body for what he did to Nina, and for now making her live a life on the run, away from her friends and normal life, I won't. Because I love her and she loves Arlo. Despite all his faults, I do believe now he will do anything and everything he can to love and protect Nina.

A few minutes later, I park the car and get out, say hello to my doorman, Larry, and grab the mail before I head up to my sprawling condo on the fifth floor.

I throw the door open to my expansive home, walk over to my sound system and turn it on. Blaring music makes me feel less alone. I don't have any pets or roommates, no one to keep me company. I prefer it this way. I like having my own space and the freedom to spend my evenings how want.

It's also one of the reasons why I stick to dates. I like being alone. I don't care about settling down anytime soon. I don't want a live-in boyfriend or a husband. Work keeps me plenty busy. I date one night a week.

My date gets one shot with me, and no matter how much we connect or how good the sex is, that's all I'll ever give him. I don't want to get attached. I don't him to develop feelings for me either, so I follow my simple rules. One man, one date, once a week.

I stretch, wishing I had time for a quick yoga session before my date but I don't. I pour myself a glass of red wine and then head to my bedroom to find a suitable dress for tonight. I strip down to my black lace bra and underwear. I always wear sexy underwear, even when I'm the only one who is going to see it, especially on days I'm in court. Racy lingerie makes me feel strong and confident, which I need in the courtroom.

I dig through my closet and find a simple black dress with plenty of sex appeal between its short length and low-cut front, giving off the vibe that I expect sex tonight and lots of it. I get dressed and touch up my hair and makeup in the mirror. I consider curling my hair but think better of it. I don't want him to think I'm trying too hard. That's not what tonight is about. If he thinks I'm trying hard, then he'll think I want to go on a second date. I don't.

I apply another coat of red lipstick as I hear a knock on the door, faintly from behind my blaring music. I glance at the clock on my phone; he's early. One positive strike for him already. Carrying my wine and phone with me, I head to the living room and turn off the music on my way to the door. We have plenty of time to have a drink together first before heading to dinner.

I open the door with an intriguing smile. My skin flushes, my lips part, and my knees grow so weak I have to grasp the doorframe to remain standing when I see how ruggedly handsome my date is. He has shoulder-length dark hair, a scar across his cheek that makes him look a little dangerous, but nothing compared to the men I prose-cute. His body looks strong and fit beneath his simple black T-shirt and jeans. He appears to be way underdressed for the restaurant he told me he was taking me to tonight, but maybe I'm the one who's overdressed. There is also something familiar about him that I can't place.

"Would you like to come in and have a drink before our date tonight?" I ask Saul. I rake my teeth over my bottom lip letting him know how much I appreciate his body and charming appearance. Jack did an excellent job setting us up.

"I'd love to come in."

He steps inside, taking up space like he owns the place as he walks.

I shut the door behind us and rush forward, leading him into my kitchen.

"Is red wine okay or would you like something else?" I ask, my voice raspy as I speak. I swallow hard, trying to remedy my voice.

He scours the room, but I have no idea what he's looking for. "Red wine is fine."

I suddenly feel nervous, my hands clammy, as I begin pouring him a glass of wine. I'm used to dating powerful, strong men, but this man is different. He walks around commanding attention, demanding my eyes to stay on him and he's barely said anything or hardly even looked at me. I'm used to sharp dressed men that give me flowers and complements, place their hand on the small my back, or link our fingers together.

He does none of these things. But yet he requires everything of me.

He walks over to the colossal windows spanning the entire length of the wall, looking out over the ocean. I walk over to him and hold out his glass of wine to him, my hand shaking slightly. "Here you go."

He takes the glass from me, lifts it to his mouth, and takes a sip before spitting it out.

He eyes the glass suspiciously. "You call this wine? It's disgusting."

I snort and raise an eyebrow as I take the wine glass back from him. "Sorry, I don't have much experience with wine, so I usually buy whatever cheap wine is on sale. I think I have some whiskey if you prefer?"

He shakes his head. "I don't think I trust your taste in whiskey either."

"I guess you'll be the one picking out the wine at dinner tonight."

He reaches out and tugs gently on one of my strands of hair. "Do you always straighten your hair like this?"

I nod. "Why? You don't like it?" I open my eyes wide and give him an 'I dare you to say you hate it' stare.

"No reason. I used to know someone who wore her hair very much like yours. It suits you well."

"Thank you. Although, straight is a trendy hairstyle. I do have a close friend who wears her hair very similar to mine. People would call us twins, or at the very least, sisters because we were so much alike."

"And what is your friend's name?"

"Nina."

"Would Nina like to go on a double date with us to dinner this evening?"

I shake my head. "No, she doesn't live here."

I swear he frowns at the news, but then again, he seems always to be frowning or grimacing or glaring. He doesn't seem like a happy, relaxed person. He seems stiff and far too serious.

I'm one to talk. I spend my whole day being serious. Maybe his work is similar to mine, and he has to take it seriously. I can understand why it would be hard for him to relax, even on a date.

"Shall we head to dinner?"

"Sure, that way we can get you a proper drink," I say smiling at him, hoping he will smile back.

He doesn't; he continues to stare at me like he has seen a ghost or something.

A knock at the door startles me, and I turn.

"Maybe it's the doorman delivering a package or something?" I say, walking toward the door after setting my wine glass down on the kitchen counter.

I open the door and see a charming man standing in my doorway in a suit, holding a modest bouquet of daisies. He grins at me as he approvingly checks out my tanned legs and cleavage.

I wince, holding the door open. "I'm sorry I think you have the wrong condo."

"You're Eden Collins, right?"

I nod. "And you are?"

"I'm Saul Lewis. Jack set us up on a blind date tonight or did I get the wrong day?" He glances behind me to the man standing in my living room.

"Wait, you're Saul?"

He nods.

"Can you show me your ID?"

He raises an eyebrow, reaching into his back pocket for his ID and handing it to me. I read his name across the top of his driver's license. Saul Lewis.

I storm back to the living room, leaving Saul standing in my doorway.

"Who the hell are you and what are you doing in my home?"

I cross my arms over my chest and give him a glare I only reserve for the worst of the criminals I prosecute.

He chuckles. "I'm surprised you don't recognize me, sweetheart."

I stare at him a second longer, and then I do. "No..."

He cocks his head to the side flashing me a grin I immediately hate. "So you do remember me. That's good; it means you'll help me."

"No, get out of my condo Matteo. Now."

He takes a sprawling seat on my leather couch instead, a couch that seems small with his muscular body dwarfing it.

My eyes fly open at the audacity of him to come here, let alone sit down on my couch, after what he did to my friend. Nina may have forgiven him, but I don't. I've barely absolved Arlo, and that's only because she loves him. I can't forgive Matteo. Besides, now he is in charge of the Carini company, so I'm sure he's done far worse things than any of the men I lock up on a daily basis.

"Should I come in or what?" Saul asks from the doorway.

"Yes, come in."

Saul walks inside. "Do you need help throwing this guy out?"

"No, I can handle him."

I turn my attention back to Matteo. "Unless you came to tell me something's happened to Nina and Arlo, I don't want to hear about it."

"Actually, I'm here to find out where they are. They call you. You know exactly where they are. So tell me, and I'll be on my way."

I hate myself for finding him attractive for even a minute. I hate myself for wanting anything to do with this monster.

"Why do you want to know?"

"Because I need my brother's help."

I search his eyes. "Liar."

He smirks, leaning forward, his eyes glued to me. "Fine. Because Arlo stole something from me and I want it back."

My heart sinks. "Nina. You want Nina back."

He nods.

I smile. "You're never gonna find them."

"And why not?"

"Because I don't know where they are. Yes, they call me and let me know they're safe every once in a while, but they never tell me where they are. Just that they're safe. They never tell you where they are either. Arlo is better than you at this sort of thing. They'll be able to run and hide from you forever."

A pinched expression crosses his face as he stares at me, then at my date, and back to me again.

"I don't think I'll have any trouble finding them," Matteo says, standing up from my couch and walking toward Saul. "Enjoy your date. Don't let her pick the wine." He's at my door in seconds, while I'm still staring at the couch, confused as to what the hell's going on.

"Where are you going?" I snap out of my stupor.

He stops short of the door, turns, and smirks at me. His eyes grow venomous.

"I'm letting you have one last date before I take you."

2

EDEN

I'M stunned as the door slams shut.

He's gone as quickly as he came. He struck fear into my heart and disappeared into the night leaving me with a thousand questions and no answers.

I close my eyes and crack my head side to side before deeply exhaling as I let all of the air out of my body. Calm. I need to remain calm. Now I wish I had had time for that yoga session to help relax me.

"Eden, what's wrong? What's going on?"

I ignore Saul. I can't handle his questions right now. I don't even have time to deal with my own fear. The only thing I can worry about is how to keep Matteo from kidnapping me.

There's a reason Nina and Arlo ran. Matteo was one of those reasons. He may be Arlo's brother, but I know what he's capable of. He's ruthless and will do whatever it takes to get what he wants.

I'm desperate for a solution and fast. I need a way to get rid of Matteo.

Nina. I rush over to the counter where my phone is lying and pick it up, ready to dial the number I memorized by heart. A number I'm only supposed to use in emergencies. Matteo coming back and threatening to steal me is unquestionably an emergency. I unlock my phone and begin dialing the numbers 376...

I stop.

I can't call Nina.

I try to swallow the lump in my throat. The one person who could help me is the one person I can't call. The one person who understands Matteo better than anyone. The one person who knows what Matteo might be planning.

All I know is I don't trust Matteo. I would be putting her in danger.

And if I tell Nina what is going on, she will come back. She will want to fight. And I can't put her through something like this again. She's happy. And even if I was able to convince her not to come back, Matteo could be tracking my calls. He could figure out that I know how to contact her. He could use the information to discover where she is. And I won't help him find her. I won't risk Nina's life no matter the cost.

Matteo didn't tell me why he wants Nina. But I doubt his intentions are pure. Nina told me almost everything. Matteo loved her as much as Arlo. She made her choice. She chose Arlo, now Matteo has to live with it. I don't want to imagine what battle might ensue if he was to find her.

I don't trust Arlo much more than I do Matteo, but Nina is as safe as she can be with him. Matteo can't find them.

Heath. I can call Heath. He is the only other person who might understand. He went through all this with Nina, and as much as I hate to bring him back into this world again, he is the only option I have.

I find his contact in my phone and dial the number. I hold my phone to my ear as my fingers drum across my granite countertops. I listen to one ring, two, three...

"Come on Heath, answer your damn phone."

Four rings... It goes to his answering machine.

"Call me when you get this. ASAP. It's an emergency."

I slam the phone down hard on the counter, not caring when the small crack forms in the corner of my phone. *Stupid phone.*

My whole body shakes. I'm not afraid Matteo's going to take me.

For one, I won't let him. But I'm petrified of what would happen to Nina if he stole her from Arlo. She wouldn't survive being ripped from the love of her life. So I have to stop Matteo.

"Eden?...Are you okay?" Saul says as he walks over to me and carefully places his hand on my shoulder.

I exhale deeply again, letting everything out. I try to find my tranquil, happy place, but his unsteady hand shaking my entire body isn't helping.

"Thank you. I'm going to be fine." I step away, causing his hand to drop from my body.

"You want to tell me what that was about?"

I turn and try to make my eyes brighten at him as I force my lips to smile. "No. It was nothing important."

He looks away as he rubs his tidy hair, making a mess of it. Sweat glistens on his forehead.

"What do you want to do now?"

I pause before answering. "Go out to dinner on our date and then whatever you had planned afterward. I want to forget about all this." I don't mention that I'm more desperate than I was before to have him. For him to fuck me and make me forget about what just happened. I want him to take me to a restaurant and then fuck me in the bathroom halfway through dinner.

"Okay," he smiles at me. He holds out his arm, and I take it, trying to focus on him as he leads me out of the condo and out to his waiting Volvo. He opens the door for me like the perfect gentleman he is, and I climb in as he goes around to the driver side. He starts up the car and turns on the radio, drowning out the silence.

"Do you like Asian food? This restaurant I'm taking you to does this fusion thing between Asian and Mexican."

Normal conversation. This is exactly what I need.

"I love Asian food."

He reaches over and takes my hand in his, holding it softly. I let my hand rest in his, despite how clammy his hand is.

I'm going to pretend like Matteo didn't walk into my life. I'm not going to run as Nina did. I'm going to stay and fight. All running did for Nina was stall the inevitable anyway. She ran and was still stolen. And in the meantime, she lived a life of fear.

I'm not running. I'm a smart, intelligent woman. I'm skilled enough to take on this asshole and win. I won't be taken.

The restaurant is impressive. It's the kind of restaurant where you sit on the floor on pillows, and they bring out food on sizable trays. The food was clearly thought out to blend aspects of Asian and Mexican cooking, with some dishes bringing a sweet heat of Korea and others the full-on spice of a jalepeño. The chef apparently had deep roots in both of the cultures, and it shows.

Saul does his best to keep the conversation light and moving, but we don't have much in common, and I'm far too distracted to be able to focus on much of what he is saying.

"Have you taken self-defense classes before?" I ask, unable to take my mind off the fact I may require his help tonight.

Saul clears his throat and blinks rapidly. "No."

"Know how to shoot a gun?"

"No."

"Know how to evade someone who is following you in a car?"

"No."

I sigh.

"But I do know how to order delicious wine. The kind that will make you turn up your nose at anything less."

My cheeks flush, and I readjust my legs loving the sound of his voice and the promises of more. "I could drink some fabulous wine. And I promise no more talk about self-defense or guns."

He reaches his hand out and holds mine again. Somehow his palm seems to have taken on even more moisture. I try my best to ignore it.

"Good, I may not own a gun, but I do know how to call the police."

I nod, and repeat to myself: *I won't let Matteo make me afraid. I won't fear him.*

I push away all thoughts of Matteo and enjoy my meal with Saul. I drink fabulous wine and eat delicious food. And I let ideas of all the ways that I want Saul to fuck me creep in like I would on any other date. His hands may be clammy, and the words that leave his mouth may be dull, but when he moves, I can see his biceps flex beneath his suit jacket. When he does grin, it reaches his deep blue eyes, inviting me in. And I have noticed his cock straining against the zipper on his pants more than once tonight. I do not doubt that he's incredible in bed.

I take the last bite of my chocolate dessert, savoring it slowly in my mouth before I swallow it down. I moan a little at the richness and glance over at Saul staring at me like he wants to eat me for dessert. I glance down at his erection that is straining against his pants. My lips part. I can't wait.

"You had your fun. Now tell me where Nina and Arlo are or I'm taking you with me."

I don't have to turn around to recognize that it's Matteo standing behind me.

"No."

My eyes cut over to Saul, whose eyes are bulging up at Matteo. Saul's scared shitless. *Why couldn't I have been set up with a Navy SEAL or something?* This man is utterly useless to me.

Matteo places his hand on my shoulder, gripping it firmly, letting me know that he's in control. I grab his hand, zeroing in on his pinky finger, and twist hard, ensuring that it breaks.

"Son of a bitch," Matteo says, pulling his hand back from me to tend to his wound.

I stand up and turn to face him with a set jaw and my chin high.

His finger is bent backward in a way that no finger should bend.

"You bitch. You broke my finger."

"I did."

"Do you know who I am? I'm a monster now. King of everything evil. Your little tantrums won't protect you from my army."

I smirk. "I put away monsters every day. I can handle you." I pick up my purse and turn to Saul. "We're leaving."

Saul stands and hurries past us, not bothering to wait for me. *Some gentleman he is.* I follow after him, Matteo won't be far behind.

I always knew that there was evil in this world. I just didn't realize evil would ever come for me.

3

MATTEO

DAMN, this woman.

My finger stings like a bitch. You'd think I'd be used to the pain, but I'm not. Living the life that I do, puts me in dangerous situations every day. But that's what my men are for, taking bullets for me. I rarely, if ever, have to deal with the agony myself. It's only a broken finger, but it still hurts like hell.

I've only ever broken a bone once before. When Arlo and I were fighting as teenagers, trying to prove who was better, stronger. He won, of course, breaking my jaw with a hard punch in my face, knocking me out cold.

I never expected Eden, of all people, to be the one to break one of my bones. I'll make her pay for it, of course.

I need Nina. I thought I was okay when she chose Arlo. I thought I could live without her, but I can't. She haunts my dreams and forms my nightmares. Everything makes me think of her. Everything makes me want her. She tortures me, and she's not even here. I'm addicted to her. I can't be apart from her.

And my idiot brother needs to be punished for what he did. I don't care that he's my brother. As the new leader, he needs to know that there are consequences to crossing me, whoever you are. For taking her from me. For abandoning me when I need him the most. I thought I could always count on him. I was wrong.

"Sir, are you okay?" a waiter asks, staring at me with wide eyes at my broken finger. His bright face changes to green, and quickly shuts his mouth to keep from puking. His eyes never leave my finger, despite the vile that's I'm sure is forming in his throat. It's like I'm a car crash on the side of the road that people can't stop staring at once they start, despite how unsafe it is to stare.

"Does it fucking look like I'm okay?"

His face is now red as he stands there, wholly incompetent.

"Get me a Band-Aid, or preferably a first-aid kit. Now," I growl.

The boy runs off toward the restaurant's kitchen. I have no clue if he's going to return or not. But he only has about a minute of my patience before I storm back there myself and find what I need.

He returns in a few seconds. He may be a fool, but at least he's fast.

I plop the first aid kit down on the table and sit down, popping the lid open. I dig through it, throwing band-aids aside, not caring about the mess I'm creating on the floor until I find the gauze and tape I am searching for.

I tape my pinky to my ring finger for support, ensuring that my little finger is aligned correctly and not flopping around everywhere.

"You should have a doctor examine that," the waiter says, turning green again.

I glare at him as I stand and he shuts up. At least I'm still able to intimidate him.

I thought Eden would come with me easily. I thought a simple threat would be enough to convince her to do whatever I wanted. I was wrong. This requires a more thorough plan.

I start walking out of the restaurant, ignoring the disgusting smell wafting off the food and the cheap wine sitting on every table. I have to steal this woman for no other reason than to show her what first class food and superior wine is.

Focus. I need a plan. I didn't bring backup. I didn't think I would require assistance. I wouldn't use it if I had it. This is personal. I want to do this alone.

I walk outside and down the sidewalk the three blocks to my car. Eden creeps into my mind as I walk.

I was dumbfounded by how similar her appearance is to Nina when she opened the door to her condo. So astounded, I thought she was Nina for a second. Her skin is the same olive color. Her hair long, dark, and straight. Her eyes just as piercing.

But my mind likes to play tricks on me when it comes to Nina. Eden, of course, isn't her. But they are best friends. They lived together. I'm sure Nina's told Eden everything. I doubt the similarities end with their appearance. Eden now shares the same fate Nina did. Eden will be captured the same way the Nina was.

I throw the door open to my convertible and calmly climb in, enjoying the smell of the leather seats. The car is brand-new. I bought it for this trip. I don't like sharing cars, and I can afford the more expensive things in life, even a new car for my single day in the US. I fire up the car and pull out of my spot, chasing after them. I pull out my phone and begin tracking Eden's phone. She may be feisty, but she's not smart enough to realize that she needs to get rid of her phone. The app on my phone instantly finds them. They are about ten blocks away, headed in the direction of her condo.

I start driving fast, weaving around car after car as I catch up to them. Each minute that passes I get closer and closer. Adrenaline rushes through my muscles as I drive almost automatically. My brain doesn't operate the car, my excitement does. The sooner I take Eden, the sooner I take Nina back and get to punish my brother.

My hands remain unshakeable as I speed through another red light. My heart beats steadily, my breathing relaxed, when I almost crash into an old Volkswagen Beetle that's driving far too slow in front of me. I dart out into the next lane and speed around it, not bothering to flip off the driver as I should. I've chased after someone in a car hundreds of times before. This is my life.

I see her douchebag of a date's car two in front of me. He thinks he's fancy driving in his Volvo S90. It's a ridiculous car, for men who are too weak to drive anything faster. His driving could use some work. I shouldn't have been able to catch up to them as quickly as I did.

I make a hard left turn, followed by two rights, looping around the block to get in front of them and stop at the light at the intersection. I lurk in the shadows of the building, waiting for them to stop at the light, perpendicular to where I sit. They do, and then I wait. I watch them from my seat in the car, talking to each other, having no idea the danger they are in. Having no clue that I hide feet away from them. Ready to take them out.

I don't know what kind of man she's dating, but he's definitely not worthy of her. He can't even protect her from a villain like me.

I keep my eye on the light and watch as it turns green for them. I step on the gas, slamming into his side of his car.

Our airbags go off, knocking the wind out of me for a second, but I'm determined. It does nothing to stop me. I want Eden, and I want her now. I'm tired of the games. I throw open my door and give myself a once-over before I examine my car. It barely has a scratch on it, while his shitty car took the brunt of the force. The entire front half is smashed in.

I walk toward the driver side of the car, knowing now my target should have been Saul, instead of Eden. If I understand anything about her, I know she will protect her stupid date. She'll put herself last.

I throw his door open and grab his arm, pulling him out of the car as I take my gun out of the back of my pants and aim it at his head.

"Now, let's try this again," I say, staring at Eden.

Her eyes bulge as she undoes her seatbelt and pushes the airbag down out of her face.

"Don't hurt him."

Her voice is slick and unwavering as she speaks without a drop of fear.

I smirk, my plan will work.

"Do as I say and I won't kill him."

She inspects me then her date. "I'm sorry," she mouths.

She throws open her door and runs.

"Damn it." *What's wrong with her?* She doesn't give a shit about her date.

I throw him hard against the concrete road.

"You can blame Eden for this." I shoot him squarely in the leg to keep him from coming after me. He has a fighting chance of surviving, as long as I didn't hit any major artery running through his leg. *I might need some help cleaning up this mess after all.*

I start running after her. She won't run far before I catch up with her. I'm far too impressive of a runner, and I'm far too motivated to not catch up with her. Her only hope is if there happens to be a police station or some place of sanctuary she can run to and hide inside.

But she seems to be out of luck. I see her turn a corner and I run after her, a second behind. She is fast, but not quick enough. I make a mental note not to underestimate her speed in the future.

She feels me catching up to her and turns to glance behind her, only to see me feet away. She darts down another road, leading her out toward a four-lane street filled with cars zipping by. She's trapped.

I slow my jogging down a little. She has nowhere to go. She won't be able to cross the busy street without getting hit by traffic. And there is nowhere else for her to hide.

She hesitates, staring out at the cars whizzing by her and then glances back at me.

I smirk.

She darts out into traffic, because, apparently, she'd rather die then get taken by me.

Shit.

I run after her, dashing out into the traffic. One car stops, honking their horn emphatically. She won't get so lucky a second time. I catch up with her, grab onto her and pull us out of the way of another speeding car.

We both lay on the cold concrete, my arms still around her, panting hard as the rush of adrenaline continues to beat wildly throughout our bodies.

"You're welcome."

She tries to climb out of my arms, but I hold her tighter to my body, enjoying having her warm body pressed against mine.

"What? You aren't grateful?"

"No."

"But I saved your life."

"You saved my life only so you could steal me, and use me against my best friend. That's not saving me."

"It's better than what you did to your date."

She scowls at me. "If I had gone with you, you would've killed him anyway."

"That's where you're wrong. If I give you my word I won't kill someone, then I won't."

"Will you kill me?"

"Not today."

She doesn't hesitate. She knees me hard in the balls, giving her enough time to free herself while I wrap myself around my wounded manhood.

She's good. But I'm better. I jump up, run the few feet after her, and grab her arm, twisting it hard behind her back.

She cries out.

"Now that I have your attention again, you will do what I say, or I'll break your arm, which trust me, from how much agony my finger is in, you won't recover from rapidly."

"You're a monster."

"I know."

I walk her back toward where my car and her date still sit, him bleeding out over the concrete.

I smirk at the weak man lying on the ground. "How does it feel that this incredible woman wasn't willing to save you?"

Her date glares back at me, too broken to even fight back with words.

"Should I kill him now since he means so little to you?"

"No, you wouldn't."

"I would and I will."

She pants hard. She makes the mistake of looking at the what is left of her date.

"Save him, and I'll cooperate."

"No, you won't."

But I walk her forward to him, still holding her arm behind her back.

"Take off your shirt," I say to him.

He squeezes his eyes shut, like that will make me disappear.

"Shirt off now," I bark again.

"Listen to him," Eden pleads.

He reluctantly removes his shirt, and I turn to Eden. "Now, take his shirt and tie it above the wound as tightly as you can."

I release Eden, keeping the gun firmly to her head as she does what I say. As soon as she's finished, I use my gun to slap him as hard as I can in the head, knocking him unconscious to the floor.

"Why did you do that?" she screams, trying to wake him up with her pathetic shakes of his shoulder.

"So he wouldn't follow us or remember any of this conversation to tell the police."

I grab her arm again, pulling her up from his limp body as I take out my phone and dial 911.

"911, what's your emergency?"

"There's been an accident at the corner of 7th and South Olive." I hang up.

"I kept my word. Now get in the car and cooperate before I change my mind and kill you both."

4

EDEN

MATTEO SPEEDS OFF, away from the accident. Away from Saul.

I glance into the side mirror at Saul's car shrinking smaller and smaller as we speed away, until it all but gets lost among the other cars driving by. Regret instantly fills my soul. *How could I have been so heartless to have let Matteo shoot Saul?* I needed to save myself. I needed to save Nina. *But will I ever be able to live with myself if Saul dies?* If he dies, it's *my fault*.

Matteo turns the corner, and I'm no longer able to see the car or Saul.

"He's going to die, isn't he?" I stare out the window as buildings whiz by, narrowly registering what's happening to me. All I can think about is Saul.

"He'll survive if he's strong enough."

I turn toward Matteo, who is whistling to himself as he loosely grasps the steering wheel. He's acting as if nothing happened. Like he didn't just shoot a man in the leg and leave him bleeding out on the sidewalk, most likely to die. Like he's not currently kidnapping me. In fact, the entire car appears that way. His convertible hardly has a scratch on it. And when I take a deep breath, I smell the fresh new car scent, when it should reek of death and gloom.

"How do you know that?"

"Stop worrying about your date. You didn't seem concerned with him before, by the way you ran off instead of trying to save him."

"That's because I didn't think you would shoot him. And I wasn't thinking about him, I was thinking about Nina."

He rapidly steps on the gas, accelerating as we go around another corner. I grab onto my seat to attempt from slamming my head into the side of the door.

"Relax, he'll survive. I missed all his major arteries, and if the emergency system is halfway decent around here, the paramedics are already at his side providing medical services. And as long as it doesn't take them hours to drive him to a hospital, he won't bleed out before they save him."

"How do you know you didn't hit any major arteries? You're not a doctor."

He rolls his eyes. "Because he would've been dead by the time we got back to him and blood would have been pouring out of his leg."

I'm not sure if I believe him. It sure as hell looked like a lot of blood to me. I'm not sure he knows anything about gunshot wounds, although he's probably been shot dozens of times before, so maybe he does.

But I also know that he is willing to tell me whatever he thinks I want to hear to get me to cooperate. He's right about one thing; I won't be cooperating. I plan on running again the next chance I get.

I rest my hand on the door handle in case he decides to stop, and I can make my escape.

"Don't even think about it."

"I'm not thinking about anything."

He shakes his head and punches the gas. My body slams against the door as he swerves around cars and goes the wrong way down a one-way street. I close my eyes and pray we don't hit anything, and simultaneously hope we do crash and die so this will be all over.

"I'll never slow down enough for you to be able to jump out of the car and run, so remove your fucking hand from the door."

My hand slips off the door, bracing myself again as he continues to speed and curse. I have to be more careful at revealing any part of my plan to him in the future. He's done this before; he's going to be able to spot what I'm planning before I carry it out. I have to make sure I don't give him any signs or clues that I'm going to bolt again. Not even a tiny hint with my body.

"Where are you driving me?" I stare at him, demanding an answer to my question but doubting he'll give me one. I'm sure the less I know, the better, in his mind.

"Italy."

My mouth drops a little when he answers me. He's taking me back to his home. I'm not sure why I didn't realize what his plan was before. I thought he would hold me captive in a hotel room, or an empty warehouse somewhere where he could torture me to find out where Nina and Arlo are. It would end with either me escaping or with a bullet through my head. Apparently, though, that's not the plan.

Italy. He's taking me back to Italy. So many memories and emotions pour through my head as I think of going back to a country I both love and hate. I love because it was the last time I got to be free.

I always thought I would do something creative, bringing more joy to the world with art and imagination. I enjoy painting and studying history. Architecture. Everything beautiful.

A life of art and creativity was the path I was headed down in Italy, and it was the last time I did things solely for the love of it.

But Italy is also where I lost my best friend. Her life changed forever, and so did mine. I realized I couldn't do things for the love of it anymore. I needed a more significant purpose. So I went to law school and then started prosecuting bad guys. I've been fulfilling my new reason to exist every day since.

We arrive at the airport far too quickly. He takes me to a private airfield, not LAX. He drives through the security gate, past the armed guards who merely open the gate without asking for ID, because apparently they already know who Matteo is. He continues right up to a plane I assume he owns and parks a few feet away.

I can't leave with him. If he takes me to Italy, I could end up trapped for weeks. Or dead. I need to escape. Now.

He undoes his seatbelt and pushes the door ajar. I undo my seatbelt and throw my door open wide and sprint as fast as I can in the opposite direction of the plane.

I don't have a plan. I move as quickly as my body will run, away from Matteo. I will hopefully find someone who can help me. A police officer, someone in the military, or any person with a car who will stop and drive me far, far away from here.

I sense him behind me. I'm a runner and in shape. I'm fast; he's faster. I hoped catching him off guard for a second would allow me enough of a head start to escape. But I was wrong.

His arms wrap around my body as he tackles me to the rough tarmac below. My face hits the ground with a thud and scrapes harshly across the tarmac while the rest of my body is stricken with the force of his body.

"You don't know when to give up, do you? You're mine. I'm kidnapping you, and there's nothing you can do to deter me. Fighting won't help, it will only earn you more punishment later."

I struggle against his arms, trying frantically to smash free, but his arms tighten more around my arms, making it impossible for me to make any of the moves I learned in self-defense classes over the years. I can't physically break free, but I can convince him of all the reasons he shouldn't do this.

"You can't take me. I never take a vacation or miss a day of work. Tomorrow morning when I don't show up for work, my boss will call and try to find me. My friend, Jules, will call the police when she can't reach me. I already called Heath and told him you are here and to contact the police if anything happened to me. You won't be able to get away with it. People will start searching for me; the police will become involved, maybe even the FBI. They will hunt you down and put you in prison for the rest of your life."

He laughs as he stands up, pulling me to my feet and twisting my arm behind my back. I try to move, but I can't wiggle free without snapping my arm in two. Maybe the pain of breaking my arm would be worth it to be free.

"I'm not too worried about the police or FBI. They can't touch me. And we all know how well Heath was able to save Nina. You do have a point though; I don't want people searching for you until I'm ready for them to find out you're missing."

His eyes rake over my body. "Where is your phone?"

"In my purse, back in Saul's car."

His hands travel over my body. Into the pockets of my pants as he searches for a phone that doesn't exist. Then his eyes burn into my chest.

"No," I say.

His hand reaches down the top of my shirt and over my breast, softly grazing my nipple as he forages for my phone. I squirm beneath his fingers, partially because I want his hand to stop invading my personal space and partly because I want to know how it would feel for him to touch me for real.

"I guess you weren't lying." He removes his hands from my shirt, reaches into his back pocket, and pulls out his phone, handing it to me.

"Call work and tell them you're taking an extended leave of absence. That you found out your mother has cancer and you will be taking care of her. And you won't be back anytime soon."

I smirk. "No."

He reaches into the back of his pants and aims the gun at my head. "Leave the message, or I'll kill you."

I stare at the gun. I should be terrified, but I'm not. "You won't shoot me. You hardly shot Saul, and you had no use for him. *Me*, you have use for. You won't kill me, or even harm me."

He glares at me as his nostrils flare and his face turns red with rage. He places the gun back into the back of his pants. "Do it, and I won't look for Nina for one week. She gets seven more days of safety."

Damn it. How was Matteo able to figure out my weakness so quickly? One week is a long time. In a week, I could find a way to escape. In a week, I could find a way to warn Nina and make sure she stays safe forever. In one week, I could kill Matteo.

"How do I know that you'll keep your word?"

"Because I'm an honorable person. I keep my promises."

He holds out the phone. I take it, not needing to consider his offer any further. I dial the number for my work. I realize as soon as it goes to voicemail I could change course. I could tell them Matteo took me and to look for me in Italy. I could save myself. But Matteo would still take me, and Nina would still be at risk.

"Hi, this is Eden. I'm calling to let you know I will be taking an extended leave of absence. I was in a car accident tonight. I'm fine, but it shook me up a little bit, and it made me realize I'm not living my life. I need a vacation. I've been working too hard for too long and not enjoying life. I don't know how long my absence will be, but I'll contact you when I'm ready to return. In the meantime, I'll be using all my vacation days I saved over the years. Jules can inform you of anything you need on my past clients. The other prosecutors should be able to handle new cases, since I closed all my current cases." I press end.

He holds out his hand, and I toss the phone back.

"You didn't do what I said."

"My mom died years ago; your plan wouldn't have worked."

He twists my arm again and walks me toward the plane, then up the stairs onto the lavish private jet. I've never been on a plane this nice before. There are leather chairs and couches everywhere. A small kitchen and bar area toward the back and doors I assume lead to bathrooms or possibly even bedrooms all the way in the rear.

I don't understand why it takes me this long for it to hit me again that I'm being stolen and I have to do everything I can to fight back. I turn, planning on elbowing Matteo in the nose as sharply as I can with my elbow, but he blocks me and grabs my other arm.

"I'm not going to deal with you fighting me all the way to Italy. I have work to do."

"Too bad, because that's exactly what I plan on doing."

The jab pierces my skin without warning before the needle burns into my neck. I don't have a chance to react.

"No, I think you're going to take a very long nap."

My body grows weak and tired in his arms. The bastard drugged me. But it will do nothing to prevent me from fighting again the second I wake up. So unless he plans on keeping me sedated the entire time he has me, he better be prepared for a fight.

———

My head pounds as my eyelids flutter wide. I'm groggy, my entire body aches, and my mind can't make sense of why I feel like I've been run over by a train.

I attempt to raise my head up, but the cloudiness is enough to knock me back down against the bed, my head hitting the soft pillow. My headache is so intense that even the pillow makes the thumping in my head worse.

Instead of raising my head up, I look around the fancy room with just my eyes. I'm lying in an oversized king-size bed made of shiny black wood, covered in a light gray comforter. The bed matches the dark dressers scattered throughout the room. I glance over to the expansive windows that are covered with opaque shades, giving me no clue to what time of day it is or where I am.

I glance over at the two picture frames sitting on the nightstand next to me. One of Matteo, Arlo, and what I assume is their sister, Gia. Nina has told me about her, but I've never met her. The other is a picture of Nina. I reach over and pick up the frame. My hand shakes as I struggle to hold onto the frame. She appears so happy in the photograph. I don't know when it was taken or whose picture it is. *Am I in Arlo's room or Matteo's?*

It would make sense if this were Arlo's room before he left. He loves her. But if this were to be Matteo's room, I don't understand why he would have a photograph of Nina. *Is it love or hatred he feels toward her?*

I set the frame back on the nightstand with uneasy hands. Still lying on my back, I work my way to the edge of the bed, let my feet dangle off the end, and finally, I gradually push my body up into a sitting position.

My eyes flicker shut as the pain and dizziness overwhelm me. I rest on the edge of the bed for much longer than I want. I want to run. I want to find out what's going on and why my memories are so foggy.

I try to remember how I got here, but I can't. I try to recall why I feel so shitty, but I have no idea. *Is Nina waiting for me in the next room? Or is something more sinister happening?* The only way to find out the answers to my questions is to stand up and walk out of this room. A room that is more like a gloomy cave than an actual bedroom.

I lean forward, over the end of the bed, until my feet touch the floor. Then, I slowly get to my feet using my arms to help push me up. I grab a bedpost to maintain my balance as I take a few steps forward, ensuring my legs are strong enough to carry me before I let go. I walk cautiously and deliberately, focusing on the walnut wood door. When I make it to the door, my body collapses against the doorknob and smooth finish.

I don't ever recall ever enduring such exhaustion in all my life. Not even after all the nights staying up studying to pass my board exams for law school. I've never felt this tired. I take a deep breath, trying to fill my body with oxygen and energy.

I force my body off the door enough to reach the doorknob. I expect to have to walk several more feet before I find another person on the other side of this door. But when I pull it ajar, Matteo is standing in the doorway looking at me.

"Surprised you were able to walk this far out of bed."

I narrow my eyes, scolding him. But then I get a whiff of what he is holding. Some type of soup. A delicious tomato-based broth I instantly want in my stomach. My stomach growls at the thought of food and my mouth waters, already able to taste it in my mouth from the smell alone.

"Sit down on the couch," he says, clearly noticing my hunger lust.

I glance behind me and see a living room on the other side of the bed, connected to a small kitchenette area by a door. I clumsily walk to the soft cushions, because I don't have any other options and because I seriously want that soup. My legs give out several feet before I make it to the couch, so I prepare myself for impact on the floor. Matteo grabs my arm at the last moment before my body hits the ground.

"Jesus, you're one determined woman," he mutters under his breath as he pulls me upright again.

Determined, yes. Determined to get that soup into my stomach as fast as possible. He guides me to the couch where I plop down, my body giving out the moment it feels the cushions on the back of my legs.

"Here," he says, placing the bowl of soup into my hands. "Eat, and you'll feel better."

I lift the spoon slowly to my lips and pour the creamy liquid down my throat. The soup is silky, creamy, with a hint of sweetness, and some flavor I can't identify. It's mainly a thick broth with a few soft noodles and tomatoes, but primarily liquid, as to make it easy to swallow. It's simple, but the most delicious thing I've ever tasted.

My growling stomach eases a teeny, tiny bit, but it's going to take me a long time to eat this entire bowl of soup and give my stomach the satisfying, full feeling it's seeking.

I lower my hand again to scoop another spoonful and lift it to my lips. This time, as the liquid goes down, my stomach burns. As mouth-watering as the soup tastes, my stomach no longer agrees.

"I'm going to be sick."

Matteo jumps off the couch and races across the room for a trashcan, but I can't wait.

"I'm going to be – "

I grab the towering decorative vase sitting in the center of the coffee table and scoot it towards me seconds before the contents of my stomach come back up. There's not much left in my stomach, but whatever was inside dispenses into the shiny gold vase.

"Jesus, Eden," Matteo says, holding the trashcan he went to retrieve in his hand.

"What happened to me?" I dry heave, grasping the vessel like it is my most valuable possession.

Matteo unhinges my hands from the vase filled with my puke and carries it out of the room ignoring my question and leaving me with the empty trashcan. He returns less than a minute later with a glass of water, a warm washcloth, and two pills in his hand.

"Clean yourself up and take these anti-nausea pills, they will help you keep the food down."

I take the washcloth from him and wipe my face before I set it down on the coffee table. Then I pop the pills into my mouth, swallow, and down the entire glass of water.

My eyes suspiciously cut to the soup sitting on the coffee table. I should try eating it again, but I don't want to vomit.

My hunger wins out over my fear. I try picking up the bowl with my hands. I manage to lift it an inch before it slips out of my trembling hands and hits the table with a thump, spilling a couple of drops onto the table's flawless surface.

Redness flushes my cheeks. I can't even lift a fucking bowl I'm so weak. I grab the spoon with my still unsteady hand, while I lean over the bowl. I scoop some of the broth onto the spoon and lift it to my lips more slowly than before. The liquid finally touches my lips, and I quickly swallow. I wait for my stomach to growl or burn again, giving me any sign that food is settling well in my stomach. It doesn't.

I smile. Success.

Now on to another spoonful.

"Fuck this. We'll be here all day," Matteo says, snatching the bowl of soup away from me.

My eyes protrude from their sockets as I glare at him. I may not have the strength to do much damage to Matteo, but I will use every ounce of strength I have left to attack him for taking away the only thing giving me any comfort.

"Sit back," he commands.

I do, but only so I can see his pupils when I tell him off.

He puts the spoon down on the table and holds the entire bowl of soup up to my lips.

"Drink."

He tilts the bowl, and the liquid gradually pours into my mouth and down my throat. He continues to feed me until all the soup is gone. My cheeks begin to warm, my head becomes lucid, and my stomach no longer aches for food. Even just moving my arms is manageable compared to before.

He sets the bowl back down. "You should climb back in bed and sleep."

I nod and stand, my legs still wobbly and weak.

Matteo doesn't have the patience for me. He scoops me up in his arms and carries me back to what I now assume is his bed. He places me down and pulls the covers back over me, but that's as far as his chivalry goes.

"Sleep."

My eyes drift closed, following his command. None of this makes any sense. The photograph of Nina. Matteo taking care of me. My body so incredibly weak. I can't process what's happening in my still foggy head. My body, nor my mind can deal with solving the problem. What I need is sleep. It's the only thing I can think about.

———

I open my eyes, and everything becomes clear.

Matteo stole me.

He knocked me out. He pretended to care about me when I was at my weakest.

I don't know how long I've been asleep, but I won't stay his prisoner. My feet hit the floor, I sprint to the door, and throw it wide to see Matteo standing there again like deja-vu.

He smirks. "Video cameras," he says, answering my unspoken question and explaining how he knows I was out of bed.

This time, when I confront him, I'm not decrepit. This time, I remember what he did. I punch him in the nose, making sure to cause the most impact to a sensitive area, as my self-defense classes taught me all these years. I don't wait to see the blood spurting out. It isn't the first time I've broken a man's nose before.

I bolt down the hallway, barefoot. He must've changed my clothes because I'm dressed in one of his T-shirts that scarcely covers my butt and underwear. I should've put regular clothes on first before I tried to make my escape, but it's too late now. I'll run barefoot as long as it takes to reach my freedom.

I round the corner and see several men standing in the hallway. They end their conversations and gape at me. I keep running, managing to slip past them and down another long corridor. This hallway has a door at the end with light shining around its edges. Could it lead outside?

I beg my legs to move faster. They do, but it's not fast enough. A man steps out of one of the rooms lining the hallway and blocks my exit.

I turn around, preparing to race the other direction, but the men I passed earlier are now storming after me.

I'm trapped, but I won't go down without a fight.

My legs are moving swiftly, preparing to slip through the men's grasps again.

I run fast past the first, but the second grabs my arm. I knee him in the balls and keep running.

I punch the next man I see and hear his nose crunch, the bones breaking.

Almost free.

My arm jolts me back as one of the men grabs hold of it. He ducks as I try to punch him, the same way I did his friend. He puts me in a headlock before I have a chance to attack. I bite down hard, tearing through the flesh on his arm until I taste blood.

He lets me go, but only for a second before four hands are on me, grabbing my flailing arms roughly.

"Where do you think you're going, bitch?" One of them asks.

"The cunt bit me. I can't wait to see what Matteo does to her," another says, staring at the wound on his arm.

I may not have escaped, but I caused damage. That's a start.

They drag me back down the corridor and out to the living room where Matteo is sitting, waiting. He has an ice pack pressed to this nose and a whiskey in his hand. His entire body tenses when he sees me.

I smirk. At least I made him bleed. He may have won now, but I'll make him suffer over and over and over again.

"Do you want us to lock her in the dungeon?" the man whom I bit asks.

"No, I need her to talk. She won't talk in the dungeon."

"The cunt bit my arm, she deserves severe punishment."

"I agree."

He stares at me intensely.

"Maximo, bring me some shackles."

The man whom I bit lets go of my arm and galavants away. "With pleasure."

Matteo stands up, dropping the ice pack to the ground, and walks toward me. My arms are still spread wide, away from my body held by the three men left.

"You have two choices, Eden. One, I drug you again and lock you in the dungeons until you learn to behave. Or two, I chain you to me so you can't run and you start talking."

Neither seems like a good option.

"Which do you choose?"

"Chained."

He nods. Maximo returns with the shackles and hands them to Matteo. He bends down and shackles my legs so close together I know I won't be able to do much more than shuffle my feet. I, indeed, won't be able to run. He then connects my right wrist and to his left wrist with another shackle.

"You can't win Eden, so stop trying. The only way you can earn your freedom is by giving me, Nina and Arlo. If you attempt to escape again, or hurt my men or me in any way, you'll remain medicated and unconscious the rest of your time here. Understand?"

I nod.

He gives his men a look, and they let me go. My instinct is to bolt over and hurt Matteo. Punch him in the face, rip out his heart, snap his neck. However, I don't want to spend the rest of my time here drugged, even though he's bluffing. He won't allow me to endure my entire time here in a coma because I would be of no use to him. I don't doubt he would at least drug me for another night though, and that could result in several days in bed recovering.

"How long have I been here?"

"Too long," he answers before he walks away. The handcuff on my wrist pulls, and I struggle to remain even with his long strides as we walk down the hallway, my feet shuffling as rapidly as I can move them in the chains.

"Slow down."

"No."

He jerks me into, what I assume, is his office before he takes a seat behind the desk, not offering me a place to sit. I'm left either stand-ing, leaning against the wall, or sitting on the floor. I decide to conserve my energy and take a seat.

I study him as he makes phone call after phone call, hoping to gain some useful information I can use against him. All of the calls are boring, none of them giving me any insight into a way for me to escape. He mostly talks numbers, men, and how many weapons are to be sent to various clients.

I sit on the floor for at least an hour with nothing to do but to listen to him talk on the phone. I try to figure a way to get out of this, but I come up empty.

I close my eyes, deciding I'll rest while he works.

My body is jerked awake as he strides out of the office giving me no warning. My eyes fly open, and I scramble to my feet.

"You could at least give me some warning when we are going somewhere."

"No, I can't. You need to learn to behave and maybe then I'll treat you with some respect."

He walks into a small bathroom, and I have no choice but to step inside with him.

"Really?"

"Don't act like you don't want to drool over my cock."

"Gross." I turn up my nose.

He undoes his pants and pulls out his penis to take a piss. And I admit I can't help but take a quick peek. His cock is long and thick, more substantial than I expected it to be. I try to keep my thoughts pure, but I can't help it. Any woman's mind would immediately think of what a cock like his is capable of doing.

He zips his pants and washes his hands smirking at me in the mirror while I frown again.

"Where are we going next?"

"Going for a run."

My eyes widen. "You can't be serious?"

"I always go for a run every day."

"I can't run with the shackles on my feet and no shoes on."

He walks down the hallway dragging me behind him without

another word. I realize we're heading back to his bedroom and I smile a little.

We step inside, and he locks the door, trapping us inside together. He unlocks the shackles on my arm and legs.

"I think you'll find the clothing and shoes you require to go running in that closet." He motions toward a closet opposite of the one he heads to.

I walk over to the closet and step inside, finding a whole wardrobe of women's clothes. They all look like they could fit me. I don't ask how or why, but I see a pair of shorts, a sports bra, and a T-shirt. I change into them quickly, along with some tennis shoes I find in my size. I change as fast as I can because I know the second he's ready, he'll put the shackles back on, regardless if I'm ready or not.

I step back out into the main bedroom in time to see him slipping a shirt over his rippled body. I notice a few tattoos covering his chest, but otherwise, his body is flawless.

He puts one of the shackles on his wrist and then looks at me with an impatient glance. I hold out my hand, offering to behave, because it would be nice to stretch my legs outside and breathe some fresh air. If this is the only way I get to do it, fine.

He snaps the shackle on to my wrist and leads me outside.

I close my eyes and inhale deeply, letting the air and warmth take over me.

But I'm jerked forward as Matteo starts running, giving me no time to warm up. He's faster than me, so I have to push myself to prevent myself falling to the ground and getting dragged.

The path he jogs is beautiful. Through the forest behind his house, a trail he has clearly carved out for himself and no one else.

We jog for a long time until my legs and lungs burn, but I don't complain. For one, I have a great view of his ass as he runs. And as much as I hate to admit it, he has a great ass. And two, I get to push myself and work on gaining speed and strength so someday I can outrun him. And three, I can bask in the warm sun.

As we return to the back of the house, a buzzing sound makes Matteo stop and pull out his phone.

"Yes?" He pauses. "You still haven't found my brother and Nina then?"

"Fine." He hangs up the phone.

I strike him on the back, frustrated.

"What was that for? And just when I thought you were learning to behave."

"What about our deal? You promised if I left those messages at work, you wouldn't go after Nina and Arlo for at least a week."

He pulls out his phone again and hands it to me showing me the date.

"You have been here two weeks."

My mouth drops open. *Two weeks.*

"How did you keep me alive for that long unconscious?"

"IVs. The medications I gave you seem to have had a particularly strong effect on you."

I look up, needing to know an answer to my question desperately. "Why? Why do you want Arlo and Nina? Why do you have a picture of Nina in your bedroom?"

"Because Arlo owes me for leaving. He's my brother. He is supposed to stay and work for me, but he left, abandoning me without a word or a goodbye."

"And Nina?"

"I love Nina. I want her back."

"You're lying. You're saying that so I'll eventually tell you where they are. You don't love Nina or care about your brother. How can you love someone that hurt you?"

His eyes shoot straight into mine as his lips pull back.

"I guess you'll find out if it's possible. Could you ever learn to love me despite how I've hurt you?"

"No. Could you if I hurt you as badly as you have hurt me?"

He shrugs. "I guess I'm a more forgiving person than you are."

He stares past me as he leads me back inside. I don't believe he loves her. He's not capable of love. He doesn't even know what love is. Matteo is evil, and I won't ever tell him where Nina is. Even if it costs me my life.

5

MATTEO

I NEED to shatter the shield around Eden.

I need to demolish her will to live so that she will tell me anything I want.

I need to find Nina and Arlo, now.

My heart has turned to ice with them gone. I have power now. I control the entire Carini empire along with hundreds of men and money at my disposal. *What good is having all this power if I can't use it, especially to deal with the one matter I care about?*

Getting Nina and Arlo back is about so much more than claiming the woman I love and punishing my brother. It's much, much bigger.

My alarm clock goes off, but I don't need it to wake me up. I rarely need an alarm clock, but I've been struggling to sleep even more since I took Eden. I climb out of bed and stretch before I dress in jeans and a dark gray T-shirt. I walk over to the small living room in my quarters where Eden is snoring on the couch.

She spent the last three days handcuffed to me, stuck following me everywhere. Her dreams are the only thing that gives her the illusion of freedom. I can't have her in my bed though. I like having my own space. And I haven't had a woman in my bed since Nina. My insomnia would get worse with her in my bed anyway.

So instead, she sleeps on my couch with her leg attached to a hook on the floor I had Maximo create to ensure she wouldn't run off or try to shoot me during the few hours of rest I actually get at night.

My head jerks back every time I see her lying on the couch in the morning when I come in. It isn't the only part of me that is drawn to attention at the sight of her. My cock quarrels with my brain for me to fuck her.

Soon. Very soon.

Eden doesn't normally seem like the kind of woman who would allow herself to let her guard down when her enemy is so close. Vulnerability is seen as a weakness to her, and she will do anything not to appear fragile. Either she's too exhausted to stay awake, or she doesn't believe I'll hurt her while she's out.

"Wake up sleepyhead," I shout, grabbing the couch and shaking it violently like I have the last two mornings.

She drops off the couch, the weight of her body crashing to the floor with a smack.

"You bastard."

"Just a bastard today? I must be growing on you then."

She bares her teeth at me as she stands up and lunges at me, trying to can grab ahold of me and cause any damage she can. But like every other morning, the chains take her by surprise, and she's pulled back to the ground.

I smirk, as her round ass hits the floor again. "You're not a very fast learner, are you?"

She pulls against the restraints, trying to pummel me. "I learn just fine. I've learned how much of a heartless ruler you are. I've come up with a dozen ways to kill you. It only takes one night of forgetting to lock me up. One time to get careless with the knives or the guns, or for me to find a way to pick the lock. That day will come soon. That's when I'll murder you."

"And that's when my men will kill you."

"It will be worth it." Her eyes taunt mine with a smugness that I want to wash away with my cock down her throat.

Patience, I remind myself.

I place the shackles back on both our wrists, joining her to me. I can't decide whether I love or hate tethering her to me. I love having the control over her, but I hate having her around me all the time. It's as much of a torture to me as it is to her. She's starting to mess with my head.

Today is when the real fun starts. Nina is Eden's weakness, but there are only so many ways I can use Nina against Eden. Eden has to have more than one fault, so I plan on finding and exploiting them to my advantage.

I turn and start walking out the door, not giving Eden any warning. She's relatively used to my abrupt changes by now, and can keep pace with me effortlessly. She's starting to anticipate my moves before I make them. Probably because I have a routine she has already learned.

Today that ends.

I sneer back at my little slave. Her face is bored and restless. Her body tired. She has no idea what's about to happen to her.

I walk into the dining room. A long rectangular table stretches across the center of the room, able to hold two dozen people, underneath the antique chandelier, which sparkles brightly overhead. Half a dozen men are at the table already eating breakfast, ready for their daily orders from me.

I walk to my usual spot at the head of the table, and Eden follows. She ordinarily takes a seat next to me at the table, but not today. I snap my fingers and motion for my two closest men to claim the seats next to me. Even when Eden isn't here, they rarely sit next to me. I like being alone in my thoughts in the morning.

They pick up their breakfast plates and move down until they are occupying the two chairs on either side of me. I take a seat knowing there's nowhere for Eden to sit. The chain, attaching us, isn't long enough for her to sit in any of the other open chairs at the table.

I wait for her to complain or make a snarky comment, but she doesn't. Apparently, she's going to pretend I don't affect her when I clearly do. I crawl under her skin like no one else.

She's giving me a dirty look, one that I'm sure is meant to display her hatred for me. It does. But her cheeks are flushed, her lips slightly parted, and, every so often, she wets her bottom lip. She can pretend to hate me all she wants, but she can't deny her body craves mine.

She's an uptight woman used to getting her way, but I have a feeling after one kiss she's going to be putty in my arms.

"Here's your coffee, sir. Would you like your usual omelete?"

"Yes, Emilia," I say, lifting the coffee to my lips.

My servant turns her attention toward Eden. "And what would you like for breakfast?"

"I'd love –"

"She won't be eating or drinking anything."

Emilia fidgets with the bottom of her apron as her eyes cut from Eden to me. I'll have to make sure that Emilia doesn't try to sneak Eden food.

"That'll be all," I say, dismissing my servant.

Emilia runs off to fix my breakfast, and I wait for Eden's reaction.

Eden doesn't say anything to me. She pretends I didn't deny her food. She pretends I didn't refuse her a place at the table and make her stand behind me like a dog. I was cruel before, but she hasn't seen my dark side yet. Her silly plan of acting like I don't affect her won't work.

She can act tough now, but I'll break her. I have to find the right button to push. We'll see how well she does without nourishment. I give her three days, at most, before she starts begging me for water, bread, even scraps off my plate. Especially in her weakened state.

Emilia returns with my breakfast. Her eyes dart to Eden before she scurries off again.

My men continue to eat silently at the table, occasionally snickering or glaring at Eden. They too realize that today is the day the real fun begins. Today is when we get Eden to talk, no matter what it takes.

"Were you able to confirm the shipment for Thursday, Maximo?" I ask.

"We ran into a few complications, but we plan on using force tonight. I think it can be done."

"Good. Once that's dealt with, we can move on to more important things like finding Nina and Arlo. After tonight, I want at least half the team searching for them.

"And as an added incentive, if you find Nina and Arlo before Eden discloses their location, I'll make sure a substantial bonus awaits you in your next paycheck. I'll even let you participate in helping me teach Nina and Arlo a lesson for running."

Maximo laughs, and it soars through the room. "We'll find them long before Eden speaks a syllable." His eyes eat up her body, which attempts to hide beneath the thin T-shirt she's wearing.

A low growl escapes my throat. A warning. Maximo stops looking at Eden.

My jaw slowly unclenches, and my vein stops throbbing in my forehead. I don't understand why it annoys me that Maximo leered at Eden. After my cock claims Eden and she spills their whereabouts, he can fuck her all he wants. All I want is to find Nina and Arlo.

Maximo shouldn't have dared to check her out. I rub my neck trying to release the tension he caused. Maybe my anger reared up because he's now my number two since Arlo left. I want Maximo to be entirely loyal to me, not pining over some woman.

I look to Dierk on my left. "You up for the task, Dierk?"

"Absolutely."

"Good. I need all of my best men on this. Now everyone get the fuck out of here and start working."

The men immediately stand and file out of the room, leaving whatever remains of their food on their plates.

Eden immediately sinks into the chair next to me that Dierk had occupied.

"I thought you love Nina? I thought you wouldn't hurt her?"

"I do, but we tend to punish those we love the most. Nina chose my brother over me. She made the wrong choice."

"Your plan isn't going to work. I don't believe that you love Nina. But even if you do, you don't deserve her. Arlo does. He has kept her safe for this long."

I shake my head minutely. "Nina hasn't told you the truth about her stay here, has she?"

Eden's pupils bore into mine as she crosses her arms and leans back in the chair. "She told me enough."

"Let me fill you in on the details she didn't tell you. I saved her life and protected her, just like Arlo did. I healed her body countless times. I provided medical treatment and nursed her back to life. So don't tell me I don't deserve her. I can protect her better than Arlo can."

"Your plan won't work," she repeats.

Her stomach growls, and I grin. "I think my plan will work fine."

I take another bite of my omelete chomping on it vulgarly, taunting her with the food in my open mouth.

Her hand darts to Dierk's plate and snatches the biscuit he left. She shoves the entire thing into her mouth, chews rapidly, and swallows before I have a chance to do anything else.

I lean forward, grinning at her. "You think you won?"

She nods.

"You lost. You showed me you have a weakness. You're not used to going without sustenance. It may take a few hours longer actually to crack you, since you took a bite of food, but you'll still break. You'll tell me where Nina is. You'll betray her, and you'll have to live with yourself forever because of it. I give you three days, tops, before you beg me for food. You're scrappy, but not strong enough."

She huffs and reaches for my omelete. I grab her wrist stopping her.

"I hope you enjoyed that biscuit, because it's the last bite of food you will get."

———

It doesn't take three days for Eden to break.

In fact, it's been almost two weeks, and she hasn't so much as cracked. She's not even close. I've tried food deprivation. Somehow, I know she is getting food from someone. Emilia is the most likely culprit, but I can't prove it.

Eden should be close to death's door. Instead, her legs simply move a little slower when I pull her behind me, her stomach rumbles a little more frequently, and sleep is more necessary.

I tried sleep deprivation, keeping Eden up for days at a time, but losing sleep did not affect her. She became delusional, her words slurred, her body slowed. It was impossible for her to think, much less talk to me, and yet she refused to give up their location.

I threatened beatings. I threatened to rape her. But it didn't scare her. Probably because she thinks I won't follow through with my threat. She thinks she looks too much like Nina for me to beat her.

Nothing works.

It's because I haven't tried the one thing that I know will.

Torture.

I wanted Nina to like me still, instead of despising me, when I got her back, but I'm running out of options. It's time to turn into the monster Eden thinks I am.

She's currently tied to the couch while I shower. I needed some time alone to think, but my hand falls on my cock, stroking it as I let Eden's body saturate my thoughts.

Her dark hair, still smooth and silky despite not washing it in weeks. Her flawless, smooth skin that my hands are about to mark. Her perky breasts with nipples that will harden, despite how hard she tries to hide her attraction. And her tight cunt that will be torn between trying to push me out and drench me, as it pulls me back in.

My erection hardens and lengthens in my hand, ready to take Eden. I smirk as I turn the water off and step out of the shower and out into the living room, not bothering to dry off or even clothe myself.

She doesn't notice me at first or even glance at me. Her eyes are half shut. Her body limp on the couch.

I clear my throat. I want Eden to look at me. I want her to feel terrified about what I'm going to do with her. I want to see the change in her eyes before I rape her.

Her head turns, and her lips slowly drop open. Her eyes go straight to my dick, but I can't tell if she's turned on, disgusted, or indifferent.

I growl. I need to feel Eden's suffering. *Soon enough, I will.*

I walk to her, grab her neck, and climb on top of her, water dripping down onto her. My body presses against hers, and the only thing separating us is my shirt she's wearing and her panties. I clench her throat with my hand.

"This is your last chance, baby. Tell me where to find Nina."

She squeezes her eyes shut, and her lips move, but nothing comes out.

I loosen my grasp.

"No." Her lips curl up into a smile.

I'm not a good person. I've raped plenty of women before. She should believe my threats.

I snarl.

I tighten my hand again watching as the blood drains from her face.

"You're so much prettier when you can't speak."

She doesn't move beneath me or struggle at all. She still thinks I'll stop. I won't.

My other hand ducks under her shirt, running up the length of her body savoring the smooth skin on her belly and up to her hardened nipples. Her body wants me, despite her hatred of me.

"You want me, baby." I flick my thumb across her nipple.

Her cheeks flush, and I loosen my grip on her throat, taunting her. Letting her deny her cravings if she wants, but she can't.

Her head jerks to the side as she bares her teeth and sinks them into the flesh of my hand. I grab her jaw, prying her mouth off my hand before slapping her across the face.

She huffs, breathing heavily in and out as the sting spreads across her face. She's angry now and is finally going to fight back. Good. I need her fighting to find out exactly how strong she is.

"You're nothing more than a rapist. I don't want you. I could never want someone that hurts me as you do. My body is human. It responds automatically to a man's touch. It doesn't mean anything."

I rip her panties down and plunge two fingers inside her, feeling the wetness and spreading it out between her legs so that she can feel how wet she is for me. Her arms fight against my body trying to push me off, but she's barely fighting at all. I've pissed her off, but not enough to become desperate.

"You feel that baby? You're so wet. Wetter than you've ever been before. Aren't you?"

I grab her chin and turn her head toward me. "Answer me!"

"I hate you." Her nostrils flare with each exhale. Her body is tense beneath mine as she does everything she can to keep me from penetrating her shell.

"I'll take that as a yes."

Her hands fight against my chest, trying to get me off. One of her nails sinks into a sensitive spot in my back, releasing a deep growl from my throat. I grab her wrists and lift them above her head, holding them with one hand as she struggles beneath me.

"Last chance. You can stop this beautiful. Tell me where to find Nina, and I'll spare you."

She bites her lip, forcing herself to keep her mouth shut. I don't scare her enough. Even the thought of me raping her isn't enough for her to give up her friend. She's a saint. I'm about to make her feel like a sinner.

I grab her thigh with my free hand and pull her leg wide, as my cock sinks between her legs pulsing at her wet entrance.

I tease her, letting the head of my cock push inside her sex and watch her eyes darken. With rage. Anger. And pleasure.

It's been a long time since she's had a man between her legs and her body is practically pulling me further inside.

I wait three seconds for her to change her mind.

One.

Two. My cock slips further inside.

Three.

My cock drives into her, feeling every inch of her slick interior. I could stay here forever, fucking her.

Her hips buck underneath mine, trying to get free. But all it does is allow me to descend deeper. I close my eyes, letting my body enjoy hers for a moment, before I start tormenting her again until she's crying and willing to give me whatever I want to make me stop. So many different ways and places I could fuck her, make her suffer.

Nina.

No, she's not here. I'm fucking Eden, not Nina.

I close and open my eyes trying to make Nina go away but I can't.

"I chose you, Matteo," Nina says, looking at me with big sad eyes.

"No, you chose Arlo."

She shakes her head. "I chose you..."

Knocking, followed by shouting, brings me back to reality and the dream slowly fades.

Eden is lying beneath me, her eyes wide with concern.

My bedroom door opens, and Maximo sticks his head in. He immediately turns his head away when he spots the two of us.

"Sorry boss, but we need you. We lost three men in a gunfight. Clive and Erick were trying to sell weapons on our territory again and—"

"I'll be right there. Drive the Rolls Royce around to the front, and I'll meet you there."

"Yes, sir," Maximo says, sticking his head back in for half a second to catch another peek. His face flushes red, and he smirks before he runs off to do what I commanded.

"This will have to continue later."

I stand up and release my hands from her, although her leg remains chained to the floor.

She exhales like she has been holding her breath this entire time, while I walk to the bathroom where I left my clothes to shower. I grab my underwear and slip it on, not bothering to wash her slickness off of me. I put on my jeans and T-shirt before grabbing my gun from the counter and stashing it in the back of my jeans. I glance in the mirror.

I punch it without thinking. My knuckles split as the glass digs deep into them. Rage is all my body registers; the pain doesn't even exist. I'm pissed that Maximo interrupted us, but also mad that even if he didn't, I wasn't strong enough to finish torturing her. Nina is messing with my head. I'm not strong enough to abuse her as I should. I didn't do enough to break her. My cock barely touched her. I have to rape her, make her fear for her life. It's the only way.

It's because you're such a pathetic little bitch, my father's voice rings in my ear.

He still has a fucking hold on me even though he's no longer in power. He's gone, or as good as gone. Last time I checked on him, he was recovering in a physical therapy center in Scotland.

I walk back to Eden who is pretending to sleep on the couch so that I'll leave her be.

"Get up."

Her eyes open thinly, but she doesn't move. I grab her arm and jerk her up, tired of her games. I unshackle her, not bothering her to shackle her back to myself. Instead, I twist her arm behind her back and lead her out my bedroom, down the hallway, and down the stairs to the darkest place in the mansion. The dungeon.

"What's going on?"

"I have work to do, and I'm tired of your games. I know that you've been getting food elsewhere. And I know that the food and sleep deprivation aren't doing enough anyway. It's time for Plan B."

"And what's plan B?"

I throw her to the dungeon floor and pull out the needle filled with drugs that will knock her out for at least twenty-four hours.

"No." Her eyes grow big and her body trembles, just enough to be noticeable. She's more afraid than she was a moment ago when my cock was buried inside her.

I should be focused on pushing the needle into Eden's neck, instead of cooking her. All I can think about is her gorgeous lips and beautiful cunt wrapped around my dick.

It gives Eden a chance to run to the door I locked behind me. She grabs the doorknob and shakes it fiercely, trying to pry it open, but it doesn't budge. I march toward her with the syringe in my hand.

"No."

"You don't have a choice. You either tell me where to find Nina, or I'll jab this needle into your neck. You'll stay passed out for hours. Weak and incapable of defending yourself if any of my men decide to get frisky with you. You won't even remember if I raped you or not."

She stares at the needle, and for the first time since she's been here, I can truly see the fear. This is her Achille's heel: being unconscious. But I don't have time to deal with her now. Maybe after getting knocked out again, she'll be ready to talk, but it's clear she is not willing to speak now.

I plunge the needle into her neck as she cries out. She tries to push my hand away, but she only fights for second before her body collapses to the floor.

Her lifeless body is lying on the ground, and I can't help myself. I pick her up and carry her to the bench in the corner of the room. It's not much more comfortable, but at least she's off the dirt. I shouldn't have touched her. I should have left her in the dirt. I don't know why I moved her.

Because Eden is so much like Nina, that's why I.

I walk out of the dungeon and pull the gun I always keep in the back of my pants out as I head to my car. It's time to kill some motherfuckers for daring to cross me.

6

EDEN

MY EYES FLUTTER open and the same familiar headache throbs in the back of my head like last time. My stomach heaves and the dizziness and grogginess consume me. My muscles ache like I just finished running a marathon. Last time I didn't know what was happening to me, but this time I do.

Matteo knocked me out with drugs.

I take my time sitting up, so I don't vomit like last time. I lie in bed for several minutes as my eyes adjust to the light and my body gets used to being awake before I try to sit up.

I don't know how long I was out. Hours? Days? Weeks? It doesn't matter. I don't have access to a calendar or phone telling me what day it is. I can hardly keep track of how long I've been here when I'm conscious.

I very carefully sit up in Matteo's bed. Careful not to move too fast, so I don't get sick.

Surprisingly, I don't feel like throwing up when I sit up. I felt much worse last time. So either my body is getting used to the drugs, or he didn't give me as much as last time.

I close my eyes, trying to regain my strength before I stand up.

Darkness and cold overwhelm me in one memory. Matteo's black eyes before he locked the door, leaving me in the filth.

The dungeon. I remember.

He locked me in the dungeon unconscious and left me there all alone. I don't remember why he was so angry. What did I do to piss him off enough to do that to me again? He's a horrible person; he doesn't need a reason to do monstrous things.

I know one thing: I will do anything not to get drugged again. Well, anything short of telling him where Nina is. But I need a plan.

I thought I had one after Matteo tried taking food and sleep from me. I thought when I found a way to get food and defy him; he would give up and realize I was a dead end. Apparently, he hasn't given up yet.

I need help. My lips curl up. I've made one ally here. I can make plenty more. Eventually, I'll have enough allies to escape or fight back. Maybe I'll find more allies as I did with the first...

———

My stomach rumbles again for the hundredth time today. I've never gone so long without food. It's only been three days but the way my stomach heaves, it feels like torture. If I don't get some food in my system soon, I'm going to become delirious, and I'll tell Matteo whatever he wants.

"I have to go meet Maximo and sign a deal for a weapons trade for next week. Watch her." Matteo undoes the shackle on his wrist and hands it to Dierk who hesitantly attaches it to his arm.

"What am I supposed to do with her?"

"Make sure she doesn't run. And if she tries to, beat her."

We both stare, as Matteo walks away from us, both thinking this is some sort of a joke. He hasn't left me alone with anyone since I got here. He's only worked at his home office. Today, though, he either needs to leave or having me around is getting on his nerves. Matteo is a loner; he likes to be left alone in his thoughts. We don't converse a lot when I'm around; he doesn't like the company. I think I remind him too much of Nina. That, or he's a grumpy ass for no reason.

When I get out of here and talk to Nina again, I need to ask her what happened when she was here. Because apparently, she did a number on Matteo.

My stomach growls again and Dierk gawks at it, like a stomach making noise is a foreign concept to him.

"You hungry?" he asks.

I nod.

"Let's get you some food then. I could eat, too."

I try not to react. My eyes gloss over, and I smile politely. But my heart is beating fast in my chest. My feet are jittering at just the thought of food. And I can't keep my lips from curling up. Matteo forgot to tell Dierk he isn't supposed to feed me or let me sleep. If I play this cool, I might get to eat.

My stomach is going to give me away, though. It's booming loudly now at the thought of getting fed. I try to calm it down by holding my belly gently, but it can't be calmed.

Dierk turns and starts walking toward the kitchen at a much slower pace than I'm used to following Matteo at. I don't like it. Especially not now, when I might be getting food.

We finally make it to the kitchen, after what seems like hours have passed. Lines at Disney World have moved faster than Dierk.

"I'd like a Turkey sandwich with fries," he says to Emelia.

He looks at me, waiting for me to give Emelia my order as well.

"Same," I say, though I really want a Turkey sandwich, fries, a burger, tacos, and a milkshake. I try to act like I haven't eaten in hours instead of days.

The woman's eyes bulge while I stare at her, biting my lip hard, begging her with my entire body to not give me away. To fix me food and not question if she should be feeding me or not.

I don't know how Matteo treats his staff. I've never seen him treat the men who work for him poorly. The worst I've seen him do is raise his voice slightly when he was frustrated with them. I've never seen him hurt them or threaten to kill them or something. But for the most part, I've never seen any of the men who work for him do anything that would deserve punishment. They practically worship him.

I'm not sure if the regular house staff would be immune to any discipline if they were to fuck up. If this cook got caught giving me food when she knew I wasn't allowed to eat, what would Matteo do? Dock her wages? Fire her? Beat her? Or kill her?

I don't know the answer, and I hate making this woman take the risk, but I'm desperate.

She nods and turns toward the grill to start preparing our food.

Dierk turns, takes a few steps, and waits for me to follow him until we are standing side by side. He doesn't go to the main dining room as I expect. Instead, he walks past it to another room, which I realize is an office.

"You okay eating in here? I like having some quiet time to think before things become crazy at night."

I nod, happy not to have to eat in the dining room where any number of people could walk in and remind Dierk he's not supposed to be feeding me.

He slowly walks me over to the small table in the corner of the room where two chairs are seated around it.

He pulls out my chair for me like we are on a date or something.

I smile at him as I take my seat. I try not to let his simple charms eat at my heart. There is a high probability this is all an act. Like a good cop, bad cop routine. Dierk is going to treat me nice so that Matteo can treat me like crap later and I'll let something slip.

"What do you do?" he asks.

I snort.

His eyes wide and his mouth parts questioningly, like he doesn't understand why I could find what he said funny.

"You're serious? I'm a slave in this house, and you want to pretend we are friendly strangers chatting for the first time?"

He rubs his neck with the hand tied to me. He stares at the chain like he's seeing it for the first time and realizes what it means.

"I'm sorry." His eyes show the sadness of the world as he speaks. He leans forward in his chair placing his hands in his lap. "I'm sincerely sorry. I know you don't understand, but I am."

I frown. Dierk can't be serious. I distract myself with the office filled with ancient wood, worn like it was made in a different time, as is the entire house. It looks old-fashioned and regal. The mahogany desk takes up most of the space in the room, leaving enough room for a bookshelf and this small table.

"This is your office, right?" I ask.

He nods.

"Then I don't think your sorrys mean very much. You decided to work for the devil. So you are just as culpable for what happens to me as he is."

A knock startles me.

"Come in," Dierk says, staring at the door past me.

Emelia comes in, carrying two plates of food and my stomach churns. The dizziness in my head aches, knowing soon it could be gone. Soon I might be able to walk straight without swerving. Soon, I might have some strength back.

"Can I bring you anything else?"

"No, thank you," Dierk says.

The woman leaves.

It takes everything inside of me not to dig into my food, stuffing everything on my plate into my mouth in one scoop.

"I know you're hungry. Eat."

I hesitate and peek at Dierk, even though I know I shouldn't. I need to eat as he said.

"You know?" my voice trembles, thinking this is some twisted game.

He nods. "I know Matteo isn't feeding you."

"But you're allowing me to eat? What game are you playing? The food's poisoned or something, isn't it?"

His lips fall, and his body seems to hunch over a little.

He reaches onto my plate, stealing one of my fries and popping them into his mouth. He chews and swallows before I'm satisfied.

I can't wait any longer. I dig into my food as Dierk nibbles on his fries.

"Why? Why be nice to me?" I ask, my mouth full of my turkey sandwich.

He stares out the large window out into the forest below.

"Because I know what it feels like to be hungry."

My mouth drops open a little. Dierk seems to have transformed into a young boy in seconds.

"I went without food many a night when I was a kid. I watched my mother starve to death. My sister cried herself to sleep every night because she was in so much pain from the stomach aches. No one should ever be hungry."

I swallow down the turkey, along with the lump in my throat.

"Thank you."

He nods. "I know Matteo wants you to tell him where Nina is. He still loves her, but he deserves better. She loves Arlo; she will never love Matteo. He needs to move on and do what's best for his family."

I shovel the rest of the fries into my mouth and Dierk places the rest of his food on my plate.

"*Matteo is a caring, devoted man. He's just lost. He's always had his brother. He doesn't have the confidence to operate on his own. He hasn't found his place in the world yet.*"

I frown. "*I don't think Matteo's a very caring man.*"

He takes a deep breath staring at me. "*Maybe you're right. Maybe he isn't a kind man. I don't know. I took this job in high school to put food on the table and ensure my family never goes hungry again. But I can say Matteo is a better boss than Enrico was. That doesn't make Matteo a saint; it makes him better.*"

"*I guess,*" *remembering all of the horrible things Nina told me about Enrico, Matteo's father.*

"*Now, tell me about yourself. I might as well get to know you if I'm risking getting fired for you.*"

I wince. "*You could get fired because of me?*"

He shrugs. "*Maybe. If Enrico was in charge, yes. No one has gotten fired since Matteo took over. But probably.*"

"*You shouldn't have risked it.*" *I don't want another family hurting because of me.*

He laughs. "*You say that now you have a full belly again. I couldn't sit back and watch you wither away.*"

"*You're prolonging the inevitable. Tomorrow Matteo will start starving me again.*"

"*He'll try, but he won't be able to, not when I'm sneaking you food.*"

I smile. "*Thank you. I wasn't sure there was a kind person in this house.*"

"*There are a lot of nice people here. There are a lot of bad people too, though. Now, what do you do for a living when you aren't here?*"

"*I prosecute the bad guys and lock them up in prison.*"

He grins. "*I guess you were right. You do have a better judge of character than I do. Any chance you will spare me when this is all over with?*" *He wiggles his eyebrows, and I laugh.*

"*What makes you think I will make it out alive?*"

"*Because you are strong and resourceful. And despite Matteo being cruel, he's not the worst kind of monster. He won't kill you. Heck, he can't even beat you or rape you as he wants. He's desperate to get answers about a woman he loves, you're the only lead he has to find her, and the best he can do is deprive you of food. I'm pretty sure he left you with me because he knew I couldn't resist feeding you. He's aware of my past.*"

I think for a minute, letting Dierk's view of Matteo in, but I'm not sure it's true. I think Matteo hides his plans from everyone he doesn't fully trust.

"You don't have a clue where Nina and Arlo are?"

He shakes his head. "Not a clue."

I grin. "I will spare you once I escape."

———

Dierk said Matteo has a soft side, that Matteo has some warmth in him, even if the evil hides it. Looking around at where I woke up, I'm beginning to think Dierk might be right. I was drugged in the dungeon, but he didn't leave me there. Instead, he brought me back to his bed.

When I was unconscious, did Matteo sleep next to me in bed or did he sleep on the couch and give up the bed to me? I'm guessing from how I was lying in the middle of the bed, I slept in the bed alone. So he gave up his bed for me, again.

His weakness is Nina, I know that, but could I also be his weakness? I remind him of her, so maybe I can find a way to use that to my advantage. All I know is I won't let him drug me again. I'd rather he starve me. I can't handle giving up substantial portions of my memory.

The door opens, and Matteo steps in, but only to make his presence known as his eyes focus on me.

"Come on. Breakfast is getting cold."

I raise an eyebrow. "Breakfast?"

"Yes, starving you only works when my staff doesn't feed you behind my back."

My heart races. "Your staff didn't—"

His face tenses, and his dark eyes protrude, threatening me. I stop.

"I'm not asking you to rat out who it was. I don't care. I know my employees are loyal to me and I can understand how a woman like you could manipulate them into doing what you want. Now get the fuck up and let's go."

I stand up abruptly, forgetting I'm still weak and need to move slowly. My knees give out, and I grasp for the post at the end of the bed, hoping it will keep me upright. I miss. I prepare for impact, my arms outstretched to catch myself. I don't hit the floor though; Matteo's arms snatch my wrists, holding me up.

He searches my eyes. "Why do I do this?"

I swallow down whatever emotions are creeping up in my throat. Matteo doesn't have to explain himself. I know what he means. *Why does he keep protecting me? Why doesn't he let me fall to the floor? Why does he care at all?* I don't know the answer, but I have a feeling it's the same reason I haven't stolen a knife from the kitchen and jabbed it into his throat while he sleeps. Something unexplainable stops me.

He lifts my body up into his arms, carrying me like a baby. My head instinctually rests against his firm chest. I breathe in, and the chills all over my arms cause all the tiny hairs on my arms to stick up straight.

He notices the goosebumps on my arms and carries me to his closet, before pulling a sweatshirt off one of the hangers. He gently places me down on the bench on one end and holds the sweatshirt above my head. I lift my arms up, and he places it over my arms and head, pulling it down to my waist. He walks back over and pulls a pair of yoga pants off the shelf and bends down in front of my leg. He puts one foot into the pants, then the other, and helps me shimmy them up my bare legs until the pants are on.

I feel much better now that I'm clothed. I don't know why Matteo always has me sleep in my underwear and one of his t-shirts.

"Why?" I ask, confused why he dressed me.

He stands up, seeming taller somehow, and lifts me back into his arms. "You look like Nina, and I like taking care of people. It's a curse."

I frown. He could have fooled me about the taking care of people. He only takes care of me after he drugs me and I literally can't function without him. Dierk is twisted if he thinks Matteo is warmhearted.

He carries me down the hallway to the dining room where two plates of food are already sitting in front of our usual seats.

He leisurely drops me into my seat. None of his men are seated at the table. I glance out the window behind him and realize it's the middle of the day, not morning.

"How long have I been out for?" I ask.

"A few hours. I gave you a much smaller dose."

I exhale. Only a few hours. I'm not sure if I believe him, but I need to if I'm going to keep my sanity.

I start shoveling the eggs and toast into my body without waiting for him to permit me. Despite having at least one hearty meal a day for the past couple of weeks, I'm still starving, especially after not having eaten for however long I was out.

Matteo stares at me, not touching anything but his coffee.

I try to ignore him, but it's impossible to ignore his presence. He's just sitting there, but I can't enjoy the eggs I'm putting in my mouth because all I can think about is him. What he wants, what he's thinking.

"What are you doing?" I ask, my mouth jammed full with toast.

He shakes his head, ignoring my question.

I keep eating. I'll need it to regain strength for whatever ridiculous plan he is scheming next. I watch him out of the corner of my eye, and I can't help but notice he's different. Tired. Worn down.

His eyes are bloodshot like he hasn't slept in a week or is high. His clothes are ragged like he hasn't showered or changed in days. I notice the spots of dirt and blood scattered over his shirt and jeans. It's not a lot, but enough to make him look like he's been through hell and back.

"What happened?" I ask, staring at the blood. I don't know if it is his or someone else's.

He doesn't answer. Instead, he glances past me like I'm not here.

Strange. He usually answers all of my questions. Today though, all I get is silence.

I don't like silence. I know from experience when the men I prosecute become quiet and stop talking, that's when things start happening. They make one last desperate attempt to get what they want. And it's never pretty. Someone ends up hurt or dead.

I need to keep Matteo talking. I need him to go back to the old Matteo, who was solely focused on Nina. He requires focus to keep him going. And I need him to keep his sights on getting Nina back to stay alive long enough to escape.

I eat the last drop of runny eggs with the last piece of bread, sopping up every last drop. I lean back in my chair trying to remain relaxed. Food in my stomach makes me calmer. But it won't last, not with this Matteo.

The old Matteo was predictable, this man sitting at the table next to me is erratic. He's dangerous. A flip has been switched, and I'm not sure how to turn the switch back off.

I have to change my plan. I have to do something daring for a chance to get out of here.

"I'll tell you where Nina is, but I have some things I need in return."

He doesn't move. He doesn't react. This is the one thing he claims he wants above everything else. The thing he kidnapped me for, but he doesn't care.

"She's in Monterey Bay, Jamaica."

I wait for him to answer. For his eyes to grow big or him to grin so widely he can't contain it. Or for him to smirk and let me know he realizes it isn't true. He doesn't do any of these things. He sits in his chair like I don't exist.

I glance around. No one is in the dining room. Most of Matteo's men are gone or are hanging around in their offices or the living room. *If I got up and walked out, would anyone stop me?*

I consider it for a second before I realize it's a stupid idea. Far too risky. If Matteo were to snap to and realize I ran off, he would probably kill me when he found me.

"Did you hear me? I told you where to find your precious Nina."

Nothing.

"Matteo!" I slap him on the cheek. It feels good to have my hand hit his rough face, even though my arms are weak and the hit was more of a light slap. So light that it didn't even make a satisfying sound when our skin touched.

It does earn me a growl and a glare.

I smirk. "Glad to bring you back to the living. Did you hear me?"

"Yes. I'm not deaf."

"You could have fooled me."

"I heard you, but it wasn't worth responding to. It was a lie. We both know it. You want some of your control back. You want to know what's going on so you can try to get one step in front of me. Well, guess what sweetheart? Not everything revolves around you and Nina. Sometimes, I have more important things to worry about."

I wrinkle my brow. "Like what?"

"Nothing that concerns you. You need to shut up. I need to be alone right now, and even though I can't be alone because I have to babysit you, I can at least pretend in the silence."

"You could let me go if you want to be alone."

"I said, shut up!" His voice beams, bouncing off the high ceilings and walls so loudly I'm sure anyone in the house could hear him.

"No."

The anger rolls off his body, but there's something else mixed with it too. I'm playing with fire, but maybe figuring out what is going on is the key to gaining my freedom. I need to know everything I can about Matteo. It's the only way I can be free.

Matteo shoves his uneaten plate of food in front of me.

"Eat. I know you are still hungry and if your mouth is full, maybe you'll stop fucking talking."

Damn it. My stomach aches at the sight of more food. I could use more nourishment. Who knows when my next meal will be.

But it's a distraction. I know that. But it's a diversion that is going to work.

I dig in, filling my belly. It will only work temporarily, and then I'll be back to questioning Matteo every second until he starts speaking.

"Matteo Carini, it's been a long time," a deep voice bellows through the dining room.

I keep shoveling in food as I turn in the direction of the man who has entered. It's not a man I recognize, but I haven't met all of the men who work for Matteo.

"Not long enough," Matteo answers.

The man chuckles and walks over and takes a seat opposite me and next to Matteo. He leans back in his chair, ignoring me completely as he stares at Matteo.

It gives me a chance to study him. He's well dressed in dress pants and a buttoned-down shirt. It fits his body perfectly, like it was hand-made for him. His hair is gelled and his face cleanly shaven. He doesn't look like the rest of the men who are employed by Matteo. They wear clothes to make them look as menacing as possible. Dark jeans, shirts, and jackets. Items they can quickly move in and store weapons in. Not suits meant for an office.

"Your sister is ridiculous," the man says, leaning back in his chair.

Matteo glares at the man. "Careful," he warns.

"What? We're friends. And you know how your sister can be. I came by to ask her to go with me to the ball my family is throwing."

"Just because we are friends doesn't mean you can say anything bad about my sister because she turned you down."

"I didn't say anything mean. I could have called Gia a bitch or cunt or something."

Matteo is going to kill him. They don't appear to be friends to me.

"What do you want Armas?" Matteo growls.

Armas grins at Matteo's foul mood. "You know what I want. The same thing I've wanted for the past couple of years."

"Gia will never go out with you."

"Why not? She should. I'm handsome, charming, have almost as much money as this family. I'm your best friend, so we already have your blessing to date."

"You don't have my permission to date my sister. Not that it matters, because she will never date you."

"Not without some help. Come on Matteo, put in a good word for me."

"And why would I do that?"

"Because we are friends and I have saved your butt plenty of times."

Matteo narrows his eyes. "When? Because all I ever remember you doing was running when I needed your help."

Armas laughs. "They were shooting at us. What was I supposed to do?"

"Stay and fight like a real man."

"And get killed? No, thank you. Where is your brother anyway? He's the one who usually saves your ass."

"None of your business."

Armas cracks his neck side to side. "Why won't Gia go out with me? She is going to my family's ball anyway. You all are. So why won't she go with me?"

Matteo shakes his head. "You are clueless. She won't go out with you because she's in love with another man."

Armas laughs like it's the most ridiculous thing he's ever heard. "You can't be serious. She doesn't fall in love. She's a Carini. Carinis are ruthless, uncaring, and controlling. They don't deal with things as simple as love."

My eyes burn into Matteo. It's not true. Arlo is definitely in love. He gave up his whole family, his entire life to live a life on the run with Nina.

Matteo doesn't mention Arlo. Apparently, no one in town knows Arlo is gone or the reason.

"Well, call it lust then, but Gia is still hung up on the last guy that took her out on a date, so forgive her if she isn't interested in letting you take her out."

Armas sighs and leans back in his chair until his feet go up on the table. As he does, he notices I'm in the room for the first time. A creepy smile slinks up on his face as he gawks at me.

"And what's your name, beautiful?"

I shovel in the last bite. "Eden." I stare at him cautiously, letting him know not to mess with me.

Armas looks to Matteo. "Seriously? You have a slave? I thought the stories were only rumors."

Matteo shrugs. "When will you learn all of the rumors are true?"

Armas cocks his head to the side. "Well, well, it's my lucky day then."

"I don't know why? You have no luck," Matteo says.

Armas turns his head toward me. "You can give me some luck by letting me borrow your slave tonight. It will help me get over your sister."

Matteo crosses his arms across his chest. "And why would I do that? She's mine."

I swallow hard, not sure about this exchange at all or what I want to happen. For one, I want both men to stop referring to me as a slave. And two, I don't know whose side Armas is on. If he takes me, maybe

I can convince him to help me escape. But if not, then I want Matteo to win. Matteo, I understand. Matteo, I know what to expect from him. Armas would be like starting all over. And he might have no problem hurting me unlike, Matteo.

"Because you owe me. And I know your little secret."

"What secret is that?"

"You just told me to trust the rumors. And the rumors are Arlo fell in love with the last slave the family brought home. He's run off with her." He cuts his eyes to me. "I have a feeling this new slave has a lot to do with fixing your little problem. But she doesn't appear too broken to me. Let me have my fun, I might be able to help you, and I'll promise to keep your secret."

Matteo growls and grabs Armas by the collar of his shirt. "Don't threaten me. You know what I'm capable of."

"Not threatening, simply offering my assistance."

Paul, one of Matteo's men, enters the room.

"Sorry to interrupt. There has been another attack," Paul says.

"I'll be right there," Matteo says, dismissing Paul.

He waits until Paul has disappeared before he gets up from the table and jerks Armas back in the chair.

"Babysit her for me, I have to go," Matteo says, walking away.

I watch him walk away from me, and I'm not sure whether to be happy or terrified. With each step he takes, I think he's going to stop, turn around, and tell Armas to go to hell. I think he's going to say I'm his slave and no one else has permission to touch me. Matteo isn't the kind of man who can share easily. He likes being in control.

But he doesn't stop. He doesn't turn around. He doesn't say another word. He leaves me alone with a man who claims to be his friend, but from the short exchange I witnessed, I know he is anything but his friend.

Matteo's gone, and I'm left with a man who is a stranger. I don't know what he wants from me. I don't know what drives him. I don't know what his weaknesses are. I don't know anything about him. I need to tread carefully.

"How long have you known Matteo?" I ask, trying to make light conversation. It might give me some clue to who he is and how to survive until Matteo gets back or better yet, escape.

He smirks. "Since the day I was born. Our families are both rich, old, and know each other well."

"So you sell weapons too?"

He chuckles. "No, we only meddle with legal things. Our family sells wine."

"So you aren't as rich since you don't do illegal things?"

His eyes narrow. "I guess not."

"Are you and Matteo truly friends? Because it seems there is more to your friendship than either of you are saying."

"Does it matter if we are friends or not?"

I shrug. "No reason. I might be able to help you if you are more enemies than friends."

He leans across the table with a smirk on his face. "Oh, yea? And how could you help me?"

"I've been here a month or two now, and I've overheard plenty of secrets I'm sure could help you take Matteo down."

He laughs. "No secrets I don't already know."

"I know his weaknesses. It's how I've ensured he hasn't touched me or hurt me."

He leans back in his chair again and folds his arms across his chest while he raises an eyebrow. "Really? He has a slave he never uses?"

I nod. "He is using me to get his brother back. Help me escape, and you'll cause him more pain than you can imagine."

He stands up and walks around the table to my side and leans against the edge of the table.

"I have a better idea."

I bite my lip and tuck my matted hair behind my ear. "And what's that?"

"I'll fix his problem."

I narrow my eyes not understanding until I see the gleam in his eyes. His eyes darken, his grin widens, and he licks his bottom lip like he's about to devour the most delicious meal he's ever tasted.

"I'm going to rape you."

7

EDEN

Rape.

I've known it was a possibility since Matteo forced me onto his private plane, but I always thought I would be strong enough to stop it from happening. I've taken self-defense classes. I'm smart and know how to find people's weak points and exploit them. I thought I would be able to escape long before anyone even attempted to rape me.

Matteo thought about raping me. I saw the glimmer in his eyes every now and again. He couldn't do it, or at least I don't remember him doing it. Something held him back. I can't rely on the same thing happening with Armas. I don't know him, but from the way he's devouring me, I think he's far more evil than Matteo has ever pretended to be.

I swallow hard.

"You're not going to rape me."

His grin widens. "You're a spitfire, huh? I'm going to enjoy this."

"No, you're going to be sitting with a bag of ice on your balls for a week, recovering from your wounds."

He purses his lips together as he studies me up and down. I don't look like much, not in my weakened state, but it doesn't matter. Let him think I'm delicate and incapable of anything; it will only make it easier for me to escape.

I have to take him down. Matteo is gone, along with all of his men, dealing with whatever latest attack. If I can get past Armas, then I might be free.

I try to decide if I should wait for him to grab me or strike first. My blood is pumping, already full of adrenaline. My legs bounce, and my mouth dries. I feel the fear, but mostly the excitement, at the possibility of being free.

Free.

I never thought I would be begging to be released. I never thought I would have to struggle for it, but that's what I'm going to do. And when I gain it back, I'm going to fight every day to ensure every other innocent, kidnapped person is freed and stays that way.

I can't wait for Armas to try and take even more from me. I have to run. Now.

I ball my hand into a fist, and then I jab it forcefully into his neck as hard as I can. My arms are weaker than usual, but the adrenaline and determination make up for the disability.

He grabs his throat as he struggles to breathe.

I jump out of my chair and start running. I don't shoot out the back of the house. I know what awaits me back there. An immense forest and rolling hills that lead nowhere. I'd be sprinting for days to get to anyone who could help me. I don't have the strength to flee more than a few hours at best.

Instead, I race toward the other side of the house, which leads out to the garage. I need a car if I have a chance to escape.

My legs stumble as I run, like they are going to give out at any moment, but I don't let the fear of falling consume me. Instead, I allow it to drive me forward. I let it fill me.

The fear of failing. The fear of giving up. The fear of what would happen if Armas caught me. The fear of what will happen to Nina if I don't stop Matteo from finding her. I let it all fuel me to make my legs move faster.

I don't know if it's enough. I know I'm not quicker than Matteo. Armas appears fit. He doesn't look like he's had a day of manual labor, unlike Matteo who gets his hands dirty protecting his business on a daily basis. Armas is used to sitting in a corporate office building, away from the action. Hopefully, my fitness will be enough to outrun him.

I don't turn around or glance behind me to see if I'm right. I keep moving, running fast.

I haven't been to the garage. I don't know if Matteo keeps the keys in the cars or nearby. I don't even know how many cars he has in the garage, or if there are any left, but it's my only hope.

I turn down another hallway and see the door at the end that I think leads to the garage.

I can make it.

My feet carry me faster as I fly down the hallway. I grab the door, hurl it open, and flip the light on.

I pause for a single breath when I see more than a dozen cars in the expansive garage. I'm clueless when it comes to cars. I don't know how expensive they all are or how fast they go. I run to the nearest one and fling the door open, begging for the keys to be inside.

Please, please, please.

The car doesn't have a spot to slide the key in. Instead, it has a button you use to start the car. I have no clue where to search to see if there is a key somewhere in the car or not.

I push the button and exhale deeply when the engine roars to life.

I press the clicker at the roof the car, and the garage door opens.

I step on the gas and speed out of the garage, clipping the side mirror of a black car parked near the exit.

I remember the long driveway that leads off the property and I know I'm not anywhere near safety yet, but getting the car makes me feel unstoppable. There is nothing Armas can do at this point to stop me.

The driveway curves and I see Armas. He's standing in the middle of the driveway, his red sports car sits behind him parked sideways across the gravel. Hundred-year-old oak trees line both sides of the road.

He's blocking my exit. There is no way out, except to run him over.

I smirk.

I don't have a problem killing him if it means my freedom. I'll hit him with my car first. Then I'll take his car if that is what I need to do to get out of here.

I step firmly on the gas making my intentions known. Armas can move or get killed.

He turns to his car, opens the back door, and grabs a woman by the arm, jerking her out. He holds her by the arm next to him in front of his car.

I squint trying to get a better look at the woman and realizing it's one of the cooks. She made me breakfast most days. She probably has a family; people that love and depend on her.

Shit.

I keep my foot on the gas, hoping if I play chicken with him long enough he'll move her out of my path. As my car inches closer, I know in my heart, he won't. I'll have to run them over and kill them both if I want a shot at getting free.

Damn it. Damn it. Damn it. I hit the steering wheel trying to figure out what I should do.

I swerve the car just before I hit them, stomping on the brake. The car doesn't stop. I was going too fast.

I squeeze my eyes shut, not wanting to see the tree the car is about to crash into.

My body slams forward, the airbag deploys and launches my body backward, and the air is knocked out of me for the second time since Matteo entered my life. I've never been in a car accident before, and it makes me never want to ride in a car ever again.

All I feel is pain as the airbag slowly deflates. Pain in my head, my stomach, my leg. I should get out of the car and start running, but I can't. I can't move, the pain is intense.

Instead, I have to wait for Armas to come to me. I try to think of what my next plan is and how I can cause the most damage. But at the moment, I'm out of ideas. The self-defense classes I took never covered how to defend yourself against someone when you've spent your night drugged and were in a car accident where you couldn't physically move.

I hear twigs breaking and leaves crunching, his presence looming nearer and nearer.

I close my eyes, pretending I'm anywhere but here. I'm back in my office going over a new case. Or I'm in the courtroom after winning a verdict.

I can't.

I hear the door pop open, and I'm brought right back to reality.

"Good thing I like my women feisty."

I gradually turn my head to him, and give him my worst death stare. "Go to hell."

He grins. "I think I'll fuck you first."

He pushes the airbag down and reaches over me and undoes my seatbelt. He grabs my arms and starts yanking me out of the car.

I cry out.

"My. Leg. Is. Stuck." Each word comes out with a cry of pain. Like somehow talking is making the torment in my leg worse.

"Stop being dramatic and get out of the fucking car," Armas says.

"I can't," I cry again, trying to wrench my leg loose. I glance down and realize the front of the car has smashed in and trapped my leg. There is no way I'm going to be able to get it out, not without damaging my leg or something that can cut the metal.

He grabs me by both shoulders and begins tugging me violently, trying to get me out of the car.

I cry out again. "Stop! My leg is stuck, you idiot!"

"I don't give a fuck." He pulls forcefully, and my skin scrapes across the jagged metal as he heaves me loose.

We topple to the ground.

I don't wait for the agony to stop or to catch my breath. I get up and try to run. My left leg works fine, but my right leg is useless. I collapse to the ground after only a few strides.

I've never broken a bone before, and I never want to again. The pain is fire, burning throughout my entire body. It overwhelms me. I can't budge it. I can't think. I can scarcely exist.

I stare down at my useless limb. I have a huge gash on the top of my shin where blood is spilling out. Not fast enough I'm worried about dying, but enough to warrant going to a hospital to have it cleaned and stitched up. The laceration looks awful, but the damage is much deeper in my leg. My leg is red and swollen. Broken, possibly in multiple places.

My eyes drift up, and Armas is standing over me. His eyes are the darkest I've ever seen, his lips curled up into an evil grin, and his face hot with desire.

My arms start moving as I attempt to crawl away. It's a useless endeavor, but I can't lie here and let him take me.

"You don't give up, do you?"

I ignore him and continue crawling away, despite every movement feeling like I'm getting thrown on a fire and then stabbed repeatedly. *Who knew breaking a bone burned from the inside out?*

My head is jerked back as he grabs my hair.

I scream.

A tear trickles out of my eye, overcoming my effort of doing my damndest to keep in. I hate crying in front of these monsters, but crying is the least of my worries.

He starts dragging me across the rough, gravel road. I strive to grab him to right myself and soften the aching.

I can't move fast enough.

Every pebble, every rock, every stick. I feel it all. And each one is like a knife being thrust into the most sensitive parts of my body.

If Matteo were here, I would be pleading with him to jab me with his needle and give me the drugs to knock me out and make this go away. I would rather give up control than be in this torment for one more second.

He pauses when we get to his car. I glance around for the women whose life I saved when I swerved and hit the tree instead of her. She should be here thanking me or on the phone with the police helping to rescue me, but she is doing neither. She's loyal to Matteo, like everyone else here is.

My heart turns dark. *I should have run her over. I should have saved myself.*

No.

I can't let them win. I can't become as evil as Matteo and Armas are. I will find another way to save myself.

He opens the back door, and tugs savagely on my hair forcing me up onto my healthy leg while my mangled leg dangles uselessly.

"I can't wait to get you back to my place."

———

The car ride to his house is long.

Either because he lives far away from Matteo's mansion or because I'm in writhing pain. But as long as it is, I wish that the car ride would never end. Because I know what is coming when the car finally stops and as much suffering as I'm in now, it will be nothing compared to the torture I will be left with when he rapes me.

I can come back from a broken leg, but I've prosecuted too many rapists. I've met with their victims. Once brutality like that happens to you, you're never the same. For some, it makes some of them stronger. Others debilitated and timid. Either way, it always makes them afraid. Fearing other people. Scared of the violence. Terrified of life.

I don't want to live life afraid of getting raped again. I've spent the entire trip trying to come up with a plan. Some way to escape. I've tried finding a way to fix my leg so that I could run, but that would be impossible even with the best of equipment. I need a doctor.

I'm surprised that Armas was okay with me bleeding all over his fancy leather seats. I guess he feels kidnapping me so that he can rape me makes it worth it.

I've tried thinking back to all my training about how to defend myself against an assaulter, but even if I'm able to do some damage to him, all my instruction was around the fact that I could temporarily injure my assailant while I ran away to get help.

I can't run.

And there is no help coming.

Armas may not be as rich as Matteo, but judging by the mansion buried deep in the woods that the car stopped in front of, Armas has plenty of money. Money buys loyalty and silence.

No one is going to help me.

Armas steps out of the car and slings my door open. I kick with my uninjured leg, trying to fend him off. Adrenaline takes over and helps with the pain.

He seizes my leg, and I fight in his grasp. He yanks my leg, and I'm pulled out of the car. I crash to the ground, not registering much of the new pain. My head hits the door, which should add a headache to the list, but a headache doesn't even register on my pain scale.

"You are just what I need."

He smirks.

Bile rises in my throat as he undresses me with his eyes. He's sick.

I won't let him win.

I narrow in on his crotch and kick with all my might. I hit my target, but it's not enough.

He laughs, a high-pitched annoying sound. He takes a step back as he snaps his fingers.

My eyes search around him, to see who he summoned with the snap of his fingers. A butler? His dogs? I could handle either.

Two men, in dark suits, start running toward us.

Damn it. I can now spot a guard anywhere. Even well dressed guards.

Both men cower by their master's side. He glances down at me, and they both automatically reach down and clutch my arms. I try unsuccessfully to get them off for only a second before they stand me up. I balance on my good leg while I glare at Armas.

"I thought you only dealt with legal things? What would you need men like this for if you were on the straight and narrow? They are experienced in handling women if all they needed was a look to grab me."

Armas steps forward, standing inches from me, now that he has his men to hold me back and I can't do anything to harm him.

"I said my business was lawful; I never said that I wasn't a monster."

"You're a coward. You won't even face me alone. I've got a busted leg, and you still couldn't take me alone."

My stomach churns looking at his devilish grin.

"Don't worry. I'll have you *alone* soon." He glances at the man on my right. "Take her to my bedroom and make sure she's secured with handcuffs."

The man's eyes widen as he stares down at my leg. "I'll confine her, but I don't think it's necessary. She's not going anywhere."

Armas glares at the man, who is going to be punished later for daring to speak out against him. "You need to use the thick handcuffs. She's not as broken as she looks. She will do everything she can to escape, even when there is no hope left."

The man nods and both men start pulling me into the house while I hop on one leg, attempting to keep up instead of getting dragged again.

They pull me inside the house, and I'm overtaken by the smell of sweet flowers. The whole house has vases of fresh flowers everywhere, sitting on almost every hard surface.

A woman lives here. There is no way that Armas would think to have flowers in his house if he lived alone. A tiny glimmer of hope flickers in my heart. If I can find the woman and convince her to help me, then I might have a chance.

I glance at the man that thought it was pointless to tie me up.

"Does Armas live here by himself?"

"Yes."

I frown, not sure if I believe him.

"Ow," I moan. My injured leg hits the bottom step as they start leading me up the stairs.

The men pause, giving me a moment to catch up with them. I do my best to lift my wounded leg up.

"It seems like such a big house for him to live here all alone. And I've never heard of a man that has so many flowers."

The man chuckles. "Trust me. He lives alone except for the staff. The flowers were supposed to be for Gia, but —"

The man stops when the man to my left clears his throat and gives him a look.

I sigh.

The men start moving quickly again, and I struggle to keep up. My leg hits more stairs than I can tolerate and when we reach the top, I collapse in their arms.

They don't let me rest though. It's like a flip has been switched and gone are the men that didn't want to bring me additional pain.

I have no energy left. Nothing left in me to fight with.

I let them drag me, despite the stabbing pain, down the hallway, and into a bedroom.

I can make out the bedroom from behind the dark spots that have formed in my field of vision. There is a bed and some other furniture, but I can't make out what color the items are or any details.

My heart palpates so loudly in my chest that I'm sure both men holding onto me can hear it and feel it. My body trembles in their arms. I blink rapidly trying to clear my head. I'm desperate to figure out a plan to get out of here.

But no matter how many times I blink, my eyes don't uncloud, my head doesn't focus, and the pain doesn't leave my body.

The men start dragging me toward the bed, and I dig the heel of my healthy leg into the ground, trying to stall them until I can come up with a plan. Once I'm tied to the bed, I will have no hope of escaping.

The men exchange glances and pick me up off the floor entirely.

I thrash in their arms determined to escape. They hold my arms and legs tightly, making it almost impossible to kick free. I move my head over to bite them on the arm, but I'm too slow. One of the men grips my head and holds it still.

I can't move.

I can't do anything to prevent this from happening.

"Please, you don't want to do this," I beg. I can't use my body, but maybe I can remind them that they have a soul. That they don't want to work for a devil like Armas.

One man laughs.

"You think we care?"

I bite my bottom lip to keep it from trembling. "Yes, I know you do. I've been held captive for weeks now. I know when a man has a heart or not. You both do. Help me escape. Find the kindheartedness inside you. I'll give you whatever you want if you do."

The second man snickers.

"We don't need your help. We get paid handsomely for the work that we do. Mr. Espocito is a fair employer, better than Mr. Carini. He doesn't ask us to risk our lives as Mr. Carini does. We deal with wine shipments and security. Occasionally, he asks more of us. Things you might call evil and wrong. But it's not wrong. We've learned that bitches like you always deserve what is coming to you."

My eyes widen at the smug expression on his face. *How could I think he had a heart?* No man in Italy has a soul. No one can save me. All these men want is money. They will do anything their masters command of them for it.

They carry me to the bed and toss me down, not caring that I scream when they do. A sharpness shoots from my leg up to my spine as the soft bed hits it, but it feels like a sharp knife instead.

My head is light, and the room spins around, making it impossible for me to fight, as they start holding down my arms and legs. I feel the familiar cold of handcuffs going around my wrists, as my arms are jerked above my head and attached to something. I don't even bother testing the strength of the metal cuffs. If they had used floss to tie my arms up, I still wouldn't be able to break through. I'm that weak.

Metal goes on my left leg, and my right leg is spread wide, but I don't feel the cold I'm expecting.

I stare down at the man looking at my broken leg. He's hesitating to put the last cuff on. He knows it's useless, but his boss commanded it, so after a few seconds of hesitation, he puts it on and attaches my leg to the bed.

I grimace as my broken leg is pulled tight like every other one of my extremities.

The men leave without a word. I close my eyes as I hear the door slam shut.

Sleep. I've never wanted to sleep so much in my life. My body needs rest to attempt to start healing. Maybe if I fall asleep, I'll sleep through the whole thing and have no memory of the rape.

Rape.

The thought of the word causes my stomach to flip in my body. I'm sick. This can't be happening.

I try to take a deep breath, but I can't. My body won't relax. It's on heightened alert. Blood races through my body as my heart pumps way too fast. Nerves fire off, alerting every inch of my body to stay awake and ready. Alerting me that something dangerous is about to happen.

The door opens, and Armas appears in the doorway.

I narrow my eyes at him, as he walks to the edge of the bed. I will not let him see my fear or pain. I may not have a chance of escaping, but I'm going to leave with as much of me intact as possible.

His hand runs over my wound, and I do everything I can to not flinch, but my leg twitches involuntarily trying to escape the discomfort.

He smirks. "It hurts, doesn't it?"

My lips tighten. I won't answer him.

He shakes his head, as his hand trails up my injured leg over my sex and across my stomach to my breast. He squeezes it tightly, attempting to invoke another reaction out of me.

I'm stoic. I don't move. I act like he is shaking my hand, nothing more.

He exhales as his eyes roll back in his head like my reaction is turning him on. "I'm going to enjoy this far too much."

My lips frown before I have a chance to stop them.

His thumb glides up over my lips, and I try to bite him, but he pulls his fingers away before I have the opportunity to.

"I can't believe Matteo hasn't touched you yet. It seems like such a waste."

"He has touched me," I say, hoping if I can convince him Matteo has already had a turn with me, he will lose interest. I doubt it will work, since I already told him he hasn't touched me, but I have to try.

Armas is right, though, about me being lucky so far. I don't fully understand why Matteo hasn't raped me or beat me yet.

His hands move back down to my shirt and rip it in two, revealing my bare breasts. His eyes burn into my plump breasts, before he bends down and takes my nipple into his mouth.

I cry out, and my back tries to sink into the bed, away from his sharp teeth, as he nibbles harshly on my nipple.

"No, he hasn't touched you. No man has been with you for weeks. If Matteo had touched you, you would already be broken. You're the opposite of lost. You are more alive than any woman I've ever had the pleasure of tying up in my bed.

"But don't worry, the hope you feel deep in your belly will soon be gone. I'll shred every bit of attachment you have to this world until you are begging me to die, only then will I return you to Matteo."

He's going to keep me alive. That's the only words I focus on. He doesn't want to kill. He can't kill me, or Matteo would kill him.

Matteo still thinks that he can crack me and convince me to tell him where Nina is. I'm beginning to believe that Armas might be part of that plan. Once he's done with me, he's right though, I'll be begging for death, and I'll give Matteo whatever he wants.

Blood pours out of my lip, into my mouth, as I bite down on my lip while Armas takes my nipple in between his teeth again. He's cruel, treating me like an object that he can do what he pleases with.

He removes his shirt to reveal his muscular body. He has a fit body, but it's nothing like Matteo's. I close my eyes, hating myself for comparing his body to Matteo's. Both men are evil. The fact that they both have hot bodies is irrelevant. It doesn't make me want to fuck them.

Hands tighten around my neck so that I can't breathe.

"Open your eyes."

I try to hold out, but I need to breathe.

I open my eyes.

"Good girl."

He stands back and pushes his pants and boxer briefs down. "Like what you see?"

I turn away in disgust.

"Look at me bitch," he says, as his hand grabs my neck again, forcing my head to turn back to him.

He smirks. "You like my body. Your pussy is begging to feel a man again."

He's insane. There is no way I could feel anything positive about this man, not even lust. My leg is shattered thanks to him. My body is tied up, and he's about to rape me against my will.

I spit in his face. His hand crashes against my face. He doesn't slap me like I was expecting. His fist was tightly balled as he punched me.

Dots. All I can see are black spots, no matter if my eyes are open or closed. My head throbs so severely that I don't want to move it. I don't even want to think.

His hands are at my pants, and my body trembles, as he rips my pants off.

I'm naked. Exposed. I've never felt so vulnerable in my life. Not even when Matteo kidnapped me. This man is going to rape me. Nothing is stopping him.

I try to squeeze my legs together, but his hands grip my thighs, pushing me wide, while his body settles in between my legs. I can feel the head of his erection pushing at my entrance, and a tear trickles down my cheek.

My arms thrash against the restraints, but I'm tied up so tightly that I can only wiggle them an inch.

My body tries to twist away from him, but his hand crashes down on my chest, putting his entire body weight on my chest.

I can't breathe. I try to move my lungs up and down to let air in, but I can't. His hand is pressing down too hard.

I stop moving. I stop trying.

Only then does he let his hands up enough so that a little air pushes into my lungs.

I don't want the air anymore. I want to stop breathing, stop living. I won't survive this.

No.

He doesn't get to win.

I will survive this.

My eyes fly open. He's going to have to look me in the eye when he rapes me. He's going to see the anger that he's causing instead of the pain. He'll see the rage that he created, and he'll know that I will spend the rest of my life coming after him. That I won't let him rest until I've hurt him like he's hurt me, and then I'll kill him.

I swear I see a bit of hesitation and fear in his eyes when he sees the fire in mine when I open them, but it's probably my imagination.

I need him to fear me to get through this. I need to fight him. And if I can't do that with my body, I will with my eyes. I'll let him know what's coming to him when I get out of these restraints. Matteo used to be my number one target, but now it's Armas.

His head drops, and he slobbers down my neck. It's because he can't look me in the eyes, the coward.

He thrusts his cock inside me with his face still buried in my neck. It's probably a good thing that he's not looking at me though, because I can't stay strong now that his cock is inside me. My eyes water and I close them to keep the tears in.

He groans as he sinks deeper, while tears burn my eyes.

He won.

I may eventually get free and kill him, but right now, he won.

"You're mine, bitch. You're nothing but a slave. You're going to spend the rest of your week tied to my bed so that I can come fuck you whenever I want. You are going to be black and blue. By the end of the week, your body will be begging for my cock."

His cock thrust in and out of me and my insides burn, my stomach aches, and vile shoots up my throat.

I hate him.

I hate him more than all the criminals I've locked up. Armas is the worst. I will make him pay for what he's doing to me.

My eyes gloss over as I try to pretend I'm anywhere but here. I try to imagine myself in the courtroom. My brain won't go there though.

I try to imagine I'm on a beach, the warm saltwater stinging my eyes, and that's why they cry. But my mind knows it isn't real.

I try to imagine Nina. I pretend we are back in college and are about to head out for a night of drinking and hitting on boys. But it only makes the tears come faster, because if I can't save myself, how am I going to protect Nina?

My mind goes to Matteo. His dark locks, his intense gaze, his sculpted body. I want to blame him for this. If he hadn't stolen me, then I wouldn't be here getting raped.

But I don't hold him responsible. Because going back to him is going to feel like a sanctuary compared to where I am right now.

8

MATTEO

It was a false alarm.

The men thought they were being set up and about to be ambushed. But they weren't. Instead, the client they were delivering weapons to changed the location and snuck up on them to try to keep their secrecy.

I had a stern talking with the client to let him know we won't be working with him again. We set the rules, not him. He doesn't get to change the location of the drop. We do. What he did was unacceptable and put everyone at risk.

We have been under attack numerous times lately. It's put everyone on edge. I know it's Clive and Erick behind the attacks.

They are still upset about us taking Nina from them. And they are testing me. I'm the new leader of the Carini family, and they want to find out what they can and can't get away with. They are trying to push me and take over some of my turf.

I won't let them. Soon, they will find out I'm more ruthless than my father when it comes to protecting my own. I will need to go on the offensive to prove it to them and end this nonsense.

My phone buzzes in my pocket, as I walk back from the wooded area to where my car is parked along the street.

"Yes," I answer, snapping harder than I mean to. I'm in a foul mood. I don't know what to do with Eden and having to deal with this idiot only made my temper worse.

"Sorry to bother you, sir. I wanted to let you know we saw Armas drive Eden off the grounds and I thought you'd like to be aware."

I growl.

"How could you let this happen?"

He doesn't answer. I already know how. I left one guard, and I've threatened them all with their lives when only one guard is on duty to never leave the premises if a Carini is still in the house. Gia must be home. She needs protection. It's my fault for calling my men here to defend our turf, without leaving more behind to protect what's mine.

I end the call, shove the phone back into my pocket, and I run to my car. I hop in, speeding off as my wheels squeal against the pavement.

Thoughts of what Armas could be doing to Eden right now cloud my head. His lips on hers. His dick inside her tight cunt, making her cry out while he breaks her.

All the things I wanted to do to her and barely got a taste of. Things that I could never entirely go through with myself.

I thought it was what I wanted. I couldn't break Eden myself so why not let Armas do the dirty work? But now that it is happening, it's not what I want.

And I need to teach him a lesson for thinking he could take what's mine off my property. He knows I'm going to retaliate for breaking my rules.

I'm not far from his house. Assuming that's where Armas has taken Eden. Maybe I can save her before anything happens.

I press my foot down all the way on the gas, my car speeds up, and I hit the apex of each of the turns that weave through the woods. I shouldn't drive so fast, not on these roads. But I push my limits to get to his house faster.

Ten minutes. That's how long it takes me, when usually it would take more than twenty. The gate to Armas's property is closed, but it's nothing my car can't handle.

I rev the engine, going full speed again, breaking the flimsy lock on the gate as my car bursts through it. I don't stop until my car is right outside the side door leading into the house.

I jump out of the car and draw my gun. Armas doesn't deal with weapons or anything illegal, but he has security guards who wouldn't have any difficulty shooting me. I didn't bring any backup of my own. I considered it, but I don't need the help. And I don't want any witnesses for what I decide to do Armas. My men have no problem with torture or killing, but they may give my actions pause when it comes to innocent rich men who could have been their boss instead of me.

"Sir, Armas is busy at the moment. If you'd like to come back later, I'll let him know you came by," one of his security guards says, coming outside.

God, he needs to train his men better. You shoot first, ask questions later.

He didn't notice my gun yet, so I let it hang in my hand casually to my side.

I smile as I walk up to him like I want to give him a message to deliver to Armas. When I'm a foot away, I draw my gun again aiming it at his head.

He puts his hands up in surrender.

I shake my head. *Idiot.*

"Where is Eden?"

"Who?"

"Don't act dumb. Where is Eden? The woman Armas stole from me this morning. I know he brought her here."

The man stares down at my gun like he's never had a gun aimed at him before.

I roll my eyes. You never hire someone who hasn't at the very least had a gun aimed at them. Preferably you want someone who has been shot before. That way you know they understand the risks and are adequately trained.

I see another man step out, out of the corner of my eye. I shoot him in the chest without a second thought. The man drops to the floor.

"How many other guards does Armas have?"

The man's eyes cut to the man lying lifeless on the floor behind him. "It's just the two of us."

"Don't lie to me or I'll kill you, like I did him."

The man swallows. "I'm not lying."

"Good. Now, where is Eden?"

He glances up. "She's upstairs in Armas' bedroom. It's the third bedroom on the left."

I smirk. "Good boy." I strike him hard in the head with the end of my gun. His body falls to the floor as I race inside. I cough on the intense flowery smell when I enter his house. If he doesn't rape her, he's going to smother her to death with the scent of roses.

I take the stairs two at a time as I climb up the grand staircase. The staircase swerves, taking up most of the space in the entryway. It's meant to be magnificent, the centerpiece of the room, but I have three staircases that trump this one in size and stature.

I get to the top of the stairs and intently listen as I slink down the hallway as quietly as I can. I don't want Armas to know I'm here until I want him to know.

I don't hear anything as I walk down the hallway counting the doors as I go.

One.

Two.

Three.

I grab the doorknob as I lean against the door listening.

Nothing.

I draw my gun ready to kill in a second if I need to.

I push the door open. The room is dark, I flick on the lights, but I already know what I'm going to find. Nothing. It's empty.

The bastard lied to me. I should have killed him.

Eden screams.

I turn and run toward her screams. The fourth door. I kick the door open without thinking about anything other than getting to Eden as fast as possible.

Armas is on top of Eden when I enter the room. He doesn't even turn his head to me. Either because he didn't hear me enter, or because he believes I'm a member of his staff, who is coming to check on him and will quickly leave.

My eyes go to Eden. All I can see though are her arms and legs tied to the bed. Her screams and cries pierce my heart, begging me to protect her.

I respond, running to the bed without thinking. I may not be any better than Armas is, but if anyone is going to lay a hand on her, it's going to be me.

Stowing my gun in my waistband, I grab Armas by the neck and fling him against the far wall as easily as I would tossing a ball. I'm much stronger than he is, and in my pent up state, he's not a match for me at all.

Anger.

Rage.

Pain.

The emotions alight deep in my belly and spread like fire through my entire body when I see Eden. I've never been so mad in all my life. I've never felt such rage. My body is red, my arms shake, unable to keep my frustration inside.

Eden is tied to the bed by her arms and legs with shackles to the frame of the bed designed with loops to attach rope or chains. It's clear Armas has done this to women before.

She's naked. Nothing I haven't already seen plenty of times before, but seeing her now makes me ache, my cock throbs against the zipper of my jeans. It makes me want to finish the job that I didn't get to finish.

It's been a long time since I've had a woman. Months. Usually, it isn't a problem, but when I look at her body, I'm tempted to pull out my cock and fuck her right here, right now.

Her eyes look straight at me, but she doesn't react. She doesn't think this is real. She thinks she's dreaming I came and saved her. She must have been desperate to get away from Armas to be fantasizing about me protecting her.

I expect her to look broken, lost, gone. But her eyes don't show that. She still has hope and fight. Her body doesn't seem beaten, other than some redness on her breasts. He's barely fucked her or touched her. No more than I did before.

My eyes continue to inspect her body until I see her leg.

Her entire leg is red and swollen with black and blue bruises all up and down it. But the coloring isn't what has me concerned. There is a large gash on the top of her shin still actively bleeding and filled with dirt and debris. It looks bad. Most likely broken.

Red. It's all I see and feel as I turn from Eden to Armas, who is smirking at me in the corner of the room. He slowly gets to his feet, wiping the blood off his forehead. I must have caused the blood when he I threw him across the room.

"Jealous much? I was having a taste and helping to break her in so she would be ready for you." Armas continues to smirk as he stares at Eden on the bed.

"She wasn't yours to touch."

He cocks his head to the side as his eyes stay locked on Eden, looking at her like he wants to devour her.

"You left her with me. You gave me power to do what I pleased with her when you left. What is she to you that you would be this upset anyway? She's only a slave."

My fist pulls back and then makes contact, hard, with the side of his jaw. His face whips around and I can see redness forming where my fist hit him, but it's not enough. Not nearly enough.

His eyes darken when he looks back at me, holding his face. He doesn't dare try to fight me back. I've kicked his ass before, and I'll kick it again.

"What the hell man?" he says.

"Eden's mine." My fist hits his face again, and this time it knocks him off balance enough so when I hit him again, he falls to the floor.

I can't think of anything other than causing him as much agony as possible for what he did to Eden. He touched her. Raped her. And broke her fucking leg. He doesn't deserve to keep breathing.

I punch him again and again, each strike harder than the previous. He holds up his hands trying to block my punches at first, but eventually, his hands fall to the side as does his body.

I can't stop though. I have to make Armas pay for what he did to

Eden. I don't understand why I feel this way. Eden is nothing to me but the key to getting Nina and Arlo back. But my stomach is in knots and my body filled with rage as I pound into his flesh over and over.

My fists are raw and bleeding, but I don't feel the pain. Only the anger. It consumes every muscle in my body, so all I can do or think about is making Armas pay.

Eden groans and I stop.

I turn to her immediately, ignoring the bloody, lifeless mess on the floor in front of me.

I run to her body and cradle her head in my hands.

"Matteo? Are you really here?" she asks, her voice trembling.

I nod. "Yes, I'm getting you out of here."

She rapidly blinks like she's trying to make me go away by blinking, but when I don't, she smiles enough to melt the anger that has taken over me.

She pulls on the shackles holding her down on the bed. My eyes go to the bedside table where I find the key. I grab it and unlock each shackle, moving quickly and efficiently.

Her eyes stay with me each time I move, her eyes narrowed like she doesn't understand what I'm doing.

She doesn't have to understand. I don't even understand what I'm doing. She can't stay here. And I won't let anything like this ever happen again.

When I've removed every single shackle from her extremities, I help her sit up. Then I gather a blanket draped over a chair in the corner of the room and wrap it around her body.

She winces when the fabric touches her leg.

I scoop her up as gingerly as I can in my arms.

"What are you doing?" she asks.

"You can't walk. I'm getting you out of here and taking you where it's safe."

I expect her to argue with me, that my own home is no safer than this place is.

She doesn't.

Instead, her head falls against my chest as her body shakes gently in my arms. The adrenaline now controlling her body has no place to go, making her tremble.

I hold her tighter against my body, ensuring she can't see Armas's dead body as I take her out of the room.

My gun is still tucked into the back of my pants as I leave the room and run down the hallway and the stairs. It's not the smartest move I've ever made, but I doubt Armas has many more guards on duty. And if he does, I don't expect them to be any smarter or more adept than the other guards I ran into.

I stare intently at Eden as I carry her out of the house, not understanding what spell she currently has over me. My erection is still stiff in my pants. My body still aches to toss her in the back of the car and rape her, now. But something stops me.

The need to take care of her. To heal her. Help her.

That's my biggest weakness. I can't stop helping others. And I'll most likely hate myself for taking care of her instead of taking care of my own needs.

Rescuing her made me a target. I shouldn't have messed with one of the wealthiest families in Italy. Now I'll have to deal with the rest of his family once they find out what I did.

I get to my car, but it barely has a second row. I start to put her in the backseat, but I don't want to let her go. It's not far back to my house, but for her, it will seem like an eternity in her condition. And I want to keep an eye on her leg to make sure she's still awake.

I reach into my back pocket and pull out my cell phone while I hold her with my other arm. Even when she is dead weight and barely able to hold herself up, she's still light in my arms.

I dial the number for Maximo.

"Yes, Matteo."

"I need you to get to Armas' place with an SUV as fast as you can and bring someone with you to drive back the sports car."

"Is everything okay, sir?"

"Yes, hurry."

"I'm five minutes away."

I end the call and pocket my phone.

Eden's eyes flicker, and I can't help but stroke the hair away from her face. I've grown soft. It's only because she reminds me so much of

Nina. That's not true, because, besides her looks and strength, she is the opposite of Nina.

Nina was soft and caring. She cared too deeply about others and was obsessed with Arlo and me. Eden is harsh. She's faced the cruel world before, and it's made her icy and closed off. She doesn't care about others as much as she cares about protecting Nina and herself.

She swallows as she stares at me and I swear I see her blush a little as her eyes rake down my body.

"How are you feeling?"

"My leg hurts a lot."

I nod. "And everything else?" I ask, unable to ask if he left permanent scars when he raped her or if he even got that far. I couldn't tell from where I was standing or when I pulled him off her. I didn't leave scars when I touched her, but I'm not sure if it's because she has no memory of it or because I didn't go far enough.

She purses her lips together as she takes her time answering me. "I'll heal."

My stomach churns. Armas did rape her; she's just not telling me. Most likely, she doesn't want to admit it to herself either. She'll have to face it eventually. But in the meantime, I'll play along and pretend the only problem that needs healing is her leg.

Maximo drives up, stopping feet from me. I pull the back door open and slide her body inside before I climb in after her. I let her head rest in my lap.

One of the men runs to my car to drive it home, while Maximo starts driving us toward my house.

The car hits a bump in the road, and Eden moans loudly, louder than I expected.

"You okay?" I ask.

She doesn't answer right away. "Yes," she finally breathes. "The pain is getting worse for some reason."

I stroke her hair. "The adrenaline pumping through you, that helped you survived, is leaving your body. It was masking some of the pain."

As we speed around another corner, she closes her eyes and winces. A tear rolls down her cheek and then another, despite her eyes being shut tight. Her face is turning redder every second. Her body shaking faster in my arms trying to distract her from her agony.

There is nothing I can do to comfort her, except hold her.

"Do you..." she starts and then stops as the discomfort overtakes her.

"Shhh. Try to relax. We will be back soon."

I glance down at her wound to make sure the bleeding hasn't gotten worse. It hasn't. I considered tying a tourniquet around it but decided against it, when I knew how much torture it would cause her, and the bleeding wasn't strong enough to warrant it anyway.

There is nothing I can do to help her until we get back and I have the proper medical supplies to help her.

"Do you have any of the drugs you've used to knock me out on you?" she asks, her voice stronger than before.

My eyes widen, and my heart stops. She wouldn't ask me if she wasn't desperate for relief. She's made it clear how much she hates it when I knock her out. The lack of control makes it impossible for her to handle when she wakes back up.

"No, I don't have any on me."

She lifts her head a little and turns to look at me, her eyes imploring me for solace.

"Please, I'm begging you, please help me. Knock me out. Make me forget. Make the pain go away. I can't stand it."

I swallow hard, uncomfortable with the way she's looking at me when I know there is nothing I can do to alleviate her pain.

"You can dig through my pockets if it makes you feel better, but I don't have any of the drugs on me."

Her tears stream down her face as she realizes she's going to have to wait for painkillers.

"Make the pain stop. Please. I know you know how."

I've seen plenty of people in pain before. Hell, I've caused most people as much or more suffering than she is currently dealing with. I've heard their cries for me to bring them relief. And the only way I ever did was with a bullet through their head.

She looks at my pants and her hands claw at my waist searching for the gun she knows is stored there.

Damn it.

She's more fucked up in the leg then I realized. Or being raped by Armas screwed up her head worse than I thought it did.

She wants me to kill her. I won't let her give up so quickly.

"I'm not going to kill you!"

She stops, her face stoic like I slapped her.

"I don't want you to kill me."

"You don't? Then why do you look like you've given up and you are reaching for my gun?"

"Because I want you to knock me out as you did to Saul. Make the pain go away until you get me some pain medication. If you don't, I'm going to chew my leg off to make it stop."

I smirk and don't tell her chewing her leg off would only make the pain unbearable.

"Please," she begs.

Knocking her unconscious will make her suffering worse later. That healing will take longer. My heart is too infatuated with her at the moment to disappoint her, so I keep quiet.

I don't use my gun like she wants me to. It wouldn't take much to knock her out. Not in her current state.

I look over to Maximo, making Eden follows my gaze to him. I wait until her head is turned to him and then I hit her hard across the back of her head. I catch her as her head drops into my arms.

Maximo looks in the rearview mirror, judging me with his eyes, but he doesn't say anything.

I stroke her cheek again, pretending she fell asleep instead of me striking her.

"Is she going to be okay?" Maximo asks.

I nod. "She's going to be better than okay."

"Do we need to go to the hospital first? We can go to Dr. Pietri; he won't question it. He owes us."

I stare down at Eden's leg for a long time. I'm sure it's broken. A woman as strong as Eden wouldn't cry in pain like that at anything less than broken. It's probably shattered.

I know how to treat most wounds and ailments. I've healed most of Arlo's injuries without any issues. I'm not sure if I can repair Eden's leg if it is broken in more than one place and requires surgery.

She could never walk properly again if I don't take her to the hospital.

But I can't. I don't want to give her up. She may think I'm her savior at the moment, but I'm not. I'm still a monster.

"No. Take us home."

Maximo doesn't question me again. He knows the decision I made might lead to her death and he doesn't care. Eden is mine to do with what I want. I stole her. Saving her was only to reclaim her as mine, not because I cared or have a heart. She'll realize soon enough when she'll never be able to walk again. At least I won't have to worry about her running away from me.

9

EDEN

MY EYES flicker wide as the sharp pain in my leg wakes me up. My head is pounding, telling me not to dare move my head off the pillow. I've been drugged enough times now to know the familiar feeling. Although, this time it's different. Achier than before.

Matteo.

He's hovering over my leg; his hands gloved as he inspects it. He stops when he sees I'm awake. He takes the gloves off and tosses them to the floor as he sits on the edge of the bed.

"How are you feeling?"

"Like I was in a car accident and raped."

He winces when I say the word rape. I don't understand why he would care. That's why he left me with Armas in the first place, so he would rape me and do the dirty work Matteo was incapable of doing.

"So you remember what happened?"

I close my eyes as the images start flooding back. Me slamming my car into a tree, Armas taking me to his place and raping me, Matteo rescuing me, and then striking me in the head as I asked.

I rub my head on the back and find the bump that has formed.

He narrows my eyes. "Still happy I knocked you out?"

"Yes," I say, despite the agony I'm in now.

He turns from my eyes to give my leg his attention again.

"It's bad, isn't it?" I ask.

He doesn't respond. Instead, he moves down the length of the bed until he's resting next to my leg.

"Can you move your toes?"

My eyes widen at his request. I don't want even to try to move a single part of my leg.

"That's what I thought." He peers back into my eyes trying to tell me something he won't tell me with his words.

I swallow hard as a lump creeps up my throat. My mouth runs dry as Matteo stares at me like I'm the most important thing in his world.

"It's broken."

I bite my lip to keep from smiling. He thinks he's delivered me bad news, but it isn't something I didn't already know. And telling me I have a broken bone is nothing when I was just violated by a man. Had his mouth on my skin. His cock inside me.

"I guessed that."

He nods.

"Can it be fixed?" I ask, hoping he will offer to take me to the hospital or at least bring a doctor to me. For one, it gives me a tiny chance at escaping from Matteo. Although, at the moment, I don't feel like running. Him rescuing me from my nightmare gave me a little bit of hope and respect for him. And two, I would love to have a working leg again, and the only way that can happen is with a doctor's help.

"Yes, but it's going to be painful." He gives me a warning look.

My heart thumps wildly in my chest as I bask in his eyes. I could get lost in them forever.

I shake my head. What's happening to me? I must be feeling guilty for him saving me, that's it.

"A doctor?"

He shakes his head. "No, your leg doesn't need surgery. It was a clean break. It needs realigning, the wound cleaned up and sewed shut, and plenty of rest. Your body will do the rest."

I stare at him wide-eyed. It's the second time he's shocked me with his knowledge of medical information. But I don't know whether I believe him.

"Do you trust me?"

I smirk.

He grins. "That's a no."

I nod.

He turns his attention to my leg.

"But I don't have much of a choice, do I? Either trust you or die."

His face scrunches like he smelled something rotten "Yes, you don't have an option but to trust me."

"Okay then." My eyes flutter down at my leg that looks rotten. I've seen worse at crime scenes, but it still isn't pleasant to look at.

He puts on some gloves and sits on the chair he was sitting on to exam my leg before I woke up. I notice the small table filled with gauze, needles, tweezers, and viles of medications.

"I need to realign the bone as best as I can to help your tibia and fibula heal. Then I will clean the wound and stitch it up before attaching a stent to your leg to keep it from moving."

I nod. His words make sense, but it isn't any more reassuring.

"It's going to hurt. Worse than before."

I swallow hard.

"I can give you some numbing shots to your leg, but it will only work on the surface. Or I can knock you out again with the drugs, so you don't feel anything until I'm done."

"Also so I don't remember anything either."

He nods. His eyes glare into mine waiting for my decision. Before I would have said give me the drugs. Make the pain go away. Make me forget.

But now, I need to be awake. I need to watch what he does to my leg because if he fucks it up, I want to remember what he did when I finally make it to a doctor.

"Give me the local injection."

He doesn't wait for me to tell him I'm sure I don't want to be unconscious. He takes the needle and carefully jabs it into my shin.

It burns slightly and then warms as the liquid fills my skin. He moves the needle to several different places, always slowing down his movements as the needle pierces my skin. I don't know why he cares if it hurts me. He could be using this against me, to torture me to find out where Nina is, but for some reason, he isn't.

He sets the needle back down on the table next to him and then gives me a look that tells me to brace myself.

I fist the sheets I'm lying on. My heart races but not in anticipation of the pain. It races when his hands touch my skin.

"Tell me something about yourself. What do you do for a living? Where is your favorite place to travel? What are your hobbies?"

My mouth drops open. He can't seriously care about any of the answers to those questions.

He waits. No longer touching me or preparing any of his supplies.

I sigh. "I'm a prosecutor. I deal mostly with murder and rape cases. I prosecute the bad guys and lock them away forever."

He smirks.

"I don't have a favorite place to travel. I've turned into a bit of a homebody since everything that happened with Nina. And my hobbies, I used to enjoy paint—"

He rips my leg off. I know it. The pain sears through my leg and then cascades through my body like a hurricane does a city. Shattering everything in its path and leaving nothing left untouched. My entire body is screaming for relief from whatever trauma he caused. I shouldn't have trusted him.

"Motherfucker!" I scream as I bend down to grab my leg, hoping to bring it some comfort. The spots return over my eyes, and my head is so light I'm afraid it's going to drift away from my body.

"Eden, breathe."

I can't.

The voice is crazy if it thinks I can focus on anything as silly as breathing. I can't exist.

Hands rest on my shoulder and chest as I'm gently pushed back down on the pillows behind me.

"Take a deep breath," the voice commands, again more sternly.

I can't. Why can't the voice get that?

"In...," his hands press against my chest reminding my lungs to breath. The traitors take a breath.

"Now out..." his hands guide my lungs again as I slowly exhale.

"In..." I take a breath in.

"And out..."

I open my eyes that I didn't realize I had shut and the pain is still there, but manageable. I don't feel like I'm about to die anymore, more like slow torture that may never stop.

"Tha—" I stop. I'm not going to thank him.

He slinks back from me to his chair. "I hoped taking your mind off what I was about to do would help. Apparently, I was wrong."

I bite my lip.

"The worst part is over. I'll rinse out the wound and then close it with stitches. The novocaine I gave you earlier should make it, so you hardly feel a thing."

I nod.

He begins to work, cleaning out the wound, flushing it with a clear liquid. When he gets the needle out, I close my eyes and grab the sheets again, preparing for a sharp sting. It never comes.

I open my eyes, shocked as I watch him thread the needle through my skin as easily as he would cloth. He's done this before. He's too experienced not to have.

"I can't feel a thing."

His lips curl up a little, in what could be a smile if it wasn't for this menacing glare.

"I used to stitch my brother up on an almost weekly basis. I got skilled at it. Now I'm always working on one of the guy's wounds. It beats paying a doctor's bill every other week, and most of the time, the wounds couldn't wait until we got them to the doctor anyway."

I continue to watch him sew up my leg. Not sure what to say or how to feel. My emotions are all over the place. *Should I be thankful? Angry? Upset?*

I feel everything and more.

He finally stops sewing and leans back to take a look at his work.

"If it isn't significantly better in a week, I'll take you to the doctor myself."

I'm shocked at his words. "Thank you," I say without thinking.

His mouth drops open.

Moments pass while we both sit staring at each other without speaking, hardly breathing. I have no doubt now he will keep his word and take me to the doctor if my leg doesn't heal. But he's done such a good job I'm not sure I can even hope for that to happen. Even if I were to go to a doctor, I have little hope for escape.

He clears his throat. "I'm going to attach this stent to your leg to help keep the bone in the correct position and to remind you not to move your leg."

I nod and watch as he removes his gloves before he attaches the stent to the side of my leg with gauze. His hands are rough and calloused as they graze my skin causing tiny goosebumps to pop up.

When he's finished, he places a pillow under my leg so that it's raised. Then he walks behind him to the closet and comes back with a thick blanket to drape over me.

I gulp when he stops just inches from my body.

"You should get some rest. I'll bring you some food and more pain pills soon."

I nod, not willing to say thank you twice. Not to him.

He turns and walks away. And the ache deep in my stomach grows stronger. I don't need any other physical comforts right now. He's made me entirely comfortable on his bed. The physical pain is all but a distant memory. But I still have needs, questions that haven't been answered, and I won't be able to get any rest without him answering.

"Why did you save me?" I blurt out.

He pauses and turns his head, but not his entire body.

"Because you weren't Armas' to take."

"Why didn't you rape me?"

He hesitates. "Who says I won't?"

I swallow. Because he would have already raped me if that was his plan. He couldn't even if he wanted to. No man that would spend that much time fixing my leg would hurt me.

I narrow my eyes and firm my stare. "You won't."

He laughs, and it sends chills down my arms, the only part of me not covered by the covers. "Don't mistake me for someone who cares about you. I don't. I'm cursed with the ability to heal, that's all. And you're mine. I wasn't about to let another man touch you. Don't think

I won't rape you, I will. Unlike Armas, I prefer my woman to have the ability to fight back."

"What happened to Armas? Will he try to come after me again?"

"No."

His lips are tight, his jaw set as he speaks, but he doesn't offer me up a further explanation.

"I'm going to need more assurances than that."

He frowns as he runs his hand through his hair and finally faces me squarely on. His eyes peer into mine, and I stop breathing again. My body reacting to him unwillingly.

"He's dead," he says, deadpanned like he was telling me the weather.

"How?"

"I killed him. Beat him to death for touching what is mine. I'll make sure everyone else in his family is either dead or made to believe Armas deserved to be killed. No one will ever take you again. You're mine."

My nipples harden, my lips part, and I feel a stirring deep in my belly begging to feel the erection I swear I see when I glance down at his crotch. If he notices me staring he doesn't comment. Instead, he turns and strides out of the room, not bothering to tie me up or even lock the door. I couldn't get far anyway, not with my leg the way it is even if I tried to crawl.

My body continues to ache, and I throb between my legs, needing relief.

The trauma from the car accident and rape must have fucked with my mind. That or the painkillers are making me delusional. There is no way I want to fuck Matteo. No way is that ever happening. I don't care if he's turned into the world's greatest saint. There is nothing he can do to make me forgive him for what he's done to me.

10

MATTEO

Fuck this woman.

Eden's turned her charm on, and I don't know how to stop my cock from falling for her ridiculous mind games. She thinks she can manipulate me into giving her back her freedom.

She's wrong.

There is only one way for her to earn back her freedom. By telling me where I can find Nina. Otherwise, I'll keep her trapped forever.

11

EDEN

Four weeks.

That's how long it's been since the rape. That's how long it's been since my life changed forever.

My leg healing was the easy part. After watching Matteo work, as I suspected, it has healed magnificently. The swelling has gone down. The skin has fused together where it was once open. And from what I can tell, my bones have begun the long road of healing as well.

My mind is haunted. Armas may be dead, but he still has control over me. I don't sleep without having a nightmare of him raping me. I jump at every loud noise or movement. I hate being alone with any man, even the servants who are only bringing me food.

Matteo hasn't visited. Not once since the night, he saved me. The staff and men have brought me food, books, and pain pills, and have told me he's busy working. But I know it's a lie. He's staying away because I wasn't the only one who changed when I was raped. He felt something too. *What? I'm not sure, but it changed.*

I hear the familiar creak of the door as it opens. I expect one of the men, Maximo, or Dierk, or Paul to be coming in to check on me. One of them normally does around this time of day. The interaction is always brief; I'm sure Matteo gave them orders not to stay long. But it's at least something to look forward to each day.

I hope it's Dierk. He lingers the longest and will sometimes make jokes or tell me about the outside world. Mainly the weather and a few current events, but it's heaven when I don't even get to look out the window or step a foot out of bed. I should try walking soon, but I need help. And I don't trust any of the men to help me. Not to mention I need a bath, a change of clothes, and a walk outside to remember what fresh air smells like again.

My jaw unhinges when Matteo walks into the room. He doesn't look at me. He seems lost in thought as he pulls his gray T-shirt up over his head. My eyes travel over his chest, six-pack abs, and down the v that disappears into his running shorts.

My mouth waters, both from glimpsing his body and from jealousy. He can run outside, while the only thing I can do is turn over in bed.

I clear my throat, and he stops, examining at me like he forgot I was still in his room. Or I exist at all. His lips tighten together, he's going to go about his business, go shower, or whatever he came up here to do, instead of engaging with me.

"Have you tried walking yet?" he asks, surprising me by speaking.

"No." I plead with my heart to stop racing in my chest. He's just a naked man. I'm excited because it's been so long since I've experienced the pleasure and release that comes with a great fuck. That's all.

He takes the shirt in his hand and wipes the sweat from his forehead.

"You should be able to walk by now. If not, we should call a doctor out here."

"I haven't exactly had too many opportunities to walk. I don't trust if I try to get out of bed by myself, that I won't fall and hurt myself all over."

He raises an eyebrow as he edges closer to the bed.

"You? Afraid of falling?" He chuckles. "I didn't think you were scared of anything, let alone a little fall."

I narrow my eyes as the anger rolls through my body. I let it escape though, as swiftly as it came. I'll prove Matteo wrong.

I throw the covers off my body and reach down and pull the gauze off my leg holding the stent in place so that I can move my leg. I scoot to the edge of the bed until my legs dangle over the edge and without thinking, I place my legs on the floor and stand up.

He claps in a slow, teasing sort of way when I stand.

My cheeks blush red, and sweat covers my brow, now more determined than ever to prove to him I'm not afraid. I take a step forward, and gradually transfer my weight to my newly healed leg. I think I have it when my knee buckles and I fall.

His arms catch me as my face and hands are about to make contact with the ground.

"Well, at least you proved you aren't frightened."

I snarl.

He laughs again. His laughter soon turns solemn as he holds me up under my arms and I clutch his shoulders.

"Try again."

I take a step forward, and this time, with his help, I'm ready to put some weight on my leg. Not enough that I'm able to walk on my own, but enough to confirm my leg is healing and gives me enough faith I will soon make a full recovery, at least where my leg is concerned.

I grin so widely I'm sure my lips reach my eyes.

Matteo grins too, in his own way. It looks as much like a smirk as it does a genuine grin.

"Take me to the bathroom. I could use a bath."

"I was going to say you stink."

I hit him playfully, and he chuckles. It's weird to be bantering like this. We seem normal. Like any two friends, or at least, close acquaintances would.

"Bathroom. Now."

He smirks, and we make our slow trek to the bathroom taking far longer than I would like.

When my feet hit the cold tile, I gaze up at the tall shower standing beyond the entrance. The shower is impressive with five different shower heads and glass surrounding all of the walls. I don't have a hope of using it again anytime soon.

"Help me into the bath. I can remove my clothes and turn the water on after you leave."

He raises an eyebrow. "No, you either strip now, or you don't bathe at all. I should receive a reward for helping you get this far. It's been a few weeks since I've glimpsed your naked body."

I blush when I remember he's already seen me naked plenty of times before.

I pull my shirt off and push my underwear down.

Matteo's eyes don't go to my body like I was expecting. Instead, his eyes stay on mine.

I raise an eyebrow.

"I thought you wanted to ogle at my body."

"I do."

I swallow hard as my breath catches in my throat and my body shivers from the cold.

He runs my arms up and down instinctively, warming me.

He's different. Kinder somehow.

His eyes drift down my body, and I bite my lip squirming a little in his arms as he studies my curves.

"You do not need to be embarrassed. You have an amazing body, even if it's a little beat up at the moment."

"I'm not embarrassed."

"Then why are you squirming and your cheeks are blushed?"

I frown. "Because I'm naked standing in front of a man who kidnapped me. I think I'm allowed to blush."

He holds my hand, keeping me upright while he leans over the tub and turns the water on to hot. The steam from it begins to fill the room.

We are both silent for a moment while we wait for the bath to fill. I don't like the silence. In the quiet, that's when Armas creeps in making me unsafe. So I don't let the silence stretch like I usually would.

"Why do you always keep the blinds closed? I've been living in a cave for weeks. I asked the men to open them for me, but it was one of the things they wouldn't do for me no matter how much I asked them to."

He chuckles. "A misunderstanding. They think I like the darkness. I often sit in my office with all the blinds closed. Every time I've allowed anyone into my personal space, it is always jet-black."

"Why?"

"Because that's what I want them to see. I want them to think I'm nothing but a monster that lives in the night. I do like the dark when I need to focus and think, which happens to be often. I'll make sure the blinds are open from now on."

My mouth is dry as he speaks. I nod instead of saying thanks.

He reaches over and turns off the faucet. I glance over at the tub filled almost to the brim with water. I take a step toward the tub, forgetting I can't walk on my own, and my leg gives out.

Matteo holds me up though. He's always holding me up. *Saving me.*

He holds my arms as I carefully take the two steps over to the tub and step in. He doesn't let me go until I've sunk into the warm water. I close my eyes as the liquid warms my body and starts melting the dirt caked on me. Along with anything remaining of Armas.

I keep my eyes closed for a long time trying to push Armas out.

I can't.

The warm water can't do it.

I should wash and get clean. Maybe, being clean will do the trick. I open my eyes and Matteo is still standing there.

"You just going to stand there and creepily watch me?"

He removes his shorts, and my heart stops. He's going to join me.

My eyes try to stay on his chest, but I can't help but sneak a peek at his cock again. His cock is hard and thick, wanting me.

My cheeks flush as I breathe and tear my eyes from his erection.

I can't.

I don't know what's wrong with me; it's like I've never seen a cock before.

"Are you just going to stare at me creepily? Because I'd be more than okay if you were."

I attempt to smile like I'm not bothered, but he knows me well enough to realize the smile is a lie. By now my cheeks are bright red as I finally meet his gaze.

His face is smiling brightly at me. For once, he doesn't seem as serious or dangerous. He seems human.

He starts walking toward me though, and I'm not sure I want him in the tub with me. My nipples may have hardened, and my sex may be aching for his cock, but it's not what I want. I don't want to have sex with a man as cruel as him.

At the last second, he turns and steps into the all-glass shower, flipping the water on.

I exhale.

He's not going to touch me.

I try to ignore him as I take the bar of soap and begin scrubbing my body thoroughly. My eyes fluttering up to his naked ass any chance I get to take a glance without him noticing.

He doesn't glimpse my way though. He showers like I'm not two feet away and naked.

I've washed every piece of skin I can find on my body, and I still don't feel relaxed, though it helps the ache in my leg. I'm clean again. I should be calm, but I'm not.

I dunk my head under the water washing off the last pieces of dirt. I don't have any shampoo to wash my hair, but dunking it in the soapy water does enough.

When I resurface, Matteo is standing over me. Naked. His body dripping with water.

My bottom lip quivers, both terrified and excited. *What do I want from him?* I don't know. *What does he want from me?* He doesn't know either.

He extends his hand to me. I take it, and he pulls me up. He hands me a towel, and I take it wrapping it around my body. I lift my leg to step out, but he scoops me into his arms, a motion I've started to get used to and enjoy.

"I don't want you overworking your leg. I'll teach you some exercises you can start doing to increase your leg strength slowly, so you don't injure it again."

I nod, still unable to speak. Nothing but a towel separate my body from his.

He takes me back to his bed.

"Why do you always put me in your bed instead of one of the other bedrooms? Why give up your bed to me?"

He gently lays me down as he stands over me, not at all embarrassed he's naked. Not that he should be.

"Because I want you in my bed."

He says it so simply like it's obvious. He grabs a pillow and places it under my leg, lifting my leg up. Then he reaches for the towel clutched to my body. He snatches it out of my grip and pulls it off my body, exposing me again.

My breathing speeds when the cold air hits, touching my warm skin. I close my eyes making an effort to calm my breathing to keep Matteo from thinking I'm into him.

Armas.

Armas' face smirks down at me. His cock resting at my entrance.

"No."

He pushes in any way. His cock burns inside me, ripping my insides apart as he rapes me. My body isn't *mine* anymore. It's *his*. He bites down on my nipple, and I cry. It hurts too much.

I can't escape him. It all hurts, but having his cock inside me is too much. His thrusts never end, and my body can't take the intrusion much longer.

"No. Please, stop."

He doesn't. Not until his cum is spilling into me. It feels like lava. I want it out.

"Eden," Matteo's voice calls out, saving me from my nightmare, as he saved me from that day.

I open my eyes, and his arms are on my arms, concern in his eyes.

"Eden, what's happening? What's wrong?"

I pant, not wanting to talk about it. Maybe if I do, I'll feel better. Armas will finally be gone.

"Armas. I can't escape him. Every time I close my eyes he's there. Taunting me. I can't stop reliving that day. I can't stop reliving him raping me. His dick tearing me open. His teeth ripping my skin. His cum—"

"Wait, he came inside you?" His eyes widen.

I swallow needing to face my fears. "Yes, he came. He was close to coming again when you stopped him."

His eyes drop to my body like he's seeing me for the first time. He notices the tiny scars still on my breasts where he bit me. And he sees my sex that is no longer mine. It's Armas'.

I don't think I can ever have sex again. It hurts to think about it.

I touch his face because he looks like he needs comforting. His somber eyes come back to mine.

"What do you need?"

I shrug. "I don't know."

"Come on. There has to be something I can do to help. Bring you ice cream, take you to a movie, give you a massage. Something to help."

The word leaves my mouth without understanding what I want myself. "You."

His face juts back like he doesn't believe what I said.

"I'm sorry. I didn't mean it..."

I grab the covers to cover myself up along with the embarrassment. His hand pushes them down before he grabs my chin and turns it toward him.

"You meant what you said."

I nod.

"You want me to make the memories go away?"

"Yes, it's stupid. It probably won't even work. You can't make the memories go away. You can't replace them. I don't even think if I was in love with you could you make the memories go away."

"I can make the nightmares go away." He says it like he believes what he is saying, and it almost makes me believe him.

I glance down at his rippling chest, preventing my eyes from going lower. I can feel him grinning at me.

"And you can't deny you want a taste of my body. What hurt would it do to try?"

I swallow. *A lot.* If it feels like he's raping me, instead of pleasuring me, I'm not sure how I will survive. I'll die of insanity if I have to deal with both Armas and Matteo haunting me. Matteo has done some bad things, but nothing like Armas. This could make it worse.

He sighs and starts to get up sensing my hesitation. He's going to leave me alone with my nightmares. I can't handle that.

I grab his neck and pull him to me, kissing him firmly on the lips.

His mouth tastes delicious, and he smells heavenly like a musky soap he used in the shower. I pull away, gently trying to give my brain time to think, because there is no way I'm going to be getting any thinking done with my lips locked with his.

I keep my eyes closed as I rest my forehead against his. "I want you. Fuck me, make me forget. I trust you, don't lose that trust. It might be the only way you have a chance to get Nina back."

He exhales like he's judging my words.

"Promise me you won't hurt me. You won't rape me. If I say stop, you'll stop."

I open my eyes to wait for his response, needing to see his eyes as he says it.

He doesn't say anything. Instead, he grabs my neck and kisses me again profoundly. His tongue sweeps into my mouth, and I forget about waiting for him to promise not to hurt me. I just feel. His tongue dancing with mine as our lips and moans collide.

He pushes me back as he climbs on top of me, our lips still locked together. I close my eyes and immediately realize it's a mistake.

"Stay with me, pretty girl," he moans against my lips. "I don't want you crediting someone else with my sexy moves."

He grins against my lips as he says it and I open my eyes, smiling a little back.

We both keep our eyes open as we continue kissing; our eyes moving deeper into each other's souls as we kiss. His eyes tell me to trust him, though he hasn't promised he wouldn't hurt me yet. I don't have a choice but to trust him.

Even if I did have an option, I would still be here, trusting him. I would choose anything over my nightmares.

His eyes change. That's what I notice first, and then a mischievous grin as he pulls away.

"What?" I ask, laughing, because it's clear he has thought of something funny.

"Nothing."

I raise an eyebrow, but he never answers me.

"Take a deep breath," he says.

I'm suspicious, but I slowly inhale, trying my best to trust him. He grabs my hands and shoves them over my head in one fluid motion while he kisses my neck.

"Matteo," I cry out, not liking my hands not having control. Even though being able to move my arms wouldn't be enough to stop Matteo if he wanted to rape me.

He kisses my neck, and I come unglued from the way he is sweetly kissing, lapping over my neck, making all the nerves in my body tingle.

"Tell me you don't like it. Tell me you want me to stop."

I moan loudly as his kissing turns to nibbling and then biting.

"Stop," I moan, but my cry isn't compelling.

He grins against my neck.

"I don't believe you."

I swallow.

His mouth drops to my hardened nipple, and I freeze thinking of the last time a man's teeth were there. How rough and terrifying it felt and how it was the final step before he plunged inside me.

He doesn't hesitate at my anxiety. He takes my nipple into his mouth, swirling his tongue around before biting, hard.

I yelp at the sudden pain, but it's not pain. Not like when Armas bit me, although I'm sure they both bit me equally hard. There's a difference; one I can't figure out.

"Tell me to stop," he says again, with his teeth still tightened against my nipple.

"Stop," I say, but it's softer than the first.

He moves to the other nipple, giving it the same treatment, my back arches against his lips, wanting him to take my nipple into his mouth deeper, to bite harder.

I feel his cock against my stomach as I arch my back, diving into my belly, pressing harder, as his erection grows. It should scare me, the feeling of how large his cock is growing. He wants me, badly. And if I genuinely begged him to stop, he wouldn't. He would hurt me worse than Armas. Both physically and emotionally.

"Grab the bars on the bed," he commands as he pushes my arms up.

I do.

"Don't let go," he orders, his eyes threatening before he releases my hands. I keep my hands on the bars like they are tied up, and I can't move them, though I can.

His dark eyes dip down as his lips travel down my neck, breasts, and stomach. His tongue tasting my skin, sending chills through my body and an ache I'm not familiar with deep in my belly.

I close my eyes, trying to gulp down my fears that are sneaking in. I know what happens next. Next, his cock drives in me. He's not a nice man. He's not going to wait for my body to adjust. He's not going to wait for me to come or even attempt to make me feel good. He's going to get what he wants and hopefully not hurt me too badly in the process.

I hold my breath, and Armas starts creeping back in while I wait for his erection to be pushing at my entrance.

Instead, I feel something much lighter and wetter. It traces slowly over my lips between my legs as hands gently push my thighs wider. His tongue laps over me and my eyes fly open to watch him.

I've never had a man lick me so intimately like he is. Most men I've been with use their fingers to get me off. It's ecstasy. Any man I'm with after this will be required to lick me if he wants me to have sex with him.

His tongue continues over my folds until he finds my clit. He flicks it fast as my juices fill my sex. He licks them up, spreading them over my clit as I moan and arch my back.

I pull at my hands wishing I could touch him. Wanting my hands free to play with his thick hair.

His eyes tease me as he looks up at me and then he plunges his fingers inside me while he keeps licking my exterior.

I expect pain. But it's nothing but pleasure. An experience I haven't felt with a man before.

His fingers slip in and out quickly while my legs begin to tighten around his head and my eyes roll back in my head. My toes curl as he continues licking me and I scream.

"Jesus," I cry as I come on his fingers, his tongue not slowing down until he's pulled all of my orgasms out of me.

My body needs to rest, but he doesn't let me rest. Not until he gets what he wants. His fingers pull out of me, and I feel my legs being pushed wider as he kneels between them, pushing his cock nearer my entrance.

He doesn't wait for permission. He pushes his cock inside me, making me cry out from the intrusion.

But I don't feel pain. Not one drop of it. My eyes widen as he smirks, holding my legs but not moving while he waits for me to realize how much my body is aching for him.

He raises an eyebrow, asking if I'm ready and I bite my lip in response.

"I got you, beautiful."

He rocks in and out of me, and my body comes alive like it had been dormant all these years, waiting until his cock reached inside and brought me back to life. I can feel everything. Every magnificent craving inside my body. Need. Excitement. Lust. It all takes over, pushing out the negative emotions I've been living with for months. Far too long to understand what's happening.

I forget about everything except being here with him. I'm willingly having sex with my kidnapper and enjoying it. *What's wrong with me? And why didn't I make him fuck me sooner?*

He thrusts, and my body responds.

"Oh my god!" I cry when he rocks deeper, hitting a sweet spot I didn't realize existed within my body.

"Tell me to stop."

I chuckle as he brings my body higher. There is no way I want this to stop.

"Tell me to stop!" he demands, his voice harsh.

"Stop," I whisper.

"Louder. Scream it."

"Stop!" I scream, and my body comes at the same time he does. Pouring his seed into my body.

I close my eyes and then open them with a goofy grin on my face while Matteo's cock still rests inside me. When I finally catch my breath again, I ask, "Why did you want me to yell stop?"

He pulls out, and the emptiness is instant. I want him again. Now.

He stares at my hands, and I realize I can let go. I'd forgotten I could let go, that they weren't tied above my head.

"Because I wanted you to realize you have more power than you think. You have control over your body. You have control of your memories. Only you have the power to get rid of the nightmares."

I swallow hard, listening to his words. He stands up, and pulls the covers over me.

"Now sleep."

"Wait."

He stops.

"Sleep with me. You're right, I have the power to make sure my nightmares don't come back, but your arms holding me might help."

I think he's going to say no. In fact, I expect it. He doesn't speak.

He walks around the bed, pulls the covers down, and climbs in still naked. He reaches down to my leg, making sure it's propped up on a pillow, and wraps his arms around me. I close my eyes, and for the first time in a long time, I don't think I will dream of Armas. Because my body is consumed with Matteo.

12

MATTEO

I WAKE up with Eden's arms wrapped around me. My body is far too warm, but I won't dare move her. I like her skin against mine too much to care about something as silly as being too hot.

What's gotten into me?

I've become a wuss in a matter of moments. Ever since I rescued Eden from Armas. Although, I didn't arrive there fast enough like I thought I did. I thought I stole her back before the worst happened. I was wrong.

I think I helped her now though. She didn't wake up in the night. No thrashing or apparent night terrors. And she's still asleep now, despite it being well past eight in the morning. We've been sleeping for over ten hours.

I saved her from Armas, but she should be equally terrified of me. I thought fucking her again would stir up the memory of me raping her.

It didn't.

I'm not sure what I want more. Her to remember me raping her and be afraid of me, or her to forget about it forever.

Her sultry eyes eventually open and she grins when she gapes at me.

"Good morning," she says, smiling like I'm her favorite person in the world.

I stroke her hair automatically. "Morning."

She bites her lip.

"How are you feeling?" I ask.

"Good. Really, good. I didn't have any nightmares."

I nod.

We both stare at each other, not sure where to take this from here. For one, I need food and coffee in my system to think straight, and then I have to get to work. I can deal with Eden later.

"You hungry? I can have one of the servants bring you some breakfast. I don't think you should walk all the way to the dining room until your leg is further along in the healing process."

"Eat with me here."

I raise an eyebrow. "Why?"

The covers slip, and I'm rewarded with a view of her perky breasts and nipples, which I can still taste in my mouth.

She doesn't cover up. Instead, she blushes.

"I know you aren't the rainbows and hearts kind of guy. I know you are still evil. But I have a proposition for you, and I think we could both use some coffee first."

I frown.

She's still my prisoner. I don't like her thinking she has any power over me. I have the control, not her. But I guess I need to listen to whatever she thinks she gained yesterday so I can put her back in her place.

I step out of bed, sensing her gaze on my ass.

I smirk.

She still wants me. I walk over to my dresser and pull out a dark pair of boxer briefs and put them on. I walk to my closet, pull a pair of sweatpants out, and put them on before walking back out.

She's biting her lip when she gawks at me.

"Coffee no sugar, extra crispy bacon, and eggs sunny side up?" I ask, although I know it's what she wants.

She nods with a grin.

Damn that grin. It's beautiful. Just looking at it makes me happy.

I dash down the stairs to put in our order and impatiently wait before I carry both of our breakfasts on a tray upstairs.

When I return, I place the tray on Eden's lap before climbing into bed next to her and taking my coffee off. I start drinking it while I wait for her ridiculous proposal I'm going to say no to.

She takes her time and drinks her coffee while nibbling on the bacon on her plate. I made sure the cooks prepared plenty of bacon for her since it's her favorite part of breakfast.

"So you going to tell me what your proposition is or what? I have a lot of work I should be doing."

She sighs and twirls the piece of bacon between her finger.

"Fine. I would like to make a deal with you."

"I figured that. What kind of deal?"

She sucks in a breath. She's nervous. Her hand is shaking slightly, and her breathing has sped up.

"The kind where I get more sex like last night."

I laugh. "Nina tried the same thing. You can't seduce me and get me to fall in love with you to help you escape. If I fell in love with you, it would only make you more trapped. Remember how it turned out for Nina?"

She blushes. "I'm not trying to convince you to fall in love with me. That's not what I want."

"What do you want then?"

"I want more sex like last night. Sex that makes me feel good but in control. I don't want to be raped. I want the kind that makes me feel stronger afterward."

I shake my head. "Not going to happen. Last night was a one-time thing. I did it because I don't want another guy in your head. Now I can talk to you. Question you. Torture you. Or rape you without worrying you are thinking about any man but me."

She laughs, but it's nervous. "You won't rape me."

I raise an eyebrow and inch toward her, watching as the breathing in her chest becomes weaker. "I won't?"

"No, you won't. I believe your story. You love Nina or are still obsessed with her or whatever your feelings are toward her. I believe that to be true. If you want to have a chance at having Nina back at the end of all of this, then you won't rape me. You know she would never forgive you for it. She'll forgive you for kidnapping me, but not rape. That's how I know you won't do it."

I frown. "Fine. But that doesn't mean I'll fuck you. I have plenty of women at my disposal to fuck when I want."

She smirks. "You might. But they aren't who you want. You want Nina. And me. Admit it."

"No. I like hurting women. Raping them. I don't fuck often. Not for a woman's pleasure."

"Fuck me, and for every time I let you fuck me, you hold off looking for Nina for one week."

I narrow my eyes chuckling softly. "That sounds like you get two things you want and I get nothing."

Her eyes hide behind her lashes. "I said fuck me how you want. Rough, dirty, filthy. Do what you want to me, and if I don't stop you, then Nina gets one more week of freedom."

"You think fucking you last night was that good for me?"

"Yes," she breathes.

She knows me too well. I don't understand it, but fucking her last night made my top five all-time fucks. Nina, making up the other four.

"I'll never get Nina that way. Why would I follow your plan? Why wouldn't I just hurt you until you talk?"

She smiles, her face light and airy because she thinks she's won. "Because you love Nina. That's why you won't hurt me because you can't hurt her. I believe you love her. I think your love might be a lost cause. But it's also the only way you can ever have her. I won't talk if you torture me. As you can see, that hasn't been working out well for you so far. I might talk if you gain my trust. Show me I'm right in my realization that you love her and will protect her. You are the better man for her and I'll tell you where she is."

I stare into her brown eyes intently. She's lying. Nothing will ever make her tell me where Nina is. Or at least that's what she thinks. I can think of several ways to get her to talk, now that I know her better.

Now, though, I don't want Nina. I need to deal with the aftermath of Armas' family. I need to make sure Clive and Erick are taken care of. That they won't come after us as soon as I get Nina back. Until then, I don't want to know where Nina is. It puts her at risk.

I won't shake her hand or promise her a deal though. That way when I want the agreement to end, it can, without renegotiating or breaking my promise. It will be like last night where I promise with my body and that has to be enough for her for now.

I want to fuck her. And she's right I don't want to deal with Nina finding out I raped Eden repeatedly. But I will, if that's what it takes to get her to talk to me.

This way I get to rape her with her permission. I don't plan on going easy on Eden. I plan on making her pay for not telling me where Nina is. Because I'm more desperate to get her back than she knows.

"Finish eating your breakfast," I say. Other than the one piece of bacon, she has hardly touched any of her food.

She bats her eyelashes at me as she lets the covers fall further down her body until only her pussy and legs are covered.

"Or...we could..." She grins, licking her lip.

I shake my head as I ignore her and continue eating my breakfast. I can't help but chuckle, though, when I see her pout out of the corner of my eye.

"Eat. You're going to need your strength."

Her eyes light up like I just told her the most exciting news. She will regret the deal she made with me. Because last night was nothing. I enjoyed fucking her, but it's not what I crave. I seek the darkness, just like I do during the day.

I drink the rest of my coffee, watching her as she digs into her food as frantically as she did after going without for several days when Dierk fed her. I watched the security tapes last week and saw her with him. She used her big eyes and seductive smile to get Dierk to do whatever she wanted. She's not going to be able to do the same with me.

She finishes her food and looks at me with eager eyes.

I glance down at my coffee, letting her know she can't rush me.

It doesn't stop her from trying. She leans into me, her lips purring, begging me to make her feel as good as last night.

I slowly, deliberately, drink the rest of my coffee and then set my cup on the tray still in her lap. She practically shoves the tray into my hands as I set it down on the nightstand next to me.

"So eager," I mumble.

She reaches her hand to grab my neck and kiss me. I seize her hand, stopping her. Her mouth parts as she stares at me, holding her wrist a little too tight. I can see the realization hit her. This won't be like last time. This time, I will be taking full advantage of her body.

She takes a deep breath while I plan in my head what I want from her body. *How do I want her? Tied up? Red? Crying my name? What do I want?*

All of it.

I want it all.

I get out of bed knowing she can't follow me, and it will drive her mad the longer I'm gone. I step into my closet and unhurriedly remove my clothes again. Taking my time and letting the image of her body, naked and tied up for me, sink into my mind. Her body red with stains where her flesh was whipped and beaten. Her eyes shed of tears all but spilled from her pain.

That's what I want. Her defeated and mine. I want her to feel like she did after Armas, but because of me.

I thought I could be kind, but the kindness has dried up.

I walk to the shelf where I keep my ties and pull two off. Usually, I would prefer something much stronger, but this will do for what I have planned.

Finally, when I know her pussy is dripping and her heart has sped to an unmeasurable speed, I step out.

Her eyes mix with concern and arousal as she looks at me.

I glare back. Her eyes reflect more worry than excitement. Her eyes drift down the ties I hold in my hand, and she grips the sheets trying to hide herself again.

"You can't hide from me. Not now."

"I'm not hiding. I made the deal remember?"

"And you are going to regret it."

"Not likely, if it keeps my friend safe for another day."

"And gives you another orgasm, right?"

Her cheeks blush her response. She wants me to fuck her as much as I want to fuck her. She just doesn't want what I have planned.

"This is your last chance to back out. You don't get a safe word. I won't stop once I start. I'll ask you beforehand each time, but once you say yes, that's it."

The fear disappears as I speak. Like my words give her confidence instead of panic.

"Fuck me, Matteo. Do your worst."

"I will."

I snatch the covers and jerk them off until her entire body is exposed and ready at my disposal.

I unroll one of the ties as I storm toward her, my gaze never leaving her and she's fighting back just as strongly, telling me she is ready for anything.

I grab her healing leg, digging my fingers deep into her skin.

She screams at my sudden touch.

My fingers continue holding pressure, loving the sounds she's making.

"You asshole."

I smirk. "Didn't think I would fight fair, did you?"

"No," she growls. "I thought you would slowly transform into a monster, not become it as quickly as I can snap my fingers."

I bend her knee, so her thigh is pressed against her stomach.

She cries again. Her leg hasn't been used to bending that way in weeks.

"I didn't need to transform. I've always been this way."

I clutch her wrist and pull it to her leg before I attach the tie around it.

She takes a deep breath. Trying not to panic. She won't be able to move when I'm done with her. She's going to remain hurting, her leg throbbing how it is, the entire time I fuck her.

I finish tying her hand tightly to her leg; then I jerk her other leg back before I grab her hand and fasten it to her leg with the other tie.

She bites her lip.

"You regretting your decision yet?"

"No, I never regret anything."

I enjoy her confidence. It will make this so much more fun when I beat it out of her.

I take a step back, admiring my work and her body tied up for me. She can't move, and there is no turning back. No words will convince me to stop, not now I've had her.

I disappear again. Needing more tools.

When I return, she's panting as she struggles against the ties, trying to break free. She freezes when she sees what I'm holding in my hand.

She closes her eyes, like that, will help her.

I hold the whip in my hand, letting my fingers tangle in the leather threads that will soon be touching her body. I doubt she has ever felt such a thing before. She would have if Armas had more time with her. But I get to be her first. I get to break her in. I get to make her mine.

"Open your eyes."

"No," she whispers.

"Open your eyes, or I'll make it extra painful."

I want to see her pupils dilate and the fear take over when the leather touches her smooth skin.

She opens them.

"Good girl."

I don't hesitate. I let the whip come down harshly against her ass that is splayed for me.

She yelps, her body swaying as it tries to adjust to the sting.

My eyes roll back as the pain I caused sinks into me, bringing me far too much pleasure.

I strike her again on the other cheek, more forceful than before.

Her yelp turns to a cry, almost a plea, that this is her limit. This is all she can take. Not a millimeter harder.

She hasn't felt anything yet.

I whip her again, this time over the most sensitive bud on her body.

She cries, and I finally see the tears streaking down her cheeks. This is what I want. This is what I crave. To see women in pain, terrified of me. I want them to feel powerless, so I feel more power. I need the darkness.

"Please," she whispers behind her tears. She doesn't say stop. She doesn't dare show she's weak so quickly. But I can still see it. I know it won't take much more for her to say it.

I crack the whip again, hitting her ass again.

Her body lurches from the contact before she rocks gently on her back, trying to calm the sting. My eyes deepen when I'm rewarded with the red mark I've left on her ass. I want more. Something permanent.

I strike her again with all the force I have. More tears spill, but she barely cries this time.

"Had enough?"

She glares at me but doesn't say anything. My cock aches watching her. She might get lucky. I'm usually a patient person, but I can't wait much longer to fuck her. My cock is growing closer to her with every moan from her body.

I hit her again, purposefully striking her pussy, needing her to tell me to stop. Needing to know I'm breaking her. That this feels like I'm taking something from her. Raping her.

She cries loudly, but her cry turns to an enduring groan.

I throw back my arm, coming down with all my strength, expecting this to be the moment she cracks. The moment where her new nightmares form that I caused.

She doesn't cry.

Or scream.

No tears fall.

Instead, she grins before her mouth falls open in ecstasy. A deep growl leaves her throat, and her body opens up more for me to hit her again.

I do.

Her toes curl, and her back arches and she pushes into the strike.

My mouth falls open. She likes the pain. She wants me to hurt her. It turns her on.

And I can't wait any longer.

I grab her ass as I stand on the edge of the bed and pull her to me, my cock plunging into her tight cunt. She's dripping and easily allows me in.

I spank her ass as I drive in and out of her. It only makes her wetter.

"Harder," she cries.

I fuck her harder.

"Deeper."

I fuck her deeper.

I don't know when I gave up control, and she took over, but I don't care. I would give her control every time if it felt this good every time.

I pound into her, loving how her body tightens around me. I lean forward so I can grasp her nipples and twist them between my fingers.

She bites her lip and like it's the most glorious thing I've done.

I stare into her eyes trying to find the woman who was raped by Armas, was so broken only a few hours ago. The woman who would have been equally shattered by me after I raped her, if she had retained her memory.

She's gone.

And in her place is a woman more powerful than any woman I've ever met. She's thriving being tied up, in pain, and in pleasure. She controlled this by making the deal. And in doing so, it gave her power over what she felt as well.

I won't last much longer, though I want this feeling to last forever. It feels far too pleasurable, and I plan on fucking her again as soon as I arrive back from work. And every day until I've had enough.

I move faster about to push my cum deep into her belly when her lips brush against mine.

My eyes fly open as I take the kiss further. My tongue sweeping into her mouth, tangling with hers. I'm not opposed to kissing her, but I wanted to deny her any pleasure. Now that I know that's not possible, why deny myself any?

I kiss her, taking in everything she feels as I fuck her.

"Oh god, Matteo!" she cries as her orgasm escapes her.

"Fuck," I growl as I shoot my load inside her.

Our eyes connect as our orgasms slowly subside. Our bodies wrench as I collapse on top of her. Neither of us understands what the hell happened. We both know that should have terrified her. It should have ripped her to pieces instead of building her back up.

"Why do I crave you?" she asks.

I smirk.

She laughs.

"Because you're fucked up. You like the darkness. The evil you have been fighting all your life is tucked inside, and you just started to let it free. You're no different than me."

13

EDEN

OH MY GOD, the sex.

The fucking sex.

Why does he have to be so good at sex?

The kissing is incredible.

His tongue massages mine in a way that makes me melt every time.

The way his hands grip my body makes me come undone.

And his cock, the way he knows exactly how much my body craves it, along with the sweet sensation of pain. I lose control with him, but also gain it. It doesn't make sense, but it's how I feel.

Sex with Matteo is *life-altering*.

He thought it would break me. Honestly, I thought it would too. I thought I would be flooded with memories of Armas. Or new painful memories with Matteo would be all I could think about.

Matteo is all I can think about. Not the nightmares. Instead, it is sweet, sweet dreams that make me forget everything else. I can't function without thinking about him. All I want is sex.

I'm an addict. One who can't survive without my drug. Sex with him has changed me. I'm not sure if it is for the better.

I feel stronger, but also less in control. I should be focused on getting free and protecting Nina. But all I can think about is sex.

Good thing every time I'm having sex with Matteo, I'm protecting Nina. I'm just not getting any closer to being free.

"Hurry up. You are using all the hot water, and you need to get dressed," Matteo says as he throws the bathroom door open.

I frown as I stand under the steaming water of the shower. I don't want to move out from under the faucet. I love the hot water and showers so much more than baths. I will never take showering for granted again.

"No! I'm enjoying my shower. Leave me alone or join me."

I expect him to join me. He likes the sex as much or more than I do and hasn't passed up an opportunity to fuck me any chance he's gotten in the last month.

His hand reaches into the shower, and he turns the faucet off.

"I mean it. Out now."

I frown. "Why?"

"Because we are going to the ball Armas' family is throwing."

My heart stops. I grab the towel and wrap it around my body not understanding what is happening or why we are just now talking about it.

"His family is still holding a ball even though Armas is dead?"

"Yes, they are arranging it in his honor."

I step out of the shower, keeping the towel wrapped around me snuggly.

"Why are you going?"

"*We*. We are going."

I frown. Matteo's never let me off the property before. The only time I've left since he kidnapped me was when Armas stole me.

"Why are *we* going?"

He folds his arms across his chest as he leans against the counter.

"Because we are letting his family know Armas deserved to die. We are making sure they understand that."

My stomach flips. "And how does going to the ball help? Couldn't you go talk to them with some of your men?"

He shakes his head. "That's not how things work. Appearances are everything when it comes to rich families."

"Why am I going?" I ask, needing to know the answer, even though

I'm excited at the thought of getting out of the house and having a chance to escape.

"Because I need a date. And I want to see what you look like in the dress I bought for you."

He nods to the dress hanging on the hook at the rear of the bathroom and my mouth drops. It's sparkly and red and divine. It's been a while since I've worn anything this fancy before and I desperately want to wear it. I want to feel pretty, which this dress would definitely help me achieve. I would also be able to seduce Matteo or any other man at the ball I want to. Possibly even make Matteo jealous.

I run my hand over the fabric already imagining it on my body when I get to the bottom of the dress and see the shoes sitting underneath. Tall, spiky heels the kind only models and women who hate their feet wear.

"I can't wear those heels."

He smirks. "If you want to go to the ball with me, you're wearing them. And preferably with no underwear underneath."

He playfully swats my ass, but there is nothing playful about it.

"I'm serious. My leg has hardly healed. I can walk, but not in heels like that."

"Fine, then I guess I'll have to find a last minute date."

I glare at him as he starts to strut by me.

"Fine, I'll wear them."

He grins. "Good. Be ready in twenty."

"Twenty minutes! I can't even do my hair in that amount of time. And did you get me any makeup?"

He nods toward one of the drawers. I pull the drawer open, and it's filled with the most expensive makeups money can buy.

"I mean it. I'm leaving in twenty so be ready, or your ass is staying here."

He shuts the door, leaving me alone in the bathroom to get ready. It's going to take a lot longer than twenty minutes for me to do my hair and makeup. And I'll make sure Matteo thinks it is worth the wait.

"Eden Marie! Get your ass out here now, or I'm leaving you," Matteo shouts.

It's the third time he's shouted at me. I apply my lipstick before I answer back. "How do you know my middle name is Marie?"

"I don't. But every American's middle name is either Elizabeth or Marie. Marie sounded better with Eden."

I smile. I like it when Matteo's relaxed with me. He's funny and charming and *human*.

I walk to the door and open it. I take two steps out before I see Matteo standing with his hands in his pockets in the most glorious tuxedo I've ever seen. It fits him snug, and his five o'clock shadow makes him appear rugged, despite how clean cut he looks in his tux. His eyes and grin are what make me weak in the knees though.

He's seen me naked dozens of times now, but he's never looked at me the way he is looking at me now. He makes me feel special, like we are going out on a proper date instead of him bringing me to a job.

"What do you think?" I ask, because I want to hear him say I'm beautiful and to fawn all over me. I like the attention.

I take a step forward so he can get a better look and I trip in my damn shoes.

He catches me.

"Why are you always catching me?" I breathe into his chest, as his cologne sneaks up my nostrils.

"Because you're always falling."

I laugh.

"You're in a good mood," he says.

"I guess something about getting out of this dark mansion and doing something fun for a change makes me happy."

His eyes narrow and I expect him to realize I could escape. After tonight, I could no longer be his slave. He doesn't say anything though.

Instead, he holds out his arm, and I take it. For once, I'm not going to worry about anything other than enjoying myself. I'm his date. I'm not his slave.

He leads me out of the house and out to a waiting limo. He holds the door open for me, and I climb in. But the limo isn't empty like I expect.

"Uh...hi..." I say staring at the two strangers already sitting inside.

"It took you long enough. We were supposed to leave thirty minutes ago," the woman says, who has a striking resemblance to Matteo.

"I'm sorry. Your brother only told me to start getting ready twenty minutes before he wanted to leave."

Gia smiles when I call Matteo her brother. She glares at Matteo when he enters and swats his leg.

"What were you thinking not telling her earlier to start getting dressed? You know it takes women longer than twenty minutes to get ready, especially for a night like tonight."

Matteo shrugs. "I thought she was my slave and she would do what she's told."

Gia hits him harder.

"Fine. I'm sorry. Next time I'll give her more time. Happy?" Matteo says.

"Yes," Gia says, smiling.

I watch the exchange happily. I can't believe Gia got Matteo to apologize. He's not usually the type of guy to give apologies, but I guess Gia might be the only one who has him wrapped around her finger.

"I'm Gia, but you already figured that out," she says.

"I'm Eden."

"And this is Stephen, my date for tonight."

The good-looking man nods at us, but otherwise doesn't seem interested in our conversation or Gia. I hope he isn't the guy she got her heart broken for.

Matteo puts his arm around my back, and I lean back into his arm. Gia stares at us intently, looking back and forth between us.

"What? Is my makeup messed up? It's been a while since I've applied makeup or done my hair."

Gia laughs. "No, you're beautiful."

I smile hesitantly, still not understanding why she is gazing at me so weirdly.

I stare out the window trying to relax until I realize where we are going.

"You didn't tell me the ball was going to be at Armas' house."

I turn to Matteo waiting for an explanation.

He shrugs again. "Must have slipped my mind."

I frown, not liking the idea of being back in his house again. Armas may be gone, but that doesn't mean he doesn't have a brother or a cousin who is as bad or worse.

The limo parks outside the house, and the door opens. Gia and her date step out while I stare at the house, not sure if I want to go inside anymore.

Matteo steps out and holds his hand out to me, commanding me to step out without pushing me.

I grab his hand, feeling calm radiate through him to me as he helps me out of the car.

I continue to hold onto his hand, grasping it for dear life, as we step inside the mansion. I expect to feel nervous, anxious butterflies flickering in my belly. I expect hauntings and terror to cloud my head. But Matteo smiles at me like he knows a secret he's sharing with me, and it all stops. I can't think about anything other than enjoying the night with him.

"You okay?" he asks, raising an eyebrow.

I smile. "Never been better."

He laughs because we both know what I said isn't true.

"Good. Now dance with me."

He pulls me to the dance floor in a large room toward the back of the house that seems it was built entirely for this purpose. With so many people laughing and enjoying themselves, and this room feeling so far from what it was like in Armas' room, it doesn't even feel like I'm in the same house.

Matteo wraps his arms around me, and we start dancing. The music is slow and classic, not what I'm used to dancing to, but Matteo is practiced and patient with me. His hands guide me until we are moving together to the music.

I step on his foot at least three times and each time he growls and laughs. I almost want to step on his foot again on purpose to make him laugh because I love hearing him laugh so much.

"Don't even think about it," he whispers in my ear.

"Think about what?"

"Stepping on my foot again."

I grin, surprised he was able to guess my next move.

He doesn't smile back. Instead, he's focused on something off in the distance.

I turn in the direction of his stare, and I see a man who looks almost exactly like Armas, but a few years older from the gray in his hair.

I swallow hard.

"Sorry, the fun needs to end. Time to get to work," he says.

My heart stops. As he hooks my arm into the crook of his and we start walking toward the man.

He pats my hand calmly, letting me know things are going to be okay, as we stroll without saying a word.

But I have a feeling everything is *not* going to be fine. My stomach is in knots, and so far since I've been captured, my gut feeling has been right. Every time.

The man strides outside to a balcony, and we follow. My throat tightens when we step outside, and we are joined by the entire Espocito family. Armas' parents, his older brother, and a younger brother, who looks to be fifteen. All are standing, staring at us like they want to kill us. They probably will. We are out numbered, and they have a vendetta against Matteo.

We are dead.

And just when I was finally accepting my new life and wanted to live.

I hear heels behind us, and see Gia, and her date walk up next to us. We are now four against four, but I still give them the better odds. The only person who would be useful in a fight on our side is Matteo.

"You had some balls to show up here tonight," Armas' older brother says.

"Why? We were invited, Bruno. It would be rude not to show up," Matteo says.

I clutch his arm tighter as I stare at the man who terrifies me with the same eyes Armas had.

"You fucking—" the young boy says, starting to run at Matteo.

I flinch, but Bruno holds his younger brother back.

"You destroyed this family when you killed Armas and don't pretend you don't know what we are talking about. You are on the security tape," Bruno says.

"Then, you know Armas deserved to die for how he treated Eden," Matteo says.

The older brother smirks and the parents hold onto each other like they can't stand this much longer.

"No. She deserved what she got and worse. And don't act like you don't treat her worse. We all know what she is - a slave," Bruno says.

I stare at the man defiantly. I'm tired of being called a slave. Matteo senses my frustration and tries to pet my hand again to calm me. It doesn't work. I want to rip his tongue out for saying I deserved what happened to me.

I glare over at Gia who appears bored with this conversation. Not the least bit worried we are all about to get shot.

"You need to drop this Bruno. All of you do. I'm more powerful than your entire family put together. I have more resources, more men, more money. Don't start a fight you can't win," Matteo says.

"I didn't start the fight. You did. I don't care what resources you have or how much money you have. We are going to make you pay for what you did to our son," the father says, breaking his silence.

Matteo ignores him, thinking he doesn't have the decision making power.

"This is your last warning. Stop this now. Go back to being old families who rule this town no matter the beef between us," Matteo says.

"No, this is not something we can forgive. This is war. So get ready because—"

Shots are fired. I duck down protecting my head as the bullets ring out around me. I don't realize where they are coming from until I see Matteo holding a gun.

I stare at the Espocito family as they begin dropping to the floor one after the other. First the mother. Then father. Then Bruno.

My eyes widen hoping he won't shoot the young boy. He's a boy. I see the fire in the boy's eyes though, and I know Matteo won't leave him standing either. He shoots him between the eyes, and he drops dead, instantly.

I can't breathe.

I've never seen a person die before. I've seen plenty of crime scene photos. I've imagined how Matteo killed Armas in my head hundreds of times, but I didn't get to witness it. I was too out of it at the time.

But this...this is like nothing I've ever imagined. I thought I would feel more, watching innocent people die. I thought it would feel cold. I thought I would feel sad or heartbroken.

I don't.

I feel nothing.

Maybe it's because this experience has changed everything for me. My heart has hardened. I no longer feel pain for other people. Because if I let the pain in, I'll never be able to survive.

Whatever the reason, I feel nothing as Matteo stores his gun and types a message on his phone.

"Time to go," he says to Gia and me.

I don't know how he will get away with killing the entire Espocito family, but I'm sure he will. He stopped the threat. Armas' family will no longer come after us because they are all dead.

We all climb back in the limo Matteo must have summoned with his text message and begin driving home in silence. Matteo hugs me to his body.

"You're safe now," he says, kissing my hair.

I smile weakly, because in my heart I know I'm thankful for what Matteo did. He killed them to protect not only himself, but me too. And for that, I'm incredibly grateful. Too thankful.

Tonight, I lost another tiny piece of myself. I lost the part that cared about innocent strangers more than I care about myself. I don't know how I can go back to work after this. I don't know how I can have any resemblance to my normal life again after this. This changed me as much or more than the rape did. I've become a monster the same as Matteo.

———

Matteo wanted sex tonight, but he respected my space when I made it clear I wanted to sleep. I wanted to fuck him, but I couldn't bring myself to do it, not when people died tonight because of us. I couldn't be that cruel to celebrate their deaths, no matter how much I wanted to.

So now I'm in his bed, his arm draped over me, as he snores and I can't sleep.

The minutes tick by, but all I can think about is the boy he killed. The white leaving his eyes as the blood spilled out. Matteo is more dangerous than I imagined. He walked into a party with over a hundred people and killed four by himself, without backup. He murdered four wealthy, well-known people in this town, and tomorrow the cops won't come knocking on his door because he paid them off.

I made a deal with the devil, and now I'm as guilty of the crimes he commits. I could have continued to fight. To hold my ground. But I caved because I wanted sex and an easier way. Now I have to live with the consequences.

I carefully slide out from under his arm and sit on the edge of the bed as my stomach grumbles. We left so early I didn't eat much, and I couldn't eat when we got back, but now I could use some food. It might help me sleep.

I stand and tiptoe over to Matteo's closet putting on a pair of his boxers and T-shirt. I have clothes in my closet, but I prefer the smell of his. It comforts me, even though it shouldn't.

But I guess I've gotten comfortable after sleeping with the devil for this long.

I walk over to the small kitchenette in his quarters that usually has at least some basic foods.

I open the fridge and find nothing but beer and moldy cheese. I open the cabinets and find it empty except for a few crackers.

I frown. I need something more substantial than crackers.

I glance over at the door that leads to the rest of the house, as I munch on a couple of the saltines. It's always locked with a key he puts in a safe, when he sleeps, with a code I don't know the password to. I'm sure it's locked, but my grumbling tummy wants food.

I walk over to the door and rest my hand on the doorknob as I glance over at Matteo sleeping. I'm sure he's going to catch me trying to get out and think I'm trying to escape rather than getting food.

My heart beats fast as I wait to ensure Matteo is still asleep before I try the door. I turn the knob and pull. Surprisingly, the door creaks open. It always makes a high pitched sound when it opens, but this time seems worse than usual.

I stare over at Matteo. He doesn't move. So I slink out between the crack before letting the door close slowly, so it doesn't make a sound.

The hallway is pitch black. I assume I'll be met with a guard right outside the door, but I'm not. I know he has security cameras, so I know it is only a matter of time before someone comes to drag me back to Matteo. I don't wait for them to come. I storm down the hallway to the kitchen.

I open the fridge and pull out leftover pizza someone left. I grab two slices and place them on a napkin before walking out to the dining room where I plan on eating before heading back to Matteo's room. I could go back and eat in Matteo's room, but I like having a moment to myself. I like having the freedom. I like that I'm being a bit of a rebel.

I freeze in the door when I find the dining room already occupied.

I wasn't expecting anyone. Least of all Gia. She has her own wing of the house, and she never bothers coming on this side. I know nothing of her life, other than she had a boyfriend who hurt her.

She's sitting at the table with tears running down her cheek and a gallon tub of ice cream sitting on the table.

"I'm sorry, I didn't realize anyone was here. I'll go back to my room," I say.

Gia chuckles. "You mean my brother's room."

I nod.

"Or I could join you?" I ask, not sure what I'm supposed to do.

She pulls out a chair next to her, and I take a seat with my cold pizza.

I start eating it, and her eyes widen and dry a little as she looks at me.

"We have an oven you know? That would taste much better warmed up."

I smile and hold out a piece to her. "You've never had cold pizza? It's an American tradition."

She wrinkles her nose and sticks to eating her ice cream.

"Are you upset about what happened tonight?" I ask, not sure if I should be asking her anything, but I might as well.

"No, I knew what was going to happen when we went. The Espocito family deserved it. I would have killed them myself if Matteo didn't."

I force the bite of pizza in my mouth down. She's as ruthless as Matteo. I need to remember that. I'll need to watch out for her and not get on her bad side.

She raises an eyebrow at me, wanting to know how I feel.

"I'm not upset about tonight either. It needed to happen. I feel guilty that I feel okay it happened."

Gia smirks. "Your first kill?"

I nod.

"You'll get used to it. The first time changes everything. Next time the guilt won't eat you anymore."

My eyes widen. I hope there isn't a next time, but I don't say that to her.

"I'm here because I'm starving and couldn't sleep, the guilt and all. Why are you down here instead of in your wing?"

"I'm all out of ice cream on my side."

"What's the ice cream for?"

She sighs. "Because I'm in love with a guy who doesn't love me back. It's ridiculous to be crying about it, I know, considering your situation, but it's the truth. I'm a hopeless romantic, and I don't know how to get over him."

I smile. "Good to know that at least one Carini has a heart."

She smiles a little.

"You want to talk about him?"

"No."

"If you ever want to, I'm here. I don't exactly have anywhere else to go."

She laughs and looks at me soberly. "Why haven't you asked me to help you get free yet?"

I frown. "You're a Carini. If I know one thing, it's that Carini's are loyal to each other. I knew it was a hopeless endeavor. Plus, I'm not sure I wanted to put siblings in that situation."

She holds out her spoon to me, and I dig into her ice cream. It's rocky road, complicated like her.

"Want to talk to me about you and Matteo?" she asks.

I chuckle and take another large bite of the ice cream. "No. What's to talk about? He stole me to get my best friend back because he's in love with her. I won't tell him where she is because I don't trust he won't hurt her, and Nina ran for a reason."

"Because of our father, not Matteo."

"What?"

"Arlo and Nina ran because Enrico is still alive. Although, I've heard he is barely hanging on in a coma or something, somewhere in Northern Ireland. They are safe from him. Matteo wants his brother back and a chance to get the girl he thinks he loves back."

I consider her words, but considering who they are coming from, I don't trust her any more than I trust Matteo. This could all be a trick to get me to talk.

"Thank you for telling me." I put the spoon down. "I guess I should be getting back. I need some sleep. "

She smirks. "Yes, you'll need some sleep to be able to keep up with my brother. "

I blush.

"He cares about you too, you know."

I freeze as I'm standing up. "What?"

"Matteo, he cares about you. He would never admit it to you or anyone, but he looks at you differently. Even differently than how he looked at Nina."

"He cares about me because he likes to fuck me and I'm his best shot at getting Nina back. That's all."

"Maybe, or maybe he's falling in love with you."

"Even if he is, it doesn't change anything. I don't love him. I don't want this life. I want to go back home to my old life."

"You sure about that? Because it would seem a woman who wasn't falling for him would try a little harder to escape, especially when given such a glaring opportunity tonight, instead of rushing back to his bed."

I ignore her and go back to Matteo's bed, but her words stay with me. I'm not falling in love with Matteo, and he's not falling in love with me. We hate each other. Sex won't change that. Killing for each other won't change that. Not even kindness will change that.

14

MATTEO

SHE THINKS SHE'S WINNING.

Ever since I killed the Espocito family, she has gotten cocky. At first, she was scared, hesitant. She didn't like that she was accepting I killed Armas's family. But now, she's fearless.

I tested her, leaving the door unlocked giving her a bit more freedom. And every night since the night I killed the Espocito family, she has snuck out.

Every. Single. Fucking. Night.

At first, I thought she was planning on finding a way to escape. I thought she was sneaking out to test my security, to find the weak points so when the timing was right, she would run to freedom.

But that's not what she was doing. It seems that merely leaving my room whenever she wanted was freedom enough, at least for now. She's happy with her life, though she will never admit it. And I can't have her happy. Happy means I'll never get what I want.

I close my eyes pretending to sleep like I always do. I wrap my arm around her naked body after fucking her earlier in the shower. She thinks I was rough then; she felt like she was drowning as she laid under the water while I fucked her. Tonight, I have even darker plans for her.

She waits for my breathing to become slow, I even fake snore for a while, so she thinks I'm fast asleep. My arm weighs her down, and I think for once, she might not sneak out tonight and my plan to tame her happy thoughts might be squandered.

But she sneaks out like I knew she would.

I grin as I throw the covers off. I'm going to enjoy tonight.

15

EDEN

I SNEAK INTO THE DARKNESS, not for any other reason than I can. I enjoy the little bit of freedom Matteo has decided to give me. I spend the night eating, walking, reading, or sitting quietly in a new room in the house. It's hard for me sometimes to pull away from his arms. I like sleeping with him wrapped around me, and I still sleep plenty with him. I don't spend more than an hour or two out of bed. And I have plenty of time while he's working during the day to nap if I'm tired.

I let the door close slowly behind me, planning on only reading for twenty minutes or so in the library and then returning to Matteo because I enjoy snuggling with him in bed.

"What are you doing out of bed?" Maximo says, as I freeze in the hallway.

"Just getting some food to bring back to Matteo. He's hungry," I lie.

"No, you're not," he says as Dierk and Paul walk up behind me.

"Matteo gave us strict orders to punish you if you ever broke his rules," Maximo says.

I smile, trying to keep it together. "I'm not breaking his rules. Ask him."

"We will," Maximo says pulling out his phone and dialing Matteo's number.

Shit.

"Matteo, we caught Eden out of bed. What would you like us to do?" Maximo says.

Please let him say take me back to his room.

Maximo grins. "Done."

I swallow hard, trying to keep the fear down. Whatever Matteo told them to do I can handle it. It won't be bad.

"I'll go back to Matteo..." I say.

"No, you'll be coming with us," Maximo says, grabbing my arm.

I elbow him as hard as I can instinctively, not liking his hands on me.

He ducks though, prepared for it this time, and I panic. More hands go on me. More hands than I'm prepared to handle. I try fighting back, but I know at least three guys are holding onto me, and there is no use fighting.

I let them hold onto me and carry me into a room. I feel the bed beneath me as they toss me. My initial thought is to panic. Fight. I'm on a bed with three men standing over me. I should be afraid. Terrified they are going to rape me. But I'm not. If Matteo has made anything clear, it's that he doesn't share. The consequences of sharing me are enormous. *Death.*

So I try to calm my breathing as they stretch my limbs wide and tie me up. Each limb. One by one until I can't move.

Deep breath. In and out. *They can't touch me. They won't touch me.*

I feel hands on my clothes though. Clothes are being ripped from my body. My shirt is torn in half, exposing my breasts. My pants are cut off.

I'm naked. In front of three men. Men I now hate. Men that had no right to try and embarrass me like this.

They all stare down at my naked body hungrily, and I'm what they are hungry for.

"You're disgusting. All of you."

Maximo grins. "We are about to get a lot more disgusting."

He holds a blindfold in his hand and ties it tightly over my eyes so I can't see.

"We won't cover your mouth. We want to hear you scream. We want you to fight. It's music to our ears. That way we know we are doing a good job when we break you. You'll be speaking about Nina by the end of the night," Maximo says.

I keep my lips closed. That's what this is about. It's what this is always about. Nina.

A fear tactic to try and get me to talk. It won't work. Nothing will work.

I've endured worse. Whatever they are going to do to me is nothing.

I still don't believe they will rape me. They might beat me though with whips and bats, anything to get me to speak.

I have to prove to them I can't be broken. I will never speak, and they will stop.

I feel the strike I was anticipating on my stomach, but I don't flinch. I'm used to the pain. I imagine Matteo doing it instead of Maximo.

I'm whipped again on my breasts, and the sting against my nipples makes them harden. Begging the attacker for more.

Next is my thighs, arms, and pussy. Each strike is hard and perfect from the hands of someone experienced with a whip.

"You're sick. You like the pain, don't you?" Maximo says.

I focus on breathing. I should try meditation after this is all over. I can see the benefits.

"You're like Matteo. Dark, sick, and cruel," he continues.

I hear the whip crack again as it hits my stomach.

"Let's see how dirty you like it." His tongue licks the side of my face, and my lips curl in disgust.

I don't want to feel him on me. I don't want him touching me.

I feel more hands. On my breasts, my stomach, my arms. They are everywhere. Exploring my body, touching me places no man should touch without permission.

"Stop," I let slip from my lips.

I bite my lip again hating that I spoke.

"You want us to stop, huh? I thought having three men at once turned you on?" Maximo says.

I deeply exhale as I feel hands twisting my nipple and I can't help but get turned on a little.

Lips on my neck send chills down my throat, and an erection is pushing at my entrance.

No.

I won't be raped.

Ever again.

But that's precisely what's happening at Matteo's orders.

I take a deep breath in again, letting the musky scent of whichever guy is on me. *Matteo?*

I try not to react. I take another deep breath as the cock pushes in. A very familiar cock to go with a very familiar scent.

The asshole was messing with me. Trying to make me think I was being raped when I wasn't.

Two can play this game.

"Stop," I scream again letting it all out as his cock pushes deeper inside me.

The other guys may have their hands on me as well, but it's mostly on the outskirts. Holding my arms and legs down, and saying dirty things to keep up the appearance they are raping me, while Matteo does the dirty work himself.

"No," I cry out as he roughly takes my breast.

"You don't get to speak," Maximo says as something covers my mouth and nose so that I can't even breathe.

I pretend to panic, my arms flailing as best as I can with everyone's arms on me. I don't panic though. I know Matteo is here and he is the one in control and if sex with him these last few weeks has taught me anything, it's he knows my limits and won't hurt me. So when my lungs start burning and aren't able to breathe, that's when the hand is removed, and I suck in a deep breath.

The hand covers my nose and mouth as Matteo thrusts inside of me, hitting the sweetest spots making me come alive like only he can.

I can't breathe as he thrusts, but it only makes it more invigorating. The fact that three other men are watching with their hands on me should embarrass me, but it only turns me on more that Matteo will let them participate to intensify the experience.

I feel my orgasm growing, and now I can't hold on. I can't keep up the ruse that this is hurting me, and I no longer care. I want my orgasm to explode out and give me freedom and pleasure.

The hand is removed so I can breathe, but I can't breathe as my orgasm explodes through my body.

"Matteo!" I cry out as I come around his dick as he explodes into my body.

No one speaks or moves. Eventually, I feel hands slowly leaving my body until I know it's just me and Matteo left in the room.

I grin widely and bite my lip as he slowly removes the blindfold.

"When did you figure out it was me this whole time?" Matteo asks.

I smirk. "The second you touched me basically. I know your scent, your touch, and I know what your cock feels like. You can't fool me."

He grins. "I thought I would teach you a lesson for sneaking out every night. I guess I need to try harder next time."

I shake my head. "Lesson learned. But I wouldn't sneak out if you locked the door."

He leans down and kisses me hard on the lips. I don't know why he kisses me. It's a gentle after fuck kiss, the kind that lovers or people who care about each other give. Not us.

"Let's get you back to bed," he says when he stops the kiss, like nothing happened.

I nod and let him undo the ties on my arms and legs before he carries me back to his bed and climbs in next to me before snuggling close.

I don't understand what we are or even what I want. But maybe that's the point. He's messing with my head completely confusing me, so I don't know how I feel or what I want. I need to get my head cleared now before I let any more confusion cloud my judgment. Or like Gia said the other night, fall in love.

16

MATTEO

I SHOULD BE FOCUSED on the new client we are delivering weapons to today. This client is enormous, and if this first delivery goes well, it could continue to be extremely lucrative for the Carini family in many ways.

But I can't focus on the trade. All I can focus on is Eden.

Damn it.

Fabio said words and I have no idea what. And now he's waiting for me to respond.

"Exactly," I say.

He smiles happily at my response. Hopefully, I didn't agree to give him double the number of weapons for the same price.

I pull out the piece of paper and slide it across his desk.

"Have your team meet us at this address in ten minutes." I stand up and walk out of the office and out to my car where my team is waiting next to their own cars.

"It's on," I say.

The men nod and get in their cars. I do the same and start driving fast to the trade location. The car ride gives me plenty of time to lose myself in ways I can fuck Eden. On the balcony, the pool, my car. Tied up, from behind, in the air. Every way makes me want her more, grow more desperate for her.

My cock can't stop thinking about her. My brain can't stop dreaming of her. And I don't just want sex. I want to drive her in my car and show her all Italy has to offer. Take her to drink fine wines with me and delicious foods. Explore the city and countryside.

I don't understand what is wrong with me. Or why I feel this way. It's been a while since I've gone on a date. Perhaps I need to invite one of my old girlfriends to do something fun with me this weekend instead of spending all my time on work or Eden. That was my father's problem. Work started consuming him until it was his entire life.

I hear the danger before I even arrive. I'm the fifth or sixth car to get to the location, but I know that we are being ambushed. And I know it isn't our new client. He was far too eager to do business, and although he is wealthy, he doesn't have the experience to launch an attack like the one I'm witnessing.

I don't hesitate, I park the car and jump out with my gun out, firing off shots into the woods at our attackers. Some leaders don't get involved in attacks like this. They hang back and let their men do the fighting for them. Carini's don't hang back and let others fight our battles. If I'm going to ask my men to fight, I better be willing to take the risk equally as much.

We are outnumbered. I know that much from the bullets whizzing past my head, but that doesn't mean we are going to lose.

I see my number two, Maximo, to my left. And I give him a look, telling him what I'm thinking without having to say anything. We've had plans like this for weeks after the last almost ambush.

We're ready.

But it's risky.

Maximo takes some of the men and starts moving them to the left side while I stay with some of the men in the middle. We need to draw them to us so that Maximo and his men can attack from behind.

I move forward out of my hiding spot so Clive and Erick's men will focus on me. I'm their target anyway. They want to take me out. Make me feel pain. They don't give a shit about my men.

They think if they can take me out, my men will switch their loyalty to them. They don't realize to join my ranks you have to be loyal. Too loyal. So loyal you'd die rather than join anyone else.

I see Clive hiding behind his men, not even bothering to attack. Letting his men do the dirty work for him.

I aim at him trying to take him out, but he's too far away. A bullet grazes my shoulder, but I keep shooting, sticking to the plan. Another hits my leg; I kneel on the ground still shooting. Not stopping until I the plan succeeds.

Another hits my hand knocking the gun out of my hand. I start to reach for it, but one of Clive's men knocks it out of the way.

A gun is pressed against my head, and I hold my hands up, not that I will surrender. I won't. I would rather die than surrender.

I glare at Clive and Erick, my body red with rage, as they walk over. They are the reason everything started in the first place.

"Ready to give up yet?" Erick asks.

I don't give him a response. He doesn't deserve one.

"Don't worry; we aren't going to kill you yet. What fun would that be?" Erick says.

I frown. The only reason they wouldn't kill me now is if they had bigger plans they thought would hurt me worse. "You can't hurt me. Arlo and Nina are gone. And I know you won't hurt Gia. So there is nothing you can do to hurt me."

Clive smirks. "Oh, there is certainly a way to hurt you."

"No, there isn't."

"There is," Clive looks to Erick both smirking at me. "Eden, your new slave toy. Except, she isn't a slave. You love her."

I growl. I don't want them threatening Eden or telling me I have feelings for someone that I don't. I will never love again. Love only makes things worse.

"My slave is nothing more than property to me. If you steal her, it would be the same as if you stole my car. I would be pissed and kill you. So go ahead and try. I'll enjoy hunting you down."

"We will. The only way to stop this is to turn over Nina, but I bet you won't do that. I think your feelings have shifted."

I open my mouth to respond but I see the gun coming down on my head, and I know it's useless anyway. I close my eyes to control the darkness before it comes. But then I don't have any control at all. I'm lost to the darkness.

———

I open my eyes and find Eden's. She's staring at me, looking at me worriedly, and I'm sure I'm still dreaming. She can't be worried about me.

I close and open my eyes again to try to force myself to wake up, but when I open them again, she's still sitting on the foot of my bed staring at me with her big eyes.

"How are you feeling?" she asks.

I frown. "Like hell."

She nods. "You want some pain meds?"

"In a minute," I say, sitting up and examining my body. My left shin is sore, along with my right shoulder and right hand. And my head is pounding like I was knocked out.

"Don't worry; I didn't stitch up any of your wounds. You wouldn't be alive if I did. Maximo had the doctor come and remove the bullet fragments and stitch you up. He said you should rest in bed for at least a week, but you probably wouldn't listen to his advice."

I nod.

"How long have I been out?"

"Since yesterday afternoon," she says, tucking a strand of hair behind her ear. "I was worried you wouldn't wake up, but the doctor said I shouldn't worry. It was impossible not to worry though."

I grin. "You were worried about me? I figured you would be praying for me to die so you could be free."

"Nah, I figured you had something written in your will that I would go to some long-lost cousin of yours or something if you died."

I smirk. "It's not written in my will, but it gives me ideas."

She laughs, but it's nervous.

I reach out my hand and take hers in mine, wanting to calm her nerves.

"What's wrong?" I ask.

She shakes her head, but I can see the tears in her eyes.

"Nothing, I just...I'm really glad you are okay." She wipes her tears. She must be on her period or something because there is no way she should be crying over me almost dying. The sex isn't that good.

"Anyway, is there anything I can get you to make you feel more comfortable?" she asks.

My eyes turn mischievous as I grab her neck and pull her into a hasty kiss that is meant to show her exactly what I want. My cock pushes into her belly as she falls on top of me.

She pulls away. "We can't. Your doctor told you to rest, and the sex that you usually are into requires far too much of you."

I pout, and she grins.

"No," she says again.

I pull her back into a kiss, and I know she won't be able to resist me. She's horny, and I'll have her tied up in this bed in no time.

Her leg hooks over my body as she sits on my lap, kissing me, as my cock hardens against her groin. Her hips grind over me making me harder and I pull her body too me. She grabs my shoulders to keep her balance.

And I groan in pain.

She pulls back.

"I'm so sorry," she says, holding her hands over her mouth.

I wince, holding my shoulder.

"I told you it wasn't a good idea," she says.

I growl. "No, it's a very good idea."

I grab her, pulling her back to me, despite the pain in my arm. All I feel is the ache in my groin.

"It's worth the pain," I say.

She smiles, but her smile doesn't reach her eyes. It's not genuine.

I kiss her trying to make her forget about anything but having me. She moans against my lips, and I think I've convinced her when she pulls away again.

I frown. "What now?"

She bites her lip in the most adorable way, and it melts my insides a little. "I have an idea," she says.

I raise my eyebrows.

"Do you trust me?" she asks.

"Are you going to let me fuck you?"

"I'm going to fuck you."

I narrow my eyes not fully understanding the difference, but I'll go along with whatever at this point if it gets me laid. My wounds are minimal, although she thinks I almost died. But regardless, my cock deserves sex for what I've been through lately.

She continues to straddle my lap while she looks around the room searching for something.

"Be right back," she finally says as she hops off my lap and runs to my closet.

I sigh.

I guess I understand how she feels every time I tease her and make her wait for sex.

She runs back, holding a couple of my ties in her hand.

"What are those for? Do I get to tie you up?" I ask.

"No, I'm tying you up. That way you won't hurt yourself, and we can still have sex."

I frown, not liking her logic, but as she hops back on my lap and my cock strains against my pants, there is no arguing with her. I want her. And if this is how I can have her, fine.

"Hold out your right arm," she says.

I do.

She takes it and begins tying the tie gently around my wrist before attaching it to the bed.

"I can get out of that you know."

She smiles. "I'm aware. I mainly want your injured arm out of the way, so I remember not to touch it."

She glances back at my leg. "Do I need to tie your leg up too?"

I grab her waist, pulling her to me as I sweep a kiss hungrily on her lips, not letting her stall this any longer.

She kisses back, just as hungrily, forgetting that I'm injured or that she needs to be careful. Her hands grab my neck and tangle in my hair, holding me to her.

I tangle my one free hand in her hair, keeping her lips locked with mine. We don't always kiss when we fuck, but when we do, it's like fireworks go off. Lighting strikes our bodies, and we can't stop kissing. No matter what.

I reach for the hem of her shirt needing her T-shirt off.

She grabs the hem and lifts it over her head, tossing it to the floor giving me access to her perfect tits. I massage the soft flesh of her breast as it fills my hand.

Her moans are like honey. Sweet and sultry and beautiful. I love the sounds she makes with her throat. Sounds that I cause.

Her fingers rake down my chest, feeling every muscle in their wake.

She's fierce as she moves her hands over my body, knowing exactly what she wants, and not being sorry for it.

I try to pull her pants down, but she swats my hand away.

I frown.

"You need to learn to be patient," she says, grinning and enjoying herself far too much.

She stands, and I pout, as I try to grab her and pull her back to me. She fights me off.

She very slowly lowers her pants like she is putting on a show for me. Wiggling her hips as the pants fall slowly to the floor.

I growl at her naked body that is a few feet away that I don't get to touch.

I pull at the tie that is barely holding me to the bed.

She wags her finger back and forth at me.

I growl.

She grabs the covers and pulls them down, before grabbing my boxer briefs and pulling them down my body, as I lift my hips to help her.

I want her on my cock now.

She winks at me, knowing exactly how desperate I am for her.

She takes my cock in her hand and pumps it up and down slowly. So, so slowly. I can't handle it.

I grab her hand, moving it faster over my cock.

"No, I get to be in control. Not you," she says, pushing my hand off.

She lowers her head, and her lips wrap around my cock as she moves just as slowly up and down, teasing and taunting me.

My eyes roll back in my head, and I let my head fall back on the pillow, at how good her lips and tongue feel over my cock.

But I'm not patient. Not with her.

I grab her hair, moving her head faster over my cock.

She grins when she can finally breathe again.

"I knew I should have tied both of your hands up."

I smirk. "No, you shouldn't have."

I grab her, as she climbs on top of me and finally sinks her pussy on top of me. My cock drives into her, and she moans against me as her hips climb up and down on top of me.

I won't last.

And from the moans she is making, she won't last either.

I thrust, and she sinks down on top of me, our eyes meeting and our tongues tangling.

"Yes," she moans, as she comes on my cock, drenching me.

Her moans take me over the edge, and I come right after her.

She grins as she climbs off me and slowly unties my arm, which is just beginning to ache again, now that the adrenaline is slowly leaving my body.

I watch her body, now flushed and glowing, as she puts her baggy T-shirt and sweatpants back on.

I get up to go shower and get dressed. I need to go to the office and make a plan for how to deal with Erick and Clive. I'm not going to let them make the next move. I won't let them hurt Eden or anyone else.

The only way to defend ourselves is to take out Erick and Clive. Destroy them and their business. I need them dead. Only then will Eden be safe. Any of us be safe.

"What are you doing?" Eden asks, staring at my naked body, as I start walking toward the bathroom.

"I'm going to shower and then get dressed. I have work to do."

She frowns and chases after me as I walk to the bathroom and turn on the shower, before stepping in. The water is chilly at first but quickly turns warm within seconds of me standing under the water.

"You are not going to work," Eden says, stripping before stepping into the shower with me.

I smirk, enjoying having a naked woman in the shower with me. I grab the bar of soap and begin running it over her body, over every one of her curves.

Her eyes close as she enjoys my hands on her body. She shakes her head, realizing that I've gotten her under my spell again.

"You are not going to work! Your doctor told you to stay in bed for a couple of weeks. You were just shot. Three times and knocked unconscious. You aren't going anywhere."

I cock my head to the side and hold down her flailing arms.

"I'm going." I glance down at my wounds that are healing well and barely ache. They are nothing compared to the pain I feel knowing that Erick and Clive want to take what is mine.

I stare at Eden. "Trust me. I'm fine. This pain is nothing."

She pouts. "Stay..."

I narrow my eyes at her. "I have to go."

"Why?"

"Because I protect what's mine."

She takes the soap from me and begins scrubbing my body with it, as she contemplates what I meant by my words. I rinse off and then turn the water off when I'm done before stepping out. I hand her a towel and take one myself before I walk to my closet to get dressed.

Eden follows me to the closet, watching me dress in jeans, a shirt, and jacket.

"I don't need you to protect me. I need you to stay alive," she says, her voice soft.

I raise an eyebrow. "You'd miss my cock that much if I was dead?"

She swallows. "Something like that."

I stare at her a moment before I make up my mind. "Get dressed. Jeans, a nice shirt, and jacket. None of those sweatpants you usually wear."

"Why?"

"Because you are coming with me."

Her face lights up, and she runs to her closet to get dressed before I even step out of the closet.

She looks gorgeous in her dark jeans, red shirt, and black leather jacket. She chose red heels to complete her look.

"I'm not going to have to hold your hand to keep you from falling in those all day, am I?"

She laughs. "No, but you can hold my hand all the same."

I do hold her hand. I hold her hand in the Ferrari as we drive with the top down on the way to the warehouse we use as an office building and storage facility.

I try to relax knowing that Clive and Erick won't launch a second attack again so soon. I spoke with Maximo before we left and I know that their team was severely injured. They don't have the manpower to launch a second attack again so soon.

So Eden is safe, for now.

I stop the car outside the building that is my whole world. The men inside are not just men. They are family. Family that relies on me for an income. For keeping them safe. And for providing them a family.

I hold Eden's hand as I lead her into the building. When we step inside, all eyes are on us. Everyone has wide eyes or shocked expressions on their faces. I've never brought anyone here that wasn't my family or an employee.

No one expected me ever to bring Eden here, yet here she is.

"I need a team ready to discuss what our plan of attack is to take out Clive and Erick in five minutes," I say to Dierk.

He nods and runs off to gather a team while I lead Eden to the long table at the far end of the warehouse.

She smiles at the men. "Hi, guys. Is Matteo working you too hard?"

"Not any worse than usual," Paul says with a wink.

"I'll put in a good word to try and get you some time off," she says back, smiling.

I pull her to me. "You know that you don't have to flirt with every guy here?"

She smiles. "Why? Would it make you jealous if I did?"

"Yes, very jealous."

"Good. You don't have to worry though. I've just gotten close to a few of the guys that have been helping me out."

"I know. Going against my rules, feeding you, and taking care of you."

She grins. "Go easy on them. I'm charming."

I kiss her on the lips, claiming her in front of everyone. "I know."

We both take a seat at the long wooden table, as several of my men start taking a seat at the table surrounding us. When the team of about six of my most trusted men arrive, all sitting down at the table, I start.

"As you all know, we are here to talk about how to handle Clive and Erick. I'm done with their games. They threatened my life. They threatened this company and all of your lives." I don't add that they threatened Eden's life. "We are going to put an end to them and their business."

"I think we should set up an ambush similar to how they attacked us," Dierk says.

I nod along just listening, not shooting down anyone's ideas yet.

"That will never work, they will be expecting that," Paul says.

"They are going to be expecting every kind of attack. The only thing they won't be expecting is one where we do nothing. So unless we plan to do nothing, then we are going to lose our element of surprise."

"What do you think sexy?" Maximo asks, running his hand up and down Eden's arms. "I know you have some brains in that head of yours. What do you think?"

I glare at Maximo, not liking him touching Eden. I don't like how she shivers at his touch. I don't like him even talking to her. I immediately regret bringing her here.

Eden looks from me to the men as I can see her brain turning, thinking of a solution to our problems.

"You use me," she says.

I frown. Yep, definitely shouldn't have brought her.

I laugh. "You're crazy. Erick and Clive don't give a fuck about you."

She raises an eyebrow at me, as do most of the men.

"They are after Eden? Why?" Dierk asks.

"Because I look like Nina. The Carini's stole my best friend from them, and now they want revenge. They think I'm the new Nina. So they want to steal me. Use me to draw them in. Use me as bait, then attack," Eden says.

Realization hits every one of my men as they listen to her speak. They like her plan. And there is nothing I can say to convince them otherwise. The only leverage I have to put an end to the plan is my claim as the leader. Their boss. Tell them they don't get a say in decisions that affect their lives too.

"No, we aren't using Eden," I say, trying to end the conversation. They know that if I say no, that's the end of it.

But instead, chaos erupts. Men start talking over each other trying to throw out plans and convince me why Eden should be involved in the plan.

This is not what I expected. At all. I thought we would come up with a plan that involved a carefully crafted attack. Not one that would involve using Eden as bait.

I glance to my right and see Maximo, with his hands on Eden. I've had enough.

I punch Maximo in the face. "Touch her again, and you're fired," I say, grabbing Eden's arm and leading her out of the warehouse.

Maximo runs after me blood pouring down his face. He grabs my arm, and I think he's going to punch me. Instead, he says, "I'm sorry."

He looks from me to Eden.

"Apology accepted," Eden says.

"Eden, go wait for me in the car," I say, tossing her the keys, knowing that she could jump in the car, take off, and I could never see her again.

She takes them with wide eyes and walks out to the car.

"I don't need your apologies. I need you to focus on work instead of on my woman. Understand?" I say.

Maximo nods. "I understand. But I need to be blunt with you. Your feelings for that woman have blinded you. Clive and Erick want Eden, don't they?"

I don't respond, giving him his answer.

"That's what I thought. So the only way to take them out is to use her as bait. She knows that. The men know that. And —"

"I know that," I say finishing his sentence.

He pauses. "So what are you going to do? Are you going to lead us into an ambush even though you know it will end in us all dead or will you use the girl?"

I glare at him. "She's not a girl."

He takes a step back, assuming I'm about to hit him again.

I glance out the window to where Eden is sitting in the car.

"I'll use Eden."

17

EDEN

THE DAY MATTEO took me to the old warehouse, where he runs his business, was the day that everything changed.

I don't know what changed. And I don't care. But my life is much easier now.

Matteo never locks the door to his bedroom. He lets me freely explore the house and the grounds whenever I want.

He even let Gia take me shopping the other day.

It's like we are a couple. Well, almost.

Minus the fact that I didn't enter into this relationship willingly. And the fact that he never takes me on dates. And when we fuck, it's borderline rape every time, somehow pushing the line, but crossing it. And I don't have access to a phone.

Otherwise, we've developed an easy relationship with each other. We may not talk about mundane things, like how our work day went, or the weather, or anything like that, but none of that stuff matters anyway.

We know how each other feels with just a glance. We know what each other craves with just a touch. We know what each wants with just a kiss.

We both like fucking each other too much. I'm not sure it's

healthy. Actually, I know it's not. I'm addicted to his body. I'd willingly have sex with him multiple times a day, and it has nothing to do with saving Nina.

I'm afraid that if given a choice between returning home immediately to freedom, or getting a day full of sex with Matteo but having to stay his slave forever, I might choose the latter.

I'm sick. And Matteo is my cure.

This can't keep going on like this. It's not healthy for either of us when we both know this sexual relationship has a time limit on it. And the longer we go, the harder it's going to be when we stop.

Neither of us cares or think about that though. All we care about is the next fuck. Like a drug addict only caring about his next fix.

Matteo won't be home for hours, which means I'm going to have to handle the familiar ache between my legs myself. He's at work, trying to figure out a plan to deal with Clive and Erick, the same single focus he's been worried about for weeks.

He hasn't brought me back to the warehouse since he first took me there weeks ago. He also won't even talk to me about using me as bait. He won't even consider it.

Which means he either cares, or he really thinks of me as his property.

He's fooling himself if he doesn't think I can help though. I know what Clive and Erick want. Me.

Matteo can deny it all he wants, but it doesn't matter. I know the truth he hides behind his eyes.

I head to the bathroom and turn on the faucet in the tub. I might as well take a long bath since I have hours to kill and nothing to do until Matteo gets home. I have free range of the house and could watch TV, read a book, or go for a run. But none of those things can hold my attention.

It seems that only Matteo can hold my attention.

I turn the water off when it fills the bath, drop my clothes to the floor, and then climb into the bath, sinking all the way down until the water hits the tip of my chin.

It's warm and relaxing. But I didn't draw the bath for relaxing. I drew it to get rid of the aches that consume my thoughts.

I let my hand drift down between my legs, rubbing gently as my bud slowly starts to awaken. I close my eyes and my thoughts immediately go to Matteo. I try to think of past boyfriends, hot celebrities, and imaginary men. Anything to make me stop thinking of Matteo. But despite trying, it never works.

Matteo is what my body wants, even when he isn't good for me.

I picture his hand replacing mine. I picture him climbing into the tub naked, as his cock drives against my stomach letting me know he wants me as much as I want him. He pinches my nipples, making my hard peaks come alive. And then he sweeps his tongue into my mouth, claiming me in a kiss that is primal, hungry, and sexy as hell.

I purr, the kiss feeling far too real.

"You wouldn't be trying to get yourself off without me, would you?" Matteo asks.

My eyes fly open, and I grin.

"No, you were there in my dreams."

He smirks. "I bet."

He climbs into the tub, still fully clothed, and I squeal from the excitement of him being here.

"Why are you back so early?" I ask.

"We figured out a solution."

"Really? What is it?"

He shakes his head and then kisses me again. "Does it matter?"

No, it doesn't matter. He's kissing me and that only means one thing. He's going to fuck me.

He reaches behind me. "I have some fun toys to try."

My eyes darken as I see the nipple clamps in his hand.

He kisses me again, and I feel the cold metal against my skin. My nipple hardens against his touch, and then he places the clamp firmly on my nipple.

I moan from the pain and the pleasure.

He does the other one, and I can't focus on anything but my breasts. It's like all my blood and focus go there. He grins as his hand goes down between my legs, tearing my focus between my nipples and the ache between my legs.

I let my head roll back and rest against the edge of the bath, no longer caring where my focus is. It's his. Just like my body. He can do whatever he wants to me, and it doesn't matter.

I feel his cock slide into me, and my body feels whole.

I open my eyes to see him still clothed except for his cock. He grabs my shoulder as he thrusts into me, sliding me down deeper into the tub. I don't care. I let him. I trust him completely with my body. Despite the fact that with each thrust, my mouth falls further beneath the water threatening my oxygen supply.

I can't breathe after a few thrusts, because my face is covered with water. His lips come down on mine giving me breath and a sweet release. I come on his cock as easily as breathing.

He grins pulling out of me and pulling me back up out of the water. He stands and then pulls me up too. He tugs at the nipple clamps, turning me on again before he pulls them off and I'm left with nothing but ecstasy and emptiness, missing his cock.

He helps me out of the tub and hands me a towel, while he finally undresses and wraps a towel low around his waist.

"I want to try something. Trust me?" he says, but all I hear is a command to my soul to which I can't say no.

I nod, my mouth dry. I love when he wants round two so quickly afterward.

"Go lie down on my bed, face down."

I don't bother to dry off all the water from my body. I walk to the bed, laying the towel down first to not completely soak the bed, and then lie down on my stomach as he asked.

He takes his time before he finally walks to the bed. I don't hear him, but I can feel him standing at the base of the bed.

I don't turn to look. I don't need to. I trust him and whatever new thing he wants to try.

He climbs on the bed behind me and gently lifts my hips up placing a pillow under my stomach.

"I'm not going to tie you up, but you can't move. Understand?" he asks.

I nod.

"I need to hear you say you won't move."

"I won't move."

"Good girl." He pushes his cock inside me without warning into my ass. He's fucked me in the ass before, but usually, I get a lot more warning and preparation. Not this time. This time he wants me to feel the pain.

Tears sting my eyes, but quickly subside when his fingers play with my most sensitive bud, and he starts thrusting, making me feel like I'm floating on a cloud.

He kisses my neck, and I moan. I love it when he kisses my neck before he nibbles. I love feeling his lips anywhere on my body.

"Take a deep breath, baby," he whispers into my ear before sucking on my earlobe sweetly. He's acting far too sweet, which means it's time for the pain. The part where I don't know if I can handle it right before I come but want more and more of the pain I thought moments before I couldn't tolerate.

I suck in a breath.

Pain.

I feel searing pain in the back of my neck as Matteo stabs me with something. I know he's drawing blood from whatever he's doing.

This.

This is my breaking point.

I can't handle more of whatever this is.

"Stop," I beg through tears.

He kisses my neck, and the pain disappears. Just like that. Did he listen to me? Or did I blackout?

He thrusts inside, and I'm back to the real world again. The world where he worships my body in the worst ways.

"You got this baby. I need this," he says, and then I feel the burning pain again against my neck.

I don't know what he's doing or why. I take his words and play them in my head again and again. He needs this. He's using my body to please himself. And as screwed up as it is, I'm more than okay with that.

The tears still sting my eyes, but less this time. My body jolts as the stabbing continues, but this time he thrusts, I focus on what his cock is doing to my body instead of the pain in my neck.

"You're mine, beautiful," he moans as he continues.

"Yours," I whisper back, knowing exactly how true my words are.

I don't care about being a lawyer again.

I don't care about returning to my old boring life.

I care about him. Because he's the only one that has made me feel alive.

He's protected me against Armas. He's taken care of me when I needed help the most. He's done everything for me. More than anyone else in my life ever has.

I can see myself painting again here. I can run. I can study history again. I'm stronger here. No longer afraid of anything. Because I know I can handle any pain or nightmares. I'm stronger than I ever realized.

Matteo showed me that.

I'm more alive here than I ever was back home. Matteo is my new home. I don't ever want to go back.

I might even love him.

It's a crazy thought.

One I shouldn't have.

I probably have Stockholm syndrome. I just fell in love with my captor, and when I get free, I'll realize how crazy these feelings are. But I don't think so.

I've seen other women who had feelings for their captor. This is different. I still despise him for taking me against my will. I won't ever forgive him for that, but I can't ignore the caring man he can be when he's not pretending to be a monster.

All the feelings in my body intensify. The pain. The pleasure. The heartache. It all comes to a head.

"Come, Eden," Matteo commands.

I don't think it's possible. I can't when I'm in this much pain. But I feel the tightening of my body. My toes curl, my breath catches. And I come like I haven't ever before.

I come hard on his cock as the pain slowly subsides and the kisses on my neck stop.

I come, and it's an experience I never want to forget. It's the first time I've come while in love. And I want to remember it forever.

Matteo doesn't let me collapse against the bed. He grabs my arm and drags me off the bed and into his arms. I'm too exhausted to walk.

He knows, so he scoops me into his arms to carry me to the bathroom, most likely to clean up.

"Look in the mirror," Matteo commands, and he brushes my hair off my neck.

I glance in the mirror, out of the corner of my eye.

My eyes widen when I see the marks he left in black ink.

Matteo Carini's.

It's a crude tattoo. Blood is oozing down my back, and the lettering isn't perfect or dark, but I wouldn't have it any other way. It's a perfect way to mark how I feel.

He doesn't wait for me to respond. He doesn't speak any other words either. He simply kisses my forehead and then carries me back to bed.

He didn't say I love you. I didn't either.

He didn't ask if I liked the tattoo or if it was okay.

I didn't want him to anyway.

He marked me as his. And it's exactly what I wanted.

Even though our relationship will never last, I'll never remain his forever. Someday another man will fuck me and have to look at his name on my neck with his name on it.

I may love another man one day. A man that treats me nicely and lets me make my own decisions in my life. A man that isn't dangerous enough. A man that won't remind me of Matteo in any way.

When that day comes, I'll be more than happy to have Matteo's name etched on my skin.

18

MATTEO

"You ready?" I ask Eden.

She raises an eyebrow. "I'm always ready for you." She throws her arms around my neck and kisses me hard on the lips.

I smirk. "I meant ready to go."

Her eyes widen as she falls off my lap. "You were serious? You're taking me on a date?"

I nod.

Her face lights up, and I really wish it wouldn't. She's wanted to go on a date for weeks, despite never asking me to take her. I've wanted to take her on a date too. Today's that day.

But as much as I wish this was just about going on a date, it's not. It's playing double duty. I've given into what Eden wants, in more way than one.

"You have five minutes to get changed."

She darts off my lap in the main living room and starts running toward my bedroom.

She pauses in the hallway. "What should I wear?"

"Jeans and a nice shirt. And make sure to wear your hair up!"

She grins and then disappears. She better fucking listen to me, for once, and wear her hair up. I need to see her tattoo today.

I thought she would make a big fuss when she finally saw the tattoo. I thought she would yell and tell me I had no right to do it.

She didn't. In fact, I'm pretty sure she likes it. More than she should.

I don't even know why I did it. It was an impulse thing. I had the equipment. Not the fancy tattoo guns that you get at the shop, but the kind that barely gets the job done, although in a more painful way.

I just knew that I needed her marked. Especially before today. I may be giving in to Eden and my men's plans, but I'm going to let the world know she's mine while I do it.

Eden leans against the wall of the living room. "Does this work?" she asks beaming, knowing how fucking sexy she looks.

I stand and walk over to her. Taking in her dark jeans, her cleavage-revealing yellow halter top, and her matching spiked heels. And her hair pulled up in a clip.

I kiss her on the lips, sweeping her off her feet, reminding her who she belongs to tonight because I'm afraid this plan is going to fail. I think it will work to take Clive and Erick out, but I'm worried I might lose Eden in the process. She might finally find a way to escape. Although, the heels she is wearing makes it a little less likely. But she can run fast. Even in heels.

"So where are you taking me?" she asks, grinning far too brightly.

"Dinner."

"It's two o'clock in the afternoon? What are we doing before dinner?"

"Whatever you want."

She bites her lip. "Anything?"

"Anything."

"How about horseback riding?" she asks, her cheeks flushed.

I laugh. "You want to go horseback riding, in that?" I look down at her heels.

She frowns. "I didn't realize we could do anything I wanted when I picked this outfit out. But yes, I want to go horseback riding. I think it will make me feel free. And then I want you to take me to a local bakery. Buy me something sweet and coffee, and then make out with me as the sunsets, before taking me to dinner. That's what I want."

"You are such a girl."

She puts her hands on her hips. "Well, what would you have us do then?"

I shrug. I hadn't really thought about what we were going to do before dinner. I just wanted out of this house with her. That was the plan.

"I guess, drive fast in my Ferrari with the top down. Then take you to one of my favorite wine bars to get a drink, and then I guess I could show you my favorite spot to watch the sunset before dinner."

She thinks for a moment. "Damn it. I like your idea better."

I smirk, surprised that she would be so agreeable to my plans.

"Let's go," she says, holding out her hand to me. I take it, and we run through the house, like two teenagers sneaking out of their parents' house.

We make it to the garage. "Which car should we drive?"

"The red one," she says, knowing that one is my favorite, despite not knowing the name of the car.

"Good choice."

We climb in, and then I spend the next hour racing through the countryside of Italy. Enjoying the twists and turns, occasionally taking a turn too fast just to hear her squeal.

Then I take her to my favorite wine bar, where I let her taste various wines and explain to her why her tastes in wine are wrong. She laughs but eventually comes to see things my way.

Lastly, I take her to an old bridge that looks out over the river to watch the sunset. I take her in my arms, wrapping my hands around her waist, while we watch the sunset. Kissing her neck, just to the side of where I carved my name into her neck a few days before.

Just as the sun is about to set fully, she says, "Why did you give me the tattoo?"

I swallow but don't immediately answer.

"Why are we on this date? Why give me the perfect day? What's going on?"

I kiss her again, giving her one more perfect moment, not wanting this to end.

"I'm giving you what you want."

She cocks her head to the side, not understanding. "You're giving me my freedom?"

I suck in a breath, not liking her response, but of course, that's what she wants - freedom from me. I'm not ready to give her that yet. I can't give her freedom.

"Using you as bait to draw out Clive and Erick."

She tucks a strand of hair behind her ear.

"Is that still what you want?" I ask, thinking I made a mistake.

She nods. "Yes, I want to help."

"Good. Because it's going down tonight. That's what this date tonight is about."

"Oh..."

I study her soft expression, but I don't understand what it means.

"What's wrong?"

"Nothing. I just thought... never mind." She smiles too brightly. "What do you need me to do?"

"Nothing. I just need you to pretend you are on a date with me and let me and my men do the rest."

She nods.

"Can you do that?"

She nods again.

"Don't be afraid. I won't let them take you. You're mine."

She melts against my side as we start walking the three blocks to the restaurant we picked out. I made reservations at the restaurant a couple of days ago under a fake name, but I know the owner likes to run his mouth, and he's good friends with Clive. He would have told him that I was coming in and bringing a date. I'm positive Clive will take the bait once it's confirmed that Eden is here with me.

He will try to steal her. And I'll take him out when he does.

We walk into the restaurant, and we are guided toward a booth at the back that overlooks the river. This is one of the most upscale restaurants in town. And I'm the wealthiest sucker in this town, so I always get the best table. They bring over a bottle of my favorite wine without me even having to ask. They pour us both a glass, and I notice Eden drinking hers faster than usual.

I take her hand in mine and try to come up with something funny

462

to say to distract her, but I can't. I can't even distract myself. Clive will give us one look, and he'll know that this is fake. A setup.

I stand up and slide into her side of the booth draping my arm around her shoulder. I may not be able to make her laugh right now, but I can make her forget.

My hand slides up her jeans, and I silently wish that she had worn a skirt instead of pants. She shifts as her cheeks finally flush pink.

I tilt her head toward mine and kiss her firmly on the lips. She melts in my arms, instantly forgetting about everything. I continue making out with her in the booth, not caring that this is a fancy restaurant and this is simply not done. I want her calm. She doesn't know that my men are all around, waiting for the signal to attack.

Food is set in front of us. The restaurant has a fixed menu so course after course will be brought to us.

The first is soup, bringing us both back to the night I fed her soup by holding the bowl up to her lips.

She laughs when I pick the bowl up to her lips, but it doesn't stop her from drinking the liquid from it.

The rest of our meal is pretty uneventful. We talk, we laugh, we eat. Clive nor Erick have made an appearance, nor any of their men. We've been eating dinner for almost three hours now, well past the time that a normal dinner would take. They aren't coming.

"I need to use the restroom before we go," Eden says.

I nod, get out of the booth to let her out, and then take a seat again, watching her ass sway as she walks away in her jeans. Loving that we are both wearing jeans, despite this being a fancy restaurant where everyone in it is wearing dresses and suits. The staff hasn't said anything to us. They know better.

I pay the waiter while I wait for Eden to return. But ten minutes pass and she still hasn't returned.

I glance back at Dierk at one of the tables a few back. He has a concerned look on his face as well.

Shit.

We both dash up, drawing our guns, as we run toward the back exit.

I find Eden with a gun pointed at her head in Erick's arms.

She doesn't look afraid though. She looks mad. And I know that she has the skills to break free from Erick's arms any moment she wants to. I don't know what self-defense classes she took, but they were good. She's taken out plenty of my men before. She won't right now. She's acting as bait. But she will when the time is right.

"Let her go," I say, acting scared. Although it's not an act. I am scared. I hate him touching her or having a gun pointed at her. Even if the plan is working.

"Nah, I think we will keep her. You seem to care about her. I think we will enjoy playing with her a bit first," Erick says, nuzzling Eden's neck. Her eyes turn to rage, matching my own.

Patience.

Don't let him goad you into doing anything stupid, I tell myself.

I sigh. "Fine. Take her. She's nothing to me." I put my weapon down pretending I'm done fighting.

Clive laughs. "You can't fool us. You love her. You won't let any harm come to her."

I swallow. I don't love her. But damn, do I care about her more than I should.

"Fine. You got me. Now make a trade."

Clive raises his eyebrows. "What kind of trade?"

"Me for her."

He laughs. "No way, what use are you to us?"

My men are in position. The only man that ran out with me was Dierk, and that's because he was acting as my usual security. Clive and Erick and the dozen men they brought with them don't know that I have more men here.

"What do I have to do to get her back?" I ask slowly and deliberately, giving Eden a look that she needs to break free now, as I give my team the cue words to attack.

Erick's hand drops just a tiny bit as he grows tired of holding the gun. Eden takes the opportunity to knock the gun out of his hand while she elbows him hard in the nose. He lets go of her immediately, grabbing his nose. She runs toward me as shots from my men ring out around us.

I start shooting as well; I won't ever leave my men to fight a battle for me.

"Get her out of her," I say to Dierk as Eden reaches me. I grab her hand and sling her over into Dierk's arms. He grabs her arms and starts pulling her. He'll get her inside.

I have a job to do. I need to kill these bastards and keep my men and Eden safe.

I glance to my right to make sure that Eden is safe after Erick & Clive's men start returning shots, but Dierk has barely made it to the door and Eden is in his arms, fighting him the whole way. I give him a look and then turn my attention back to Erick who now has his sights set on me.

He fires, but I'm faster. I hit him hard in the chest watching him fall to the ground. Most likely dead, or he will be soon enough.

I hear Eden scream, and I feel the bullet in the back of my arm. I try to spin to turn and shoot my attacker before he gets another shot off but I know I won't be fast enough. I can only hope that he doesn't have great aim and hits me in my extremities instead of my head or chest.

The shot has gone off, but I make it all the way around before I realize what happened.

Eden.

She took the bullet for me and is lying on the ground at my feet.

I aim my gun at the guy that shot us both, and hit him in the head, watching him drop dead instantly.

And then I fall to the ground, scooping Eden up in my arms before I run. I never run. I stay and fight with my men. Maybe I would have in the past, but not now that I'm their leader.

But tonight is different. Eden could be dying in my arms, and I need to save her.

I run as fast as I can to my car, toss her in and then start driving, not thinking about anything other than getting her to a hospital as fast as I can. She took a bullet that could have easily killed me. She saved me.

I stroke her lifeless face as I drive. I'm pretty sure she stole more than a bullet meant for me. She stole my heart.

Erick may not be right about many things. But he was right when he said that I love her. I do. I love Eden. I would do anything for her.

I only hope I get the chance to tell her and earn hers in return. Because there is no way, an angel like her could love the devil in me. I need to give her her freedom and hope it's enough to keep her.

19

EDEN

I WAKE up and immediately know I'm in a hospital. It's far too bright to be anywhere in Matteo's home. The only other place it could be is heaven, but I know that the bullet just barely grazed my arm, so that can't be it.

Although, why I'm in a hospital is lost on me. I can tell from how my body barely aches that I'm not injured enough to be here.

I look over and see Matteo holding my hand like I'm about to die, staring at me with relieved eyes when I open mine. He exhales deeply, reaches over the hospital bed, and hugs me.

"I'm so glad that you are okay," he says.

I scrunch my nose. "Did I miss something? Because I don't feel that injured."

I move my arms and legs around, realizing the only part of me that is even taped up is my arm, and it barely hurts. I have an IV that could be feeding me pain drugs, but they wouldn't make me feel this much better.

"You were shot in the arm."

I smile. "You brought me here because I was shot in the arm?"

He nods, still frowning and not understanding while I'm smiling.

"Yes, you were also passed out, and I was afraid you might die."

I bite my lip to keep from smiling brighter as I stroke his cheek.

"You do know I survived an injury to my leg that was a lot worse than this without going to the hospital?"

"That was a mistake," he says coldly.

I raise an eyebrow. "Did the doctor say that something was wrong with my leg?" I'd be surprised if he did. My leg feels amazing.

"No, he said it seemed to have healed nicely."

"Then, what's the problem?"

He sighs.

My heart falls in love a little more, seeing him risking losing me to bring me here.

"How did...?" I ask, not being able to ask how many men he lost when he saved me instead of staying and fighting.

"Clive and Erick are taken care of. We only lost two men. It's going to be hard for the men to lose them. But their sacrifice wasn't in vain. Just like yours wasn't."

I swallow. I hate that anyone died, but I'm glad it's over. We're safe. For now at least.

I hear the knock and look up to see a doctor walk in smiling at me brightly.

"Can I have a moment alone with Eden?" she says, looking at Matteo.

"No, I'd like to be here for whatever you have to talk to her about," Matteo says, glaring at the woman for even suggesting that he leave my side for a moment.

I don't care if he stays or leaves, but I like that he wants to stay.

The woman gives him a snide look back. "I'm not asking. I have private information that I need to discuss with Eden, and I will not have you here when I talk to her."

He doesn't budge. "I'm her husband."

She laughs. "No, you're not. Now get out of here, before I call security and have you thrown out. I don't care if you are the king of Italy, I want you out."

He looks from her to me, and I nod, encouraging him it's okay that he leaves.

"I'll be right outside the door if you need me." He kisses me gently on the lips and then storms out, flipping off the doctor as he does.

The doctor ignores him and walks over to my bed. "I'm Abigail Faustino. I've been looking after you while you are here. How are you feeling?"

"Great actually."

She smiles. "Good. I know that you were involved in a gunfight with Mr. Carini. I'm not here to ask questions or get involved. But I am here to help if you want a way out. Do you need a way out?"

I swallow. I may never get another chance like this again. She's offering to help me. I should take it. My heart thumps loudly. I can't.

"No, I don't need your help," I finally say.

She nods. "I figured you'd say that. Mr. Carini seems to be especially fond of you, so I hope he treats you well."

"He does."

"Good, well now that that is out of the way, I have some news to share with you. When you were admitted, we ran some regular tests and well...you're pregnant."

I gasp and then I can't breathe. I can't move. I can't think. Of all the things she could have said, that was the least expected.

The door is thrown open, and Matteo runs in, clearly having heard what the doctor said.

The woman sighs but doesn't object as Matteo runs to my side and holds my hand.

"I think she might be in shock," the doctor says, coming to my side as Matteo stares at me.

I suck in a breath as the doctor puts her hands on me.

"How far along?" I ask, coming to.

"We don't know for sure without an ultrasound, but it could be a couple of months."

I swallow, staring at Matteo, silently telling him that it could be Armas' baby.

Matteo frowns. Grabbing my cheek and forcing me to look at him. "It's mine."

I swallow. It should make me feel better. It should make me feel happy to know that it's most likely Matteo's, but it doesn't. I don't know how he will feel about having a baby. I don't even know how I feel. Should I get an abortion? I shouldn't have a monster's baby while I'm captured.

But I haven't really been captured in a while. He has given me freedom without actually telling me I was free. I just turned down freedom. He's shown me he loved me without telling me.

And I know I love him. Is this the worst thing? Maybe him having a kid would change him. Make him softer, get out of this life and live a whole new life with me.

"Could you leave us alone for a few minutes, doctor?" Matteo asks.

The woman nods and leaves.

I stare at Matteo, still not understanding how I feel. Matteo smiles at me softly as he holds his hand over my stomach.

"We are going to have a baby," he says, giddily kissing me firmly on the lips, seemingly happy with the idea.

I take a deep breath and close my eyes as he kisses me. He's happy to have a baby with me, so I'm not going to fret. Not immediately anyway. I'm going to just be. And see what happens.

I open my eyes though, needing to talk about so many things. But what I see when I open my eyes isn't the Matteo I've gotten used to these last few weeks.

Instead, a darker Matteo is here with much darker intentions. His hands are on me touching me without permission. His cock burns inside me, and his eyes see red.

I close my eyes and open them again, and I'm back in the hospital room instead of the couch in his room. It was a memory. A memory I had forgotten or tried to push out of my head. Whichever it is doesn't matter.

What matters is that I remember. I remember the worst of Matteo. And I realize I should have taken the doctor's offer to help me escape.

20

MATTEO

EDEN'S PREGNANT.

That should send my heart into a panic.

I've stolen a woman, made her mine, and now I've knocked her up.

She hates me. There is no way she will want to carry my baby. Even if she does, there is no way that afterward, she will stay. That she won't try and steal the baby away from me.

Eden deserves to be free. I can't keep her trapped. Not anymore.

But I can't let her go. Because if I do, if she gets that chance, she will never stay. I won't ever see the baby.

And this baby is already mine. I need an heir. I need a family to continue my legacy just like my father needed me. And more than that, I want a family. I want someone to love and take care of. That's who I am. I take care of people, and I want to take care of a family.

I stare at Eden. I have no idea how to keep her. I have no idea how to set her free, but convince her to stay. I have to try though. And it starts with telling her how I feel.

"Eden I—"

She slaps me hard across the cheek before throwing the covers off and stepping out of hospital bed. She rips the IV out of her hand before she starts gathering her clothes in the corner of the room and starts putting them on, one by one.

"What was that for?" I ask, trying to keep my anger out of my voice.

She pulls up her jeans before grabbing her top and jerking it on before she answers me.

"You raped me," she says.

I freeze. The one thing I didn't want her to remember is rushing back into her memory. I stare at her, not sure how to continue. I don't see fear when she looks at me. I don't see the same broken woman I saw with Armas.

Instead, I see a strong, fierce woman, that won't put up with my crap.

"Eden, let me explain."

She laughs. But it's not a funny laugh. It's a 'you're ridiculous for trying to explain rape to me' laugh.

"I don't need you to explain. I was there. I remember. You raped me."

"I stopped!"

"You stopped because you were interrupted. And stopping doesn't matter anyway. You should have never started!"

"I'm sorry! Okay? Is that what you want to hear? I'm fucking sorry."

She shakes her head. "You can't just apologize for rape. That doesn't make it any better. It doesn't take away any of the pain."

She starts walking toward the door, and I grab her arm.

"Where are you going?" I ask.

"I'm leaving," she says, before realizing her mistake. She doesn't have freedom. She doesn't get to leave because she wants to. I tell her what she gets to do and what she doesn't.

She freezes, as does my heart because I know what I have to do, and it risks losing her and the baby forever.

I reach into my back pocket and pull out my wallet. I dig out my cash and my credit card along with my cell phone and hand them all to her.

She takes them hesitantly, not understanding what I'm doing.

"You're free. Use the money, the phone, to get you wherever you want to go. Tell Dierk to take you if you prefer. But you're free to go. You're not my slave or my captive. You're free."

She studies me for a moment and then she walks to the door.

"I love you, Eden. I love this baby. I still want you to be mine," I say.

She doesn't hesitate at my words. She simply walks out, leaving me alone.

I thought raping her would break her. I thought it would change her and force her to give me what I want.

Instead, she broke me.

———

One week after Eden left, I could barely get out of bed.

Three weeks after she left, I was so drunk all the time I couldn't even think straight.

Six weeks after she left, and I'm now a broken man, not worth anything.

"I found her," Dierk says, while I lie on the couch staring out the window.

"What?" I ask, sitting up abruptly.

"I found her," he says again.

"Did she go back to her condo in Los Angeles? Or did she get a new apartment?"

"She didn't go back."

"Huh?"

"She didn't go back," Dierk says again, getting annoyed at having to repeat everything to me. "She's staying in a hotel in the old downtown area. She's working at a coffee shop as a barista. She stayed."

She stayed.

She fucking stayed.

That must mean something. She still has feelings for me. She still wants me. She wants me to fight for her. Or she still has unfinished business. Whatever it is, I'm going to find out. Today.

I get up off the couch, needing to go to her immediately.

"Where are you going?" Dierk asks.

"To get Eden back."

He runs in front of me, blocking my path to the garage.

"You aren't going anywhere. One, you are drunk and are not driving a car. Two, Eden will not take you back in this state. You'll just piss her off further. You are going to have to work hard to earn her trust back."

I glare at him, but even in my haze, I know he's right.

I sink back down onto the couch, hating myself for getting drunk again today. It takes me far too long sitting on the couch to realize what my next move should be.

"I need you to get me the number to the florist. I should at least send her flowers," I say to Dierk, who has been standing over me to ensure that I don't do anything crazy.

He nods. "It's going to take a lot more than flowers to get her back."

"I know, but it's the best place to start."

———

After I sent her flowers every day for a week, I decide to step foot inside the coffee shop. I figure it's safer to show up during the day, instead of waiting until she goes back to her hotel room where she's alone. She'll probably shoot me without a second thought if I show up there.

The bells chime as I step inside the quaint tiny shop that only has two small tables, both of which are occupied. Most people just come in to grab a cup of coffee and then go out to the local park to drink it or head off to work.

There is nowhere for me to hide in the shop and take my time by studying her first.

She spots me the second she hears the chimes.

Her face is expressionless. She doesn't react. She must have been expecting me after all the flowers. She looks good, despite her expression. Her body is curvy, just beginning to show signs that she's pregnant.

She's still pregnant. My insides warm seeing her still pregnant. I thought she would have gotten rid of the baby by now if she hated me.

I walk slowly to the counter, not sure how to handle this. I haven't asked a woman for forgiveness, ever. I don't date. I don't know how to make up with her. I don't know how to make any of this better.

"What can I make for you?" she asks, when I get to the counter like I'm any other customer. I understand now what the expression on her face is - indifference. That's at least how she's trying to appear. Like she doesn't care about me.

But if she didn't have any feelings for me, whether it be love, or caring, or hatred, she wouldn't still be in Italy.

"I'll have an espresso."

She types it into the computer and then turns to make my coffee. When she finishes, she sets the mug down with a thud, letting a couple of drops of the coffee spill out onto the counter.

She takes my credit card and swipes it, before handing it back to me.

"Why are you still here? Why haven't you gone back to the US yet?"

She frowns. "Because they won't let me back without a passport. And since I don't have one of those, I'm stuck here for a while."

I sigh. A passport. Of course. "I'll have Dierk get you a passport by the end of the day."

I take the espresso to go drink it on the small patio outside when I see, out of the corner of my eye, the flowers that I sent her sitting in the far back of the coffee shop. She didn't immediately toss them. There is still hope for us yet.

———

I show up at her coffee shop every day for a week. Every day I go, I expect her to be gone. She has everything she needs to leave now. A passport. Money. I even bought her a suitcase and packed up all her things from my house so that she had whatever she needed to leave.

And yet she still hasn't left.

She hasn't spoken more than two words to me or smiled at me, either. But I figure it will take a long time for her to be accepting of me, let alone start to forgive me for what I've done.

I stole her from her life.

I've threatened her life and her best friends.

I raped her.

I knocked her up.

I shouldn't ever be forgiven.

Today, though, I have to try. I can live with myself if she leaves, as long as I've tried everything I can to keep her, while also giving her her freedom.

"I'm sorry," I say when she hands me my cup of coffee.

She doesn't look up. She keeps staring down at the cash register.

"I'm sorry for being a monster. I'm sorry for stealing you. I'm sorry for hurting you. I'm sorry for raping you. You shouldn't forgive me, ever. But I'm not going to lie. I want you back. And I'll do anything to make that happen."

Her breath catches.

"But I won't steal you again. I won't take you against your will. I love you, Eden. I don't know what that means or even how to love you, but I will work hard every day to love you more than I did before. I will become the man that you deserve."

I take my coffee, walk out, and then I pull out my cell phone. She needs a grand gesture to come back. I know that. This phone call is the first step in making that happen.

21

EDEN

I DON'T KNOW what I'm doing at Matteo's doorstep with my luggage in my hand. All I know is I won't run. I don't know what's going on between us. I doubt we can ever work through the damage we have caused each other, but if I leave without trying to figure this out, it will feel like running.

He will come after me eventually. He might be trying to change, but he hasn't changed that quickly. And he will continue to haunt my dreams as he has for the past few weeks.

Our child will grow up without a father, and I won't have a reasonable explanation as to why, other than he was a monster once and I never gave him a chance to change.

So I guess that's what I'm doing knocking on his door. Seeing if he can change. And seeing if I can forgive.

I'm not sure if one or either is possible. But the growing baby in my stomach convinces me I need to try at least.

The door opens, and I'm shocked Matteo is the one that opens the door, but then I remember he has plenty of security to tell him who is standing at his door.

"Hi," I say, my voice sounding weaker than I'd hoped.

"Hi, would you like to come in?" he asks, his voice just as weak.

I nod.

He takes my suitcase from my hand and holds the door while I step in. It's strange walking in the front door instead of the side from the garage. It was strange ringing the doorbell. His house had started to feel like home the last time I was here.

"Can I get you anything? Something to eat or drink?" Matteo asks. He's nervous.

So am I. I wanted to pretend he didn't affect me when I stepped inside this house. That's not possible.

"No, I'm fine."

He tries to be patient with me, but it's clear he can't be.

"What do you want then?" he asks.

"Let's go out back and talk."

He nods and places his hand on the small of my back as he leads me through the house to the back patio. I like having his hand touching me, even if his hand has done wrong, monstrous things.

We take a seat on couches, opposite each other. I want him sitting right next to me, touching me, comforting me, but it's not what this conversation needs.

I sit in silence, watching him squirm, trying to remain calm and patient with me. I like watching him squirm, so I take my time before I speak.

"I can't forgive you," I say.

He sucks in a breath, and his eyes turn sad.

"But I can try. Maybe I can't forgive you, but we can start from here and grow into something better. Or maybe we can't. I don't know. I just know I don't want to run. I want to stay and figure this out. I want to see if the man that sends me flowers and love notes every day is possible of actually loving this baby and me. I think he can."

"I can. I love you more than I want to keep breathing."

"I have a couple of conditions."

He nods, his eyes glaring into mine as his hands grip the armrests to keep himself glued to his seat.

"I'm not a slave. I'm free—"

"You're free. It's not something I want anymore. I don't want to trap you or kidnap you ever again. I don't ever want to hurt you."

I smile and nod. "Good. You don't get to tell me what to do or boss me around in any way. We make decisions together. Understand?"

"Yes, together," he says, smirking a little as I smile at him, giving up a little of my authority.

"And you give up searching for Nina. You leave Nina and Arlo alone."

This is the one condition I expect to be the hardest for him. I don't understand what his connection is to her. I don't know if he still wants her or wants revenge. I don't know.

When I was free, I called Nina a few times. I didn't tell her what happened. I pretended I was still back in the US and had just been busy working. But she didn't seem that shocked I hadn't called in a while. She understood I was busy with work.

"I won't go after Nina or Arlo. I give you my word," Matteo says without hesitation.

I listen to his words looking for any deception. But I believe him. I have to if I'm going to give whatever crazy relationship we have a shot again.

It doesn't mean I won't want him to continue proving it to me over and over.

But to be honest, something changed when I found out I was pregnant in the hospital. Matteo changed. He set me free. And I realized what I wanted, more than my freedom was to be with him. How fucked up is that?

"Can I show you something?" Matteo asks.

I nod.

He holds out his hand, and I take it automatically, feeling his warm grip comfort me with just his touch.

He leads me inside, and we walk to his bedroom. I smirk, he's going to show me his cock. He's such a guy.

He opens the door that isn't locked and holds it open while I step inside.

It's so bright. Light shines in through the large windows that he usually keeps hidden beneath the drapes. The bed and furniture are gone and replaced by white antique furniture with a light gray comforter and turquoise and pink pillows.

"Pink?"

He shrugs. "I had Gia help. She said you would like the pink."

I laugh. But my laughter soon turns to tears when I see the bassinet he put in the corner next to the bed. I walk over and run my hand across the white lace fabric draped over it.

I turn to Matteo who has his hands in his pockets. He does that when he wants to touch me but won't let himself do it.

"I started clearing out the room next door for a baby's room, but I thought I should wait to see if you'd come back before I decorated it. I thought you might enjoy doing that. And I had no idea what color you would want it to be."

"Pink."

He chuckles. "It can be pink, or whatever color makes you happy."

I shake my head because he doesn't understand what I'm saying. I walk over to him swaying my hips just to torture him.

"There is a reason I want it pink, and it's not because I like the color."

He frowns. "Why?"

I bite my lip to keep from laughing hysterically. He's so clueless; he doesn't even understand what I'm saying. "I'm having a girl."

I don't know how he will respond. If I had to guess which gender he would prefer, it would be a boy. A boy to follow in his footsteps and his father's before him. A boy that will become as ruthless as him. He would have taught him how to shoot a gun at the same time he learned to walk most likely.

He grabs me by the waist and twirls me around before kissing me firmly on the lips. "*We* are having a girl."

I nod. "*We*." I like the sound of that.

He kisses me again, and his hands are all over my body, feeling my curves like he hasn't felt them in years instead of weeks.

I moan because I've missed his hands just as much. Honestly, I've yearned for everything about him. Even the darkness.

I throw my hands around his neck, not thinking of anything but Matteo. I want him, and he wants me. I don't care that I haven't forgiven him yet. I don't care that I still don't know what I want and he's still the devil. I don't care about any of our problems.

I want him. Naked. Worshipping my body. Making it so that all I can think about his tongue, his hands, and his cock.

He gets the message immediately and pushes us back on the bed. We fall in a heap, our arms and legs tangling together, refusing to let go of each other.

I grab for the hem of his T-shirt, jerking it off his head so that I can see and taste his hard skin. He helps me pull off his shirt before his lips land back on mine again, not giving me enough time to ogle his body as I want, but when his tongue sweeps over mine, I forget about hot his body is. I can look later. I only want this. So much more of this.

His hands slide under my shirt, careful over my belly, and push my flowy tank up, as his hands caress my swollen breasts.

Every time he touches me it feels like more. More intensity. More caring. More energy. More love.

He pushes the shirt off my body and stands to remove both of our pants until we are both naked, our bodies pulsing with blood and filled with aches that need satiating.

"Tie me up. Spank me. Whip me. Claim me," I beg, needing to see the darkest side of him again. He might think that is one of the reasons I ran, but it's not. It's one of the things I surprisingly like about sex with him. He's not afraid to be himself with me. Even the darkest parts.

But his darkest parts allow for me to be free.

His eyes deepen, and his throat growls. At first, I think he's going to give me what I want.

Instead, he spreads my legs wide, and his head buries between my legs, licking my most sensitive of areas as he worships my body. I grab his hair, needing to touch him, as he drives me wild with his masterful tongue.

"God, yes, Matteo. I forgot how good that feels."

He grins against my lips as he continues to lick until I'm screaming his name and coming around his tongue.

My legs fall to the bed, exhausted from coming. But I know we aren't done. I need his cock, and he needs me.

"Do you trust me?" he asks.

I stare up at him with wide eyes, not sure what he's asking, but if it has to do with tying me up or spanking, then yes. I trust him completely.

"Yes," I whisper, still in my sex coma from coming once already.

He scoops up my body and starts carrying my naked body. I think he's going to carry me out of the bedroom to another room where he thinks he can fuck me better. He doesn't.

He takes me to the couch where he raped me.

I close my eyes and take a deep breath as he forces me to face the worse in him. I expect the butterflies and the pain in my heart to overtake me. I wait for the tears to pour. But they don't come.

He lays me down, ever so gently on the couch and then carefully nests himself between my legs.

"I want to fuck you. Make love to you," he says, waiting for me to respond.

"Fuck me," I respond, knowing we both need this if we are ever going to have a shot at moving forward together.

He leans down and kisses me tenderly as his cock slides into my pussy. I arch my back at the invasion, wanting him deeper as he intensifies the kiss and tangles his hand in my hair.

His eyes are open as he kisses me and thrusts inside. I keep my eyes open as well, not willing to miss one moment of the emotion oozing out of his eyes.

His eyes tell me everything as he fucks me sweetly. I'm sorry. You're beautiful. You're my everything. I love you.

I never thought that someone could say so much and my heart would melt so quickly.

He kisses my favorite spot on my neck making my toes curl before he says, "I love you, Eden. More than anything."

I suck in a breath as he starts bringing me to my climax again.

My body convulses exploding around him as he comes inside me. "I love you, too."

He stays inside me holding me on the couch for what must be hours as we both drift to sleep. The couch used to represent so much pain. He tied me up here. He raped me here. But now, I can't think of this couch without thinking about what just happened. We made loved and found the first step toward what could be a forever kind of love here. The beginning of forgiveness.

———

Our love and forgiveness continue to grow over the next month, as our baby grows large in my stomach, making it clear how pregnant I am when I'm wearing anything other than a baggy T-shirt to cover up my bump.

Our days are filled with normal things that normal couples do. Dates. Fights. Cooking. Sex. And a lot of decorating the baby's soon to be room.

Matteo painted the walls pink for me. I hated it, so he painted it this beautiful gold sparkly color. But then I saw this gorgeous crib that was a silver color that would have been perfect, and he offered to paint it again. He might have to, but for now, I've settled on gold with pink accents.

Our life has been simple. Good. But we haven't talked about any of the big stuff. I figure if we can get through the little things like what we are having for dinner and what movie we are watching on our dates, then the big stuff will come.

Am I ever going back to the US and my old life? Do I want to start a new career here? What are we going to name this baby? What life do we want for her? Is Matteo going to continue killing people? Am I okay if he does? Are Nina and Arlo ever going to be safe to come out of hiding?

I don't know the answers to any of those questions. All I know is that I'm desperately in love with Matteo. And he's equally in love with me. And both of us are smitten with our baby that's due in a few months. *What else could we need?*

It's early in the morning when Matteo slips out of bed, throws on some clothes, and sneaks out of our bedroom without kissing me goodbye or letting me know he was leaving.

He rarely does this. But he has done it a handful of times over the last month. He doesn't tell me where he is going and I don't ask. But I know what he is doing. Working.

Just one of the many topics we should discuss and be honest with each other, but we don't. I guess we aren't doing as well as I thought we were.

I try sleeping, but I know it is a useless endeavor. I can't sleep with him out of bed.

I get out of bed and put on a robe, deciding I should head downstairs to get some coffee and drink it out on the back balcony to watch the sunrise and think about how we should handle all the things we are too afraid to talk about.

I make it to the kitchen and start pouring myself a cup of coffee when I hear Matteo's voice ringing through the hallway before it drops to barely a whisper.

I frown. That's weird. He's working in his home office instead of the warehouse.

I decide to go give him a kiss, bring him a cup of coffee, and let him know I'll be out on the balcony if he wants to join me when he is finished with his phone call. I pour another cup of coffee and then carry them both down the hallway to Matteo's office.

"I have them. I know where Nina and Arlo are," Matteo says.

I freeze outside the door, my heart sinking.

"Yes, I remember our deal. I'll be ready to bring them to you by the end of the week."

I try to calm my breathing and heart, but both are beating so speedily I'm sure that Matteo can hear me lurking outside his door.

"Yes, father. You can do whatever you want with Nina and Arlo. I'll even help you kill them if you want. But you have to keep your end of the deal. I expect to be paid well for this, and you promise to leave Italy and never return. I don't want you messing with what is mine now."

I can't listen anymore. He's making me sick. I thought he had changed. I thought he cared about me, loved me. I didn't think he was ready to give up his entire life and I never asked him to. All I asked was for him to give up Nina. That's all I wanted. To keep her safe.

He told me he loved her once, but it was never about love. It was always about revenge and money. That's how he and his father both think. That's why Nina chose Arlo.

I need a phone.

I run through the house, needing to find a phone to call Nina. The thing that I've spent my entire time trying not to do, I now have to do. Matteo figured out where Nina and Arlo are. He might already have men there, ready to take them. I have to warn them.

The problem is there are no fucking phones in this house. I know because I've looked countless times.

I see Maximo round the corner. He must be on duty this morning. He's not my favorite. He doesn't usually want to help. But today, I'll force him to help me.

"Maximo," I shout.

He stops.

"I need to use your phone," I say, panting heavily.

He stares at me a moment, and I think he's going to say no. He's going to revert back to the slave talk and say I don't get such privileges.

Instead, he pulls out his phone and hands it to me.

"I need to go patrol outside for a bit. I'll make sure to buy you your own phone after I get done with my patrol. I'm sure Matteo meant for you to have a phone but hasn't gotten around to getting you one yet," he says.

Even Maximo thinks highly of Matteo. Matteo has fooled everyone, his trusty employees included.

"Thank you, Maximo," I say. I don't tell him that the new phone won't be necessary because I won't be staying. I need to warn Nina and then get out of here as fast as I can.

When Maximo has walked outside, I pull up the keyboard and begin typing the number I memorized that Nina gave me for emergencies only. I wait impatiently, pacing back and forth in the hallway hoping that Nina answers. If she answers, she's still alive.

I hear the phone click over, "Nin—"

The phone is snatched out of my hand, and Matteo speaks, "I have Eden. I've had her for the past year. If you want to save her, I suggest you and Arlo get to Italy. Fast."

"No," I shout, hoping she hears me before he hangs up the phone.

"She won't come. You won't get her."

He shakes his head, and I swear I see tears in his menacing eyes.

"Nina will come. She loves you. She will do anything to protect you," Matteo says.

He's right. And I hate him for it.

"You won't hurt her. You promised. You won't turn her over to Enrico. You can't."

He swallows. "I'm sorry."

I back up, sick and tired of his apologies.

"If you do this, we are done. I won't forgive you for this. I'll run. And I'll take our baby with me. You'll never get to see her."

"If that is what you think is for the best, then I will let you go. You won't have to run; I won't come after you or our daughter. You can be free."

I narrow my eyes, not understanding him. He's fought so hard to get me back only to let me go now? It doesn't make sense.

"When this is all over, I'll let you go."

I see the syringe in his hand too late. I feel the sting, and then my eyes grow heavy. If this fucks up our baby, I'll kill him. He catches me in his arms, and the last thing I remember is him saying, "This is for the best. It's the only way to keep you safe."

He could have said those words. Or my brain may have imagined them because I was too desperate to hold onto the thought that he still loves me and we can be a happy family someday. He could have said those words. He could have been protecting me. Or he could not have given a fuck at all.

22

NINA

SHE'S BEEN GONE A YEAR. And I did nothing. I didn't even know she was gone.

I don't know why Matteo took Eden. The only thought I can come up with is because he is pissed at me and looking for revenge. He wants to hurt Arlo and me for what we did to him.

He's had Eden this whole time. Tortured her. Raped her. And now he might kill her if we don't do exactly what he wants.

I swore I would never go back. That Arlo and I had started fresh. We would run forever if it meant we would never have to go back. But I would do anything for Eden.

I'll go back to her in a heartbeat if she can be free.

"Can you drive any faster?" I ask Arlo, who's barely breaking the speed limit as we drive through the curvy roads of Italy.

He rests his hand on my lap trying to calm me. "Dying in a car crash won't help Eden. Besides, he won't touch her until we get there. He wants us to suffer," Arlo says.

I swallow the lump in my throat. "I was a horrible friend. I was living this amazing life with you, while my best friend was suffering in agonizing pain."

"No, you didn't know. And from what you've told me, Eden's tough. She will get through this. Just like you did."

I nod. She's made it a year. That's a lot longer than I was locked up for.

Arlo speeds up, and we finally pull up in the driveway of the Carini house. It's long and dark and equally as hauntingly beautiful as I remember.

But we aren't here to admire the beautiful architecture. We are here to do whatever it takes to get Eden back.

Arlo takes my hand as we pull up in front of the house, both of us knowing that the security team already knows we are here.

"Ready?" he asks.

I pull the gun he gave me and taught me to use, out of my purse.

I nod.

He pulls his gun out, and then we step out of the car ready for an attack at any moment.

Arlo still has hope that he can negotiate with Matteo. Get him to talk to us, and we will get out of here without a scratch. I don't think we will be so lucky.

Arlo also thinks that the men that now work for Matteo will still show him some loyalty because he used to work with them. Was friends with them. They were like family.

He's delusional. I remember what family does to each other.

We step into the house and don't hear anything. Not a person talking. Not the TV or radio on. Not even a deep exhale of breath. Nothing.

We hold onto each other's hands as we slink through the house, trying to hide in the shadows, but it quickly becomes apparent that there is no one to hide from. No one is here.

"Why would Matteo call us here and then not be here?" I ask.

Arlo gives me a dark look, and I know what he's thinking.

Dungeon.

He's in the dungeons waiting for us. I don't want to go back to the dungeon. It holds too many mixed memories for me. It's dark, and Matteo will have the upper hand. But we didn't exactly get to pick the place where the fight will happen.

It will also be harder for us to talk calmly with Matteo.

We don't have a choice. We have to go.

So we slink down to the dungeon. Trying to be as quiet as possible.

But when we open the unlocked door and it creaks loudly, we know that it was the wrong approach.

I scream as Arlo is knocked out from behind before he even has a chance to fight.

"Seems you've lost your touch brother," Matteo says.

"Matteo, please. Just let us go. I'm sorry I chose Arlo. We never meant to hurt you."

"It's been a long time. You don't understand the trouble you have caused," he says.

I drop the gun, knowing it's useless against him. My only hope is to find his weakness.

"Let Eden go. She doesn't deserve to be here. Take me instead," I say.

"No!" I hear Eden cry behind me.

I turn and see Eden locked away in one of the cells behind me. She's still alive. Her eyes are still full of fight. I exhale a little seeing her, but I don't run to her as much as I want to. I need Matteo to make the trade first.

"You're right about one thing. Eden doesn't deserve to be here."

He grabs me by the arm, and he motions for his men to pick up Arlo's lifeless body that I can barely look at. I know he's still alive, but I still hate seeing him like that.

I hear Eden continue to scream behind us, but I tune her out as Matteo walks me away from the dungeon.

"Where are we going?" I ask.

"To make you good on your end of the deal. Eden will go free, in exchange, I'm turning you and Arlo over to Enrico."

Everything stops. I would die for Eden. Do anything for her. But I will do anything not to be taken by Enrico again. He raped me. Did unspeakable things. I will not let him be the one to torture and eventually kill me. I'll die before I let him touch me again.

23

MATTEO

I HAVE Maximo take Nina in one of the cars. I can't be near her and do what I need to do.

I sit in the back of one of the SUVs while Dierk drives with Arlo tied up next to me.

He slowly wakes up. I knew he would on the way to the warehouse.

"You asshole. Nina gave you all this power, and this is how you choose to use it, by turning us over to Enrico?" Arlo asks.

"It beats running," I say.

Arlo glares. "Running kept us alive."

I smirk. "For how long. I was able to track you within a month. Even with Enrico weak and with limited resources, he wouldn't have taken much longer to find you even without my help. You were dead anyway."

"So that makes this better? We were going to die one way or another so you might as well make some cash off of this and get on Enrico's good side?"

I shrug. "You know me. Only looking out for myself. You aren't worth much to me after you abandoned me."

"Why wait so long? Why not turn us over the second you found us?" Arlo asks, struggling against the ropes, but it's useless, he isn't getting free.

"I thought it would be more enjoyable if you and Nina had a chance to bond. Fall in love truly and all that shit. It also gave me plenty of time to have my own fun with Eden. Now Nina will die knowing that I have her best friend who also faces her same fate."

"If you love Nina, let her go. She's yours. I'll back off. You can have her. She loved you once; she can love you again. Just don't turn her over to Enrico. Keep her alive and safe," Arlo begs.

I stare at him, my brother who has no idea who I am or what I want. I laugh. "You really are clueless."

"I'll do whatever you want. Just don't hurt Nina."

"Then you should have stayed. You should have been loyal to me. Instead, you ran. Now deal with the consequences."

I pull out my cell phone and dial the number. "I have them. We are making the trade tonight. At the warehouse."

Arlo's eyes grow big as he realizes he's lost. That soon I'm turning him and Nina over to Enrico, and there is nothing he can do.

Welcome to my life brother. How does it feel to have no power and know there is nothing you can do to protect the woman you love?

24

EDEN

Nina and Arlo came. Nina was feet away from me, and there was nothing I could do to protect her.

Matteo took them, and I'm afraid it was the last time I might ever see either of them ever again.

"Dierk!" I shout to the man standing guard outside my dungeon cell.

He casually walks over to the door that has bars and a small window at the top.

"Where is Matteo taking them?" I ask.

He looks at me sadly. "To the warehouse. He's turning them over to Enrico. But if it makes you feel any better, I really think he will let you go free when this is all over. He told me not to hurt you no matter what. He wouldn't do that if he wasn't going to let you free."

What is it with everyone thinking that Matteo is a good man? He's a cruel, manipulative, monster. He wants power and money. He doesn't give a shit about anyone else.

I sink down on the floor terrified Nina is going to die, and it's my fault. I should have protected her. I should have called her and told her what was happening when I was free. Now I'll never get the chance.

My body shakes and trembles as I sit on the floor, sobbing. My voice cracks, a high-pitched cry that encompasses everything I'm feeling. Heartache. Terror. Fear. Love. Useless.

"Eden, are you okay?" Dierk shouts through the bars.

I open my mouth to say yes, but an idea forms.

"No, I think...god, my stomach, I think something is wrong with the baby..."

I don't know what instructions that Matteo gave Dierk, but if Dierk thinks that Matteo still cares about the baby and me then Dierk will think he has to do everything he can to protect me.

Dierk pops the door open and runs to me holding me in his arms.

"Let's get you to the hospital," he says, helping me to my feet. "Can you walk?" he asks.

I nod as he puts his arms around me and starts leading me to the garage. He walks me to the car that is parked nearest to the exit of the garage. Just as he's lowering me into the car, I say, "I'm sorry," and elbow him hard in the nose.

Dierk falls to the floor, and I grab the keys, race around to the driver's side, and speed off. I may not be able to save Nina, but I have to try.

————

The warehouse is dark when I pull up, but there are dozens of cars scattered around the parking lot. I know they are here.

I don't have any weapons. Nothing to get Nina back or protect myself with. I have no idea how I'm going to get her back. But I have to find a way.

I rub my stomach reminding myself that I'm not just risking my life when I try to save Nina. I'm risking my baby's life too.

It just makes me more determined.

I choose the back entrance to enter, hoping that I can sneak in without being noticed. I do, but I hear a man's voice that brings fear to my soul.

Enrico Carini, I assume.

I slink down the hallway to the large room that serves as everything; weapons hold, meeting room, office, and now as a trading place. A place to trade my best friend for money and the promise of Enrico to leave Matteo alone.

I duck down behind a desk when I see Matteo. He's standing in the center of the room across from a man that looks twice his age. He's shorter than Matteo, but also somehow crueler looking. It's Enrico.

Behind Enrico is a dozen men on his side.

At least a dozen stand behind Matteo as well.

I search, but it doesn't take me long to see Nina and Arlo with their arms tied behind their back, standing behind Matteo with a gun pointed at their heads by Maximo and Paul.

My fingers tremble, and my legs ache as I squat down. I want to jump over the table and demand Matteo to release Nina and Arlo, but I know that won't happen. All I can do is stay here behind this dusky desk and hope that an opportunity presents itself to save them.

"You brought them. I didn't think you had it in you, Matteo, to betray your own brother, but maybe you are my son after all," Enrico says.

"I did. Now you need to hold up your end of the deal," Matteo responds.

Enrico nods to one of his men, who brings forward a large brief-case. He opens it presenting it to Matteo. Matteo flips through the cash quickly and the nods, accepting the cash.

The man closes the briefcase and sets it next to Matteo.

"And the second half of our agreement?" Matteo asks.

"You won't see or hear from me again. I won't return to Italy. I've been staying in Northern Ireland setting up a new turf there. That's where I'll be returning," Enrico says.

Matteo nods. "Good."

"Now one last thing to meet my terms," Enrico says.

"You didn't have any other terms," Matteo says, the corner of his lip twitching, upset.

Enrico cocks his head to the side as he smirks. "I always have additional terms when needed. You brought me Nina and Arlo so I could get my revenge. I'm still not convinced you've completely turned on your brother and are now on my side, however."

Matteo narrows his eyes, clearly annoyed with his father's requests. He doesn't argue though. Instead, he turns and walks toward Nina first. He grabs her chin as she struggles against the ropes, which keep her from lashing out at Matteo.

"I love you, and you betrayed me. You deserve what's coming to you," Matteo says. He tightens his grip on her chin and then kisses her lips. It's not like a kiss he's ever done with me. It's all tongue as he slobbers over her lips and forces his tongue into her mouth. Suddenly, he ends the kiss, as quickly as he started it, and then slaps her, knocking her to the floor.

I was expecting him to hurt her. I knew he hated her, but I can't stop the tears from flooding my eyes, seeing her drop to the floor in pain. And I can't stop the ache in my heart from forming when I see Matteo kissing another woman. Even Nina. Even under these circumstances. I know that he loves her and hates her. Unlike me, who is nothing to him.

Matteo turns his attention to Arlo, who is writhing with anger after watching the woman he loves hurt by Matteo.

"You're no brother of mine," Arlo says growling.

Matteo stands expressionless in front of his brother. He stands still for a long time as he stares at Arlo. I don't know what he's doing. He doesn't talk. He doesn't move. He just stands there.

Suddenly, he pulls something shiny out of his pocket and quickly jabs the object into Arlo's stomach.

I gasp at the sight of the blood pouring out of Arlo, not expecting Matteo to actually stab him.

Everyone's eyes turn toward me. My gasp was far too loud not to be discovered, but they can barely see me as I'm still crouched behind the desk.

I have two choices. Run away. Or try to save Nina.

I choose the latter.

I run around the desk and race toward Nina, hoping if I distract Matteo's men long enough, Nina will be able to escape. I'm fast, but not as fast as I used to be, now that I'm pregnant.

I run straight toward Paul, who is holding Nina back, and I kick him as hard as I can in the shin. He jumps back, and I grab her.

"Shoot her," Enrico says to his men.

I hear the shots and Nina and I both duck down instinctively.

Abruptly, I'm gripped by strong hands, and I know that my plan to try to free Nina is short-lived.

I glance up and see Matteo shielding me from the bullets. Not Nina, me.

I frown, not understanding. I thought he only had love-hate feelings toward Nina. I thought he felt nothing toward me.

"Stop," Enrico says, and the bullets stop. He chuckles loudly.

"Now, this looks familiar. Fallen in love again so soon have we? I thought I taught you better than to get attached," Enrico says.

Matteo glares at him as he slowly lets me go, realizing his mistake.

"I don't love her," Matteo says. "I was trying to protect Nina. I don't want you thinking I planned this and to renege on our agreement."

Enrico narrows his eyes and lets his lips fall as he studies Matteo and then each of us.

"Time to make the swap, then. You won't mind throwing in the bitch then will ya? An old man like me doesn't get many opportunities to taste two beautiful women in one night," Enrico says.

"It will cost you more," Matteo answers.

"Well, of course," Matteo says, snapping his fingers and more money is brought to Matteo's feet.

Matteo grabs both Nina and my arms and starts walking us toward Enrico, he glances to his right, and I swear I see Matteo wink.

And then bullets. I duck again, getting far too used to covering my head at the sound of bullets.

People start running, and my feet start moving instinctively.

Matteo's hand falls from my arm.

"Eden!" Matteo screams, but I don't stop running. He doesn't love me. He won't protect me. I can only rely on myself to keep my baby and me safe.

I run, trying to get as far away from the bullets as I can. I don't wait for Nina. She's smart, and I know that she's running back to Arlo.

Together, they will be able to escape now that all hell has broken loose. I have no doubt.

I have to worry about myself.

I dart around a lifeless body and then make it to the back door. I need to make it to the car and then drive straight to the airport and never look back.

I grab the handle of the door as I feel a hand grip my shoulder, jerking me back.

"Hello, beautiful," Enrico says, tossing me into two of his men's arms. "I came for revenge, and I got something better, a chance to ruin true love."

"You're wrong. Matteo doesn't love me. He doesn't want me."

He laughs. "Of course he loves you. He did everything he could to protect you and keep you out of harm's way, even giving up his brother and old fling for a chance to keep me far away so that I would never discover you."

Matteo loves me. I try to search for him to see if it's true. To see if I was the idiot that missed the signs, that this was somehow all an elaborate plan to save me. I can't find him. Enrico's men start dragging me away. And now I'm afraid I'll never know.

25

MATTEO

SHIT.

Enrico took Eden. I felt it the second she was gone. The bullet fire slowly started to subside, and Enrico was nowhere in sight. He stole her from me. I won't let him live.

I'm going to kill Dierk for not keeping Eden locked up where it was safe.

I race back to where Arlo lays on the ground, with Nina over him, trying her best to close his wound and undo the rope around his wrists.

I bend down and place my hands on him, but Nina tries to fight me off.

"Get the fuck away from him!" Nina yells.

"Calm down. I'm helping him."

"Get away!" she cries again.

I turn to Arlo. "Will you tell her to stop so that I can help you?"

Arlo studies me a minute and then looks at Nina. She stops screaming, and I look down at his wound. I pull thread and a needle out of my pocket I always keep with me when we are going into battle, and I start closing his wound.

"You did this all on purpose, didn't you? Why?" Arlo asks, finally understanding I was scheming this whole time.

"Because Enrico was alive after you left. And he wouldn't stop until he got his revenge. You protected Nina by running. I protected her by setting a trap for Enrico."

"By using us as the bait?" Arlo asks, his voice raised.

"Yes."

Arlo head butts me. "You put Nina's life at risk!"

"I had to; it was the only way to get Enrico to come to me. I needed to ensure that he was killed."

"You stabbed me and didn't include me on the plan."

I roll my eyes. "I barely stabbed you, and you know I missed any major organs. You'll be good as new in a few weeks."

Arlo growls, and Nina crosses her arms with a pissed expression.

"Why did you steal Eden? Why keep her so long?" Nina asks.

I wince, not wanting to answer. "I found you guys within a few weeks of you leaving. I needed it to look like I hadn't though so Enrico would think you were so off the grid, he wouldn't bother looking. So I pretended that I needed Eden's help to find you. I planned on using her to get him to think I was struggling to find you and keep you safe until I came up with a plan. But then..."

"Then you fell in love with her," Nina finishes.

I nod. "And now she thinks I hate her."

Nina places a hand on my shoulder. "You'll earn her love back."

She slaps me across the cheek. "But don't ever hurt her or stab my boyfriend again."

"I won't," I say, rubbing the spot that barely stings.

"He's headed north. We think he has a cabin he's renting about thirty miles from here," Clive says as he jogs over to me.

Nina's eyes grow big as she takes a step in front of Arlo, who still has his arms tied behind his back.

"What the hell are you doing here?" Arlo asks, looking at Clive.

Clive cocks his head to the side as he grins as Nina. "Matteo needed my assistance."

Nina and Arlo turn their gazes to me.

"I needed more help to ensure that Enrico was dead. I've been busy with Eden and the baby—"

"Baby?" Nina squeals.

I smile. "Eden's pregnant."

"Oh my god! I'm going to be an aunt!" she screams.

"Baby, that's great, and all but our lives are still in danger, and we need to get Eden back and kill Enrico," Arlo says.

Nina stops squealing.

I turn to Clive. "I found out Clive and Erick were still alive after I almost killed them in an ambush. They have doubled the size of their team, and I thought I could use all the help I could get going against Enrico.

"Enrico thinks Clive and Erick would be the last people I would ever work with, so I knew if they planned this operation, it would mean Enrico would have no clue of the plan. I was afraid some of my men might still be loyal to Enrico."

I grab Clive by the collar of his shirt. "But it seems that Enrico isn't dead. And Eden is gone. Your plan didn't work. You have one hour to fix your screw up, and we'll be right behind you. Enrico needs to be dead, and Eden needs to be safe. Otherwise, we have no deal. Understand?" I say.

"Yes," Clive smirks.

I release him, and he runs off.

"What deal?" Arlo asks.

I shrug. "It doesn't matter. All that matters is killing Enrico and protecting Eden and our baby."

I pull a knife out of my pocket and cut the ropes holding Arlo back.

"Thanks," he says, as the ropes drop from his wrists.

Then he punches me in the jaw.

I close my eyes as the pain radiates through my entire head and down my arms.

"That was for stabbing me," Arlo says.

"Seems fair."

He laughs. "I'm not done yet. I still get a jab for risking me and my fiancé's lives."

"Fiancé?"

"I haven't asked yet, but yea, I'm hoping," Arlo says.

Nina gives him look that says 'yes' and then jumps into his arms with a kiss.

I sigh. "It's good to have you back. And as much as I'd love to watch you two make out, can we please go save Eden?"

26

EDEN

My hands are tied in front of my body, and my mouth is taped shut as I sit in the passenger seat of Enrico's car. He had one of his men throw me in the car so he could drive off alone with me.

He talks nonsense as he drives. Things about honor and what it means to be a man. How his sons have both disappointed him and just want him dead. But now that he has me, he will destroy Matteo, and then go back to obliterate Arlo by killing Nina.

I can't listen.

I feel sick, and not just because he's speeding around turns far too quickly. I'm sick that I left Matteo and didn't have confidence in his love for me. He was trying to protect me in his own way. I'm sick he doesn't understand that I trust him. I'm sick I'm going to die, along with our baby. I should have been thinking about our baby first, instead of trying to play the hero.

Enrico finally stops in front of an old cabin. I glance in the side mirror to see if there are any other cars behind us. There aren't. There will be soon though. I have one shot.

My hands grab the door, and I jump out, running down the gravel road toward the street. A street we only passed one car during the entire ten plus miles we drove down it. The odds aren't great that a car will pass when I reach the road, but it's my only shot.

Enrico chases after me, and as much as I beg my legs to move faster, he catches me. He grabs my arms and jerks me backward, lifting my legs off the ground.

I try to beg through the duct tape, but it comes out mumbled. I can move my hands up enough to reach the duct tape, barely. So that's what I do. I focus on getting the tape off. I can't fight him physically, but I can fight with my words. I can hope that this man has a heart or soul in there somewhere. He might show some compassion if I could only speak to him.

He drags me away from the street and into the cabin, which isn't much more than a fridge, couch, and bed. My eyes widen when I see the bed already set up with ropes to tie me down. He will not rape me. He might kill me, but he will not rape me. I won't let him. I will fight to the death.

I finally rip the tape off my mouth.

"Please don't do this," I beg.

He tosses me to the ground, and I'm barely able to catch myself with my hands before hitting the floor.

"I'm pregnant!" I shout, pissed he just risked my baby's life. Again.

He freezes, staring at me, finally seeing the small bump beneath my T-shirt.

"It's Matteo's. He's going to be a father. You are going to be a grandfather. You can be in this child's life. But you have to stop hurting your family. Stop. Ask for forgiveness and let's move past this."

He continues to stand over me, speechless, while I take several deep breaths, glancing around me for the nearest escape. There isn't one. Unless breaking a window counts. The only door is the front door he carried me through.

He squats down to look me in the eye. This is it. My last shot.

I hold his gaze, trying to get him to see my humanity. He doesn't need to hurt the baby or me. He can change.

If Matteo can change, so can he.

He cocks his head to the side and grins. "You're not going to be pregnant for long. Not when you're dead."

I scramble to my feet to run, but he grabs my hair, jerking me backward.

He yanks me toward the bed, but I dig my feet in, making it as hard as possible for him.

He punches me hard in the stomach.

I see stars. I can't feel anything. I'm dizzy, and sick, and pissed off. If he hurt my baby in any way, death will be his preferred option when I get through with him.

He grabs my hair again and starts dragging me to the bed. My eyes are barely open, but I see the shiny object sticking out of his shoe.

He's not paying attention to me, so I quickly and quietly snatch the knife and hide it in my hands. I could stab him in the leg, but then he'd just shoot me. I have to wait for the right moment.

We get to the bed, and he scoops me up, tossing me to the bed.

His body crashes down on top of me. His weight feels like an elephant sitting on my chest. I can't breathe. If I'm lucky, he might suffocate me before he has a chance to rape me.

His tongue licks my face, and I scream, "No."

He pauses a second at my unexpected outburst. He laughs and does it again.

I scream again.

If he touches me, it won't be enjoyable for him. I'm going to scream and yell and bite and fight. Do anything I can to try and stop him.

"I like fighters. This is going to be more enjoyable than I thought." He sits back. "I'll rape you here on this white bed. Then I'll cut out your baby and let you bleed to death, before Matteo finally arrives, too late to save his one true love. It's perfect."

"You disgusting bastard! You won't touch me."

He licks my face again, simply to show his dominance. As his body presses in again, I remember the knife in my hand, the metal cutting into my grip. Somehow I must have grabbed the blade instead of the handle.

I need to turn the knife around. I need to stab him in the chest. Before he ties me to the bed.

I try to keep my pain focused on Enrico, as he continues to slobber all over my face, down my neck to my breasts. He rips my shirt open, giving him access, as his disgusting cock presses into my belly. I try to ignore him as I slowly turn the knife around, cutting my hands and side in the process.

"Your breasts are going to taste delicious in my mouth," he says, lowering his mouth.

I jab the knife as hard as I can into his stomach. He cries out, but grabs my neck, tightening around me, trying to suck the oxygen out of me. I have limited mobility, but I jab the knife into his stomach again and again, until finally, he releases me.

I roll out from underneath him as he grasps his stomach, lying on his back, holding his wounds.

He thinks I'm done. That I will try to run off and his guards will capture me. But I can't let him live.

Matteo and Arlo made that mistake before. Enrico threatened everyone I love: Matteo, Arlo, Nina, and even my baby. I gave him the chance to change, but he didn't take it. He has to die.

I don't think twice. I take the knife and jab it into his throat will all my might.

Blood spurts out and his body jerks. I pull out the knife and stab him again, blood spraying everywhere. I stab him one more time until the blood slowly stops pouring out and his body is lifeless. I stare at him a few minutes, ensuring there is no way he is still alive. Finally, I get off the bed and head to the door, still holding the knife with my bound hands.

I don't have time to untie my hands. I need to get out of here.

I throw the door open, and I'm met with gunfire.

I know I should slam the door shut, run back inside, and wait for the winner to emerge, but then I see Matteo. He sees me, and I see the pain in his eyes. I can't lose him. I can't risk his death without telling him I love him and I trust him.

So instead, I stupidly run toward him. He runs toward me with a pissed off expression on his face.

I don't see the bullets. I don't see the men dying. Only Matteo.

He catches me in his arms, wrapping them around me tightly, and dives us down to the ground as he takes a bullet in the back.

"Oh my god! Matteo!" I cry, needing him to live.

He strokes my face, and I know he's going to be okay.

"Are you hurt?" he looks down, seeing the blood covering my body. His hands start searching for my wounds, but other than the small ones on my hands and stomach, he'll find none.

"I'm fine. But..." I pause, not sure how Matteo will take my news. He was trying to protect us all from Enrico, but he was still his father. I'm not sure if he would have killed Enrico if it came down to it. "I killed Enrico."

Matteo's eyes widen. "You're sure?"

"I stabbed him three times in the neck and waited until blood stopped spewing out of his neck."

Matteo grins. "That's my baby," he says, kissing me firmly on the lips.

"I'm so sorry. I should have trusted you. I love you. I want to spend forever with you," I say.

He grins. "That's my line. I'm sorry. I should have trusted you with the plan. I should have told you."

I shake my head. "I don't care. I just want you safe."

Matteo kisses me as men continue to fight around us. We should move somewhere safer, but we can't. So instead, we lie on the ground making out, tongues swirling together as we wait for it to be over.

"I think we need to get you two to the hospital," Arlo says over us.

Matteo looks over his shoulder. "Nah, I'll have you stitch it up, and Eden is fine."

Matteo helps me up, and I hold my shirt closed, Matteo wrapping his arms around me.

"I just checked the cabin. Enrico's dead. I made sure this time. He's really gone," Arlo says.

"Eden killed him."

"Thank you," Arlo says.

I smile.

"You're safe!" Nina cries when she finally gets to me.

We throw our arms around each other, hugging tightly as tears stream down our cheeks.

"You're pregnant! And happy?" she asks, eyeing Matteo behind me.

I glance behind me to Matteo with a grin. "Very happy. Or at least we will be."

Matteo pulls me back to him. "We need to talk," he says, pulling me away from Arlo and Nina.

"Okay," I say, not liking his tone.

"We haven't talked much about our future. Whether we will be together or separate. Whether I will get to be part of our child's life or not. And how to keep our family safe, while still doing what we want."

I nod. "I don't know the answers to most of those except that I want us to be together."

"I have answers for a few."

I raise an eyebrow.

"I made a deal with Clive and Erick."

"They are still alive?" I ask.

He nods. "I needed help to try and take out Enrico. Although, apparently, I just needed you."

I smirk.

He holds me tighter against his body. "I gave up everything."

"What?"

"I gave up everything. The house. My job. The weapons. I gave up being a monster."

My eyes widen and my pulse freezes, not understanding. "But it was your whole life. You loved being a Carini, ruler of Italy, and weapons trader. What will you do if you don't do that?"

He smiles. "I'll love you, and I'll love this baby. We can live in America, or in Italy. I don't care. Although, you might have to work and I'll be a stay home dad for a while, until I figure out what I'm good at, other than killing people."

I laugh.

"I love you, Matteo, but you will always be a bit of a monster to me. The kind with a big heart."

He kisses me. "A monster that gave up everything for love."

27

MATTEO

I GAVE IT ALL UP.

Everything.

The guns. The lifestyle. The mansion. My security team and employees. Everything.

It's gone.

None of that mattered anyway. The only thing that mattered was Eden. I was addicted to her from the moment I took her. I thought I was obsessed with Nina, but it was nothing compared to what I feel now for Eden.

The only thing I kept is money, but Eden will hardly let me spend it. We moved into her condo in Los Angeles, which is beautiful, light, and airy, but it's not very big. Not when we are about to bring another life into this world.

"Matteo?" she moans on all fours, her gorgeous ass in the air, begging me to enter her.

I grab her hips and press my cock to her entrance. Eden is due to have our baby any day. But she's insatiable. I didn't think we should, but Eden begged for my cock, and I'm always happy to oblige.

"I love you, baby," I say, kissing down her back.

"That doesn't sound like fucking," she snaps back sassily.

I laugh as I begin to push my cock inside her.

"Wait...ow..." she moans.

I stop and move to her head.

"Are you okay?" I ask.

"I think that was a contraction."

I grin. Yes. Finally. I don't think I can take much more of a pregnant Eden. I love her. I want to spend my life with her forever. But her mood swings are killing me.

I help her off the bed and put a T-shirt and sweats on so we can go to the hospital in a few hours, since her contractions just started.

"Matteo, I think we need to get to the hospital. Now," she says, gripping my hand tightly at a contraction.

It shouldn't be this painful this early, should it? I think.

"Um... are you sure?"

Her look tells me she will kill me if I don't get her to the hospital ASAP.

"Okay," I say, as I grab the bag she packed, and then take her hand and lead her out of the condo, with her stopping every few feet to rest as another contraction hits her.

It takes us twenty minutes to make it to the elevator, and our car is parked in a garage three blocks away. I'm afraid we won't make it.

We step into the elevator, while I try to figure out how to call an Uber.

"The baby is coming!" she screams. "The baby is coming, now!"

Shit, shit, shit.

"Okay, stay calm."

She lies down on the floor, and I see the baby's head crowning.

"This baby's coming!" I shout.

She half laughs, half screams.

"Breathe baby. You got this. You are a fighter. You have survived much worse. Push our baby out."

I've never helped deliver a baby before, but I know enough. As long as nothing goes wrong, I just need to catch the baby and keep it warm. If nothing goes wrong.

This is us. Everything bad will go wrong. But we didn't survive everything we've been through for Eden to die in childbirth. Not going to happen.

"Push, baby," I say.

Eden pushes and our daughter lands in my arms. I wrap the baby in my shirt, and hold her up to Eden's chest.

My heart stops until I hear her cry. It's a magnificent sound.

Eden cries, as well, as she holds our daughter. I wrap my arms around both of them, knowing I need to call an ambulance soon, but right now I can't. I just want to be happy with Eden.

"That was one of the scariest moments of my life," I say.

Eden smiles. "Me too. But we're fine. And we have a daughter."

I stroke our daughter's cheek.

"What should we name her?"

She thinks for a moment. "Nora."

"It's beautiful."

I reach into my pocket, pull out my phone, and call an ambulance. Then I call Arlo to tell Nina and Gia to meet us at the hospital to meet their new niece.

Everyone is living in LA now. None of us have jobs at the moment, but we will figure all of that out soon enough. We have each other, and we are safe.

I look down at my daughter and the woman I love. They are safe. I ensured their safety by giving up my life as a criminal, and by making Clive and Erick happy, giving them my empire. I knew they would always be running after us if I didn't. We would never be safe. This was the only way.

I did everything I could to protect my family and today was still the scariest day of my life. Because I realized that sometimes we can't save people. Sometimes they die anyway.

Today we beat the odds. Eden lived. We get to keep being a family for another day.

I was afraid to love Eden because I knew what it meant. Especially after loving Nina. I loved her, and she was taken from me. Eden could be taken from me just as easily. But it is still worth it to love her.

I may live my life afraid of losing her, but that is what love is. Love is fear. But that fear can't keep us from living.

EPILOGUE

GIA

"Yes, Matteo, I'll be careful. I'm just in Paris to see friends for a few days. How much trouble could I get in?" I say, stepping off the plane.

"Don't get upset with me for caring about you. I love you. I'm your big brother; I'm supposed to look out for you."

"I know, I know," I say, my heels clicking against the floor as I walk toward the exit of the airport to a taxi.

"When will you be back? Your niece, Nora, already misses you, and Nina is due any day now."

"I'll probably be gone a month," I say, knowing he's going to be upset.

"A month? Gia! You can't be gone that long. Do you understand how much Nora will have grown in a month? And Eden needs your help."

I laugh. "Eden does not need my help. She's a wonderful mother. And as much as I love her offer to work for her at the law firm, I need to find my own way."

I hop into a cab and hand the driver the address.

Matteo pauses. "I understand."

I raise my eyebrows. My brother never understands. Eden has really changed him.

"I love you. Don't worry about me. I simply need some time to figure out what I do next, now that I don't have to worry about the Carini enemies coming after me all the time."

"Did you take security? It's not completely safe. It won't be for a while, but it is safer."

"Of course, I brought security," I lie.

"Good. Who did you bring? Because Dierk isn't bad, but don't even get me started on Paul," Matteo rambles.

"Um...oh sorry. I have to go; I just got to the airport, and the girls are waiting. Kisses. Love you. Bye," I say, ending the call before I have to lie anymore to my brother. Lying to him used to be easy. But now that he's turned into a saint, I struggle lying to him.

I ignore the cab driver, who is looking at me with suspicion after hearing my lie about arriving at the airport.

The cab driver finally parks the car in front of the Carini mansion.

"Thank you," I say, before stepping out. The cab driver gets my bags and then drives off leaving me alone in the only home I've ever known. It may have sucked at times growing up, but it was still home. It's hard figuring out what my life might be without it.

I stare at my phone in my hand. I can't keep it. Matteo or Arlo could be tracking it. They could find out exactly where I am and come after me.

I drop the phone to the gravel driveway and stomp on it as hard as I can with my high heel, watching the phone shatter.

I smile, and stomp off to the front door. I ring the doorbell, feeling strange ringing my own doorbell. But it's not my doorbell anymore. This house isn't mine anymore. I have to stop pretending otherwise.

I wait no more than a couple of seconds before the door opens, and Roman stands in the doorway.

My grin reaches my eyes, elated when I see him. He's just as handsome as I remember. Tall, dark, and beautiful.

"You came," he says with a bright smile.

"You doubted me?"

Roman shrugs and pulls me into a tight hug. "After how I treated you, yes. I didn't think you would show up."

I take a deep breath, smelling his cologne I've missed so much. He may have hurt me, but all can be forgiven if he treats me right this time. I'm tired of being alone. That's all I ever am, alone.

"When did you move into my home?" I ask, staring at Roman.

"About two weeks ago. I'm just living here while my company renovates the property for Clive and Erick to move into."

My smile falters. I don't like the thought of my home being renovated at all. I like it as it is. Darkness and all.

"You okay?" he asks.

I nod. "Of course. I'm here with you."

I reach up to kiss him, but he turns, and my kiss hits his cheek. I frown. "What's wrong?"

"Nothing. Just don't want to move things too fast."

I raise an eyebrow and step out from under his arm. "Since when?"

He puts his hands in his pockets and shrugs. "Since we want a deeper relationship."

I study him. I want his words to be true, but I don't believe him. People change. Arlo and Matteo are proof of that. But not this fast and not without a lot of help.

"Why did you invite me here? If it wasn't for sex?"

"Everything doesn't have to be about sex."

I glare at him. "I want the truth. I know you. All you see when you look at me is sex. I'm hoping that can change with time, but right now, it can't."

He blushes, and I think he's about to tell me the truth, finally. Tell me why I haven't ever been more than just a sex object to him. Pour out his heart to me and tell me how sorry he is, but he'll do better.

Instead, he glances behind me as a dozen men fill the room.

"What's going on?" I ask, looking around behind me.

"I needed money Gia. I was in a lot of debt. I got five million out of the deal."

My eyes widen, already understanding. It's the world I grew up in. But I can't fathom it's happening to me.

"You got five million for what, Roman?"

"For you. I sold you."

DIRTY REVENGE

PROLOGUE

GIA

I'M the princess of darkness.

My father was the king. My brothers, princes.

I thought being a princess meant I would live in an extravagant world. Princes would be knocking at my door every day, wanting me. Or at least that's what happens in all the fairy tales. In reality, I sit locked away in the castle, and wait. Men are terrified to date me unless it assists them in doing a deal with my family. The Carini name holds too much power in this town.

I want out of the tower I've been locked away in for far too long. Dating isn't an option unless my brothers have vetted the man and deemed him worthy first. To ensure him dating me doesn't fuck with their empire. That's all they care about.

But things are changing. I'm not the girl they can lock away in the tower anymore. They can't keep me hidden from the world. I want to be free. If prince charming won't come to me, then I'm going to knock down walls to find him.

I'm a grown ass woman now. I can make my own decisions about what I want to do with my life. Just like everyone else in my family.

Father has been knocked off his throne. He no longer belongs in this town.

Arlo is gone. He ran away with his own love, and I have a feeling he won't be back. Ever.

And Matteo, he has a new plaything he's already falling for. He may be the ruler of the Carini empire now, but soon the Carini empire will fall to love.

And when it does, where will that leave me? Alone, without even a tower to hide away in.

I apply my red lipstick and fluff my hair. I'm beautiful. I know that. I have deep olive skin, bright green eyes, and dark, flowing hair that falls down my back and stops just before the curve of my ass. I have striking features any woman would pay good money to have. My looks alone should be able to land me a handsome prince. If only I didn't have my damn name to go with it.

It's not fair. My brothers carry the Carini name with pride. As soon as a woman hears the Carini name fall from one of my brother's lips, any woman falls at his feet, worshipping him, begging him to date her, fuck her, marry her.

Not me; men hear I'm a Carini and it sends them running. Well, the good guys at least. Occasionally, there is a man who hears my name, and it makes him want me more. Because he thinks dating me will get him an in with my brothers. Those men are disgusting. They are old, gross, and twisted. They are involved in a dark world where stealing, rape, and murder are everyday occurrences.

I don't want to belong to the dark world I grew up in anymore. It served me well when I was a kid. I had a dozen rooms to myself. I never had to lift a finger to do a chore, make myself food, or go to the store for anything as simple as a toothbrush. I got to go on the best vacations to the most exquisite places in the world. France, Bahamas, Greece, Australia, Maldives, Botswana - you name it, I've seen it all.

But now, I want my own life. I'm tired of being the dark princess. I want a normal life, with a normal boyfriend who has a normal job.

I frown, there is no way Matteo is going to let me date a normal guy with a normal job like a teacher or mechanic or something. He will say no normal guy will be able to offer me the protection I need to keep myself safe.

But maybe, normal is exactly what I need to escape this life. No one in Matteo's world is going to care about me if I'm with a boring man who makes no money. I have plenty of money saved, what would I do with more money, anyway?

Tonight, I'm going to find an ordinary man. I look down at my dark black dress, fit for Cinderella to wear to the ball. Or at least, for Cinderella's wicked stepsister. A dress like this isn't going to work to find a normal man. A dress like this will attract a prince.

I step into my closet, although 'closet' isn't the best word to describe it. It's more like a dressing room filled with all of Italy's designers' most expensive dresses. Complete with a different high heel for every occasion. I love my collection of dresses and elegant shoes. But if I keep wearing them, I'm going to remain trapped in this world. I need to change.

So I slowly slip out of the sparkly dress, until I'm standing in my black heels, stockings that attach to my garter belt, and strapless bra complete with dark embroidered roses.

What do ordinary Italian women wear when looking for a man to take them home?

My hands run over the different fabrics. Silk, lace, chiffon. So many gorgeous fabrics cut to fit my body. I stop when I get to my dark jeans.

Jeans.

I've never worn jeans out of the house. I always wear a dress or a skirt. Jeans are meant for bumming around the house. Relaxing, not gaining the attention of a man.

I grab my darkest, nicest pair. One I don't think I've ever even worn before. I slip it on and then scour my shirts. I settle on a simple black tank top with a little lace around the bust. This is the most underdressed ensemble I've ever put on. I feel wrong to be wearing something so informal.

This is what I want. I want to fit in. I want to be seen as more than a princess. No one will ever suspect me being anything but ordinary.

Now for slipping out my house unnoticed.

I walk to my bedroom and stare down at my phone lying on my dresser next to my black purse. I grab the phone to slip it into my purse, but then think better of it. Matteo can track me with my phone. I can't bring it with me.

I leave it on the nightstand, slip my purse strap over my shoulder, and strut out of my bedroom.

I walk straight to Angelo, my security team lead and prison guard, for all intensive purposes.

"I'll be ready to leave in twenty minutes."

"Of course, Miss Carini."

My lip twitches when he calls me Carini. I need to think of another name when people ask what my last name is tonight.

"First, can you fix the door lock to my bathroom? It keeps giving me problems."

"Of course, Miss Carini. I'll have it fixed and then meet you at the Lamborghini in twenty minutes."

I purse my lips. "Thank you."

I strut by him like I'm headed to the bar to fix myself a drink before I leave. Angelo thinks I'm meeting with friends at the local bar tonight. But I don't plan on doing anything typical. I plan on taking the least flashy car we own and driving it at least an hour away to the farthest, yet practical, town I can find. Then I plan on going to the busiest bar and find a man who wants me.

When Angelo enters my room, I make a hard turn to my right and head straight for the garage. I walk to the large, black Suburban. It's not mine. It is a car the security team uses to drive around on the grounds when they need to get somewhere fast. I stare at my Lamborghini that I really want to drive. It's fast, expensive, and a joy to drive. This thing is a tank that burns fuel for no reason, unlike my Lamborghini that brings fuel to life.

I can't drive the Lamborghini.

I don't want people to treat me differently. I can't show up in it.

So I climb into the tank and drive off before anyone in my family can stop me.

And for the first time in my life, I don't feel like a princess.

I don't feel like a villain.

I feel like me. A woman in seek of a man.

I smirk, staring into my rearview mirror without seeing a security team following me. *A first.*

I'm free.

———

This bar is loud, stingy, and smells like sweat. I love it.

I can't stop smiling as I slowly make my way through the crowd, trying to find the bar so I can order a drink. I've been elbowed in the face, shoved, and had my foot stepped on. Not once did anyone apologize or cower and bow after possibly hurting a Carini. No one has run away scared I'm going to have my brothers hunt them down and shoot them for hurting me.

I'm just me.

I make it to the bar, but not without some serious effort. And when I lean against the bar and raise my hand to get the bartender's attention, nothing happens.

He doesn't even glance my way over the throng of people.

"Hey, I would love to order a drink!" I holler down the long bar, which should only hold about a dozen people, but has at least three times as many crowded around it now.

I frown when nothing happens.

"Hey!" I shout again. My voice can be loud when I want it to be, but apparently, it's not enough to grab anyone's attention.

I hear a deep chuckle, and I turn to give the man my best side-eye stare.

"You don't come here often, do you?" the man asks me.

I look him up and down. He seems my age, or at least close enough. He's not dressed up at all. He's wearing jeans with holes in them, tennis shoes, and a dark grey T-shirt. He didn't even bother shaving. His dark hair covers his chin and neck, making his sparkly white teeth shine even brighter when he smiles.

I try to contain my grin. I don't want him to think I'm too anxious, but he's exactly what I'm looking for. He doesn't come from my world of fancy balls, thrown to hide the murders and evil occurring behind the scenes.

"You caught me. I'm not from this town. How do you get the bartender's attention?" I ask, giving him a tiny smile and turning entirely to face him.

His eyes drop down to my impressive cleavage. He swallows hard and shifts his legs back and forth, most likely trying to hide the jaw-dropping bulge straining in his pants.

"Like this," he pulls out a wad of cash, holds it out, and whistles loudly. The bartender turns and glides down the bar to the mysterious man who holds out the stack of twenties. The bartender takes it, pockets the large wad of cash, and then places two bottles of beer in front of us.

The man winces. "You probably aren't a beer drinker, are you? I could get you something fancier than a beer, but it's going to take a while. All the bartender will do quickly is get you bottles of beer."

I eye the bottle and pick it up. I rarely have a beer, and never out of a bottle, always a glass. But tonight, I'm not a princess. That girl is gone. Tonight, I'm wild, adventurous, and going to go home with this man who keeps eyeing me like he wants to take me to the bathroom and fuck me.

I drink from the bottle, and the man grins like he's just won the biggest prize.

"I'm Roman Alfonso," he says.

"I'm Gia," I say, leaving off my last name intentionally.

"Well, Gia with no last name. I would love to dance with you."

I look out at the crowd of people smashed together. That doesn't look like dancing to me. They press against each other, but are barely moving anything except their hips as they grind into each other.

"Or, I could take you back to my place, and we could talk. I'd love to learn more about you somewhere where we can actually listen to each other talk," Roman says.

I'm not naive. I know what he means when he says 'talk.' He doesn't mean talk. He means fuck. And I know whatever electricity pulsing between us isn't a love attraction. *It's lust.*

But I can't ignore the way he looks at me. The way his grin softens when I return his stare. The way his hand brushes against mine, and I feel a jolt of emotion rush through me.

This may not be the man I'm going to marry, but he might be the first man I'm with who doesn't treat me like a princess. He can fuck me, leave me, and rip out my heart as any normal man would.

Roman could be the first guy who treats me like a one-night stand, instead of royalty. I want a man to help me escape my atypical world. But I could use sex with a normal guy. The last man I was with was selling weapons to Matteo. I'm tired of dangerous men.

"I live three blocks from here."

I grin and chug my beer. "Your place sounds perfect."

––––––––

Roman's place is anything but perfect. It's tiny. It's messy. And it has a weird smell, a mix of burnt coffee and old pizza.

"You're beautiful, Gia. The most beautiful woman I've ever seen."

I roll my eyes. "How many times have you used that line?"

He chuckles. "A few times, but I've never meant it like I do right now."

His eyes twinkle when he talks. I like it.

He takes my hand and leads me toward his kitchen containing two cupboards and enough counter space to fit a single plate.

He pulls two beers out of the refrigerator and hands one to me, after popping the top off on a bottle opener stuck to the fridge.

"Thanks."

"So where are you from, beautiful?"

I narrow my eyes as I drink. "We don't have to do this. You don't care where I'm from or what I do for a living or where I went to school. You want in my pants, and that's it. So let's not pretend you are this perfect gentleman and get to the sex part."

He smirks as he leans against the counter not more than a foot from me. He cocks his head lazily to one side like he's studying me.

"What if I want more?"

My heart catches. *Stupid heart.* He doesn't want more. It's just another line.

"You don't know anything about me. How could you know if you want more or not?"

He licks his lips, and I can't stop staring. I want his lips kissing me. I want more than a kiss. I want it all with him. I want the fairy tale. I know all I'm feeling is lust. This isn't real. I don't know this man. But yet, he's perfect.

Roman reaches out and touches my flowing hair gently. "How could any man, not want you? I wasn't lying when I said you were gorgeous. You are the most beautiful fucking woman I've ever seen. I saw you from the moment you entered that bar, and I followed you. I didn't even need another drink. I was already drinking. I was dancing with a blonde bombshell, but she had nothing on you. I had to talk to you. See you. I couldn't explain it.

"You have a smart mouth. No other woman I've been with has called me a liar for saying that line."

My lips fall open as I listen to his every word.

"I'm not like most women."

He stares at me with seriousness in his eyes. "You aren't like most women. You're special."

I bite my lip, trying to control myself. But I want to throw my arms around him, kiss him, and tell him I'll marry him and have his babies all in the same breath. I don't understand what's happening. Every word he speaks is dripping with sex. His eyes are oozing with sincerity.

I know I shouldn't believe a word he is saying. It's all an act. He says this and does this with every woman he brings home to get them into bed with him. Tomorrow, he'll flip. He'll be an ass who doesn't even makes me coffee before he sends me home in a cab.

I can't stop myself though from falling instantly in love with Roman. Maybe it's the freedom he represents, but I want everything with him. I should walk away now. But I can't. My feet are cemented to the floor.

I can't move.

I can't breathe.

I can't think.

I'm lost in Roman.

"I want you Gia. So fucking badly. In my bed. As my girlfriend. As my *wife*."

My eyes shoot wide. *What the hell is he talking about?*

"I know who you are, Gia. Jeans and a tank top can't hide who you are."

Fuck.

"You're Gia Carini."

I nod.

"And I've never wanted a woman more. You're beautiful, royal, and powerful."

I bite my lip again as he grabs my neck and pulls me into a kiss. I'm lost forever as his tongue brushes against mine. I've never been kissed this hard or this passionately before. I've never been wanted. *Not for being a monster.*

Because that's what I am, a monster. I may pretend I'm a princess who hides away in a tower and has no control over my life or what my family does, but it isn't true. I have power. I could change my life if I wanted to. Stop participating in the evil my family partakes in.

I'm a Carini though. Carinis are powerful, dark creatures, incapable of real love.

Roman knows who I am. I don't know how, and I don't care. He wants me as I am. And I plan on giving him everything I have. The light, the darkness. My heart, and soul. And maybe with him, I'll find a way to be the real Gia Carini. The one I've kept hidden beneath the pretty dresses. With Roman, I can learn to love.

1

GIA

Months Later

I sold you.

Roman's words play over and over in my head.

The light trickles in, striking my face, so all I can see is the light. I can't see the arch of the doorway overhead made of dark gray marble stone. I can't see the sharp edge of the windows next to me that open up the living room to the garden below. I can't see the beauty of the green oak trees that have been here for hundreds of years, the only things on this property entirely untouched by darkness.

All I can see is the weak shit standing in front of me. *Asshole, cunt, manwhore, gold-digger, scum of the earth, piece of shit...* Words keep coming, but they make no difference. I can call Roman whatever I want in my head, but it doesn't stop what's happening. And I won't give him the satisfaction of seeing my anger.

Roman doesn't get to see my pain. My regret. Or my anger.

He means nothing to me.

He used to be my entire world.

Now, he's nothing.

I sold you.

Roman was the one. He's sexy, charming, and despite how he dresses, he owns a string of wineries. He has money, not Carini level money, but he isn't poor. I thought he loved me. I thought I was special. I thought I was his everything.

He fucked it up once.

I thought today was about fixing his mistake.

Instead, he's fucking my life up forever.

I shield my eyes, as I see the men approaching me. I stand stoically because I know there is nothing else to do at the moment. Running is useless, I'll just end up hurt. I've seen it happen to too many women before.

I will look for an opportunity to escape once they have me, but I know that won't be more useful. In this world, there is no escaping. Even Nina and Eden didn't escape. They remained. They just changed their circumstances in their favor until this world no longer terrified them.

My only hope is that Matteo and Arlo save me. That they realize I'm gone and still have enough power in this world to save me. If they can't, I'm as good as dead.

I feel the cold, rough hands on my arms as they are jerked backward.

I sold you.

Roman's words play again.

I should focus on the men tying rope around my wrists. I need to learn as much about them as I can. Find their weaknesses. Study their faces so when I'm free, I can come back and get my revenge. But I can't focus on anyone but Roman.

Roman stands stoically as he watches the men tighten the rope around my wrists. He seems pleased with himself. His lips curl up into a wicked grin, while his eyes deepen with a mix of lust and greed, watching me lose my freedom. He thinks he's won. But the war has only just begun. He may have won the battle, but the war is long. Carini's hold grudges, and we always get our revenge in the end.

I smirk.

"Happy to be taken? Oh, that's right. You are desperate for a man's attention. Any man. Even a demon like Dante."

Dante. That's the first time my captor has been mentioned. It doesn't ring any bells. He didn't run in our immediate circle of friends.

I continue smirking, shaking my head. "I'm not smiling. I'm smirking. You think you've won, but you forget that I'm a Carini. My days aren't numbered, but yours are."

Roman narrows his eyes at me and laughs, glancing at the men holding onto my arms. Arms that are now firmly tied behind my back. I pull at the rope, and I know there is no way my hands will break free.

"I don't think so. You are the one whose days are numbered. I'd bet good money you don't survive the week where you are going. I not only made sure to get the highest price for you, but I made sure you went to the most ruthless owner in all of Italy. Dante Russo will beat you, rape you, and kill you when he realizes how ordinary you are. You have no fight in you. Your brothers will quickly forget about you. No one will save you. And when you are dead, no one will come after me."

I search his eyes, and I find exactly what I would expect from scum like him.

"Then why is there fear in your eyes?"

Roman clears his throat and then walks toward me. "If there is any fear in my eyes, it's simply the reflection of your own."

I spit in his face.

My head whips to the side as I feel the sting of the slap against my cheek. I take a deep slow breath as the bite spreads across my cheek and to my eye.

I will not cry.

I will not show anger.

I will not show my pain.

Roman will get nothing from me.

I slowly turn my head back. I can't stop my hand from reaching instinctively to calm my cheek, which is no doubt turning redder as the seconds pass. The ropes stop me before I remember my hands are tied behind my back.

Roman's jaw spasms as he notices my hands squirming against the ropes. I know the rope is digging into my delicate skin, and will undoubtedly leave a burn in its wake, but I can't stop fighting against it. Not now that Roman has me so worked up.

He takes a step back, while the men hold me back. One of the men's hands clenches my arm so roughly the pain pulls my attention away for a second from Roman. I feel the nails digging into my flesh, and I want to cry out in pain. Tell him to stop, but I don't.

Instead, I keep all my wrath for Roman. Giving him my full attention assures him I will come after him. I will watch the whites leave his eyes as he slowly slips away from this earth to hell. Everything that happens to me from this point forward is because of Roman. And I will make him hurt for every prickle of pain I endure.

"Everything going okay in here?" a man says from behind Roman.

I force my eyes away from the snake before me and stare at the man who just entered. Clive is standing in the entryway with a cup of coffee in his hand, like this is a typical morning. Erick enters behind him, and he smirks at me.

"Yes, just about to have the garbage taken out," Roman answers.

I snarl. I can't help it. At this point, I want the men holding onto me to drag me out, so I don't have to look at Roman for another second.

Clive stands with a raised eyebrow, no doubt waiting for me to beg him to rescue me. He'll be waiting forever. I will never ask for his help. Matteo may have been willing to ask for his help to save Eden and kill my father, but I'm not willing to ask this slime for help. The cost would be too high. Matteo had to give up everything he worked for to get Eden. If I asked for Clive's help, I would merely be trading my life from Dante to Clive. I still wouldn't be free.

Roman turns from me and walks into the kitchen before returning with a stack of money. He holds it out to Clive who isn't surprised to see the money. He takes it from him eagerly.

"Thank you, Clive, for assisting me. I wasn't sure if the pull of old love would be enough to persuade Gia to come back. But I knew she couldn't resist coming back to her old home." Roman turns his head to me, and the evil oozes out of his dark eyes. "But then again, I think Gia is desperate enough that she would have come back just for a chance at my attention."

The men chuckle as if he made the funniest joke.

I hold my tongue, keeping my snark remarks to myself. Whatever I say won't help. But I will remember every word. And every bone I break on his body, every cut I inflict into his flesh, every bullet I shoot into his body will be my revenge. I will not let him live. I'm a Carini. It may take me a week, a month, or even years to escape my fate, but when I do, revenge will be sweet.

I pull on the ropes again as Roman turns away. Maybe if I can get free for a second, I can inflict some pain right now. I can't wait.

I get one arm free of the man's grasp, but the other man holding onto me jerks me back.

"Gia's feisty. She won't go easily, but it won't take long to break her. Tame her. She's already broken."

"You fucking asshole!" I yell, no longer caring what Roman thinks. I can't contain myself any longer.

Roman turns around and walks back to Clive and Erick. None of them pay me any attention as I continue to curse and yell out my threats. I will come for them all. They think my family was evil before. That Enrico was the worst, and my brothers were demons that would fight to the death. They have no idea I'm worse than all of them.

Roman, Clive, and Erick ignore me as they turn the corner and disappear into the shadows of the house. *My house.* They may occupy it now after Matteo gave it to them in exchange for their help, but I'm getting it back when I take all their lives. I'm not as forgiving as Matteo and Arlo. Clive and Erick may have little to do with me being taken, but they could have done more to prevent it. They didn't. They are just as culpable.

"Time to go, whore," the man on my left says. He has dark eyes and a scruffy beard. His biceps bulge, covered in a sleeve of tattoos. He's meant to look menacing, but he doesn't realize I've dealt with men like him my entire life. Grew up around them. His looks don't scare me. He's nothing but muscle working for his boss, Dante. He follows orders, nothing more. He won't touch me or hurt me as long as I behave.

He thinks a word like 'whore' will degrade me. Make me feel like I'm nothing. Start the process of breaking me. He doesn't realize I've been called much worse. I don't easily break, despite what Roman says.

Roman was an important lesson. One I learned far too late, but will never repeat. I will never fall in love with a man. I will never be that vulnerable again.

The other man holding my arm doesn't say anything as they start leading me to the back door of my house. This man isn't the leader. He's smaller and therefore seen as weaker. I need to wait until I'm left alone with the weaker one, then I'll make my run for it.

They don't have to pull me hard as we walk. I go willingly. Or at least that's what I make them think. Really, I'm planning in my head for when I return and slaughter all of them.

We walk out into the hot sun. Will this be the last time I see the sun? For how long? Days? Weeks? Years?

Will I be locked away in a dark dungeon? Or will I be given the freedom to walk around the house like my family always gave their slaves?

I have no way of knowing. So I lift my face up and soak in every drop of warmth. Letting the sun warm my heart and provide a memory of something positive I can take with me.

The door to the back of an SUV opens, and I'm quickly tossed into the back, just before the door is thrown shut behind me. I take a deep breath and wiggle myself up into a sitting position, recovering from falling on my face on the chilled leather seat.

Both men climb into the front without a word to each other. The car is started, and we drive off. I don't dare turn around or look in any of the side mirrors to get a last glance of my home. I refuse to let it be my last glance.

My heart beats rapidly in my chest, but other than my heart, I can't feel anything. Not fear or pain. Nothing.

But they made their first mistake. They tied my hands together, but not my legs. They sit in the front and not the back. They don't think I will run. They believe I'm already broken as Roman said. That I've relented to being someone's slut already.

I try to keep my lips thin, my expression blank, as if I'm in shock. It doesn't matter though, because the men in front pay me no attention. They think there is no way for me to escape. They're wrong.

2

CASPIAN

*

I LIFT the cup of coffee to my lips, scanning for any signs of Dante Russo or his men. I spot one man at the bar, out of the corner of my eye. Another member of his security team strolls down the quaint, brick sidewalk that has been here for hundreds of years.

I shake my head. Dante's men stand out like a sore thumb. They need to learn to at least wear clothing that helps them to blend in. Look inconspicuous. Otherwise, they might as well stand at Dante's side and look as menacing as possible to try to keep people away.

"Mr. Conti, a pleasure to meet you. I've heard many great things about you. Although, I'm surprised to learn you didn't bring a security team with you since that's what you specialize in," Dante says, towering over me at my table.

I resist the urge to roll my eyes at this man. I simply stand and hold out a hand. "Just because your men haven't identified my security team, doesn't mean I don't have one."

"Touché, Mr. Conti," Dante says, as we both sit back down.

He scans me up and down, and I wait for the comment about my age.

"You seem young to have become such a leading voice in security, Mr. Conti."

Yep, there it is. I do roll my eyes this time. I'm sick of men like him thinking because I'm young, and I didn't inherit my company from my father like he did, that I'm not capable.

"Why did you take this meeting with me, Dante, if you didn't think I was capable of delivering?" My eyes burn into his as I speak. I hate men who waste my time.

"I never said you were incapable, just young, Mr. Conti." He repeats my formal name. He wants me to give him the same respect, but he hasn't earned it. Dante Russo may be a powerful man, but that doesn't mean I'm willing to cower at his feet like everyone else in this country. I may not have his money, but everything I earned, I built on my own. I was given nothing.

I take another sip of my coffee while I wait for him to speak again. I'm anxious, too anxious. And if I let him know that, he will realize this is more than just a deal for me. So much more. Dante doesn't understand I know exactly who he is.

"As I said, I've heard many great things from you, Mr. Conti. And as you know, security and discretion are of utmost importance to me. Money isn't an issue. I will pay you well, if you are, in fact, the best."

I don't care about his money. But I don't tell him that. It's time to impress. "You have two men at the bar. One on the street. Four in cars around the perimeter. And one sniper on the building across the street. They all use a Retevis RT21 system to communicate with, which can easily be dismantled..." I pull out the device from my pocket and press the button. "With the touch of a button."

Dante scans his men, all grabbing for the earpieces in response to the loud fog sound blowing out their eardrums.

I nod at my sister behind me, and my team moves in on all of his men. His men drop to the ground, put there by my team. My team knows how to blend into the shadows.

Dante freezes as a gun presses against his temple, but only after his gun in the back of his pants is pulled free and tossed to the side.

I smirk as I lean back in my chair, and Dante glares at me. "Meet my sister, Mr. Russo," I say, using his last name to make a greater impact.

Dante lets out a breath and chuckles.

I nod to Adela who slowly lowers her gun.

"I'm impressed. I didn't realize your team was here, or that you had a sister." Dante eyes Adela with lust. This is why I never tell anyone I have a sister. She is fully capable of taking care of herself, but I can't handle creeps staring at her like a piece of meat.

"That's all, Adela," I say.

She nods and disappears again.

"Like I told you when I contacted you last week, I'm the best. I believe in being discreet and working with the best technology around. Technology that no one but me owns."

"How long to get your systems and my team up to your level?"

"I can have my system installed in your home as soon as payment hits my bank account. A week. Shorter, if you prefer. And your team? I would recommend firing them and starting over. If I hire your team, I can have you the perfect team within two weeks."

Dante frowns. "My men are good men. They have been with me for a long time. I trust them."

I glance over at the man slowly dusting himself off after my team tackled him to the ground. "Ezio there? He's been stealing money, drugs, jewels, anything he thinks he can take from you without you noticing for years."

I glance toward the man at the bar. "Gareth has been getting paid by Domenèc for any interesting tidbits about you. Do I need to continue?"

"No."

"Would you like me to find you a better-qualified team and fire your current team?"

"Yes, hire me the best you can find. No women, though."

I snigger. I wouldn't expect anything less from a chauvinist like him.

"It's not good for the business I run. Women bodyguards are too emotional to handle the work I require."

I nod. I don't doubt women get too emotional when they realize he smuggles women like drugs. Although, I bet most women, if they worked with Dante, wouldn't say anything. They'd be too afraid they might face the same fate if they told anyone.

"No women. Got it."

Dante scowls as he looks at his men with his hands folded on the table like this is a simple business meeting, and we aren't talking about men's lives. "No need to fire them. I'll take care of it."

A chill creeps down my spine at his words. I know how he will 'handle it.' They will all be dead by morning. Not that they don't deserve it, or that I disagree with his tactics. I would do the same if he left the firing to me.

His phone buzzes, and he pulls it out. "One moment, Mr. Conti. I need to take this. Then, we can discuss your price."

I nod as he stands, leaving me alone at the small table on the edge of the sidewalk. I sip more of my coffee as a black Escalade pulls up outside. The man in the driver's seat rolls down his window as he speaks with the man on the sidewalk.

I narrow my eyes. These men aren't part of Dante's security team. They do other work for him. I don't have time to deduce precisely what work, before the back door is thrust open and a beautiful woman falls to the stone drive.

I can't take my eyes off of her as she pulls herself to a standing position. Her arms are tied behind her back, and I have no doubt what she was doing in the back of the SUV or who she belongs to. She's one of Dante's women. He hasn't touched her yet, that much is clear. She has fight and determination in her piercing green eyes, visible even though we are several feet apart.

Her eyes shine brightly beneath her black hair that cascades down the sides of her face. When my eyes find her breasts, I bite my lip and groan. Perfectly round mounds spill out over the top of her shirt. And I don't even dare let my eyes travel down her long, lean legs or heels I want digging into my back as my cock slams inside her.

I don't know who this woman is. But I will. My cock aches at the sight of her. I have to have her. I have to know her. Go near her. Touch her. Taste her. Fuck her.

It's clear from her designer outfit and the way she holds her head high that she comes from money. Old wealth, no doubt. I don't know how Dante got her. Is she payment for an old debt? Did he steal her?

I would understand the urge if he stole her. I'm very much feeling the same, and I've only just seen her.

The dark beauty considers her next move. I see it in her eyes. She wants to run. Is desperate to. But she glances down at her spiky heels and the men who are slowly becoming aware she is no longer in the back of the car. *Amateurs.* How hard is it to keep a woman retained in a car? It's clear the ropes will do nothing to contain a fire like her.

Her eyes search quickly for any chance at escape. For freedom. For help.

Her eyes stop when they find mine. For a flicker of a second, I think I see lust in her eyes as she checks me out. But realize it is most likely my own lust reflected in her eyes. No woman in her predicament would think about such silly things as lust at a moment like this.

She runs toward me. She's choosing *me*. Thinking I'll be her salvation.

She's wrong.

She may think she sees some kindness in my blue eyes, but there isn't any caring left. Any kindness I once had was taken from me years ago, as easily as her freedom is being ripped from her now.

She stumbles, approaching me. My arms go out automatically, catching her as she falls into my aching lap.

She smiles, catching her breath. She thinks she's safe in my arms.

I smirk. *She couldn't be more unsafe.*

"Help. Please."

I raise an eyebrow as I get a whiff of her shampoo and perfume. It's strong, just like her. But not overwhelming. Just strong enough. Not overly flowery, but feminine nonetheless.

I stroke her hair, resisting my urge to grab the long strands roughly and drag her to my car waiting on the next block so I can fuck her in my bed.

What the hell?

I shouldn't want to fuck her. She's Dante's. Fucking her would ruin everything I've planned and worked on for years.

I push her up until she's standing again. Hoping that some distance between us will ease my discomfort and need for her. My cock only strains harder in my jeans.

Jesus, she's gorgeous.

Her eyes widen. She thinks I was helping her when I helped her stand. She believes that was kindness. She may be strong, but she has no idea how to read people. She needs to learn fast if she's going to survive a year with Dante.

"Help me. Please. A man named Dante has kidnapped me."

She glances behind her and sees the guards approaching. I think she's going to change her mind and make a run for it. It's instinct. Any person would run.

But not her.

She keeps her feet firmly planted, as if she knows exactly what's coming and is ready to face it. She does everything she can to show no fear. Her body stands tall, robust. Her body doesn't quiver or shake. Her breathing is steady and calm. Her lips are pulled back into a thin line. Even her eyes do everything possible to hide any fear.

I read people for a living though. So I know, despite how calm she appears on the outside, her pulse is racing. I grab her wrist.

She smiles a tiny bit, thinking I'm offering to help her.

I feel her pulse racing fast. It's one of the signs she can't hide. No matter how tough she tries to act on the outside.

"Help. They are going to take me. Call my brothers. They will help me. I'm Gia Ca—"

Her voice is cut off by Dante's. "You've stopped my new whore from escaping, Mr. Conti. You are well worth your asking price."

I take Gia's hand and hand her over to Dante.

Gia. It's a beautiful name that fits her well.

Her eyes widen when she realizes she fell into the lap of the devil instead of a saint. She wasted her one chance of escape on me.

She swallows hard, trying to keep her calm facade, when Dante pulls her into his body. He takes a deep breath, letting her know he smells her, unlike when I tried to hide my desire to smell her.

Dante grabs her chin and forces her to look up at him. He licks his lip like he can't wait to get her back to his house.

My insides burn, seeing her in his arms. She's mine. I found her first.

"I think I underpaid for you, whore. You are trying to hide it from me. But you are most definitely a spitfire I will get the pleasure of breaking. I look forward to it. Not many women would attempt to break free this quickly. Most are in too much of shock to even react."

"Go to hell," she says.

He grins, tightening his grip on her. But she doesn't react, other than a glare.

Dante turns to me. "As you can see, I have some things to attend to. I'll have the money to you by the end of the day. Call my secretary to discuss when you can set up my new system. Maybe I'll even let you play with my new toy?" Dante licks her face, and she shudders.

I growl, but it's so low I'm not sure either of them heard me.

Dante is too focused on Gia. He grips her tightly as he walks her to the waiting Escalade, where his incompetent men wait. He shoves her in the back and, I have no doubt, will be climbing in, right next to her, to ensure she doesn't attempt an escape again.

Gia looks at me one last time. I was her only hope, and now that hope is gone. But I don't see that reflected in her eyes. Instead, I see fire. She studies me, and I know I've just been added to her list. She wants revenge, to make me suffer like she is going to suffer.

I can't take my eyes off her until the door is shut, blocking my view with the tinted windows. Even then, I don't stop watching until the SUV drives away.

Gia wants her revenge on me for not helping her. For turning her over to a barbarian. I do not doubt she will one day get her revenge. But if I'm going to be punished by her, I'm going to do something worth getting punished for.

Dante invited me to his house to share her. I don't share, but I can't stay away. I'll fuck her, get her out of my system, so I can forget about her and return to my own revenge. While I happily wait for the day she carries out hers. It will be worth it, if only to see her piercing eyes again.

3

GIA

MR. CONTI.

That's the name of the man I put my faith in. I don't even know his first name. But I risked my only hope of escape on him. I thought he would go to the police. Call my brothers. Figure out who I am and realize the reward my brothers would give him would be more than generous. Instead, I'm pinned in the back of the SUV with Dante and his men.

I thought I saw kindness in Mr. Conti's eyes when I stepped out of the SUV. I knew I couldn't outrun the idiots who drove me. My guards may not have much of a brain between their ears, but they are built. All muscle. I couldn't outrun them with my hands tied behind my back and my high heeled shoes, so I chose a man; a man with tired, gray eyes and what I thought might be warmth hiding behind those eyes.

I was wrong.

Whatever I saw, it wasn't kindness. Mr. Conti is friends with the devil.

I made the worst mistake I could. I trusted a stranger because I thought I could sense something more than cold indifference oozing off of him.

Mr. Conti turned me over to Dante without a second thought. I am nothing to him. Not even a woman, just another way for Mr. Conti to show his loyalties to Dante.

I swallow down my regret, trying not to think too hard about the gorgeous man sitting back at the quaint coffee shop I've been to hundreds of times before. Amante. I love the place. I never realized monsters hung out there.

Beautiful, handsome, dark beasts. Mr. Conti may be evil, but if I were free, he would have been precisely the type of man I went after. Tall, muscular, wealthy, and hiding a dark past beneath his grimace. When his eyes soaked into me, full of want and desire, I saw the hunger in his eyes. I even let myself feel it for one second. One full second, and then I stopped myself.

It might have been the last time a man looked at me with a hint of lust where I had a choice in what happened afterward. From now on, if any man looks at me that way, I won't have a choice to say no. They will take whatever they want from me.

Mr. Conti was supposed to be my savior. But he won't help me.

My brothers don't have a clue I'm missing. And by the time they figure out I'm gone, it will be too late.

I have to save myself.

Dante grabs my chin and forces me to look at him again.

"Such a beauty."

I growl and jerk my head out of his grasp.

He grabs my chin and pulls me so close to his face I can smell his breath; a disgusting mix of coffee, cigarettes, and rotting flesh.

I glare at him as I lean away from him.

"I will enjoy breaking you, whore."

"My name is Gia," I say, although I don't know if he used my name if I would feel any better. Gia feels more personal. But it's better than 'whore.'

Dante cocks his head to the side and glances up at the man in the passenger seat, perplexed, as if to say, "Can you believe this?"

"I've never had a woman quite like you. Usually, the women I take are in too much shock to say anything, especially nothing that snarky."

"That wasn't snarky. You haven't seen me be snarky yet."

"I don't doubt that. I will enjoy slowly snuffing the fire out of you as the days pass. Usually, I need a new woman within a week. None of my previous conquests have lasted long, and I'm not into necrophilia. I once had a woman last a month. She had a man she was living for, fighting for. You don't have a man you are fighting to get back to, do you, whore?"

I don't react when he calls me a whore. It's just a word. I need to prepare myself for much worse.

"No, I don't need a man. When I escape, I will be returning with an army to kill every single one of you. But don't worry, I'll kill you last, slowly, for payback for everything you do to me."

His eyes blaze, and his nostrils steam. I've just turned him on.

Shit.

"So you have relented I will have my way with you then, whore?"

"No."

He strokes my hair slowly and gently, before grabbing my hair forcefully, jerking my head back as his lips hover over my ear.

"I will have my way with you, whore. Lucky for you, I don't have any clients to see this week. So you and I will have an entire week to get to know each other. And you can wish you had a man in your life who might rescue you, or at least to cloud your memories when I fuck you."

I suck in a breath. I hate how his hot breath breathes down my neck. My body freezes, hoping he will stop. But I need to fight my urge to stop moving. Not fighting back won't get me anywhere. I need to fight to get free. Even if it means I might get more injuries until I finally break free.

Dante jerks me away from his mouth so he can look me in the eyes.

"I think you are going to be my greatest conquest of all, whore." Dante turns his attention to his men in the front seat who have largely ignored our conversation. "How long do you think my new whore will survive?"

"You are the greatest master, sir. You will tame her within the week, and then how long she survives will be up to you."

"Two weeks, sir."

Dante licks his bottom lip slowly as he turns back to me.

I squirm back against the door, trying to get as far away from him as possible.

"I'm feeling generous. I'll give you two months. I think you are stronger than the rest. You have spirit and fight, and you fight all for yourself, not for the love of a man. I admire that, whore. But in the end, it won't help you. You're mine now. The sooner you learn to behave, the sooner this will all end."

End.

He means this will only end when I die.

I may have made some mistakes in choosing my escape, but this will not end with my death. Even if I do die, Arlo and Matteo will never stop until Dante is dead. They will get my revenge. He underestimates the Carini bloodline if he thinks he will survive this.

I don't say any of that to him. It won't help. For now, I need to prepare myself for what's next. Good thing I've had years of practice.

The car slows, and I stare up with wide eyes at the house which, I assume, will soon become my prison. It's a large house, almost as big as the Carini mansion, but unlike the warm, ancient, and inviting Carini mansion, this house feels cold and indifferent. The building has high, light-gray brick walls. The front door is a dark wood that looks like it's meant on a dungeon cell, not the front door of a home. But then again, this isn't a home; it's a prison.

I swallow and feel my heart beating rapidly. Maybe I'll die of a heart attack before I even get inside. That would be the easy way out. No suffering.

I'm used to suffering; I remind myself.

Whatever Dante has planned for me, I can survive. I always survive.

I don't realize the men are already out of the car until my door is thrust open, and I almost fall to the concrete ground below.

A burst of thunder sends a jolt through me, almost as if restarting my heart. I take a deep breath, and I feel stronger than I've felt in a long time. My heart rate slows to a much steadier pace.

I'm a Carini. There is nothing I can't face.

I step out of the car as hands clasp around my bicep again. I won't be forced into the house. I won't be dragged. I will walk in proudly like I own the place. I'm different than his other whores. And therefore, I have an advantage. I can't change and start acting scared.

Raindrops pour down as I walk the few feet to the front door. I feel every drop. I love the rain, but today the rain mirrors my mood. Thunder rolls again, but this time I don't jump. It sounds more like a chorus beating loudly in the background, reminding me I have someone on my side. I'm as strong as the thunderous sound.

Dante opens the door, and I step in with one of his men still gripping my arm. I quickly scan everything in sight. I need information if I'm going to survive. I need to know every exit. Every security camera. Every guard. I need to know every person in this house. Every car. Every weapon. Only then will I be able to escape.

"You never cease to surprise me, whore," Dante says as he takes over for his guard, whom he quickly dismisses.

I raise an eyebrow. It's just him and me.

He either thinks he can easily overpower me. Control me. Or he has more security guards waiting to take me out if I run.

Dante isn't stupid, unlike his men.

He won't leave himself vulnerable. He wants me too badly to give me a chance to escape. He's testing me. Seeing if I will run so he can punish me.

Think differently.

My instinct is to run, but that's not what I need to do. He wants me because I'm a spitfire, and he would enjoy breaking me.

I won't let him win.

I need to be different.

I need to pretend I'm into him. That I want him to fuck me. That I've been so desperate for male attention, I'd even fuck a man like him. It's going to suck, but it might be the only way for freedom. I can pretend. That's all this is, pretend.

I took acting classes in high school. I was good. I can do this.

"You have a beautiful home, Mr. Russo."

He raises an eyebrow.

"Thank you, whore. It doesn't have the views you are used to, but then again, you haven't lived in a home like this for several weeks now. I'm sure you are aching to know what it feels like again."

He strokes my face, and I do everything I can to not react negatively to his touch. I don't miss the double meaning of his words. He doesn't think a man has touched me in weeks. He's right. I need to let him know just how right he is.

"I'm looking forward to it," I say, my eyes meeting his, challenging him to call me out on my words.

He smirks, pleased with my response.

So I continue. "You're right. I haven't been with a man in months. I thought Roman was the one. I thought he loved me and wanted me. I was wrong. Roman is half the man you are."

Dante doesn't respond. His eyes deepen though at my words. He grabs my wrists, bound with rope behind my back. He spins me until my back is to him.

I resist the urge to glance back at him. I need to show him I trust him with my body.

So instead, I focus on studying my surroundings, but it's impossible with him breathing down the back of my neck again.

I feel something sharp and cold against my wrists.

Shit.

He's going to cut me. I should never have turned my back to him.

My breath catches as he cuts the rope from my wrists. My hands pull apart, and I rub them gingerly, examining the red bumps and abrasions which have formed a perfect circle where the rope used to be.

I turn slowly, trying to show appreciation in my eyes, as I look at Dante.

"Thank you."

He stows the knife in his back pocket. I try not to look too eager to know where he hides a weapon. As much as I want to go over to him now and steal the knife, I won't. It would be easy enough to distract him with a kiss while retrieving it from his pocket. I resist. It won't get me anywhere. Even if I killed him, his men would attack me. I would never get out alive. And if I missed, I would have to deal with his wrath. I would have played my cards too early.

No, I need to wait. Have patience. Get him to trust me and let his guard down.

"This way, whore," he says, snapping his fingers.

I follow, still getting used to having my hands free again. When I catch up to him, I hook one of my hands around his arm.

His lips curl up a little, but otherwise, he doesn't react. I'm used to hanging onto men I don't have feelings for. I've played the interested, hot woman too many times for my father or brothers. I know how to distract men.

And I do just that as Dante leads me around his house, showing off various pieces of art or views he thinks are impressive. They aren't. Nothing in this house is remarkable.

"I have one more room to show you. I think it will be your favorite," he says, his voice deeper than it's been.

I know what room he is talking about. *A bedroom*. I know what's coming. Dante isn't a patient man. He wants what he paid for. He wants to fuck me. This is the moment that will define our relation-ship. I need to jump on him, seem needy and wanting before he has a chance to rape me. I need to be the one to initiate the sex. Even if it destroys me to pretend.

We walk down a long hallway, and I try to pretend I'm walking down a hallway in the Carini mansion. I try to think of my niece. How beautiful she is. I need to fight to get back to her. She deserves to have me as an aunt who will spoil her and take her shopping.

But even thoughts of the most precious creature on the planet can't hold my attention when he opens the door to the room at the end of the hallway.

It's not a bedroom.

Well, there is a bed in the room, but I wouldn't call it a bedroom. It's a torture chamber.

Whips line the walls. Ropes, chains, handcuffs. Poles topped with metal hoops stand throughout the room, for restraints to be tied to. Walking around the room, inspecting the equipment, I stop when I get to sharper, bloody devices. Blood from other women tortured in this room. I can't think about this.

Dante is darker than I ever imagined. He has a twisted soul.

Fucking him won't be enough to save me. I have to be willing to let him beat and torture me.

I turn back to Dante, with a wicked smile on my face, and walk calmly toward him.

I wrap my arms around his neck, and he raises an eyebrow while staring down at me. His eyes are burning with dark desire.

I run my thumb over his bottom lip. "You're into BDSM. Good thing, I'm the queen of BDSM."

This goes well beyond a healthy BDSM relationship. This is a sick fetish. Even if he was doing these things to women consensually, there is something very wrong with a man that wants to torture a woman this badly.

I continue my plan though, keeping my breathing and heart steady as I raise my lips to his and kiss him.

I try to keep pleasant thoughts in my head so that he won't sense my disgust.

Mr. Conti pops into my head. He's a good-looking man. He's a fiend, but better looking than Dante.

I pretend I'm kissing Conti. I drop the mister from my head because it seems too formal. Conti kisses me harder, sweeping his tongue into my mouth, letting me know how much he needs to be in control of my body.

I can't hold the image long in my head, and slowly I pull away when Dante returns to my vision. I keep my hand on his neck, trying my best to show affection. I bite my lip and watch his eyes burn into my lip.

"I must admit, this is a fantasy of mine. Being taken by a handsome man like you. Tortured, fucked, like only a man like you can fuck. I want this. Tell me what you want me to do, and I'll do it, master."

Dante grabs my wrist, and I think he's going to give in to my words and body. His eyes and cock pressing hard into my stomach say as much.

I smile seductively. Trying to force him to give into his desire for me instead of the darker, controlling side.

Before I realize what's happening, I'm thrown hard into the wall behind me, and I crumple to the floor.

My head is pounding, and I feel the blood oozing down my back.

I don't know what I hit my head on, but it was hard and sharp.

Dante takes his time strutting over to me. He has more patience than I thought.

"Stand up, whore."

I don't know how he expects me to stand. I can barely see. He's merely a haze of a shadow in front of me.

I try to scramble to my feet, but the dizziness drops me back on my ass, and I hit my head again.

"I said, stand," he commands.

I try, but it's an impossible task.

He grabs my wrist, jerking me to my feet, and I swear I feel bones cracking in my wrist.

"I don't play games with my whores. You aren't my first. I've had hundreds, and I know every game in the book. You will not win. I will destroy you."

I nod because I think it's what he wants, and I can't take another hit. I know I have a concussion. Possibly a broken skull or wrist. I can't think straight. I can't see. I'm not even sure if I exist, or if any of this is real.

I'm either dead or about to be raped. And I pray I'm already dead. Either way, I'm in hell.

4

GIA

DAYS. Weeks. Months.

I have no idea how much time has passed since Dante stole me.

Time means nothing anymore.

I thought I was a force to be reckoned with. I thought I would fight every second of every day for my freedom. Dante taught me how mistaken I was.

Most seconds I can't even lift my head up off the ground. I can't stand. I can't see.

Seconds are how I measure my life. I can't think beyond that.

This second, I'm lying on the cold floor of the torture room. I haven't left since I arrived. There are no windows. No bathroom. No light.

It's a dark room, but I welcome the pitch-black. It helps me sleep at all hours of the day, which is the only reason I'm still breathing.

Sleep has been my savior.

I hear footsteps outside my door. Dante said he had a surprise in store for me when he returned. Was that hours, or days, ago?

Dante's surprises aren't surprises. He's given me half a dozen surprises already, and they all involved bringing in more men to share in the 'fun,' as he calls it.

Dante talks like he hasn't broken me yet. Like I still have a fighting spirit he hasn't figure out how to tame yet.

He's wrong. I'm broken. Physically I know I have dozens of broken bones. My left wrist flops when Dante ties me up, my right knee shattered when Dante whacked me with a bat. I'm not sure I have any ribs left intact after Dante kicked me numerous times in the chest.

I have nothing left to fight for.

Even if I did survive, I would be a hollow shell compared to the woman I was before. I would go through my days staring into the abyss, my mind most definitely stuck in the dungeon my body is trapped in now.

Yes, occasionally I gather enough strength to spit in someone's face, bite a finger, or give a swift kick to a groin, if I'm really in a fighting mood. But it's not fighting. It's *revenge*.

I don't care if I die anymore. I just need Dante and Roman to suffer.

The door crashes open, rattling the doorframe, as steady boots stomp inside my cage.

I used to shutter at such sounds, but I no longer do. I don't care if Dante is here or if he's gone. It makes no difference. I no longer feel pain. I feel nothing.

Lights flick on, and I close my eyes. The light too bright for me to keep my swollen eyes open.

"Such a good whore. You are exactly where I left you."

I don't answer. Where did Dante expect me to go? I have a broken leg, and he tied my legs with shackles to the post behind me. I didn't have any options but to stay exactly where he left me: naked and slumped on the floor.

"Stand, whore."

I can't stand, idiot.

I feel Dante's eyes burning into me. I expect the kick will come soon, but I don't brace myself for it.

"No," I spit back. Maybe I'm feeling more defiant than I realized.

The kick jerks my body backward and hard against a wall. Other than my body moving, I don't feel the pain I would expect from being kicked with solid boots at full force. It's all the same pain to me.

It benefits me. I no longer whimper or groan. I give Dante none of the sounds that turn him on. Now, he tries harder to evoke those sounds from me. He'll keep attempting until I'm dead.

Maybe today will be that day?

No.

That word has hovered around in my head and heart every time I've wished I was dead.

No.

I don't know why. I don't know where the hope or strength comes from, but it floats through my body, filling my soul, all the same.

No.

"Stand, whore."

"No."

"I told you she had a spirit, unlike any woman I've ever had. She's been here a month, and she never breaks. In fact, she may have grown stronger. She controls her whimpers for the most part, but today, I think that will change."

Another kick to the ribs. This one doesn't send me flying back. I'm already against the wall. I hear something cracking in my body. What was it this time? More ribs? My leg? Or my skull cracking?

No. No. No. Don't focus on the tiny slivers of pain creeping in. I'm dead. Nothing can hurt me.

I feel the tears starting in my eyes. I don't know how they formed. I'm dehydrated from crying so much when I first got here. I thought all my tears were empty.

One month, Dante said. Have I really been here that long?

It seems like longer and shorter at the same time.

One month. Has Matteo or Arlo realized I'm gone yet? I told Matteo I would be gone for a month. After not hearing from me, or my security team, for this long, would he come for me finally? How much longer do I have to hold on?

Another kick.

A low growl.

Wait...a growl? Did I make that sound?

My puffy eyes flicker open, as wide as I can bring them. I don't have access to a mirror, but I don't doubt I look bad. My face has to be all sorts of shades of reds, blacks, and yellows, as different parts of my face are in different phases of healing. And my cheeks, in particular, are at least twice the size they usually are.

I see men. At least five standing over me. I don't bother to count the exact number. That should scare me. It doesn't.

One more kick.

And this time I definitely hear the growl. It's not mine. My head darts in the direction of the sound. My eyes are too clouded to see clearly, but I swear I see an angel.

"Mr. Conti, would you like a turn?" Dante says, lust dripping off his voice.

Mr. Conti. A vision creeps in, one I've played over and over in my head. Mr. Conti barges into the dungeon with my brothers. He apologizes profusely, telling me he never wanted to turn me over to Dante. He had to, to save me later. But now that Conti's here, standing over me, I realize it was a stupid dream that will never become a reality.

Mr. Conti moves forward, and he still looks like an angel in my eyes. A cloud of fog forms around his head, shining brightly in the darkness of the world I'm trapped in. I know it's just my eyes playing tricks on me, but he was the culprit. He was the one who growled. He didn't like what Dante was doing to me. This man won't hurt me. I don't care why he's here; he won't hurt me.

A sly grin forms on Conti's face, and it warms me a second.

Then I'm kicked. Hard into the wall.

And the illusion of Conti being an ally shatters. He's as much of a monster as any man in this room.

"Now stand, whore," Dante says.

"Don't you think if I could stand, I would? I want nothing more than to look you all in the eyes so that when I do get free, I will know who to torture and kill."

Men chuckle. Not Conti. His eyes never leave mine. His jaw twitches and I swear his eyes are trying to tell me something, but I have no idea what.

He's not on my side. No one is. It's just my imagination.

Dante snaps his fingers, and I'm on my feet. Hands grip my arms too tightly, and I try to balance on my uninjured leg only to realize it's just as useless as my other leg. *When did Dante break my other leg? How did I miss that?*

"Oh whore, today I share you, but tonight, you're mine alone," Dante says in my ear before biting my earlobe.

He's never gentle. Not even for a second. He's relentless in his pursuit to cause me harm. It never stops. I don't know how he has the energy to hurt me while still keeping up with his job.

"On the bed," Dante orders.

Hands drag me to the bed. Shackles release from my legs. No longer needed with five powerful men in the room. Not that it was needed before. I couldn't walk, but I guess Dante thought I would crawl.

I'm spread open, something that used to embarrass me now seems like nothing.

Look at my body you disgusting cunts! Look at what a beautiful woman you are breaking, and tell me how you would like your karma handed to you for what you've done. The words form in my head, but I don't think I have the strength to make them leave my mouth.

"The guest of honor can have his way with her first," Dante says.

I don't care who the guest of honor is. They will all rape me. Defile me. Break me.

No.

I won't let them break me.

Conti moves in close, settling between my legs, grabbing them with his hands. He's going to be the first to rape me. I pull hard once. It's all the energy I have. One of my legs gets free, and I kick Conti in the side. He doesn't move. It was a weak kick. I'm surprised I even had the strength.

The grips on my arms and legs tighten as I'm spread wider for him. His clothes are still on, but the men don't usually reveal anything but their cock to me. While I'm naked. Always.

I watch as Conti begins to undo his pants and a single tear trickles down my cheek. I hate the damn tear. And I don't even have arms to wipe it away. Every man here can see my weakness.

It's been a long time since I cried. Or felt anything. But watching as my angel turns back into the devil has done it.

I close my eyes tightly. I won't open them again. I need to find a happy place to survive. But there is no memory or dream left which can take me away from here. I need to sleep. But I can't.

I open my eyes again. I can't help myself. I need to see Conti turn into the monster I knew he always was. I need to make sure he's added firmly to my revenge list, instead of living in my fantasies.

Smack. A hand shoots fire against my face. One of the hardest assaults I've ever experienced. My head is spinning, and I can't open my eyes.

Conti punched me in the face. He's too much of a coward to rape me fully conscious. *Asshole.*

I start drifting in and out of consciousness, but I won't fully let sleep consume me. I'll remember every moment of this, while I play brutal images of what I will do to Conti when I get free. He's a bigger monster than all the rest. And now I know I'm really on my own.

5

CASPIAN

"LEAVE," *I say.*

The men in the room stutter, not sure what to do as they look to Dante to give them orders.

"Leave!" I shout.

The men let go of Gia's hands and legs and leave the dark room. Dante is the last to leave, but he doesn't say anything as he eventually leaves me alone with Gia.

I rest between her stretched legs that are no doubt broken, but it doesn't stop me from pushing her wider.

She moans.

I lean down and kiss her lips. Lips I've been desperate to taste since she fell into my lap weeks ago.

Her lips are soft and delicious, but it's not what I want. I want her to kiss me back.

I lower my lips tasting her neck, breasts, and stomach.

And then I pull my rock hard cock out of my pants. I shouldn't do this. I shouldn't fuck her, but I can't stop myself.

I'm desperate for her.

She's all I've thought about for the last four weeks. I almost did something incredibly stupid. I wanted to steal her from Dante before he touched her, but it would have fucked up all my plans. So I didn't. I let him touch her.

I growl.

That was a mistake I won't repeat. She's mine.

I'm not a better man than Dante. In fact, I might be worse. I let an innocent woman suffer when I could have done something to stop it, but I chose not to.

"*Gia Carini, you will be mine. You don't belong to Dante. You belong to me.*"

She whimpers.

She hates me, just as she does Dante. And I deserve her wrath.

I should stop, but I have to have a taste of her. I have to fuck her. I can't stop myself.

My cock sinks into her slit; wet and welcoming. I don't know what she's dreaming about, but it's dirty if her cunt is this slick for me. I sure didn't do anything to turn her on.

Beautiful.

The most beautiful, fierce woman on the planet lies beneath me, encircling my cock. I should stop. But I can't. Dante didn't break her, but I can. First, I'll steal her; then I'll destroy her.

———

I walk up the stairs to the front door with my team encircling the house. My sister and second best, Terence, stand behind me.

Today, everything changes. Dante's team will be taken out and replaced by a team I hired for him. Dante wanted to do all the killing himself, but he realized he couldn't. So instead, he took out his most valuable men in the darkness of last night. Today, everyone else dies in the daylight.

Then, my first phase will be complete. I'll be able to monitor everything he does and be able to make my move on Dante whenever I want. Once I confirm what I already know about Dante.

And then I can steal Gia.

No.

I can't steal her. It will ruin everything.

But I have to have her.

My inner conflict never stops. Not since I had her in my grasp.

Today, I need to focus on my job. I'll decide what to do about Gia tomorrow.

I knock on the door and am surprised when Dante opens the door. I expected one of his guards. Did he jump the gun and take out all his men himself? I do not doubt Dante is capable enough of doing the job. It doesn't matter to me. Killing demons like Dante's men pleases me. I'll admit it. But I'm just as happy to have someone else do the bloodshed, as long the task is done.

"Mr. Conti, come in," Dante says, not giving anything away.

I see his men out of the corner of my eye. Dante told them I was here to work on the security system I installed a few weeks ago. It's a lie. My security system is running flawlessly. Right now, it's allowing my team to know the precise location of Dante's men, so they can all be taken out at the same moment.

I follow Dante into the living room with Terence and Adela following behind me.

I freeze at the entrance when I see Gia. I wasn't expecting her. It is clear from the security tapes that Dante never allows her to leave the room she was locked in. But today, she's lying on the black leather couch. A rope is tied around her hands and legs. She's naked and bruised, but not broken. I'm not sure if anything can truly break her.

I can.

I don't know why Gia is here, but she's going to distract me, and most likely Dante, from doing the job.

"Want to put your whore away before we get to work?" I ask Dante, not liking using the word 'whore' to describe Gia. She is anything but a whore. *Warrior, gorgeous, precious, angel.* All those words describe her so much better.

Dante laughs. "Don't worry. She won't distract us from our job. I want her to watch."

My lips thin, but otherwise I don't give away my disgust. Dante wants Gia to watch, in an attempt to break her. If she sees the carnage, it might scare her. Death has a way of doing that to people.

I suspect Gia isn't one of those people. For one, she seems completely prepared for her own death. And two, she's a Carini. My understanding about Carinis is they are as ruthless as Dante. She may not have killed anyone with her own hands, but she's seen death before.

And she won't care if men, who have held her captive, die. In fact, she will rejoice at the sight.

I nod and glance at my ready sister behind me. I stare at Dante, letting him know this is his last chance to stop this.

He smirks and sits down on the couch next to Gia, pulling her into his lap. Using her as a shield in case this goes badly.

Coward.

He won't partake in what is about to happen, and he'd prefer his whore get shot, rather than him, if a bullet goes awry.

He doesn't think I'm the best if he thinks that's even a possibility of that happening.

"Dante, I'll get to work then," I say, giving my team the signal.

All at once we reach for our hidden weapons and begin taking out our targets one by one with silenced pistols. Most of Dante's men shout out and surround him. That's why my best people are with me. I take out three as I head toward the kitchen, knowing there are two more in there.

A bullet whizzes by my head as I duck and shoot the bastard dead with one quick shot to the head.

Another gets a bullet to the heart.

I hear my team all confirming their targets are down, but it doesn't make me drop my gun. Not until I get the all clear from Steward, my man monitoring the security system to ensure every man is down.

"You have one more in the hallway," Steward says.

My heart races, and my lips curl into a wicked smile. I enjoy this more than I should.

I move to the wall as I slink down the kitchen counters to the hallway where my last target awaits his death.

I turn the corner and fire before he has a chance to move or shoot. I watch his body drop to the floor in front of me.

"All clear," Steward says.

"And our team?" I ask, hoping my team has kept our flawless record of being injury free.

"All good. No injuries reported."

I let out a deep exhale. I take pride in not losing anyone on my team.

I walk back to the living room where Adela and Terence are waiting for me.

"It's done?" Dante asks.

I nod. "All of your men have been taken care of. I'll have my team dispose of the bodies and get your new team ready to go within the hour."

Dante grins as he fondles Gia's breasts much too hard. She doesn't move or flinch, if she notices his touch.

"What do you think, sweetheart?" Dante asks Gia, calling her an endearment for the first time; his tone conflicting with the dead men covering the floor.

"I think you are a coward."

I smirk. I can't help it. I agree with her assessment.

Dante doesn't notice. He's too intrigued by his plaything to notice me.

God, I have to have Gia.

It will fuck up all of my plans if I steal her from Dante. Plans I have been working on for years. I no longer care.

I stare at my sister out of the corner of my eye. I will need her help. I can't do this without her. She will hate me for doing this, but I can't help myself. And in the end, my sister will do anything for me.

But will I make her?

Yes.

I stare at the stunning brunette, who deserves so much better, but she will never get it.

I will steal Gia. I just have to be careful, so Dante doesn't realize I'm the one who stole her. And then, when I need to get in Dante's favor, I will return her. Pretend some other bastard was the culprit of her disappearance.

But how can someone steal her and my security team not be blamed?

"I'm taking my whore to my work while you finish. Call me when it's done."

I smirk. I have to steal her. *Now.* I'm not responsible for his security at his office. I have no cameras or security set up there. He can't blame me.

Dante forces Gia up. I don't know how she's standing. I'm pretty sure her legs are broken. She's fucking amazing, that's how.

And she's *mine*.

Gia will think I'm saving her when I steal her from Dante. But really, she'll be trading in one monster for another. One with the power to actually break her.

6

GIA

WORTHLESS. That's what Dante thinks I am. That's what my brain tells me my body is. My legs, my arms, my eyes; all broken, futile, and useless.

It's not the first time I've heard the word used. Enrico used to call me worthless all the time. I was no use to him. I was a daughter, not a son. I wasn't built for this world.

Enrico said I'm too stupid to understand the business.

Not strong enough to handle the bloodshed.

Not powerful enough to control a team of men.

Not smart enough to make high paying deals.

And I'm too pretty to be taken seriously.

My entire life I've been 'worthless.'

My brothers never said it, but they kept me out of the business as much as possible.

Now, Dante is saying the same things. I'm worthless. Nothing but a whore.

My mind believes him. I'm too broken to remember any of the reasons I am worthy. All I can think about is my faults. My body doesn't work. I'm so bruised and beat up no one would consider me beautiful anymore. I don't have a college degree. I don't have a career.

I don't even own a house or car anymore. I live off my inheritance. Inheritance I gained from a father who never loved me and brothers willing to do anything to keep me safe.

I should be defeated, but every time I hear the word 'worthless,' it sparks something in my heart. Something that keeps me alive. Makes me fight.

I think Dante knows what the word does to me, which is why he keeps using it.

Dante had his entire team killed in front of me. It was a warning. The same fate awaits me if I don't do as I'm told. But it didn't scare me.

It just made the fire in my heart grow with the need of my revenge. I don't know what the men did to deserve death, but I know if they willingly worked for Dante, they deserved their fate.

It didn't make me sad. It made me happy to see their karma repaid.

And now, I have a chance at freedom and my vengeance.

Dante is in the driver's seat of his white Maserati while I sit in the passenger seat with my head against the window, soaking up every drop of sunlight hitting the window. I won't move my head no matter how uncomfortable the crick in my neck grows, or how much my forehead burns from the light. Dante thinks I'm resting my head against the window because I'm too weak to move my head, but I'm drawing as much strength as I can from the sun's warmth, preparing for the coming battle.

This is the first time I've been out of the house since Dante stole me. He doesn't have any guards with us. They are all dead.

He didn't use any ropes to tie my arms or legs.

He carried me to the car because I can't walk.

We are headed to his office so he can enjoy me, while Conti and his team prepare a new security system and team of guards.

We will be alone. I may not be able to walk, but I'll fly when the opportunity arises for me to escape.

I sigh. Large trees block some of my sunlight as we drive through a wooded portion of the road, but it doesn't stomp my hope. The trees are picturesque Italian. The vines climbing up their trunks remind me of my homeland. I was never meant to be an American like my brothers have accepted. I'm meant to be an Italian. Whatever faces me, at least it will be here, in the motherland.

My eyes begin to drift shut, but I force them to stay wide. I don't want to miss a second of the beautiful countryside or the quaint cottages we'll pass on the side of the road. I try to memorize the path we are taking. All the houses and villages we pass become ingrained in my mind. If I get a chance to escape, I need to be able to find my way to help.

Dante pulls the car to a stop in front of a row of office buildings, and my heart sinks. Surely, there are going to be people everywhere. I won't have a chance to escape. I could make a run for it now, but I have no shot against Dante, not in my state.

He would punish me worse if I ran. And I don't think I can handle any more broken bones.

Dante gets out, without a word, and then walks to my side of the car, opening the door and lifting me gently into his arms.

I let my body remain limp. I will not use an ounce of energy that isn't necessary. But I don't know why he is acting so cautiously with me. Are we being watched?

I look around for a sign of a video camera I can make a plea for help to, but I find none.

No, Dante wouldn't work at a place where there are video cameras he doesn't own.

He pulls a key out of his pocket and unlocks the glass doors.

Why does he need to unlock a door, if this is an office building full of people?

"Don't worry, whore. It's Saturday. The building is closed on Saturdays. We are all alone. No one will hear your screams."

I bite my lip as if he's going to make me scream right now. He's not. He's gentle so that when he beats me, it will make it feel so much worse.

My arms and legs dangle as he pushes the door open, and we step inside the building. The smell of paper and air fresheners overwhelms my nose. It's such a stark difference to the smell of blood and musky men.

This place is clean and sterile. Dante doesn't bother to flick on the lights as he carries me down the hallway. He doesn't look at me or speak as he stomps. He's a man on a mission. I don't have to look into his eyes to know the carnage that happened only minutes ago turned him on. Dante loves the blood, the pain, the wrath. It's who he is. He enjoys killing.

He wants to take that all out on me. All of his lust and aggression.

Just as Dante said, we don't pass anyone as we head down two hallways, then into an elevator, and up five floors. I don't know what Dante does to make his money. This building doesn't add any clues. But if I had to guess, Dante's business is similar to my own family's business. Dante just isn't as good at selling weapons as we are. This building is a front; something he can point to when his more nefarious dealings are revealed to the police.

It's stupid. The police will never believe him. He needs to have the cops on his side as the Carinis have for years.

Dante opens a glass door to a large office. Glass walls surround us, while large windows open the office up to the outside light.

My eyes widen, and my mouth hangs open, as I stare at the office. It's so normal, bright, and airy. This cannot be Dante's office. He likes dark. He likes to hide in a cave. He would never work somewhere so open.

I glance up as Dante's eyes are searing into my body. I'm wearing clothes for the first time in weeks. It's just a T-shirt and his boxers, but I'm still thankful to be wearing clothes instead of being naked. But I know from the look in his eyes I won't be wearing them for much longer.

My body stills as he tosses me onto a leather couch. He removes his jacket, slowly, as he walks over to his desk. He's going to rape me again. I can't take it. Not even one more time.

My eyes scan his entire office in seconds, looking for a weapon. Scissors, a knife, a hidden gun. Even a stapler. I'll take anything I can use to inflict pain on this man.

Dante begins rolling up the sleeves of his crisp white shirt while he stands behind his desk. He bites his lip, and his entire face tightens as looks at me. But he's not really looking at me. He's envisioning his sick fantasy in his head. I've seen the disgusting look before.

I pull my legs up against my chest, wrapping my arms around them. It takes a lot of effort to move this little, but it's worth it to bring myself some level of comfort.

"Oh, so many things I could do to you, whore," Dante says.

My bottom lip trembles as his eyes go wild. I bite my lip, stilling it. *I will not be afraid.*

Dante opens a drawer at the bottom of his desk. I try not to focus on what he's pulling out. It's meant to frighten me, as is everything he does around me. I will not let him win.

I try staring out the beautiful glass windows, filled with the warmth of the sunlight from the cloudless day. But I still see the items out of the corner of my eye, as he lays them on his desk.

A whip. Metal handcuffs. A butt plug. A ball gag. And a knife.

The knife is the only item that makes me react. He used it before on my back. It terrifies me. But it also excites me, for some reason.

My breathing speeds to unthinkable levels. My eyes water with both fear and excitement at seeing a weapon I could use against him. And my hands tremble in my lap.

The day he used the knife was the worst day. Unlike the pain of broken bones or rape that I can easily hide away within the cloud of overwhelming pain. The sharp edge of the blade can't be hidden. When it pierces my skin, there is no escape.

I cried. I screamed. I begged.

It was Dante's best day. My lowest point.

I can't relive it.

But it's a weapon. If I was able to get hold of the knife, I could kill Dante. I could get free.

I purse my lips and let all of the air out of my lungs, sinking into the couch and allowing all my muscles to relax. I haven't sat on anything this comfortable in weeks. I'm going to savor it.

I hear Dante's footsteps getting closer from behind the desk. I should pay attention to his movements so I can react and try to prevent an injury. My reflexes aren't what they used to be, though. So even if I know a punch or kick is coming, I can't move out of the way fast enough. I've learned to not spend any energy on avoiding his movements.

"We have hours together, undisturbed. We have an empty building. And new toys to play with."

I see Dante spin the knife in his hand. It's bigger than the last one he used.

Good. It will be easier to kill him with it.

A haunting song jolts us both out of our fantasies as his pocket rings and vibrates. He reaches into his back pocket and pulls the phone out. I think he's going to end the call without answering.

Instead, he answers.

"Perfect timing. I need an update before I turn off my phone for a few hours," Dante says, his lips curling up into a wicked grin to match the darkness in his eyes.

I grab the throw pillow on the couch and place it in front of my stomach, squeezing hard, like the pillow will somehow protect me from the dangers ahead.

Dante smirks, lifts the phone from his ear, and says, "That pillow won't save you, whore. I need to step outside to take this call. When I return, I expect you will be naked, and your cunt dripping wet, waiting for my cock."

I grimace as a low growl escapes my stomach.

Dante's stare intensifies. "If not, I will punish you." His eyes shine with a new level of hatred as he speaks. It would ruin his fucking plans if I were naked and my cunt was dripping for him.

He steps out the glass doors, and I almost consider stripping and doing everything possible to make my pussy wet for him. It would be worth it to see the surprise on his face, but he'd probably punish me anyway.

I watch as Dante paces outside the glass door. *Stupid, fucking glass.* What was so beautiful a minute ago has quickly lost its appeal. If it was sheetrock, then I could slink across the wooden floor to his desk and retrieve the knife without him noticing.

Maybe I still can?

If I had the knife, I could kill him. Or at the least injure him.

But if he caught me, it would be so much worse.

I try to still my body and become invisible. Dante isn't paying me any attention. Whoever is on the phone has Dante captivated.

Dante frowns and then keeps walking, out of view.

My heart stops. He left me alone.

He didn't tie me up.

I'm alone with a weapon.

I don't know how long he's going to be gone, but I won't wait to see.

This is my chance.

I force my body up from the couch. I expect unthinkable pain to roll through my body and drop me back to the couch, but I feel nothing.

Adrenaline or hope has filled my body, making it impossible for me to feel pain.

I grin, my cheeks flush, and my body moves. *This ends today.* I'm either going to be free or die trying.

I race across the room to snatch the knife. I move too fast and too slow at the same time. In reality, I have no idea how fast I walk.

I keep one eye on the glass wall, expecting Dante to return into view at any second. When my hand grasps the smooth surface of the black handle of the knife, I feel hope. Real *hope*.

I can escape.

I grip the knife firmly in my hand as I face the door. I could wait for Dante to return and stab him the second he enters. Or I could take my chance and run.

I tiptoe to the door, keeping the knife hidden down by my side as I lean against the door to see if Dante is just outside the door.

The hallway is empty.

My hands are sweaty as I work to hold onto the knife. I don't have much strength. I'm standing purely on adrenaline.

If Dante returns, it will take everything I have to stab him. It will just be luck whether I kill him or not.

I'm not waiting.

I glance back at his desk and notice a pair of keys. When did he toss his car keys onto his desk?

I don't bother trying to remember. I grab the keys with my other hand, and then, after taking one breath filling my body with every drop of air in the room to give me the courage to step into the hallway, I push the door open.

I open it slowly, ensuring any creaks of the door remain silent.

Silence.

I step out, holding onto the door as it carefully closes.

Silence.

I look to the left and then right. Dante disappeared to the right. So my feet move left.

Slow at first. Careful, cautious. But after two steps, I can't wait to get to freedom. I run or fly. I don't know which. All I know is my body soars down the hallway and to the elevator. The doors open the second I press the button, and I step inside. My pulse fires through my body as my mind flutters with thoughts of everything that could go wrong.

I press the ground floor button and catch my breath while the elevator descends. I don't know what is waiting for me when the doors open downstairs, but I hold the knife out, ready to attack.

The doors finally open, after what seems like years to my anxious body.

Nothing.

I don't have time to revel in another win. My feet run again. Legs, which aren't broken, compel my body forward, step after step. And even if my legs are broken, they work anyway.

I zero in on the door, only glancing to my left when I pass the final hallway before reaching the door.

Nothing. No one.

I don't hesitate as I push the door open and step out into the sunlight. I want to lie flat on the concrete and let the sun heal me, but I'll have to wait until I'm somewhere safer.

My feet keep moving quickly as I grab the door handle of the Maserati Dante drove me here in. I pull on the handle, but it doesn't open.

I frown.

Dante has one of these keyless entries. The kind that you don't have to press a button to enter the car. You only need to have the keys on you, and the doors unlock automatically.

I fidget with the keys, find the fob, and press the unlock button. Then, I grab the door handle again and pull.

It doesn't budge.

Shit.

I press the button over and over, but nothing happens. I try inserting the key into the door, but it doesn't fit.

These keys don't belong to the Maserati.

I look around the parking lot, but there is only one other car. A Fiat. I press the unlock button again, but the car is silent as well. It doesn't come to life.

Dante didn't pull these keys out of his pocket. These keys belong to a different car or a different owner.

I throw the keys at Dante's Maserati, watching as a tiny dent forms.

I smile a minuscule amount. The first smile I can recall in a month. A dent in his precious car is sure to enrage him.

My feet start flying again, as I move out of the parking lot to the road. I don't see or hear cars coming in either direction. I have two choices. Run along the road and hope I run into someone who can help me, or disappear into the woods.

I chose a man last time to help me. It was a mistake. This time, I choose me. I choose the woods. I'll disappear into the woods. Hopefully, Dante will think I chose the road. I'll hide in the woods for a couple of days until I can find a way to get to a phone.

I run across the road and disappear into the woods. I glance behind me but don't see anyone following me.

I'm free.

I take another step though, and my legs give out. It's almost as if they only had the strength to make it to the edge of freedom, but not enough to finish the job.

NO! *Get up.*

I grab onto a tree trunk and force myself to stand again. I can't keep running. I have to take things slowly. Very, very slowly. I hate it, but I don't have a choice.

It's okay. I have time. Dante will look here last. I need to find a place to hide in. I could gather some leaves and cover myself and hide until dark falls. Give my legs some rest; then I might be able to move again.

Or I could freeze or starve to death.

I need to keep moving for as long as I can.

"Stop."

My legs stop at the command. It's what they are desperate for: a reason to stop. They've done so much and gotten me so far, but they aren't enough to take me miles from here.

I grip the knife tighter in my hand as it rests by my side. I don't know if the man behind me has seen the blade or not. I don't know if the man behind me is my foe or friend. I lean toward foe.

I settle my breathing, trying to appear natural, but there is no way any person would take a look at me and think something isn't wrong.

I hear the crunch of leaves behind me as the man approaches me.

My jaw ticks, while the rest of my body remains still. I purse my lips again, letting all the anxiety out of me. One stab. I can get one stab in. It will give me an adrenaline rush again, and then I'll be able to run. I just have to wait until the man is close enough to stab.

More crunching of leaves, and then a hand on my shoulder.

I turn as fast as my body will allow me and bring the knife up to jab into the man's shoulder. I don't care if he is a friend. I don't trust anyone.

My knife dives toward him, but his hand grasps my wrist, inches before it plunges into his chest.

My eyes flicker to his.

Conti.

Fuck.

His eyes are unreadable as he stares at me, still holding onto my wrist.

I'm going back to Dante.

"Please," I whisper.

Conti's eyes narrow, but I don't have a clue what that means.

"Drop the knife."

I stare up at the knife. At my *salvation.*

"I can't."

He nods as if he understands.

"I'll let you run if you want to run, but Dante will find you before morning. He knows you are missing. That's why I'm here."

I nod.

"Or you can come with me."

I laugh. I don't know why. Maybe because I need the release. "I will never become Dante's again."

He nods. "I wasn't asking you to go back to Dante. I was asking you to be *mine*."

"I don't want to belong to anyone. I want to be free."

"No one is ever free."

Sadness. That is what I see, mixed with lust, in his eyes.

"I was."

"No, you weren't. You belonged to the rich, the powerful. You belonged to your family. You never belonged to yourself."

"Why would I go with you? Why would I trust you? Last time you turned me over to Dante."

"Last time I didn't have a choice. I didn't know what I was giving up. Now I do. I want you, Gia Carini."

He knows my name, and it feels good to hear something other than cunt or whore. But he turned me over. He's raped me before.

"You're no better than him," I say, unable to speak the devil's name, or even think it for another second.

"No, I'm not better than him. In fact, I'm probably worse. I'm not saying I'm offering you deliverance. I'm not saving you. Just offering you a new master."

He speaks the truth. Every one of his words. I believe him.

"What will happen if I go with you, Conti? Will you rape me, torture me, and beat me?"

His jaw twitches.

"Maybe. Maybe, I'll do worse. And the name is Caspian. Conti is my father's name."

My face softens when I hear Caspian. I try to reread this man. Last time, I saw kindness. I saw hope. This time, I'm realistic. It wasn't kindness I saw before. It was pain and sadness. I see it now. Now that I've felt it.

This man is broken, same as me. He's not evil like Dante is.

Caspian may not treat me well, but he won't hurt me in the same way Dante did.

Caspian may rape me, hurt me, beat me, but not with the same hatred. Caspian's rage comes from a place of pain. Pain can weaken, hate can't.

"Choose Gia. The woods, where Dante will find you, or me."

Nothing can be worse than Dante. I don't trust Caspian, but I believe him. I don't know what faces me, but I don't have a choice.

"You."

7

CASPIAN

I SHOULD BE OVERSEEING the security team. I should be at Dante's house ensuring the system I set up is working flawlessly. I should be on the phone with Dante, schmoozing him, and making sure he thinks everything I'm doing is to make him more secure.

Instead, I'm standing at the edge of the woods, while the most entrancing woman I've ever met tells me she will come with me.

I shouldn't be here.

I shouldn't steal Gia.

It could ruin *everything*.

Gia isn't the type of woman who is barely noticed. She blazes in, knocking down walls, and setting fire to everything in her path. Some people survive and are made stronger because she was in their life, but most dissolve into ashes.

Gia takes one step and her leg trembles. I've studied her body for the last three minutes, and I know her leg is broken. She can walk on it, but only because there is so much adrenaline pulsing through her veins. Adrenaline is the only thing keeping her moving. And it is almost gone. She won't be standing much longer.

I rush to her side, my arms finally able to wrap around her body again. I grab onto her waist, and her hands grip my forearms.

Gia is filthy. Covered in layers of dirt and mud. Her face is swollen, and about ten different shades of black and blue. The only thing left of the Gia I saw that day outside the coffee shop is her eyes. Her eyes still blaze with life.

Her hair, once straight and shiny, is now tangled and matted. I don't know if she will ever be able to get the knots out, except by cutting her hair. I can't even let my eyes travel over the rest of her body. My anger rages too fast in my chest at the number of cuts, bruises, and broken bones.

I can't think about what Dante did to her. It will destroy me.

I don't let Gia see my rage, instead, I still in strong solitude.

"I can walk," Gia says, her voice so fucking determined.

I chuckle. This is not the time for chuckling. If Dante changes his plans and decides to search these woods, he'll find us. And I won't have a choice, but to turn her back over to him.

"No, you can't."

I don't give her a choice. I scoop her up in my arms and start jogging back to my car, hidden under a large oak tree on the edge of the street.

Gia stops fighting once she's in my arms. She doesn't have a choice. I try to do anything to keep from looking at her. In just a few minutes, she'll be mine. Dante will have no chance to get her back. I can look at her all I want then. Do more than look at her.

Having Gia in my arms makes it impossible for me to focus though. All I can do is breathe in her scent. Before she smelt like roses. It still lingers in her hair, but now she reeks of Dante. Musky, sweaty, and manly.

I need to change that.

I bite my bottom lip to keep from growling as my legs move faster to get her away from this devil.

Gia doesn't move in my arms. She lays her head on my chest, and I know her eyes are open because I can feel them burning into a spot on my chin. Don't look at her.

I make it to my Fiat, and though I know she would be more comfortable in a backseat where she could lie down on the journey ahead, I'm glad my car doesn't have a backseat. I need her near me. I need to be able to touch her and keep my eyes on her as we drive. Otherwise, I'll lose my damn mind.

So that's where I put her, before hopping in the driver's seat. My heart pounds half from stress and half from anger. It's been a long time since I cared so much about a mission working out like this one. It takes everything inside of me not to call Dante and drive straight to him before pulling out my gun and shooting him dead.

How could he ever think it was okay to maim such a beautiful spirit?

"You going to drive or do I need to?" Gia says. She's slouched in the chair, not even able to hold her head up. There is no way she can drive. Her sly smile and rosy cheeks warm my heart.

He didn't damage her spirit. It's very much alive.

I speed out of our spot, slinging Gia against the window as I do.

"Much better," she says, as she slowly pushes herself off the window into an upright position.

I should drive her straight to the hospital. Her body is beaten so much; she no doubt needs countless surgeries to fix her broken bones.

It won't be safe.

The hospital would be one of the first places Dante looks. That's what I keep telling myself anyway. The truth is I'm a selfish bastard who wants Gia all to myself.

"Where are we going?" Gia asks, her voice weaker than before. Everything she does drains another quarter of her energy. She should conserve it. Another sentence or two and she'll pass out from exhaustion.

"Shh, you should rest. You don't need to worry about anything. You're mine, now."

I expect her to listen. I know she feels safer than she did with Dante. And for the time being at least, she's right.

She doesn't listen.

"I'm not anyone's. I belong to me."

Focus on the road. There is no reason to argue semantics with her right now. She's mine, even if she won't say it.

But I see her damn lips curl up. She knows her not saying she's mine fucks with me.

I try to figure out what gave me away. Usually, only my sister can read me. My grip is loose on the steering wheel. I'm driving fast, but not excessive. My body is relaxed, sunk into my seat. And my facial expressions are blank.

Gia looks at me dreamily.

"What?" I snap a little too loudly.

This earns me a full smile. *Damn it.* She likes getting under my skin.

"Gia, I don't like being disobeyed. You will learn that soon. So when I ask you a question or give you a command, I expect you to follow it. Understand?"

She giggles. "Yes, sir."

I glare at her, unable to hold in my rage at her little mistake.

"Why are you giggling? You think me risking my life to take you is funny?"

She takes a deep breath, calming her giggles. "No."

I hesitate before asking my next question, but it's the one I want answered the most. "Are you afraid of me?"

She pauses. "No."

"Why not?"

"Because you call me Gia."

I shake my head. "That won't stop me from raping you when I get the chance. It won't stop my temper from beating you when you disobey me. It won't stop me from breaking you."

She nods. "Maybe not. But you call me Gia instead of whore. You see me as a human instead of property. That's a start. You can't be worse than him."

I shake my head. *She has no idea.*

My phone buzzes, right on cue. My car has the ability to answer calls hands-free, but I don't want Gia to hear; nor do I want Dante to have a chance at hearing Gia next to me.

So I retrieve my phone from my pocket and answer the call privately on my phone.

"Hello, Dante. What can I do for you?" I answer, loving how much it pisses him off to use Dante instead of Mr. Russo. It will never get old.

"You can get your fucking team to my office ASAP. My whore is missing. Stolen, no doubt. Your fucking fancy security system and team did nothing to stop it!"

I grin. I can't help myself at hearing his panic on the other end of the line. Even if I didn't want Gia for myself, I should have stolen her to listen to his panic.

"My team wasn't responsible for you or your whore's security this afternoon. I told you, you shouldn't have left the house until the team was set up to escort you."

"You don't get to fucking lecture me, Caspian. Not today! Fucking fix it, or your whole team is fired."

"I will have my team meet you at your office. We will find her. If she's still in Italy, we will find her."

"And if she's not?" Dante's voice trembles as he speaks.

"Then, we will find you a new whore while we track down her kidnapper and kill him."

I end the call. Pocketing my phone.

Her eyes are huge as she stares at me. Her smile has vanished. And she's now as far as she can get from me in her chair.

She's afraid of me. I don't have to ask her to understand that.

"You're going to return me to him..." Her lip quivers and tears threaten in her big green eyes, clouding the sparkle there before.

"No."

"I don't believe you. You turned me over to him before. You want to wait a few days. Get your fill of me, and then pretend you found me when it's most convenient to get back on Dante's good side."

"N—"

"I'll tell Dante. I'll tell him everything if you give me back to him."

I pull the car over abruptly to the side of the road. I need to focus on her if I'm going to win this fight with her.

I grab her shoulders and pull her, so she is staring straight at me. I tell myself it's so I have her full attention, and she can see into my eyes that I'm telling the truth, but it's because I need to have my hands on her.

"If you believe one thing about me, believe this. I will never give you back to Dante. Even to save my own skin. You will never see Dante Russo again. He will never touch you again. Never beat you.

Never rape you. Once I claim something as mine, it's mine. I don't share. I don't change my mind. I will never let Dante have you again."

"Dante won't stop looking for me. Ever. You can't assure that."

I cock my head to the side and give her a wicked smirk I'm sure reaches my eyes. "I'm Dante's security now. He wiped out his old team. He trusts me. Dante will never find you unless I want him to find you. I control Dante now. And I'm the best damn security in the country. You are free of Dante."

My eyes scan hers, trying to decide if she believes me. I don't know why it matters to me that she believes me. It's frustrating me that I can't read her.

"Do you believe me?"

Nothing. No answer on her face or from her lips.

"Gia?" I ask, with a warning to my voice.

"I don't know."

I sigh.

"Why? Why would you never turn me over to Dante? I don't understand."

So many heartbreaking images fill my head, and I almost forget where I am.

I shake my head, pushing the memories away.

"It doesn't matter why. Just believe me when I say Dante will never own you again."

I release her, and her body falls back into the chair, unable to hold herself up. I start driving again while we both sit in silence.

I do everything I can to not think about the gorgeous, feisty woman sitting next to me. When my mind starts counting her breaths, I change to counting the road signs we pass. When my eyes cut to the glow of her filthy skin, I punish them by playing images of Dante. When my nose takes deeper breaths, trying to get a whiff of her sweet smell, I roll down my window as we pass a cow pasture.

It takes us forty-five minutes to reach the small turnoff for my house. Gia fell asleep shortly after driving again. Her breathing has been slow and steady since.

I reached over around minute ten to tuck her hair behind her ear so I could see her pretty face better. She didn't stir. I punished myself by digging my nails into my skin. I'm going to need a better way to keep Gia out of my thoughts when I'm on the job. This won't work.

Now that we are almost to my house, it doesn't matter if I think about her. I can act on my needs. Fuck her if I want.

No. I will not fuck a woman who was so recently touched by another man. He probably fucked her in his office before she ran.

I slow my speed as the car sways over the gravel path leading to my house. There is no sign for this road. There is barely even an opening among the trees. It's how I like it. No one knows my house even exists back here.

Slowly, my black roof starts peaking out over the trees. The small cabin-like feel of the siding comes into view.

"Your house is tiny."

My head jerks to Gia. I thought she was asleep, but the bouncing of the car must have woken her.

I raise an eyebrow. "I can return you to your previous owner. Just say the word, and you'll be back in his giant mansion."

She stills. "I'll give your tiny house a try first."

I narrow my eyes. "I forgot. You're a Carini. You care about things like houses and cars and money."

She looks out the window, suddenly more solemn. I said something wrong.

"I'm not sure if such things matter or not, but I miss them." The way she speaks with regret stirs my deep feelings. It's clear she doesn't want to miss mansions, money, and expensive cars.

I shrug. "I don't think it matters if you prefer giant mansions or not. I prefer my excluded house in the woods."

"Our house was excluded. Hidden. But it had enough rooms we could all live under one roof. My entire family. We could have extravagant parties and lush rooms. Why wouldn't you want that?"

I shake my head. "You may think the Carini mansion was hidden and private. It wasn't. Trust me. I've been doing security for a long time. I've seen hundreds of houses. My house is private. Yours wasn't."

"I doubt you have been doing this for a long time." She rakes her eyes over my body as she takes in my appearance and age.

"Security is all I've ever done. Even when I was a kid. Don't start judging me because I don't come from a long line of Conti's who work in security. I made my money on my own."

Her face brightens at my admission. *Damn it. How do I keep revealing so much about myself to her so easily?*

She nods. "I wasn't judging you for not inheriting money. I admire that. It seems like a simpler life, where nothing is expected of you, and you can choose your own path. I envy you for that."

"Don't. My life is no more perfect than yours is."

She raises an eyebrow. "You can't be serious. Your life is a lot better than mine. You've never had your life threatened. Your ownership of your body, taken. Never been violated by another person."

"Don't speak unless you know the words you are saying are truthful. You know nothing about my life. In some ways, my hell is much worse than yours."

Her eyes cross in confusion and her luscious red lips open to speak again. I climb out of the car before she starts firing off her questions. This is one area she won't be getting any answers to her questions. I've endured more pain than she can ever imagine. I would easily trade paths with her to get rid of my own omnipresent pain.

I walk to her side, but her door is already open, and her feet are swung to the side as she prepares to step out.

Not fucking happening.

I scoop her up roughly.

"Put me down. I can walk! There is no threat at the moment. Dante isn't lurking behind one of the trees. Let me walk. It doesn't matter how long it takes me."

"It does too matter how long. I have work to do. I can't just sit around waiting for hours as you stumble into my house."

She pouts. "What did you mean back there about your hell being worse?"

I refuse to answer her or even acknowledge her words. I enter my code on the front door and wait for the door to unlock after it has scanned my face and recognized me as the owner. It opens, and I carry her in. The door shuts and locks automatically behind me.

"Caspian, it's good to have you home. Can I get you anything, sir?"

Michi, my assistant, and the owner of the house on paper, asks. He oversees everything that has to do with the house when I'm not here.

"We would love some food. Something light, please Michi."

Gia looks from me to Michi curiously. I expect her to open her mouth, but she doesn't.

"Yes, sir. I'll make some soup and grilled cheese."

"Thank you."

Michi heads to the kitchen.

"Wow, I'm surprised you can fit a third person into this shack," Gia says, with a hint of teasing in her voice. I don't know what it is that allows her to feel comfortable teasing me, but I like it.

"Watch it, or you'll be sleeping outside."

I carry her to my bedroom. The house is small, with only two bedrooms; one for me and one for Michi. The living room couch folds out into a bed when my sister stays over. But that isn't often anymore. I didn't think about it much when I was planning on taking Gia, just that I wanted her here.

I'll figure out the rest later. I place her on my bed before I realize my mistake. My cock comes to life straining hard in my pants at the sight of her on my bed.

The T-shirt she is wearing doesn't hide her glorious tits. Her nipples are hard against the thin material. And the boxers she is wearing cling to her far too skinny legs. Legs that were not this skinny before, but after a month of hardly eating, I'm sure she has lost a lot of weight.

I frown. I need the clothes off of her, but I don't want this to be a fight. She's exhausted, and my temper is tired of being tested. I'm not used to anyone disobeying my commands. She will learn to follow my demands, but it will take time.

Today, I want her clean, in new clothes, and fed. Then I will busy myself in work or spend my night jerking off while I try to be patient and not claim her pussy tonight.

I leave her on my bed, knowing full well she will try to get up and make a run for it. My bathroom is good sized. Not huge, but it has a large clawfoot tub I never use. Now I'm glad I never got rid of it to make more space in the bathroom.

I turn on the faucet in the tub and stick my hand under the water until it is warm, but not hot. I don't think her skin can handle hot. I take my time returning to the bedroom. I lean against the door frame watching her as it takes everything in her to scoot herself to the edge of the bed.

"What is your plan once you are standing?"

Her body jumps at the sound of my voice. She looks up with a frown.

I smile. "What's your plan? I know you don't have a weapon. You haven't figured out where I keep my guns yet. You can barely walk. If you run, I'd get you back in five minutes. What's your plan?"

"Dante didn't find me in five minutes when I ran."

I nod. "True, but then you weren't the one that planned your escape. I did."

Her frown deepens, and the determination in her eyes grows stronger. "You did not plan my escape, *I* did."

I smirk. "I had my team call, Dante, to distract him so you could escape. I made sure no one was in that building or parking lot. I made sure he didn't find you."

"I escaped on my own."

"Fine. You made it down an elevator, through a parking lot, and into the woods. If it weren't for me, you would have died in those woods or Dante would've found you."

She folds her arms across her chest, hiding her view of her breasts from me.

My lips thin, but I don't frown. I don't want her to see my disappointment at her hiding her body from me.

"What's your plan? You aren't escaping. You aren't strong enough. So I would recommend you let me help you clean up, you eat some food, and you rest. And then, when you've healed, you can try an escape again. Okay, sweetheart?"

Her jaw twitches when I say 'sweetheart.' She clearly doesn't like nicknames. But she doesn't say anything.

"I'm going to remove your clothes and help you into the tub so we can clean the filth off you."

I walk to her not giving her a choice in the matter as I grab the hem of her T-shirt. She keeps her arms crossed and I give her a stern look.

"Do you want to waste energy fighting me on this? You want to be clean. And I can't leave you alone in the bathtub. You'd drown. So let me help you."

Slowly, she lifts her arms and lets me remove her shirt. She doesn't shudder or hide when my eyes rake over her body. She's used to being naked in front of men.

My cock grows, but it stills every time a new bruise or injury is revealed. I don't think there is one area of her skin that hasn't been touched by that monster.

I kneel down in front of her as I grab the waistband of his boxers. She lifts her hips the tiniest bit as I pull them off her. My eyes go to her beautiful cunt. Needing to see it. It's glorious. But then my eyes see the large bruise on the inside of her thigh. I see the red cuts around her ankles and wrists where she's been tied up too tightly. I see the way her knee bends at an awkward angle, clearly not set correctly.

Fuck.

Her body is more damaged than I ever imagined possible. I don't know how her body hasn't already shut down from the pain.

I hoped to see the naked body of the beautiful woman who fell into my lap and begged for my help. Now that body is so scarred, there are only remnants left. She needs to heal.

My cock stiffens at the sight of her nipples hardening in the brisk air.

Damn, cock.

I can't fuck her. Not here. Not now. I'm better than this.

Our gazes meet, exchanging too many feelings. I hate feelings. I don't do feelings. Not anymore. I've spent the last few years shut off from the world. The only emotion I ever felt was anger and revenge.

Now, looking at Gia as I stand over her, she stirs a feeling I haven't felt in years. I can't quite place it. I don't know what the feeling is called. I hate it. I want it to go away. But I need to wash away any sign of Dante from her body. Or at least, what I can wash away. I know I can't remove the bruises or scars. Or the mental images from her mind.

I see the same emotion in Gia's eyes. Revenge is what she runs on. It's what has kept her alive, but there is something different now.

"Thank you," she says quietly.

I still. She shouldn't thank me. Not until she understands what I require of her. Not until she knows who I am. But I recognize it as the feeling in her eyes. She's thankful. Her eyes say she's scared to say the words, but she says them because it releases her from any guilt over what comes next.

I feel the reflection of emotion in myself. I'm grateful I have her. That I could save her, whatever that means.

I will accept that I did save her. Dante was set on killing her. Doing everything he could to get to that point and push her over the edge to darkness until her body stopped working, her mind shut down, and she vanished into nothing. If I hadn't saved her, I'm not sure she would have survived another week. Definitely not another month.

"You're welcome," I say, finally admitting what I've done.

Gia moves to get off the bed but then stops herself. She looks up at me with her dopey sad eyes. Her eyes say sad, but her long curling eyelashes say beautiful. I could get lost in the length of her lashes.

She exhales deeply, but it comes out more of a huff of frustration.

"Caspian, will you please help me to the bath?"

I catch my breath in my throat. Of all the things I expected her to say, I never expected her to ask for my help. I don't know what I did to earn her trust, but at this moment, she's giving it to me.

I don't say a word. I put one hand under her frail legs and the other under her arms. I lift her, feeling every bone in her body pressing into my chest as I carry her.

I've fantasized about carrying her naked since I first saw her. But this is the opposite of what I wanted. This is me taking care of her. This will hurt her worse than any physical thing I could do for her. She can't feel anything when it comes to me. She can't like me, or be grateful for me, or love me.

I place her into the warm water of the bath, carefully lowering her as her hands grasp onto the side of the tub to keep herself upright. I turn the faucet off as the water covers her breasts.

I kneel next to the tub. I can't leave her alone because she could drown, I tell myself. No matter how weak Gia's body is now, she would never let herself drown. She's too strong for that. Her spirit won't allow it.

Gia closes her eyes and lays her head against the back of the tub, letting the warm water go to work on her body and soul. The water immediately turns a light brown color as the caked on dirt washes off her skin.

I hold out a bar of soap and wait until she opens her eyes to take it from my hand. She begins moving the bar over her arms and chest, shakily rubbing her skin with the soap. She winces with every tiny movement, either from the energy it takes to move her arm or the pain the bar of soap causes as it moves over her skin.

I can't keep watching.

My hand reaches out to grab the soap from her, gripping her hand over the soap resting against her chest.

Her eyes meet mine, and I think she's going to fight me. Tell me she can wash herself. But she slowly relinquishes the bar of soap to me.

My teeth clench together, and my cock is hard as a rock as I move the soap over her chest to wash off the dirt. She watches me a moment. Staring into my eyes like she will find the greatest treasure if she keeps looking. Luckily, my waist is hidden from her view by the side of the tub. She can't see how hard I am for her and how desperate I am to become Dante. To rip her from the tub and fuck her. If Dante hadn't already hurt her so much, I would probably be doing just that.

Slowly, Gia closes her eyes and rests her head back while I move as slowly as I can to wash her. Applying just enough pressure to clean away the dirt, while careful not to press too hard and cause her more pain.

Every once in a while she bites her lip, winces, or lets out a low moan when I press too hard. But for the most part, I feel like I'm in more pain than she is.

"I need you to sit up so I can wash your back."

She opens her eyes slowly, as if even doing something that simple hurts. I've never been in that much physical pain before, so it's hard for me to understand. I do understand emotional distress, however.

She grabs onto the side of the tub again and starts pulling while I put my hand on the smoothness of her back and push her into a sitting position. Her entire body trembles as I wash her back. I move quickly so she can relax again.

I put the soap away and grab the nearby bottle of shampoo. It's not a feminine scent. It's the kind I use. Fresh and manly. She will smell like me if I use it, and I can't resist.

She notices the shampoo and dunks her head under the water to soak her long tresses. I squeeze a couple of drops of the shampoo into my hand and then massage it into her hair, hoping it will work on the tangles as well as the dirt.

Gia moans loudly.

"Am I hurting you?" I ask, stopping, afraid she has an injury covered by her hair.

She smiles up at me sweetly. "No, sorry. You massaging my head like that feels incredible."

My jaw falls open a little when I massage the shampoo into her head again, and the same sound escapes her lips. It sounds like I'm doing much more to her body than just shampooing her hair. It sounds like I'm rubbing an area much further south. I can only imagine the sounds she makes when she comes.

I sigh. I need to wait days, weeks, months until I try to hear those types of sounds from her. And even then, I don't think she will find sex with me enjoyable enough to gasp and moan at my touch. She will probably fight me off, instead.

I finish shampooing and help her dunk her hair back, rinsing the suds from her hair.

She runs her hands through her hair, working to untangle the strands.

"Give it time," I say when I see the disappointment at her hair not untangling.

She nods.

We both need to give ourselves time.

I grab a towel from the cabinet while we wait for the water to drain out of the tub. When the tub is empty of water, I wrap the towel around her and carry her back to my bed. I sit her on the edge of the bed and help her dry her body and hair before I head to my drawers and pull out one of my T-shirts and boxer shorts. It feels strange to be giving her the same thing to wear Dante gave her.

But when I hold out the clothes for her, she takes them with a warm smile.

I help her put the clothes on and climb into the bed.

Her eyes fall closed the second her head hits the pillow.

"I'll have Michi bring you food soon."

"Mmm."

I crack a tiny grin. I don't know why you are in my life, Gia Carini, but you have turned all my plans upside down. I'm not even sure what I want with you, beautiful. My cock knows what he wants. But what do I want? Why did I take you? Why did I save you? And what happens next?

———

I sit in my favorite chair in the living room with a scotch in my hand. It's late. Almost three in the morning, but I prefer the night. I like the darkness. It hides my emotions well. No one can discover any of my secrets if they are buried beneath the dark blanket of night.

I stare at my bedroom door I closed hours ago. Gia slept for two hours before I woke her to eat the soup and grilled cheese sandwich Michi cooked. She's been asleep since after she finished her dinner. I considered sleeping in the bed next to her, but I stopped myself. I didn't care if she was comfortable or not, but I knew if I slept in the same bed with her I wouldn't be able to control myself. Fucking her will be so much better when she's healed.

Instead, I sit in my chair drinking my scotch. It's not an expensive brand. I don't drink it for the taste. I drink it because it dulls my emotions. So why bother buying an expensive bottle?

I have a theory about Gia Carini. I think I know her better than she realizes. I've barely spent any time with her, but I know enough. My job is about reading people, and I can read her like an open book. The signs are all there. I don't have to read the file I had Adela do on her to know who Gia Carini is. She may have thanked me for helping her escape this evening, but that was then. I don't expect any more thank yous. From now on, the real Gia will come out. The one that will do whatever it takes to save herself.

I don't have a TV, and even if I did, I wouldn't turn it on to help the minutes pass. I don't open a book or play music either. All that I have to pass the time with is my scotch and the ticking of the clock in my living room. It's enough. Just thinking about Gia is enough.

I hear the familiar crick of the door.

I don't react. I don't smile or frown. I don't gasp or growl. This was what I was expecting.

The door cracks open further until I can see the shadow of Gia standing in the doorway holding onto the doorway like it's a lifeline.

Anger and annoyance roll through me. Gia may be brave, but she's also stubborn and relentless, both will eventually get her killed.

I nurse my drink while I watch Gia in the darkness gather her strength. She holds onto the wall as she takes careful steps, trying to quiet her feet on my old battered floors. It's an impossible task for the talent of a ballerina floating across the floor, let alone someone who is injured. Gia can't control her legs. She's off balance, and every step sounds like an elephant tromping through my house.

She falls. I hear the thunderous sound vibrate through the entire house, her body hitting the ground.

I wince and curse under my breath. My instinct is to run to her and help her up. I'm desperate to help her.

That's what I'm doing, I remind myself. By staying, I'm helping her.

So I wait and force more of the cheap scotch down my throat. She gets back to her feet, but it takes time. I've already finished my drink, poured myself a second, and finished all but a drop of that before she manages to stand again.

I close my eyes. I feel her heavy breathing. I hear her bones aching with each movement. My floor bends and cracks with each shift of her weight.

I grip the armrests, trying to restrain myself. *Stay. Wait.*

I glance up at the clock above my fireplace mantel. It's after four in the morning. She's been at this almost an hour now. *Enough.*

I spring off of my chair and walk silently into the hallway.

"Fifty-five minutes and thirty-four seconds, that must be a world record for the slowest attempt at escaping my house," I snarl. I can't keep my anger and frustration out of my voice, though I know it will provoke her temper.

Gia glares at me, her anger reaching the deepest parts of her frown.

"If you've been listening to me this entire time, you could have at least helped me back to bed or told me there was no point."

I laugh in a twisted way. "Would you have listened or would you have just postponed your attempt until tomorrow?"

She crosses her arms across her chest as her mouth prepares to tell me off, but the movement knocks her off balance.

I grab her before she falls again. I sigh. "Stop trying to escape. Stop trying to save yourself. It won't work. You're too weak."

She chuckles in defeat. "Would you stop fighting? How can I stop when it's all I have? I have my freedom, my honor, my name. That's all I am. I'm Gia Carini. Wealthy, powerful, and beautiful. If I lose it, then what?

"I have nothing left. I have to fight. I can't spend tonight giving into you when tomorrow you could be beating me half to death. If that happens, I need to know I did everything I could to try and escape tonight. Understand?"

"More than you know."

"So don't lecture me about trying to escape."

I shake my head. "You need to stop trying to escape. No matter what happens next, you are still Gia Carini, the most powerful, intelligent, beautiful woman in all of Italy. Nothing I do will change that. But you have to stop trying to escape. You'll never heal."

"Why would I want to heal when you will just break me again? I see it in your eyes. I know you are just as bad as Dante, even if you can control yourself better than him. Why wait for you to lose control?"

"Because like you said, I can control my monster. I won't hurt you. For one month."

Her eyes widen, and her mouth falls open. And all I can think about is what it would feel like to shove my cock into her glorious mouth. Her long pink tongue massaging me, bringing me to the brink.

"Caspian?"

She must have said something.

"Yes?"

She shakes her head. "I thanked you for saving me, or whatever it was when you took me from Dante. But that doesn't make you a saint."

"I never said it did."

"Then let me go. You have no use for me. You are a good-looking man. I'm sure you can get plenty of women. You have enough money you can pay a nice woman to live out your fantasies. You don't need me. Call my brothers. Tell them I'm safe and for them to rescue me. You don't need the hassle. If Dante finds out you have me, your business will be ruined, and you will probably end up dead."

I don't disagree with her. She's right. But again I think too much with my cock, and all I can think about is she called me good-looking. I think back to the day we first met. The look of lust in her eyes I thought I imagined. Was that real?

"No."

It's a simple word that answers her unspoken question.

She doesn't react to my word. She knew it would be my answer. It's why she never asked the question. It's why she tried to sneak out in the middle of the night.

"I can promise you this, Gia. I won't touch you. I won't hurt you. Nothing. For one month.

"For one month you can move about this house as if you aren't enslaved. For one month you can have as much freedom as you like within these four walls. Come and go in any room as you please. Ask Michi to make you any food you want. Ask me to do anything within reason for you in this house. Heal. Stop trying to sneak out.

"Then, after the month is up, you are free to try and run as much as you want. But when the month is up, attempting to run will be as useless as it is now. Your body can't handle running now, but even if you were healed, I have the best security system installed in my house. Better than ones I install in any of my clients' homes. You will never escape without my permission."

"Why?"

I shake my head. I just told her she was safe for an entire month, and she asks me why. She's too curious for her own good. She should accept my offer and work for the next month to figure out my weaknesses, instead of using all her strength to stand in this dark hallway and talk to me.

"Does it matter?"

"Yes," she says without hesitation.

"I don't play with broken toys, even partially broken."

She narrows her eyes into thin slits. Her eyes are the only thing I can see in the dark of the night, and now they are barely visible.

"I'm entirely broken."

"No!" My voice is louder than I wanted when I opened my mouth, and her body jumps. I slow and calm my voice. "You are not broken. Just injured. You can heal."

She shivers under my gaze. "When the month is up, will you hurt me?"

Yes. No. I don't know. I can't tell her any of those things. I don't even know what I want myself. But the answer is most likely yes.

"I have a track record of hurting women. I've never failed."

"Neither has Dante. Dante always ends the lives of the women he captures within a month. He failed."

She's hoping I'll admit I, too, will fail. But hurting her isn't my mission, unlike Dante. I will wound her whether I want to or not. Her being in my life will mean she will end up fatally injured, forever.

"Dante never played with your heart."

She gasps. I got the reaction I wanted, now time to close.

"He fought to get it, but he never had it. You can't take a heart by force. It has to be given, *willingly*. I don't just want your body Gia. I want all of you. Your heart most of all. And I'm the type of man who won't give up until I have it."

"And if you claimed my heart?"

"I would never give it back. I don't think you've ever lived without your heart. It's like living in the dark shadows, never being able to step into the light. It's not a particularly enjoyable way to live."

She silently nods like she understands. She doesn't. I've seen women lose their minds by the time I'm done with them. They leave me more broken than the woman leaving Dante's side. Death is the only answer for someone who has lost the will to live.

"Hold onto your heart, Gia. Don't give it to me. And don't let me steal it. If you want to live after you leave here, then keep yourself guarded. And when the month is up, find a way to escape."

8

GIA

A MONTH IS A LONG TIME, but at the same time, not long enough. Especially when I've spent most of my month in bed. I've never slept so much in all of my life.

When my body hits the bed, I'm out. It doesn't matter what plans I had before. Once I'm in Caspian's bed, I'm out.

When I leave, I'm stealing this bed. Caspian doesn't spend much of his money on anything in his house, but he didn't scrimp on this bed. It has the thickest mattress, the silkiest sheets, and the fluffiest pillow I've ever laid on. It makes it impossible to get out of bed. Even more impossible when my body feels like it's gotten repeatedly hit by a truck.

Caspian spent most of his time away since he gave me his proclamation weeks ago. Most likely because he has a fancy house elsewhere, he enjoys staying at. But even this tiny cabin is beginning to grow on me. I might even fall in love with the simplicity of it, if it wasn't just another form of a prison.

The forest surrounds the cabin on one side, with a small vineyard on the other. Nothing to hear but birds chirping for miles when I sit out on the small deck overlooking the forest and vineyard. But I can understand, if he has a larger, more extravagant house, why he spends most of his time there instead of here.

I don't know what to think about Caspian. We spent a lot of time together the first day when he rescued me, but we haven't spent any time together since. Michi takes care of my every need. He brings me food. It started out simple, just a broth or soup, but now he feeds me more extravagant meals like pasta and meats, both have put some much-needed fat on my bones.

Michi brings me clothes. The small closet now contains almost half as many clothes for me as it does for Caspian.

And he brings me pain medications when I can't take the pain in my legs any longer.

Most of the bruising and swelling is gone. If I wear pants and long sleeves, no one would realize what I have been through. And my leg has healed, mostly. I can walk, but I have a limp. Michi brought me a cane, and that makes walking more comfortable. But I don't want to be using a cane the rest of my life.

It's only been a few weeks, I tell myself. My leg will continue to heal. Even without a doctor.

My month is almost up, and I have no idea what awaits me when my time is up. More importantly, I don't know how to escape. I've tried not to obsess about escaping as I did with Dante. It made it so much harder when I realized I would never escape on my own.

I haven't found a phone or a computer. I have no way to contact Matteo or Arlo, but surely they are looking for me by now. They have limitless resources. They will find me. I just need to give them more time. And in the meantime, pretend I'm in a quiet spa. That's all this is. A peaceful, secluded spa where I heal, uninterrupted.

I hear a door shut, and I quiver. I can never get used to the loud unexpected sounds. Michi is good about trying to be quiet. I don't know how he lives here by himself in the silence. It's nice for a while, but I'm not sure I could live here indefinitely.

I hold my breath and pull the covers up tighter against my chest. I'm wearing yoga pants and a tank top, but I need more protection against whatever is lurking in the hallway.

Caspian is here. He's only come home a handful of times since I've been here. And he's usually pissed. He yells and stomps like he needs a break from the world and uses this place as his escape.

As long as he doesn't use me as an escape.

He treads heavily through the house, not hiding his anger, while I can barely breathe. All I can do is focus on his footsteps and hope they stay away from this bedroom.

They grow closer, and my heart is in my throat. Caspian may have been nothing but sweet to me when he stole me, but that doesn't mean he will continue to be kind to me. He belongs in Dante's fucked up world. I know what that means. I know what he meant when he said he would break me when Dante didn't.

Caspian is better looking than Dante. Caspian has a charm Dante doesn't. Caspian has a sadness I can connect with. Caspian will still rape me, but when he does, I will make excuses for him. I will want him because sex with him will be better than Dante. I'll fall for him in the same way Beauty fell in love with the Beast. But unlike the Beast, Caspian won't turn into a prince.

Caspian's footsteps get louder, until I know he is pacing outside my door, trying to decide if he will keep his promise to me or not. He's pissed and probably wants a release. He promised he wouldn't touch me for another week, but his reserve seems to be slipping. Whatever happened today has pushed him over the edge.

It wouldn't matter if he broke his promise. I don't get anything if he breaks. I just lose my ability to trust him. Not that I believe him anyway.

I can't do anything but wait and grip the sheets to my chest like holding on and sinking heavy into this bed will save me.

I wait for him to burst through the door and beat me.

He doesn't.

I wait for him to rip off my clothes.

He doesn't.

I wait for him to thrust his cock into my unwilling cunt.

He doesn't.

Nothing happens. I don't know why he made the promise not to touch me for a month. Maybe he was testing his ability to control his urges. Or maybe, he's breaking down my walls so it will be easier to hurt me when he finally does touch me.

Either way, it doesn't matter. He won't touch me. I know that now. Even though he's still pacing, his steps have slowed. He's calmed down. He won't break his promise.

Slowly the door opens, and Caspian enters.

His shirt sleeves are rolled up haphazardly. His blue tie hangs loosely around his neck, and the first few buttons of his once crisp white shirt are undone. There is a hint of red on his shirt, not enough to be blood. Or is it?

I continue my scrutinization of his body. His pants are slightly wrinkled from wearing them too long. And his body hunches slightly, like he doesn't even have the strength to stand upright anymore.

His hair is disheveled. He usually styles his hair in a purposefully tousled way. He's got the perfect bed hair down. But this is more. It's not styled. Just messy. It matches the chaos in his eyes.

He looks like a disaster, but despite whatever he went through to make him look like this, his mouth and body don't give away any distress.

He hasn't said anything since entering the room. He puts his hands in his pockets, most likely to remind himself he can't touch me.

I let go of the sheets and toss them down to my waist. Caspian both scares me and electrifies me. His eyes travel to my breasts, and I ache for more. I see the promise in his eyes, that he will do more if I say the word.

I don't.

I won't give in to his steamy stare. He saved me, but I'm still not free. I will never let a man touch me again until I'm free.

"What happened?" I ask, after several minutes pass of nothing.

He stares, and I see everything. It was bad. Blood everywhere. But he's used to seeing blood and death. The same as me. He lost someone. Not a close relative or friend, but someone he was responsible for. He never fails.

I see it all in his eyes. I'm used to not being able to read people, but Caspian reads like an open book. I'm not sure if I'm not usually observant, or if I prefer not to know. Because if I were able to read the people in my life, I wouldn't like what I found.

Caspian doesn't answer, except with his eyes.

"What do you want with me, Caspian? Let me go. Let me call my family."

He doesn't answer. He stares at me. His jaw eventually ticks familiarly. He does it to hide his real emotions. Because he doesn't want people to know what he's feeling. But I notice.

"Seven more days," he says.

I stare at him, trying to decipher the meaning of his words. He'll let me go in seven days, or he can finally touch me in seven days? He doesn't clarify.

"What do you want with me, Caspian?" I half whisper, half scream.

I expect a smirk or a half-hearted grin. I expect him to think of some deliciously, naughty thing he wants to do to me that I only get a hint of in his eyes.

I get none.

His mind doesn't leave the room. His thoughts stay in the present. And his quietness scares me more than any dirty thoughts ever could.

"Nothing, I should have never taken you," he says so quietly, I'm not sure he said it.

Caspian turns and walks out, leaving me alone with my thoughts. I will never admit my thoughts turn dirty when it comes to him. That Caspian stars in my fantasies. It's just because I've been without a man for so long. It has nothing to do with the man, and it has everything to do with me.

One day left.

Days left in my month is how I keep track of time. It's better than counting seconds, like I was doing before at Dante's.

My body wants to spend the day in bed. It's so comfy, and even though I've healed tremendously in the last month, I still have a long ways to go. Another day in bed would do my body good.

I won't lie around my last day though. I need to get up and out. I need to enjoy my last day, if it is, in fact, my last day of 'freedom.'

I stretch, before moving to the edge of the bed. I'm wearing pajama pants and a tank top. I consider changing, but I'm not allowed out of the house except to sit out on the deck, so there is no reason to change. I brush my teeth and comb my hair, which finally has all the knots out of it. And then I walk to the kitchen, smelling the delicious french toast cooking on the stove.

I pour myself a cup of coffee, before Michi realizes I'm awake.

"Wow, I wasn't sure you knew how to get out of bed for breakfast," Michi says.

I smile softly as I lift the coffee to my lips. I don't know what Michi does to the coffee but every time is different and mouth-watering.

I take a sip. "Mmmhmm."

Michi lifts an eyebrow as he holds a spatula in his hand to flip the toast.

"Good?"

I nod. "Delicious as always. Where is this roast from?"

"Hawaii. I thought you deserved a bit of a vacation. And since you can't go to Hawaii, I thought I would bring a tiny part of Hawaii to you."

"Thank you. Is that french toast?" I ask with too much excitement in my eyes and voice.

He nods. "Your favorite."

I bite my lip. French toast was never my favorite. It's always too sweet. But anything Michi makes has quickly become my favorite.

I glance out at the sunlight covering the deck. I want to eat outside, but I want to talk more with Michi first. I glance around the small house and open my ears as best I can, trying to hear if Caspian is here.

"Caspian is at work; you have the house to yourself," Michi says.

I stare up at him incredulously. He can read my mind as easily as I can read the word on the side of the coffee cup.

Buona giornata; "have a good day" in Italian.

I warm. I will have a good day, whatever awaits me. It will be good.

"I put a copy of *Treasure Island* out on the deck for you to read."

"Thank you." Michi has gotten me countless books since I've been here. They are always amazing. Books about adventure or travel. Never about love or family. He's careful with the books he chooses for me. He makes sure they are enjoyable, without reminding me of anyone I might miss.

I drink more of my coffee while Michi cooks. I usually eat my breakfast in bed, and then come out and talk to him for lunch. We never talk about anything serious. He takes my mind away from my life, but I'm running out of time if I want to know anything about Caspian.

"What is it like to work for Caspian?" I ask. I rarely even say his name in front of Michi, so it's weird to say it now.

"He's a good employer. I'm happy, and he's more than generous."

"You live here all the time?"

He nods. "I like the seclusion. I've only taken a handful of vacations in the five years I've worked for him."

"Are you allowed to leave?"

He chuckles with his back to me as he flips my french toast. He finally turns back. "Of course I can leave, Gia. I'm not a slave. How do you think I get this tasty coffee and french toast for you?"

I blush. "What can you tell me about Caspian? How did he get into the security world? Does he date? Does he have any family nearby?"

Michi freezes. "I don't think I should talk about Caspian's personal life. Any questions you have about Caspian need to go to him."

I frown, but I was expecting he wouldn't say much about Caspian Conti. The man will remain a mystery to me, for at least another twenty-four hours.

"Why don't you take your coffee outside and enjoy the sunshine?" Michi says, dismissing me. I don't ask him if he also knows today is my last day of 'freedom,' but it appears from the sadness in his eyes, he knows.

I take my coffee and walk outside to my favorite chair, but it feels more like I'm walking to the guillotine. Or at least my last meal before death finds me.

I don't know what tomorrow brings, but I won't dwell on it. I'll eat my yummy food. I'll read my book. I'll tan in the sun. And I won't think about tomorrow.

My breakfast and lunch are delicious. Michi is an excellent cook. I don't know why Caspian doesn't have him cook wherever Caspian stays when he isn't here.

I hear shouting, and my heart does its usual freeze. I hear Caspian's voice, but I also hear the faintness of a woman's voice.

A woman?

That can't be. Why would Caspian have a woman here?

He wouldn't want to bring a date to see me. I glance at the large glass door out of the corner of my eye, and I can see Caspian standing in the living room as a woman sits on the couch.

What the hell?

I don't move, afraid the couple might notice I'm outside. So far the pair seems to be locked in an argument.

I can't hear the exact words they are saying to each other. But they are yelling.

I turn my head more fully to watch them, not caring if they notice I'm watching. They shouldn't be here if they didn't want me to snoop.

That's when I get my first look at the woman. She's wearing regular clothes. Jeans and a black T-shirt. But her face is puffy from crying. Her auburn hair is matted. And then I see the bruise on the back of her arm.

She was taken, just like me. I don't know if Caspian saved her, the same as me, or if he was the one who stole her in the first place.

Could he not wait one more day to have me? Did he need a release today, and that's why he stole this woman?

Oh, God. I can't be responsible for Caspian hurting another woman. Before I realize what I'm doing, I'm off my chair. I'm at the glass doors trying to listen to the conversation, but the doors are extra thick. I'd guess even bulletproof, and definitely soundproof.

Caspian grabs the woman's arm over the bruise, and I wince, feeling the pain in my own arm. He starts pulling her down the hallway to the bedroom. I can't let him rape her. I can't.

I jerk the door open and shout. "Stop!"

Both of them freeze and stare at me. The woman's eyes are huge, as she realizes Caspian has another woman here. She looks at me like I might be able to free her, but she doesn't realize I am just as much a slave as she is.

Caspian looks at me with rage expanding from his eyes. It's clear he forgot I was even here. And now that I've interrupted, he's even more pissed.

"Stop? What are you going to do to make me stop?" Caspian asks, his voice void of any emotion.

"Please, don't. You promised you wouldn't hurt me for one month. My time isn't up yet, and this would hurt me." I don't think this falls under the rules of our agreement, but I have to try.

He shakes his head. "That's not how our deal works."

I swallow hard, trying to push any fear down. "Please, don't rape her."

The woman's eyes grow larger at my words. But Caspian holds up a hand to silence her. She goes silent, before a word can leave her gaping mouth.

"What does it matter to you if I raped this woman? I promised you a month, and you have one day left. This woman is nothing to you. If she satisfies me, you might even get longer than a month to be free of me."

My eyes cut from Caspian to the woman. I see the fear I've felt too many times. And I see Caspian's rage. I don't think I've ever seen him this pissed before. I've seen a similar look in Dante's eyes. He will beat her within a second of life. Only then, when she has no fight left, will he use his cock to finish her. She will be dead by morning. At least her spirit will. Her body will follow quickly.

"Please?" I say in barely a whisper.

"Why should I?"

Caspian stares at me, not letting me have a moment alone with my thoughts. I can't think. I will do anything to prevent him from hurting her. I can't protect myself, but I can protect her.

"Rape me instead."

9

GIA

WHY DID I just tell Caspian to rape me?

Because I can't help myself. I can't watch another woman deal with even a drop of the violation and pain I've felt. I won't let Caspian hurt this woman.

I don't know who she is. I shouldn't feel guilty for any pain she might endure. I shouldn't feel responsible for saving her from the same fate I've faced. But the way her dark eyes bulge wide when she stares at me, with a sadness I didn't think was possible until I was taken, made me want to do anything to save this woman.

I don't care what happens to me. This woman is fragile. She couldn't survive the same things I've been through. She's too kind. One crack of a whip would break her.

Caspian lets go of, and ignores, the woman, as they both stare across the living room at me: his new prize.

I haven't moved since I pleaded with him to take me, instead of her. He hasn't either. We are both locked in a staring contest which might never end. The intensity flowing between us has us locked together in a wind that will never stop blowing.

Neither of us realizes it, but Caspian starts walking toward me. His feet stop automatically, just in time to prevent his body from crashing into mine. God, his eyes are so beautiful. And dangerous. And kind. And mysterious. And bright, but with specks of dark.

I don't breathe. I don't move. I don't back down. I try to lock down everything I'm feeling tight away in my chest so Caspian won't have a clue how to break me, while I try to figure out what he's feeling. He's a walking contradiction. He has equal parts light and dark. But that can't be true. He has to have one side of him that is stronger. Is it the light or the dark?

Right now, dark.

His chest rises and falls sharply as he sucks in all the oxygen in the room with each breath before exhaling deeply enough to blow me over. The beauty I saw on his face turns to a painful stare. All the light from his eyes evaporates until I'm not even sure his eyes are blue anymore.

He's decided. He'll take me instead of the woman behind him. He wants me. And I'm giving myself to him willingly. He doesn't have to tell me his decision. His body does.

I smile. It will probably be my last smile. So I savor it. I let the tiny bit of joy from winning cascade through my body, warming me all the way to my fingertips. My cheeks pink and my eyes soften. I saved her. I don't know who she is, the woman still standing behind Caspian, staring at us like she doesn't have a clue what's happening.

You're safe, I whisper in my head. Run. Hide. Find joy in your last days. I'm not playing games though. I'm not that type of woman. I prefer reality.

"I'll be in the bedroom," I say, turning. Happy to get one more word in before Caspian lets his inner demon out. I can see the evil in him growing stronger and stronger as every second ticks by. Dante lets his monster out freely. Caspian keeps his locked away. It's how he has so much control.

But now I'm permitting him to let his true self out. And it appears it takes Caspian time to unlock the door to the dungeon in his soul. I'm not going to stand here and watch the darkness cloud him, as fear starts creeping up my own body. Caspian doesn't get to see my fear.

My instinct is to wrap my arms around my body as I walk back. Holding myself to bring me comfort and keep Caspian's negative energy away. But I won't let him see me cower. So I strut with my hands by my side. My legs are steadier than they've been since I arrived here.

I open the door to his bedroom. I don't know whether to hope he will follow me immediately, or he will take his time. Immediately, I decide, before I lose my nerve. I want this over fast.

I get my wish.

Caspian presses my body against the wall before I even realize he's in the room. I don't know how he's able to walk in this house without making loud steps.

I wait for the hit. Or for him to choke me. Knock me out again, like he did last time. Or like Dante has done countless times.

I know Caspian is a brute. I see it fully in his eyes now as he pants over me. His breathing may be unsteady, but he is perfectly in control of himself.

I close my eyes slowly and deliberately, trying to find a happy place for my mind to go to. I imagine Caspian's deck, where I've read so many books this last month. What was the name of the last book I read? It had a blue cover, I remember, but the title escapes me. It was about a prince going on a grand adventure to save his kingdom. I try to remember the book, but it's easier to remember the feeling of the sun burning my skin. The smell of the pollen scattered over the deck, making me sneeze. The cool breeze is making me shiver in the early morning, before the sun fully rose.

"Open your eyes, Gia," Caspian says.

I won't. I don't care what he does to me, but I need my happy place. I need to go somewhere that isn't reality. It's the only way I've survived this long.

"Open your eyes, Gia, or I'll go back and—"

I open my eyes. He doesn't have to finish that sentence. I don't want him to hurt that woman. He knows it. And now I've obeyed him, he knows he can use it to get me to do almost anything.

I hate him. Maybe even more than Dante. I could deal with the physical pain as long as I had my escape. I don't know if I can daydream with my eyes open. I need to get under Caspian's skin, so he'll punch me. If my eyes are swollen shut, then he can't ask me to open them.

Caspian shakes his head slowly, side to side.

"You, Gia Carini, made a big mistake."

I swallow hard. I don't disagree. If I cared only about myself, then it was a mistake.

I saved her, I repeat to myself. That's what I need to hold onto. *I saved another woman.*

"You want me to rape you?" he asks, his voice deep and rumbling in his throat.

"Yes," I say, without hesitation or fear.

"Good."

I blink, but force my eyes back open, before the blink turns into shut eyes again.

Caspian licks his lip, like he is deciding the best way to devour me.

And, damn it, my nipples perk up at the thought of his tongue licking me like that.

Caspian will not turn me on. It's just because he's good looking. His body is strong and fit. His hair is luscious and dark. His eyes are what I like most about him, but they've changed. This isn't the same man I had fantasies about. This man is dangerous.

I am not turned on by Caspian, I repeat over and over to myself.

Caspian backs away from my body. He hasn't even touched me yet. Not really. Other than moving me to the wall, but I'm pretty sure my body moved voluntarily.

"Undress me," he says, standing a few feet away from me.

"What?" I ask, not expecting him to give me a command. Dante commanded, but he preferred to use his fists to get me to do what he wanted.

"Do you need your hearing checked?" he asks.

"Um...no...I just...don't understand." I would have expected him to tell me to undress. Dante always kept his clothes on when he raped me. I'm wearing a T-shirt and sweatpants. Not exactly real clothes, but it at least hides my body.

Caspian sighs. "I'm not a patient man, Miss Carini. If you'd prefer I use alternative means to persuade you to behave, then I can. If not, I prefer to give you a command, and for you to follow it as soon as I've said it. Understand?" His voice is threatening. He will hurt me if I don't behave as he says, but if I do, he might not beat me. Can I do that? I hate following men's directions. I've dated a few men that thought they could control me in the bedroom and my normal activities. It never worked out for long.

I just healed. I don't really want a broken bone again. Not so soon. Not when I haven't had a chance to run yet.

And he's asking me to remove his clothes, not mine. He's not asking me to suck his dick or fuck him, yet. I'll behave, as long as it's what I want. Then, I will fight.

I walk over to Caspian. He's wearing a buttoned-down shirt and slacks. I grab the top button at the top of his shirt. My hands tremble at little as I grasp the button. *What the hell is wrong with me?*

I take a deep breath, as I slowly undo the first button.

"Today, Miss Carini," Caspian says, eyeing me firmly. I don't know why I'm Miss Carini, instead of Gia. But I like both of my names rolling off his tongue. Either name he calls me sends chills down my arms and warms my core.

I move my fingers faster, but my stupid fingers stumble at every button, unable to get the tiny buttons to move properly. Caspian doesn't scold me again though. I finish the last button and pull the bottom of his shirt out of his pants. Then, I push the shirt off his broad shoulders, as Caspian shrugs out of the shirt.

My jaw unhinges, staring at Caspian's naked torso. Rippling abs cover most of his body, before forming a perfect V that disappears into his pants. I've never seen a more toned body. But the shock is in the tattoo which winds around his body.

It's a thorn from a rose bush. I know it's a rose bush because he has one in his backyard I've stared at for weeks now. But unlike the rosebush in his backyard that is full of flowers, his tattoo has one single flower on his chest, over his heart. I want him to turn around so I can search his back for more flowers, but I know from the pain in his eyes, there are none.

"What does the tattoo mean?" I ask. I don't expect him to answer me, and honestly, I'm not sure I need him to speak to tell me. It's pretty clear he lives a dangerous life with plenty of thorns. I would guess the thorns represent his kills, and the flower is his heart, slowly withering away.

"The thorns are every time I've felt pain. And the flower is the only time I've felt love."

I catch my breath as he speaks. Love. Caspian is capable of love. He's capable of feeling pain. Dante wasn't capable of either.

"I will never love you; remember that."

Goosebumps cover my body, and I shiver. I don't know why his words affect me so. I don't want him to love me. I know him loving me won't help me escape. I will remain trapped in this house forever, if he loves me. And my only hope at feeling happiness would be for me to love him back. I don't want love. Love is just its own form of a prison.

I want freedom. I never realized how wrong I was in thinking I wanted a boyfriend, before Roman sold me. I'm done with guys. I don't need a man. I just need me.

Caspian's eyes drop to his pants, and I know he wants me to continue undressing him, as he requested.

I squat down in front of Caspian, refusing to kneel. It would feel too much like I'm submitting, and I've had Dante's cock shoved down my throat in that position too many times for me to ever voluntarily get in that position again.

I untie his shoes, careful not to look up at him as I do. I don't need to stir any other feelings, whether pleasant or scary, inside me.

When I've untied his shoes, I carefully remove them. I stare at his shoes a second longer, before I realize they aren't designer shoes. In fact, I would bet they didn't even cost him a hundred dollars. They look nice, but anyone who knows fashion wouldn't be fooled.

I toss the shoes aside.

"Careful with those," Caspian snarls.

I chuckle. "Why? The shoes are cheap. You don't spend any of the money you supposedly make."

Caspian grabs my arm and jerks me up. "I asked you to undress me, not comment on the amount of money I do or don't have. I don't have Carini money, that's true, but I wasn't handed money like you were. I earned every penny. How much money have you actually earned?"

I narrow my eyes, and my anger pulses through me. "You don't think I earned every dollar I was given? I may not have had a traditional job that brought in new money, but I earned every dollar of my inheritance. Being a Carini isn't easy. Especially being a daughter. There was a reason I was so desperate to find a man on my own. I needed a way out. And the only way to leave was by marrying a wealthy man. Even after my father was gone, it didn't change anything. I was still a woman living in a man's world. Seen as nothing but charming arm candy.

"You don't think my leg was the first broken bone I've ever experienced? Those bruises on my face weren't my first either. My father used to call me a whore. And Dante's men, you killed in front of me to try and scare me, are just a few of hundreds of deaths I've seen before. Don't tell me I didn't earn the money I have! I've spilled more blood and tears earning my money than you have."

My body trembles as I speak. Not from fear, but from the passion in which I speak. I've always felt like I was nothing. Not important. I never brought in any money. I never went to college. I have no special skills. But I do know, unlike other heiresses, I've earned everything. And I won't let Caspian take it away from me with a few words.

"My pants," Caspian says after a few seconds pass.

I glare at him as I roughly remove his belt, then undo the button of his pants, before shoving his pants down. Ensuring to scrape my nails against his legs as I push them down.

I cross my arms, taking a step back now that I've finished undressing him, still steaming.

But then I get a glance of his body. His thighs are bigger than both of my legs combined. Muscles meant for hard work. But it's what's between his legs that has all of my attention. His cock is long and thick, pointing directly at me. He wants me.

I should be disgusted by his cock. I've seen enough of them since I was sold to know it doesn't matter how beautiful of a cock the man has, or how gorgeous the man is, I still don't want a dick inside me that I haven't invited in willingly. But his...

I'm drooling thinking about his delicious cock. I want to feel his dick. I want his thighs pounding it inside me. I've dreamed about sex with Conti. I've imagined it, but even in my imaginations, I never thought his body would be this perfect. I try to think back to the last time he raped me, but he never showed me his body then. Maybe if he did, that time would have been more enjoyable.

No. No. No.

Caspian still wants to rape me. He wants to hurt me. Force me to have sex with him. It doesn't matter if I'm attracted to him, this is still wrong.

My body doesn't understand the difference between right and wrong right now. All it knows is that there is an incredibly attractive man with a cock straining to be inside me. My nipples are hard peaks beneath the thin T-shirt that I know Caspian can see. My cheeks are flushed, and my eyes tell him exactly what I want his cock to do.

I wish this were different. I wish I weren't his captive. Then I would be flirting with him, happy to have a one night stand with him. Instead, I'm doing everything I can to make the walls of my pussy clench up tight, instead of dripping with desire to welcome him in.

Caspian smirks.

And my mouth drops. The bastard knows exactly what he's doing. It's why he had me undress him first. He knew I would find him attractive. He knew I would be conflicted.

Fucking bastard.

"Now, it's my turn."

I gasp as his mouth comes down on mine. His hand cradles the back of my neck, and his lips smash into mine. I haven't been kissed since Roman. Dante and the rest slobbered, but those weren't kisses. And before I realize what my traitorous body is doing, I'm kissing him back.

His lips are so soft and sweet. So different than the way the rest of him is behaving. I can't help but moan as we kiss. I've been so deprived of anything that feels like love. I'm desperate to keep the kiss going. My tongue massages his. My lips push hard against his, needing more and more of the kiss. My hands wrap into his thick hair, keeping his mouth against my lips.

But just as I get what I want, he pulls away, stopping the kiss. I'm breathless, but I will never admit I liked the kiss, or want him to do that again. Never.

He doesn't smile, but I see the hint of pleasure on his swollen lips after our kiss. And I can see in his eyes, he knows I'm reacting the same way.

Damn.

I need to gain control again.

How?

"On the bed," Caspian commands.

Think, think, think. I need to follow his command, but I need to do something that also breaks it at the same time. I walk over to the bed, lie down on my stomach with my feet in the air, making it as hard for him as possible to get what he wants. It's not a great plan, but it's all I have at the moment.

Caspian walks over to the edge of the bed. Not even surprised by my tiny bit of rebellion, and flips me over.

"Undress."

I purse my lips. "I undressed you."

"Fine."

He grabs my ankles and pulls me to him. "I don't need you naked to have you."

My legs dangle over the edge of the bed, as he steps between them, before grabbing my neck again and pulling me into a kiss. This kiss has more passion than our first. His teeth nibble on my lip, but not in an excruciating way. I've soaked my panties by the time he's done kissing me. I fall back to the bed. My lips numb with pleasure.

He kneels down in front of me, his mouth attacking my pussy over my sweatpants.

I gasp and grip the comforter. *What the hell?*

I can't think, as he kisses my most sensitive area over my pants. I haven't experienced any pleasure in months. And I groan and moan, far too loudly for what he is doing.

I bite my lip to keep the sounds from coming and tighten my grip on the comforter. *Why is he doing this?*

He's playing with me. Making me enjoy him. It will make me hate myself later for finding any pleasure in this, but I can't help what my body feels.

He stops.

"Now, remove your pants."

I shove my pants down without thinking, my body already begging for his tongue on my pussy.

"Much better, Miss Carini."

He lowers his mouth over the lips between my legs. What I wouldn't give to have a razor to shave. But his tongue stops, just short of tasting me.

"You don't deserve it, Gia. You don't deserve to feel my tongue flick over your clit, or into the deepest trenches of your pussy. You must learn when you follow my directions, you get pleasure; when you don't, pain."

He flips me back over and smacks my bare ass with the palm of his hand.

"Fuck," I cry out, surprised the small amount of pain caused anything to leave my mouth.

The sting spreads, as he smacks my ass again. I yelp, but it doesn't really hurt. It's nothing compared to Dante. Caspian's smacks won't even leave a mark.

I start panting, anticipating the next smack, but he spreads them out, never letting me anticipate his next strike.

He strikes again and then lets his hand slide slowly down my ass to my dripping slit.

"That turns you on, doesn't it, Gia?"

I bite my lip, not wanting to answer him.

He slides two fingers inside me as he moans. "It does, doesn't it?"

"Yes," I barely whisper.

"God, there are so many things I want to do to you, Gia. But I don't want to break you too fast. Fuck waiting for a taste though."

He flips me again, and his mouth is instantly on my cunt. I cry out in pure ecstasy. I've never felt so much pleasure from a man's tongue pushing into me. My body writhes underneath his touch. And my fantasies become a reality. Caspian Conti is making me orgasm. He knows it before I do. His lips curl up as he makes me come.

"Fuck you, Conti," I cry out, as my body trembles my orgasm.

"I will gladly fuck you."

He stands up with an amused expression on his face. He grabs my legs, jerking my body to him.

"I've waited too long for this." His cock rests at my entrance, and for a second, I think he is going to ask me for permission. Ask if I want him to fuck me.

My answer would be yes. I want Caspian Conti to fuck me. After what he just did to my body, I want to know what his cock would feel like. Sex with him would be amazing. Incredible. I know it without even experiencing it. I know my body craves his. I don't understand it. Other than saving me, he's done nothing to earn me. He doesn't get to fuck me without earning it.

"No," I say, as defiantly as I can. I pull myself back on the bed away from his cock.

He cocks his head to the side and his face tenses. He's not used to being disobeyed. He's not used to being defied. And I prepare for a fight that rivals Dante.

But I refuse to be raped again. I will protect the woman that Caspian brought home, but I won't let him violate me. I can't.

He moves to grab my ankles, but I scoot further away.

"No," I say, louder.

He doesn't stop moving. He crawls up onto the bed, as I continue to scoot back. My head turns to the door. Did he lock it? Could I escape? He's much faster than me. But if my adrenaline is running, could I get free?

"Try it," he growls.

My head snaps back to Caspian. Him reading my thoughts is getting really annoying.

"You can't rape me."

He raises an eyebrow, as he climbs further up until his body is over mine. "I can't?"

"No, you can't. You won't. You're better than, Dante. You won't hurt me like that. You just made me come. You aren't cruel," I say, hoping my words are true.

"Am I?"

"Yes, you're kind."

"No, I'm not kind."

I take a deep breath, and all I breathe in is him. His sweat, his cologne, and my cum on his breath. And it drives my womanhood wild.

"You won't rape me," I repeat.

He frowns, and I see in his eyes that he won't. I don't know why. He's raped me before. He might have assaulted other women before. But I know he won't rape me, now.

"No," he finally says, defeated.

"Will you rape the other woman you stole?" I ask.

He chuckles lightly like he knows something I don't. "No."

I frown. His word doesn't give me much confidence.

"Why?"

He lowers his face until it's directly over mine. "I guess you will have to trust me."

He leans back, and his eyes scan my body with hunger. He still wants me, and my body is craving for his touch again. I feel empty, cold. I want to feel the warmth of his body pressed against mine.

My back arches and my breasts graze his chest. One spark changes everything.

I don't know who kisses who, or whose body crashes with the other first, but our lips lock, and I know nothing will stop us this time. This time, I said yes. I will say yes. This isn't rape. This is the best goddamn sex of my life.

Our tongues dance again, both pushing harder into each other's mouths, both needing more. My fingernails dig into his back sharply as his body presses hard against mine. He settles between my legs automatically, his cock resting at my entrance, and then suddenly, he stops.

"No," I say because I don't want him to stop.

Caspian takes it in the same way as I said before. To stop. With pain in his eyes, he slowly inches off my body.

I grab his neck.

"No, I meant..." *Shit, I can't say it.* I can't tell him to fuck me. He's holding me captive. He wants to rape me. *What's wrong with me?*

But I'm not thinking with my brain. My body is trembling with need for a release. I've been raped, but I haven't had sex. The kind that makes your toes curl, and your body whole. Not in months. I need it. I need it to make all the horrible memories go away. I need it to be my choice. I need to tell him what I want.

He hesitates, not sure what I'm about to say.

"Fuck me, Conti."

His cock slides inside me the second the words leave my mouth. I'm soaking wet, so his passage inside me is easy. But I still stretch around him, as he pushes further in sweet agony.

But the second he does, memories come back. Of him raping me before; of Dante.

"I got you," Conti says. His lips come over my hardened nipple, a move that was only met with rough teeth before, and I calm.

My body comes alive then, pushing out any stray memories. Caspian may have raped me before, but Conti hasn't. Conti was my savior. Conti is who I want to fuck. I want this.

So I don't let the twisted-ness of the situation ruin how I feel.

I arch my back as Conti kisses down my neck, like I had imagined so many times before.

I moan loudly when his cock brushes against a spot deep inside me. A spot no man has ever hit before.

"Yes," I cry, as he hits my clit over and over with his body.

His lips cover mine, silencing me. But my purring continues with his every movement. I can't get enough. My body can't take much more, and yet I want this to never stop. I've never had sex that made me lose my mind like this.

I no longer care about anything terrible Caspian has done before.

I don't care he didn't save me when I ran into his lap from the car.

I don't care he killed a dozen men in front of me.

I don't care he raped me.

I don't care he's holding me captive now.

I'm sick. Sex with him has changed me, and I don't know what to do with myself now.

"Come," he says in a deep, commanding voice. A voice I'm not sure I hate or love. But even if I wanted to disobey his command, there is no way my body could disobey.

"Yes, Conti." I come, screaming his name. Pretending I didn't just let a man who raped me, fuck me.

We both finish, completely spent, but nowhere near sated. The exhaustion gets the best of us, however. We don't talk. We don't fuck again. We drift slowly off to sleep with our arms and legs entangled together.

I realize nothing I thought about Caspian was true. Everything has changed. He's not who I thought he was. *Or he is*. Maybe he is exactly who I thought he is.

10

CASPIAN

"No!"

"No, No, No."

"No!"

I don't know who's screaming. *Is it me?* No, I'm not screaming. I open my eyes and feel the wetness on my face. I'm crying from another nightmare. Another reliving of the worst day of my life over and over again.

But with my eyes open, the screaming continues. I turn to my left and see a naked woman flailing next to me, screaming 'no' over and over again. It takes me a minute to realize who the woman is in my arms. I haven't had a woman in my bed in years. At least none whom I allow to stay after the fucking is over.

Gia, I finally realize. I remember. *The sex. God, the fucking sex.* What I did to deserve such a beautifully strong woman, I don't know.

Last night started as a disaster. I considered raping her. That's not who I am, but that's how desperate I was to fuck her. I would do anything, including turn into the type of man I hate, to have her.

She told me, no, and my heart broke. I didn't even realize I had any of my heart left capable of breaking. But then she grew deviant. And I could tell from the gaze in her eyes, she was as torn inside as I was.

She wanted me to fuck her, and when she finally said yes, I lost my damn mind.

I only fucked her once, but I already can't imagine fucking any other woman. I loved her mix of strength and sweetness. She fought me every step of the way but then gave into my commands with some persuasion.

Gia isn't my type. I like obedient woman. Women who do exactly what I say without arguing. I like women who don't have a clue what I'm thinking, but Gia seems to guess my every thought.

"Gia," I whisper, afraid if I wake her too abruptly, I'll end up with a broken face or something.

She stirs but doesn't wake.

"No! Please don't..." her voice gets quieter as tears drip down her cheeks.

"Gia, it's okay." I put my arms around her, strategically trying to calm her while ensuring her flailing arms don't find me as a target.

"No! Conti, don't rape me!"

I let go of her when she says my name, and I get smacked in the face by one of her thrashing arms. I don't feel the impact though. I'm too shocked by what she just said. Is she having a dream about last night, when I almost raped her? I didn't, but am I now a bigger nightmare than Dante is to her?

I deserve to be. I'm no better than him. I have different desires than him, but I'm just as capable of permanently scarring her.

Gia's eyes slowly flicker open. They are soaked with her tears. And she cautiously looks around like she doesn't know where she is. I sit on the edge of the bed, staring at her like she's a tiger that made its way into my bed. And if I get too close, I will get clawed.

"Caspian? What are you doing in here?" she asks, moving her body up as she leans against the headboard. She's completely naked, lying on top of the covers, but she doesn't seem to care. I guess weeks of being naked in Dante's world would make her not care.

"We must have fallen asleep after I fucked your brains out," I say.

She blushes, and a slow grin creeps up on her tearstained cheeks.

"Oh, I remember now," she says, smiling like a silly teenager.

"What was your nightmare about?" I ask.

Her smile drops in an instant and small lines form around her eyes, thinking too hard.

"You," she finally says.

I nod. "I thought so. You said my name. Was what happened yesterday that bad, you had a nightmare about it?"

She cocks her head to her side and opens her eyes wide like I'm crazy. Her hand drums up and down her smooth stomach while she waits for me to realize my mistake. I have no idea what mistake I could have made.

"What aren't you telling me?" I feel anger again. She doesn't have to tell me anything, but I want to know everything. I want her to trust me with her everything. I haven't earned it, but that is what I'm used to. We will have to talk later.

"I didn't have a nightmare about last night. Last night was well... last night was pretty great. I had a nightmare about when you came to Dante's."

I frown, not understanding. "I thought when I killed those men in front of you, I didn't upset you?"

"You didn't."

"Then, what the hell are you talking about? The only time I've been to Dante's in the last month was to kill his men and install the security system. I didn't see you when I installed the security system."

"I'm talking about when you fucking raped me, you asshole!"

Tears, so many tears, flow down her cheeks. She's pissed and angry and hurt. But I still don't have a damn clue what she's talking about.

I can't stand women crying. It might be one of my biggest weaknesses. I reach my thumb up to her cheek, to brush the tears away, so I can focus on this psychotic conversation, but she slaps my hand away.

"Don't touch me."

I jerk my hand back and rub my neck, while staring at her, forcing my eyes to stay on her face instead of perky breasts like my cock wants.

"I don't understand. I've never raped you, Gia. I think I would remember raping a woman like you. The only time I've fucked you was last night."

"No, you raped me. It was one of the worst ones," her voice trembles as she speaks.

"Tell me," I say, hoping her telling me her nightmare, which is most likely just that: a nightmare she dreamed up.

"Dante said he had a surprise for me. Five of his closest friends he owed. Each would get a turn with me. You were first."

She stops, pausing as her eyes shut. She's remembering. And it chills my heart knowing her words are true, even if I'm not the one who committed the crime.

"I was on the bed, spread wide for you. I was cold and warm at the same time. You looked so calm and collected. You wanted me, and I would have given myself to you if you asked. You had saved me."

I bite my lip. Her story can't be true if I had already saved her.

She grasps the end of her long dark hair and twists the strands together in her fingers. "You were my fantasy. My last hope at freedom. When I ran into you that day in the street, I thought you were hot. And somehow your face and body were what I imagined every day when Dante was fucking me. Any chance I could, I pretended he was you. I dreamed about fucking you, instead of him. I fantasized about you coming to save me."

She sucks in a breath that rattles in her throat through her shaky tears. "But then you were there. You were as bad as Dante. You weren't my savior anymore. You wanted to rape me."

"Gia, I—"

"No, let me finish."

I close my mouth.

"You settled your body between my wide, open legs. I couldn't move, I was so badly beaten. You kicked me rougher than Dante ever had. And then, just before you entered me, you realized you couldn't have me watch. You couldn't let me watch you hurt me. So you knocked me out."

I bite my lip to keep from talking. This is her time to talk, not mine. I will have a chance to tell my story.

"And as I was slipping into unconsciousness, you started raping me. I didn't even wake up until after the four other men had violated me. The only way I even knew that it had happened was because of the soreness and cum that kept dripping out of me. The additional bruises that my body earned, even though I was knocked out."

The green in her eyes turns red as she spits her words at me. "You may have thought you were compassionate. But not being awake, not being able to fight, not knowing who has violated my body, is worse than knowing. You are nothing but a coward!" Her voice breaks.

I want to hold her, comfort her, but she doesn't want that. She doesn't need that. She is fully capable of taking care of herself. And me holding her, would only make things worse. But I need the comfort. I have to wait to get it though.

I open my mouth, wanting to say words to make her feel better, but I'm not sure how to start so she will believe me. I'm not sure she will ever believe me.

I decide right now isn't the time to try.

I get up off the bed while she is still shaking with her anger.

I grab her favorite pajama pants and shirt and place it on the bed next to her. I walk over to my dresser and put on some boxer shorts and sweatpants.

"What do you want for breakfast?"

She doesn't answer. Just stares at me with a gaping mouth at my balls to ask if she wants breakfast when I haven't addressed her story. But I can't tell my side of the story. Not without a lot of help.

"I know you like french toast and eggs. I'll make that and some coffee. Join me out on the balcony when you are ready."

I don't wait for her to answer or yell at me. I walk out and head to the kitchen.

Michi jumps to attention when he sees me. "I haven't started the coffee yet, because I wasn't sure when you'd awake. What should I make for breakfast?"

"Take the day off, Michi."

"Sir, I would be happy to make you breakfast. I don't need a day off—"

I take a deep breath before speaking so that I don't take all my anger and frustration out on him. "Take the day off, Michi. I am fully capable of making breakfast today, and you haven't had a day off in months."

Michi stares at me a moment. I don't think I've ever asked him to take a day off. He's taken only a handful in all our years together. He's like a father to me. He would do anything for me. And I know he sees the pain in my eyes right now. He wants to help me. But I won't let him.

Michi finally nods and then leaves me alone in the kitchen. I make coffee, french toast, and eggs. I pile everything up on plates and carry it outside. Gia hasn't left the bedroom yet, and I don't know if she's going to or not. But this is the only way to earn her trust.

I set the plates down at the table and then take one of the seats.

The french doors open and Adela steps outside. "Did you make some for me too?"

My lips thin. I want to talk to my sister, but I also want Gia out here. I nod, and Adela takes one of the seats behind a mound of french toast.

Adela takes several bites of her breakfast while studying me. "I guess you aren't going to tell me what last night and this morning was all about?"

I shake my head. "You will find out soon enough."

She shrugs. And I know she already knows more than she is letting on. The walls in my house are thin, so she probably heard plenty of our conversations. And she is more skilled than I am at finding information when she puts her skills to use.

I sit silently, watching Adela shovel in her breakfast.

"You've gotten better at cooking, bro. This is almost edible."

I glare at her. "You seem to be eating it just fine. My cooking is as good as Michi's."

She laughs. "No, it isn't. You aren't the best at everything."

I roll my eyes. I am the best at everything, but I'm not going to argue with my sister about it.

The door slowly cracks open behind me, and my heart stills.

Gia.

I know without turning my head that it's her. The only other person it could be is Michi, and he knows better than to come back after I gave him time off.

Gia walks toward us. Her feet loud on the deck floor, it creaking below her steps, and then she takes a seat next to me, across from Adela, at the table.

"I'll let you two talk," Adela says, winking at me.

"Stay," I say.

Adela raises an eyebrow, but she eases back into her chair.

I put a plate of food in front of Gia. "Eat. Then, we will talk."

I want her fed before I speak and she storms out without eating. Dante left her far too skinny.

She rolls her eyes at me. "No, talk."

"No, not until you eat."

She pouts, sticking her bottom lip out roughly toward me.

"I'll eat while you talk."

I sigh. "Fine."

I wait until she has eaten a couple of good bites, and then I start.

"Gia, this is Adela, my sister," I say, gesturing toward Adela.

Adela jumps in, like the good sister she is, and holds out her hand. "It's so nice to meet you, Gia. You are such an amazing woman, and I've heard so many great things about you. I've always wanted a sister. I know you aren't exactly my sister, but I hope you don't date this guy," she says, pointing her thumb at me. "He's a bit of an asshole, but you already know that. I'm just so happy to see a woman in his life at all."

Adela speaks without taking a breath. But Gia smiles as she shakes her hand.

"It's very nice to meet you too, Adela."

Gia lets go of Adela's hand and turns to me with an evil grin on her face. She slaps me hard across the jaw.

"You are worse than an asshole. You are a motherfucking jerk-bastard-man who deserves to get shot repeatedly in the leg every few weeks, just after you heal."

I nod. "Jerk-bastard-man?" I smile a little at her new nickname for me.

"Yes, that's what I said, and I stand by it."

She crosses her arms. "I can't fucking believe you. You led me to believe you were going to hurt her. She's your sister! I know you are a bastard, but I don't think you would ever rape your sister."

Adela eyes me suspiciously.

"Really, Adela?"

She laughs. "No, I don't have to worry about that. You would never rape any woman." Adela glances between Gia and me, her smile faltering. "Wait! Did you rape Gia?"

I turn from Adela to Gia. "That's what we need your help with Adela."

"What? Did you rape her last night?"

"No," Gia and I both say in unison.

Adela visibly relaxes in her chair, her body sinking into the wicker and cushions. "Thank God! If I had thought you would have actually have raped her last night, I would have never left you alone with her."

I shift my weight in my chair, not letting her know I almost did rape Gia. But Gia again saved herself. I'm not as good of a person as Adela thinks I am. I don't deserve any of the affection Adela gives me.

"How can I help then?" Adela asks.

"Where was I last Tuesday?"

Adela narrows her eyes. "What time?"

"Three PM."

"You were running on the boring ass treadmill at the gym, twenty minutes from here on Ratonni street."

"How about last Sunday at ten AM?"

"You were installing a security system in Milan."

"And how about three Saturdays ago at six PM?"

"You were getting a manicure."

Gia laughs at that.

"Adela has a photographic memory. Everything she reads, sees, or hears, she remembers. It's quite annoying, actually." I give a dirty look to Adela, who laughs at me.

"It's true; I remember everything. My husband, Rodolfo, hates it. He never wins a fight."

Gia continues her careful laughing.

"And how do you know everything about my schedule and daily life?"

"Because it's my job to know. I protect you. I work for you and so most of the time I'm with you, and when I'm not, I have access to all of the security. It's my job to keep you safe."

I turn to Gia. "Satisfied she knows my whereabouts at all times?"

Gia nods slowly.

"Eat," I command, looking at her still full plate.

Gia lifts her fork and cuts off a bit, before sticking a bite in her mouth.

"Tell Gia every time I was at Dante's house while she was captive there."

"The first time was Tuesday, the second of May. You were there to install the security system. I was with you the entire time. I don't trust Dante, and I thought he might try to backstab us. As soon as the system was installed, I was able to monitor every part of the house. Including you Gia..."

Adela's voice grows sad when she says she could see Gia. I've watched enough of the security feed of what Dante did to Gia to want to go over and strangle him with my bare hands, bring him back to life, shoot him, and then bring him back to life again and continue until he can't survive any longer.

"Any other times?" I ask, prodding Adela.

"Yes, the day you rescued Gia."

Gia's mouth falls a little. And I can see her un-chewed food in her mouth. It doesn't make me stop wanting her.

"Do you have any questions for Adela?" I ask Gia.

Gia shakes her head, although I'm sure Gia will eventually have a million questions for Adela.

"Adela, give Gia and me a few minutes alone."

Adela smiles sweetly and nods. "Of course." Adela gets up and walks over to Gia, squeezing her in a comforting manner on the shoulder. Then Adela looks at me, and I know she is going to be listening to every word of our conversation. At least Gia doesn't have to know that.

I wait until Adela walks back inside.

"I never raped you, Gia."

She looks up from her plate, staring at me like staring at me is the most important thing in her life. Like her life depends on finding my secrets.

"I believe Adela. I believe she thinks she knows what you do at all times. But she can't possibly know. You could have snuck away for a few minutes that day."

I nod. "I could have."

"So why would I believe you? Why would I believe you when you say you didn't rape me?"

"I'm not asking me to believe me. I'm asking you to believe yourself."

She bites her lip.

"You already know it wasn't me that raped you. You just said it was *pretty great* when I fucked you. Although, I'm sure it was far better than *pretty great*."

She blushes and sits back in her chair like she's trying to hide.

"Do you think if I had raped you, sex with me would have felt that amazing?"

She doesn't answer.

"Do you think you would have wanted to have had sex with me if deep down you truly believed I had raped you?"

Nothing.

"Do you believe I'm capable of raping you?"

She glances back up at me. "No, I don't think you raped me. I don't think you've raped anyone or are capable of rape."

My lips twitch. If she only knew the truth, she wouldn't be saying I'm not capable. But as much as I wanted to, I never touched her without her permission.

"I just can't make sense of what I remember," she says, staring down at her french toast again as she uses her fork to move the food around on her plate before taking a bite.

"Is it possible it was another fantasy? That whoever was hurting you was too much for you? So you changed the image of the man hurting you to me, so it was easier for you to take?"

She nods. "It's possible."

"If you need, Adela can find the security tapes and try to find the tape of the rape you are talking about. If it will help."

She nods. "I'll think about it."

I nod. I'm sure Adela has already scanned the images in her head and found the exact instance Gia told me about earlier.

But it will be tough for Gia to watch. It was impossible for me to watch without punching the display.

Gia finishes every bite of her breakfast, to my surprise. "This is better than Michi's." She pauses. "But don't tell him I said that; he'd be crushed."

I chuckle. "Don't worry, Michi will love you no matter if he finds out you prefer my cooking to his or not."

Gia's eyes warm as she wipes her red lips with a napkin.

"So what now?" she asks.

I raise an eyebrow. "I'm not sure what you mean?"

"When will you let me go? It's clear you aren't the monster you said you are. When will I be free?"

I sigh. "I'm still the monster, Gia. Just not the same monster Dante is. You'll figure out my darkness soon enough."

"When will I be free?"

"Never."

Her hope drops. "Why? Why not just let me go?"

"I can't."

"Why?"

"The why doesn't change what is. You will never be free. So start finding ways to enjoy your life here with Michi, Adela, and me. You enjoy your books. We can get you more and—"

"No, I am not your captive."

I smirk. "It seems like you are."

She crosses her arms stubbornly. "I won't have sex with you again. You will have to rape me." Her voice is defiant, but her eyes are half filled with lust. She can't hold out. She needs sex with me as much as she needs air to breathe.

I lean forward and sweep a hair off her face. She doesn't move, but her eyes fill higher and higher until I know she is imagining me naked.

"I think you can be persuaded."

11

GIA

CASPIAN IS SO CONFUSING.

He's sweet and charming. He's menacing and a liar. He's truthful. He's every personality that has ever existed. And it turns me on and pisses me off at the same time. I don't know what's wrong with me. But I can't live like this. I need to know what he wants with me, other than sex. The sex is amazing, but it won't last. He will get bored with me. *So why keep me forever?*

Above everything, he's kinder than he thinks. He's saved me more times than he realizes. I just wish I could break through his control and figure out what's going on in his head. He's so careful with what he tells me I think he could point back to always telling me the truth, but he's clearly hiding something. A lot of things, actually.

There is only one bad thing he's ever really done. Denied me my freedom.

I know now he never raped me. I trust his words. I trust Adela, even though I'm pretty sure I'll want her to show me the video later. I need to know what happened to me when my mind was weakened. But after having sex with Caspian, I know he didn't rape me. That's one line I don't believe he would cross. At least not with me.

I haven't moved from my chair on the balcony after Caspian left. I finished my coffee almost an hour ago, but I can't bring myself to go inside and get another coffee. The warm sun is too cozy to leave, even for a minute. And when I go back inside, it means this is real. I'm his captive. He saved me to make me his.

Forever.

That's the word he used. Forever.

I just have to figure out to change forever to a month. I could use a month longer healing here. Hiding out from Dante where it's safe, and fucking Caspian whenever I get a chance. Then, when the month is up, I could seek my revenge. I'd be strong enough by then, and have Caspian out of my system.

But then what? What life would I go back to? The aunt who doesn't have a life of her own? Who has never had a life of her own? I'll worry about that once I get out of here. First, I need to get Caspian to agree to my plan.

I jump up, now that I have a plan. I can agree to all his darkest sexual fantasies, in agreement for him letting me go in one month. He won't be able to resist. If I'm here any longer than that, I will just become a headache or a liability. At least that's what I convince myself my argument is as I race inside his small cabin.

I listen, trying to hear where he or Adela is. I look down at the couch that is now stretched into a bed where Adela must have slept. But I don't see any other sign of her.

I do smell coffee. I can't resist getting another cup. I assume I will find Michi in the kitchen, but he's gone. Adela or Caspian can't be far away. Someone must have refreshed the coffee recently. I pour myself the steaming liquid gold and then walk through the house.

It takes me all of two minutes to walk through the entire house. I will never understand why he has such a small house. He must have another house somewhere else. He might even have a family, a wife, children he is hiding from me.

No one is in the house.

I consider my next move. *Could I run?*

My leg is mostly healed. Enough that I could walk, or even jog, for miles. No one is here to stop me.

I know Caspian has a security system. *Is one of his employees watching me right now?*

I sigh.

I'll try running if my plan fails. I'm safe. Caspian won't hurt me. Dante doesn't know I'm here. And I can keep having mind-blowing sex. My life could be worse at the moment.

Still...

I move to the front door and rest my hand on the door handle. *What would happen if I opened the door?*

My pulse raises with anticipation. I bite my lip as I grin. I like playing devil's advocate too much.

I turn the knob, surprised the door even opens. And then I step out on the small porch of the cabin. Nothing happens. No alarms sound. No men come racing out of the bushes to pull me back inside. *Maybe Caspian was lying about the security?*

I sigh. He's not lying. Just not telling the whole truth. He knows I'm out here.

I walk down the three steps and sit on the bottom step, my feet hitting the gravel outside of the house for the first time since I arrived. I sip my coffee and wait.

I don't have to wait long. Five minutes later, maybe, I see Caspian running up the drive. *Shirtless.*

My mouth falls open seeing his rippling muscles contract. I lift my cup of coffee to my mouth to cover my gaping. I glance over at the side of the house and realize his car has been here the whole time. I could have searched for his keys and tried to escape.

He would have found me. I'm sure his car has a GPS system.

I turn back to the gorgeous man sparkling under the sun reflecting off of his glistening skin.

Damn, maybe I should agree to stay for two months. I could stay locked up in this tiny cabin if it meant two months of fucking him.

"You wouldn't be trying to escape, would you?" he asks.

"Nope, just drinking my coffee on the front porch." I take a sip of my coffee to prove my point.

"You don't listen to music when you run?" I ask, noticing he doesn't have any earbuds in.

"No need. I have voices in my head far too often. I prefer to run alone."

I narrow my eyes. "What does that mean?"

Caspian stretches his arms over his head, and my insides are putty. My nipples perk up, thinking they are about to get attention. And my core burns with desire.

He shrugs. "I have earbuds in often to communicate with my security teams. I prefer to be alone when I run."

I nod. That makes sense. But again, I get the feeling that although it's true, it's not the reason he doesn't listen to music.

"I have a proposition for you," I say, letting the previous topic go.

He bends down, stretching at the waist. "So you were trying to escape. Just with propositions this time, instead of running."

I frown. "How do you know what my proposition is about?"

He straightens. "Because I know you. "

I pout. "No, you don't."

He cocks his head to the side. "You're Gia Carini. Third born. You are the child your mother thought would save her marriage to your father. She was wrong.

"You weren't exactly neglected as a child, but you were not praised like your brothers. You never fully belonged in their world. You were just one more child to split the inheritance with.

"You just floated by in school. Never really pushing yourself, but getting mostly A's all the same. You never went to college, didn't even apply. Why would you? You are the beautiful woman your family uses to distract other men when it suits them.

"And then you met a man, Roman. You thought he was different. He could give you a real life. A purpose. So you fell in love, and now you're here. How'd I do?"

I set my coffee cup down on the step before I stand calmly. "Like you had Adela do a background check on me and figure out the basics. That doesn't mean you know me."

He takes a step closer to me, closing the already tiny gap and setting off an electrical pulse. It starts off slow, as his hand grazes my fingertips accidentally, and then races faster as it hits every major nerve in my body.

"You're incredibly stubborn. You won't take no for an answer. You hate to be controlled. You're naïve. You're a bit of a princess who is used to other people taking care of them. Your beauty has gotten you far in life."

I glare at him, hating where he is going with this.

"But you are also an incredibly strong, intelligent, and fierce woman. One that could put me on my knees with one word. That's how I know you what you are about to propose."

He's right. He knows me better than I want him too.

"And that's why I'm not going to stick around and listen to it."

"What?" the word slips out of my mouth more in shock than an actual question. He slips by me, jogging inside.

It takes a second for the shock to wear off and the annoyance to set in. He will too listen to me.

I stomp inside, not even bothering to pick up my coffee mug. I slam the door behind me and then I listen, waiting to figure out where Caspian went.

Shower. I can hear the water on. I smile; the benefits of having a small home.

I take loud steps, making my presence known as I make my way to the bathroom.

Caspian has kicked off his running shoes and is standing in the bathroom with the water running. He sees me, smirks, pushes down his running shorts and flicks them in my direction before stepping into the shower.

I gape for a second as his body disappears behind the glass doors.

"Caspian! You don't get to end a conversation like that!" I yell when I regain my composure.

He ignores me and grabs the bottle of shampoo.

He doesn't get to win without even hearing me out.

I stomp to the shower door and throw it open. "Talk to me, damn it!"

Nothing. He pretends I'm not even here. He massages the cream colored liquid into his hair until it begins to lather.

I don't think. I want him to talk to me, and this is the only way I know how. I rip the clothes off my body and step into the shower.

He continues to ignore that I'm here. Instead, he tilts his head back and closes his eyes as he rinses the shampoo. I stop thinking for a moment while I watch the suds drip down his hard chest.

I shake my head, forcing myself to focus.

"Look at me, Conti!" I yell.

He finally does with an amused expression.

"Yes?"

Damn, I can't think. All I can do is stare at his lips. I forgot how inviting they are. I want him pressed against mine. And then sucking on every sensitive part of my body.

No.

Focus.

"I want to make a deal. You don't want me here forever. I'm a liability. I'll drive you mad. It's clear you are a loner."

He shrugs. But he's listening closely.

"Let me go in two months. I mean, one month. You can have me for one month. Do anything you want. All those dirty thoughts floating around in your head can be a reality. For one month. Then let me go. You don't want the trouble I bring anyway."

He leans forward until his lips brush against mine, the water dripping down his face and rolling onto mine. I shiver.

"No."

My heart stops. He said no, but I don't care about his answer. I care about what I want. I want sex.

My lips close the gap, needing his lips on mine. He doesn't hesitate. He kisses back with the force of the universe pushing us together. I don't understand the attraction between us. It's not like the attraction between Roman and me. This is different. Very, very different. It's all-consuming.

I can't think about escaping when I want to go deeper into his abyss. I want him more and more until I no longer feel like myself except when our lips are locked. I've never felt like myself until now.

I should have learned my lesson. Relying on a guy to make me whole is what landed me in trouble. I was raped and abused because I trusted a man with more than he had earned. But Caspian saved me. He's not evil. And it's just sex.

The sex will eventually get boring. We aren't together. We aren't a couple. Eventually, Caspian will let me go. And then I can find my own life, without a man.

"What do you want, Gia?" he asks as he presses me against the back of the shower. The cold tile presses against my back. He's asking if I still want my freedom. How can I say it's what I want when all I can think about is his body? I'm not sure when I will be ready to give him up. One month won't be long enough. I don't even know if two months would be long enough.

"Freedom, I want freedom. I just don't know how to get it," I whisper.

"I do. Let me take you away from everything." He doesn't wait for me to respond. He kisses down my neck as he palms my breast. I've never had shower sex. Never felt the slick water racing down my face. Never been with a man who is half monster and half angel.

But that is exactly who Caspian is.

My body comes alive under his touch. I forget about everything but him. He's right that it feels a lot like freedom. At least it does in my head, even if my body isn't really free.

His eyes rage with lust as I writhe under his touch.

"You have the body of a princess," he says, lowering how mouth to my nipple to lick the sensitive bud.

I arch my back, needing more of the flickering he's doing with his tongue.

"And the heart of a warrior." He releases his latch and sinks his hand between my legs. He hits my favorite spot without even trying.

I see the look of something darker in his eyes. He wants more than what he's about to do to me. This time is for me. But if I want to win this game we are playing, I will have to give into his desires. Is he as twisted as Dante?

No, but he said he was worse. I still don't know what that means, but I plan on figuring it out.

Right now though, I just need the release of freedom he promised.

His cock pushes into my stomach, and I ache to have him inside me.

But he's patient. As much as my body presses against his, needing to feel his slick length inside me, he won't let me until he says so. He may not seek everything he wants when he's with me, but he still has the control.

"Come, Gia," he commands as his fingers slide inside my slit while his thumb presses the button to build me.

"Conti!" I cry as an orgasm rolls through me.

His eyes blaze as he watches me follow his command. I pant for several seconds, trying to get my hold on reality again.

"How do you do that?" I ask breathing slightly more regularly, but his hand is still buried inside me.

"The question you should be asking is why. Why do I do that when I should be punishing you?"

"But—"

I don't get to speak. His mouth covers mine, taking my voice and any thoughts with me.

His cock replaces his fingers inside me, stretching me to my brink. He pumps quickly in and out of me, not giving either of us time to say anything to each other.

He lifts my legs up, and I dig them into his back as my hand grips his neck, holding on for my life as he moves us faster and faster.

"I can't," I cry, knowing his body is begging me to orgasm again, but there is no way my body can handle that again so soon.

Caspian stills, and strokes my face, running his thumb across my bottom lip. He smiles sweetly, even though his cock is still inside me. There is nothing sweet about Caspian.

"Beautiful," he says simply.

I blush at the simple compliment I wasn't expecting in the midst of quick shower sex.

His sweet smile turns wicked. And then he thrusts. My body clenches around his cock. My soul contracts to the beat of his breathing. And I know I'm going to be lost to Caspian forever.

"Conti!" I cry again, loving the way his name rolls off my tongue.

I hold onto him with everything I have as he slams his body into mine. He's not gentle as his own orgasm takes over him. My body hits the shower tile over and over.

It's hard. It's primal. And it's something that has been missing from my life for a long time: passion.

I clutch onto him knowing I don't know when I will have to let this feeling go, let Caspian go.

"It's Caspian, by the way," he says as he slowly stills, both of our breathing still frantic.

"I like Conti better. Conti saved me from my nightmares."

He frowns. "Conti doesn't exist. You saved yourself."

Jesus, my heart stops. Can Caspian say anything more perfect right now? While at the same time moments ago, say all the wrong things?

It's a good thing my heart is stopped right now, because I don't trust it. If Caspian gave me my freedom right now, I'm not sure I would take it. He treats me well. Then he treats me horrible. He can say the sweetest compliments and the most awful insults. Sex with him is incredible, but also intense. His house is homy but also feels like a prison.

I like Caspian. More than I would ever admit to him or myself. But like isn't love. And even if I loved him, the thought of that feeling got me in trouble before. I can't stay here forever. Whatever this is, needs to end. It would be so much easier if I hated him.

Why don't I hate you, Caspian?

12

GIA

CASPIAN NEVER SAID yes to my proposal. He also never gave me a definitive no. Neither is surprising. We don't really talk. We fuck.

I'm not complaining. The sex is amazing, but I need to figure out what is going on in Caspian's head to have a chance of getting free.

I woke up this morning without a nightmare. Which means Caspian slept in the bed with me last night. He only has twice. Usually, he sleeps on the couch in the living room. He hasn't said he doesn't like sleeping with me. But I assume it crosses some line in his book. Makes whatever this is, too relationship-y. But I want him in my bed every night. He keeps my demons away.

I put on some jeans and a fitted white shirt that makes my boobs look fantastic. I comb my long hair and then hurry out to see if I can find Caspian before he leaves for work, or wherever he goes when he isn't here.

"He's not here," Adela says, stopping me as I reach the kitchen.

She sits at a barstool eating her breakfast. Michi is in the kitchen cooking omelettes.

I frown as I glance at the clock on the microwave. It's seven in the morning. I didn't exactly sleep in, but I have no idea what time Caspian usually wakes.

She smiles at me. "Don't worry; he didn't run out on you on purpose. He had a meeting. That's why I came over so early: to keep you company."

Adela's voice is strong and happy. She reminds me of myself before life destroyed me.

I don't have the heart to tell her even if he was here this morning; it wouldn't mean we would have some romantic moment. Her eyes seem too hopeful for a relationship that will never happen between us.

"You mean you are here to make sure I don't run away."

I take a seat next to her as Michi pours me a cup of coffee. He's whistling to himself, ignoring my sharp words.

My words don't faze Adela. "I don't need to be here to make sure you don't run. You won't run."

I shake my head. "You Contis underestimate me."

She chuckles. "I don't think Caspian underestimates you at all. I think that's why he's fascinated with you. He doesn't know what to do with you. And I'm not a Conti by the way, so don't group me in with him."

"I thought you were his sister?"

"I am. I'm just married. I'm a Caruso now."

I stare at her in disbelief. I never expected her to be married. To have some resemblance of a normal life.

She smiles. "I've shocked you."

I nod.

"Good, I didn't think that was possible."

"Omelette, okay?" Michi asks.

"Of course."

He places the omelette in front of me. "My cooking may not be as good as Caspian's, but mine is more reliable."

I chuckle. "Caspian told you?"

He gives me a wink. "Yes, I guess I will have to work harder to gain your approval."

"Your food is amazing. It's just—"

"Caspian's is better. You're wrong, but I get it. When you love someone, it's easy to look past their faults."

"I do not love Caspian! He's holding me captive. How could I love someone who took away my freedom?"

Adela sinks in her chair, as her and Michi exchange knowing glances.

Michi shakes his head at me. "Love is strange. You don't get to choose it. It chooses you. I believe you if you don't love him now, just be careful. Love sneaks up on you when you least expect it to."

I take a bite of my omelette. I'm not going to argue with Michi about loving Caspian. It's not possible for me to love a man who took my independence away, my choices away, for even one second.

I turn to Adela as Michi starts cleaning the dishes in the sink.

"You have the security footage of Dante's house?"

She nods slowly, only looking at me out of the corner of her eye as she tries to sip her coffee casually.

"You had a camera in the room where I was kept?"

She nods even slower.

"I need to see. I need to know Caspian never touched me."

She swallows her coffee, hard. "Are you sure?"

"Yes."

She stands and walks slowly toward the front door, like if she walks slowly I might change my mind. She exits, and I think maybe she is leaving, rather than getting the recording. But a few minutes later, she returns with a computer in her hand.

She walks back next to me and opens the computer. She glances at Michi.

"I think I'm going to go for a walk down to town. Get us some nice wine to enjoy with our pasta tonight," he says before walking out the front door.

Adela turns to me. "What do you want to see?"

"The night that five men came."

She nods. She starts typing into the computer searching files, and then she clicks on a video.

She turns the computer back to me. "Do you want me to stay or give you some time?"

"You've already seen it?"

She nods. "I spent most of my time since Dante captured you

639

monitoring you."

"Why?"

"Because Caspian couldn't. He wanted to make sure you were still okay."

My heart hurts. How could he think I was still okay when he knew what Dante was doing to me? How could he wait so long to rescue me?

"It killed Caspian to leave you there. I know he hasn't told you why yet. I've told him he needs to tell you why soon. I don't know if he will, but it's not my place to explain. Just know he had a reason, and it tormented him every hour he left you with that monster."

Her words don't make me think any better of Caspian.

"I don't care if you stay or not." It's the truth. She's already seen the horror. I've experienced it. Watching it can't be worse than feeling it.

I turn the computer toward me so I can have a good view. And then I press play.

"I think I'll stay," Adela says softly, sitting next to me.

I don't look at her. I can't take my eyes off the completely broken version of myself lying in the room.

There is no audio. It's a good thing, because I could probably hear my broken heart beating so weakly, if I weren't sitting here right now I would think the woman on the video was about to die. I would have.

Dante enters with five men on his tail. All look strong and defiant. He makes a joke and they all chuckle as he kicks me hard. That part was real. Then a man with a similar build to Caspian steps forward. The man has a similar build and similar eyes. But this man is skinnier than Caspian. He's weaker. He could pass as a distant cousin of Caspian, but he's not him.

I watch as he kicks me and I feel the ache in my ribs. I watch as I'm dragged to the bed. It's like I'm there, but I'm not. I'm floating in a cloud looking down at my naked and bruised body, helpless to save myself from the fate that awaits me.

I'm tied to the bed. And then the coward settles between my legs before knocking me out. He could see my need for revenge in my eyes. He knew I would come after him if I remembered what he did. So he tried to take away my memories.

But I will never forget his face. Not until I've killed him.

I continue watching. I watch each thrust, each grab of my breasts, each punch to the gut.

A tear escapes my eye as I watch. It's painful and horrible, and exactly what I needed to remember Caspian isn't much better. He wanted to do the same thing to me. He's locking me up, keeping me from seeking my revenge.

My tears turn to flames fanning an invisible fire growing stronger as each second of the video passes. I watch each man climb on top of me and use my body like they use a piece of exercise equipment. Like I'm not human.

Finally, it's Dante's turn, but I don't need to see what he does to me. I remember every second of him.

I close the computer. I'm not sure if I'm stronger or weaker for watching it.

"Stronger," Adela says as I wipe the tears from my cheek on the back of my hand.

"What?" I whisper, my voice hoarse.

"You are strong, Gia. The strongest. No one can take that from you. That's one of the reasons you stayed as long as you did. You were strong. You survived until we could get you out. And you're stronger now."

I smile weakly. "You are definitely a Conti, no matter what your last name is now. I don't know how you guys do it, but you are always able to read my mind."

"I've been watching you for a long time. I have a good idea of what you are thinking."

I nod.

"I need something to drink," I finally say.

She jumps up. "We have wine or whiskey or vodka or..."

"Whiskey."

She fixes an overfilled glass and slides it to me.

"You aren't going to join me?" I ask. It's eight in the morning. It's not surprising that she won't drink with me.

"I would, but I can't."

"Work?"

"No." She pauses. "Can you keep a secret?"

I shrug. "Sometimes."

"I think you will be able to keep this one. I'm pregnant!"

"Congratulations!" I say staring down at the invisible bump under her dark grey T-shirt.

"But why is it a secret?"

"Because if I told Caspian, there is a chance he wouldn't let me work as hard or would put me on desk detail instead of helping him. He's never denied me the ability to do what I love before, but I'm afraid if I tell him I'm pregnant, he won't let me continue working for him. Caspian has always trusted me with my safety. He's let me make my own choices. He knows I can take care of myself and kick anyone's butt when need be. He's never told me I can't before. That's what is so great about our relationship: we are a perfect team working together. He's not my boss. We work together."

I hate it, but I respect Caspian more for treating his sister this way. My brothers were always too protective of me. Never let me do anything without security and protection. I guess they were right to worry because of where I am now, but maybe if I had had the skills Adela has, I wouldn't be here.

"But I'm afraid when Caspian finds out I'm pregnant he won't be able to resist keeping me away from all of this to keep me safe."

"I won't tell Caspian. I promise."

"Thank you. It's so exciting to tell someone. I'm excited to be a mom, but I love working security." Her arms go around me before I realize it.

And I melt in her arms. This is exactly what I needed. A hug from a friend.

Caspian might be dark, but there is nothing but warmth in Adela. She loves her brother, and it's not her fault he has an evil side. I won't fault her for that. She's a friend. I just don't think I can trust her judgment of Caspian.

There is no reason he should have left me with Dante if he could have saved me. If her words are true, there is nothing he could do to ever earn my forgiveness. He might have saved me, but nothing can save him from what he's done.

13

CASPIAN

TODAY SUCKS.

Worse than sucks. Today destroyed me.

It knocked me on my ass time and time again. Beat me until I have nothing left. Ripped out the tiny bit of strength I have left, leaving me weak and vulnerable.

I need today to be over. It's gone on far too long. I'll take a fifth of whiskey to my bedroom and drink until I pass out. Tomorrow will be better. It has to be. I know from experience.

It's been five years since I lost my will to live. Each year on the anniversary of my life ending, I think it will get better. I plot my revenge thinking this year it will be different. This year, I will finally kill them all for taking my life from me. But instead, I realize I have a tiny bit of life left in me when another piece of it is taken.

I slam my front door, not caring if I startle Michi. He's used to me coming home angry. He knows not to linger today. He'll be hidden away in his room. I'm sure he made dinner and left it warming in the oven as always, along with a new bottle of whiskey.

I head to the kitchen. I don't care about the food, but I need the whiskey.

I exhale when I see the bottle of whiskey on the counter. If I didn't have the bottle, I wouldn't survive another second. I smell the chicken warming in the oven, but it makes my stomach churn at the thought of food.

I snatch the bottle off the counter as I stomp to my bedroom, loosening my tie as I walk. In a few more minutes, today will be over. I'll have drunk enough to wash my memories into oblivion. And I won't wake until the sun has risen.

I throw my bedroom door open as I kick off my shoes. All I can think about is getting the bottle of whiskey into me as fast as possible. I unscrew the top and lift the smooth bottle to my lips, tilt the bottle up, and begin gulping the liquid, feeling it burn down my throat and welcoming the feeling.

When I lower the bottle though, the pain is still there. I glance at the amount of liquid I drank. Almost a fourth of the bottle. It's going to be a long night if that amount did nothing to make me numb.

I take a step forward and stub my toe on the corner of my bed.

"Fuck," I curse, as I toss the bottle of liquid against the wall without thinking.

The bottle shatters as the liquid sprays everywhere in the dark room.

"Caspian?" a tiny voice asks gently from the bathroom.

I close my eyes and grab my head. I forgot Gia was here. Usually, she is all I think about when I'm working. Her breasts bobbing up and down as I push inside her. Her swollen lips begging for me. Her raspy voice as she comes at my command. I can't get her out of my head on a normal day.

But today is different. Today, Gia didn't even exist.

I can't handle her today. *Not today.*

I should call Adela and have her take Gia to her house. Or tell Michi to take her to a hotel. I need Gia anywhere but here.

I walk to my ensuite. The door is cracked, and the light peeks through the bottom of the door into the dark bedroom. I never bothered to flip the lights on.

I open the door and step from the darkness into the light of the bathroom. Gia is sunk into the tub with bubbles dancing on the surface, hiding her gorgeous body from me. A candle is lit sitting on the ledge near the tub, along with a glass of red wine and a book.

My mind goes back to the first time I bathed her in the tub. And for a split second, I think I want to join her in the tub and then fuck away the dark memories clouding my mind. It won't work though. The memories will remain.

When Gia looks up at me, she doesn't look afraid. Her eyes are big, but more out of concern than fear.

"What happened? I heard a loud crash," she asks her voice calm.

I ignore her question. She doesn't need to know I just threw away my only hope at getting any relief tonight. Hopefully, Michi stocked the liquor cabinet well, and I can find another bottle to drink.

"You need to leave," I say, staring down at her nipples piercing through the bubbles.

She narrows her eyes as she takes the glass of wine off the shelf and brings it to her lips slowly.

"Leave?" she asks calmly.

Her calmness is annoying me. I'm not calm. I know she can feel the rage emanating from me. Her eyes tell me she knows exactly what I'm thinking. She always knows what I'm thinking. It's the weird connection between us I can't understand. Like we've known each other for a lot longer than the few weeks she's been here.

"Yes, leave." I snatch the towel off the hanger and hold it out to her, assuming she will stand and take it from me.

Instead, she flicks her big toe up, playing casually in the bubbles.

"What happened?"

"I need you to leave, Gia. You can sleep in Michi's room. I'll get him a hotel room for tonight. I need you away from me."

She nods, and I think she will agree. "I'll leave after I finish my bath. I just got in. I was planning on soaking for about an hour while I read my book and finish my wine."

"No." I can't handle her defiance. Not even for a second.

"Then, talk. What. Happened?"

"No."

I grab her arm and pull her up, shoving the towel around her body. "Out. Now." I growl.

She smirks, and her eyes gleam with her defiance. Her dark eyes scan my body looking for a clue to what happened. Her mouth falls open when she finds it.

"Oh my god! You're bleeding."

"It's nothing," I say, although I know it needs stitches. Adela only let me go after I promised I would go to the hospital. But I can't go to a hospital today. I'll put a bandage on and go in the morning.

"Out, Gia," my voice rings out its final warning. I can't handle being near her for one more second.

She ignores me as her hands pull the buttons of my shirt apart. Her hands go to my wounds, and she carefully examines it.

"You were shot," she says calmly. Her eyes slowly moving back up from the wound to my eyes.

I don't answer her. She didn't question me anyway. She's been around enough bullet wounds to know the answer without me explaining.

She sees whatever she is searching for in my eyes, and then she steps out of the tub brushing past me and disappearing out of the bathroom. Finally listening to my command.

It's what I wanted, but I'm left in the cold, empty bathroom by myself, and I suddenly wish she would have continued to disobey me. At least it would give me something to focus on.

"Sit," her voice rings through the bathroom as she places a first aid kit on the counter.

I sink onto the edge of the tub. I don't know why I listen to her. Probably because I have no fight left in me.

She opens the first aid kit and starts digging through it. She sighs and pulls a few items out of it.

"The hydrogen peroxide is expired, and there is nothing to stitch the wound closed. Let me clean it for you, and I think I can use these band-aids and gauze to at least stop the bleeding until Michi can get us some better supplies."

My eyes stay on her body, only a towel covering her naked body. Her hair is pulled up in a bun on top of her head, but a few curls hang down dripping water down onto her chest. The only part of her hair that got wet when she took a bath.

I don't say anything, and neither does she, as she kneels next to my body so she can examine the wound on my stomach. She pushes my shirt open, and I let it fall off my body.

She takes out the expired peroxide and some gauze.

"This is going to sting," she warns. Her big eyes fill with something I wasn't expecting to see. Kindness.

I don't move as she pours the liquid onto my wound. It doesn't sting. Maybe on another day, I would feel the burn, but not today. Today I'm too overwhelmed with my grief to feel something as minute as a tiny sting.

Gia bites her lip as she works. Her careful fingers work quickly as she uses the band-aids like a stitch pulling my wound closed. She then takes the gauze and places it with a larger wrapping to protect the wound.

When she finishes, she sits back examining it, but I know she did a good job. The bleeding has slowed and will eventually stop. She did so well I may not even need stitches to keep the wound closed.

She doesn't ask me what happened. She doesn't ask how I ended up with a bullet wound.

And I don't ask how she knows how to heal a wound so well.

We both come from the same world. We know. We both deal with evil every day. We create it and harness it. I don't have to explain what happened. But the bullet isn't what is causing my despair. On any other day, I would be angry. I don't like having my life, or any of my employees' lives, threatened. But today, it was just a blip on the never-ending pain I feel.

I didn't even realize I had been shot until Adela pointed it out to me and made me promise I would go to the hospital. At least now that Gia has fixed me up I won't bleed to death tonight.

We both sit on the edge of the bath for a while, neither speaking or looking at each other. Occasionally she glances at me in the mirror out of the corner of her eye. She wants to say more. I can see it, but she knows I won't answer.

I can't answer even if I wanted to.

Slowly Gia stands. She licks her lips, turning to me with a wicked gleam in her eyes.

Any other day I would revel in that look. I would do almost anything to see it. But tonight it does nothing for me.

She drops the towel. I watch as it puddles on the floor.

She clears her throat, and my gaze travels upward over her thin legs that used to be scattered with heavy bruises. Now the bruises have lightened to the point of almost disappearing. The red cuts have turned to thin scars.

My eyes hover for a second over her pussy that appears to already be swollen and dripping. I don't allow my eyes to linger. If I had sex with her right now, I would destroy her. But as my eyes travel further up over her perky breasts and her red lips, I'm lost to my own darkness.

I couldn't get my revenge tonight, but I'm desperate to take it out on her. I can't drink the whiskey, but maybe if I drink her, I'll be able to forget. If only for a few minutes. Or I'll pass out afterward from the ecstasy.

"Use me," she says, her voice strong and determined.

Her words are exactly what I want to hear, but I know if I give in, I won't be able to hold back. I will ruin her. Destroy her. She will hate me more than she hates Dante.

"No." My voice rolls through the room bouncing off the walls. It took everything inside me to say it, and I don't have the strength to repeat it. But my voice tells her that. If she doesn't leave, I will demolish her.

She swallows hard, considering my unsaid words with every breath.

"I want to see your monster."

"Why?"

"Because I don't think you are one."

"Last chance." My voice is heavy with my final warning.

"Show me the darkest part of you. Show me the worst. Show me how bad you truly are."

She's testing me. Trying to release me, thinking if the worst part of me is out, then when my best returns, I'll let her go. It's a horrible plan because she won't survive the night.

I grab her smooth, slippery body and force her against the bathroom wall.

She gasps, her mouth wide and open as her head hits the wall roughly bouncing off.

I know it hurt, but the darkness doesn't care. I like the pain, the suffering, the agony. It matches my own and stops me from feeling alone.

"Your darkness doesn't scare me."

"It should."

I squeeze her neck tightly, watching the tiniest bit of panic in her eyes. But she doesn't struggle against me. She lets me suck the oxygen from her throat. I squeeze until she is on the verge of panicking. I've seen the look in her eyes before.

I saw it the first time she was with Dante. She didn't fight because it turned him on, but her eyes said she was defiant. She would survive.

She's wearing the same look now.

An idea forms in my head. A dark and dangerous one.

"Stand here and don't move." I turn and walk out of the bathroom, heading to my living room. I pull a security camera from a box I keep under the coffee table and carry it back to the bedroom. I flick the light on but don't actually turn it on. Gia won't know that though.

Then, I start gathering everything. A whip, rope, candles, and a knife. I lay them out on the bed so she will see them all when she enters. She wants the worst. She's about to get it.

"Come here, Gia."

My voice is loud and dominating, but I don't yell. And I know Gia will comply. She wants me to hurt her, so she can use it against me to get me to give her up later. She won't fight me tonight. She wants the worst.

I hear her careful footsteps against the tile and then she's standing in the doorway of the bedroom. Her eyes flicker to the bed and then to me.

Fear.

I see it in her eyes this time, but she blinks, and it's gone.

She takes deep breaths in and out, and I can't take my eyes off her breasts as they rise and fall.

I glance at the clock on the wall. Nine PM. Three hours until this day is over. And I plan on using every single one of them fucking Gia.

She doesn't know it yet, but tonight will be the longest night of her life.

"You can't hide your fear, beautiful. I can see it in your eyes. Hear it in your breath. It oozes out of you."

"I'm not afraid of you."

I shake my head as I walk to her.

"Yes, you are."

"No."

I stop in front of her, watching as her breathing picks up speed, and she tries to anticipate my next move.

I touch her cheek letting my finger travel slowly down her neck. Goosebumps form over her arms. I love mixing calm with roughness. I like the extremes. I like being rough with a woman and seeing her limits.

In a split second, I change. I grab her body roughly and slam her to the bed. Her eyes close to keep in the pain. I expect her to tell me to stop at any point. I know she will last longer than this, for no reason other than her pride, but I know there will be more fear when she opens her eyes.

I walk slowly to the edge of the bed where I laid out my toys for tonight, so she could anticipate what is coming next, and her fear would intensify.

I grab the rope in my hand, feeling the threads, as I wait for her to open her eyes.

She does, and I get the most beautiful view into her soul. It's not fear I see. It's lust, and my darkness reflecting back at me. Being rough with her turned her on.

I smirk, knowing it won't last.

She eyes the rope in my hand, and she licks her lips slowly.

I grab her wrist and stretch her hand to the end of the bed, tying it to the bedpost. She tests the rope as I move to her second hand. It's only when both hands are tied up, does the panic start to creep in.

My lips lower to hers, and I kiss her roughly, enjoying her arms tied up, knowing she can't get free. At least, she thinks she can't get free. All she would have to say is one word, and I'd stop: "no." The second she says it this ends. I'm a monster, but not a rapist. I like hurting my victims by pushing them to their limit and not letting them know the rules.

When I pull back, her mouth lingers trying to kiss me further. I grab her ankle and tie it to the bedpost and then spread her other leg wide and tie it to the other bedpost.

She pants, both wanting me to come back and scared of what comes next, as she looks over at the items lying next to her. I take my time walking over to the dresser where I placed the camera.

I press the top, and the red light comes on, indicating the camera is on.

"I have clients tomorrow I owe a large debt to. They would love to see a video of my hot new slave."

I would never show your body to any man.

"I owe them for saving my life. They might cancel my debt if I share you with them."

I would never share you with anyone.

Her eyes flicker with every word.

"I don't believe you," she says, but her eyes focus in on the camera. She thinks she knows who I am, but she's never seen what turns me on. *What I crave more than anything.*

I walk toward her, my mind racing with all the horrendous things I want to do to her body. Whip her, bite her, suffocate her, cut her, fuck her. I want to mark her body. I want her to know she is mine. I want her to follow my every command. I want to know every inch of her body.

"You should," I say, grabbing the whip and hitting her smooth stomach with it.

She arches her back against the sharp pain, and she groans quietly, low in her throat. It's enough to make me hard in an instant and forget everything shitty about this day.

I strike her again, this time over her throbbing pussy. I get the reaction I need. A sharp cry followed by her body writhing against the rope keeping her body in position for me.

Normally, I would be able to be patient with her. Take my time to bring each strike. Take my time with each method of torturing her body. But today, I'm too worked up. I need to do everything to her body all at once. Afterward, I will take my time. My breathing has quickened, and my pulse is a venom shooting through my body with the need to own her body as no man has before.

She's going to hate me.

She raises her eyebrow like she knows I might back down. I might stop. We both want me to continue, just for entirely different reasons.

I can't stop. Not unless she says no.

"Please," she begs. It's not a plea to stop; it's a plea to continue.

I toss the whip on the floor after striking her body several more times, watching her perfect flesh turn pink in every place I hit her. And every time I'm rewarded with a cry, a groan, and, once, a tear. It hurts, but she doesn't tell me to stop.

I love her cries, it feeds the darkness, but when I climb up on the bed and find her thighs wet with her desire, I lose my fucking mind. She likes my darkness.

I can't wait to be inside her. So I grab her hips and take her all at once, my cock driving inside her.

She winces from the pain, but I don't give her time to rest. I fuck her hard as my mouth devours her breasts. I bite hard on her nipple.

And I know she would have slapped me if her hands were free. Her body jerks at the sharp pain.

"Want me to stop, princess?"

I lick her nipple, softening the pain before I strike again.

"Never," she whispers, but I'm not sure even she believes her own words.

I grin before biting down hard again. I move my mouth up, needing to leave a permanent mark with my teeth, branding her as mine. I bite down hard on the fleshy part of her breast.

"Fuck you, Conti!"

Just the reaction I was hoping for. My dick grows harder inside of her, reaching depths I haven't explored yet.

I've tied her up, beaten her, exposed her to other men, and bitten her. But it's not enough. She feels the pain. She's experienced what I'm capable of. But she's not been terrified.

I kiss her roughly, our tongues tangling and fighting with each other, telling me everything she is feeling. She's feeling a lot of emotions right now, but the main emotion she pushes through is determination. Don't stop.

Never.

The words she spoke earlier ring in my head. *Never is a long time.*

I grab the knife, the last of the toys for tonight. I bring it to her neck, and she freezes. The knife scares her. I knew it would. I've seen the fear in her eyes when Dante used it on her before.

I let her feel the cold metal against her neck. Let her know her life is in my hands. How easy it would be for me to kill her if I wanted to.

"You're so beautiful," I say, surprising us both with my compliment at this moment.

I swallow hard, needing to see her bleed.

She bites her lip, still holding her breath as she stares at me, realizing how big of a mistake she just made. I still my cock inside her.

"I want to make you bleed. I want you to know your body is mine to do as I please. And now that you've offered your body so willingly to me, you're mine, forever."

She sucks in a breath when I say forever, and I take the moment to scar her body. The knife pierces her skin at her neck, spilling red blood onto her glorious neck.

"Fuck!" she cries out as the pain hits her. I drive my cock inside her, hitting the glorious spot inside that will mark this moment not only with pain but pleasure.

My tongue laps over the cut, moving the blood over her neck while I continue to fuck her.

Tears trickle down her cheek, but she doesn't tell me to stop. She doesn't tell me to go to hell. She doesn't curse me at all.

She lets me fuck her.

I grab her neck, smearing the blood across her perfect skin as I do. I squeeze and watch the panic rise in her eyes as she can't catch her breath.

I fuck her harder, faster until she is mine completely. Mine to keep alive. Mine to make come. Mine to let die.

"Come, princess."

"I—"

"Come." I don't want to hear any words except her glorious screams as she comes.

I loosen my grip on her neck and dive my head down to kiss her and bring her back to life. She moans into my mouth taking my oxygen from me. And then she comes, screaming my fucking last name. The only name she knew to call me for all those weeks when Dante thought she was his. She was never his; she was always mine.

I shoot my cum into her tight cunt. Marking her again as *mine*. As soon as I finish, I take the knife and cut her arms and legs free.

And then I wait for the slap. I wait for the curse. I wait for the yelling.

Instead, she cries.

Shit.

I really did break her.

I run to the bathroom, grab a wet washcloth and some band-aids to heal her.

I sit carefully on the bed next to her as she cries more tears. Her hands are gripping her neck where blood still oozes.

I slowly push her hands down as I press the washcloth to her skin.

"I'm sorry. My monster is horrible. I'm sorry I hurt you. You should have told me to stop, and I would have."

Gia stops crying almost instantly. "You didn't hurt me."

I frown. "Your neck is bleeding. Your body is pink and red where I struck you. Your pussy is battered after how roughly I fucked you without making sure you were ready for me. I hurt you."

She pushes my hand down.

"No, you didn't. I thought you would. I was prepared for it. I thought after talking with Adela that I hated you. I just needed you to push me a little harder, and I would hate you forever. I knew you would push me far and rip me to pieces. I thought doing so would fill me with enough anger, all I would focus on going forward is the need to get my revenge on you."

I nod, understanding her need for revenge. I used her tonight to get my revenge.

"But I don't hate you."

"How? You must hate me." *I hate me.*

"What Adela told me about you, hurt. I thought I could never forgive you, but just now I realized something. You were my guardian angel."

"Huh?"

"You watched me the entire time I was with Dante, didn't you?"

I suck in a breath, not liking where this is going.

"Didn't you?" she presses again.

"Yes, I watched you."

She smiles, and it's the most beautiful thing I've ever seen.

"You watched me and made sure I could survive. I don't know why you left me with him for as long as you did, but as soon as you realized I couldn't make it one more day, you got me out."

She takes a deep breath.

"Tonight, you repeated every horrible thing Dante did to me. But you didn't take anything from me. You didn't hurt me. You gave me my life back. You gave me my freedom. You let me choose the darkness. And you helped me replace the negative memories with something beautiful."

My mouth twitches, not agreeing or disagreeing with her.

"You made me stronger."

I look her up and down. I can't disagree with that. She looks stronger. Her eyes are clearer. Her body sits more upright. And when she smiles, she really smiles.

"And you made me fall in love with the darkness. I've been fighting it my entire life. But I've always been the princess of darkness. This is my home. And you gave me the power for that to be okay."

She leans forward and kisses me softly on the lips. "Thank you."

She pulls me to her and hugs me. Of all the ways I thought this was going to go, I never thought this was a possibility. I don't know what just happened, but I want it to happen again. I'm addicted to her body now.

"Again," she whispers into my ear before releasing me.

I grin. "You sure?"

She laughs. "No, but I want you. You excite and terrify me, and yet, I've never felt so free as when I'm with you."

I nod. I understand. I've only ever felt that way once, and then it was taken from me. I won't let Gia ever leave my side.

I still see the need for revenge in her eyes, but it's lessened a little. And when she looks at my body, I see the lust for more. She wants me, monster and all.

She thinks I didn't hurt her. I hope she's right. But I'm afraid I have, she just doesn't know it yet.

14

GIA

I'M SICK.

That's what last night made me realize. I'm one sick and twisted motherfucker. I loved what Caspian did to my body last night. I loved every mark, every scar, every sharp intake of pain.

I loved every kiss, every tease, and every thrust.

I loved it all.

I've never felt so free, and yet so trapped. I had a plan before. Find the hate and the need for revenge to free myself from him, but now, I can't live without our messed up sex.

I'm not sure I would ever come again with plain missionary sex. I want more.

I know yesterday was a bad day for Caspian. Something happened beyond just getting shot. He didn't tell me what, and honestly, it doesn't matter. He shared something much more precious with me. His true self.

He thought I would run afterward. He thought I would hate him. But now, I'm afraid I might love him.

I love his dark.

I love his light.

I need to find my place in this mess. Find a way to live in this world when I'm still consumed with a past that won't let me go. And the only way to truly stay with Caspian is if he grants me my freedom. Lets me choose whether I want to stay or go.

I don't know what I would choose if he gave me a choice at freedom right now. I want to explore Caspian more. See if he is the missing piece in my life. But I also want my revenge. I want to find my own way. I want to see my family.

"Good morning, beautiful," Caspian says, kissing me softly on the lips.

I smile and stretch; my body is completely sore from the twistedness of last night. This morning, the darkness is gone, and I see nothing but light in his eyes. Today he's Caspian, while last night he was Conti.

Conti is his darkness, while Caspian is the light. He may not realize it, but I love both parts of him. I couldn't take one without the other.

"Morning, Caspian."

"I'm Caspian again, huh?"

I nod. "Yes. Caspian is the person you are in front of most people. Conti, you reserve for the most intense situations."

"Which do you prefer?"

I shrug. "I like both parts of you."

He squeezes me, pulling me to him. It seems so normal. Something any couple would do in the morning after having sex all night. The difference is last night. It was the opposite of normal. But it was also everything I never knew I wanted.

"Come with me today."

I sit up, staring at him like he's just turned into an alien.

"What?" I ask even though I heard him perfectly well.

"Come with me to Rome. I have a client I have to meet with for a couple of days, so I have to go to Rome."

I half smile as I bite my lip, trying to keep my feelings under wrap. I don't want him to know I love what he is asking me. To go with him.

"Why?" I ask even though I know why. He doesn't want to be apart. And he's giving me a tiny bit of freedom. A reward for last night. No, maybe reward isn't the right word. Appreciation, maybe? Or he's claiming me as his.

"Because I'm selfish and don't want to be separated from you. I need you with me. Always."

Always.

I love that word.

God, I've got to stop saying, love. I don't love Caspian Conti. I don't even know him. And the parts I do know about him scare me.

I'm just infatuated with him. Especially after what happened last night.

There is still a part of me that is pissed at him for not saving me right away. I need to hold onto that part before I let the part that adores him consume me.

It's clear last night affected him the same way it did me.

"I'll go with you," I say. I want to ask him questions. I want to push this. I want to ask if this is the first step toward him granting me my freedom. But I don't.

It's enough for now. Soon, I will take my freedom, whether he grants it to me or not.

———

"I'm not playing a game with you," Caspian says for the hundredth time in the ten minutes we've been in the car.

I pout. "Why not? If you don't, I'm going to sing horribly along to the radio the entire time."

He frowns. "How about we sit quietly in the car on the way?"

"No, that's not fun. We always sit quietly. We never talk. We hardly know anything about each other."

"I know plenty about you."

I roll my eyes. "Only things you or Adela have looked up about me. Nothing directly from me."

I reach for the radio and turn it on. A Demi Lovato song comes on, and I start singing at the top of my lungs about having daddy issues. The irony is striking because I do have daddy issues.

Caspian turns the radio off, but I keep singing.

"Fine," he relents.

I grin from ear to ear. "So the rules are we get to take turns asking each other anything. And we have to answer each other's questions to get another turn."

"And if I don't want to answer?"

"Then, I win the game."

"And the winner gets?"

I've thought about this carefully. I could offer him something sexual, but he already knows I will do anything he wants without this silly game. I could ask for something worthy of playing, like my freedom, but then he wouldn't play or would just lie. I have nothing to offer him, but I know he's competitive. He hates losing. It's enough. I want this game to be light anyway. I'll only ask the tough questions when I want the game to be over.

"Bragging rights."

He narrows his eyes. "And how we will know if the other is telling the truth?"

"We will know." I have no doubt we will be able to tell.

"Okay, I'll go first. What is your favorite place in the world?"

"My house." He answers quickly. My first questions are meant to be light and easy so he will play along, but I didn't expect this answer.

"Seriously? You like your cabin? You're not talking about a bigger house you own somewhere else?"

"That seems like a second question."

I glare at him as his lips curl up. He's teasing me. I like it. I'm not used to this playful side of him.

"I'm talking about my only home. The house we share."

Share, that's a strange word to use when we don't share it. It's his; I'm just a captive there.

"Your turn."

"Why did you fall for a man like Roman?"

My mouth falls and my fingers, that were drumming along still to Demi Lovato in my head, still. I stare at him, and he stares back with the same intensity. He's not playing games with me. He won't ask any lighthearted questions. Only serious ones.

"Because I was desperate to be loved. I wanted an escape from the

Carini family, and I couldn't do it on my own. Or at the time at least, I thought I couldn't. Roman paid attention to me. He offered me a chance at freedom, and I was stupid enough to think freedom was love."

Caspian stills for a second before he nods. "Your turn," he says as if I didn't just bare my heart to him.

"Why don't you buy expensive things? You make good money. Why don't you have a mansion?"

He raises an eyebrow as if he can't believe how easy my questions are, but this one I really want to know the answer to. "Because things mean nothing to me. I don't need a large house to relax at night."

"Then what do you spend your money on?"

He chuckles. "You don't know how to keep to your own rules, do you? That's a second question again. But if you must know, I spend it on Adela. I pay my employees more than fair to make sure they are loyal to me alone. And I use it to get my revenge."

I swallow hard at the word revenge. I know he needs revenge the same as me. I don't know what happened to him, but I won't be asking him any questions about revenge today.

"Your turn."

"What do you want in life? What's your passion?"

"Jesus, you don't ask easy questions do you?"

He shrugs. "This is the easiest question I will ask. It should be easy for anyone who knows themselves at all."

I frown. "I don't know myself. That's my problem. I don't have a passion because I've never been allowed to be anything but a Carini."

"Do you like being a Carini?"

I smile smugly. "Now who isn't playing by the rules?"

He doesn't smile. He stares at me seriously waiting for me to answer. I guess it's only fair.

"Yes. I love being a Carini. There was once a time I hated it, but I think being a Carini made me stronger. It made me strong enough to survive these last few weeks. Without it, I would have dissolved into nothing."

He nods.

"My turn. Tell me about your first kiss."

He chuckles. "You know how to ask the tough questions," he says sarcastically.

I laugh and grab his hand. He lets me. This is normal. "First kiss was in the third grade on the playground with Luisa Pellegrini."

I smile, loving his normal answer. But my smile falters as I see the look in his eyes. He's about to ask me a question I won't want to answer. He's about to end the game. I can see it.

And then he smiles deviously. "Tell me who your favorite sexual partner was."

I laugh, blushing brightly, hating him for making me answer his question he already knows the answer to.

"This smug ass who doesn't deserve me, but managed to find all the buttons to my body within seconds because he secretly crept on me for weeks."

"Hmm, he sounds pretty incredible. What's his name?"

"You, you fucktard."

His grin reaches his eyes. "Fucktard? That's a new one."

I try to pull my hand out of his, but he tightens his grip before kissing the back of my hand.

We continue on, asking silly questions back and forth, just trying to make each other laugh until we reach Rome.

Caspian gets us settled into our hotel room. The room is huge. He may not spend his money often, but he did tonight. I expect him to start talking to me about all the security he has installed before he leaves. I expect him to talk to me about the guards I'm sure he will have placed outside our door. Or the tracker he secretly placed inside my clothes when I was sleeping.

He doesn't.

Instead, he kisses me on the lips and says, "Come with me to my meeting."

I raise an eyebrow at him. "Why?"

He shrugs. "I want you by my side."

There is more he isn't telling me. But I won't get my answers unless I go. "Okay, I'll go with you. What should I wear?"

"Something that makes you feel powerful and strong."

His words have me worried I'm going to need all my strength to get through the meeting tonight.

But I do as he says. I change into a scarlet dress with plunging cleavage, while Caspian changes into a tuxedo.

His eyes never leave me as we dress, and mine never leave his. We both give promises of what we are going to do to each other when we return to the hotel room. But we keep our distance, or we will never leave the room in the first place. And as much as I want to stay in and let Caspian fuck me, I also want to leave. I want to enjoy a night with Caspian that isn't about sex, especially after our fun game in the car. I want a light, care-free night where I get more insight into his work.

"Ready, princess?" Caspian asks, holding out his arm to me as I finish applying red lipstick.

"As ready as I'll be when I don't know what we are doing or where we are going."

He stills, and I know he is considering telling me more, but then he changes his mind.

I grab his arm. "I promise it will be a pleasant surprise."

This has me even more intrigued, but I don't ask. I will find out soon enough.

Caspian leads me out of our hotel room, and to my surprise, no guards are sitting outside waiting for us to leave. We head down only one floor to where the hotel restaurant sits below our penthouse.

"Mr. Conti, your guest has already arrived. I'll show you to your table," the maître d' says.

Caspian leads me through the beautiful restaurant. At least I'll have a nice dinner in a gorgeous place.

Caspian leans down and whispers in my ear as we walk. "You want your freedom. After last night, I think I can give you a tiny piece of freedom. Revenge is freedom."

I don't understand what his words mean until we approach the table, arm in arm looking like the king and queen. I recognize the man at the table, and I realize immediately what Caspian is offering when he says I can get revenge.

Because sitting at the table is one of the men I hate most in the world.

Roman.

———

"Roman," I say, letting his name hang in the air.

Roman looks up at me. He recognized my voice, but he doesn't recognize the woman standing in front of him. I've been tortured, beaten, and raped. I should be weaker, but Caspian showed me how strong I am. And tonight, Roman is going to understand as well.

Caspian pulls out a chair, and I take a seat. Caspian takes his own seat.

"Gia, what a wonderful surprise to see you," Roman says, looking from me to Caspian. There is no fear in Roman's eyes, but there should be.

"I didn't realize you owned any women, Caspian," Roman says, using Caspian's first name instead of his last, like I've heard all of Caspian's other business associates address him.

"I don't," Caspian answers.

Caspian's answer shocks the hell out of me, but I don't let Roman know. *If Caspian doesn't own me, then what the hell are we doing?*

Roman chuckles. "Whatever you say. I'm glad you brought us some eye candy while we discuss our deal."

"I'm not eye candy," I say, glaring at Roman, trying to figure out how I'm going to kill him. Right now, cutting out his tongue so he can't speak to me like that is my first step.

"Really? Because that is what you look like to me," Roman says.

I don't wait for Caspian to give me any permission to start a fight with Roman. I can't wait.

I slam my heel into Roman's groin.

He cries out, like I just stabbed him, and grips his balls in pain.

I smirk. It feels good to cause him some pain. My eyes see Caspian out of the corner of my eye, looking at Roman like he's scum. I guess we won't be doing much eating after all.

Caspian gets up and grabs Roman's arm while he's still writhing in pain. He pulls him toward a back room while I follow. I'm not going to miss a second of Roman's pain.

When we get to the back room, Caspian slams the door shut behind us as he tosses Roman to the floor.

Roman takes his time getting up, still not realizing what danger he's in. It will make it all the better when I kill him.

"Our deal is off. I won't pay you anything to protect me when you let your whore disrespect me like that," Roman says.

"Gia didn't disrespect you," Caspian says, his eyes red.

I stomp toward Roman, knowing he could strangle me, snap my neck, or pull a gun on me before I realized what was happening, but I need to be close to him to say what I need to say.

"I am not a whore," I say, kicking Roman again.

He cries out but doesn't fight back. *Why doesn't he fight back?*

I glance behind me and see Caspian has a gun pointed at Roman. I smirk. This is where Caspian and I understand each other the most. In the darkness.

"I am not yours. I never was. You didn't own me. You didn't have the ability to sell me."

I kick him again and again after each sentence, needing to get my frustration and anger out on him. He lets me and takes each punch and kick with a grunt or a groan. I watch as the blood slowly pours down his face.

"You are a fucking coward. A weak, shithole that didn't have the balls to hurt me yourself. So you sold me. You sold me and pretended it was just a business transaction. That it didn't bother you what happened to me next.

"Well, guess what? I was raped. I was beaten until I couldn't move. I was violated until sex became torture. My life was threatened every day because of you."

He cowers on the floor beneath me, curling up into himself.

"You are nothing to me. Fucking nothing!"

I take a deep breath, trying to get oxygen in my body as I keep yelling.

"You think you won. You got your money. You sold me, and I was no longer your problem. I told you I would come after you. I said you would pay for what you did. Today is that day.

"You think I'm weaker because of what you did, but I'm stronger. I'm your fucking nightmare."

I kick him again, watching the blood spill from his eyes where my heel clipped him.

My body shakes with anger. I thought I wanted to torture Roman, make him suffer for hours or days, but he isn't worth my time. I want him gone.

Caspian steps forward when I've finished all I need to say.

I think Caspian is going to shoot Roman. Eliminate him. Wipe him from my nightmares with one bullet.

Instead, Caspian thrusts the cold metal into my hand. I stare at the gun for a second. I don't know if Caspian realizes how dark I am. The things that I have done in my past. He calls me princess, but I'm not a princess. I'm just as evil and twisted as him.

Roman won't be my first kill. Not by a long shot. But I will remember this kill forever.

Caspian steps back, knowing I don't need him by my side to do what has to be done. Roman needs to be killed, if for no other reason than to protect other women from the same fate.

But that's not why I'm killing him though. I kill him for me.

"Goodbye, Roman."

I pull the trigger and watch the blood spill. The light in his eyes leaves, and then he's nothing.

I watch him a second longer before I walk back to Caspian and hold out the gun to him.

"Keep it," he says.

I don't question him. I put the gun in the back of my dress and underwear. And then I kiss Caspian with everything I have. I've never needed a kiss so much in my life. This kiss is everything I've ever needed. I need it more than air.

My stomach grumbles, and Caspian pulls away. "I should feed you."

I smirk. "No, you should fuck me."

15

CASPIAN

GIA CARINI IS A BADASS.

That's all I can think about as I carry the sexiest woman I've ever met back to our hotel room. Her heels are digging into my side. Heels that she used to kick that son of a bitch in the balls.

It was amazing to watch. I always knew she was strong and fucking incredible. But I never realized just how fucking badass until now. I know Gia's brothers didn't let her get too involved in the business side of things. They wanted to protect her and for good reason. So I doubted she would kill Roman when I handed her my gun.

I knew she was angry. I knew she needed revenge, but I thought if she found the strength to pull the trigger, she'd miss and I'd have to finish the bastard.

She aimed right for his heart and killed him without a second thought. She's more like me than I could have ever imagined.

She was just dark and dangerous, but earlier in the car she was the sweetest, funniest woman. And that makes her even sexier. One moment she could live out my fantasies, and the next she could kill me. Especially since I let her keep the gun.

She won't use the gun to kill me. I know her well enough to know that. Her feelings for me are too strong. She's not pissed at me like the others, even though I'm just as much of the reason she is in this mess as Roman or Dante is. I've hurt her the same. So if she does decide to use the gun against me, I deserve it.

But she needs the gun for her protection. Now that I know she is capable of proficiently using a gun, I trust her with it. She could kill an intruder as easily as I could. And it will make her feel better protected now that she is starting to make enemies.

I've planted the story that Roman stole her back. He was the one that stole her from Dante. Dante will be looking for her with a greater intensity now. And I'll be the one to find her. She will want to help me.

I can't focus on Dante now. Now I have the sexiest, most incredible, amazing, awesome, badass woman in the world. And I plan on making good use of her wanting me while I have the chance.

We burst through the door of the hotel room I sprung for. I never buy anything this expensive, not anymore. I only told a half-truth when I told Gia why I don't have anything nice or expensive. I don't find much use in more expensive things, it's true, but I also don't feel worthy.

I got this hotel room for Gia. She's worthy of a penthouse. She's worthy of a lot more.

Her hands claw at my neck, desperate to put the adrenaline and high she is feeling to use. And she wants to use me.

"Slow down, princess," I say as she kisses my neck and starts undoing my tie.

"Why?" she purrs.

"Because I want to savor you."

"You can as long as it's dark and dirty, as fucking messed up as it was last night."

Last night was incredible. The best night of my life by far when it should have been my worst. I've never gone that far with a woman before. No woman has ever been able or willing to take on the sadistic side of me. The controlling asshole that lives in the dark.

But she craved it, same as me. And now she wants more.

"Be careful what you wish for, beautiful."

She grins. "I want everything. All of your darkness. I want to feel it all."

Her words are what I've wanted to hear all this time. I've needed to hear them for so long, but no woman has ever measured to her. Now the woman of my fantasies finally exists. She's real.

She rips my tie off. "I want to know all the darkest parts of your soul."

I smile. "You already do."

She cocks her head to the side and whispers in my ear. "You haven't found my darkest places yet. So find them."

Damn, my cock is hard.

I'm the one who is going to need to fucking slow down. I'm still holding her in my arms, and we both grow wild at the same time. She rips off my tie, and I kiss down her neck, hungrily until I reach her cleavage, which is far too exposed in this dress for going in public. I want her to myself. I don't want to share, even a glimpse of her.

My tie is off, my shirt is unbuttoned, and my cock strains against my zipper about to burst through my pants. I remove the gun from the back of her dress, toss it to the nightstand, and let our bodies fall to the bed. I don't have any of the dark toys I had before to play with her, but that doesn't mean this session is going to be light. I don't know how to go back into the light with her.

Her nails dig into my chest, and I know that she is still in the dark with me. If I don't tie her up, she's going to be just as rough with me as I am with her. I welcome it.

Last time, I needed control. This time, I need her with me.

I grab her dress and rip it down the middle, the sparkly sequins scattering to the bed as I rip.

She glares at me. "I loved this dress. Why did you ruin it?"

"Because you can't wear it in public anymore now. I can't stand to see other guys looking at you in it."

She blushes. I think she's going to scold me. "Are you jealous, Caspian?"

"No, jealous would imply you look at other men in a room. You don't. I'm infuriated with any man that looks at what's mine."

Her eyes darken, her breath catches, and her nipples stand at attention waiting for me. My caveman words turn her on, instead of turning her off.

"Fuck me, Caspian," she says, growing impatient with our pause.

I grab her legs and pull her cunt to me so I can taste the sweet pleasure I know is dripping there. My tongue darts inside her, and her body sings.

"God!" she moans, unable to even say my name, as I make her body wiggle beneath me.

I smirk, pushing my tongue deeper inside her and bringing her right to the brink. She wants to come so badly, but she also wants what comes next.

I push her, moving my tongue deeper inside her body as I hit the sweet spot that will make her do anything I want.

She explodes around my tongue.

"Yes, Conti!"

Her screams still me. She's called me Conti several times before, and every time she does, it reminds me of someone else. And it melts my cold heart. This time it shatters the ice holding it together until there is nothing left.

I sit up abruptly, not believing what I'm doing.

"Conti?" Gia sits up slowly, feeling the coldness in the room. The chill that won't go away until I start talking.

I feel tears burning my eyes. Tears I haven't cried in almost five years.

"I should have saved you."

Gia shivers as she wraps the ripped dress around her body.

"You did save me."

"No, I should have saved you the second you fell into my lap."

"You couldn't. Dante would have killed you."

"No, I could have saved you. It would have ruined my relationship with Dante, sure, but I could have prevented every horrible thing from happening to you, and I didn't because I was selfish."

Gia scoots closer to me but doesn't touch me as we both sit half naked on the edge of the oversized king bed. I never expected to spill my heart to a woman again, but here I am, ripping my own heart to shreds. Gia doesn't say anything. She waits until I can speak again.

"I needed revenge more than I wanted to save you. You shouldn't want to fuck me. I'm a bigger monster than Dante and Roman combined."

She nods. "I know you could have saved me. I know you were torn and wanted to. Adela told me. At that moment, I hated you, but I knew you had to have a reason for not saving me. And last night I realized you were watching over me, making sure I never got hurt so badly I couldn't recover. You saved me the second you could."

"No!" I grab Gia's face as tears stream down my face. "I let that disgusting excuse of a man hurt you. I let him touch you. I let him rape you, and I did nothing. There is no excuse good enough to let you go through that."

Tears burn her eyes, but she doesn't let them fall. "Just tell me why."

"I had the perfect wife—"

She gasps when I say, wife. And then she realizes she shouldn't act surprised and relaxes.

"I had the perfect wife. She was beautiful, smart, determined. She was a nurse. She devoted her life to helping kids that didn't have any money to pay her. She only took enough money to feed and clothe herself. She was a saint."

The tears will never stop now that I've started.

"She was my light. She kept me pure. She knew there was a darkness inside me, but she kept the darkness at bay."

"She sounds wonderful."

"She was. She was heavenly. Purer than an angel. She saved me, helped me find my purpose in providing security systems to protect the innocent from the evil."

I can't look at Gia as I talk about my wife. It's too much. So I stare at my hands. Hands that have done so much wrong.

"But security isn't pure. I got mixed into a world of evil. I tried to stay away, but it sucked me in like a vacuum I couldn't get free of.

"We'd been married two years when she was taken in the middle of the night. My security system had failed us...failed her. Yesterday was the anniversary of her being taken."

I roar out my anger needing the pain to go away. I've been numb for too long to be able to handle this pain now.

"I searched every day for her for a year. One year I searched. I found her, but it was too late. She was dead and gone, tossed out like trash. I brought her back to my home in the woods and buried her in the garden, but it wasn't enough. I needed to get her revenge."

Gia nods but keeps her hands in her lap, even though I can tell she wants to comfort me, she knows I won't accept it right now.

"Dante Russo was the one who took her. I vowed the day I found her, I would torture and kill him the way he did her. I needed the best security system to get a way in. I needed a system he would want. So I became the best. And then I needed something Dante would truly mourn when I stole it."

"Me," Gia says.

I nod.

"I'm not valuable to him. I'm just a body he can fuck. He doesn't care about me any more than he does any other woman."

I shake my head. "I planned to install the system, watch him, and find his weakness. But the second I saw you run out of the car, I knew it was you. You would become his weakness because you instantly became mine."

She sucks in a breath.

"I've watched him every day since I took you. He's gone mad. He would do anything to get you back. And now that I've tortured him with your disappearance, I can kill him."

Gia takes a second to herself and then grabs my cheeks, wiping my tears with her thumbs. "I forgive you."

More tears fall. Of all the things she could say now, I never expected her to say that.

"You can't forgive me."

She smiles carefully. "I just did. You don't get to tell me how I feel. I forgive you. I can't understand what you've been through. I've never lost someone like that, but I've experienced pain and if there were something I could do to make that pain lessen for someone I love, then I would. Even if it meant hurting someone else."

I grab her neck and kiss her firmly on the lips, sucking all the air from her.

"How can you be this perfect?" I ask against her lips.

She kisses me again, needing our lips together. "I'm no more perfect than you are. We are just kindred spirits, both searching for the same thing. Revenge."

I devour her lips now. I need to be inside her as quickly as possible. She needs the same thing. Her hands are at the waistband of my pants, trying to push them off.

I rip her panties down and push inside her without waiting to see if she is ready for me or not. From her wince, her body wasn't prepared, but her moans and clawing on my back tell me she doesn't care. Her soul can't wait.

I rock in and out of her, gripping her tightly as I fuck her. But I'm not just fucking her. There is something different happening, but I can't find the word to describe it. Because no word can describe the connection between us. No matter what happens next, it's unbreakable.

"What was her name?" Gia asks, and that's when I realize what's happening. This is for my wife. For a connection I had with a woman that was stolen from me too soon. A woman I never deserved. Whatever beautiful connection is happening now is because of her.

"Clara Conti."

Gia pauses for a second, honoring her, and then she kisses me hard on the lips. And I fuck her like tomorrow might never come. And it might not.

I don't know how this ends with Gia and me. How am I going to give her up? Because I can't keep her.

16

GIA

CASPIAN TOLD me his darkest secret, but I can never tell him mine. I forgave him. He would never forgive me.

Everything has changed since I killed Roman. We've been home a week, and it's almost like we are a normal couple. We don't talk about me leaving, or giving me my freedom anymore. I already have my freedom. I got it the day he tracked down Roman for me to kill and then let me keep the gun. Any time I want to use it to leave, I could.

But I don't want to leave.

Caspian's home is becoming my home. His desires are becoming mine. We both want the same thing.

Revenge on Dante Russo.

We want him to hurt as much as possible, and then when he's done hurting, we want to kill him.

We don't talk about it. Instead, we talk about normal things. The weather, food, drinks, our day. But it's always on our minds. Even when we are fucking.

Our desire for revenge is too strong for anything else. And I'm tired of not talking about it. Once it's done, then we can focus on what the hell we are doing together. What our future could hold. Until it's over, we are trapped in our revenge.

At one point revenge was my freedom, but now I'm afraid it's starting to hold me back.

Caspian is sitting outside on his computer. He usually sits there after dinner, soaking in the last drops of sunlight on his computer. I usually sit next to him reading a book. But today, I helped Michi clean up the dishes first. So when I finally join Caspian outside, the sun has all but set.

"You ready to go inside?" he asks when I join him.

"No."

He glances up from his computer, sensing the trepidation in my voice.

"When are we going to kill Dante?" I ask. I know he has a plan, he just hasn't shared it with me yet.

He closes his computer, and I'm afraid he's closing our conversation.

"Soon, but I'm not sure I can bring you with me, or if I do if I can let you kill him. I've been planning this for five years. I need to be the one to kill him. I can't just hand you the gun like I did with Roman."

It hurts that I won't be the one to kill him, but as long as he's dead, it doesn't matter. "I understand."

He narrows his eyes. "How could you? My wife was taken from me, but you were the one who went through so much. And I let it happen."

I grab his face and kiss him softly, annoyed even though I've forgiven him, he still hasn't forgiven himself.

"Stop. I understand. I didn't die. I didn't lose anything. You did."

He turns away, not able to look at me. I hate it when he does this. Shuts me out. I know he doesn't owe me anything. We aren't in a real relationship. I don't even know what "we" are. But it still hurts.

He turns back. "Take your revenge out on me."

I frown. "No, I forgive you. I don't want to hurt you."

His thumb strokes my cheek before he pulls me onto his lap. "I need you to. I can't forgive myself. My nightmares are no longer about Clara. They are about you. Every night I have a nightmare about what Dante did to you. I hate myself for letting him lay a hand on you, much less hurt you every night. I can't live with myself. Take out your revenge on me."

I search his eyes and find him near breaking. He needs this. And when I search my heart, I realize I do too. I may have forgiven him, but it still hurts. I need to let the pain go. And this might be how.

"Okay."

He lifts me and sets me down on my feet. Then he gathers his computer and empty wine glass and walks inside. I follow after, both terrified and exhilarated with what is about to happen.

He sets the computer and glass down on the counter where Michi is still cleaning.

Caspian looks at Michi, and he knows. Michi really needs his own place if Caspian is going to keep kicking him out. Michi heads out without a word.

Then, Caspian walks to the bedroom. My feet can barely move, but I make it somehow. Must be muscle memory that moves me.

I stand in the doorway and watch as Caspian gathers items. Whips, chains, floggers, knives, anything destructive he can find. He lays them all out on the bed. And then he starts undressing. Removing his shirt slowly, then his pants, until he's standing in nothing but his underwear. He considers his next move for a second and then he removes his boxers too. It's not sexual. He's baring his all to me.

And I've never seen a stronger man.

"Please," he whispers, and I know what he's asking. Please make the pain go away, for both of us.

Then he lies down on the bed and waits.

I take a couple of deep breaths, letting go of the compassion I have for Caspian and let the hate I've pushed away back in.

He could have saved me but didn't.

I repeat those words over and over until I'm lost in them. Then I stomp toward the chains, knowing I have to tie him up. No matter how much he says he wants this, as soon as the first crack of pain hits him, he will try to stop me. For this to work, he has to be completely vulnerable.

So I pick up the metal cuffs and loop one around the post and then attach the cuff to his wrist. He looks at me with sad eyes but doesn't say anything. He just watches. I feel the fear oozing off of him, but know it has nothing to do with the pain he's about to feel. It has everything to do with us. Where will we be when this is over?

I walk to his other arm and attach it to the bed, doing the same to his legs.

"Try to break free," I command.

He pulls hard with his arms and legs, but he can't move.

I nod and then close my eyes. Filling everything in me with the memories of Dante. Him striking me, beating me, raping me. His cock driving into me is what does it the most. So I focus on the image. Of what it felt like to have a cock push into me when I'm dry and unwilling. The burn, the violation, the pain. I let it consume me, and then I open my eyes.

I don't see Caspian lying on the bed; I see Dante.

I grab the first item I can find. A bat. I bring it high over my head and then I beat down on the broken body in front of me.

"I fucking hate you!" I scream as I hit the body hard in the stomach. I can't see anything but rage.

I lift the bat and strike again and again. I'm rewarded with a loud groan each time, but it's not enough. I want the screams I let out every time Dante hurt me.

I strike his chest one more time with the bat before I move onto the whip.

I don't know if it will hurt more or less, but I plan on using every instrument I can until I hear the screams.

I'm not as skilled with the whip, so my first attempt misses, hitting the bed. But my second strike hits my target's legs. His legs jump at the sting, leaving bright red welts.

It's not enough.

I've formed the bruises on him with the bat. I've formed the redness with the whip. I need the scars. I need the cries.

The cock inside me was one of the worst. The absolute worst. I don't want to fuck this man. He doesn't deserve a second of my pleasure. But the next worst thing was the sharpness of the blade. Knowing he could take my life if he wanted with a slip of the knife.

I grab the sharp blade, and then I climb onto Dante's body. I straddle his hard chest as I hold the knife to his neck as he has to me so many times before.

"Do it. I deserve it," he says.

I freeze the knife over his artery. He does deserve it. He deserves to die.

I shove the knife hard against his neck until I see blood. But I still don't hear screams. I need his screams! I need to know I hurt him as badly as he hurt me.

I remove the knife from his neck and aim for his heart, stabbing his chest.

He screams. It's high pitched and terrifying, and it feeds my soul. I want more.

I stab him again. He's going to get a slow torturous death.

"I'm so sorry, Gia. I'm so sorry. I deserve this."

His voice makes me stop. That isn't the voice of Dante.

I stop the knife and close my eyes, trying to push the hate back down. When I open again, I see Caspian on the bed. Bleeding to death.

"No! Oh my god! What did I do?"

I jump off of him, dropping the knife and race to get the first aid kit.

When I climb back on the bed, his breathing has slowed, and his eyes have grown heavy.

"Shh, you did nothing wrong. You did what had to be done. And if I die, it's what needs to happen," Caspian says.

I pull out gauze, covering the wound to attempt to stop the bleeding.

"Don't talk like that. You aren't going to die."

But I'm not sure. There is a lot of blood. I don't think I hit his heart, but I hit something major.

"Michi!" I yell, hoping he's in the house or nearby. I get no answer.

I glance at the handcuffs I used to restrain him. I need the key to release him. He's going to die restrained to his bed if I don't help him.

Fuck.

But if I worry about releasing him, he will definitely die.

I dig through the first aid kit while I keep applying pressure with my other hand. I find the stapler and drugs I requested Michi stock after the last time Caspian was injured. I don't have time for morphine though.

"It's going to be okay," I say calmly. I take out the stapler.

"Look away," I tell him. He turns his head and bites his lip knowing more pain is coming. I staple the wound over and over. Each time the pain ripping into his heart. Each time I pray he doesn't die because of me. *What was I thinking? I have no control over my demons.*

"One more," I say as the last staple goes in.

I press the gauze back, and the bleeding has reduced greatly.

I exhale deeply. He's going to be okay. He needs a hospital, but he's going to survive.

"I'm so sorry," I say.

I look at him, but he doesn't respond.

"Caspian?"

Nothing.

I lower my head over his chest. He isn't breathing.

Shit.

I blow into his mouth and start doing compressions.

"Please, Caspian!"

I keep compressing over his heart, praying his staples don't pop open and the bleeding doesn't start all over again.

"Don't you dare die, Caspian!"

More compressions, but he's not breathing.

"You are going to be an uncle. You hear me! You can't die!"

More compressions.

"I need your help to kill Dante. Clara can't be avenged without your help."

Two breaths.

"I love you. Please don't leave me."

More compressions.

Then, coughing.

"Caspian!" He's alive.

I ease off him, letting him get some good breaths in.

"Thank god, you're alive," I cry. Tears are streaming down my face. "I've never been so scared in my life."

"Liar," Caspian teases.

More tears. "I can't believe you let me do that. What were you thinking? I could have killed you! You should have stopped me."

"I couldn't exactly stop you with the cuffs. And I would have deserved it."

"No! You don't deserve to die."

He tries to comfort me but can't because he's still tied up, but I can't leave him for a second right now to grab the key from the bathroom.

So I lay my head on the uninjured side of his chest. I need to get Michi to help me get him to a hospital soon, but right now I can't move him.

"I'm so sorry," I whisper as tears stream from my eyes to his chest.

"You have nothing to be sorry for; you saved me."

"No, I didn't. I almost killed you."

"No, you killed Dante. You killed the pain in me for what I let happen to you. You let go of your own trauma. And now, we can survive so much stronger. We helped each other heal."

I nod, not believing he is comforting me right now after I just killed him.

"I almost let you die; you almost killed me. I saved you; you saved me. I think we are even now. We can move forward and decide our future without anything holding us back."

I know his words are true. And I wish he was right. That we are even now. But we aren't even close to even. He might have been selfish, but everything he did was for Clara Conti, a woman who deserved his love. I may love Caspian Conti, but I don't deserve to be loved in return. I don't know if he heard any of my words when he was out. I hope he didn't because I don't want him to love me in return.

He may have hurt me, but I'm the real monster.

17

CASPIAN

GIA ALMOST KILLED ME. Sometimes I wish she had. Then the pain would finally be gone.

She has taken care of me these last few weeks. Life has been normal. My wounds have healed, and we don't talk about that night at all. We don't talk about Dante or the pain we caused each other.

All we do is heal, together. It's taken time, but we are finally healed. At least as healed as we can be.

But we can't continue like this.

"We need to talk," I say to Gia. She's sitting next to me on her patio chair reading. The last time we talked out here, it ended in her stabbing me. This time, I hope it ends better. But I'm still dreading the conversation I'm about to have because it's the beginning of the end.

She looks up from her book, her eyes big. "Maybe we should go somewhere else to talk first. The last time we talked out here, it didn't end well."

She kisses me softly on the cheek. "What's up?" she says more calmly.

"I have a plan to kill Dante."

She folds her book and puts it on the end table before turning her feet to the side to give me her full attention.

"When?"

"Next week."

She nods then smiles. "Good, I can't wait to have him out of our lives for good."

"I need your help though."

Her smile brightens. "Anything."

"I want to fake your death. That will make him suffer the most. You may not realize he loves you, but he does."

"He does not love me."

"Not in the typical sense. He loves owning you. He loves hurting you. He would hate if anyone else were the one to break you."

She thinks for a moment. "Okay, I'll do it."

I suck in a breath I've been holding. I want to fake her death not only to make him suffer but also because it will keep her safe if my plan fails. He can't come searching for her if she's dead.

"And next week after I kill him, you can finally be free."

Her body freezes at the word *free*.

I give her time to recover, not pushing her to understand what she's feeling in her head.

"What do you mean by *free?*"

"I mean you can leave. Go home to your family. Start your new life away from here."

She nods slowly, like she can't believe the words she's hearing. She stares at the ground for the longest time, before staring back up at me.

"I love you, Caspian."

Fuck.

My worst nightmare happened. She can't love me. I will break her when she finds out I'm incapable of love. Clara took my heart with her when she died. I haven't loved since. I can't.

"When I kill Dante next week, I will have Michi pack your things and make sure you are on a plane to see your brothers in the US."

I stand up, needing to be done with this conversation. If I stay and talk, it will only make this worse.

"Seriously? That's all I get. I tell you I love you and you leave? This can't be happening!"

"I told you I would hurt you. I don't love you. In one week, you should go."

Her face drops like I just told her her puppy died or something else horrendous. All I did was tell her I didn't love her.

"No. I'm not leaving. You love me too you big jerk, even if you won't say it now. You wouldn't have saved me if you didn't care about me. You wouldn't have let me hurt you if you didn't love me. You wouldn't do everything to protect me if you didn't love me. You love me!"

I stand firm. "I'm incapable of love, Gia. Even you. I'm sorry. I know I said you would never be free, but I meant that figuratively, not literally. You will never be free of your past."

"You love me."

I grab her body and jerk her to me. "No, I don't. I never can. I'm sorry for being nice to you. For saving you. I knew I would hurt you. I was afraid you would fall in love with me, but I couldn't stop it and keep you. I'm selfish, but then you already know that. I used you to get what I wanted from Dante. That's it."

The last part stings the worst. I can see the devastation in her eyes. The drop in her body. The loss in her face. I hurt her worse than Dante ever did, and it kills me. But this is for the best. This must end. If she stays in my life, she will end up dead. And she deserves a man who can love her like she needs to be loved. Not constantly saved by a selfish asshole like me.

Gia looks at me for one more moment with tears in her eyes. But she doesn't let them fall. I've watched her many nights in Dante's room where she was able to hold back her tears, despite the pain she was in. She's had plenty of practice holding her tears in.

I want her to stay, to fight because I don't want to lose her, but I need to let her go.

She makes the right decision. She walks out the door. Most likely to sulk in the bedroom or in Michi's room.

I give her a minute before I head inside and grab a bottle of whiskey and then head back outside. I'll drink myself into oblivion and pass out on the couch. I'll be doing a lot of that in the near future.

I may not love her, but it won't stop me from missing her. I'm not good at missing people. I'm destructive and cruel. But after Dante's dead, it won't matter because I'll have nothing left to live for.

———

Gia's gone.

The words float around in my head but don't really land. She's not gone. She can't be.

But she will be soon, and when she is, I don't know what to do with myself. I'm not sure I will survive without her in my life. I've grown used to her light-heartedness. Her beauty. Her smart mouth.

I will miss her too much.

"Caspian!" my body falls off the chair and lands with a thud. *Damn it, that's going to leave a bruise in the morning.*

I open my eyes and see Adela standing over me, but there appears to be four of her.

"What?" I snap, annoyed she brought me out of my sleep. When I'm asleep, I don't have to remember Gia is leaving me in less than a week.

"Gia's gone," Adela says.

"No, she's not. She's in my bedroom."

"Caspian, she's gone."

I shake my head as I sit up carefully, trying to not puke.

"She ran out. She looked upset. Did you fight?"

I nod. It was close enough to a fight.

Adela's body shakes, and she finally has my attention. "Where is she? Who followed her?"

"I'm so sorry, Caspian. I was on duty. But I've had an upset stomach all day, and I stepped away from the feed for a few minutes. You were with her; I thought she was safe."

"Adela, what happened?" My heart freezes as I already know what happened.

"Da—" She doesn't get the word out. I know. Dante took her.

I jump up and race inside, grabbing my gun and running to my car with Adela on my heels. I don't know how Dante found out she was here, but he did. And I will do anything to get her back.

"Caspian stop! You're drunk! Let me drive," Adela yells.

"Get in the car. I've never been more sober in my life."

Adela frowns but jumps in the passenger seat. She starts calling in any member of the team she can get ahold of to help us as I drive to Dante's place.

Gia ran out because of me, and now she's his. I can't lose her. I can't lose another woman I love.

Love.

Shit, I love her. I didn't think it was possible, but now that she's gone, I'm lost forever.

18

GIA

My arms are tied behind my back as the light tickles into my eyes again. I don't have to open my eyes fully to know where I am. I can smell the rotten flesh, taste the blood, and feel the cold floor beneath me.

Dante stole me, again.

And now I'm back in the same room of his house; I swore I would never return. But this time, I will escape after I kill Dante.

The door opens, and I feel Dante's presence before I see him. He smells of sweat and blood and fear.

I stare at him as he walks in without a word, and I've never seen his face redder. His nostrils flare wide, and his teeth grind together, striding toward me.

I won't cower in the corner though, no matter how much my head hurts.

I stand slowly, even though my hands are tied behind my back, I'm ready for a fight. He will not touch me again.

Dante chuckles, watching me. "You think you are going to be able to stop me?"

"Yes, I will. And by the time I leave here, you will be dead. If not by my hand, then by Caspian's."

He smirks. "Oh yes, Caspian. The man who stole you. I thought he stole you because he wanted you as his slave. But you look very well taken care of."

I frown. I don't want Dante talking about Caspian.

Dante walks closer to me, and I stand tall, ready to fight as best I can if he touches me.

"I have a feeling we will be meeting your new lover sooner rather than later. He won't like that I get to touch you, not now that he's had you. He will realize what a good prize you are."

"I'm not a prize. I'm a person."

Dante shrugs. "No, you are mine." His hand clenches tightly around my arm, and I wince at the touch. Before a touch like that wouldn't have affected me, but now it's all I can think about. The pain shoots through me, making me realize how weak I am compared to him. If Dante wants to rape me, there isn't much I can do to prevent it.

"And this time, when I'm finished with you, I will kill you before any man has a chance to take you again."

I shiver at his words. He's wrong. He will be dead long before me.

The door slams open, and Caspian stands in the doorway. His gun is drawn, and it's pointed at Dante. I knew Caspian would come for me. He hurt me worse than Dante ever thought about hurting me, but he will do anything to protect me, even if he doesn't love me.

Dante chuckles. "Nice of you to finally show up. I thought you were supposedly the best at security, but I was able to snatch her up with ease. It took you hours to even realize she was gone. I almost thought you weren't coming, which would have been tragic, because then I would have had to hunt you down and kill you for taking what's mine."

"Let her go, Dante. Then we can work this out man to man," Caspian says, his eyes searching me for signs of any trauma.

I'm fine, I mouth to him.

His shoulders relax when he realizes my words are true. Dante, on the other hand, hasn't loosened his grip on my arm. I can't move. And I don't know how good of a shot Caspian is. Can he shoot Dante while missing me?

"You seem to be missing your partner though. Where is she?" Dante says.

"I'm here alone," Caspian answers, and my eyes widen. I don't want Adela here, but I'm not sure Caspian can take Dante and his men out on his own.

Dante chuckles. "You're a terrible liar, Caspian."

My heart stills at Dante's words.

Dante's phone buzzes, and he pulls it from his pocket casually, not acting like his life is currently in danger.

"Do you have her?" Dante asks.

There's a pause.

"Good," Dante says ending the call. "It appears my guards have your sister. They are under strict instructions to kill her within three minutes if you don't arrive to save her. My insurance that I remain alive."

Caspian's eyes widen in fear. Sweat drips down his face as he tries to decide if Dante is lying or not. He can't risk Dante not lying though.

"You're lying," Caspian says, and my heart stops. He can't choose me over Adela. He has to save her first.

"Stay here, and we will find out," Dante says.

"Adela's pregnant," I whisper through tears. She can't die. She has a husband who loves her. She has a baby on the way. She has a future. She deserves to be happy and live.

"Please, save her," I continue. I don't add first. I doubt there will be time to save us both.

Caspian swallows down tears I see in his eyes. He looks at me, and then Dante, and then back to me. His eyes tell me he will be back, soon. And then he disappears before either of us have a chance to change our minds.

"Now that he is taken care of, where were we?" Dante asks.

"Your guards won't kill Caspian. He'll fight them off. He'll save Adela. And then he will be back to kill you. So I suggest you spend your time running as far away as you can."

He turns me toward him, his disgusting cock pushing against my stomach.

"I hired new men. I have faith they will be able to handle Caspian. You should have said your goodbyes."

Dante's cocky as he says his words, but he's never been more wrong. He doesn't know how Caspian feels. He doesn't realize Caspian needs his revenge for killing his wife.

I struggle against the rope tying my arms together as Dante smirks, his slimy hands groping my body.

Please hurry back, Caspian.

No, I need to find a way out of this. I can.

"You're nothing but a coward. You always have been. I'm surprised you don't have four men in here holding me down like before. You can't even rape me like a man."

Dante's eyes are searing into mine. "You want a fair fight?"

"Yes."

His grin widens. "Then, let's fight."

He pulls out his knife, and I close my eyes afraid he's going to stab me. Instead, my arms pull free of the rope.

I'm in so much shock I don't anticipate the kick to my ribs. It knocks me over, and I hit the wall before sliding to the ground.

"It doesn't matter if you are tied up or not. I'm stronger than you, slave. I will win. I will rape you. And then, I will kill you. Submit now, and I will make sure your death is painless."

His words drive me, just like before. I want revenge and here is my chance to take it.

I'm stronger than Dante. Not physically, but mentally. I'm a survivor. I'm scrappy. And I know more about his world than he realizes.

He kicks me again, and my body recoils.

Think.

I need a solution. A way out.

I need a weapon. He's still holding the knife. I won't be able to snatch it from his hand. But I bet he has a gun.

And there is only one place a guy like him would keep a gun. In the waistband of his pants where he can access it quickly.

Stand, I command myself.

I do.

Dante kicks me again, but I don't let him knock me down no matter how much pain I'm in. As I stand, he grabs me, forcing my arms down to my sides.

I frown as I try to wiggle out of his grasp. His mouth comes down on mine, slobbering roughly over my mouth.

"You're mine, bitch. Don't forget it."

He tosses me down on the bed and jumps on top of me. I freeze. My mind goes to my happy place with Caspian, as my survival mechanism sets in.

No.

Focus on the gun.

He grabs my shirt and starts ripping it open as his mouth comes down on my body. It takes everything in me to not fight him off. To let his mouth take my nipple in his mouth. I need him close to me and not holding my arms down, so I can reach his gun.

I move my hands slowly, trying not to draw attention to them being free as Dante bites down hard and making me tear up.

But I can't wait. I won't let him rape me.

I grab for the waistband, find the metal gun, and shoot him in the leg.

Dante curses as he falls off of me. I scoot my body out from under him and stand to point the gun at him. Dante holds his hands up as he writhes in pain.

"You don't have the balls to kill me," Dante says.

I smirk. He doesn't know I was the one who killed Roman. That I would kill him in a second without thinking if I didn't think Caspian needed this more.

Caspian may not love me, but I love him. And we need to know that Adela is safe before we kill Dante. We may need him to get her back.

"You don't think I will kill you?"

"No."

I shake my head, tightening my grip on the gun. "If you move an inch, I will shoot you."

"I don't think you will."

He moves, and I shoot him in the other leg.

"Fuck you, bitch!"

I grin. "I'm not a liar. I will kill you if you move. I've killed plenty of men before. And even if I hadn't, the things you did to me would have made me strong enough to kill you in an instant. The only reason you are continuing to breathe is that Caspian needs to kill you more than I do."

Dante laughs. "You aren't strong enough."

"Gia's plenty strong enough. Adela's safe. Kill him, Gia," Caspian says as he enters the room.

His words should be enough for me to pull the trigger, but I can't do that. Caspian needs this more than me. He's needed this for five years.

I lower the gun and hold it out to Caspian. "You need this more."

Caspian holds onto the gun and then tries to push it back into my hands, but I won't let him.

"I love you. Let this be my final gift." I give him the gun, and then I step back. I may not get to kill Dante, but I can watch the white leave his eyes.

Caspian lifts the gun and aims it at Dante, and for the first time, I see fear in Dante's eyes.

"You took Clara from me. You deserve to be tortured over and over for the pain you caused her. You stole her, tortured her, raped her, and then killed her. But I'm a compassionate person. I will kill you swiftly if you apologize for what you did."

Dante shakes his head. "I never stole a Clara."

Caspian's finger tightens around the trigger. "You took her from me five years ago. And then threw her out with the trash like she was nothing. You were about to do the same thing to Gia and hundreds of other women. You remember her."

"I don't because she doesn't exist."

I can see Caspian's rage grow as Dante admits he doesn't remember Clara. Caspian has a lot of control, but he doesn't have much control left.

"Admit what you did, you fucking cunt."

Caspian's hand shakes as he stares at Dante with all the pain he's felt for years.

691

Dante turns from Caspian and looks at me with his lust-filled disgusting eyes.

I jump as the bullet leaves Caspian's gun without warning. It hits Dante in the head, and he falls to the ground, dead in an instant.

Caspian runs to me and throws his arms around me, both of us shaking.

"Did he hurt you?" Caspian's voice trembles as he speaks and looks me over.

I close the shirt he ripped around my body. "He barely touched me before I snatched his gun."

Caspian exhales. "You promise?"

I nod.

"Thank you for coming back and saving me."

"I didn't save you; you saved yourself."

I smile weakly.

"Is Adela okay?"

He nods. "Yes, she's shaken up, but she's fine. She will be popping a baby out in six months without a problem."

I smile. "You knew."

He nods. "I knew, but it still killed me to leave you here not knowing if you were going to live or die."

"You made the right decision. I wouldn't have forgiven you if you had saved me and anything had happened to Adela."

"I know. It still killed me."

Tears fill my eyes. I won't let him see me cry over him again.

"I'm going to go call my brothers. I'm sure they are worried sick. They will send a plane to get me."

Caspian steps in front of me, stopping me from leaving.

"Your brothers know where you are. They've known the entire time I've had you."

"What?"

"They trusted I would keep you safe. If you were with them, you would have jeopardized their lives, and it would have been one of the first places Dante would have looked."

"I should still talk to them, now that he's gone."

"Stop. Stop running."

I freeze.

"I'm sorry. For everything, but most importantly for breaking your heart. And for not telling you I love you too."

"What?"

Caspian grabs me and kisses me with everything he has. He dips me, holding me in his arms as he deepens the kiss, his tongue tasting every drop inside my mouth.

When he pulls back, I see the love in his eyes. He loves me, and I love him. This should be our happily ever after. Our perfect ending, but it isn't. I can't start our lives together on a lie. He has to know my darkest secret. Only then, can he decide if he loves me.

"There is a reason Dante didn't admit to killing Clara."

Caspian steps back, he can sense what I'm going to say.

"Dante may have stolen her, but he sold her to my family. To my father."

Caspian takes another step back, and I can feel him slipping further away from me.

"Your father? Enrico Carini?"

I nod. "He was the one who raped her. He broke her."

"He killed her?"

I swallow, trying to keep the words from leaving my mouth, but he has to hear them. He has to know the truth.

"No, I killed her."

19

CASPIAN

Gia couldn't have killed Clara. It's not possible. Gia has to be lying or misunderstanding what happened. I know Gia's past is dark, but she couldn't have killed an innocent woman.

"No," I say.

Tears stream down her pink cheeks. Whatever happened, I can forgive Gia. I love her. I almost lost her to Dante again. I won't let her go again.

I force my legs forward toward her to show my support. She needs to know there is nothing she can say to make me leave her.

"I remember Clara. She was a beautiful, strong, innocent woman. She loved life, but my father broke her almost instantly. She was so fragile, so naïve that it was easy for him to break her.

"I thought I could help her. So one night after father had gone to bed, I snuck into her room. I couldn't sneak her out; her body was too broken to run. And I couldn't lift her on my own. But I could bring her a weapon. I couldn't kill my father myself, but she could. She just needed the gun.

"So I provided her one. But she was too far gone to keep fighting. She just wanted the pain to end."

She doesn't continue, instead, her voice cracks. Clara used the gun

694

to end her life and her suffering. I don't blame Clara for what she did. I couldn't rescue her, and she didn't grow up in the world that Gia did. Clara didn't have the same fight that Gia has.

Rage and pain hit me again. And I have nothing and no one to take it out on.

"I need revenge."

"Enrico is gone. He's already dead."

I turn, needing to find something to take out my anger on.

She races in front of me. "Take it out on me. I deserve it. I never should have given her the gun in her condition."

I look away. I can't look at her. It hurts too much.

She grabs my face and turns me toward her. "Take out your revenge on me."

"I can't. The last time we did, one of us almost died."

She wipes her tears. "It's worth the risk if it means I have a shot at keeping you."

She's right. It's worth the risk.

She smiles weakly at me and then walks to the bed and lies down offering her body to me.

This room is filled with the darkest of items. Items I could use to destroy her. But it's not what I want.

I want rough. I want fast. And I want to know if we can find love in the dark. Or if we are meant to wander this world apart.

I grab her body and rip her pants until she is naked.

She moans as I do, but this isn't about pleasure. This is about releasing my rage.

I flip her over and find her sweet ass. I spank her hard, watching as her flesh turns red. She cries out, but it just sparks my deeper rage.

I hate her for what she did.

I'm not sure I can forgive her.

I'm not sure if I can forgive myself.

Or if the love I felt a minute ago was even really love or just worry.

I spank her again and again, watching the pain spread as I undo my pants. I need to be inside her whether she is ready for me or not. I need to fuck her ass and show her how much pain I'm in.

I push my pants down, and then I push my hard cock against her asshole, and in one movement, I thrust in. She screams in pain but doesn't try to stop me.

I want to do worse. More spanking. Slam into her body harder. Grab instruments to mark her body.

I settle for slamming hard into her while I slap her ass.

"Conti!" she cries out.

I still. *What am I doing?*

My rage immediately disappears as she moans my name. She sacrificed herself to save my sister. She's sacrificing her body now for a chance at love. And I'm repaying her by hurting her after I've already done more than enough horrible things to hurt her.

I pull out and flip her over before thrusting my cock back into her.

"I'm so sorry, princess," I say kissing her lips as hard as I can. Tears sting both of our eyes as we kiss harder. Gia wraps her arms around my neck as I slowly rock in and out.

"I love you," I whisper against her lips. "I'm so sorry. I'll never screw up again."

Gia smiles. "You will, and I'll forgive you. Just like I'll screw up as well. I love you."

I smile. I don't think I'll ever stop smiling as long as I have her. But right now I need to focus. I have the love of my life to make love to, and I want to rock her world.

She bites her lip as she sees my expression change. "I want to love you forever, Gia."

"I'll never stop loving you, Conti."

I laugh. "But I might stop if you keep calling me by my dad's name."

She laughs too, but her laughs quickly change to moans as I take her perky nipple into my mouth and rock against her clit. I know exactly how to play her body. It doesn't matter we are in the darkest place, where Gia was raped and with the dead body of her rapist a few feet away. We won't remember any of that after tonight. Because tonight we are reclaiming it as ours.

I never thought I could love again after Clara. Clara was my light, and Gia brings out my dark. I thought I needed to stay firmly in the light, but Gia has taught me that it's okay to live in the darkness. Because even in the darkness, there is light. And together we can always find our way back out through our love.

EPILOGUE

GIA

"I HAVE SOME EXCITING NEWS," I say into the phone where my sisters-in-law Nina and Eden are on the line.

"Oh my god, you're engaged!" Nina shouts.

"No."

"You're pregnant!" Eden says.

I laugh. "No."

I can hear the audible sadness in both Nina and Eden's voices.

"Don't worry, Caspian and I are still going strong, I just don't think either of us is ready to settle down and have kids." I don't add that I don't think we will want kids ever. Our lives are too dangerous to add kids to.

"So what's the exciting news?" Eden asks.

"I've finally found my passion! I'm officially a partner with Caspian and Adela in the security business. We install security systems in the worst of the worst homes and businesses, and then use that information to turn them over to the police or to kill them."

Silence.

I knew my news wouldn't go over well, but finally, I get a response. "That's amazing!" I hear them both say at the same time.

"Really, it's amazing! I'm so proud of you. You are really going to make a difference. You are such a badass. You have the skills, and you know this world so well," Nina says.

"Thank you."

"Just wait a little until you tell your brothers. They won't take the news well. They will probably try to ring Caspian's neck for letting you do such a dangerous job, but you are going to do amazingly well."

I smile. "I'll wait until we come to your house Christmas to tell them."

I hear a baby crying in the background. "We need to go. Be safe and visit soon. We all miss you." The line is disconnected as the cries get louder in the background.

I smile. I miss them too.

Caspian comes into the living room carrying a plate of sandwiches. "How did it go?" he asks even though I know he heard every word of our conversation. The cons of living in such a small home. The pros far outweigh the cons though. I love being so close to Caspian all the time. This house feels cozy, like a real home, instead of the coldness of the mansion my family used to call home.

"Well, my sisters think it's a great idea."

Caspian raises his eyebrows. "And your brothers?"

"We agreed it was best to wait to tell them."

Caspian laughs. "Good, that means I can live another day."

I curl up next to him on the couch and snatch a sandwich off his plate.

"I love our life. And I love you for letting me risk my life, same as you."

"It's hard. Maybe one day it will get easier. But I can't stop you from being the badass, warrior you are."

I kiss him on the lips, smiling widely. I can't get enough of him.

"I overheard your sisters-in-law though. Do you want to get married and have kids? Have the typical life?"

"No. I don't have a need to get married. I already know I'm going to spend the rest of my life with you without a piece of paper telling me so. And kids, our lives are too dangerous to bring kids into the mix. All I need is you."

"I feel the same way." He rubs his nose against mine.

And I lean into the crook of his arm while I chomp down on my sandwich.

Arlo and Nina travel to stay safe from the dangers our family has put us in. They never stay in one place for long, and that keeps them safe.

Matteo and Eden use the distance of the US and Eden's job as a prosecutor to keep them safe.

But Caspian and I confront the darkness head-on. Our lives are the riskiest, but it's worth it to live the life we want.

Italy is my home, and I would never leave it. As for my childhood home I love, and for Clive and Erick, the remaining men on my revenge list, maybe one day I'll face them and get my home back. As for now, I've realized I don't need revenge to be happy or free. Love already set me free.

DIRTY EPILOGUE

PROLOGUE

"Hello?"

"Hello, Mrs. Carini."

My heart stops at the voice on the other line. A voice I never thought I would hear again.

"Clive."

I can feel him smirking on the other end of the line.

"What do you want? Whatever it is, the answer is no," I say.

"No? I don't think you are in any position to tell me no."

"We gave you everything. Our house. Our company. *Everything*. We needed your help, and we traded everything to get it. Now we are done. You live your life, while we live ours. We aren't friends. We aren't enemies. We are nothing."

Clive laughs. "Maybe that was the promise, but you broke the rules."

"We haven't broken any rules, because there were no rules to break. We had no agreement. We are nothing."

"I doubt you will think that way anymore."

My breath catches as I race to think about every worse case scenario. My husband and kids are playing in the other room. I can hear their laughter. They are safe, for now. What about my the rest of my family? What about Eden, Matteo, Gia, and Caspian? Are they safe?

"What did you do?"

"We didn't do anything. We didn't start this war. You did."

"We didn't start anything. If you remember, you were the one that kidnapped me. You helped Roman sell Gia. You are the monsters who started this, not us. One cooperative moment helping us save Eden doesn't redeem you."

"We don't hold grudges. I'm not talking about the past. I'm talking about the present."

"We haven't done anything. We don't give a shit about you. We don't think about you."

"Well, that is about to change. Because I think you will be thinking a lot about us from now on."

Clive's bluffing. This is ridiculous. I shouldn't even be listening to this conversation. Clive and Erick can't hurt us. We have taken every precaution. We have twenty-four-hour security. Caspian installed the highest level of security equipment in all of our homes. And we all hired the best bodyguards in the world.

We have made many enemies, and we don't take the threats we receive lightly. But Clive and Erick are weak. We could squash them in a second. We don't so they can be out there making enemies, which takes a large target off our backs. We no longer need to be involved in the dangerous life the Carinis grew up in. We can exist on our own without our dark pasts.

"I'm done playing games, Clive. Tell me why you called, or I'm ending this conversation," my voice vibrates through the entire house, and Arlo strolls down the hallway to where I'm standing. We exchange a glance, and I know whatever Clive says, won't matter.

I have Arlo. I have my kids. And whatever happens, Arlo will face it with me, by my side.

"We took..."

1

NINA

I HEAR A SCREAM, and my heart stops.

It does this every time one of my children scream or cry. It skips a beat at any loud noise.

It's been five years since there has been an attack on our family. Gia was the last victim, but since Caspian helped free her, our life has been mostly quiet. Normal. Exactly what I wanted.

But this scream from my youngest child has my blood pumping. I lower my sunglasses as I sit up on my lounge chair to scan the beach in front of me. It's a private beach. We are the only ones here, but that doesn't mean it's easy to spot my little ones, who like to run off whenever they get a chance.

I spot them playing in the sand near the edge of the ocean. Doherty is supposed to be watching them, but I don't see him.

Shit.

My sunglasses fall down my face as I jump up and start running on the warm sand. I step on a seashell and its sharp edges drive into my flesh, but I don't let it stop me. I keep running. I'll deal with the cut and blood later.

I grab my babies, pulling them tight into my arms. Although, they aren't babies anymore. My oldest is almost five, and my youngest is three.

"You're safe, mommy's got you," I say, gripping my children like I just saved them from a monster. I probably won't stop holding them the rest of the day. The blood-curdling scream is embedded in my brain forever, now.

I hear laughter out of my youngest, but it doesn't calm the sweat that is beading off my skin. My heart still flutters. My arms still clutch them. I carry them back to my lawn chair where I can examine them for any injury from underneath the umbrella, instead of in the scorching sun.

I sit them down on the edge of the lawn chair and examine my youngest first. He was the one who gave out the scream.

"What happened?" I ask.

Samuel laughs. I search over his body for any sign of injury. I don't find any, but it doesn't keep me from hunting for one.

He giggles louder like I'm tickling him instead of trying to save his life.

"Mommy, we are fine. Samuel saw a jellyfish and screamed. I told him it wouldn't hurt him as long as he didn't touch it," Layla says.

I frown as I examine his hands and feet for signs he touched the creature. I find nothing, not even a hint of redness.

"Mrs. Carini, I'm so sorry. I was playing hide and seek with the kids. I made sure I could still see them from where I was hiding just a few feet away. I yelled out to you when you snatched the kids up that they were safe, but I don't think you heard me," Doherty, our nanny, and head of the kids' security, says.

I let out a breath. I should feel better, but I don't. My lungs feel closed, and I can't get enough oxygen.

I grab my oldest and begin searching her for any signs of injury.

"Mommy, I'm fine," she giggles.

I sigh as I sit down on the sand in front of the two most precious things I have in the whole world. They are safe. No one is trying to hurt them. They saw a jellyfish.

I look up at Doherty, my security. I give him a stern look that tells him we will talk later. Hide and seek isn't the best game to play when his job is to protect the kids.

I turn back and grip both of my kids' hands. "I'm sorry, your scream worried me."

"Why? We were perfectly safe."

I smile weakly. *Why?* That's a loaded question. Because your grandfather used to be the evilest person on the planet, and who knows how many people he pissed off. Because your father used to follow in his footsteps and worked with some of the most heinous men in Italy. Because we have money. Because I've been taken before, and will never let my kids go through similar pain. Because I know exactly what horrors are out in the world. Arlo used to be one of those atrocities. Now, he's my prince who protects our children and me with his life. I desperately hope he never has to.

I'm paranoid. I know it. But when I talk to Arlo later tonight, I know he won't see it that way. I'll have to leave out the part about Doherty playing hide and seek. Arlo will fire him if I don't, and despite one misstep of judgment, Doherty has done a fantastic job protecting our kids.

"How about you go play? I'll see if we can get daddy to bring us lunch here. How does that sound?"

"Pizza?" Layla asks.

"Of course," I say, stroking my daughter's sweet face.

My children hop up and start running back toward the ocean. I give Doherty one look, and he runs until he catches up with my children. I know he won't let them out of his sight again, but it doesn't ease me. Nothing will. I chose darkness as my husband, and that comes with a risk. Danger could lurk around every corner. Or it could stay just on the edge of our existence, and never creep back in. Either way, I will protect my family from it, no matter what.

I call Arlo, who agrees to bring us pizza, and then decide to go for a swim with my children. I wouldn't be able to retake a nap if I tried. So I run straight into the water with my kids splashing next to me. I may not be able to protect them from evil, but I can teach them how to shine in the darkness.

2

ARLO

"What's wrong?" I ask my beautiful wife, brushing against her as we both clean up the dishes from our dinner.

Nina hesitates for a second, before careening her neck to kiss me harder than I would have expected. Our kids are currently playing in the next room, and nothing can happen for another hour until they are tucked in bed.

She pulls away and smiles wickedly at me. She knows that kiss is going to leave my dick hard until I can have her later tonight. She returns to doing the dishes without giving me an answer.

No.

I can't let her use sex against me. She knows me well enough to know sex is her only tool of distraction, but the look in her eyes all day at the beach had me concerned.

"That's not an answer, Nina. What's wrong?"

I grab her waist and turn her to me as my cock smacks against her belly. She squirms in my grasp, making it clear her concerns are giving her the need for a release that much more.

"Nothing—"

"Nina," I interrupt with a stern tone. I don't want to hear nothing's wrong. I know every centimeter of her body. I know what every look she gives means. I know the meaning of every sound. Every motion. Everything.

She can't hide anything from me, and I can't hide anything from her.

Her eyelashes flicker past me to our children playing in the next room. They can't hear us. She has no excuse not to tell me.

"Nothing—"

I hold my fingers up to her lips to silence her words again.

"You can't lie to me."

She grabs my finger and slowly lowers it. "I know. I'm not trying to lie to you. Let me finish."

I lower my hand and nod.

"Nothing happened at the beach, but it doesn't stop me from feeling like something is about to happen. Samuel screamed when he saw a jellyfish on the beach today. I panicked, but it was nothing. There was no danger. Doherty was right there to protect them. It still just made me uneasy."

Her body trembles in my arms and I can tell exactly how uneasy it made her. All these hours later, she's still shaken up over a jellyfish. Samuel screams from the other room, and it sends chills down both our spines. We turn, but he's perfectly fine as he jumps on Layla's back.

I can understand how one scream from our son could send Nina into a panic. Samuel has strong lungs on him. We were lucky Layla wasn't a screamer. She was quiet and patient with us. Our son - not so much. He's a terror, always looking for adventure. Today won't be the only time he sends fear into my wife.

I hate seeing her like this. This is because of me. Because of who my family is, and what I did to her.

Some days I regret ever letting her into my life, even though she's my match. I was meant to be loved by her. Our children are the greatest gift I could have ever imagined. But she still struggles with the pain of what I did to her and who I am. And I grapple with watching her deal with that pain.

Right now, though, I can do something about her pain.

"No," she says, reading me as easily as I can read her.

I raise an eyebrow. "You were the one who kissed me like that."

She blushes. "Our children are in the next room," she hisses quietly so that no one can hear us.

"Doherty is here for another hour right?"

She nods.

I smirk. "Good, we will be back to read them a story and tuck them into bed."

I don't give her another option. I scoop her up in my arms and carry her out of the kitchen. We are renting a villa in Sydney on the beach, and I'm not acquainted with where everything is in this house yet. This is only our second night here. We spend our time traveling. I occasionally trade art or sell some of the pieces Nina and I have painted.

She starts to protest again, but I kiss her, pulling her tongue deep into my mouth, and I start to feel her forgetting her worries. We've attempted therapy. We've tried meditating. We've given exercise a shot. But truly the only thing that can calm my wife is me. We might have an unhealthy relationship and reliance on each other, but it warms me to know I'm her cure.

She kisses me hungrily as we stumble down the hallway. I know our bedroom is several doors down, but my wife needs me, desperately, and I will do anything to make her pain go away.

I open the first door I find and stumble inside, too focused on my wife's perfect kisses to notice the Lego toy I just stepped on. The pain radiates up my foot to my leg as I curse and kick the toy away. How can something that small be so painful?

Nina pauses looking at me in the dark, her dark eyes shining even though it's dark in the room.

"Wuss."

I frown. "You did not just say that."

"I did. What are you going to do about it?" Nina's voice is smooth as silk as she speaks. She's goading me. As much as she pretends our lives are normal during the day, she becomes as dark as me at night. She seeks the thrill of a romance she can never anticipate and leaves her panting for more.

Tonight, she won't be panting for more though. She'll be demanding more.

My eyes scan the room, trying to figure out which room we've landed in. There is a bed, not that missing a bed has ever stopped us before, but as we've grown older, I realize the importance of having a bed.

I toss her onto the bed and remove my shirt over my head. I push down my pants and underwear as I bend down and pick up the tiny toy I stepped on earlier.

I glance at my wife on the bed who I can barely make out in the dark. I consider turning the lights on so that I can see every one of her reactions, but I decide against it. The dark is better.

Her eyes glaze, as I step closer so she can get a better look at my body.

A cry draws her attention away from me and toward the door. I grab her chin and force her to focus on me as I taste her sweet mouth again, sucking all of her attention away from the door. The next rental we stay in is going to have a soundproof room.

As soon as my lips release her, she turns her attention back to the door, carefully listening for another sound coming from our children.

I sigh. I can't even distract her from her motherly duties these days.

"Nina?" I ask, hoping to God she's still with me and not about to jump off the bed to chase down our children.

She slowly turns her head back to me. "I'm sorry. I know Doherty has them. He'll come find us if he needs us."

My body covers hers as I roughly take her in my mouth again. "He'd better not, for the next twenty minutes, if he still wants a job."

"Only twenty minutes?" I can hear the disappointment in her voice.

I kiss down her smooth neck next, watching as the tiny goose-bumps form on her skin. I would love to have more than twenty minutes with her. I would love to be selfish and have her all to myself all night long. But that's not our life anymore. We have responsibilities besides ourselves. But maybe it's time for just the two of us to take a vacation by ourselves, even just a long weekend. Some time without the kids would be good for us.

Nina moans. I'll worry about convincing her later. If I already book the tickets, she can't argue with that. I'm sure Eden and Matteo would love to watch the kids for us for the weekend. Our kids love getting to see their cousins.

Focus.

I rip open her shirt and find her smooth skin bare. "Nina, you naughty girl. No bra."

I tuck my hand into the thin material of her shorts. "No underwear either."

God, my wife is the sexiest woman in the entire world.

I bury my face in her breasts. I love how swollen they are, and how stayed that size, after she gave birth to Layla. Motherhood fits Nina in every way. Except for the stress. The worry it causes her everyday creeps into her beautiful eyes, forming tiny lines on her face.

I want to take the worry away from her permanently, but I can't. All I can do is distract her for a few minutes.

"Arlo, make me forget," Nina says.

I suck in a breath, hating she has anything that needs forgetting in her past.

I kiss down her stomach, and then over her shorts.

She arches her back as I do, begging me for more.

"Patience, baby."

"No."

I smile as I begin slowly undoing her pants. If I don't take my time, this won't even last twenty minutes. I pull her pants down to reveal her smooth pussy. My eyes widen at the sight. Every part of me grows weak looking at her. Wanting her. Begging for her.

She's the woman I dreamed about for far too long. And even though she's here now, it doesn't feel real. These last few years have gone by too fast. I need time to slow down so I can enjoy every moment.

I hover over her pussy and then start torturing her by kissing down her leg. I feel the tiny hairs sticking up on her leg as I kiss. She hasn't shaved in a couple of days, most likely from being too swamped with taking care of the kids. She puts herself last now. The hair on her legs doesn't bother me, but I'm booking her a spa day tomorrow. She deserves to put herself first, always. I can handle the kids tomorrow.

I kiss down to her ankle and then press the Lego into the bottom of her foot.

"Damn you, Arlo!" she cries out.

She can curse and pretend she's upset all she wants, but I know the truth. She likes the pain. It turns her on.

I press it into her other foot, as I kiss her ankle, and I feel her blood pulsing inside of her. The blood shoots through her body like it's racing to get to the painful spot faster.

"A Lego toy doesn't exactly turn me on," Nina pants.

I smirk, pressing it on the inside of her thigh. It may not exactly be the same as a whip, or the wax of a candle, or any of the other devices I've tortured her with before, but it does provide the nip of pressure I'm looking for.

"Liar."

She smiles at my words.

I toss the toy down. I've learned to improvise. We don't exactly keep the whips out for the kids to find.

I grab her thighs and thrust into her. Her tight lips welcome me in like an old friend. It's only been a week since we've last fucked, but it feels like years. I never thought we would go this long without sex. But life has a way of changing everything.

Nina cries out as I rock inside of her. She opens more for me as I lean down to kiss her.

"What would I do without you, Nina?"

"Be lost," she whimpers, as I crash into her body again.

Our eyes never leave each other's as we come, wrapped around each other. I can never get enough of Nina, and I don't know what I'd do if she were taken from me.

Die.

I wouldn't survive without her.

I hear another playful cry from one of the kids. I might be able to hang on for them. Keep breathing, keep my heart beating. But I wouldn't really be present. Just going through the motions.

I look into the woman's eyes that keeps me existing. I would have given up a long time ago if it wasn't for her.

Another cry brings us back to life. Nina looks at me, and I know that as much as she needed this, she also needs to check on the kids. It kills her not to know they are safe every second of every day.

So I roll off her and gather our clothes. She smiles at me, like she has the greatest secret, as she covers her smooth skin with clothes.

Even though I'm a few feet away from her, I can still breathe in her scent. She smells like the ocean. Our next trip should be near an ocean too. It's our favorite. I used to think we traveled so much because we were concerned about our safety. If we were always on the move, it would be harder for people to find us. But we don't travel so much because we are running. We travel so much because it makes us feel alive.

"I like it here," Nina says.

"I like it anywhere with you," I pull her back to my arms and snuggle her against my chest.

She moans into my chest. "That's cheesy."

"It's true."

"I love traveling the world with you. I don't want anyone else by my side."

"Mmm-hmm."

Her eyes are closed, and I'm pretty sure she could fall asleep standing up, while I hold her in my arms. She hasn't been getting much sleep lately. Nightmares have tortured her every night with fear that something terrible is going to happen to our kids. She doesn't know me very well if she thinks I would ever let that happen.

"Come on, let's go play with the kids for a few minutes, so we can get you all to sleep."

She nods against my chest. I hold her close to me as we walk. We are tackled to the ground by playful kids as soon as we enter the large living room. It's clear our kids don't plan on going to bed for hours. We need to remember to cut back on the sugar.

I start wrestling with Samuel, while Layla jumps on my back. Nina giggles at us, and pretends to help the kids gang up on me as well.

I give her a 'we will wrestle more later' look, and her eyes immediately darken. She winks at me, agreeing. Damn, I love my life. I never imagined I could have such a normal, happy life. I thought, for sure, I'd die of a bullet wound before I turned thirty. Instead, here I am, living out my most wonderful dreams.

A buzzing stops Nina, who pulls her phone from her pocket. She smiles at the kids and then gives me a 'we are putting the kids to bed when I get back' look.

Fine with me, I mouth back. I want her alone in our bed again.

She rolls her eyes rascally and then takes the phone out into the hallway where she answers it.

I continue wrestling the kids until I hear Nina's voice. Whoever is on the call with Nina has her terrified. I know Nina better than I know my own body.

"Doherty, watch the kids," I say slowly, trying to keep my voice calm, so they don't notice my abrupt change. I don't need them freaking out.

Tell that to my heart. It's pounding too loudly in my chest, not giving me a second to rest. I walk to the doorway where I can look at Nina and my kids. I want to run to Nina now that Doherty has the kids occupied, but Nina would never forgive me if I left them alone for even a second.

She ends the call and turns to me. Her eyes are full, but it's not just fear I see, it's determination. She's already begun to form a plan to fix whatever problem just crashed down on us.

This feels like déjà vu to both of us. The last time we got a call like this was when we had found out Eden was taken. My idiot brother, Matteo, took her, but just like me, he fell in love and realized his mistake brought him the greatest treasure.

My voice cracks as I speak. "Eden?"

3

EDEN

MY HANDS ARE clammy as I clasp them together, resting them on the table in front of me. I feel the beads of sweat dripping down my back, beneath my blue blazer jacket. My foot taps rhythmically beneath the table to a rapid beat in my heart. My breathing is shallow, and my vision is clouded with a fog that can only focus on one person: the judge sitting in front of us.

I've never been this anxious to hear a verdict before. Usually, I know without a doubt I've won before the judge opens their mouth.

Today is different. A man's life rests in this decision. A man I locked up wrongly.

Fuck.

It still hurts every time I think about what I did. The pain wraps around my body and squeezes me tight, like a python suffocating its prey. I locked up an innocent man because I was so focused on keeping the criminals off the street, I didn't pause to realize not all men are monsters. And even the monstrous ones are still worth redeeming.

I hear the creak of the rusty chair next to me. Jake squirms in his chair, unable to sit still as the judge reads over the papers he was just handed with the verdict on it. I promised him I would do everything to get him out the second I realized my mistake, but getting him out has been incredibly difficult.

It's been almost five years. He's had to sit in prison that entire time, even though the main witness recanted her statement. Even though there isn't any physical evidence against him. No blood, no DNA, no weapon. Nothing to prove he is a murderer.

It doesn't matter in the eyes of the law. He got a fair trial. He was proven guilty. And he looks like a criminal. He's covered in tattoos. He didn't have a steady job. He smoked marijuana. He was in a gang. Why believe him? Even if he was innocent of this particular crime, the numerous opinion articles in the papers said he was probably guilty of other crimes. Because of who he is.

I used to think the same way. Then I met Matteo, and my view of the world changed. He showed me the heart of a criminal; the reasons behind the crimes. People can't choose the world they are born into. Sometimes they get lucky and can escape it, other times life can be quicksand holding onto them and eventually sucking them in until they slowly die.

Jake was young when I sent him to prison. He never even had the chance to escape.

I grab his hand and give it a gentle squeeze. I promised him I would never stop fighting for his freedom. I haven't told him this, but if I can't get him out legally, I will illegally. Matteo has been itching to do something dangerous and bad again. If the verdict is guilty, I will give Matteo the green light to get Jake out at all costs.

He will be free, even if I have to give up some of the freedom my family has been given to do it.

"The jury finds Jake..."

I missed much of what the judge said as he begins talking, but now I'm focusing on every word.

"Not guilty."

Jake and I exhale at the same time, as all the oxygen we had been holding in leaves our lungs. Tears stream down both of our faces as his sister gasps in joy from behind us.

The judge continues reading, going through all the procedures of the court.

"I'm free? I can go home tonight?" Jake asks.

I smile, wiping the tears from my face. "You can go home in about five minutes. I'm so sorry you had to be in prison in the first place."

More tears fall until I can barely make out his features beneath the tears. "Don't be; you got me out. I forgive you."

"Thank you," I mouth, because I can't get the words out.

The judge finishes, and then his sister runs to him, engulfing him in her hug.

This.

This is what I wanted. There is only a handful of times I have felt this much joy in my life. This is one of the only times that didn't involve a family or friend.

I gather my things and walk out of the courtroom before I'm swarmed with reporters. "Mrs. Carini, how confident are you Jake is actually innocent?"

"Very confident."

"But if he isn't innocent, how will you be able to sleep at night? He is the only suspect."

"Jake didn't kill anyone. He was just proven innocent today. I made a mistake, and I own that. I will sleep well for the first time in five years knowing an innocent man isn't paying for my actions."

"Will you go back to prosecuting now?"

I glance back at Jake, who is now standing behind me with a large smile on his face.

"No, I will continue to fight for the innocent, but in a different way. I will do pro-bono work to make sure the innocent get free."

I hadn't decided until this moment, but it's exactly what I want. I'm tired of being the judge that fights to lock guilty men away. Helping the innocent get free is what I love doing now. Matteo wasn't guilty when I found him; he just needed a way to get free. To find his innocence. I enjoy giving a man his life back better than taking it away.

I walk to my car and smile when I see what is sitting in the front seat: a large bouquet of flowers. I climb in and read the sweet note from my husband.

. . .

My Wife,

Congrats on winning the case! I knew you would win. I ordered these before the verdict was read. You are amazing, a badass, and the strongest person I know. Now get your cute ass home so we can celebrate in our bedroom. Naked.

—Your Impatient Husband

I smile reading his note. Matteo's too good to me. I don't deserve him, but I do plan on showing him just how much I love him tonight. I need to swing by the liquor store first. Then call and get a babysitter for tonight, so I can spend the night rocking his world.

4

MATTEO

"One, two, three..." my voice trails off as I listen to the footsteps of my kids running through the apartment. I don't have to open my eyes to know exactly where the kids are hiding. They always hide in the same spots. Not that they have many choices. Our two bedroom apartment is barely big enough to contain all of us.

I hear a small cry from Perla, our youngest who is almost six months old. I crack my eyes the tiniest bit to check on her, even though I know she's safe in her crib sitting against the wall in the living room. The cry was one checking to see if I would give her attention, not one because she needs anything.

I snap my eyes shut quickly when I see her smiley face. I can't help but smile myself.

"Ready or not, here I come!" I shout through the apartment. I grab Perla first, snatching her out of her crib, and placing her on my hip.

She laughs as I carry her down the hallway to Eden and I's bedroom. I hear giggles as soon as I throw the door open. I shake my head from side to side and hold my finger up to try to quiet Perla. I take my time walking around the room, pretending I don't have a clue where my little squirts are.

"Found you!" I scream as I jump down and look under the bed to find four pairs of eyes staring up at me. They all laugh and run out from under the bed before tackling me to the ground.

My oldest goes for my head, while the triplets tackle my stomach, and Perla stays cradled in my arm.

My head hits the dresser behind us, wobbling it hard. I snatch up the kids and roll us out of the way before the dresser comes crashing down. My heart skips a beat as I realize just how dangerous that could have been if I didn't move the kids out of the way in time. They continue giggling and laughing, not realizing the danger something as simple as a dresser could cause.

I've changed my whole world to give them a safer life. I'm not going to let something as silly as a dresser hurt them. I need to talk to Eden about getting a bigger place. I've loved having everyone close in this small apartment, but it's time we get something bigger where the kids can have their own rooms.

The front door opens.

"Mommy's home! Go get her!" I shout. The kids leap off me and start running, while I take a second to calm my heart and scoop Perla up.

I walk into the living room where Eden is hugging the kids. I lean against the doorway watching her. I can never get enough of her. This is what I wanted. To be surrounded by people I love. Forever. I don't need anything else, but this.

I step over the Barbie dolls and blocks, a skill I've perfected, before I get to Eden and kiss her firmly on the lips.

"You won your case."

She nods as she bites her lip, blushing.

"How did you know?"

I grab her ass, sweeping her off her feet, as my tongue parts her lips to slip further into her mouth. I can hear the kids laughing and yelling, wanting me to pick them up too.

She laughs and pulls her lips from mine, leaving me aching and hard beneath my jeans. I shouldn't get excited so quickly when I see my wife in front of the kids, but I can't help myself. The second she enters the room I can't think of anything but her.

"Put me down, you oaf."

I growl. "No."

She rolls her eyes, seeing the determination in my eyes and knowing I won't back down easily.

"I have a surprise for you," she whispers in my ear, knowing if she says anything too loudly, our children will think the surprise is for them. But the way the words roll off her tongue and vibrate through my body makes it clear the surprise is a dirty one.

I raise an eyebrow, as my wife smiles seductively.

The hoods of my eyes fall as all I see is her. *Damn, even after all these years together, she still makes me insane.*

I move my head to kiss her again, but her fingers pressed against my lips to stop me.

I whimper like a fucking girl. *God, this woman.*

A knock on the door startles me. I slowly ease Eden to the ground. I don't know who is at the damn door, but it pisses me off. I want my surprise now. I don't want to be patient. The faster we get the kids fed, bathed, and in bed, the faster I get to unwrap Eden. Devour her and remind her of what she's missing every time she goes into work. Whoever is at the door is just delaying my plan.

I stomp to the door and open it, ready to chew the interrupter out, but when I spot the young woman on the other side of the door, my body changes.

"Meghan, what are you doing here?" I ask our usual babysitter. She's in college and has no security skills, but she's great with our kids. We have a security team that monitors the apartment and travels with us whenever we leave the premises, so Meghan doesn't need any skills other than loving our kids and CPR.

She glances behind me to where Eden is walking up, carrying a kid on each hip. *Damn, that's sexy.*

"She's watching the kids so you and I can celebrate."

My eyes widen, and my heart stops. How lucky of a man am I? I should have thought of hiring the babysitter for tonight myself. I knew Eden would want to celebrate if she won, which is why I was going to cook her a fabulous dinner with our favorite wine. But fuck cooking. I can cook for her another time.

I grab Michela and Rosa from Eden's arms and hand them to Meghan. "You remember where everything is? All the emergency numbers?"

Meghan smiles and nods.

"Good." All I care about is that she knows how to dial 911 if the kids get into trouble. I don't care if she feeds them sugar and doesn't put them to bed until after midnight. As long as they are safe, that's all that matters.

I grab Eden's hand and start jerking her out of our apartment.

"Bye, kids. Have fun," I shout as I pull Eden through the door.

"I was going to change, but I guess that isn't happening now," she laughs.

"Nope, no time to change. I don't know what your surprise is, but I'm hoping it's a hotel room. We can order room service for food or go out later."

"Matteo," she says cautiously, as she eyes me up and down. Her eyes half laugh and half say 'I want to rip off all your clothes.'

"What?"

She bites her lip as her hand tries to hide the smile creeping up her cheeks.

I glance down where she's staring. A ketchup stain has caught her attention on the bottom of my shirt. My eyes travel higher to the breast milk stain.

She shakes her head as her eyelids grow heavier. Her hands travel over the muscles on my chest. She's no longer smiling. Her body is dead serious now.

"Good thing I didn't make dinner reservations anywhere. I plan on getting dirty with you," she moans.

Hot.

My mouth parts, and I know I'm drooling at my wife. I get a chance to take her in finally. She's in a black pencil skirt and a red blouse that she's unbuttoned one button too far. I know she keeps professional in the courtroom, but around me, she always undoes an extra button because she knows it makes me crazy. She has all the control.

Our bodies collide at that moment in the hallway of our apartment building. Our lips locking, our tongues dancing. Eden is so much better than me in every way. She's kinder, smarter, sexier. She's driven to do good in a way I never could. The only good I ever do is protect my family. I would do anything for her or my kids.

We stumble down the hallway, as I'm already trying to undress her and slip my hand under her shirt.

She moans and whimpers against my lips but doesn't try to stop me. We could have a camera televising us to the world, and it still wouldn't stop us. A door opens and then quickly shuts as the person I recognize as our neighbor, Mrs. Finker, spots us making out like teenagers in the hallway.

I wave at her just before she shuts the door, making Eden giggle. I hit the elevator button and sigh in relief when the doors open immediately.

I shove Eden hard onto the elevator, and the doors close behind me. She rips open her shirt, revealing her perky breasts encased in a dark black bra.

Fucking beautiful.

I pull a card out of my back pocket and flash it under the light on the elevator, and then press the button for the garage. The card gets us an express trip to the garage without having to stop at any other floor. One of my requirements for staying in Eden's condo. I love the city life. I love our condo. I never thought I would. I thought I wanted another mansion in the countryside, like what I had back home. But it turns out I fell in love with the damn condo, almost as quickly as I fell in love with Eden.

I love the views. I love how close our family is from sharing such a small space. I freaking love being able to order takeout at any hour of the night. But it just isn't working anymore.

Later. First, I have the most beautiful woman in the universe to fuck.

I devour her. Unable to decide which part of her I want to kiss the most. Her lips, neck, or breasts. So I take my time, over every area of exposed skin I can find.

"You are so fucking amazing," I say as the elevator stops and I grab her ass. She wraps her delicious legs around my waist, driving her tall heels into my back.

She blushes and moans. *Speechless.*

I smirk as I carry her to the Porsche. I don't even bother going to the passenger side; I just put her in through the driver's side. She tries to crawl over to the passenger seat, but I grab her and pull her back to my lap, so she's straddling me.

"What are you doing?" she asks, running her hand through her hair and panting heavily.

"Fucking you."

"Not here, you idiot."

I frown. Nothing can stop us now. "Yes, here."

"We are not teenagers who have to fuck in the back seat of your car. There isn't even a back seat to fuck in. We can be patient and wait until we get to our destination."

"No, I've missed you. You've been busy working on your case, which I'm incredibly proud of you for, and in no way am saying you should stop doing. Because you are a badass, who deserves to be doing amazing fucking things. But I've waited long enough. I'm not waiting any longer."

She cocks her head to one side as she straightens her arms, trying to keep me away, like that will help. "It's been two days since we had sex. It's not like we've been on a drought or something."

I growl. "Two days is too long when it comes to us. I want you every day. Every minute. Every second."

She rolls her eyes and tries to climb off me again, but she's not going to win this fight. Because I don't fight fair.

I slip my hand up her thigh to the button I know will make her give into me. She's not wearing panties. She never does when she has a court case she is trying to win. She wears the sexiest bra and no panties because it makes her feel invincible. Works for me.

She arches her back against the steering wheel and gasps, as I find the sweet button already swollen for me.

My thumb flicks over her clit and her legs clench, quivering around my body.

"You were saying?" I snark, as I slide a finger into her wet slit.

"Umm..." she moans.

I slide another finger in and massage her clit faster. Teasing and taunting her, before I stop. She doesn't get more unless she agrees to give me everything. I want her entire body. Now.

Her head whips to glare at me when I stop.

"Fucking bastard," she says with a smile on her face and a thrill in her eyes.

I shrug like I completely agree I'm a bastard.

"Fine, you win." She grabs the buckle on my pants and starts to undo them. I continue making her moan as her pussy drenches my fingers with her desire.

Neither of us gives a shit that this is a public garage. Our parking spots are in a secure area of the parking lot, but there are still video cameras. Other VIPs can still park near us. They could walk by at any time and see us. Not that I would let them see any part of Eden. She's mine.

She jerks my pants down and expertly slips her body onto my rock hard cock in one motion. I glide in, finding my home inside her. I would never leave if I could. This is when I finally feel alive. Here buried inside of her. Without this, I'm nothing. Without her, I'm empty.

"God, Matteo. Why does it feel like it's been too long every time we do this?" she moans as her hips start slowly rocking over me.

"Because it has."

I bury my face in her breasts. Breathing in all of her sweet, sexy scents. The hint of spilled breast milk in her bra, the sharp scent of her perfume, and the sweet smell of her sweat rolling down her mounds. She's my queen. I never knew the combination could be sexy, but damn I think she could roll around in the mud after running a marathon, dripping with sweat, and I would still find her sexy.

Her walls clench around me as she rocks slowly. Too slowly. She knows it too. It's her revenge. Trying to taunt me and punish me for fucking her in the front seat of my Porsche like a horny teenager.

Too bad.

She wants this too; she just won't admit it. Beds are great and all, but I'll take her anywhere. Any chance I get.

I grab her hips, and I thrust. Hard.

She cries out as I stretch her tight cunt. Her nails dig into my shoulders while I pump in and out of her glorious body. I'll fuck her again later when I can savor every inch of her body. But now, I'm just desperate to hear her moan my name.

I flood her body with feelings. I can see it in her eyes rolling back in her head. I can hear it in the sharp intake of breath as she tries to keep pace with me. I can feel it in the heat rippling from her body.

It matches my own. I never thought I'd be a one woman kind of man, but Eden Carini is now my life. I don't see other women. *Only her.*

Eden pants harder as I hit all the spots in her body. I know every part of her. I know when to speed up and when to slow down. I know when to change the angle to hit the deepest part of her. I know when to be rough and when to be tender. I know Eden better than I know myself.

"Matteo," she cries, her body wrenching forward and her orgasm spilling out. Her teeth sink into my shoulder as the intensity takes over her body. My orgasm rolls through me seconds later.

We both pant in unison. Unable to break apart after the intensity we feel after we fuck.

Slowly, she leans back and looks at me shaking her head like she can't believe we just did that.

"What?" I ask innocently.

"You know what. You are bad."

I wink. "Would you prefer I be nice?"

She sighs and rolls off of me, situating herself in the passenger seat and starting to button her shirt. "No."

I tuck myself back in and zip my pants up.

"Where are we going to have our next fuck?"

She scowls, but behind the scowl I see her eyes light up with the thought of round two. "Is sex all you think about?"

"No."

She gives me a stern look.

"I think about you and our family. Which speaking of—"

"No more kids!" she says laughing. Although, we both know it's not true. She said the same thing after the triplets were born. We both love sex. And we both love having a big family. The more love we can share, the better. We might be done having kids, and we might not. I'm not sure it will ever be off the table.

"Where to?" I ask more seriously, knowing she won't let me fuck her again in this car. The faster we get going, the faster we get to have sex again.

"Oh! One second!" she hops out of the car and throws open the driver door of her red Ferrari, which is parked next to mine.

I wince when the door scrapes against my car. I want to scold her for hurting my baby. She has no respect for cars, but I want to enjoy the night more, so I keep my mouth shut.

Eden hops back into my car holding a grocery bag. I eye it suspiciously.

"What is that?"

"Part of the surprise."

I smell lasagna in the bag. At least she picked up food from my favorite Italian restaurant. Although, it doesn't matter because it will be cold by the time we get where we are going.

I take her hand in mine.

"Where to?" I ask for what feels like the millionth time.

"Just drive Matteo. I'll tell you when to turn."

I don't ask questions. I've learned there is no point. Eden is the boss in almost every way. And I trust her to make the most important decisions. I prefer it that way. I take charge of the things that matter. Safety and fucking. Otherwise, I let her decide.

"Eden, why are we in the middle of a neighborhood? Please tell me we aren't going to a baby shower, or a birthday party, or something?"

She ignores me completely.

"Okay, pull in this driveway."

I groan. Whatever she has planned, I'm not sure I like it. If we are headed into a party, I'm going to kill her. I want her alone. Not surrounded by people.

She grabs the bag and bounds out of the car. I notice a Honda Odyssey mini-van parked in the driveway in front of us. A typical suburban car. What has she gotten us into now?

Eden pulls me toward the front door, practically galloping as we head to the front door. The door opens before we reach it and a woman in her early fifties steps out.

"So sorry we are late! We had to get the babysitter settled before we left," Eden says, smoothing her skirt. Her skirt isn't what she should be worried about though. Her hair is what gives away the real reason for our delay. Her hair says 'just fucked.'

The woman smiles sweetly, glancing between us. "I completely understand," she says winking at me. I wrap my arms around my wife's waist, liking this woman a little more.

"Your timing is perfect, actually." She slips something into Eden's hand I don't see and then whispers something into her ear before brushing past us and walking to her car.

So many questions race through my head. But Eden's bubbly excitement brushes them away as she pulls me into the house.

The house is gorgeous. It was built a least a hundred years ago. It's old brick exterior and hardwood floors aren't built like this anymore. But it has been recently updated to make it more modern and homey. Eden lets go of my hand and spins around in the empty living room.

"Well, what do you think?" she asks, batting her eyelashes at me.

"You are sexy as hell."

She wags her finger at me like I'm naughty. "I'm not talking about me. I'm talking about the house."

I frown, not understanding. "The house? It's beautiful. That fireplace is something else, and I love the big modern kitchen behind you."

She wraps her arms around my waist. "I knew you would love it."

I raise an eyebrow. "Eden?"

She holds up a key. "This is our house!"

"What?"

She nods excitedly. "I know I should have asked you first before I bought it. But it has the exact number of rooms we need for each kid to have their own room. This living room and the kitchen are perfect. And it has a pool. It feels like your old home, but also new."

I kiss her lips, loving her even more for reading my mind.

"You're not mad at me, are you?"

I laugh. "I could never be mad at you. I fucking love this house! I thought I was going to have to beg you to leave that condo. I love the condo, but we need more space."

She frowns. "I love the condo, too."

I tilt her chin up. "Don't worry; we will keep the condo too. It can be our fuck pad." I wink.

"You are ridiculous, but I love you." I see the heat in her eyes and know she loves the idea.

"Wait here!" she squeals as she races back out of the house. Most likely to retrieve our dinner.

I take a deep breath, taking in the scent of the house Eden bought for us. It reminds me of the house I grew up. Just smaller and with less darkness.

Eden saunters back into the living room holding up the bag of our dinner.

"Where are we going to eat? There isn't any furniture."

"On the floor," Eden says, sitting down on the hardwood before she starts taking the styrofoam boxes out.

I sigh and sit down across from her.

"Don't act all high and mighty. I know you have eaten plenty of dinners on the floor with the kids."

She's right. I have. I'm not sighing because I don't want to eat on the floor. I'm sighing because I want to show my wife how happy she made me with her surprise. I want to take her on the hardwood floor, then on the kitchen counter, then in every room and surface of the house. But she's so happy with her meal, I know I need to behave and let her feed us first.

She pulls a bottle of wine out, along with two plastic cups.

"Really?" I say, eyeing the cups.

She blushes. "I thought it would be fun to drink from plastic cups like we're having a picnic or something."

I snatch the bottle from her hand and pour what I know, without tasting, is going to be the most disgusting wine I've ever drunk. I hand her a glass.

"To our new house and my incredible wife for making it all happen," I say.

She knocks her plastic cup against mine, and it doesn't clink because, well, it's plastic. She giggles like she is purposefully annoying me the best she can.

I lift the cup to my lips, but I can't get more than a drop down before my lip curls up in disgust.

She starts laughing hysterically.

I glare. "Your taste in wine is horrible. It's like you don't pay attention at all when I try to teach you about wine."

She keeps laughing at my turned up nose. I've changed a lot since I met Eden. Wine is not something I will ever change about. I know good wine, and this isn't that.

She digs in the never-ending bag again and pulls out a second bottle and two wine glasses. She blushes as she holds them out to me.

"I stole these from the wine cellar. You picked out the bottle, so I know you will like it."

I snatch the bottle and glasses from her hand. "Much better."

I work to get the cork out, after finding a bottle opener at the bottom of her bag, next to a chocolate dessert. The first bottle she bought didn't even have a cork; it was screw top.

Her phone buzzes and she snatches the phone out of her bag. She stares at the number, apparently not recognizing it.

"Let me just make sure it's not the babysitter."

I nod and start pouring the wine that tastes like real wine, instead of sour grape juice.

I don't listen to Eden as she speaks on the phone. I'm too busy envisioning our new life in this house.

It's not until her face goes white I realize something is wrong. The phone drops out of her hand and shatters on the floor.

"Eden?" I ask, moving to her side in less than a second.

She doesn't answer.

"Eden? Who was on the phone?"

Nothing.

"Are the kids okay?"

She nods, and at least my heart is working again. But I know someone is in trouble. I've seen the look on her face before. Eden is strong and invincible. She doesn't get scared easily.

"Who is it? Nina? Arlo? Gia? Caspian? Who?"

5

GIA

"WE CAN'T DO THIS," I squeal, as Caspian kisses down my neck.

"Why not?" he says, kissing the tender spot.

I moan. I forget all the reasons.

We are on the job.

We are in the house of a well known criminal and psychopath.

We are risking our cover and ability to put away a dangerous family.

If we are caught, we are as good as dead.

Caspian pushes me backward, and shuts the door behind us, as we enter a dark space. A closet, I realize as my head hits clothes before pressing against a wall.

Caspian's hand moves up my shirt, lifting it higher as he bends down and kisses my stomach. He unbuttons my pants and kisses over my panties.

"I don't hear you arguing anymore," he smiles against me.

I bite my lip to keep another loud moan from escaping.

"Because I don't want you to stop." This is still stupid. We could still get caught. And Rasmus is definitely not the kind of man who will go easy on us if he catches us fucking, instead of protecting him like we are supposed to be doing. But it doesn't matter.

Our job is dangerous. Our lives are dangerous. But that is how we like it.

This...

Caspian tears my shirt off. This is for fun. This is what we wake up every morning for.

Each other.

We can never get enough. *Ever.*

Even though we live together and work together.

"Fuck," I let out, letting the word roll off my tongue and bounce off the walls in the closet.

My nails claw at his head as my legs wrap around his body. His cock presses into me, needing to be inside me. And the familiar ache inside my core tells me the same thing. I will explode if Caspian doesn't fuck me.

"Caspian," I pant, needing him now.

I'm not patient. Not when it comes to him.

He pushes his pants down, freeing his cock to enter me. His lips close around my mouth as his hips thrust.

I stretch and moan as he fills me. The world disappears when I'm with Caspian. He is all I see, feel, or hear.

It's only him.

Caspian's eyes still as he looks at me, his body slowing as well to drag this moment out longer.

"I love you," I whisper because I can never miss an opportunity to tell him those words.

He grins. "I know, baby."

He thrusts again, picking up speed. "As I love you."

Our bodies move in perfect synchrony as we fuck. Risking our lives for a moment of connection.

"Jesus, Caspian," I growl as his body hits the spot deep inside that makes me orgasm.

I feel the warmth of his orgasm shoot through me. We both laugh as we slowly come down from the high.

A thud outside the door makes us both jump.

"Caspian!" Rasmus shouts.

Shit.

We both scramble to get dressed.

"What are we going to do?" I whisper, my eyes wide, and my heart pumping blood much too quickly through my veins.

Caspian kisses me, and I instantly relax.

"Go get him," Caspian says, shoving me out of the closet by myself.

Rasmus stares at me with wide eyes. I'm flushed, and I'm sure I look like I've just been fucked. He angles his head to the side as he stares at the closet I just exited.

"What were you doing in the closet?"

I smile and walk up to him, letting my body brush against him as I speak. "Making sure to install security in every nook and cranny. I don't want anything to go unnoticed."

He smiles at me instantly, forgetting anything that might be wrong as he stares down at my cleavage beneath my black T-shirt. I hate using my body to get ahead in life. But around dangerous men like Rasmus, I know I'm doing the right thing. I need to use every advantage I have.

I steer him away so Caspian can sneak out of the closet.

I talk to Rasmus.

I flirt.

I pretend if he plays his cards right, I will cheat on Caspian with him.

He doesn't know that I plan on killing him as soon as the opportunity arises. The only thing keeping him breathing right now is his knowledge of the whereabouts of his brother, who also abuses women.

"We are all set here," Caspian says to Rasmus, saving me from having to talk to him any further.

Caspian eyes Rasmus' hand, which has found its way around my waist. He hates the game we play as much as I do. But it's for the best. This is how we rid the world of evil.

"Excellent. Gia was just showing me all the hard work you've put in. I have no doubt I'm safe with you watching over me."

He gives me a tight squeeze, and I give him a fake smile in return. I hate him. I want to rip out his insides and watch them burn.

"We should get going. We have another job we need to get to," Caspian says, putting his hand on my waist and pulling me to him. He doesn't usually show his jealous side. But something has made him act out his feelings.

I don't argue. I'd much rather be on Caspian's arm than Rasmus'.

"I understand, although I hate to see you go," Rasmus says.

"We'll be back soon. We are just a phone call away if you need anything," I say.

He nods.

Caspian leans down and kisses me softly on the cheek and then pulls me towards our car.

"What was that for?" I ask.

"I can't stand the way these sleazeballs look at you or touch you. It makes me mad."

"You have nothing to worry about. I'm yours." I grab his neck and kiss him like he's mine.

His eyes glow wickedly as I pull away.

"Now let's go home so we can do something about that look in your eyes."

He blushes. "Actually, I have a surprise for you."

I narrow my eyes. "Your penis?"

He laughs. "No, that's not really a surprise. That's expected. I got us another job."

I raise an eyebrow. "Why is that a surprise?"

"Because the job is with Erick and Clive."

A slow smile creeps up my face.

"Why? How?"

"It doesn't matter how. What matters is you can finally get the one thing that still gnaws at you..."

"Revenge."

6

CASPIAN

THE LOOK on Gia's face when I told her that we had a job at her old home was precisely the reason why I arranged the job in the first place. Gia deserves to get her final revenge. She deserves to get her home back.

Which is why I've spent months having Vincent infiltrate Clive and Erick's organization. So when the opportunity presented itself, we would be ready.

I've spent the afternoon installing a new security system in the house Gia grew up in. It's strange being here. Knowing the history of everything that has happened in this house. But Gia loves this house, and I will do anything to make her happy. Whole again.

I let Gia work on her own, giving her space to get reacquainted with her house. I'm not sure her need for revenge is healthy, but I don't care. Maybe when this is over, she can finally let go of all the ghosts of her past.

But I need her near now.

I pull out my cell phone and text her.

Meet me by the car in five minutes. I miss you ;)

. . .

I pocket my phone and head to the car. If I'm lucky, I can convince her of a quickie in the back of the car before we head home.

I lean against the hood of the car as I stare up at the mansion. I never understand why people want such large homes. Not when they can have a small quiet house in the woods.

I stare at the side door, waiting for Gia to exit. But she takes much longer than five minutes.

I sigh, pulling out my phone to call and see what the hold up is when I notice a text message from her.

Gia isn't going anywhere. She's ours now. I know what you planned. To take our house and kill us. We won't let that happen. Leave now.

I can't breathe. They have Gia.

I don't think. I race to the door. It doesn't budge.

I pull with everything inside of me, willing the door to open. But it doesn't open. Not even a budge.

I scream as loud as I can, cursing the door and them for taking her. My everything.

If they think I will just leave, they don't know me at all.

"Clive! Erick! I know you can hear me. I'm not leaving without her!"

I kick the door with everything I have. I pull my gun out planning on storming inside and getting her back. I'm nothing without her. I have no will to live.

I move to the window next to the door and kick as hard as I can. The glass shatters, as instantly as my heart would. Our lives are risky, but I never thought I would have to say goodbye to Gia.

I jump through the open glass and storm through the house, searching for her. It's not the smartest thing I've ever done. I should have a strategy. Call my sister first to let her know I need backup.

But with Gia ripped from me, I can't think. She is what makes me whole. She is who I can't live without.

"Drop the gun," I hear a man say from behind me.

I can't drop the gun. The gun is the only chance I have at getting Gia back.

I turn, ready to fire at the man before he gets a shot off. I'm not fast enough.

I'm not strong enough to save her.

I can't even save myself.

7
___

ARLO

I WOULD DO anything to save my sister. Anything for my family. I just never thought the way to rescue my family would be returning to my old life.

I never thought I would return to this house. When I left with Nina, I thought it was for good. I thought we had escaped this life. But somehow every time I think we have left our dark past behind, it sucks all of us back in again. I'm afraid we will never be free of it.

"Ready for this?" I ask Matteo next to me in the passenger seat, as we pull up in front of the Carini mansion. A house that, at one time, belonged to us both. But now it serves Erick and Clive.

He growls as he looks at me. "Let's go get our sister."

I nod as I park the car in the driveway like a visitor. By the time we leave, this house will be ours again. Back in the Carini family. And Gia and Caspian will be safe again.

We could have hired our security team to handle this. But this is personal. We needed to handle this ourselves. Ensure that our sister is safe and our families are safe forever.

We both step out of the car, slamming the doors loudly so we can be heard. We aren't going to sneak into our own home like thieves in the night. We are going to use the fucking front door.

We walk to the door. Each step loud and demanding. This is our house. We may have let Clive and Erick rent it temporarily, but now they've taken Gia, this is personal. We are getting the house back.

I thought running and staying away was the solution. I thought the only way to keep my family safe was to keep our distance. But running from our pasts won't keep our families safe. We are Carini's. This is who we are.

We stop at the front door, now decorated with a fucking wreath filled with red roses like this is an ordinary home. It's not.

Matteo grimaces at the change as well. The door is a beauty, no decorating is required.

He takes his fist and pounds on the front door three times.

This may be the stupidest thing we've ever done or the best. Either way, we are either going to live or die in this house. The kids are hidden with Caspian's sister. She will make sure they are taken care of if anything happens to us. But it is also why I know we will win. Matteo and I will do anything for our kids.

We hear footsteps, and we both brace ourselves for what we will face on the other side of the door. We both give each other one simple glance, letting each other know whatever happens we will be here for each other. We'd die for each other.

It can't come to that.

The door opens, and guns are pointed in our faces.

We both hold up our hands, anticipating this greeting.

Our hands are jerked behind our backs as the men tie our wrists together.

Matteo doesn't glance at me. He's focused on our mission. He's back to his old self. Ready for a fight.

Good, we are going to need all of our old skills to get out of this mess.

We are shoved through our house. Through the dark hallways, now littered with paintings that don't deserve to be seen. Past gaudy furniture and fancy crystal that doesn't fit in with the rest of the house.

We stop in the large living room where Clive and Erick sit.

"We've been expecting the two of you, although I didn't think you would be stupid enough to just walk in the front door unarmed," Clive says.

I shrug. "We were never the smartest in town."

"No, but your wives are plenty smart. Where are they?" Erick asks.

"Home, watching our children," Matteo says.

Clive smirks. "I don't believe you."

"Call them, see for yourself," I say.

Erick pulls out his phone and dials a number.

"Hello Nina, your husband is here, claiming you don't have some big scheme to come save your sister-in-law."

There is a pause, and I can barely hear Samuel crying in the background.

Erick hangs up, confirming our wives aren't here.

"Now, let's talk," I say.

Erick cocks his head to the side. "I don't think we have anything to talk about. You are tied up. You have no room for negotiation."

"We want a trade. Us for Gia and Caspian."

They both laugh.

Matteo growls, and I know he is losing his patience.

I hate this plan as much as he does, but it's the best plan we have. I never wanted to end up tied up, but so far the plan is working perfectly.

"This is your last warning," Matteo snarls.

Clive walks to us. "No trade. We are going to kill you all. End the Carini line, forever."

8

EDEN

MY HAND TREMBLES as we sneak in the back of the house. I shake it out, trying to keep Nina from seeing. But when I glance back at her, I can feel her heart beating out of her chest.

We both have everything riding on the line. Our husbands are both risking their lives to try and keep us safe, so we have a chance to rescue Gia and Caspian. Our kids are safe, but we both know we would be horrible mothers without our husbands. We need them to feel whole.

Footsteps creep down the hallway toward where we are hiding behind a dresser in the bedroom we snuck into. It used to be Matteo's bedroom.

Nina pulls out her gun, and I do the same, watching and fearing that the door is going to swing open and we'll be caught.

Neither of us moves. Or breathe. Or let our hearts beat.

The footsteps grow farther and farther away.

Nina exhales. "We need to get going. The faster we get in and out the better. I'm not sure how long our boys can keep Clive and Erick distracted."

I nod.

Every second longer this takes, the more at risk Arlo and Matteo are. We race to the door. I push my ear against it, listening and trying to ignore my feelings creeping back in from being in this room. My core sparks with a need to be near Matteo.

I shake it off. The best way to get back to him is finding Gia and Caspian. Then I get Matteo back. He's going to survive. We all are.

I glance back at Nina who holds her gun like a pro. We've both been taught by the best, but hopefully, Arlo and Matteo are providing a big enough distraction that we won't need to use our guns.

I open the door and slip into the hallway with Nina on my heels. We inch our way down the hallway looking for any sign of Gia or Caspian. Instead, we find an empty corridor.

"The dungeon maybe? Or..." Nina says.

I know what she's thinking. Enrico's bedrooms. Chills run up and down both of our bodies as we think about that. Neither of us wants to enter Enrico's side of the house. In fact, if we get the house back, I'm sure those rooms will be destroyed. But we will do anything to get Gia and Caspian back.

I nod.

"Let's start with the dungeon."

Nina breathes again.

We start slinking down the hallway in that direction when we hear footsteps again.

We both freeze. Nina moves next to me as we both hold our guns out, ready to fire the second the person comes into view. It feels good to have my best friend by my side, even if we both end up dead at the end of this.

Breathe deeply in and out, I remind myself. Matteo always said you can aim better if you are calm.

The footsteps grow closer, and I close my eyes to steady myself. When I open them, I'm calmer. Ready.

I watch as the shadow appears in front of us. I freeze for just a second, and I know it's all over.

The person standing in front of us lowers the gun aimed at our heads.

"Eden? Nina?"

"Gia!" I cry, wrapping my arms around her.

"Thank God you're okay," Nina says with tears in her eyes.

"How did you get free?"

Gia smiles. "Caspian taught me plenty of skills. I will never be captive again."

"Are you okay?" Nina asks.

"Yea, barely a scratch on me."

I grip her tighter. "Where is Caspian?"

Gia drops her head. "Somewhere in this house. I know he tried to save me and they caught him."

"We will find him. Arlo and Matteo are serving as a distraction. And with your help, we will find him in no time."

Gia nods. "I think he's in Enrico's old room."

"Of course he is," Nina says with a fierceness in her eyes I wasn't expecting to see.

"We will follow you," I say to Gia.

She gives me a tight smile and then leads the way down the hallway.

Shots ring out, and we freeze.

"What kind of distraction are my brothers doing?" Gia asks.

My heart stops. "Whatever it takes."

We use the distraction to run to the other side of the house. We pause for a second as the hallway passes the living room. Matteo glances our way. His hands are tied behind his back, but he has a gun in his hand firing away.

He winks at me and turns back to aim his gun.

I swallow hard keeping the anxiety deep in my stomach from coming up. *Please don't let that be the last time I see him.*

I run to catch up with Gia and Nina. Nina never glanced Arlo's way. I know if she did, she'd run to his rescue. Arlo and Matteo don't need us right now. This is where they are at home. Caspian needs us.

Gia fires her gun just as I reach her and Nina. She shoots again, and I watch as two men drop to the floor in front of us.

"You are such a badass," I say.

Gia nods. "I know. Come on."

We race through the house, and when we reach Enrico's bedroom,

Nina is the one to open the door. She's just as badass for facing her fears.

Gia races inside, and we run after her.

Gunshots ring out, and we all duck down. I raise my gun and fire, hitting a man square in the chest. A few more minutes of gunshots continue, and then Gia suddenly stands up.

"Caspian!" she yells. Her voice full of the fear of someone losing the only thing that matters in the world.

Gia runs at a full sprint to the other side of the room. I can barely see in the darkness.

Nina and I follow after her until we find Caspian tied up. Gia flings her arms around him, and that's when I see the blood trickling down his body.

"Caspian, please! Wake up!" Gia undoes the ropes tying him up, and he falls limp into her arms. Tears stream down her face as more blood flows from his stomach.

I rush over and place my hand on his throat trying to feel for a pulse.

"He has a pulse," I shout, looking from Gia to Nina.

"Oh my God!" Nina cries.

I pull off my jacket and apply pressure to his stomach wound, while Nina pulls off her belt and uses it as a tourniquet around his leg. Gia works on the wound on his head.

"Keep breathing, Caspian," Gia whispers.

"We need to get him out of here," I say.

Gia nods.

"Text the boys to get out of here, and we will meet them at the car," I say to Nina.

Nina pulls out her phone, while Gia and I start lifting Caspian. He's stable, but we need to get him to a hospital. His body got hit with too many bullets, and it's clear Clive and Erick weren't as kind to him as they were Gia.

Nina pockets her phone and helps us lift Caspian. It takes all of our energy to haul him out of the house. None of us breathe as we carry him, afraid he will die at any second. We get him to the car and into the backseat before he finally wakes.

"Gia?" he whispers.

"Shh, I'm here," Gia says, crying, as she climbs into the backseat with him.

Nina and I scan the yard, waiting for Arlo and Matteo to appear. But after five minutes of waiting, we fear they aren't coming.

Gia appears standing next to us. "My brothers aren't back yet?"

"No," I whisper, feeling the loss already. A loss I have no idea how to handle.

"We should go in after them," Nina says.

I nod agreeing.

"We need a distraction. We don't have enough people to rescue them if they are captured," Gia says.

"What sort of distraction?" I ask.

Gia pulls a lighter out of her pocket. "Fire."

GIA

I SET the house on fire.

What the hell was I thinking?

I love this house more than anything. And now I'm watching it burn.

"Let's go," Eden says to Nina, running off to save their husbands. They don't expect me to go. They assume I will stay to make sure Caspian is safe, but I can't let them go on their own. If my brothers really are captured, they will need my help. I'm the most skilled.

"I'll be right back," I say, kissing Caspian on the forehead and hating leaving him when he's this injured.

He moans. "I know."

I blink back my tears. "Hold this on your stomach and don't let go."

"Go," he says, holding his hand on his stomach like I asked.

I nod and run before I change my mind. I'm not going to lose anyone. Not my brothers. Not my sisters-in-law. Not Caspian.

The fire has been burning free for a few minutes now. The flames start shooting through the house, spreading faster than I ever imagined. If people don't start running out soon, they will die from the smoke or the flames. We decide to lay in wait for any escapees before running into the house.

Men start running out, and I pick them off one by one with my gun. It's my fault we are in this predicament. I'm going to be the one to end it.

Nina and Eden fire their guns, occasionally hitting a target, but it's up to me.

Nina and Eden run into the house first, and then I finally do. Smoke fills the house, and I'm afraid I made the biggest mistake. I thought the smoke would give us an advantage, but now I may have just sentenced my brothers to death.

"Arlo!" Nina screams.

"Matteo!" Eden yells.

My soul suffers from their heartache. My heart feels the same. Because even though Caspian is out, it doesn't mean he'll survive. I may have gotten to say goodbye, while they may not get the same chance.

I run after them, searching the smoke as it fills my lungs. I cough, and I know we don't have much time left to find them. If we don't get out soon, we will all die. I can't let Nina and Eden die. They have children at home who rely on them.

"Nina! Eden! We need to go!" I shout.

But they keep running forward. Searching for their loves, the one person who makes this world worth it.

I cough again and know I'm going to have to start dragging them out of here. I will if I have to.

"Gia!" Nina screams.

I run to her and see Arlo passed out on the floor with a bullet in his leg.

Shit.

Nina examines him quickly, but there doesn't seem to be any other issues.

I slap him hard, trying to get him to wake up.

He startles.

"Get him out of here! I'll get Eden," I shout and run over to Eden, hoping she's found Matteo.

Nina nods and pulls Arlo up to his feet. They will make it. Now I need to find Eden and Matteo.

"Eden!" I shout.

I run as I see her through the smoke.

I stumble, though, as someone grabs my ankle.

"Clive," I say through a cough.

"I knew you would die here," he says.

"No, you will die here," I say, ripping my leg from his grasp.

I cough again, and I know if I don't want his words to be true then I need to get out. Now.

I run to where I last saw Eden and find her clutching Matteo's hand.

We don't have time. The smoke and flames are closing in, but I won't leave my brother here. Even if he's already dead.

Without a word, Eden and I scoop under each of his arms and start dragging him out. It takes everything out of us to get him out. We all collapse onto the ground as our home behind us goes up in flames. We may have saved everyone we care about, but the house is gone.

I turn my attention to Matteo, who is starting to cough. Arlo is standing next to Nina. I run back to check on Caspian.

He smiles at me when he sees me approaching and sits up in the SUV.

"You save the day?" he asks.

I grin and kiss him firmly on the lips.

I climb into the back with him, holding him tight as we watch the house burn and my brothers and their wives slowly approaching. We're all wounded, but I have no doubt we will all survive and be stronger than ever.

Everyone is free. Erick and Clive will go down with the house. And we are all free of our pasts.

Nina and Arlo stop in front of the car. Matteo and Eden limp up. We all need to get to a hospital. But we all watch for a moment as our pasts die with the flames.

"What now?" Nina asks.

"Hospital," Eden answers.

"That's not what I meant," Nina says, glancing back at me. In fact, everyone is staring at me. Knowing how much I wanted this house back. Everyone else wanted it gone, but I wanted it.

"We can rebuild," Arlo says looking from me to Matteo who nods.

We could. We could rebuild a mansion on this land. Build the perfect home for all of us to come back to when we were missing home.

Except this isn't our home anymore. The Carini mansion is gone. Over.

Our past will never haunt us again.

"No," I say, staring at my brothers and their wives. I never thought the piece of paper mattered. I never thought I needed to get married. I was always a Carini. I never wanted to be anything else.

Until I watched the Carini house burn. In that moment, I realized I'm more than a Carini. I want to be more. I want what my siblings have. I want everything.

I turn to Caspian. "No, I don't want to rebuild. I want a new start. Our past is over. But I'm ready now for our future. A real future. I thought I could escape my past. Our pasts. I will always be a Carini, but I'm ready to be a Conti now. I want to marry you, Caspian."

He grins as he pulls me to him and kisses me firmly. "I thought you'd never say yes."

The girls squeal behind me, and when I glance back, I see the tears in their eyes.

"Here. I want to get married here though. I don't care the house is gone and will never get rebuilt. I want one last positive memory to replace all of this. And give us a fresh start."

"I'll marry you wherever you want, whenever you want. I never thought I'd convince you."

I grin. "I've been yours since you laid eyes on me."

"I know. But if we don't get your brother to the hospital fast, he's going to pass out," Caspian says eying Matteo.

"Speak for yourself," Matteo jokes at Caspian.

"Everyone in!" I shout, ready to leave this place. Nina jumps in the driver's seat and, after everyone has jumped in, starts driving off away from the home. A home that has all the memories of our pasts. It's where Arlo found Nina. Where Matteo trapped Eden. And I was sold to be saved by Caspian.

It has bad memories and good.

It holds the mistakes we all made.

A tear falls down my eye, despite the pain I've felt in that home. A pain we all felt. It's what made us who we are. It's what brought us all together.

And now, it's gone.

It's how it should be. The flames set us free. Despite what we felt before, we were never free. We could never forgive ourselves for our mistakes. I look at Arlo and Matteo, knowing the three of us have committed a lot of sins.

I look from Nina to Eden, to Caspian. We could never forget the pain that the Carinis caused them.

But now we are healed.

The flames brought us together. They saved us.

Finally, I know we are all free because we have the most important thing: family.

THE END

Thank you so much for reading the **DIRTY** series! I hope you loved this dark romance as much as I loved writing it! I'm currently writing another romantic suspense series. **Sign up to get notified when the books release and get a FREE book here**>>>EllaMiles.com/freebooks

Want to order signed paperbacks? Visit: store.ellamiles.com

ALSO BY ELLA MILES

DIRTY SERIES:

Dirty Beginning

Dirty Obsession

Dirty Addiction

Dirty Revenge

ALIGNED SERIES:

Aligned: Volume 1 (Free Series Starter)

Aligned: Volume 2

Aligned: Volume 3

Aligned: Volume 4

Aligned: The Complete Series Boxset

UNFORGIVABLE SERIES:

Heart of a Thief

Heart of a Liar

Heart of a Prick

Unforgivable: The Complete Series Boxset

STANDALONES:

Pretend I'm Yours

Finding Perfect

Savage Love

Too Much

Not Sorry

ABOUT THE AUTHOR

Ella Miles writes steamy romance, including everything from dark suspense romance that will leave you on the edge of your seat to contemporary romance that will leave you laughing out loud or crying. Most importantly, she wants you to feel everything her characters feel as you read.

Ella is currently living her own happily ever after near the Rocky Mountains with her high school sweetheart husband. Her heart is also taken by her goofy five year old black lab who is scared of everything, including her own shadow.

Ella is a USA Today Bestselling Author & Top 50 Bestselling Author.

Stalk Ella at:
www.ellamiles.com
ella@ellamiles.com

CPSIA information can be obtained
at www.ICGtesting.com
Printed in the USA
LVHW021909151120
671496LV00001B/69